ROMULANS IN PURSUIT

"The Romulans continue to pursue, Captain," Spock reported. "And they are increasing their speed."

"Can we outrun them, Mr. Spock?"

Spock hesitated, studying readouts as fast as the battle computer could supply them. "Indeterminate, Captain. With three ships in pursuit, prediction becomes extremely complex."

"Captain," Uhura interrupted. "I've received an incoming transmission from the commander of the Romulan force. He seems anxious to talk to you."

"I'll bet," Kirk replied. "Put him through . . . I've got a couple of things to talk over with him!"

By Alan Dean Foster
Published by Ballantine Books:

THE BLACK HOLE

CACHALOT

DARK STAR

LUANA

THE METROGNOME AND OTHER STORIES

MIDWORLD

NOR CRYSTAL TEARS

SENTENCED TO PRISM

SPLINTER OF THE MIND'S EYE

STAR TREK® LOGS ONE–TEN

VOYAGE TO THE CITY OF THE DEAD

. . . WHO NEEDS ENEMIES?

WITH FRIENDS LIKE THESE . . .

The Icerigger Trilogy:
ICERIGGER
MISSION TO MOULOKIN
THE DELUGE DRIVERS

The Adventures of Flinx of the Commonwealth:
FOR LOVE OF MOTHER-NOT
THE TAR AIYM KRANG
ORPHAN STAR
THE END OF THE MATTER
BLOODHYPE
FLINX IN FLUX

The Damned:
Book One: A CALL TO ARMS
Book Two: THE FALSE MIRROR
Book Three: THE SPOILS OF WAR

STAR TREK®
LOG FOUR
LOG FIVE
LOG SIX

Alan Dean Foster

Based on the Popular Animated Series Created
by Gene Roddenberry

A Del Rey Book
BALLANTINE BOOKS • NEW YORK

A Del Rey Book
Published by Ballantine Books

STAR TREK LOG FOUR copyright © 1975, 1993 by Paramount Pictures.
STAR TREK LOG FIVE copyright © 1975, 1993 by Paramount Pictures.
STAR TREK LOG SIX copyright © 1976, 1993 by Paramount Pictures.

ISBN 0-345-38522-5

Manufactured in the United States of America

First Ballantine Books Edition: July 1993

Cover Art by David Mattingly

Contents

Log Four   1

Log Five   209

Log Six   405

STAR TREK
LOG FOUR

CONTENTS

PART I
  The Terratin Incident   7

PART II
  Time Trap   97

PART III
  More Tribbles, More Troubles   163

STAR TREK LOG FOUR

Log of the Starship *Enterprise*
Stardates 5525.3–5526.2 Inclusive

James T. Kirk, Capt., USSC, FS, ret.
Commanding

transcribed by
Alan Dean Foster

At the Galactic Historical Archives
on S. Monicus I
stardated 6111.3

For the Curator: JLR

PART I

THE
TERRATIN INCIDENT

(Adapted from a script by Paul Schneider)

I

The view Kirk was studying at the moment differed little from the one normally projected on the main screen up on the *Enterprise*'s bridge. Except the brilliant specks immersed in the sea of shifting black were a uniform white instead of the variegated spectrum of a normal universe. True, the floating motes did vary in brightness and intensity, as did the pale swirls of chalcedony-colored nebulae that formed a backdrop for the white spheres. But it remained a universe singularly devoid of color.

Kirk made a movement with his right hand and a cascade of new stars permeated the void. Contemplating the result, he smiled.

Perhaps the theologians were right after all and there was some idle omnipotent force Out There that treated the real universe with the same studied indifference he was now lavishing on this private one. He moved his hand holding the instrument once more, and the tiny circular cosmos became a maelstrom of white particles and cream-colored cloud-shapes.

"Come on, Arex, play something for us."

Kirk recognized the voice of Sub-lieutenant M'turr and glanced up from his dreams.

M'turr stood off in the far corner of the Officers' Lounge. She and several of the other younger officers had cornered Arex and were gently pleading with him.

The Edoan navigator, like most of his kind, preferred his own company to that of others. This was the outgrowth of a natural shyness and strong sense of modesty, not of any feeling of awkwardness around other beings.

Ordinarily, the crew respected Arex's desire to keep to

9

himself. Kirk wondered what would have prompted them to intrude on the navigator in an off-duty moment of privacy. Curiosity astir, he moved closer to the group; and when one of the belligerent officers moved aside, the reason for the sudden assault on the Edoan's privacy became obvious.

Arex had his sessica with him, and the rest of the crew around him were exhorting him to play. They were not being especially courteous, but Kirk found it hard to be angry.

Arex usually played in the isolation of his cabin. The fact that he had brought his sessica out with him was a hint that he was half-willing to offer one of his infrequent concerts. His sense of humility, however, required that he be suitably harangued until he couldn't escape without playing.

Arex owned several of the slim, flutelike instruments, keeping each one in its own special case. Certain sessicas were used for different songs, others only on special occasions or days of the week.

Sipping his coffee, Kirk studied the one the Edoan was half-consciously fingering now. It was made of some light, ivory-colored wood that shone like fine Meerschaum. Delicately inscribed designs flowed like crevices in the bark of a tree along the instrument's sides and baffles—Edoan trees and mammals and flowers—the work of some master craftsman.

"Do play us something," Ensign Yang implored.

"Anything at all—even improvisation," another urged.

"Really, my friends, I . . .," Arex started to protest, but his companions didn't give him time to finish.

"We've got you trapped, Lieutenant," an ensign wearing the insignia of the Quartermaster Department insisted with mock warning, "and we're not letting you go until we hear at least a one-movement Edoan cycle." The threat was echoed enthusiastically by the rest.

"Well . . ." Arex spotted Kirk hovering in the background and appealed to him. "Captain Kirk, can you not explain to my friends that I have to be in a certain outgoing frame of mind in order to be able to play for others?"

"I would, Lieutenant," Kirk said slowly, "except I'd like to listen myself." He thought a moment, then suggested, "Why not tell them the story about the Edoan contortionist who operated on Earth for nine months as an incredibly successful pickpocket until the police discovered he had a third arm?''

Arex hesitated, but once Kirk had mentioned the subject, there was no way the others were going to let the navigator go without hearing the story. So he told it, letting the absurd, amusing tale unravel in his lilting, sing-song tones. Then he seemed as embarrassed as pleased by the resultant laughter.

His nervousness abated—besides, he had run out of excuses—he shifted the sessica in his hands and moistened the curved mouthpiece. Residual chuckles faded into respectful silence, and a respectful hush absorbed the assembly. The Edoan blew a couple of experimental notes, adjusted several openings in the body of the instrument, then paused. He appeared to be looking at something in the distance. Even his voice changed, growing slightly rougher, charged with something out of his past.

''This song,'' he told them, ''is in the form of an ode, in tripartite mode, and is called 'The Farmer and the Road.' ''

A recording enthusiast in the group, who seemed to know several Edoan folk ballads, murmured appreciatively.

Arex set the mouthpiece firmly to his lips and his boney, rather homely face assumed an expression at once sad and noble. He played.

Despite the inescapable alienness of the song, there was no atonality or sharpness about it. What stood out immediately was an ineffable sense of longing coupled with some mild, admonishing irony. The sessica produced long, deep tones of winsome mournfulness, rather like those of an oboe, but having much greater range in the upper registers.

Arex played easily, almost indifferently. At times he seemed to be falling asleep, then he would suddenly waken in a burst of rapid, calling notes. The delicate fingers shifted in triple patterns that grew ever more complex as he piled variation on variation on top of the basic melodic line.

Like the others, Kirk stood entranced and just listened.

Arex played for many minutes. When the last bit of honeyed sound slipped from the multiple mouths of the sessica, no one broke the mood with rude applause. But there were satisfied smiles all around.

''You liked it, then?'' the Edoan asked hesitantly, when no one spoke. Ann Sepopoa of Engineering nodded softly, once, for all the listeners and asked, "More?" Arex made a gesture of agreement, obviously pleased. Another moment of thought, then: " 'The Song of the Orchard-Master and the Twelve Polor Trees,' to be sung to children as they rest on their knees, provided they each see fit to ask, please?"

Supple fingers commenced rapid tattoo on the wood and Arex's head began to weave from side to side on his thin neck. The new tune was the emotional opposite of the one that had gone before. Lively, catching, expressing an inter-species joy which soon had the little group clapping in time, awkwardly at first but with increasing confidence in the peculiar skipping rhythm.

Kirk put cup to lips and became aware that he had ignored his coffee completely during the previous playing. It was cold now. Well, no problem. Coffee was an especially efficient recycler. He moved off and poured it into the proper disposal, drew a fresh cup nearby. Adding more cream and sugar, he stirred idly, listening to the music.

"Plays grandly, doesn't he, sir?" Kirk looked around.

"Hello, Scotty. Yes."

"Interestin' fellow, our Arex," Scott went on. "I'd like to know more about him, Cap'n, but . . . well, you know. It's not that he's standoffish, but he dinna have the sort of personality that encourages intimate questions."

"You know how shy the Edoans are, Scotty."

"Aye, Cap'n." He nodded in the direction of the concert. "It's just that to me, Arex seems more so than most. I'll give him this, though—passive he may be, but he's the best damn navigator in the fleet."

"Not everyone's naturally as nos . . . curious as you, Scotty."

They moved to a table. Scott drew a drink of his own, Darjeeling tea, with a touch of nutmeg. He also picked up a hot muffin with loganberry jam before sitting down next to Kirk.

"You wouldn't be implyin' that Arex is normal and that I'm hyper, Cap'n?"

"We all know how ridiculous an assumption that would be, Mr. Scott."

"Aye," Scott nodded vigorously, "and if sometimes I do seem to. . . ." He noticed Kirk's slight smile, responded with one of his own. "All right, so I'm not as restrained as Arex but then, who is, Cap'n? Except Spock, of course."

Kirk nodded agreement, but found himself drifting away from the conversation. Back to the music. The wild piping had turned positively rambunctious. He considered the generally held opinions the crew had regarding Arex. Shy. Introverted. Quiet. Restrained and relaxed and inoffensive. Scott and the rest of them would have been interested to know that Arex had not won his commission as Lieutenant by passing a number of exams, but in the field—during a skirmish with the ever-present Klingons testing the Federation borders. When all the officers aboard a small Federation cruiser were killed, Ensign Arex took command. Retreat, concealment, and then a re-engagement with the much larger, far more powerful Klingon ship. The Klingon ship was damaged and taken as a prize—charged with violating neutral space.

Arex was entitled to wear three separate decorations for bravery, under his Starfleet citation for conspicuous valor. Kirk had seen the medals once. Arex kept them in a plain bag at the bottom of his personal-effects drawer in his cabin. He kept them at all only because he was required to wear such things to formal Starfleet functions, events that he shunned with dedication. Had Kirk told anyone else on board about the medals, the navigator would have been embarrassed beyond recovery.

So though Kirk thought it was unnecessary modesty on Arex's part, he kept the secret and told no one, not even Scott.

Everyone had to admit that it was this unassuming posture which enabled the Edoans to coexist alongside belligerent races like the Klingons and Romulans and Kzinti while remaining in loose alliance with the Federation. The isolation of their home world also helped. Edos was located in the Triangulum Cluster at the very edge of the spiral arm and was a jumping-off point for scientific expeditions studying the great energy barrier at the galaxy's rim. The planet was not in the path of expansion of any of the would-be galactic empires.

A very long-lived people, the Edoans were able to adopt

a relaxed outlook on life. Their civilization revolved around home and family rather than around intersystem politics. Natural neutrals, their loose alliance with the Federation was a matter of convenience only.

One of Kirk's fondest wishes was some day to meet Arex's parents. He always wondered if the remarkable things rumored about them were true. . . .

A harsh buzz, doubly so in contrast to the sweetness of the sessica's song, broke his thoughts. One of the lounge speakers blared.

"Commander Scott, please contact Engineering. Commander Scott, please contact Engineering."

"Now what?" the chief engineer rumbled. He took a quick bite out of the half-devoured muffin, washed it down with a hurried draught of tea. A quick touch of a button in the table and a small intraship communicator appeared in front of him. He pressed for Engineering, was rewarded with picture and sound.

"What is it, Gabler?"

The voice of the second engineer reported back from distant regions of the ship.

"Commander? It's those extra radiation shields again. They're still not responding properly to external adjustment."

"Are they goin' over into the danger zone?" Scott asked.

"No, sir, but there's some peculiar fluctuations I don't recognize. They may be harmless enough, but I wanted to know if you want us to try and set something else up to compensate."

Scott took a deep breath.

"All right, Mr. Gabler. You did the right thing in tellin' me. I'm comin' down." He flipped off the communicator, and the little screen submerged once more.

"Excuse me, Cap'n, but we've been takin' all kinds of strange stuff from outside lately, and some of it's gettin' through the ship's shields. I've had secondary shields rigged to protect the anti-matter nacelle, just in case, but they seem to be givin' us trouble, too."

"Sensible," Kirk concurred. "In the region of particulate debris from an unmeasured nova you can't tell what sort of radiations you're likely to run through. Better not take any chances with engine shielding.''

"Aye, Cap'n.'' Scott downed the rest of the muffin in one gulp, following it with a sip of tea. He dumped cup and plate into the table disposal.

"Besides,'' he muttered around the mouthful, "we're gettin' close in now.''

"All right, Scotty.'' Kirk rose. "I'm going, too.'' He glanced back over a shoulder. "Anyway the concert seems to be coming to a close. I recognize that crescendo. Arex is winding himself up for a finish.'' The two men started for the elevators together—Kirk to go to the bridge, Scott back to Engineering.

"It's been a fairly standard scientific run so far,'' he continued. "I don't expect we'll run into any difficulties, Scotty.''

The chief engineer looked hopeful. "And so far I tend to agree with you, Cap'n, except I seem to have heard that sentiment expressed on too many occasions before. . . .''

The door to the bridge slid open, and Kirk stepped into a realm of constant but controlled activity. As long as he had been Captain of the *Enterprise*, as long as he would be, he would never fail to feel that slight tingle of excitement as he stepped into the control center of the great starship—into the control center of one of the most elaborate and powerful constructs ever built—and realized once more that its simplest movements had to be duly authorized by him, by James T. Kirk.

Little Jimmy Kirk, whose secondary-school physics instructor had assured him he would never get past second year University, let alone into Starfleet Academy. He smiled and wondered, as he took his seat in the command chair, what had ever happened to that counselor.

If the bureaucracy ran true to form, he reflected, the man was now probably a top economic advisor in the High Counsel. Kirk's musings took on more immediacy as he shifted thoughts to consider the brief discussion with engineer Scott.

He heard a brief hum behind him, and seconds later Arex strolled past to take up his position at the navigation console—minus sessica. The bridge of the *Enterprise* was now at full strength. Overstrength, he reflected, when Dr. McCoy suddenly appeared beside him. The good doctor held a portable life-systems pickup aimed at him.

"I wish you wouldn't stick that thing in my face all the time, Bones." McCoy assumed a put-upon expression.

"Just the usual health checks, Jim. Considering our position, I think it's a good idea. Why does this bother you? We're taking more radiation from outside than the 'Lizer puts out."

"I know that, Bones, but the damn thing still makes me nervous."

McCoy chuckled, carefully passing the detector over Kirk's form.

"Why Jim, you sound like the natives who refuse to have their pictures taken because they think the camera's going to capture their souls."

"Don't lecture me when I'm being obtusely dogmatic, Bones." Kirk managed a grin. "I'm really worrying about the chat I just had with Scotty. We *have* been picking up some heavy, unusual radiation recently and he's concerned about its affecting the engines in some impossibly unpredictable way."

McCoy nodded knowingly. "That's just like Scotty, Jim. He worries twice as much when there's no evidence for it. A good, solid crisis hardly bothers him at all, because he knows what the problem is. It's the nonexistent difficulties that he *really* agonizes over!" He sighed.

"I wonder what his wife must go through when he's home. I can picture it, I can picture it. Can't you see him rolling over in his sleep and muttering something like, 'Darlin', your drive components need an overhaul and lube in the bearings.' " Kirk smiled in spite of himself, looked over to where Spock stood at his science station.

"Speaking of radiations again, Mr. Spock, let's take a look at our immediate environment."

"Very well, Captain." Spock touched a switch. The main viewscreen immediately came to life. Murmurs of appreciation were heard from those on the bridge. The Arachnae nebula had been painted by one cataclysmic, searing stroke from a pallette filled with ruptured atoms and annihilated energy. A star had gone supernova and become a glistening memory. In so dying it had raised in its place one of those strange nebulae that constitute the most spectacular head-stones in the universe.

A sprawling, fiery mass of radiant gases and particles streaked across the screen—millions of kilometers of color, mostly electric white, tinged throughout with iridescent shades of crimson, azure and purple. The arms of fire were vaguely spiderish in shape and design, hence the name.

Kirk took time to study the fluorescent panorama, over-whelmed for the thousandth time by the infinite beauty and endless spool of glory the universe unwound. Returning to prosaics, he thumbed the recorder switch set into an arm of the command chair.

And spoke easily. "Captain's Log, Star Date 5525.3. We are approaching the remains of the supernova Arachnae." He paused a moment, studying the scene ahead, then continued: "Initial close-in visual observation correlates with advance telescopic probe-pictures.

"We are moving deeper into the nebular region at standard observation speed. Location survey will commence, as requested, with extensive measurements of expansion rate and radiation levels." Another pause, then: "Certain new types of radiation have already been detected. At present they exist in minute amounts and constitute no danger to either ship or mission. Engineer Scott is taking precautions."

Kirk clicked off the log recorder. That was that. A few days traveling through the region under study with the ship's automatic and manual monitoring systems operating at full capacity, and then they would be on to the next scientific station. Everything pointed to an uneventful yet interesting cruise.

No wonder Scotty was nervous.

"Mr. Spock," he said casually, "what do you think of Mr. Scott's unusual radiations?"

"They have been measured and recorded, and the results are now being analyzed by the computer, Captain. Some of the shorter wavelengths are indeed peculiar. But we have been receiving them now for several hours and have no hint of any debilitating effects. I cannot yet view them as a threat—Mr. Scott's precautionary actions notwithstanding."

"Have we any indication that this radiation might increase as we move deeper into the nebula?"

Spock, having turned back to the computer readout at his console, spoke while studying it. "On the contrary, Captain, there are signs that certain wavelengths are peaking now and, if anything, they should decrease in strength. Arachnae is entering a cycle of very strong emissions, but we should be long gone before any strong bursts reach this area." He hesitated.

"There *are* occasional brief bursts of a wave-form that does exhibit extraordinary characteristics. Extraordinary because they appear to be totally out of synchronization with the normal pulsations of the nebular center. These do seem to be growing stronger. But they are still too faint and of too brief duration for intensive analysis."

"Keep on it, then, Mr. Spock. That's the most interesting discovery we've made so far. Any chance the source might be other than natural?"

"Again, Captain, it is too early to form any definite conclusions. But I am working on it."

Kirk nudged another switch. "Stewart?"

"Here, Captain," came the voice of the head of the *Enterprise*'s Astronomical Mapping Section.

"What have we got on the rate of expansion?"

"Preliminary reports only," the voice replied evenly. "We're just now starting to receive information in bulk. Thus far the rate appears consistent with what we know of other nova and supernova remnants, though it seems to be high. A good deal higher than the Crab Nebula, for example. Too early to say if it's anything remarkable."

"Very good, Mr. Stewart. Let me know if anything unusual crops up."

"Aye, Captain."

Kirk switched off, considered possible details as yet unfinished and turned back toward Uhura. "Lieutenant, inform Star Base Twenty-three that we are now officially on station and commencing reconnaissance."

"Yes, sir." She turned full attention to her console, edged a little to one side and gave McCoy an irritated look. "Please, Doctor, can't you keep that thing out of my face while I'm working?"

"It's the only way I can effectively monitor the condition of your exquisite eyes, Lieutenant," McCoy replied, juggling the medical recorder and trying to keep it in line with the communications officer's face. She continued to move around at the console, but no more objections were offered— for all of two minutes.

"As you and others have repeatedly told me, Doctor, they're in perfect condition. Now, if you'll let me complete this call, you can then point that thing at me all you want."

McCoy moved away, shaking his head with an expression of exaggerated disgust. "I wear myself out trying to make sure everyone on this ship stays in perfect health and what are my rewards? Indifference, obstruction, lack of cooperation . . ."

"It is not that, Doctor," Spock suggested helpfully, "but rather that the desire to insure our health sometimes appears to be overridden by an exaggerated sense of what I would call the mothering instinct."

McCoy stopped short, looked up quickly from the recorder's readouts.

"*Mother* instinct?"

"Your constant solicitude sometimes laps over into an empathic condition of such a degree that it can only be properly defined as such," the first officer continued blandly. "If you will objectively analyze some of your actions, you will clearly see that. . . ."

"Now just a minute. Just a doggone minute," McCoy began hotly. "If anyone's going to do any analyzing of reactions here, it's. . . ."

Uhura broke in, "Excuse me a minute, Doctor." All three officers turned to face her. "Captain, I'm getting some strange interference on the subspace radio, everything in the upper registers."

"Any trouble in getting through to Star Base?"

She shook her head, a puzzled expression on her face. "No, Captain. I'm sure they got the message, albeit a little fuzzily. But this interference is . . . patterned. If it's a signal, I don't recognize it. It doesn't conform to any *known* pattern, though, distress or otherwise."

"Can you pinpoint the source."

"Just another moment, I think. . . ."

There was a long pause while the communications officer

worked busily at her console. Occasionally she would trade questions and answers with Sulu or Arex.

"There's a record of a star, with a single planet, in the region the interference appears to be coming from, Captain. Drone records on the system are slight or nonexistent, but . . ." She looked thoroughly confused.

"There's no mention of the area producing any kind of radio emissions. Nothing beyond the normal electromagnetic discharge of the star itself, and it shouldn't produce anything up in these wavelengths. Nothing about them in either the drone records or," she glanced away for a moment to scan another readout, "or in standard radio-telescope surveys of that area."

"Step up amplification and put it on the speakers," Kirk ordered. "Let's hear them. Maybe it'll strike a response in someone else."

Uhura shrugged, looked dubious, but turned back to her instruments and made the adjustments. A minute later the bridge was inundated with a sound like a million electrified shrimp all chattering at once. Normal star chatter, it seemed.

But at ordered intervals they heard a definite, harsh, though modulated screech that pierced the standard static with a regularity that fairly screamed *"Intelligence!"*

Uhura was right when she said it corresponded to no known broadcast signal—at least, not that of any civilization Kirk was familiar with. Nor anyone else, for that matter. While they listened and wondered, Spock worked at the computer. Great insights were not forthcoming.

"Signals appear random," he said, watching the flow of figures and words across the readout. "There are a number of possibilities. We may be receiving only disjointed parts of a more complete message and that may be why the pulsations make no sense."

"Could it be a radio mirage?" Kirk ventured. "There's certainly enough energy flowing for light-years around to transfer an awfully distant one."

"An interesting possibility that cannot be ruled out, Captain."

"Radio mirage?" McCoy looked properly blank.

"They've been known only for a century or so, Bones," Kirk explained. "They happen when a broadcasting civilization shoots signals in the direction of a highly active electromagnetic energy source, which then boosts and bounces them all over the cosmos, though usually badly distorted. Primitive radio-telescopes on Earth were picking them up for years without ever knowing what they really were.

"And the high cycle of activity Arachnae is entering would be particularly conducive to such," he finished. "It's as good a guess as to what these unknown pulses are as any."

"Correction," Spock put in laconically. "There is one identifiable word detectable in the pattern." Kirk quieted, leaned forward slightly and listened intently. After another minute of trying to sort something recognizable out of the blare of noise, he shook his head.

"I still don't recognize anything, Mr. Spock."

"That is because it is in Interset code, Captain. If you grant the fact that someone may still be using it."

"Interset," Uhura repeated. "A standard deep-space communications code—but one that has been out of use for nearly two centuries. A contradiction within a puzzle. I'm not conversant with *all* the old codes, Mr. Spock. What's the one word . . . help, hello . . . what?"

"It would seem to be in phonetic English, Captain; but the word itself has no meaning. It may be an archaic term. When decoded, the signal spells the word *T-e-r-r-a-t-i-n* . . . Terratin."

Kirk considered a moment. "Try your directional receivers, cued to the code frequency being utilized, Lieutenant. See if we can't pick up more of that message."

Uhura promptly returned to work at her instruments. But before she could make any readjustments the tiny screech which constituted the single burst of interpretable energy had faded abruptly from the speakers. Only normal star hiss was heard on the bridge. She tried the directional pickups anyway, in hopes of regaining that one elusive attempt at communication—if it was that—but with no luck.

"No use, sir. It's gone completely." More adjustments, then a long pause while she studied various readouts. "I just broadcast multiple queries in the old Interset code for further information. No response at all to our signals."

Kirk turned his attention back to the science station. "Spock, anything on that code word yet?"

"No, Captain," the first officer replied, still staring into his hooded viewer. "The computers show no ancient interpretation of the word. Nor do exhaustive scans of all variants of Interset code give any clue to what it might mean."

"Was it a random broadcast, Mr. Spock? A radio freak, perhaps?"

"No, sir. That signal was repeated at least twice, on a patently non-natural frequency . . . and possibly more often. It is difficult to be precise considering the amount of background interference."

Kirk paused thoughtfully, the other officers watching him, waiting. The only noise on the bridge now was the muted hum of instrumentation, the steady babble of interstellar static over the speakers.

"Two times . . . one too many for semantic coincidence. It has to be of human origin, then. Mr. Sulu," Kirk said crisply, swiveling back to face the helm navigation console, "lay in a course for . . .," he hesitated until the name of the obscure star came to him, ". . . Cephenes."

"Aye, sir," Sulu acknowledged, bending over his controls.

That decision caused McCoy to lower his health scanner and walk over to stare uncertainly at Kirk.

"Jim, you don't mean you're going to abandon the survey mission to check out some coincidence of stellar electronics that might or might not be part of a two-centuries dead code? At the outside, the most it might be is the dying gasp of some forgotten deep-space drone probe. Meaningless stuff. Ships run across that kind of junk all the time."

"Maybe meaningless at the moment, Bones. But there's no record of anyone having come across any old Federation artifacts anywhere near this region. It's well away from the historical exploration routes. And I'd sure like to see any 'old dead probe' that can put out a traceable signal this far from Cephenes. Must have been *some* probe. No, it doesn't make sense. There are other possibilities, too, that we haven't fully considered."

"Such as?" McCoy challenged.

"An intelligence someplace that somehow picked up the Interset code and is trying to contact us." He gave a soft shrug. "There are a host of possibilities."

"We've no indication that the signal—if it was a signal—was even directed at us."

"True enough." The Captain nodded. "I admit it's a long shot, Bones. But if there's even a chance of it being anything more, we're bound to check it out . . . even if that means deviating from our planned course. I'm rather surprised at you. Where's your spirit of adventure, Bones?"

"On top of a three-centimeter microscope slide. That's far enough off course for me, Jim."

Kirk glanced to his right. "Mr. Spock, continue intensive research on the word 'Terratin.' Check pre-Interset codes, too. There's always the chance the word may be a carry-over from an earlier, more primitive version of the code."

"I've been doing so, sir," Spock replied. "No significant historical references have been revealed as yet. I suspect that if any do exist they are certainly pre-Federation."

Kirk looked disappointed. McCoy merely turned away, muttering under his breath. "Waste of time if you ask me." Hefting the health recorder, he moved toward the helm. "Sulu, you're next."

"I'm in perfect health, Doctor."

"That's what they all say," McCoy countered, "until they show up in Sick Bay complaining of internal pains, vomiting, headache and irregularity and want to know why I didn't spot something two weeks in advance of symptoms."

"Precautionary checkups are an excellent idea, Lieutenant Sulu," came sudden advice from Spock's station. "It is illogical to object to the doctor's informal checks."

"Well, thank you, Spock," said McCoy, surprised and pleased at support from a totally unexpected quarter.

"Although," the first officer continued mildly, "I see no reason why they could not be performed with considerably less frequency than at present."

"I'll keep that in mind, Spock," McCoy said, "because you're next. . . ."

II

Actually, McCoy's concern for the mission was exaggerated. They were not too far from Cephenes, so they could examine the source of the mysterious signal and return to the scientific mapping of the huge nebula with little time lost.

Cephenes' lone planet proved to be a world of constant upheaval. Considerably drier and somewhat smaller than Earth, it resembled a convulsed Mars. The atmosphere was in continual motion, as unstable and violent as the surface.

Sulu set a low orbit and the bridge complement stared at the screen as one external viewer after another provided varying closeups of the planet below. Telescopic subviews revealed shimmering flares of crimson and yellow, occasionally blending into violent orange eruptions as volcanoes belched forth the globe's insides at sporadic intervals.

"Cephenes One . . . and only," Sulu reported formally.

"Doesn't look very hospitable," McCoy observed prosaically.

"Mr. Spock, any information on conditions below?" Kirk asked.

"Our only data are from that single early drone probe to this region, Captain, and it passed through the system very fast. Clearly there was nothing to trigger its automatics for a longer stay. We have no record of anything beyond the lower life-forms existing on the surface. Nor, indeed, mention of anything beyond a few basic statistics."

On the viewscreen an enormous orange-red flare temporarily obliterated the view.

"Two items of interest, though. The atmosphere is high in rare gases, but breathable—and surface conditions are indicated as being approximately normal."

24

Kirk studied the screen. Another gigantic flare tinged distant clouds with hellfire. "Normal, hmmm? So either the probe's instrumentation was at fault, or else these eruptions are a fairly recent phenomenon." He looked at once satisfied and disappointed.

"That probably accounts for our strange 'signal.' Natural source after all. Volcanic eruptions can produce great bursts of short-lived electromagnetic discharge. I still think it's a mighty peculiar coincidence, but it's possible. Still, we're here. We might as well run a more thorough survey. Keep scanners on and recording, Mr. Sulu?"

"Yes, sir. Anything in particular you'd like to see on the screen?"

"There doesn't seem to be anything particular. No . . . ," he watched the changing images of tectonic belligerence. "I see nothing we haven't observed on a half-dozen similar worlds before. We'll run an equatorial survey. If our 'signal' doesn't repeat itself—and I'm not optimistic—we'll return to our planned mission." He glanced back at McCoy.

"You were right, Bones. There's nothing to waste our time on, here."

Actually, this was not entirely so. But at that point Kirk had seen no reason to think otherwise. Had he utilized the starship's high-resolution scopes on a certain area, however, he might have seen something interesting. A particularly protected, barren-looking valley, for example, dominated by towering crags of black and dirty gray, some of which were more ragged than others. Thick streams of viscous molten rock poured down their slopes. Occasionally a crisped-over river would crack, and harsh yellow light would flood the jumbled cliffs and crevasses.

A valley of utter desolation, then, no different from dozens the *Enterprise* had already passed over . . .

From an area to the north of a portion of rugged basalt, a beam of intense light suddenly leaped across the valley floor. Instead of a shard of broken, twisted stone, it struck a hemispheric, concave dish studded with curvilinear projections.

The dish was camouflaged, hidden, but the polished metal was clearly the work of something other than nature. Seconds, and then the twisted protuberances began to glow brightly. Slight motion and the dish readjusted itself. From the omphalos a powerful beam probed the ash-laden sky.

Simultaneously, the dish generated another beam, a twin of the one still locked on from across the valley. It disappeared into the distance. Kilometers away, another sky beam replied immediately. Another, and yet again as a webwork of light sprang up across the valley.

Soon the blasted landscape was a bouquet of cloud-piercing beams, all entwined in the atmosphere in a mysterious, purposeful pattern—a photonic macramé.

All the while, the lava fountains played on in more substantial counterpoint to the sudden eruption of light.

Kirk relaxed and turned, bored, from the viewscreen. He had orbited over plutonic landscapes before, over hell-worlds far more spectacular than the one below. He had toured with an Academy class through the Nix Olympica thermal power station on Mars. No, there was nothing here to hold them. The survey would take but a few minutes more.

"Let me know when we've completed initial orbit, Mr. Sulu. A single circuit should be enough."

"Aye, sir." Sulu studied instrument readouts, announced moments later: "Coming up on primary termination, sir."

Involved in winding up their scan, no one noticed the unusual frown that came slowly over Spock's face. Nor the even more unusual gesture that followed. He squinted. His attention was focused on a small readout set just above the main computer screen at the science station.

A gently weaving line there had abruptly produced a violent visual hiccup which sent the line shooting off the top of the screen. Spock jabbed a switch and the moving line froze instantly. Another dial was gently turned and the monitoring gauge ran the readout backwards.

Undeniably, something had given the scanner involved a severe jolt. A powerful jab, as if something had kicked into it from below.

He allowed the dial to snap all the way back. Once again the screen showed a pattern of standard wave disturbances, the easy flowing line. Spock touched another control and a still picture of the violent distortion appeared on the main screen. Isolated, but just possibly. . . .

"Captain, I have registered a prodigious wave-disturbance. An electronic impulse of some sort has just passed through the ship."

All hint of relaxation or lassitude gone, Kirk sat up straight in his chair. "Type and source?"

"Unidentified, unknown," the science officer replied tersely, still studying the readout. "It was a single brief burst, very sharp. If the source is still active, it's extremely faint and diffuse. Too much so to pinpoint while we continue orbit." He looked away from the viewer.

"I suggest we synchronize orbit with the surface at the impulse reception point, Captain, until the effects can be analyzed. Though there is no evidence of damage." He exchanged glances with his fellow officers.

"Bridge reports?"

Sulu made a quick check of the helm monitors. "All instruments functioning. Ship's condition is normal. All status lights green. No damage calls from any sections."

"Warning sensors stable," Uhura said, and Arex added, "External scans detect nothing abnormal, sir."

Kirk drummed fingers on the arm of his chair. It was a definitive rhythm which Sulu had been trying to identify ever since he had joined the *Enterprise*. Some day he would get it.

"You're sure it passed through the ship, Mr. Spock?"

Spock appeared mildly miffed. "Absolutely, Captain. A rapid burst of an unknown type of energy. It is the apparent generative power behind it which impels my concern."

Kirk grunted, hit a switch on the chair arm. "Bridge to Engineering." A wait, then, "Scotty, we just took an energy impulse of unknown type. How are your engines?"

"A moment, Cap'n." A longer wait while everyone on the bridge visualized Scott hurriedly checking half a hundred lights and gauges. The chief engineer's voice came over the bridge as he worked the intercom multiple.

"Davis?" he asked, talking to an unseen subordinate.

"Chief?"

"Any problems?"

"Problems, Chief? What kind of problems?"

"Thanks, Davis . . . that's what I wanted to know." Back

on the main com, now. ''Purrin' like kittens, Cap'n. Why, what's going on?''

"Probably nothing, Scotty, but keep a close eye on your telltales just the same.''

Scott sounded confused, but willing. "Will do, sir.''

Kirk tried a final possibility. After the inanimate machinery, there was one other component that required checking.

"Bridge to Sick Bay. Bones?''

"Here, Jim.''

"We've just taken an unidentified energy impulse. Any effect on the lab animals or crew?''

"No sudden sicknesses, if that's what you mean, Jim. Just a second and we'll check the lab animals. Christine?'' He looked around for his assistant.

"Doctor?'' she responded from her station.

"Time to check the guineas.''

Leaving her station, Nurse Chapel followed McCoy into one of the interconnecting lab rooms. This particular chamber boasted a double thick door. It was designed for holding both alien and domestic life-forms, from beings the size of a horse down to new viral strains. The present population was starship standard, small, and quietly spectacular.

To doctor and nurse, however, the flashy experimental animals were everyday acquaintances. McCoy went first to the modest aquarium.

Nothing could look more ordinary. Small stones, waving water plants and even a few decorative bits of coral offered naught to tease the eye. One had to look much closer to see that the sole occupant was most definitely not ordinary.

Rather like a cross between the tropical trumpet and angelfish of the warm Terran ocean, the single fish was beautiful enough. What turned it from beauteous to breath-taking was the extraordinary ring of rainbow light that encircled it completely from top to bottom, floating centimeters away from the body proper.

No one had yet figured out how the halo fish produced its remarkable Saturnian ring. Its brilliance shaded the phosphorescence of Terran deep-sea dwellers into dullness.

The importance of the tiny swimmer derived not from its ornamental value, however, but from its touchy disposition.

At the moment it swam placidly—and healthily—through its liquid abode.

McCoy examined the fish carefully while Chapel peered into several connecting cages filled with small creatures, paying particular attention to the large specimen in the far corner. The cages themselves were worthy of note, not just for their inhabitants, but because they were constructed entirely of black materials. Had they been of a lighter color, observation of any kind would be difficult if not impossible.

The little mammals inside were nearly transparent, to a far greater extent than the albino, sometimes translucent cave dwellers of Earth. Here was a true transparency, like fine quartz.

McCoy mumbled something at Chapel, and she shook her head. He pressed the lab intercom.

"McCoy again, Jim. Nothing in the experimental animals indicates anything out of the ordinary has happened. The gossamer mice show no signs of shock, and our halo fish . . ."

"Halo fish, Bones?"

"We acquired them two visits ago at Star Base Science Center. The ones that lose all color at the least environmental shift? They're as radiant and healthy looking as ever."

"You sure, Bones? Isn't it possible that something subtle could affect them without their showing any signs?"

"Not in these two species, Jim. But wait a second and I'll double-check." He beckoned to Chapel and indicated the aquarium. She walked over, rolling back one sleeve on her uniform.

Carefully, she slipped her hand into the water just above the slowly swimming fish. As soon as her fingers contacted the surface, the multicolored ring vanished and the zebraic array of colors on the body turned a pale white to blend in with the white sand bottom of the tank. When she pulled her arm from the water, both ring and colors returned.

"No, Jim. The animals are healthy. No sign of any disturbance."

"Good to hear. Thanks, Bones." He clicked off and turned to Spock, more relieved than he cared to show. "Your mystery wave seems harmless enough, Spock. You may as well continue your analysis while we conclude orbit. We'll hold here another few minutes.

"Mr. Arex, summarize sensor sweeps, please."

"Commencing condensation, sir. Condensation completed."

"Further detail on surface conditions?"

Arex studied his viewer, now linked to the *Enterprise*'s elaborate system of computer cells. "Sensor scans show a far more unstable surface than the old drone probe reported, Captain. Activity appears to be increasing almost exponentially. We may have arrived in time to witness a major blowup, though we do not have enough information to know for certain whether such a cataclysm is cyclic or extraordinary.

"Both eruptive and steady-flow disturbances are present. Given the current rate of tectonic activity, the emission of subterranean noxious gases will render the oxy-nitrogen atmosphere unbreathable in a few decades."

McCoy had hurried to the bridge, curious as to what had prompted Kirk's tense check of their life-systems status. Now he studied the main viewscreen and commented, "Not that it looks very inviting right now."

"What about composition, Mr. Arex?" Kirk went on. Pronounced seismic activity often brought other, more interesting things to a planetary surface than poisonous gases. Heavy metals, for example.

"Composition appears normal, Captain," the navigator replied, turning his gaze back to the viewer. "As far as evidence of ore-bearing formations is concerned, I believe . . . ," his voice changed unexpectedly, "Captain . . . a light below. It appears to be shifting. I think . . . ."

And then he was staggering back from his console, clutching at his narrow face. "My eyes . . . !"

The suddenness of the outburst had shocked everyone into immobility . . . doubly shocked them, coming as it had from the near-whispering Arex. Then Sulu rose to help his friend. Grabbing at the steadying support of the helmsman with one hand, Arex kept his other two over his eyes.

Meanwhile, Spock's eyes had been affected, too. The reason Sulu had been first to Arex's aid was because the science officer had been stunned by the abrupt explosion of lines on the upper screen—lines similar to the one that had so troubled him when it first passed through the ship moments ago.

Now the sensor in question was receiving that subtle, powerful impulse at a steady, unwinking rate.

"Captain," Spock said anxiously, "we are now under a non-communications beam of some potency. Its effects cannot . . ."

"Sound red alert!" Kirk ordered before the first officer could finish. He had no access to Arex's viewer, no sight of Spock's gauges. But the reaction of his navigator coupled with Spock's sudden announcement was sufficient to tell him something was definitely wrong.

"Uhura . . . !"

The lieutenant was moving too rapidly to obey. Her hand shot toward the alarm switch, stopped before she could reach it. Something froze her in her seat. Froze Kirk in the command chair. Froze Arex and Sulu standing together, Spock at his station—froze everyone on the *Enterprise*.

Simultaneously the crew, their instruments, even the walls of the ship flared with a pale white luminescence. It was as if the ship were burning in the grasp of a cold white flame. They could hear a deep ringing sound, like the single toll of some great ancient bell.

Scott and Gabler were discussing the repair of a recalcitrant section of the ship's reclamation machinery when that awesome groan rolled through the ship. They stopped arguing—and moving.

In the main mess hall, hundreds of diners from the second shift were at mid-meal when all motion ceased and the light turned to creamy white.

It was the same from one end of the starship to the other—from Hydroponics to Astrophysics, from recreation rooms to sleeping quarters, from the salvage hold to the synaptic study center.

The *Enterprise* had been neatly pinned like a metal butterfly on a blackboard. It hung enveloped in an icy radiance produced by many beams erupting on the surface, forming an intricate webbing around the pinioned ship—a webbing woven by the multiple dish antennae that pockmarked the floor of a certain barren valley far below.

Trapped in that spectral radiance, the *Enterprise* drifted for long moments. Then the tired landscape below convulsed in a tremendous eruption. Several of the beams vanished as automatic antennae were thrown off their mounts. Others were buried by a steady avalanche of magmatic material.

With its interdependent, complex pattern broken, the rest of the beams shut down. On the *Enterprise*'s bridge, the last reverberations of that thunderous peal died away. There was a brief moment of uncertainty as the ship lights flickered and finally steadied. They were somewhat dimmer than normal, but showed no sign of weakening further.

In the absence of sound there was motion, as those on the bridge began the comforting routine of checking first themselves and then their instruments for internal malfunctioning. Even Arex, still blinking away streaks from his sensitive eyes, was back at his station, hunting for the source of the surprise assault on their senses.

A good conductor keeps an eye and ear on tempo and rhythm but lets his players play. Kirk waited until his people had had a little time to sort themselves out before asking formally, "Anyone hurt here?"

A stream of murmured "No, sirs" came back to him from various seats. Uhura, Sulu, Arex, McCoy, Spock. He considered, made one concerned inquiry.

"Are you sure, Lieutenant Arex?"

The navigator looked back over his shoulder, the assurance of a dozen years in the fleet showing in every syllable. "I'm quite all right now, sir. I was only temporarily stunned, and most of that was surprise. There appear to be no lingering effects."

"All right, Lieutenant. Just the same," he continued firmly, "as soon as we revert from alert status, I want you to report to Sick Bay for an eye checkup."

"I was just about to order that myself, Jim," McCoy added. He looked over at the navigator. "You're positive there are no aftereffects, Lieutenant? No blurring of vision, strong retinal images?"

"No, sir," Arex told him. "I think—evidence supports it—that if there were any dangerous radiations in whatever hit me, the scope's sensors automatically screened them out."

"Let's hope so," the doctor muttered. Behind him, Kirk could hear Uhura talking rapidly over the intership com.

"All sections report in. Damage and casualties. All sections report in . . . damage and cas . . ."

Kirk had a sudden thought, caught Sulu's attention. "Mr. Sulu, any deviation in our orbit?"

"No, sir. Maintaining standard elliptical orbit. All instruments functioning normally." He looked back worriedly. "But we've been operating on impulse power since that whatever it was hit us."

Uhura broke in before Kirk could pursue the power situation further. "I have first damage reports coming in, Captain."

"Put them over the main speaker, Lieutenant."

"Aye, sir." In a second the bridge was filled with the consecutive voices of various section chiefs, some confused, some slightly panicked, some admirably calm—all uniform.

"Mess section, no damage."

"Repair section intact."

"Cargo hold here, Captain, no damage observed."

And so on. Everyone had seen the white glow, recoiled under the ringing drone, been frozen in place. But there had not been any real damage. Not a broken eardrum or loosened plate seam. Odd.

Spock glanced up from his console, spoke quietly. "Captain, we are still receiving radiation from the surface, but it is greatly reduced—and altered. A most peculiar type. Our deflector shields are proving ineffective."

Kirk nodded quickly. "We just had ample demonstration of that. Let me know the second there's any increase in the intensity, Mr. Spock."

"Very well, sir." Spock returned to his instruments.

Kirk considered. After making sure to his own satisfaction that Arex was at least temporarily fit, McCoy had headed back for Sick Bay. He ought to be there any minute. Kirk pressed the intercom switch.

"Nurse Chapel here, sir," came the instant reply. "The doctor . . . he's coming in now, Captain." McCoy's deeper voice on the com, now.

"Sorry, Jim. Just finishing a quick check of my own.

We've no casualties reported at all. Arex appears to have been the only one even slightly affected by the attack.''

"Why 'attack,' Bones?'' Kirk wondered. "We've suffered no damage and no casualties. It might have been a natural phenomenon.''

"Call it my inherent pessimism, Jim. Anyhow, ineffectuality of method doesn't negate intent. Though I'll admit to the chance that it was some random freak of tectonic activity. If that's what it was. I don't suppose . . .''

"As yet we've no idea what it was,'' Kirk told him.

"So then it wasn't completely harmless.''

"Not hardly,'' Kirk observed. "Let me know if anyone walks in with any strange symptoms, Bones.'' A light was flashing on the arm console. "Scotty wants in. Kirk out.''

"Sick Bay out.''

McCoy flicked off the intercom and turned to Chapel.

"No one seems to have been injured, Christine. Let's hope it stays that way. Meanwhile, you can dig out the tape file on Arex for me. Also the ophthalmological standards and charts for adult Edoans.''

"Yes, Doctor.''

Engineer Scott turned and yelled instructions, liberally laced with suitable comments on certain probable ancestries, up at the four technicians who were running on the catwalk above him. Then he turned his attention back to the intercom as a beep told him it was clear.

"Engineerin' here, Cap'n.''

"Let's have the details, Scotty. I know we're running on impulse power. Anybody hurt?''

"No casualties, Cap'n,'' Scott reported, breathing heavily. He had been doing considerable shouting and running, often at the same time. "But trouble aplenty with the engines. Every dilithium crystal's smashed in the warp-drive circuitry. Damnedest thing I ever saw. We're trying to rig a temporary bypass for them now.''

"The main circuits, too?'' Kirk asked incredulously.

"*What* main circuits?'' Scott countered tiredly. "You have to see it to believe it, sir.'' He shook his head. "The big crystals in there have all come apart. Each of them fractured and re-fractured and re-re-fractured along its natural lines of cleavage until there's nothin' left but powder. Try to imagine an elephant steppin' on an opal, sir.''

"What about spares, Mr. Scott?"

"I said *all*, sir. Even the spares. Whatever it was took a whack at us didn't seem to much care whether they were activated or not.''

"And the other drive components?" Kirk asked, determined to know the worst.

"Nothin', sir. Only what shorted out when the activated crystals were pulverized. No problem replacin' them. Whatever hit us was damnably selective, Cap'n.''

Somewhere in Scott's report, Kirk mused as he switched out, was the answer to the impulse beam they'd absorbed—and were still absorbing, according to Spock. He looked across the deck, found the first officer watching him.

"Though couched in emotional terms it would appear that Dr. McCoy's supposition may have some basis in fact," Spock ventured. "If this is truly a natural phenomenon, it has certainly chosen a sensitive portion of the ship to attack. Nor have I ever heard of dilithium crystals being affected in the way Mr. Scott described.''

Kirk rose from his seat and started for the elevator. Spock followed. "We haven't *seen* it, either, Mr. Spock. But it seems that we're going to.''

The chief engineer was waiting for them. They went to a small open hatch, stared into one of the dilithium holding cases for backup supplies.

"Not only is this situation different from anythin' I've ever seen, Cap'n," Scott was telling them, "but even if I had ever imagined dilithium breaking up, I wouldn't have visualized it happenin' like this.''

"How so, Scotty?" Kirk asked.

"Well, sir, I would expect them all to go at once. Instead, whatever blasted us appears just to have initiated the process. The crystals are still in the act of disintegratin'. It's a steady process.''

Moments later they stood before one of the operative grids. Scott made sure all activating circuits were inoperative, opened the double door and stepped back. Tiny crackling sounds, like glass popcorn, issued from within.

Staring inside, Spock and Kirk could see clearly what was

left of one of the large dilithium crystals that not long ago had helped power the *Enterprise*. It had been reduced to a small pebble. And what was left was shedding tiny curlicues of itself, adding to the growing pile of dust in the grid. The curlicues were unique. Dilithium was the only mineral known subject to spiral fracture.

Kirk reached in, extracted a pinch of red-white powder. He studied the dust and tried to feel optimistic. The dust mocked his best efforts.

"This isn't going to power a toothbrush, much less the drive." He put the powder in Spock's outstretched palm and turned, heading for the engineering library. While Kirk and Scott looked on, Spock dropped the bit of dust into a depression set into one console. One switch sealed the depression; others activated the computer. Instructions were given.

"Any hope of recombining the powder into one or two usable crystals, Mr. Scott?" Kirk asked as they waited for the computer's verdict.

The chief engineer shook his head. "I know what you're thinkin', Captain, but the physicist who did that made a one in a million combination of heat and pressure work and he wasn't sure afterward exactly how he'd done it. It might take us a hundred years to grow one crystal from this powder.

"You can't play with dilithium like modeling clay. Too much of its peculiar potential is locked in sub-atomic structures. Even if we wanted to try it we haven't got the facilities here.

"No, Cap'n. Our only hope of gettin' out of here and back to a refuelin' station is a recirculatin' impulse from our stored emergency power cells—what's left of it. But before we can try that there are broken connections and linkages all over the place that have to be fixed."

Kirk looked thoughtful, considering their options. "Could we possibly . . . ," but he was interrupted by an anxious voice at the computer console.

"Captain, this is quite unprecedented."

For Spock to say something like that it would have to be, Kirk mused, as he and Scott moved close to the instrumentation.

Spock had removed the sample of powdered dilithium from its holder and, following the directions of the computer, placed some of it under an electronic scope. He was peering into it now, but stepped aside so Kirk and Scott could have a look. Kirk put his eyes to the scope . . . and sacrificed a breath.

What had prompted Spock's typically understated comment was instantly apparent under the brilliantly illuminated circular field.

Dilithium was the only metallic substance whose molecules were arranged in helical instead of linear or linear-variant form. Now, even as he watched, the molecules were unwinding in various places, the chains spinning apart. In other molecules the chains were winding tighter and tighter until they broke apart, and then the fragments would begin to unwind or tighten.

In either case the resultant substance was no longer active dilithium.

This made his thin hopes of a minute ago obsolete. Even if they did manage to stumble across the near-magical process for recombining dilithium, soon there wouldn't be any honest dilithium shards left to recombine. Almost as remarkable was the fact that the breakdown was occurring without a hint of subsidiary radiation. It was a clean disintegration.

"Fracturing is spiroform," Spock went on, "as it has been theorized it would be. But it has never been observed to occur in an inorganic material like dilithium before—only in similarly built organic molecules."

Kirk leaned back from the scope, came down off his tiptoes. His mind was occupied by the impossibility just observed—otherwise he might have noticed what he had just done. He could be pardoned. It was the spiral structure that made dilithium the most rigid, stable. . . .

III

Kirk's thoughts were broken by the nearing voice of second engineer Gabler. He spoke while walking quickly toward them.

"Mr. Scott, more trouble with the circuitry clearance. It's just that . . ."

"Blast," the chief engineer muttered. "What now?" He moved to the railing, looked down across the floor. "Now what, Mr. Gabler?"

"It's the tools, sir," Gabler yelled back up at them. "They're too big for us to handle."

Several other members of the engineering section came into view. All held up wrenches, pliers, liquid circuit welders and sliders and molly-pugs. All appeared awkwardly large in their hands.

Scott didn't know whether to be confused or furious. If this were some kind of elaborate joke on the part of his section, at a time like this . . .

"You sound like you're all of you blatherin' . . . no, wait a minute. Let's have a look." After what they'd just learned about dilithium molecules fracturing, he wasn't about to deny the possibility of anything. He moved to the nearest ladder and started down.

"That's an odd thing for Gabler to say," Kirk mused. Then he found himself frowning, staring. It seemed as if something were not quite right about Spock, all of a sudden. Nothing obtrusive—the first officer looked perfectly healthy.

Then why this sense of vague unease when he looked at him?

For his part, Spock's reaction was a dulled mirror of Kirk's

38

own. He was eyeing the captain, both eyebrows raised, an expression he reserved for more than idle occasions.

Kirk's frown deepened. He gestured at the computer console Spock was standing by, blinked. The light that had momentarily blinded Arex—was there some subtle variant of it at work in the ship now?

"Spock, are you slumping?"

"I've never slumped in my life, Captain," the science officer replied with considerable dignity. "But it is most peculiar. I was just about to ask you the exact same . . ."

"Security!" The violent call issued from the open intercom. "Any security, respond!"

Kirk rushed to the comm, reached to turn it to broadcast and had to stand on tiptoes to do it. What was wrong with Spock, what was troubling Gabler—he was astonished at how calm he was in the face of the dawning catastrophe. Maybe it was the fact that, physically, he still *felt* fine. Or it might be shock.

"Kirk here. What's the trouble?"

His steady tone apparently reassured the voice at the other end of the line. It responded crisply, less hysterically.

"Mess Officer Briel, sir." The young officer was clearly trying to calm herself with the captain on the line.

"What's going on, Briel? Speak up—what's that noise behind you?"

"It's the second shift, sir. They're nervous and frightened and so am I. We need psycho assistance in the main dining area. At least, I think we need psycho. Maybe it's just me. Or maybe I just . . ." The voice was rising again and Kirk's tone turned hard, sharp, no-nonsense.

"Easy, Briel. I think I know what you're experiencing."

The voice was still tense, but the relief was audible.

"You do, sir? I wish you'd tell me. Tables, chairs, silverware—everything seems to have grown larger, too large to use. Women are losing their rings, hairpins . . . everything. The people here are near panic, Captain, and I don't know what to tell them. I'm the ranking officer present and I . . ."

"Do your best to quiet everyone, Sub-lieutenant. Get up on a table—if you can still reach it—and make an announcement. Tell everyone we're passing through a distorting field phenomenon. We don't know how far it'll reduce us, but we will eventually return to normal. Meantime everyone is to improvise. Tell them to use their imaginations.''

''Thank you, sir,'' came the much-eased voice of the mess officer. ''I'll do that. Frankly, sir, I was beginning to get more than a little . . .''

''Don't waste time, Briel, or you'll have your full panic. Relay the information to Lieutenant Uhura and instruct her for me to broadcast it throughout the ship. Quicker dissemination that way.''

And also, he thought, the responsibility would take the sub-lieutenant's mind off her own fears.

''Aye, sir. Mess out.''

Kirk clicked off, noticing Spock still staring at him.

''Well, what are you goggling at, Spock?''

''You lie with great facility, Captain.''

''You have this constant aberration in which you persist in confusing diplomacy with prevarication, Spock,'' he shot back. ''Let's get back to the bridge. Scotty will have to handle things by himself here.''

Having absolutely no idea what to expect, their shock as they returned to the bridge was magnified severalfold.

At first glance it appeared that the *Enterprise* was being manned by a group of well-drilled children. All crew members were sitting on the fore edge of their seats. It was the only way they could still reach the controls. Heads swiveled as Kirk and Spock entered.

Uhura started in immediately. ''Captain, reports are coming in from all over the ship. The most incredible thing is happening.''

''We know,'' he broke in. ''The whole ship and every*thing* on board has apparently expanded.''

''An equally good possibility, Captain,'' hypothesized Spock, ''is that the ship's personnel have contracted.'' He moved toward his library computer station and surveyed the abruptly oversized surroundings thoughtfully.

''And are probably continuing to shrink.''

A moment of shocked silence on the bridge—somehow the idea that the *Enterprise* and its inorganic components were growing larger was merely ridiculously inconvenient, while the concept of the crew growing smaller held terrifying portents.

There was an element of grimness in Kirk's voice that hadn't been heard in some time as he turned to Sulu.

"Take us out of orbit, Mr. Sulu. Take us far out of here. Shut down all unnecessary systems . . . everything but defense and life-support. Draw on every ounce of remaining impulse power. We've got to get away from this planet."

Sulu and Arex worked furiously at the helm-navigation console. Occasionally they were forced to shift awkwardly in their seats to reach a particularly distant control. There was a mild rising hum as fresh power was fed to the ship's engines, then a tense pause.

"Mr. Spock?"

"We're shifting position, Captain, but slowly."

A red light appeared on the console to the right of Sulu's hand. He eyed it, ignored it.

"Still moving, Captain," reported Spock patiently.

Gradually, painfully, the single red light by Sulu was joined by others. A brief hooting whistle sounded near Arex. He slapped a hand down on a switch and the hooting stopped. Sulu gave his companion a questioning glance. Arex bent to his hooded viewer, studied its contents for a moment. Then he pulled away and gazed at each of the watching, expectant faces in turn.

"It's no good, Captain. The engines are completely dead."

"Confirmed, Captain," Spock added, studying readouts. "We simply do not have enough dilithium left in the holding grids to activate the matter–anti-matter annihilation sequence. We retain enough emergency power to maintain basic life and internal ship functions, but nowhere near enough to drive the ship."

"Not even enough for a last try?" Kirk asked desperately.

"It would be foolhardy, Captain. The chances are on the order of thousands to one . . . and we would surely lose life-support."

"Then that," Kirk murmured fatalistically, "is that." He glanced down toward his feet, shook his head and mumbled something Uhura strained to hear but couldn't. Then he thumbed a well-worn switch in the chair arm.

"Captain's Log, 5525.4. Our attempt to escape this world's gravity on limited power has failed after the ship's dilithium

supplies have been wiped out. We are currently in a . . . ,''
he glanced over at Arex. The navigator hid several controls.

Up to now the image on the main viewscreen had been a
moving panorama of the planet's glittering surface. Now it
shifted briefly to show a dull chart of the world with a blinking red dot floating nearby—the *Enterprise*. Kirk nodded and
Arex banished the chart back to distant cells of memory. The
roiling surface picture returned.

". . . low but stable elliptical orbit. Main engines and
circuitry are one hundred percent incapacitated.'' Again a
look to the library station.

"Mr. Spock, what about that diffuse wave bombardment?''

Spock checked his viewer, barely able to reach it now.
"We're still receiving a light amount, Captain, but it shows
no sign of thinning further.''

"Thank you, Mr. Spock.'' He spoke into the Log pickup
again. "Unidentified radiation bombardment continues, resulting in either a contraction of our bodies or an expansion
of the ship by a factor of . . . ,'' he glanced to Spock again
and the science officer held up three fingers, ". . . by a factor
of three.'' He switched off the recorder.

"Lieutenant Uhura, broadcast a general mayday.''

"Aye, sir.''

"Lieutenant Sulu, I know how precarious our reserve
power situation is. But see if you can't compute something
that would give us a little higher orbit without risking a fatal
drain on the reserves.''

"I'll try, sir.''

"Arex,'' Kirk's voice remained brisk and businesslike,
"give me a power reading on all backup cells.''

As everyone on the bridge busied himself about his immediate tasks, Kirk sat back in the command chair . . . and
discovered he couldn't even do that. He'd shrunk—or the ship
had expanded—to the point that the chair no longer fit him
easily.

He glanced over at Spock and studied the first officer in
relationship to his surroundings. Assuming he was right and
they were contracting, they now averaged about a meter and
a third in height.

Then he stared tensely up at the main viewscreen and the

glowing, angry landscape brought in close by the telephotos. Normally it would have been enough to examine the giant volcanoes, the lava lakes and strange movement in the burning, tortured crust. But now he found himself straining for sight of something more.

His first theory—that they'd been subjected to some unexpected burst of natural radiation—was being rapidly eroded. What natural effect would hit them for a microsecond with no discernible effect, come back full force, and then suddenly change to a steady low-power beaming?

But what if Bones was right and they were under attack? What kind of an enemy were they up against—and why? What could their tormentors want? There had been no attempt to contact the *Enterprise*. The only explanation that seemed logical was that the world below held a low-population race—living underground, perhaps—that was inherently inimical to all outsiders. They are other than us, therefore they are to be destroyed was the usual rationale of such races.

Yet how could they know that the *Enterprise* contained creatures different from themselves? A problem, he reflected, that had plagued mankind throughout much of his own history. If they were under assault by an intelligent civilization, its founders must have a philosophical orientation radically different from the Federation's. Kirk watched the surface they hovered over, watched it trying to tear itself to pieces, watched and tried to visualize what kinds of beings it could support.

What they must look like.

Sulu's voice roused him from contemplation. "New parameters established, sir." The helmsman sounded pleased with himself. Considering the miniscule amount of power he'd had to draw upon and the effect he'd achieved with it, he had reason to be.

"Our perigee has been raised by a significant amount."

Kirk made a positive gesture. At least they didn't have to worry about losing altitude until they crashed into the boiling crust below.

They could sit up *here* and rot.

Uhura's report was less encouraging. "No reply to our universal mayday, sir. I don't believe we have enough power left to push a signal to Star Base Twenty-three. And there's no reason to expect any other ships to be in this region.''

Kirk nodded somberly. "All right. Keep trying, Lieutenant." He glanced to the library. "Spock, anything new on the wave bombardment we're taking?"

The first officer looked up and shrugged slightly. "Only that it is complex beyond anything in my scientific experience. As a weapon it would appear to be not only extraordinarily effective, but the product of a devious mass mind. And yet, there are psychological overtones that make me wonder. . . ."

"It's the physical ones I'm concerned with at the moment, Mr. Spock."

Scott's voice came over the ship com.

"Engineering to Captain Kirk."

"Kirk here," he acknowledged. "How are you doing back there, Mr. Scott?"

The chief engineer didn't try to hide the exhaustion in his voice. "We've replaced all the damaged circuitry and by-passed what we can't replace or repair."

"Will they hold up if we have to press them, Scotty?"

"Well enough, Captain. That's not the problem. We can only run so long on impulse power before the emergency cells go. Then it's restart the reaction chambers or . . . The well will run dry soon enough, sir."

"I know, Scotty. You've done what you can. Kirk out." He considered. Somehow they had to conserve even more power. They might have to try a last breakout, Spock's warning notwithstanding. Then they would need every erg the reserve cells could muster.

"Uhura, reduce mayday signal repetition. One broadcast per ten-minute cycle."

"Reduce range, too, Captain?"

"No." Frequency would have to do. "Maximum signal strength for the isolated broadcasts . . . otherwise they'll be worse than useless."

"Yes, sir."

"Mr. Arex, cut down on all sensor sweeps of the planet."

"Visual sweeps are already impossible, Captain," the navigator told him. He gestured at his finder—*up* at his finder. "My eyes no longer properly fit the optical pickups."

"And I can't reach the dial I turned five minutes ago," added Uhura, a rising note of alarm in her voice. She was reaching for the control in question, stretching on tiptoe and still falling short.

Damnation! If they didn't shrink much more they could cope. But if they continued to lose height? He had had no compunctions about having the deflector shields turned off—they had proven useless anyway. If they couldn't break out of orbit and remained under the influence of the mysterious radiation, would they contract to the point where they could no longer operate the controls?

He was hunting for a miracle in a fog. What do you do in a fog first? Stay in one place, he reminded himself, and establish some reference points.

He hit the intercom again. "Kirk to Sick Bay."

"Sick Bay," came the familiar response, worried now. "Sick Bay . . . McCoy here, Jim."

"Bones, I've *got* to have some answers. I know what's happening to us—what I must know is how, and why."

"Come down to the lab, Jim. Spock too. I was just going to call you. I may have something . . ."

Despite the fact that they ran, Kirk and Spock took much longer than usual to reach the lab. Not that they moved any more awkwardly, or that their strength was sapped, but they were now less than a meter tall. Sheer distance was making it more time consuming simply to get around the ship.

McCoy had to call out before they spotted him. The doctor was standing part way up a metal stepping stool, necessary now if he was to reach the instruments on the counter above. The cabinets above the counter proper were as much out of his reach as the planetary surface.

He gestured at the laser scope on the counter, then stepped down to make room for Kirk. Fortunately, the device had a swivel eyepiece which could be tilted down as well as up. Kirk glanced in, feeling uncomfortable at the unnatural size of the scope lenspiece.

The slide was a hybrid, two sections joined side by side. The difference between the healthy stable tissue and the radiation-poisoned tissue was obvious.

Nonetheless, McCoy explained helpfully: "That's the test

tissue I've been using on the right, Jim. From my arm, not that it matters. The stabilized normal tissue is on the left.''

Kirk studied the accusing slide a moment longer before muttering, ''Then Spock's theory is confirmed.'' He didn't look away from the scope. ''We're contracting.''

''No question about it, Jim. That's why our weight remains about the same, and why we haven't gone floating up to the ceiling with every step. The number of atoms remains the same. The wave bombardment is simply causing them to tighten, reducing the diameter of electron orbits. Just like the dilithium. Not to the shattering point, though—I guess organic structures have more resilience. Otherwise we would start breaking up like glass figurines. At least, I don't *think* the shrinkage will get that extreme.'' He looked uncertainly to Spock.

''Though I can't really make any assurances about an effect that's never been observed before.''

''Agreed,'' the first officer said. ''A most unique phenomenon. It is quite interesting. I should like to study it at more leisure . . .''

''Except that we haven't got any leisure time left,'' McCoy finished grimly.

''An accurate if not particularly scientific description, Doctor. I believe the process is accelerating.''

Kirk finally turned away from the depressing evidence displayed by the scope. Obvious perversions of nature held a horrible inevitability about them that no amount of rationalizing could dispell.

''How long could it keep on?''

Spock stared around the lab as he reflected on the captain's question, the lab which had assumed the proportions of a coliseum.

''Perhaps infinitely. Considering that the distance between electron orbits and nuclei is relatively as great as the distances between suns, even if the rate of reduction continues to increase it should take some time before we . . . disappear entirely.''

There was numbed silence in the lab.

''Dr. McCoy.''

They turned as Nurse Chapel appeared from behind a row of cages. ''It's the experimental animals, Doctor. They're getting too small to be contained by some of the cages, the ones with wire mesh walls. All the gossamers are out already.''

She held up one of the transparent quasi-rodents for them to stare at. It was perfectly proportioned and the proper size compared to the rest of them.

''Look how tiny they've gotten,'' she went on. ''Just like the halo fish. It's tadpole size now.'' She looked back and pointed up toward the aquarium. They could still discern the sensitive swimmer, spectacularly colored as always, its satellite circlet fluorescing brightly—though now it was barely the size of a finger ring.

''And that,'' noted McCoy sarcastically, ''is supposed to be a creature sensitive to the tiniest changes in environment.'' He snorted. ''So much for the confident dictates of Starfleet Medical Center.''

''Don't be too hard on them, Doctor,'' Spock advised. ''No one could have foreseen our present remarkable situation.''

McCoy took several deep breaths and eyed Spock significantly. The science officer's attention had been diverted elsewhere, however. He was staring at a large band of metal which dangled from nurse Chapel's arm. He fingered the double twist of shiny alloy curiously.

''Christine, what is the composition of this decoration?''

Chapel blinked, looked down at her arm. ''It was made for my by the Knight Smiths of Libra IV. It's a common piece of costume jewelry.'' She lowered her arm and the now greatly oversized circle of metal slid off easily. The arm bracelet was more like a necklace now.

''What about it, Spock?'' queried McCoy. ''I didn't know you were interested in jewelry of any kind.''

''A moment please, Doctor. It is not its aesthetic qualities which intrigue me at the moment. Knight metal alloy,'' he repeated cryptically. ''An artificial construct. Yet the uniform on which it rested fits as well as ever. Your uniform, all of our uniforms, is woven from algae-based xenylon, I believe.''

''Naturally. All regular Starfleet-issue work uniforms are made of xenylon,'' McCoy observed, still not seeing what the first officer was driving at. But Kirk was only a couple of steps behind Spock and catching up rapidly.

"I think I see what you mean, Spock. They've all been shrinking proportionately with us, so. . . ."

"Exactly, Captain. I would be assured my theory is fact . . ." He was staring up at the aquarium, suddenly started towards the table it sat on. "One more example, I think."

Then he was climbing up the stool. Stretching, he reached into the water and brought out a small piece of floating coral which had become detached from the main mass. He examined it briefly before nodding to the others.

"The animals, the living corals, have contracted along with us—and so have their organically based limestone homes. Yet the rest of the material in the aquarium, the rocks on the bottom, remain unchanged and normal sized."

"I see. So that confirms it, then—only organic matter is affected," McCoy said. "But then how . . . ?"

"Remember, Doctor," Spock went on, climbing down from the stool, "the wave impulses cause only spiral molecules to wind tight. The only inorganic spiral molecular chains we know of are those which form crystalline dilithium. Which is actually analagous in structure to one we are quite close to."

"The doubled DNA helix in the nucleus of every cell in our bodies," Kirk recited, echoing a line from Academy biology. The remembrance was small comfort. He frowned. "I suppose we ought to consider ourselves lucky, Bones. Some of the dilithium crystals self-destructed when their internal structure unwound instead of contracting. If we were subjected to the same stresses we would all be puddles of jelly on the deck by now."

McCoy shrugged. "It's all the same in the end, Jim. I'm not sure that I wouldn't prefer that to being a candidate for a flea circus."

Kirk had a thought, hiked over to the computer console. "Bones, what happens when DNA is compacted to its ultimate limits?"

"I don't think the strands would break, Jim, as Spock says." He walked over to stand next to the Captain. "I guess they just stop winding."

"Well then, if that's the case, we can calculate the limits of our shrinkage. It shouldn't be infinite."

"It is possible," conceded Spock. "I'll feed the question to the library."

Kirk and McCoy wrestled with the stool set near the scope until it was set close to the computer console. Spock climbed up, carefully walked out onto the sensitive keyboard. The keys were now hand instead of thumb size. But he had no trouble depressing them.

"Something else that we had better calculate just occurred to me," Kirk yelled upward. "How long can we expect to maintain effective control of the ship?"

"I have considered that question also, Captain. The computer will project a point beyond which the systems switches and controls will be beyond our ability to operate efficiently.

"I might also add, Captain, that we had better take care where and how we walk. Remember, our weight remains approximately the same despite our smaller size. It is therefore concentrated on a smaller supportive surface. It would be dangerous to walk out on a glass surface, for example. We would tend to go right through it.

"It appears the calculations will take some time."

"Stick with it, Spock. I'm going back to the bridge."

"And I think I'd better make some preparations, Jim," McCoy told him. "At the rate we're contracting there're going to be some accidents soon. Maybe not quite the kind Spock is thinking of, but related."

"Check, Bones. Spock, report the moment you have some results."

"Yes, Captain."

The walk back to the bridge felt like a hike of kilometers, even though Kirk was expecting it. He was also expecting a new view of the bridge. Even so, his first glimpse of what had become a giant's playground was shocking. He walked slowly toward the towering command chair, thinking furiously . . .

While minutes and centimeters continued to tick away, the entire scientific complement of the *Enterprise* worked overtime trying to find a way to reverse, or at least halt the contraction that was literally taking their mastery of the ship away from them.

They knew the cause . . . the strange faint radiation from the surface they could not run away from. They could now calculate their rate of shrinkage. But no solution offered itself. They couldn't even identify the type of radiation.

The intercom buzzed insistently for attention. Kirk reached over to acknowledge the call, missed and had to readjust his reach. His arms had grown shorter in the last hour. That was the most frustrating aspect of the shrinkage effect. You had to constantly readjust your senses to a new size. A few crewmembers were reacting so badly to the constant change they had to be sent to McCoy for sedation.

"Spock here, Captain," came the voice at the other end. It was totally unreasonable to hope that the science officer had found any miracle solutions, but Spock had done it before. Unfortunately, this didn't look to be one of those times. The report was consistent only in its pessimism.

"Not only does our rate of contraction show no sign of halting, Captain, but it appears it may continue beyond our ability to adapt to it."

Still thinking about missing the intercom switch a moment ago, Kirk shot back, "How long can we anticipate retaining ship control, Mr. Spock?"

"I would say," the thoughtful reply went on, "that even with our most intensive miniaturizing measures and ability to design new compact backup systems, we will loose effective control of this vessel at the point when we become approximately one centimeter tall." There was a pause, then, "My present height is something like a third of a meter, Captain.

"I am coming forward to utilize the fuller resources of the library computer station . . . for as long as I can continue to operate it. Spock out."

"Kirk out."

IV

The next hour was a hectic race against rapidly increasing odds—reducing odds, actually—as the *Enterprise*'s construction engineers worked frantically to fashion an endless stream of ingenious, yet ultimately useless miniaturized apparatus.

Ladders mounted on wheels and built of metal strips; long clamp poles and flex tubes for manipulating simultaneous dials and switches now far out of reach—a host of intricate devices.

It was, expectedly, a losing battle. Eventually all operations and energies above bare life-support maintenance were directed toward retaining control in two sections . . . the bridge and Engineering.

Kirk leaned back and stared up at the cliff of the library computer station where Spock was running back and forth manipulating controls with tireless energy. But even with adroit manipulation of the new, miniature handling tools, Kirk could see that the first officer could not keep it up much longer.

Eventually he would grow so small he wouldn't be able to read the gargantuan printouts. He was minutes from losing the ability to use the hooded viewer.

"You said one centimeter was the critical point, Spock?"

Spock came to the edge, leaned over carefully and shouted down, "I beg your pardon, Captain?"

"When will we reach the critical one centimeter point?"

"At the present rate of compaction I should estimate in thirty-two minutes, Captain."

Kirk nodded, acknowledging the inevitable, then remembered an as yet unanswered question.

"How small will we ultimately shrink, Mr. Spock?"

"One moment, Captain." Spock turned his attention back to the instrument panel. Surveying the angular field of levers and switches, he mapped out a plan of attack. Starting with a red triangle close by he hopscotched his way across the controls. His only real worry was that his concentrated weight might shatter them, but fortunately the high-impact styrene remained intact.

Seconds passed. Then a billboard-sized series of figures appeared on the first screen in front of him. Spock studied them briefly, then marched back to the edge of the console. It wasn't the kind of answer he liked to give.

"There is not sufficient information to calculate our final reduction limit with any precision, Captain. I do have a projection on the time required for full analysis of the spiroid wave phenomenon, though, which could lead to a solution and method for reversing the process."

"That's great, Spock . . . follow it up!"

"I would, Captain, but there is one difficulty. The time required for such analysis is estimated at between seven and eight years. As we have perhaps several hours remaining to us . . ."

Across the vast valley of the bridge deck, Sulu heard Spock's fatal pronouncement and clenched his fists in helpless frustration. Sulu turned back to the helm console on which he now walked, the controls growing more and more difficult to manipulate. He stared up at the main viewscreen. It still showed the same quarter of fractured land below them.

This was not the way the men in his family had died! His ancestors would be ashamed to see one of their blood go down without fighting, without striking back. There *had* to be some way, *any* way . . .

"Bypass that analysis, Mr. Spock," Kirk instructed his first officer. He turned, looked over at the huge clock balanced carefully against the base of the command chair. The clock had recently rested on his wrist, but like all other inorganic material except the dilithium, his watch had remained normal size.

Hours—they didn't even have hours if the rate of shrinkage continued to accelerate. They had twenty-nine minutes. Twenty-nine minutes before they were too small to control the *Enterprise*.

Cupping his hands, he shouted to the busy cluster of crewmen moving around on the deck.

"Everyone continue to jury-rig control systems. There's nothing more we can do."

"But there is, Captain."

As the rest of the crew continued with their tasks, Kirk and Spock turned in the direction of the voice, staring up at the overhanging edge of the helm console. Sulu stood there, looking down at them. His tone was one of desperation.

"Sir, request permission to direct phaser fire at the surface immediately below," he implored, and then turned back to his own task at hand before the captain could reply.

Sulu shoved against a waist high needle set in a timing dial, pushing it back several notches. With his concentrated body weight he had no trouble manipulating the huge lever. But his mind was on something else.

When no reply from below was forthcoming, he turned and moved to the edge of the console again. "Ten seconds, sir, just let me set it for ten seconds and we'll destroy . . ."

"Destroy what, Mr. Sulu? Sensor studies have shown that the unknown waves originate from an area kilometers in diameter. We could assault that region for hours without disrupting whatever is generating the bombardment of the ship. We haven't got hours worth of power to divert to the phaser banks. We haven't even got minutes."

Sulu stood at the bottom of the circular timer, now clicking back along its present path, and continued to argue with the captain.

"What good does it do to wait like this, sir. Wait for a death *reductio ad absurdum* in the truest sense? Just one quick blast, Captain, to see what will happen."

In his concentration on winning Kirk over, Sulu had forgotten the timer completely. It clicked through the final notch . . . to club Sulu behind the knees. Both legs were taken out from under him.

Falling forward, he rolled once, took a wild, desperate grab at the edge of the console and fell floorward. There was a disproportionately loud thump as he hit. It sounded convincingly fatal, but wasn't.

"Sulu!" Kirk and Arex rushed to the injured helmsman's side. The same gestures that showed them he was still alive indicated he was far from uninjured. He was clutching his right leg and grimacing with the pain.

"Damn . . . mmphh!"

"Easy, Lieutenant." Kirk forced Sulu's hands away from the damaged area. He felt the leg gently, winced himself when he put miniscule pressure on a particular spot and saw the helmsman's face contort in pain.

"Leg's broken," he murmured to the watching Arex.

"Call Sick Bay for a bed?"

"No . . . the sooner we get him down there the better. Besides, Bones doubtlessly has his hands full already. Let's make a temporary splint." Arex made an expression of understanding, moved off to locate the requisite material.

"Try not to move it, Sulu. We'll have you down to Sick Bay as soon as possible." The helmsman tried to smile back up at him, managed a slight grimace.

"Good thing I fell on my head, Captain. Beyond fracturing, I think."

"Something about you is." Kirk was studying the deck nearby. Sulu's heavy, compacted form had put a noticeable dent in the smooth metal.

"These should serve, Captain." Arex showed him a couple of small metal strips of the kind being used to make miniaturized holders and grips. He had also appropriated a couple of organically based belts from several crewmen.

Kirk straightened the leg slowly, while Sulu fought to stifle the pain. It couldn't be helped, they had to get the leg straight. He set one metal strip behind the leg, the other in front, and proceeded to tie them tight with the belts. The thick straps were awkward to work with.

"Couldn't you find anything better in the way of binding material, Lieutenant?" he grumbled.

"I'm sorry, Captain," Arex replied. "None of the cordage in the bridge storage lockers would work. It is all inorganically based and therefore has remained normal size."

"Of course." Kirk pulled harder on the bottom belt. Interesting how certain small items had suddenly become indispensable—and unavailable. While others, like these belts, were proving invaluable. He found himself fervently wishing that, of all things, starship's stores had included a couple of horses.

He finished the improvised splint. With the help of the captain and the navigator, Sulu managed to struggle to his feet. Arex slipped a pair of arms under him—one across his shoulders, the other across his front—and finally put the third around his waist. Kirk added an arm to the other side.

"Let's get him to Sick Bay." He glanced around. A small crowd had gathered. "Everyone, back to your stations."

Moving as quickly as they dared, they half dragged, half carried the injured helmsman toward the bridge doors. They seemed kilometers away.

"How are you doing, Sulu?" Kirk asked awkwardly as they struggled toward the elevator. He was at his best giving orders, not comfort. For all his sometime brusqueness, that was Dr. McCoy's specialty.

"Lousy, sir," Sulu replied, grinning. "I'll make it." His expression twisted as he accidentally put pressure on the injured member.

"It would have been nicer, sir, if our ability to feel pain had diminished along with our size."

They reached the elevator doors—and came to a grinding halt. Nothing happened, even when they moved to stand right up against the metal. The now Brobdingnagian portal refused to open. Arex looked frankly puzzled. It took Kirk long seconds to recognize the reason.

"The body sensor. We've grown too small to activate it—beam's over our heads now." He left Sulu to Arex's support while he hunted around for something long enough. Everything seemed too big or too small, until he nearly tripped over a strangely shaped piece of metal.

It was barbed, thin, and bent in the shape of an elongated U . . . one of Uhura's fallen hairpins.

Hauling it back to the doorway, he hefted it carefully, then made a sweeping motion forward, overhead. Nothing. Another sweep, coupled with a little jump—and this time the colossal doors slid apart.

Slipping the hairpin over his right shoulder, ready for use at the next doorway, he resumed his support of Sulu. Together, he and Arex helped the injured helmsman through the door.

Even more depressing than the situation on the bridge was the situation in Sick Bay. Kirk was shocked by the number of injured there, many lying on the deck on makeshift pallets of bits of cloth and sponge. The fact that many of the blankets and sheets were woven from natural-based substances alleviated the problems somewhat. They'd remained in proportion to the growing number of patients, all of whom now averaged about eighteen centimeters in height.

McCoy and nurse Chapel were doing their best to care for the injured. When the number of cases began to grow alarmingly, he had distributed the rest of the medical personnel to the various sections of the ship. That, he had decided, would be more practical in the long run than trying to bring all the injured to Sick Bay and would insure medical care throughout the ship no matter how small they shrank.

And though some areas of the *Enterprise* were more injury-prone than others, a large number still made their way to Sick Bay for treatment.

Chapel spotted the new arrivals immediately, nudged McCoy. The doctor bestowed a reassuring smile on a communications tech with a shattered collarbone and went with Chapel to meet the others.

He directed them to lay Sulu on an empty bed and knelt to examine the helmsman. "What happened? No, let me guess . . . another falling incident—people aren't taking heights seriously, Jim."

"Broken leg," Kirk informed him. "He fell all right—from the helm console." Turning slowly and surveying the room, he counted the number of injured. "I might ask you the same question."

McCoy was bent over Sulu, moving an improvised miniature medical scanner over the leg.

"A lot more of the same, as I said. More and more fall injuries being reported all the time." He clipped the scanner on his belt, started to undo the makeshift splint. "Compound fracture—how did you straighten it?"

"Pulled," Kirk said curtly.

"Bedside-manner-wise you leave something to be desired, Jim. But it was the right thing to do."

"If we could only use a bone-knitting laser," Chapel was muttering. At Kirk's questioning glance, she explained, "We miniaturized all the medical instrumentation we could, Captain, but we just didn't have time for everything. We've been so busy.'' Her expression brightened.

"Wait a minute, Dr. McCoy, what about the tiny laser set in the auralite? The one designed to work on the inner ear? Could it be used for bone work?''

McCoy looked away from his examination of the leg, considering. "It ought to be easy enough to detach from the 'lite—it's a self-contained, replaceable unit. But bone work— I don't . . . no, it's better than splinting. At this stage anything's worth a try.'' He looked back down at Sulu.

"I haven't mixed a plaster cast since first year Med School. I'd sure hate to start relearning now—even if the supplies are still manageable.'' He was getting excited. "Sure, let's try it. The 'lite's up on the shelf with the semi-surgical supplies.''

"I'll get it,'' Chapel told them. She left while the others turned their attention back to Sulu. McCoy started to explain what would happen if the badly broken femur were allowed to heal by itself.

The lab room had taken on the appearance of a metallic replica of Zion Canyon on Earth, with sheer cliffs of white and gray closing in on narrowing channels. Chapel didn't need a map to find the shelf.

Up one of the movable stools to the tabletop, from there up the angled base of the aquarium, and then an easy hike to the open shelf. Miscellaneous supplies were scattered about, hastily removed from containers as the people had begun to shrink. Spools of thread, small surgical devices now the size of shuttlecraft, all were strewn haphazardly about.

Several minutes of fruitless searching made the nurse think McCoy had been wrong about the location of the auralite. Then the long polished tube came into view near the far edge of the shelf. The laser module was in the front of the device. A couple of simple twists on a pair of screw clamps, a click, and it was free. She held it easily in one hand—an extraordinary piece of medical engineering about the size of a small button.

It had its own self-contained meters. She stepped back to check the reserve power gauge in better light and stumbled. Her feet slipped onto a couple of large plastic skin-patches, now the size of folded tents, and the laser began to shift in her grasp. Clutching at it anxiously, she went over backward into the glass-sided lake of the aquarium.

The fall knocked the breath out of her and she had to fight for air as she swam back to the surface, still holding the laser. At first the incident seemed only embarrassing. The laser was well sealed and the water wouldn't bother it. She would climb out . . .

Only after regaining control of herself and her breathing did the first touches of panic set in. The towering glass sides of the aquarium proved unclimbable. And she was far from being the best swimmer on board the ship. She had to struggle to keep from thrashing about in the water and screaming in panic. Instead, she treaded water steadily and screamed at regular, controlled intervals.

Many of the patients in the main room were under sedation, so it was relatively quiet. Otherwise Kirk and the others might never have heard her.

Arex had returned to the bridge, but Kirk and McCoy heard the screams clearly enough. Kirk left the exhausted doctor attending to Sulu and ran toward the adjoining lab.

Chapel was already growing tired—she had no place to rest her legs and one arm had the double task of helping to keep her afloat while holding onto the laser—when Kirk finally located her. Following the same path upward he was soon standing on the shelf above the aquarium, looking over and down into the water.

He could hardly go in after her—that would leave two of them in need of rescue. Nor was there any miniature climbing gear in evidence. There had to be something on the shelf . . .

A now-enormous spool of metallic surgical thread caught his attention. Unwinding a sufficient number of loops—the thread looked and felt like electrical cable in his hands—he made a strong ring at one end and dropped it to Chapel.

She half swam, half flailed her way over to it. Maneuvering carefully, she put her head and arms through the loop. Using the spool cylinder as a brace he slowly hauled her up. A minute later she was standing next to him, gasping and coughing. Kirk found a shrunken lab smock that had somehow found its way onto the shelf, slipped it over her. Her shivering abated somewhat. The halo fish was a cold-water denizen.

"No more mountain climbing for you, Nurse. Understand?" Chapel ignored the warning. She was hunting through her pockets. Holding onto the laser and treading water had proven too difficult, so . . .

"Agreed, Captain," she panted as she produced the instrument, "but I've got it."

She insisted on carrying it herself as they made their way first to the floor and then back to the main room. McCoy studied it without speaking. Kirk watched him worriedly, waiting.

Finally, "What's the matter, Bones? Don't you think it'll work?"

"If you mean by work, will it still operate effectively, the answer is yes," McCoy responded. "That's not what concerns me. Normally this device locks into a much larger mechanism which in turn has standard size switches to operate it. I've never handled it directly—the contacts, of course, are far too small for our hands. I'm worried about getting the settings right." He looked at the deck, over at Sulu.

"No way to know without trying it, though. Nurse Chapel, shift the lieutenant's other leg to one side, please." Chapel did so. Then, while she and Kirk watched, McCoy improvised a stable stand for the laser. Hesitantly at first, then with growing assurance, he manipulated the tiny control contacts.

Eventually he sat back on his haunches and looked up at Kirk.

"That ought to be right, Jim, though I still can't be sure. I've replaced this component with tiny handlers often enough. It feels awfully strange working it directly." He directed his next words to the helmsman.

"Sulu, if there's any pain—anything that doesn't feel right to you—you tell me immediately, understand? Don't go overboard on stoicism—anything twangs out of tune, yell good and loud!"

Sulu responded with a quick, nervous shake of his head. No jokes, now. McCoy took a deep breath, exchanged an infinite glance with Kirk, then touched a tiny recess in the side of the circular instrument. A beam of bright blue abruptly took up the space between lens and leg. It touched the injured limb on black and blue skin, where McCoy had cut away the tunic.

"Nothing so far," Sulu reported without being asked.

McCoy bent over the laser, squinted at the screen set in the back of it and made a couple of adjustments. An infinitesimal shift in the beam was the only noticeable result. Thirty seconds, forty—McCoy touched another hidden switch and the beam vanished.

"All right, Lieutenant, move your leg." Sulu looked at him uncertainly. He gritted his teeth and started to pull his leg up. The grimace disappeared as it moved easily. Now he flexed it slowly, then with increasing confidence, moving it from side to side.

"It still aches a little, Doctor." McCoy moved over and started feeling the treated area.

"Here?"

"No . . . no . . . yes, there . . . that's the spot."

McCoy made sure of it, had Sulu straighten his leg again, then returned to the laser. Readjusting the device he activated the beam again, played it on the helmsman's leg for a couple of seconds.

"Try it again, Sulu."

The helmsman did, moving his leg at the hip, then at the knee, and finally raising it completely off the deck in a high arch.

"No pain now, Doctor. Only a kind of dull throb and a warm feeling."

"That's natural. No," he warned, as Sulu showed signs of getting up, "just stay there and rest for awhile Sulu."

"I'm going to need him, Doctor," Kirk said softly. "How soon before he can come forward?"

"You mean you'll need him at the helm?" McCoy gave Kirk a look of admonition. "Isn't there a bit of wishful thinking there, Jim?"

"I try to think positive, Bones. If we have a second's opportunity to blast free of here, I'll want my best people at the controls."

"Sorry, you can't have Sulu for a while yet. I'm not worried about the bone—it has fully knit. But sometimes rapid repairs have their own effect on the body. Severe injury isn't the only thing that can initiate shock. It will take time for the nerves and blood vessels in that area to readjust to the fact that they're suddenly not on a crisis footing. After that he'll be as good as new. But he needs to rest for a little while, at least." He lifted the laser carefully off its improvised platform.

"Christine, move the base, will you? Let's try Solinski's hip next." He looked at Kirk. "Excuse us, Jim, there are a lot of other casualties here I'd like to try this on."

"Of course, Bones." Kirk turned his attention back to Sulu. "I'm tempted to call Chapel's thinking of the ear laser a lucky break, Lieutenant, but . . ."

"Comments like that could result in a breakdown of command." Sulu smiled broadly up at him. "I understand, sir. Right now I'm too pleased with the results to care."

Kirk started to reply but was interrupted by a new voice. He turned to see Spock moving toward him.

"I have other results available now, Captain. Figures on the ultimate molecular contraction rate have come through."

"What are they?" Kirk asked, at once intensely curious and fatalistic.

The latter emotion turned out to be justified.

"Reduction factor of thirty-two-point-nine." Kirk did some rapid upstairs calculating, commented somberly.

"That means we're going down to one-sixteenth of a centimeter."

Spock nodded, spoke matter-of-factly, "Yes, Captain. While it is in a sense comforting to know we will not be tripping over dust motes, it is still well past the point at which we can exercise operative control of the ship. An interesting height from which to contemplate the world—and the remainder of one's life."

Kirk stood silently, watched by both Sulu and Spock. He thought back to Sulu's request of minutes ago. Everything was happening too fast. If they could spare the power from life-support, maybe by closing off all but a few remaining sections of the ship, maybe he should try phasers on the surface below.

No, they simply didn't have that kind of reserve energy left. Not enough for the phasers. But they did have power for something else. For one last choice.

If he was going to die, then the location didn't much matter.

"You have decided on a new course of action, Captain," Spock commented, evaluating the familiar thoughtful expression of his friend's face.

Kirk didn't even hear him. "Mr. Spock, can you calculate the approximate center of the wave-emitting region?"

"A simple enough task, Captain. But that will not necessarily be the point at which the waves are produced."

"I know that, Spock."

"May I ask the purpose then, Captain?"

Kirk shrugged, stared over to where McCoy and Chapel were busy repairing a yeoman's broken ribs with the laser.

"That is as good a place as any to beam down."

While Spock stood digesting this remarkable statement, Kirk moved to a nearby metal boulder. It had a flexible face bordered by projecting studs—a huge hand communicator. It would be quicker than climbing to a console and trying to operate the wall comm unit.

Putting his compacted weight behind the push, Kirk had no trouble opening the grid. Making his voice strong enough for the pickup to be activated was another story. He had to bend and shout into the mouthpiece at the top of his lungs.

"Kirk to Engineering! Scotty, can you hear me?" A pause, then the chief engineer's voice acknowledging, filtered, faint, and weak—but comprehensible.

"Just barely, sir."

"Get a crew down to the transporter room!" Kirk yelled. "We have twenty minutes left in which to operate ship's controls—including the transporters."

"How many beamin' down, Captain?"

"Just one, Mr. Scott. Me!"

"Aye, Captain," Scott replied solemnly. "Dinna worry . . . we'll rig somethin'. Scott out."

Kirk stop, kicked at the deactivation switch to shut off the communicator.

"I'll meet you in the transporter room, Mr. Spock. Meanwhile, see what you can manage in the way of a doll-sized communicator. Anything at all, even something that just broadcasts a pulse signal. I'll send in code, if I have to."

"Yes, Captain."

"I won't be long. I've got to make one more check of the bridge and issue final instructions."

"I understand, Captain."

Uhura, Arex, and the others took the announcements with typical calm. They had an advantage—nothing Kirk said came as any surprise.

As he headed for the distant transporter room, Kirk kept their faces, reactions in mind. There wasn't one among them who felt those last instructions would not be implemented in a dozen minutes or so. He still retained private hopes, though.

There was one last thing they could try to halt the lethal bombardment. If an intelligence was behind it, then one had to assume the waves could be shut off as competently as they had been turned on the *Enterprise*.

In the absence of any attempt at contact from the surface, Kirk had to assume paranoid reluctance on the part of any such intelligence. In which event a personal appearance might be the only thing that could convince "them" of the peaceful intent of their visitors. He would beam down and search them out.

Alternatively, they would reduce him on sight to something considerably less than a centimeter in height—a thin layer of smoking dust, for example.

With admirable foresight, the doorway to the transporter room had been locked open, and a metal plate had been secured over the sensor eye. As Kirk walked toward the transporter console he spotted Scott and Gabler working at its base. Chief Kyle was busy with a crew nearby. They were rigging a doubled-back piece of strong wire to the console, bracing it against an empty wire spool secured to the deck.

A rapid examination revealed that the other end of the doubled-back cable looped around the first manual lever of the transporter control. Fortunately, that crucial switch moved vertically. If a horizontal control had been involved they would have had all sorts of problems, requiring at least one and possibly more miniature pulleys.

The other end of the wire was being played out to a crowd of patient crewmen. Each was taking up a firm stance and a tight grip on the wire.

Kirk placed a hand on Scott's shoulders. Sweat dripping

from his face, the chief engineer turned quickly, even managed a smile.

"We'll be ready in a minute, Captain. We can still manipulate the switches properly. It's workin' them at the proper speed that's goin' to be touchy, but I think we can manage it."

"Good, Mr. Scott." Kirk looked up, following the wire into the heavens to where it looped tightly around the handle of the transporter lever, now looking like a gray sequoia angling over the console cliff.

"I estimate our height is now down to about five centimeters," Scott ventured. "With maximum leeway I think we can manage controls for another fifteen minutes—no more."

"That will have to do, Scotty."

Kirk noticed Spock hunched down over a pile of material. He walked over as the science officer stood, trailing microscopic wire and hastily reduced hand tools.

The crudely made boxlike instrument he handed the captain looked ready to fall apart any second. Kirk hefted it, was gratified to see it was more solid than it looked.

"Unattractive but functional, Captain," Spock informed him. "This is the best I could do in rigging so small a communicator in such a short time."

"It's fine, Spock. Thanks."

"It is proportionately about ten times the size a hand communicator should be, Captain," Spock went on, still apologizing for the incredible feat of improvisational engineering he had just accomplished, "and its range cannot be guaranteed. How shall we locate you for return if it fails?"

"We haven't much time anyway, Mr. Spock, so that problem solves itself." He called back over his shoulder. "Scotty, set an automatic return for me. If there's anything to be found down there, ten minutes should do it."

"Aye, sir," Scott agreed. "We'll set it now." He turned, yelled to several crewmen hanging on another wire. "You there—Johnson, Massachi, Nikkatsu—let go of that wire and give me a hand with this servopole." The men hastened to obey as Scott started to take up a grip on the long hollow tube.

"A disconcerting thought, Captain," Spock ventured,

"that I have been pondering while working here. The transporter relies on a banked record of the body's molecular structure. Will that record adapt as well to your present height?"

"There is a chance, I suppose, that it can't adjust to the transporter pattern," Kirk admitted, "in which case, either I simply won't go anywhere—or else I'll go everywhere, in pieces.

"We'll know shortly. And in fifteen minutes it won't matter whether the transporter can bring me back or not. Prepare to energize." Kirk started for the transporter platform. Spock took a step to head him off.

"Captain, may I wish you all . . ." Spock hesitated, unusually. "I hope logical eventualities prove that . . . good luck, sir," he finally finished awkwardly.

He and Kirk exchanged shoulder claps. Then Kirk hurried off down the endless metal plateau toward the alcove.

Spock watched him for a minute, then moved to take up a place along the doubled cable. There was a short wait while Kirk scrambled up the low cliff on the single step leading to the platform proper. The super-strong wire made an excellent "rope" ladder.

Once on top, Kirk ran to the center of the nearest disk, turned, and waved both arms.

Scott, lost in other thoughts, eventually became aware Spock was speaking to him.

"What?"

"The captain instructed us to energize, I believe, Mr. Scott."

Energize. He had a job to do. First wire one, then the two servopoles were adjusted, turned. Spock took up a place in front of Scott, both hands on the wire. Speed was critical now. Five seconds, ten . . .

"Heave, lads, heave! Heave for your lives!"

The line of tiny figures on the floor started backward. As the slack in the cable was taken up the line grew taut, held. Straining, straining, for millimeters at a time, they pulled on the wire. Pulled until triceps howled with the demand and shoulders threatened to pull from their sockets.

The lever began to descend. Slowly, condescendingly, but

it moved. Servopoles made minor adjustments again. A dial was turned as men broke their backs on twin wires.

On the transporter platform a waterfall, a cascade of color, splinters of a rainbow, began to form. It was normal in shade, normal in flickering speed, normal in shape—normal in all respects except for its incredible, abnormal *thinness*.

It completely enveloped the near-invisible figure standing at its base. The figure wavered, blurred, became a standard transporting silhouette . . .

. . . and was gone.

V

Even though he had seen it only from kilometers above, the landscape was far from alien to Kirk. He was studying it even as he materialized on the plutonic scoria.

What was surprising was the amount of vegetation holding its own against the threatening tremors underfoot, green-brown roots and branches offering defiance to lack of moisture, promises of sulfuric rain.

Kirk was aware of this, of the constant intrusive growl of smoking peaks all around—and something else, something indefinite and undefinable. Not the ash-filled purplish sky overhead, nor the thin layer of pumice that crunched under his boots. Something much more immediate. Something like . . .

A lessening of weight, weight on his right arm, weight that should have been nestled in the crook of arm and ribs and no longer was. Instead it rested neatly in his palm, a miniscule shard of badly worked metal and plastic.

The communicator Spock had presented to him only moments ago. He smiled.

Spock's suspicions about the touchiness of the transporter memory bank had been justified—only not in the way he had imagined. Instead of the transporter pattern adapting to his smaller size, it had operated on the old pattern stored in its cells, had forced Kirk's body to adapt to *it*. He was back to his normal size.

From a distant peak, an intense beam of light shot like a yellow bar across the valley and disappeared in a far-off crevice. To his right was another, beginning lower down but also meeting somewhere over a nearby ridge.

Turning a slow circle he saw that a network of light converged at one point just beyond his vision. He started walking toward it.

As he started up the slight grade he raised the communicator, handling it carefully. If it slipped out of his grasp he doubted he would find it again in the loose gravel and detritus. Peering at the tiny device he used his fingernail to put the lightest pressure possible on the activation lever.

A violent rumbling began in the distance, grew rapidly loud. There was a throaty ripping sound, like an underground freight-liner rushing past. A flank eruption burst the side of one of the volcanoes behind him.

He spared it only a brief glance. At the moment he was more concerned about the tiny beep from his palm. He spoke at the communicator, hoped Spock's improvised pickup would modulate his voice properly at the other end.

"Kirk to *Enterprise*. *Enterprise* . . . do you read?" No reply from the tiny speaker. Maybe they were trying to talk to him, and his ears couldn't pick up their minute voices. He continued on the chance they were picking him up.

"I think we have the answer to the height problem. It seems the transporter beam returns our molecules to normal spacing. Nothing to indicate that once realigned and transported back aboard the whole compaction process wouldn't start all over again, but at least we've got a stop-gap now."

Still no reply. He tucked the communicator away in a pocket. The slope grew steeper here and he wanted to concentrate on keeping his footing. Also, the eruptions on the valley fringe were growing in violence and he wanted both hands in case of a fall. One particularly sharp tremor almost did knock him off his feet.

Once the dust and volcanic ash in the air grew so thick he had trouble breathing. And then, without sound or warning of any kind, the beam of light he was paralleling abruptly winked out. He looked around, across the valley, up the slopes of distant mountains. The network of lights he had observed on beam-down had been completely extinguished. He brought out the communicator, tried again.

"Kirk to *Enterprise*, do you read me?" This time there was an answer. Faint and unnaturally high-pitched, but for all that immediately recognizable.

"We read you, Captain," Spock told him. "It was necessary to readjust power flow to the main communications board to boost your transmission to audible levels. Your makeshift communicator carries less power than I believed.

"A most interesting thing has just happened. If sensors are to be believed, wave bombardment of the ship has just ceased."

"I think I know why," Kirk told his astonished listeners. But before he could elaborate he felt an agonized heaving underfoot and the ground bulged. A crack like a sonic boom followed, and this time Kirk was knocked completely off balance.

Bracing himself he landed without being more than dazed, but something he had feared had come to pass. Despite his best efforts the tiny communicator had gone flying. Flaming bits of ash and lava started to fall around him as he searched for it on hands and knees. The fiery fallout was dense behind him, though less so in the direction he had been headed.

Several minutes of fruitless searching failed to locate the lost communicator. The rain of lava was growing worse and the sharp-slivered pumice had nearly butchered his knees. It seemed a good idea to move on. He was nearly to the top of the ridge and he ought to find some protection from the sizzling hail on the other side.

Scrambling to his feet he started upward again. Occasionally a hot ash would land on him and he would beat frantically at the ember as it smoldered on his clothes. But he still found no sign of whatever existed at the center of the vanished lights.

Once, a lava bomb—a tear-drop shaped dollop of molten lava cooled to hardness during its fall through the cooler atmosphere—shattered near him. It must have weighed a hundred kilos at least. It would take a far smaller bomb to make a real mess of him. No use wishing for a solid duralloy umbrella, nor could he dodge the unexpected missiles.

But it was hard not to think about them.

Another sharp tremor. Ready for this one, he kept his feet. A meter-wide crack opened in the ground to his left, forcing him to change the direction of his climb slightly. Even without the time limit imposed on him he didn't think an unarmored man could spend much time roaming this surface. Sooner or later the steady assault would either batter him unconscious or cause him to break an ankle in the plethora of tiny crevices and cracks.

He topped the rise, ready for a sight of the unexpected—but not ready for the mental shock he received.

Down in a steeply walled hollow, not five meters from the base of the slope he stood on, rose the walls of a city. Graceful towers and arching branch structures were brilliantly lit from within, the whole metropolitan network intersected by a complex webwork of covered highways.

To one side were stadiums and a huge amphitheater, while another boasted a large factory complex. Parks and lakes studded the landscape throughout, while the entire city was surrounded by concentric rings of cultivated land, farms and dairy country. In all respects it was one of the most thoroughly planned yet exquisitely wrought cities Kirk had ever seen. It differed from the great cities of Earth and Vulcan and the major colony worlds in only one respect.

The whole metropolitan area was just large enough to fill the floor of an average-sized room aboard the *Enterprise*.

He stepped over the ridge, sat down in the grinding pumice, and stared at the scene from a book of children's stories. The tallest spire of the city came just about up to his waist.

As he sat frozen with fascination, another cycle of tremors shook the ground. He was certain that the delicate towers and bridgeways of the tiny city would be shattered, yet they barely moved. Obviously those spires were built on some kind of flexible foundation, constructed to give with the constant quakes.

But this series of shakes opened a branching canyon near the outskirts of the farthest agricultural section. Kirk could have stepped over the largest crevice in the crack, but it would swallow the biggest building in the city with room to spare. Even as he watched, one arm of the canyon moved like a bolt of lightning in slow motion toward the city.

It was easy to conclude that despite its miniscule size, he had come upon an intelligent civilization which possessed enough science to immobilize and threaten the *Enterprise*. Despite the threat to himself and his crew, he still could experience a sudden fear that he might have crushed some outlying farmhouses on his approach. He resisted the urge to retrace his steps.

Right now he had to make contact with the inhabitants of the city. Clearly, their intellect was in no way proportional to their size. He studied the plan of the metropolis, decided the best thing to do was get as close to the city center as possible.

Rising, Kirk started carefully down the slope, edging around toward what appeared to be a section of farmland lying fallow. He could do the least damage by approaching the city center from there.

Even as he did so, a familiar tingling started on his skin.

No, no . . . ! He repressed the shout. There wasn't a thing he could do. The ten-minute time period was up and the automatics were bringing him inexorably back to the *Enterprise*. And then he had a moment to consider a horrifying thought.

Was this pattern the one the transporter computer would retain? Or would he be rematerialized back aboard ship in his smaller size?

Too late to stop the action, too late to change, too late to worry. His vision blurred; he felt a second of total disorientation and nausea, and then the tingling left him and his vision returned. He was back on board.

Kirk looked down at himself, around the room. He was still his proper size. He stepped off the disk, glanced around urgently.

"Scotty, Spock . . ." No answer, no gratified replies. Maybe they could not shout this far.

Moving rapidly to the transporter console, he examined the place where the crew of straining wire-pullers and pole-handlers had worked alongside the first officer and chief engineer only ten minutes before. No sign of them.

He took a moment to examine the whisker-thin wire still looped around the transporter lever, marveling from a new perspective at the ingenuity of Scott and his assistants. Dropping to all fours he commenced a detailed survey of the area, but found no sign of the crew.

Surely they could not have shrunken to microscopic size! That would be far beyond Spock's projected lower limit of a sixteenth of a centimeter.

Knowing the automatics would return him, they had probably gone to another part of the ship in need of their attention. The bridge, for example. He got to his feet.

After covering kilometers of scaled-down corridor, it was a pleasure to make it to the bridge at what seemed like superhuman speed. The door was still locked open, the metal plate still taped over the sensor.

A quick look showed all panels and instrument consoles still operating. Impulse power was still keeping the basic functions of the ship operational, then. But still no sign of any of the crew.

There was plenty of evidence of their activities, though. Discard remote handler poles, wires running to dials and levers, doubled-over cables attached to other controls in the same fashion used to manipulate the transporter lever, tiny ladders and stilts made of metal bands.

But an uncanny silence. Clicks and snaps of relays going over. The hum of still-powered machinery. And—he strained to hear it—something more?

High-pitched, barely audible, like the mewing of a small kitten tucked away in a drawer somewhere. Bending, he tried to follow the sound, finally saw the line of ant-sized figures emerging from behind one edge of the helm console.

Dropping to hands and knees, he looked closer. The figures took on familiar shapes and forms and even individual features. But they were so *tiny*, so incredibly tiny.

"Scotty, is that you?"

Scott was staring upward, past the towering peninsulas of Kirk's fingers, up into the monolith of his overhanging face. It hung in the sky like a great pink thundercloud.

He cupped his hands and shouted, "Aye, Captain, for the love of heaven, be careful where you step!"

Kirk nodded slowly, then dropped his face to the floor in an attempt to get as close as possible to eye level with his miniaturized crew. Scott and the others backed up nervously. It was like a mountain falling.

"IS EVERYONE SAFE?"

Scott staggered backward, hands clapped to his ears. "Easy Captain, you'll deafen us for sure."

Kirk dropped his voice to what he thought was a bare whisper. To the shrunken crew his voice still sounded like distant thunder. "Everyone accounted for?"

"All but the regular bridge complement, Captain!" Scott yelled back. "They were all at their posts, when according to the ensign who witnessed it, they were suddenly beamed away. Every living one of them. That's why I moved my people up here, to keep things runnin'.

"No warnin', no indication of what was comin'—and not a blessed hint of what did it! Only that something was using standard transporter technology."

That was the end, the final assassin of somnolent diplomacy. Now they would not deal so amiably with the inhabitants of the miniature city. Considering their attitude toward the *Enterprise* thus far, Kirk didn't think their treatment of the captured bridge staff would be very benign. Sulu would get his wish, if he were still alive.

Kirk put the tail end of that thought out of his mind.

Turning his head, he had another look at the main viewscreen. He could still see the same quadrant of tortured surface seething below. Transporter records would show precisely where he had been set down. He could pinpoint the city easily. He whispered downward again.

"All personnel away from the helm area. Move to the far bulkhead. I don't know if those people down there—I think I flatter them—have any kind of defense other than their compaction beam, but they might have a more physical way of jolting us. I'd hate to fall on anybody."

As the crew moved at top speed, with infinite slowness, to scatter across the floor, Kirk got to his feet and walked to the helm. His gaze went to certain boldly marked controls—controls which the now-vanished Sulu had pleaded to use before.

Kirk set the phaser control thoughtfully, pressed a couple of attendant switches, read the results of his request on the appropriate gauge.

Yes, the phasers were lined on his desired region. Yes, they still retained enough impulse power for a couple of mild bursts. But that was all it would take to melt the jewel-like little metropolis with its belligerent inhabitants into a shining puddle of metal slag.

Anyone else in Kirk's position might have done that immediately, on the chance of being whisked from the bridge by some irresistible transporter effect himself. Anyone else might, but *they* would not have been a starship captain.

Kirk's anger was moderated by one overriding factor—the chance that Sulu and the others might still be alive somewhere in that honeycomb of towers and roadways.

With the phaser controls set, he moved to Uhura's communications console, checking to make sure Scott and his companions were far from his path between there and the helm. After a second's thought, he selected the general interspecies frequency, composed his thoughts, and addressed himself to the pickup.

"Message to the inhabitants of the city on the planet below. I hope you can receive this frequency and understand my words. Your continued survival depends on it." He paused, gave any listener a chance to fine tune.

"All this ship's armament is locked in on the coordinates of your city. In case you doubt our ability to operate effectively, I've timed a demonstration." He checked his wrist chronometer, counted seconds, looked up at the screen.

The brilliant beam of the secondary phaser bank vanished into atmosphere. On the surface, another steep-walled valley appeared in the ground alongside the one which held the city. Reduced in strength as it was to a trickle of its usual self, the beam was still powerful enough to annihilate the entire city at one touch. The illumined towers and gilded rectangles trembled slightly from a new, artificial quake.

Kirk turned back to the pickup. "You have one minute to restore my bridge crew unharmed or you will receive a full barrage from my ship's armament."

Opening the speakers and setting part of the instrumentation to *Receive*, he moved back to the phaser controls, set one switch, and put his finger on the fire button. He had reversed the field effect in the fluid switch. Now, if he took his finger off the button—if he were suddenly beamed away—the phaser would fire.

He considered the possibility of destroying an entire city. He found it impossible to be objective, yet the situation had come to the point where someone below had to make the ultimate decision. It was no longer his responsibility. He told himself that, repeatedly. Sulu, Uhura, Arex, Spock—all might be dead already.

A glance at his wrist. Half a minute gone, forty seconds—and then a rapid series of high beeps and sputters filled the bridge, pouring over the main speakers. On the main viewscreen the image of the surface fluttered, was consumed by static, and then suddenly sharpened.

Kirk saw the interior of a huge room—huge on the screen—with a vaulting roof soaring far overhead. Highly intricate machinery was set nearby, and tunic-clad creatures were clustered around it.

One of the beings stepped suddenly into the visual pickup from the left side, blocking out most of the view behind. Kirk thought he had seen enough aliens to be prepared for the sight of almost any creature imaginable—any creature unimaginable.

This was unimaginable and shocking. Overpowering.

The alien was male, tall by the standards of its people, vigorous-looking and topped with gray hair. If it resembled anything Kirk had seen before, it was his own father.

Gulliver had been right all along—only his geography was inaccurate.

Kirk underwent some localized tremors of his own as he tried to readjust his thinking.

The man spoke in a high-pitched but nonetheless impressive voice, a voice filled with a dignity and earnestness that bespoke long experience as a leader of men living in desperate circumstances.

"In the name of the Terratin people," he said formally, "I forbid you to take offensive action against this city, Captain Kirk."

Kirk spoke into the helm pickup mike, trying to put as much sarcasm into his voice as possible. "You forbid me, after what you've done to my ship and to my friends?"

"I am Mandant of all this city," the figure told him with assurance, "superior in command to yourself."

"Sorry," Kirk informed the speaker grimly, his finger quivering on the fatal button, "Mandant is not a recognized Starfleet rank."

At this point the leader's tone softened noticeably.

"We are a people of considerable pride, Captain. Equal in pride to your own. We neither suffer insult, nor give apology for actions we deem necessary, but . . . ," and here he hesitated, obviously struggling with himself to find the words for something he was quite unused to saying, "I give apologies now for the inconvenience done your ship and crew."

Inconvenience!

"To make amends I may tell you that this world contains . . ."

"I'm not interested in what your world contains just now," Kirk replied angrily. "Where are Mr. Spock, Lieutenant Sulu, and the rest of my officers?"

"I order . . . ," the Mandant began and then he stopped, glanced away. "No . . . no. Not order. Please try to understand, Captain Kirk. Our adopted world is dying, has been dying for many years. No ship of an intelligent race had passed this way until yours came exploring.

"We tried to tell you of our plight as you entered orbit, but our great communications antenna was buried too deep by sequential flows of lava and ash. We were, we are, desperate, Captain. We *had* to make some kind of contact with you. The only device we had remaining to us which conceivably could have made you take notice was our invasion defense system, and . . ."

"You still haven't answered my question," Kirk interrupted him. "Either you tell me what's happened to my people . . ."

The Mandant abruptly moved aside . . . to reveal a healthy Sulu and Arex. Both were carrying tools of unfamiliar design, yet vaguely familiar in outline. Neither showed any sign of mistreatment.

"Here we are, Captain." Arex speaking, normal, relaxed.

"We're in the capitol building of the Terratin city, sir," Sulu explained. "As you've probably guessed, they beamed us down with their transporters."

Now why didn't they just do that in the first place? Kirk found the answer immediately after the thought occurred. If the Terratins had tried to make contact by transporting down members of the *Enterprise*, even one person would have obliterated not only the transport station but probably half the city as well.

That's why they had to use their invasion defense system first, to reduce the crew sufficiently in size to where they could be brought into the city.

Kirk wondered if the Terratin engineers knew that the members would return to their normal size once transpo..ed back to the *Enterprise*. That was a question best side-stepped for the moment. The important thing was that Sulu and the others were all right.

But he didn't let himself relax until he had reset the phaser controls to normal and lifted his finger from the red button.

"What's going on down there, Lieutenant Sulu?"

"See for yourself, sir." He stepped out of view, favoring his injured leg. Arex and the Mandant did likewise.

As the pickup panned the great hall, Kirk saw McCoy and Chapel tending to a mass of people scattered on beds about the chamber. The room was packed to overflowing with people. Normal, human-type people, except for their size. Many of them appeared to be burn victims. Kirk rubbed idly at a hole on the shoulder of his own shirt where one of the flying embers had burned through. He did not need to be told what the sufferers in that hall were experiencing.

Even as he watched, the picture shook visibly and the people in the building reacted to the new quake. There was no panic, however, only a few gasps and the shushing of crying children. These people were used to such shocks by now, if not resigned to them.

Panning further, the pickup finally settled on Spock. The science officer was working with several Terratins. They appeared to be struggling to repair what resembled a video-broadcast unit of extremely ancient design. His anxiety over the condition of his companions now satisfied, Kirk permitted his curiosity full flow.

"Mr. Spock!" The first officer looked up. "Who are the Terratins? Where did they come from?"

The first officer of the *Enterprise* spoke toward the screen. Kirk could hear him clearly.

"An intriguing historical sidelight, Captain," he began, with typically scholarly reserve. "From the records I have had time to examine, they appear to be the descendants of an early lost colony ship. They are, despite differences in size, of the same Terran stock as yourself.

"Believing their colony to be the tenth to be founded, they named this world Terra Ten—which over the years has become the present corrupted form, Terratin."

"All very plausible, Mr. Spock, except for that slight difference in size. I doubt we would find any records of Earth ships carrying colonists a sixteenth of a centimeter tall."

"The original colonists were normal-sized humans," Spock continued. "The remarkable radiation which they have incorporated into their unique defensive system is present naturally in a transuranic element quite common on the surface here. This defensive system intensifies the compaction effect of that radiation tremendously.

"The naturally present wave effect took several hundred years to reduce the colonists and their descendants to their present size. Once aware of what was happening, they were able, as were we, to predict the ultimate dimensions of the compaction. And to plan far in advance for it, designing all the miniature machines and devices they would need for survival."

Suddenly the Mandant reappeared on the screen, now standing beside Spock. "The colony ship was well equipped, Captain. But even with many years to prepare for this, our current state, our ancestors were forced to direct all their energies to insure their descendants' survival.

"In concentrating on survival technology, many other abilities were lost or degenerated—our ability to build deep-space communications equipment, for example. Nor could we escape, since the material inherent in a colony ship's construction is designed to be incorporated into the colony itself. Colony vessels were designed for one-way trips only. Once our ancestors began to cannibalize it for material for the first city, there was no hope of using it for travel again.

"We had to build a new way of life on this world, Captain Kirk. We had to adjust to our changing size, create a new form of defense against any potential attackers, master this planet's unstable ways. We encountered no outsiders, had no help of anyone." The screen shook again, more violently this time. When the shaking had stopped and the cries of the children in the hall had faded once more the Mandant continued, his voice growing thick with emotion.

"But as you now see, Captain, we are forced to seek outside help, for we are about to lose everything. The geologists of the original colony selected what they believed to be one of the most seismically stable regions on the surface. Yet even here we were never wholly immune to quakes and tremors. Their intensity has grown alarmingly in recent months.

"We began to hunt frantically for outside aid. And we began to despair of contacting another vessel. When your *Enterprise* went into orbit here we were hysterical with hope, despite the earlier destruction of our communications system. We are only able to contact you now," he made a gesture off screen to his left, "due to the knowledge of your Mr. Spock.

"We had to contact you and request if we could, compel if we must, your help. Many thousands look to me to preserve their lives, Captain Kirk. Even so, I hesitated before ordering the defense system brought into play. I apologize again if in gaining your attention we caused any anguish to you or your crew."

"Your actions all but lost us our ship," Kirk responded, his tone turning milder even as he spoke the words. "If I hadn't accidentally discovered that our transporters could return us to normal size, we would have lost total control of the *Enterprise*. That would have been the end of us and any help we could have given you."

"Again, I am sorry, Captain Kirk," the Mandant replied, torn between natural pride and the utter desperateness of his situation, "if in gaining your attention we utilized the first rule of politics—do that which is expedient rather than that which may be right. Really, we had no other choice." He paused, and all traces of arrogance vanished in a naked plea.

"I do not know how to beg, Captain Kirk. I can therefore only request, ask you to save as many of my people as you can. My counselors and I decided to use our defensive system to contact you. If you bear any grudge against us, we will submit whatever judgment you deem fit.

"In any case, we of course insist on being the last to be taken off."

"Don't be idiotic," Kirk found himself mumbling. He was vaguely aware that the Mandant was manipulating his emotions with a skill born of long practice, but somehow it didn't seem to matter. Not with the lives of a city at stake.

Uhura had entered the field of visual pickup and was looking out at Kirk. "They had no other way left to them, sir. They meant us no harm."

Kirk had already arrived at that opinion independently. But there were other things that had to be done first, no matter how it made him look to the anxious Terratins.

"I can help no one under present conditions," he told the Mandant, staring firmly into the pickup. "I can't run the *Enterprise* myself. All bridge crew, prepare to beam aboard. See to it, Lieutenant." She nodded, disappeared from the screen.

"Oh . . . and Uhura?" Her face reappeared. "The Terratins are an Earth colony. That means they have Federation or at least pre-Federation technology. Is their city by any chance powered by . . . ?"

"Dilithium, Captain?" The communications officer smiled. "Lieutenant Arex has already checked on that. It sure is, Captain." Kirk allowed himself to mirror her grin.

"Mandant, are you still there?" The leader of the Terratin colony reappeared a moment later.

"Yes, Captain Kirk. This difficulty, at least, has been anticipated. Your officers informed us of your difficulty in this regard. This world contains substantial deposits of dilithium. The natural wave radiation here is not strong enough to affect its internal structure in the way our defensive beams do. We have a certain amount of refined crystals on hand not essential to the operation of the city. It was this I tried to tell you before.

"My people have been transferring a stock of the largest crystals to a storage area near our main transporter. The move is nearly completed. They will be made available to you for whatever use you require."

"You realize, don't you," Kirk ventured, "that once I have the rest of my bridge crew aboard and the engines repowered, we might easily destroy your defense system and leave you stranded here."

The Mandant looked solemn.

"This is all obvious, Captain Kirk." That was all he said.

The directness and openness of his reply made Kirk feel uncomfortable he had even considered such a thought.

"Okay then. Lieutenant Uhura?"

She reappeared on the screen.

"Captain?"

"As long as we retain power I'd just as soon use our own transporters. The Terratin computer has patterns of you only for your present size. As long as you're coming back aboard you may as well do so at the proper size.

"It's going to take me a minute or two to get down to the transporter room. The dilithium crystals are ready to come aboard?"

"Nearly, sir."

"Tell the others to stand by."

"Yes, *sir*!"

He had one bad moment in the transporter room. It looked as if he had misjudged the amount of reserve power remaining and would not have enough to beam them back aboard. But by shutting down all life-support in several unoccupied storage compartments, plus the shuttlecraft hanger, he was able to divert a fair amount to the transporter. It wouldn't run forever, but by the time reserve power ran out they should have the Terratin dilithium aboard and the engines powered up.

Kirk studied the image in the transporter console viewscreen as he prepared to beam the bridge crew up. They were in another chamber of the capitol building. This one was also filled with refugees from the rain of hot ash outside.

The picture jerked a couple of times. Not from a planetary, but from a human-induced tremor, as Terratin technicians moved the pickup around. It finally settled on Spock and the rest. They were arranging themselves for beam-up while the Terratins divided huge masses of crystalline dilithium among them.

At least, they appeared huge beside the compacted crew. Actually, they were normal-sized crystals and Kirk knew he could hold the entire amount in one palm.

Terratins driving powered carts continued to arrive with more and more of the vital mineral. Kirk allowed them to heap the crystals around the feet of Uhura, Sulu, and the others until it was overflowing outside the range of transporter pickup.

"That will have to do, Mr. Spock. We can get more the next time. Prepare to beam up."

"Very well, Captain." The first officer turned away for a moment and said something to one of the Terratin technicians. He nodded and backed out of range, but Kirk could hear him speaking to the crowd.

Immediately both colonists and the cart unloaders moved away from the waiting crewmembers. Spock turned to take up his place in the group, stared straight ahead as the Terratins moved their visual pickup further back.

"We're ready, Captain. You may energize at any time."

Kirk worked the transporter controls in proper sequence, his gaze moving constantly from the console to the viewscreen. Familiar sparkling cylinders formed around the crew as the transporter effect took hold. His gaze moved to the empty alcove in front of him as the whine of shifting energies filled the chamber.

The multiple shapes were materializing in the alcove, full-size, along with irregular clumps at their feet. Dilithium, visible as gravel now instead of boulders. He shifted down, turned a dial, and the effect faded around darkening silhouettes.

"Nice to be back aboard, sir," Uhura murmured with undisguised relief, "and back at one's natural size."

Kirk nodded, spoke quickly. "Everyone watch where you step. We had enough trouble finding this dilithium. Before you move off those disks, gather up those crystals." As they all bent, he turned his attention back to the console, flipped on the ship-wide com.

"All crew personnel report to the main transporter room immediately. Prepare to beam down to the surface. Beamdown and return will bring you back to normal size. Repeat, all crew report to the main transporter room immediately. Move along the walls. Normal-sized personnel will take proper precautions."

Spock came over, both hands cupping the precious load of accumulated dilithium. It looked appallingly small compared to what he had seen on the viewscreen.

"The Terratins are making available every crystal they

can spare, Captain. The specimens are small, but I believe they will provide enough power to operate the ship efficiently until we can get a mining crew down to the surface.''

Kirk made a sign of agreement, looked past Spock. "Mr. Sulu, take over the transporter, please. Mr. Arex, you will move to B deck to handle transportation problems there. See that Mr. Scott and his engineers are in the first round trip, Sulu." The lieutenant nodded.

"They can handle the rest of the transporting, then," Kirk continued. "As soon as everyone has made the circuit and is restored to proper size, see that Mr. Scott gets a geotech crew down to dig out a sufficient supply of dilithium." He grinned.

"At least we won't have to go prospecting for it. That's another way the Terratins can be of help."

"Excuse me a moment, sir." Sulu was beginning to adjust the transporter controls for the next beam-down . . . but slowly. "What *about* the Terratins? The people in the city are in a state of barely surpressed panic and . . ."

"You have your orders, Mr. Sulu."

"Yes, sir." All hint of expression disappeared from the lieutenant's face as he turned full attention to the instrumentation.

Kirk took half of the double handful of vital crystals, eyed Spock. "Ever on-loaded an active dilithium reaction chamber by hand, Mr. Spock?"

"No, Captain. But the process is reputed to be fail-safe. As I evaluate the steps involved, I forsee only a very small chance of our destroying the ship."

"Thank you, Spock. I can always depend on you for a feeling of security and reassurance. Let's go." Together the two officers started for the elevator doors.

"Slowly, Captain," Spock advised his friend, as Kirk started off at a run from the elevator. "It would be awkward to drop the crystals—or not to see some of our still compacted companions until too late . . ."

"Don't worry, Spock. I'll choose my steps with as much care as you choose your words." The first officer jogged silently alongside as they neared the door to engineering section marked in bold red characters . . .

DILITHIUM REACTION CHAMBER—AUTHORIZED PERSONNEL ONLY!

VI

His disclaimer of experience notwithstanding, Spock managed the loading of the new supply of raw dilithium into the minutely balanced chamber with all the skill of a reaction specialist—just as Kirk had known he would.

Impulse power was fed to the chamber to spark a greater reaction. A number of gauges on the nearest monitor immediately jumped upward with gratifying speed.

Spock was ready with the results by the time Kirk had reestablished life-support and power in the sections he had shut off earlier.

"We will not be able to travel to the nearest starbase, Captain, but essential functions no longer have to be checked as closely and we could break out of orbit at any time.

"And the next load of dilithium should make us fully secure until Scotty and his mining crew can get to work." He let out a sigh of relief, moved to the intercom.

"Mr. Sulu?"

"Main transporter room here, Captain; but it's Third Transporter Engineer Lefebre in charge. Mr. Sulu has returned to the bridge, sir. I was directed to take charge here as soon as I was returned to normal size."

"Carry on, Mr. Lefebre. Is Mr. Scott there?"

"Mr. Scott left some minutes ago for Engineering Central, sir. Said something about working on the engines. He did request that I inform you when you called in that Second Engineer Gabler and a party of five have beamed down to the surface with appropriate equipment and are already engaged in extracting an adequate supply of raw dilithium for future needs—under the direction of geologists from the Terratin city."

85

"Thank you, Lefebre. Kirk out."

"Transporter Central out." Kirk started for the elevator, Spock at his side.

"It appears that we shall soon be fully powered up once more, Captain."

"Yes, Mr. Spock. As soon as we've taken on all the dilithium we'll need, we can leave this place."

Spock raised a questioning brow, but Kirk had moved slightly ahead of him and didn't notice it.

Or if he did, he chose to ignore the suggestion behind it.

The ship's transporter facilities worked overtime for the next several hours, beaming ant-sized humans down to the Terratin city and rematerializing them on board in their normal guise moments later.

The Mandant stood in the crowded chamber, watching humans come and go via transporter. Now and then he leaned to confer with one of his aides or to eye the visual linkup which had been hastily set up in the room.

It showed several views of the city outskirts, now menaced from three directions by abysses and crevices which grew with even the slightest of tremors. Another screen revealed the interior of the Terratin science center where worried geologists hurried back and forth. They paused only long enough to deliver increasingly desperate reports.

The Mandant acknowledged every report, spoke steadily and reassuringly to his aides . . . all the while trying to keep a calming hand on the metropolis itself. The macropsychosis of the city was fast approaching chaos proportions.

Already a mob was forming outside, threatening to storm the hall and hold the next group of aliens who beamed down as hostages until guaranteed rescue was effected. What kind of rescue was not specified, but that made the demonstrators no less virulent in their demands.

The Mandant smiled sadly to himself. Such people would always exist, never to be calmed, never to be satisfied.

We exist for such a minute time, he mused. We perform a great many inconsequential nothings and call them Acts of Significance, realizing the futility of our lies all the while. Yet we constantly strive for the postponement of the inevitable end which would bring peace to all. Such is the nature of man, and it does not change with his physical stature.

For himself it mattered not what the captain of the starship chose to do. For the young adults and children it mattered a great deal. Some of his aides still had confidence in the remnants of their defensive system. The Mandant knew better. Now that the location of their city was known, they were completely helpless.

Their eventual fate depended on the whim of a man whose ship and command they had nearly destroyed for their own need. Even so, if he were forced to go back he felt he would be compelled to do everything exactly as it had been done before.

But while he could control his fear of death he still had a responsibility to the people.

So when the next group of crewmen appeared in the room, he moved rapidly to stand next to them before the transporter took hold and asked, "Please inform your captain that the reports from our remote seismic research stations are very discouraging. It is apparent now that the former stability of this area is fast diminishing. We doubt we can survive continued quakes much longer without some form of aid.

"Our entire city is constructed on an interlocking series of precision bearings and gimbals mounted in a viscous fluid. These serve to keep us upright and steady despite the severity of successive jolts. Though we are rocked a little from time to time, as your fellow crewmembers can attest.

"But while we can withstand the most violent shakings we cannot withstand the peril that faces us now. A number of enormous—by our measurements—cracks in the ground are forming outside the city . . . and are expanding with each new quake. According to predictions from our science center, they will undercut the city in a very short time and drop us to our doom.

"Your captain must tell us—shall we prepare to be rescued, all or part of us? Or to die—all or part of us."

The young yeoman who stood nearest looked back at the Mandant with wide eyes. "I don't know, sir, but. . . ." The air began to glow around him. "I think I have a pretty good idea what Captain Kirk's decision will . . ."

His words were cut off as the transporter energies surged around him and stole him from sight.

Kirk glanced at his wrist chronometer again before turning

his attention back to the gauges, dials and readouts he was inspecting in his walk around the bridge. The *Enterprise* was back to battle efficiency again—fully manned and fully powered.

More than fully powered. If the dilithium Gabler's hastily improvised crew had brought back was anything less than a mother lode, the Terratin world might one day become a major source of that fabulously valuable material. Though he doubted it would ever be much of a colony world.

"How's the helm now, Mr. Sulu," he asked.

The lieutenant looked back at Kirk. "Fully responsive, sir. All instrumentation appears normal once again. All readings are up to red-alert capabilities."

"Subspace radio now operational too, sir," Uhura put in from over at communications. "I have had contact with Star Base Twenty-three and have informed them of the situation prevailing here. They are recording currently."

"Very good, Lieutenant. You might also relay to them tapes of everything that has taken place in the past twenty-four hours."

"Yes, Captain." Uhura turned back to her mike, began talking into it low and steady.

Kirk heard the elevator door hum, turned to see Scott step onto the bridge. All questions about the state of the ship's engines were answered by the broad smile on the chief engineer's face.

"The last of the crew has been through the double transporter trip, sir. Everythin' runnin' smooth as a mother's lullaby. To look at the power levels you'd think we'd never had any trouble here."

"Almost, Mr. Scott." There was one last problem to be dealt with. He turned to face the helm. "Mr. Arex, prepare ship for immediate departure from this region."

Arex looked ready to say something but another listener beat him to it.

"I beg your pardon, Captain."

Kirk turned to the science station. Spock was staring at him evenly. His voice was a monotone. "What about the people on the planet?"

"I haven't forgotten them, Mr. Spock. I know exactly what to do. I thought about it while the rest of the crew were beaming up. It's the only thing that can be done." He looked to the helm.

"Mr. Sulu, direct forward phasers to the region of the Terratin city."

"Captain, I . . ."

Kirk moved to stand next to him, smiled reassuringly. "It's all right, Mr. Sulu. We'll require pinpoint fire control. There are some precision adjustments necessary—but believe me, this is the best way."

Using the computer linkup to phaser control, he proceeded to trace with the electronic stylus a certain pattern of fire on the targeting screen. Behind them, Uhura, Scott and Spock had all turned from their responsibilities of the moment to watch. All but Arex, who continued with his part of the preparations for leaving the area. Of all of them, only he had some idea of what Kirk was going to try.

"Can you handle that, Mr. Sulu?" he asked when he'd finished with the computations. The helmsman studied the carefully wrought fire pattern and nodded slowly.

"I'm sure I can, sir. I would like to incorporate a fail-safe into it, if I might."

"No time, Mr. Sulu," Kirk objected firmly. "We'll have to do it right on the first try. Those people down there must not be made to suffer any longer."

"Very well, Captain," Sulu acquiesced. He turned and commenced programming the phaser control computer. Once he stopped, to request some information from Spock. When that was granted, Scott and Uhura grew more curious than ever—since Spock now appeared to know what was going on, too.

Neither dared interrupt what was clearly a harried operation. But when Spock was finished relaying Sulu's needed statistics, Scott moved to stand next to the first officer.

"For the love of Loch Lomond, what's happenin', Mr. Spock? What's the captain up to?"

Spock turned unblinking eyes on him. "Nothing more than what the captain has already stated, Mr. Scott, though I confess to having been somewhat mystified as to his intentions at first, myself." He turned back to his console. "I suppose one might describe it by saying we are about to embark on a program of long-range geologic dentistry."

Scott mulled this over a moment and then his face twisted into a quizzical expression. "There are some people down there I think I could grow fond of, Mr. Spock, from what I've seen of them. Don't play word games with me."

"We are attempting an extraction, Mr. Scott," Spock elucidated.

"An extraction?"

"Only instead of removing the infected region from the healthy, the captain is simply reversing the process."

Scott's expression of uncertainty lasted only long enough for a few seconds' concentrated thought . . . and then his face settled into a pleased highland grin as the truth was revealed.

On the west side of the city two yawning crevices—soil-sided, rock-toothed—pierced the outlying farmland. The atmosphere behind the tiny gilt spires and soaring steel buttresses had turned orange with the burning hills in the distance. Thunder rattled the valley and sharp slivers of blue flame broke through the orange at distant intervals.

The continued existence of intelligent life on this world was becoming impossible.

"Now, Kyle!" Kirk yelled into the intercom. Long pauses while everyone held his breath and waited—until Transporter Chief Kyle's voice sounded over the com. with an air of exhausted accomplishment.

"Got 'em, Captain."

"Are you sure, Kyle?"

"Aye, sir. It took a helluva lot of power for so broad a subject, but we're holding."

"Outstanding, Mr. Kyle. I'm on my way down. Hold it in stasis until we get there, just in case."

"Will do, sir."

Kirk and Spock hurried from the bridge. They moved impatiently through elevators, down corridors, heading for the bulk transporter room near the Shuttle Bay.

Minutes later they were standing beside Chief Kyle, staring at the considerable object which had appeared in the cavernous chamber. It was the Terratin city, neatly sliced from the planet's surface.

The city proper rested on about a half meter of crystalline bedrock, it's gimbal-bearing support system buried within and keeping it steady as always.

An astonishingly efficient system, Kirk mused, which when increased in size and adapted to other Federation colonies on active worlds would save thousands, perhaps millions of lives.

At the moment, the city was still enveloped in the shifting spectral phosphorescence of the transporter effect.

"Set it down, Chief."

"Aye, sir," Kyle replied. He activated the necessary instrumentation, pushed slowly up on a certain lever. The three men watched as the fairyland of towers and domes materialized on the deck. The city, complete to farmlands and forest belt, fitted neatly into the chamber.

If the city had appeared unusual on the surface, Kirk reflected, here on board it was thoroughly unreal. Unreally beautiful, too. No, he wasn't worried about the Terratins finding a useful niche in Federation society. Any people who could construct a habitation of pure loveliness under the incredible stresses imposed by the world below would contribute more than their share to any society they joined.

If anything, their participation in Federation affairs would be outsized.

He took a couple of steps closer, peering into the depths of the transported metropolis and wishing he could see and hear the inhabitants clearly. Spock again proved himself open to suspicion of mind-reading—or perhaps clairvoyance!

"I took the liberty of having this made up in bioengineering as soon as I divined your intentions toward the Terratins, Captain." Kirk turned and saw that Spock was bringing a large device out from behind the transporter console. It looked very much like a telescope pointing the wrong way. It was all of that—and a good deal more.

There seemed to be a great deal of activity around the open platform which girdled the tallest tower in the city. Kirk helped Spock aim the narrower end of the device toward it.

"Speak normally, Captain. The instrument will project and mollify your tones simultaneously." Kirk cleared his throat, adjusted the focus on the visual. One of the people on the platform looked familiar, though more composed than Kirk remembered him—which was understandable.

"Mandant?" The figure smiled, nodded. "We welcome your people on board the *Enterprise*."

The leader of the Terratin colony stared up at the monstrous machine. Behind him, his counselors and aides grew gradually less timid, moved out to stare up in their turn, look 'round in wonderment. To look at the Mandant, you would have thought he traveled with his city by starship at least once a year. A very cool individual, Kirk thought. He had no more worries about the Terratins' ability to handle themselves in Federation politics.

"Captain Kirk, we welcome your eye upon our city and hope you find it fair."

"I would tend to say stunning rather than fair, Mandant," Kirk responded honestly. "Right now it's about the most gorgeous thing on the *Enterprise*. Much as I hate to lose you, I'll have to admit my ship's not a sufficient setting for it."

"What do you have planned for us then, Captain?"

"There is a small world named Verdanis in a system ten days' cruising from here, Mandant. Verdanis is a lush world, much like Earth itself, but devoid of any animal life. It is also about the size of the solarian asteroid Ceres. Too small and too far away to support a normal colony, but I think more than sufficient for your people. Under Federation protection I think you will thrive and grow there—in a relative sense, of course."

The Mandant smiled back at him. "It sounds idyllic, Captain. I do not know how to begin to thank you."

"Thanks are not in order, Mandant. However, it may please you to know that while your adopted world will never support a large population, it looks to become a mining world of considerable importance for its dilithium deposits alone."

"The rescue of a portion of our population was all we could ever hope for, Captain Kirk. To be saved such, with our homes and city too, and then to be given a new, friendlier world, is beyond prayer."

Someone whispered in his ear—one of the aides—and the Mandant paused to listen to him. He turned and appeared to engage in conversation with several of the counselors.

When he turned back to Kirk, the counselors could be seen smiling in the background.

"I believe it is appropriate for me to make a very short speech, Captain." Kirk waited quietly. "People of the *Enterprise*," the Mandant intoned importantly, "we have no way we can possibly pay the debt we owe you. But this one little thing we can give, and upon this one thing we are all agreed." He gestured around, his arms taking in the city surrounding him. "We name you all honorary Terratins, now and for all time to come."

"A singular honor," observed Spock drily, "insofar as we came rather close to making it more than merely an honorary title." Kirk looked away from the eye piece.

"Somewhere along the lines of one sixteenth of a centimeter close?"

"I would say about that, Captain." Kirk grinned back at him.

Maximum attention was paid to the Terratins as the ship moved toward Verdanis. Once Starfleet deciphered the first reports on the lost miniature colony, a flood of requests for information kept Uhura and M'ress bound to the communications console.

A missing link in Federation prehistory was filled in as the ship's historian took tape after tape from the city's miniscule library stacks. Ship geologists spent days in conference with their bug-sized brothers discussing living under constant quake conditions. And all the engineers marveled over the construction of the city itself, with particular marveling reserved for the remarkable Terratin city gimbal support system. Nothing like it existed anywhere in the Federation.

There was a brief ceremony of departure when the *Enterprise* went into orbit around Verdanis. The world was officially renamed Verdantin, good wishes were exchanged, formalities of possession signed, and then the city was transported down onto a broad plain filled with miniature streams and—to the Terratins—Sequoia-sized fungi.

"What do you think will become of them, Jim?" McCoy wondered. He was staring at the main viewscreen, which showed the city nestled in among the towering vegetation. A

nearby pond formed a broad lake at the far end of the trans-
planted metropolis.

"Their location will be on public file with Starfleet Central, of course. Eventually it will become common knowledge throughout the Federation. But from what I've seen I
don't think the Terratins will be satisfied with protectorate
status for very long. They'll want full membership. That
means trade, the exchange of ideas and material. With first
settlement rights to their original home planet—and its mineral wealth—they'll wield considerable financial clout."

"That's fine for the immediate future, of course . . . but
what of the day after tomorrow?"

Kirk looked over from the command chair, considered.
"One's tempted to say they'd be in trouble, Bones, but I think
not. You should hear what the engineering people are saying
about some of their quake-resistant machinery. It looks as if
they're going to become a much sought-after group. Some
of their techniques and references are badly dated, but skill
and ability do not go out of fashion." He returned his attention to the screen.

"Why, I'd be willing to predict for openers that when
population controls are released, Verdantin is going to become one of the biggest exporters of precision machinery in
the Federation." He looked at his wrist and smiled.

"Do you know, Bones, that the Mandant and some of his
counselors wear wrist chronometers every bit as accurate as
the one I'm wearing? It takes a forty-five-hundred credit instrument under the control of a master timemaker nearly an
hour to properly adjust the timing pin where it sets into the
vibrating crystal. One of the Terratin engineers fixed it for
me before the city was transported down . . . in a couple of
minutes.

"Do you know what precision, super-miniaturized tool he
used, Bones?" He eyed the doctor challengingly. "A crow-
bar."

"I see what you're driving at," Bones confessed, suddenly
excited. "In fact, I begin to see some possibilities myself.
Damn! If I'd only spent some time with their best surgeons,
instead of setting bones and treating burns . . . !" He was
thinking furiously.

"I wonder, Jim . . . do you suppose some of the Terratin

doctors might consider a little experimental surgery . . . wearing diving suits?''

Kirk didn't comment, but McCoy rambled on, his voice taking on a reverent tone.

''Wouldn't it be wonderful, Jim, if we could perform heart operations as an inside job . . . ?''

PART II

TIME TRAP

(Adapted from a script from Joyce Perry)

VII

Kirk tossed uneasily in his sleep. Strange, unknown energies were buffeting the *Enterprise*. No matter what maneuver, no matter what speed, no matter what altitude change he ordered, she seemed unable to break the grasp of the malignant invisibility.

Around them, space was solidifying, tangible tendrils and fingers and ropy tentacles materializing out of the black depths. All reaching out, out, for the ship.

An inky pseudopod looped itself tightly around an unsuspecting engineer. A long finger folded crookedly over the bridge itself, while somewhere in the distant well of infinity a mad voice giggled.

He ordered full phaser fire, but the beams simply assaulted space itself, the ravening fire passing harmlessly through semisolid members. The *Enterprise* rolled, pitched, shook, unable to loosen the slowly contracting grip of those gigantic digits.

Two of them entered the bridge, one from either wall. They started to move toward each other. Kirk, frozen in his command chair, was in the exact middle. Someone screamed. He tried to rise from the chair and discovered he couldn't.

The black thumbs moved nearer and nearer, closing off his view of the rest of the bridge, blotting out Spock and Uhura and Arex and Sulu and the main viewscreen and the phaser controls and the black cat slinking along the deck. Spock and the others had shown no sign, no awareness, of approaching oblivion.

Didn't they see? Couldn't they feel the massive claws flowing in upon them like black glaciers to crush and squeeze and pinch? He tried to call to Spock but seemed to have lost his voice along with his mobility.

All ignored him as he tried to shout; all went about their usual tasks as the life was taken from them. Only Bones turned, once. Incredibly, his gaze went right through Kirk as if he weren't there.

The black fingers tensed tighter. The harder he struggled, the more firmly rooted he was in the chair.

And all the while the ship continued to shake as dozens of other cyclopean tendrils and fingers pulled and wrenched at it. No one paid the least attention. Pressing hard now the fingers dug in. Now they were at his very shoulders, squeezing, pressing tighter and tighter. Compression started a ringing in his ears and he felt pressure on both sides of his head.

Ringing . . . a mocking, insistent ringing that grew and grew as he tried to shut it out. Struggled to shut it out. Fought to shut it out.

And failed.

He shot to a sitting position in bed, hands behind him, eyes wide and unwinking—instantly wide awake. Then he slumped ever so slightly and ran a hand across his forehead. He rubbed at both eyes, but the buzzing and ringing didn't go away. Instead, they were transformed into a steady, almost familiar hum. It pulled at his attention insistently.

Thought . . . he turned, saw the winking red light set over his bunk. Pressed the *acknowledge* button. At the same time a strong tremor jolted the covers around him.

"Kirk here."

"I think you had better come forward, Captain. We have just impacted the perimeter of the Delta Triangle. As you can tell from the recent shake, things are beginning to happen already."

"All right, Mr. Spock." He paused while another, more violent vibration rattled his living quarters. "I'll be forward in five minutes."

He dressed rapidly. His mind raced as he hurried toward the bridge.

Following the establishment of the lost Terratin colony on the tiny world of Verdantin, the *Enterprise* had received orders to proceed to the Delta Triangle. The order had been transmitted and accepted with a quiet assurance at both ends of the transmission that neither broadcaster nor receiver felt.

There were too many unanswered questions about the Delta Triangle, none of them inspiring to a starship captain.

Kirk leaned against a corridor wall as yet another jolt shook the *Enterprise*. Noticing the uneasy, almost frightened look of two young yeomen who were walking the opposite way, he smiled confidently at them as he passed. Their incipient fears vanished, but not his own.

The Delta Triangle had a reputation that was well known. It was a vast, uninhabited, unexplored sector of the galaxy in the outer reaches of the Federation's influence. Its reputation stemmed from the number of disappearances occurring there of both manned and unmanned starships. Some dated from ancient times. Nor were they all Federation ships. Whatever was responsible for the multitude of disappearances made no distinctions as to race or region.

For awhile it had been enough simply to prohibit ships from entering the area. Nonetheless some persisted. Miners, traders, religious fanatics—the Delta Triangle was an irresistible magnet for them all.

Sometimes they came out, unharmed and having seen or found nothing. Often they disappeared, without a message, without a trace.

Now the expanding Federation found its frontiers pressing hard against the Delta Triangle. Should they avoid it and grow only in other directions? Or were there worlds within worth exploring . . . and exploiting?

Starfleet Command studied, thought, considered the problem. They decided the time had come to risk a full-scale exploration of the sector with a major research vessel. That meant a ship of the *Enterprise*'s class.

That meant, specifically, the *Enterprise*.

The alarm lights were flashing to suitable aural accompaniment as he stalked onto the bridge. His first glance was for the helm navigation console, where Sulu and Arex were working frantically. Moving near, he peered over the Edoan's shoulder.

An area roughly triangular in shape was projected on the navigation grid. A tiny, regularly-flashing blip sat just inside the bottom edge of the triangle. Neither blip nor triangle were to scale, but it was enough to show how little of the mysterious region they had managed to penetrate.

And trouble already.

Kirk nodded to nobody in particular, turned and took up his position in the command chair. Sulu cut off the alarm lights and sound. Another jolt rocked the ship as the captain took his seat. The jolts were getting stronger. For a second he thought he was back prowling the unsteady surface of the Terratin world.

It was time for facts.

"Situation, Mr. Spock?"

Spock spared him a brief glance before returning his attention to the library computer console. He looked more than usually preoccupied with his instruments.

"Indeterminate, Captain. Many of our sensors have become completely unreliable. Some continue to function, while others give readings which are patently impossible. And this wholesale disruption of detection sensors shows no internal pattern.

"The phenomenon commenced the moment we entered the Triangle sector. I do have one positive external reading, however. A solid object lies directly ahead, though it barely registers on the long-range sensors."

Kirk considered this information thoughtfully. "And this object is the source of the instrumentation disruptions, Spock?"

Now the first officer did take the time to look away from his readouts. "That is the odd thing about it, Captain. This newly detected mass appears to have nothing whatsoever to do with the addled sensors. Interesting."

"Very," Kirk agreed. "Has visual identification been tried?"

"Not yet, sir," Sulu volunteered. "The object Mr. Spock refers to has just come within range of our maximum visual scan."

"Let's see if we can't pick it up, then, Lieutenant. Magnification ten on forward scanners."

"Magnification ten, sir," Sulu echoed, working the controls just to the right of the phasers.

Kirk's gaze shifted to the main viewscreen. It showed the speckled blackness of deep space just ahead. Another of the

unexplained jolts rocked the ship. The static that momentarily appropriated the screen was of unique and unfamiliar
nature.

It sputtered out, leaving a grainy, pebbled picture behind.
Despite the lack of clarity, there was no difficulty in identifying the object picked up by Spock's operational detectors.

A Klingon battle cruiser.

It appeared to hang motionless against the distant starfield, hovering against the emptiness like the great bird of
prey it was vaguely patterned after, though Kirk knew it was
anything but motionless. The scanners compensated for its
actual speed.

It was a surprise to see an Imperial Klingon vessel here.
The Klingons were not considered to be among the more
adventurous races where abnormalities of time and space
were concerned. The Delta Triangle was one of the last places
Kirk would have expected to encounter them.

Somehow he had a feeling that their presence here was
unrelated to neutral exploration.

"Klingon battle cruiser," he announced, his tone becoming brisk. "Deflector shields up, Mr. Sulu."

"All deflectors up, sir."

"Recognize her, Mr. Spock?"

Spock studied the screen. "No, Captain. *Klolode*-class
ship, though." Kirk nodded.

"Equivalent to our own." He directed his next order backward. "Lieutenant Uhura, open a hailing frequency and . . ."

Further conversation was cut off as several pulses of lambent color suddenly erupted from the front of the Klingon
ship. The scanners were momentarily blinded. A soft rumbling was heard, and the deck trembled slightly underfoot as
the barrage of disruptor bolts impinged on the *Enterprise*'s
deflector screens and were repulsed. A moment later the
screen cleared, showed the image of the battle cruiser shrinking rapidly with distance.

"Mr. Sulu," Kirk began angrily, "will you . . . ?"

"Following, sir," Sulu said tightly. The helmsman was
obviously controlling his voice and emotions with difficulty.
Kirk didn't have to ask why.

No doubt the Klingon commander had hoped to catch the

Enterprise unprepared, her screens down, with that first attack. Seeing that it had failed, he was running now.

The Klingon's logic was not hard to follow. Were the *Enterprise* to disappear in the Delta Triangle, her demise would be recorded as just another in the age-old series of mysterious disappearances. Clever . . . and thoroughly slimy.

"He's running in a high warp arc, Captain," Sulu reported, handling the pursuit course, "but we've got her. She won't get away."

"Plotting confirmed," added Arex in his usual calm, soft tones. No sign in his voice that anything out of the ordinary had occurred.

"Ready phasers," Kirk ordered.

If the Klingon commander expected his surprise attack would go unanswered, he was badly mistaken. Letting such a provocation go would be tantamount to an admission of cowardice. That was something the Klingons would immediately rationalize as *carte blanche* to try similar adventures in other sectors—perhaps against less well-defended Federation vessels. If nothing else, a strong response was required as a deterrent to such thoughts.

"Phasers ready—approaching attack range, Captain," Sulu told him. Minutes later, "Phasers locked on target, sir."

Intolerably intense beams of deep blue lit the blackness between the *Enterprise* and the Klingon cruiser that sat squarely in the center of the main viewscreen.

The Klingon had looked normal to Kirk until just before the phasers were fired. Then he had noticed—or thought he had noticed—a peculiar wavering of space around the alien warship. A suggestion of motion where there should have been no motion. A hint of light where light was absent.

Probably a trick of the eyes. In any case, he had no time to consider it. The two bursts from the ship's forward phasers impacted on the Klingon's deflector screens.

One of two things should have happened.

The shields should have flared brilliantly with the strain of absorbing the phaser energy or, if the bursts were strong enough and contacted the shields at a weak enough point, the ship should have shown damage from the powerful attack. Neither took place.

Instead, the Klingon cruiser vanished.

Not in a burst of incandescent flame, not in a sudden supernal explosion—it just vanished. One second the ship was there, awaiting the counterattack of the *Enterprise*—and then there was only the silence of space in its place, nothing to indicate the cruiser had ever existed.

At least, that's how it appeared to a flabbergasted Kirk.

The first step was outside confirmation of his own observations. His attempt to secure same was not subtle, but had instead the virtue of directness.

"Mr. Spock, did you just see what I think I just saw?"

"Not only did I just see what you think you just saw, Captain, but I am now observing what you think you don't."

"So we concur on analysis if not on grammar. Explanation?"

Spock's attention was divided between the main viewscreen, numerous gauges set above the computer keyboard, and his double-hooded viewer. Several moments of intense study of all three areas produced a reply tinged with the faintest hint of uncertainty.

"I can offer nothing plausible at this time, Captain. However . . ." Studying yet another new bit of information, he hesitated. "Playback of sensor readings taken just prior to the disappearance of the Klingon ship, when examined at ultraslow speed, indicate that the ship was not destroyed, repeat, *not* destroyed, by our phaser fire.

"Replay further *implies* that the enemy vessel's shielding was operating at full strength and successfully deflected both phaser bursts though no direct evidence of such shielding was detectable."

Kirk paused a moment, asked, "What about the possibility they're using a variety of the invisibility shield we've encountered before?"

"I do not think so, Captain. That produces definite, detectable reactions, measurable stresses in the fabric of space. Nothing of the sort has been observed."

"Ummm." Kirk thought back to the strange phenomenon he *thought* he had noticed just before the battle cruiser vanished. "Seconds before we counterattacked, Mr. Spock, I think I saw a certain—well, a kind of fluttering around the Klingon's hull."

"I observed a similar field-effect, Captain," Sulu said excitedly. "I thought it was a distortion in our scanners, an after-effect of the disruptor bolts."

"It is not a distortion, of either our eyes or the scanners," Spock added. "I saw it, too."

"I'll assume visual confirmation, then," Kirk went on. "We should have a record of the effect, Mr. Spock. Sensor analysis?"

Spock returned to his computer, made demands on recently employed tapes. "The instruments are still not registering with regularity, Captain—a disruption still unaccounted for. But I believe I can say with assurance, after scanning the pertinent information, that the Klingon ship was not in any way responsible for the effect we observed and exercised no control over it.

"As there have been numerous ship disappearances in this region, I would venture the opinion that . . ."

"Whatever caused the disappearance of the Klingon ship was a natural phenomenon," Kirk concluded. "Clearly the Klingons were expecting it no more than we were. But what kind of natural phenomenon absorbs starships without a trace?" He turned his gaze back to the viewscreen.

"At least we have some idea what to expect . . . instant, quiet annihilation. How comforting. All duty personnel, yellow-alert status."

Sulu touched the necessary switches.

"Give me a three-hundred-sixty-degree visual scan, Mr. Sulu. Horizontal plane first, then forty-five degrees, then vertical."

"Aye, Captain," the helmsman replied, making adjustments. "Scanning three-hundred-sixty-degrees horizontal." The starfield on the screen began to move from right to left as they watched.

The scan was barely a fourth completed when the scanners picked up a new phenomenon. Unlike the odd fluttering that had appeared around the vanished battle cruiser, this one was immediately identifiable. The moving blot could be only one thing.

"Captain, we have another vessel on the screen," Sulu reported. "No, make that a double pickup, sir. Both vessels moving toward us at cruising speed, angle of approach . . . ," and he spat a rapid stream of threatening figures at Kirk.

"Visual pickup holding . . . stepping up magnification, sir," the helmsman continued. The image on screen shifted, changed, held.

Two Klingon battle cruisers appeared on the screen now, and they were between the *Enterprise* and her entry point into the Triangle.

Spock had moved over to stand next to the command chair, eyed the screen. Kirk's voice was grim as he studied the pursuing vessels.

"Mousetrapped." He glanced up at his first officer. "If the surprise attack by the first ship doesn't succeed in blasting us out of existence, they have a pair of reserves ready to make sure we don't get away to tell the story."

"Speaking strictly from the standpoint of objective tactics," Spock commented drily, "an excellent idea. They are apparently most concerned that word of this altercation should never reach Starfleet Central."

"With good reason," Kirk noted. Both men turned to face the communications console as Uhura spoke up.

"Sir, we're receiving a Class Two signal from the nearest Klingon ship. Shall I acknowledge?"

"One moment, Lieutenant." Kirk looked to his helmsman. "Mr. Sulu? On my command, I want you to turn us from our present course and head for the exact coordinates where the Klingon cruiser disappeared. Warp-eight."

"Yes sir." Sulu puzzled over the order even as he made the necessary preparations. Sometimes he wished the captain would be a bit more communicative about his intentions. It occasionally seemed to him that the *Enterprise* was governed as much by surprise as by forethought.

"All right, Lieutenant," Kirk told Uhura. "Put the visual on the main screen. And I'll want this entire exchange recorded and beamed back to Starfleet Command." Uhura looked doubtful at this last.

"It will take three weeks to reach the nearest Star Base, sir. And additional time before it can be boosted and relayed to command headquarters."

"Nonetheless, let's have it on the records . . . provided the Klingons don't try to jam it."

"Aye, sir." She turned back to her board, fiddled a moment. "Signal coming in." The main viewscreen flickered briefly. Then the view of the two Klingon cruisers was replaced by a portrait of a high-ranking Klingon officer.

This particular Klingon was heavy-set and stiff-faced. He also affected a beard and mustache, the latter a thin, drooping kind once favored by Oriental mandarins on ancient Earth. It gave him an especially displeasing appearance. His eyes were impressive, his manner standard for a Klingon commander who believed himself to be in a position of incontrovertible tactical superiority . . . blunt, overbearing, irritatingly condescending.

"You have been identified as the Federation Starship *Enterprise*, Captain James T. Kirk commanding at last record." The words came out clipped, accusative.

Kirk shifted slightly in his chair, making sure the small visual pickup trained on him was giving the Klingon as good a picture of himself as they were receiving. His voice he held carefully neutral.

"Your information is correct. This is Captain Kirk speaking."

A grunt of satisfaction, then the Klingon went on. "I am Commander Kuri of the Imperial Klingon fleet. We have just witnessed the destruction of our sister ship, the *Klothos*, and we hold you responsible. Surrender immediately or we will destroy you."

Nothing like getting to the point. Diplomacy figured in Klingon requests about as much as semantic inventiveness . . . meaning not at all.

Kirk took a pained breath, hoped Kuri was enough of a reader of human expression to know what it meant; and he continued, his voice tinged with just the proper amount of exasperation.

"We did not destroy the *Klothos*—and you are well aware of it, Commander."

"Surely you don't expect me to believe it just vanished," Kuri replied furiously.

Spock leaned over, still staying out of range of the visual pickup, and whispered, "The Klingons are not good poker players, Captain. From this one's attitude and expression, I would say he is as confused as we are—and not a little bit frightened.''

Kirk had no time to consider Spock's observations in detail. He went on sharply. "You may believe what you like, Commander. We were fired upon first, without warning of any kind. Naturally we returned fire. Our instruments record that the *Klothos* successfully turned back our phaser attack . . . and then disappeared. I have no more idea than you what caused it.

"But, as you are no doubt aware, we are now in the Delta Triangle. You are familiar with this region's reputation?''

Kuri suddenly seemed unsure of himself. Clearly he had believed the *Enterprise* was responsible for the disappearance of the *Klothos*. Kirk's explanation sounded plausible.

"Yes, certainly, that was why . . .'' He hastily took another tack, aware of what he had almost confessed openly. "I am familiar with the numerous ship disappearances recorded in this sector, yes. But that it should happen now, at such a time, is a coincidence of proportions I am not prepared to accept.'' He confessed the last in such a way that Kirk couldn't be sure if it was meant for his ears or for those of unseen persons hovering invisibly around them.

Kirk was the only one who responded, however. "Frankly, Commander, what you accept is of little concern to me. *Enterprise* out.'' He flicked a switch in the armchair console which shifted the viewscreen back to external scan. Once more the two battle cruisers dominated the picture.

At the same time he said, "Now, Mr. Sulu.''

The Klingon ships vanished as Sulu drew power from the engines. Kirk called for further magnification, but the Klingons had been lost in the starfield. That wouldn't last for long.

The view on the bridge of the lead Klingon cruiser was reversed, where it was the *Enterprise* that seemed to disappear.

"Fools, idiots!'' Kuri shouted. "Thinking they can escape.'' He had already forgotten Kirk's protestation of innocence. It was confession enough that the Federation ship was running. He turned to his own helmsman.

"Accelerate to maximum . . . use emergency power if necessary—but *do not let them escape*! Prepare to open fire.''

Moving in tandem, both cruisers leaped forward in pursuit

of the *Enterprise*. Using emergency power, they sprinted, closing on the Federation craft.

Range had been reduced from excessive to marginal and several minutes had passed when the gunner on board the lead Klingon cruiser looked back at his commander wonderingly.

Kuri was aware of the scrutiny. Undoubtedly the officer was wondering why the order to fire was being withheld. Kuri fully intended to give the order, but he had just the least bit of hesitation, the tiniest touch of uncertainty, at the back of his mind.

He did not know Kirk personally, but he knew both his reputation and the reputation of his ship. It was not like the *Enterprise* to turn and run, no matter what the odds. A quick frontal assault, at least, a passing attempt to damage one of his two remaining ships—but instead, she had turned and run.

Nevertheless, they *were* within range.

"Both ships, fire at will," he ordered, waiting expectantly for the *Enterprise* to do . . . what? What if Kirk had been right about the disappearance of the *Klothos* being due to natural phenomena? Might not the same be waiting out there, poised to capture yet another vessel?

Disruptor bolts fled across the intervening space. A feathery nimbus flared repeatedly around the fleeing *Enterprise* as her screens handled the assault.

The steady barrage of disruptors blanked out the rear scanners. Kirk switched to the forward pickups. By now he was more concerned about where they were going than what was behind them.

Scott was working the engineering console on the bridge. He had held off speaking as long as he could. Now he felt it was time to speak up.

"Sir, aren't you going to defend ourselves?"

"Your deflector shields are doing that quite nicely, Mr. Scott." Scott struggled to maintain a respectful attitude. This wasn't like Kirk.

"But sir, just to . . . run away, sir. We *were* attacked . . . and there are only two of them left."

The chief engineer might have felt better if he could have seen how Kirk was fighting his own instincts. "We'll turn and fight if we have to, Mr. Scott.'' He looked to the helm. ''Mr. Sulu, are we on course for the exact spot where the *Klothos* disappeared?''

''Dead on, sir,'' Sulu responded, checking his readouts. ''We'll arrive in . . . ten seconds. Mark, nine, eight . . .'' He counted down the seconds. At six, Scott whirled from his console to announce in a stunned tone, ''Captain, our deflector shields have just gone out.''

Sulu commanded his attention before Kirk could reply. ''Sir, the helm instrumentation has gone haywire. I can't orient myself.''

''Everything is quite abnormal, Captain,'' Arex added. ''None of the navigation readouts are behaving sanely.''

''Subspace radio channels are all dead, sir,'' put in Uhura.

By way of mechanical afterthought, alarm lights began flashing, blinking on the bridge. None of them could see, of course, the gentle shimmering light which had suddenly appeared around the ship.

For several seconds the *Enterprise* lay enveloped in a faint, ghostly halo. Then the halo winked out, and with it, the *Enterprise*—both presumably gone to the same unimaginable, unknown destination.

Not too far away in the relative sense, a senior Klingon officer suddenly jumped halfway out of his seat, staring in disbelief at his main viewscreen. A Federation vessel had been depicted there only seconds before.

''Where did they go? Where did they run to? Navigator!'' The officer in question examined his gauges and telltales, looked back helplessly at his commander.

''I do not know, Exalted One. Their ship has vanished from range of every one of our detectors—as did the *Klothos*.''

Kuri sat down slowly.

It was not permitted a cruiser commander to appear frightened before his men. However, nothing in the manual of battlefield posture prohibited him from sounding concerned.

''Slow to minimum speed. Spread out, search this area. And remain in contact at all times. The second any abnormal phenomena are detected, both ships are to retreat at battle speed to the perimeter of the Delta Triangle.'' He turned to his communications officer.

"Keep all hailing channels open." The officer nodded. "Federation and Imperial frequencies." Now there was nothing more he could do.

First the *Klothos*—and now the *Enterprise*. Kirk had been right, then, in his explanation of the *Klothos'* disappearance. Little good it had done him!

Unless . . . unless this was another Federation trick. If there was one thing Kuri had learned through the years it was never to underestimate the deviousness of the Federation mind. But he was grasping at *f'korr*. Some gross abnormality of space-time was at work here.

It was time to proceed with the utmost caution.

On the *Enterprise* something had happened to the vision of the bridge crew. Or else something had affected the atmosphere in the room. Whether the thing was in their eyes or air, it caused everyone to see his neighbor through a faint haze. One couldn't judge distances, discern outlines; and whatever it was made the eyes hurt—and the brain, which had the responsibility of trying to sort out the distorted images and reconcile them with known memories.

No one was having much success. Those who had not fallen from their seats were hanging on for dear life. The sudden displacement was not due to any violent shaking or tumbling, although a weird vibration was running through the metal underfoot and in the hull walls. Rather, everyone was experiencing an abrupt and disquieting loss of balance. Something was causing a gross distortion within familiar surroundings.

Sulu had both arms around the back of his chair and was leaning crazily around one end, staring back in Kirk's general direction.

"Captain, coordination's gone . . . dizzy."

Even Spock spoke without his usual assurance. "Captain, we appear to be suffering from a sensation akin to mass vertigo. Remarkable."

"Sulu," Kirk managed to mumble, "are we still locked into the same course?" The effort to concentrate on the weaving outline of the helmsman was making him feel sick. Somehow he controlled it.

"I can't tell, sir," was Sulu's reply. "I can't read the instruments clearly. They're all running together. Running, blending, and . . .''

As abruptly as it had begun, the strange haziness abated. Vision and balance returned with unnatural speed. Only the lingering queasiness gave any indication something unusual had happened.

Spock, characteristically, was the first to recover. His gaze was directed not to Kirk or any of the others but to the main viewscreen.

"Captain . . . ahead of us."

Still feeling slightly ill, Kirk looked over at his first officer and followed his gaze to the main viewscreen. His first reaction was that somehow the two Klingon battle cruisers might have gotten ahead of them. But that was not the explanation. *Oh, no.*

There were other starships ahead of them, though. Several starships. Dozens of starships. Starships of every age and origin. Starships representing every known civilization—and some unknown.

Some looked so ancient it was difficult to believe they contained even the most rudimentary form of star-drive. Others were sufficiently advanced looking to boggle Scott's mind.

All drifted motionless against an alien starfield, tightly packed, a chaotic confluence of uncounted relics in overwhelming numbers.

There was unconscious awe in Kirk's voice as he studied the slowly shifting panorama. "It's a graveyard. A graveyard of ships from every part of the galaxy—maybe from Outside, too. Ships I've never seen before. Look at that one."

He was indicating a monstrous jumble of spikes and pylons bound together by a webbing of translucent arches. Not in his considerable experience nor in the recognition tapes Starfleet issued regularly had he seen anything remotely like it.

Nor, he ventured to guess, had he ever encountered anything like its unknown builders—wherever they were.

"Where are we, sir?" a voice asked hesitantly. Uhura's.

"I have no idea, Lieutenant," he said huskily. "I don't *think* we've traveled very far in space." He nodded toward the screen. "Some of those farther constellations looked unchanged. It's the nearer ones that look distorted. That means we may have traveled a respectable distance . . . in time."

He broke off to stare at another vessel passing close by to starboard. It showed a more familiar outline—an interstellar cargo transport of a type and design discarded as obsolete some three hundred years ago.

"If we check," he went on, "I'll bet we'll find that many of these ships are ones designated by history as having been lost in the Delta Triangle."

"Where . . . ," Uhura started to say, but Kirk had other concerns in mind.

"Mr. Arex, can you give us any idea of our present spatial position?" Arex worked at his console for several minutes. Eventually the bony skull swiveled round on its thin neck and he stared back at Kirk out of deep, soulful eyes.

"I'm afraid not, Captain. Our sensors are operating properly once more, but the star-field is not cooperating. I cannot place our position with any certainty, given the apparent position of the nearer stars. Nor can I pick up anything like a navigation beacon."

Kirk was nodding. "I suspected as much."

"An alternate universe, Captain?" Uhura wondered.

"Perhaps something of the sort, Lieutenant. If we were in the same universe but behind some form of energy screen then we ought to be able to plot our position. But as Mr. Arex says, everything is changed around here. Same universe, different continuum—it's all a matter of semantics."

Alternate universe, different continuum . . . amazing how easily the words came when you were presented with an astrophysical *fait accompli*.

"Observations and comments, Mr. Spock."

"I can find no fault with your evaluation of the situation, Captain. I would add a thought, however.

"It must be remembered that many vessels which enter the Delta Triangle traverse it with no incident whatsoever. It would seem therefore that the contact between the two continua is erratic, the point of tangency shifting. In this case the *gate* remained open long enough for us to follow the *Klothos* in." He momentarily turned his attention back to a readout.

"Possibly it closed before our pursuers could follow us on through."

"I'm not sure they tried," Kirk ventured.

Scotty added a heartfelt "Aye."

"Speaking of the *Klothos*, Captain, I've been scanning for her ever since we threw off the lingering effects of the entry." Sulu continued to probe the space around them with full scanners. "But there are so many ships here, it's near impossible to locate a specific one."

"Stay with it, Mr. Sulu."

"Yes, sir."

Kirk studied the viewscreen. Somewhere in that sargasso the *Klothos* drifted, perhaps disabled, perhaps as intact as the *Enterprise* seemed to be. The *Klothos*, which had sprung a totally unprovoked, premeditated surprise attack on them, he found himself looking forward to meeting again . . .

VIII

At slow speed the *Enterprise* moved deeper into the swarm of dead ships—and dead they surely were. Not a sign of life or hint of motion from any of them.

Every member of the bridge complement experienced related reactions to the sight of so many abandoned vessels, the thought of so many vanished crews. But for Chief Engineer Scott the experience bordered on the religious.

Naturally the man to whom starships themselves were reason for existence was most profoundly moved of them all.

"Sir," he told Kirk, his voice hushed, "there are ships here I've only seen crude drawings of. Pictures in museums. Ships I've only seen bare outlines of on the Federation's unconfirmed-sightings charts. Ships hinted at by rumors."

Spock added additional information, his library working overtime. "Sensor scans have provided a rough approximation of the age of the metal in some of the hulls, sir—those hulls which are metallic in composition. I have already catalogued several whose base is plastic. There is also one of a unique ceramic-metal alloy and even one of wood."

"Wood! Come on now, Mr. Spock!" Scott admonished. But Spock remained confident in the findings of his sensors.

"That is what the detectors reported, that is what the spectograph confirmed, Mr. Scott. A wooden starship. The hull was composed of a celluloid material of a density not believed possible in an organic substance.

"As to the age, Captain," he continued, turning his attention back to Kirk, "while none of the vessels here have deteriorated, of course, there was sufficient degeneration of some material to indicate that many have been here for centuries. That may be a conservative estimate."

Scott's voice rose in a yelp of sudden recognition. He pointed at the screen. "My Great Aunt McTavish's haggis, Captain, isn't that the old *Bonaventure*?"

Kirk looked at that hulk. He had no question which of the myriad ships on the screen Scott was gesturing at.

Among the alien helical, parallelopiped, and conic ships floated a metal shape much like that of the *Enterprise*, only smaller. Its hull was not as smooth, festooned with awkward-looking projections and tubes, its design not as sleek—but nevertheless, a powerful vessel in its time.

Scott's voice was reverent. They were looking upon a piece of the interstellar cross. "The *Bonaventure*, the first ship to have warp-drive installed. The first of us all."

"She vanished without a trace on her third voyage." Spock spoke from over by his hooded viewer. "The crew's descendants could still be living, Captain."

"Their descendants?" Kirk threw his science officer a look of puzzlement. "But I thought . . ."

"The vessels in our immediate vicinity are indeed dead, Captain. But there is a chance some of their crews could have transferred to other ships. Specifically, to the cluster directly ahead of us, from which I am picking up faint energy and, I believe, life readings. They are increasing in intensity as we move nearer."

While Spock and Scott and Kirk studied the *Bonaventure* and this new possibility, the *Enterprise* was being observed on another screen.

With its life-systems screened out, and nestled carefully into the melange of empty hulks, the *Klothos* waited like a trap-door spider at the edge of its hole—all systems poised, only its eyes showing.

Senior Officer Kaas looked back from his station at the main sensor console. "It is the *Enterprise*, positively, Exalted One. Scanners indicate her shields are fully down."

"Excellent!" Commander Kor viewed the hated silhouette on his bridge viewscreen with satisfaction. He still did not understand what had happened to him and his ship, and for awhile it had seemed as though nothing good could come of it.

But now . . . "All hands to battle stations, quietly. Prepare to open fire on the *Enterprise* the moment she comes within range. Full disruptors—let's get her the first time, this time.

"First Engineer, I want minimum motive power to the engines. Navigator, intercept course. And rotate the ship slightly. It is imperative that we resemble one of these derelicts as much as possible."

Spock turned away from his loaded viewer for a quick glance up at the screen. His gaze started to turn back . . . and lingered. One eyebrow rose a millimeter. Then he returned his attention to the viewer.

"Strange," he muttered.

"What, Mr. Spock?" asked Kirk idly.

"I had thought that the only sign of life here was in the cluster of ships lying directly ahead of us, but there appears to be . . ."

Before he could finish, Sulu was leaning forward in his seat, staring at the screen. His eyes suddenly bugged as he recognized one shape in the crowded scene, and his brows went even higher than Spock's.

"Captain . . . the *Klothos* . . . twenty degrees port!"

"Sound red alert," Kirk ordered sharply. "All deflectors on full—phasers locked on target."

"Aye, sir," Sulu responded, his hands moving faster than his reply. "Screens up . . . phasers locked on."

On board the *Klothos*, sirens and horns suddenly howled in warning. Commander Kor shouted an obscene word, made a violent gesture.

Every disruptor that could be brought to bear immediately cut loose with a tremendous discharge of destructive energy. The *Klothos* shook with the release.

The wave-particle tide got halfway to the *Enterprise*—and the enormous charge shimmered and dissolved into nothingness. First Officer Kaas stared at his gauges with an expression he might have used if they had suddenly confronted a Kalusian sand serpent a hundred *kuvits* long.

"Sir, I don't . . . our entire weapons system . . . it's frozen."

Kor started to rise from the command seat, an appropriate comment on his lips—then there was a sudden crackling in the air. A brief whiff of ozone, the commander was outlined in a sharp flare and then he was gone. Utterly dumbfounded, the rest of the crew stared at the chair where their commander had sat seconds before.

On board the *Enterprise*, Kirk had a brief comment of his own, directed in this case to the helm. "Fire, Mr. Sulu."

"Firing phasers." It was the *Enterprise*'s turn to tremble with the release of annihilating energies.

Seconds passed before Kirk prodded Sulu. "This is no time for daydreaming—report, Mister."

"There's nothing to report, sir," the dazed Sulu finally managed to blurt. For a moment he thought the sensors might have gone berserk again, but no, they were operational. But the readings made no sense.

"No indication of damage, or even that the deflector shields of the *Klothos* registered contact. All instrumentation appears functional and . . ."

A sharp report, like the discharge of an ancient projectile weapon, sounded on the bridge. Sulu whirled in time to see Kirk outlined by a radiant nimbus. It closed over him, and was gone.

So was Captain Kirk.

For once, Spock had nothing to say.

The chamber conveyed a vastness of spirit rather than mere space. To a Terran it would have seemed more like a gothic cathedral rendered in pastel tones than anything else. A curved wall backed one end of the chamber, fronted by a raised dais.

Twelve beings sat behind a sloping table running the length of the dais. Male and female, humans, humanoid, and other—no two members were of the same race.

A Klingon sat next to a Tallerine, who seemed tiny compared to the huge Berikazin on his right. Next to the representative of that warlike race sat a beautiful woman from the Orion system. An Edoan was near her, from the same world that had given Lieutenant Arex birth. A Vulcan rested at ease beside him. One could also see a Gorin and a human in the assembly.

There were also three aliens representing races no one in the Federation would have recognized, for they were as foreign to Federation knowledge as was the Tetroid ship the staff of the *Enterprise* had observed here. Yet they waited in harmony with their nine spiritual brothers and sisters.

There was an air of purposefulness about this place which transcended mere species. No seat was more prominent than another, no being of the twelve higher than his neighbor. At the moment an air of expectancy hovered over them, though none could say what they awaited.

A peculiar electrical discharge appeared in the room immediately before the dais. The flickering vanished and a large simian shape stood there.

Kor's reaction was typical of a Klingon warrior suddenly thrust into an inexplicable situation. He reached for his side arm.

The clutching hand never touched the handle of the pistol. A secondary discharge formed in the region of the gun and he stumbled backward. The electrical shock he had taken was not strong enough to hurt him badly. The import, however, was sufficient to discourage him from trying it again.

Near the center of this alien collage, a tall Romulan stood. His eyes were oddly sunken for a Romulan and his voice soft yet firm.

"My name is Xerius." He nodded in a way that was unmistakably directed at the weapon, and his voice turned cold. "That will not be needed here, Commander Kor."

Before Kor could offer the objections that occurred without thought, a golden cloud of charged particles formed at his side. He stepped hastily out of range of the tingling field. A moment, and Captain Kirk had materialized beside him.

Kirk spared Kor a barely contemptuous glance. Other things claimed his attention.

"My name is Xerius," the aged Romulan repeated. "Welcome to Elysia, Captain Kirk." Turning, he gestured at the exquisite Orionite woman who sat next to him.

"This is Devna, our interpreter of the laws. She will speak to you both, now."

As the woman stood, she cleared her throat—the first sign Kirk had that while remarkable, this place was not Olympus and its inhabitants not gods.

She bowed formally, her gaze shifting from one starship commandant to the other. "Gentlemen," she informed them in clear, bell-like tones, "you stand now before the ruling council of Elysia. Our nation, confederation . . . call it what you will. Our world without a world.

"Representatives of one hundred and twenty-three races participate in our government. Our existence dates back over a thousand Terran years. During this time these diverse peoples, many of whom were bitter enemies on the Outside, have learned to live together in peace. Learned to do so because they must.

"Any act of violence is strictly forbidden here and will be dealt with swiftly and with utmost severity." This directed primarily at the scowling Kor, though she didn't neglect Kirk.

The ritual speech ended abruptly. She smiled. "You are now each permitted a question. Captain Kirk?"

Kirk considered a moment before asking, "Are we in an alternate universe, truly?"

"It is not certain, but we believe otherwise," Devna told him. "This tiny universe has no stars or planets, though we can see many such. Exploration here has been most extensive. There is a barrier that cannot be pierced to the outer galaxy." Her smile grew wider, her attitude sympathetic.

"Those who were first here have had much time to explore. The finite limits of our environment is one reason why all must cooperate. This place is best described as a pocket in the fabric of normal space-time."

"A restrictive Elysium," Kirk murmured, but to himself.

"Never mind all that," Kor broke in roughly. "How did you freeze my weaponry?"

Overlooking his tone, Devna endeavored to explain. "We have among us many individuals gifted with psionic powers unknown to most races. On the Outside such people were often required to use their powers to exploit, terrorize, and kill. Here those powers are employed only to preserve the peace.

"All our energies are directed to the maintainance of that peace. You, a moment ago, were attempting to break that peace, Commander Kor. We will not allow that."

There was a significant pause while she stared at both men in turn, then a look at Xerius.

"Pronounce the law," the Romulan intoned solemnly.

Once more the Orionite bowed, this time to the Romulan, then turned back to the two commanders. "Under our law, as ship captains you are each responsible for the behavior of your crews at all times. Should a crew member engage in any form of violence against another intelligent being here, you will suffer the maximum penalty. Total immobilization of your ship and selves for a century. There is no lesser penalty for such an abomination.''

Something had finally taken a little of the cockiness out of Kor, Kirk noticed. His startled reply carried little of its natural bile.

''A century!'' he exclaimed. ''We will all be dead by the end of the penalty period.''

''No, Commander Kor, you would not.'' Kirk looked closely at the Romulan. ''This small universe of ours is a most curious trap, you see. Time passes here other than it does Outside. It moves with a most extraordinary patience. A century means nothing to us.'' He gestured at his colleagues.

''Our council appears fairly young, yet all of us are centuries old.''

And *that* took some of the self-assurance out of Kirk. ''No war, and near immortality,'' he murmured softly. ''Your life here must be almost perfect.''

Xerius smiled wistfully. ''The same laws that enable us to exist here over the decades in peace compel me to tell you the truth, Captain Kirk. At one time or another, not one among us has not experienced a desire to leave this place, to return to the normal universe. Such desires can be tamed.

''We have made the best possible existence here, Captain, our lasting peace, because we have found there is no choice. There is no escape from Elysia—as you will find.''

Each word of the Romulan's last sentence fell like a steel weight on Kirk. It had a similar effect on Kor. Incredible as it seemed, the confidence in Xerius' pronouncement belied any attempt to deceive them.

And with a thousand years in which to explore and attempt, it was possible that he was right—though every molecule of Kirk's mind rejected such a possibility.

''No escape . . . no escape . . . no escape . . .'' The words rattled around in his head maddeningly. There had to be a way. He'd seen little enough of this paradise, but one thing he did not doubt was Xerius' contention that everyone had tried to leave it at least once.

It was like the children's fable of the man who became a billionaire, had himself transformed into the handsomest man in the galaxy—and then found himself trapped on an empty world. Money is valueless with naught to spend it on.

The same was true of life. Yet . . . it might be merely years of practice, of concealing truth, but as he read those expressions he could on the faces of the twelve, there were none that looked mad or unbalanced. These people had come to believe in their isolated immortality. It wasn't surprising, really.

Sanity dictated it.

Well, they could swim in it if they liked. He wanted no part of it. Right now all he desired was to be back on the bridge of the *Enterprise* where . . .

. . . Spock, Scott, and Sulu suddenly entered from the elevator, Kirk between them, still talking.

Otherwise the bridge was empty. The viewscreen remained on, still showing a panorama of the metal constellation swirling about them.

". . . and that's the whole of it, gentlemen," he finished, sitting down in the command chair. Spock and Scott arranged themselves nearby while Sulu took up his position at the helm. Kirk gestured at the screen.

"They may not be able to get out of here; they may be resigned and even happy with their *perfect* society—but *we* are getting out."

"Then we'd better do it pretty quickly, Captain," Scott said warningly. Kirk eyed him uncertainly.

"I'm afraid speed may not be possible," Spock ventured. "As the captain has told us, these people have been here for centuries, and their escape plans have failed. We'll need time to find an answer." Typical Spock, Kirk thought admiringly, understatement and complete confidence in the same breath.

His confidence did not rub off on the chief engineer. "Time is just what we haven't got."

"What's wrong, Scotty," Kirk said calmingly. "I thought time was the one thing we had an unlimited supply of here."

"Only in the abstract sense, Captain," Scott replied

crisply. "Not in the practical. No wonder no one's been able to work out an escape plan from this continuum.

"It's the dilithium crystals. They're deteriorating again, breaking up—and rapidly."

"But how . . . ?" Kirk began, and then looked exasperated. "I sometimes wish, Mr. Spock, that Professor Jenkins and his associates had found a more stable substance on which to base their successful warp-drive."

"It is this very instability that gives dilithium crystals the triggering power necessary to drive starship engines, Captain," reminded Spock.

"I don't know how it's happenin', sir," Scott continued. "It's not like the last time . . . the breakdown is fast, but not as bad. And it's a basic atomic breakdown, it's not in the molecular links this time.

"I've no doubt it's somehow connected with the same energies that slow time here. At any rate, I calculate that we've another four days our time before the power goes completely."

"It's a gradual breakdown, then?"

"Aye, Captain. That's the odd part of it. The crystals lose power uniformly."

Kirk nodded. "Otherwise we would lose every function on the ship. Be unable to maintain life-support. I wonder what the other ships here use as substitute for dilithium. Their drives don't appear radically different from ours."

"There are other races here whose engineering abilities we know nothing of, Captain. Think of the unique transporter, for example, which took both you and Commander Kor at a moment's notice. Clearly they possess an alternate energy system sufficient to keep them alive, but not sufficient to drive a ship at a decent rate of speed."

"Four days to get out of here, then." He threw his science officer a questioning glance. "Got any miracles in your physical-science tapes, Mr. Spock?"

"The basis for producing miracles does not exist in the system, Captain."

"I'll settle for a natural solution, then. You'll start work on the theory immediately, Spock. When you have something worked out, talk it through with Scotty. If his objections get too strenuous, go back and start again.

"Requisition whatever you need. Work around the clock until you arrive at a formula for getting us out of here." He looked away, back up at the screen. "If you can't find one in ninety-six hours, you'll have plenty of time to catch up on lost sleep . . ."

On board the *Klothos*, in the pseudo-barbaric chamber that was the commander's quarters, Kor looked up suddenly from the sheaf of forms he was studying. His attention was focused on the erect figure of First Officer Kaas, who stood stiffly at attention.

"You call yourself a science officer!" Kor sneered, suddenly throwing the forms and printouts in Kaas' face. The first officer flinched only slightly.

"These computations are useless. You couldn't compute your way out of the defecatory." Standing, he jabbed a finger at the other officer's nose. "Get out of my sight and don't come back until you have a plan that will work. Not one that delineates at length the reasons for your ineptitude."

Kaas saluted smartly, his upper lip trembling only a little. "Yes, Exalted One." Then he knelt, quietly gathered up the scattered forms, and left the cabin.

Kor watched him go. He paced nervously for long minutes before throwing himself on the circular sleeping platform. Rolling over, he stared up at the multidepth picture set into the ceiling. He felt caged—by this room, this ship, this accursed pocket in time and space.

His sole consolation was that Kirk must be as frustrated as he was.

Only three of the twelve who had welcomed the newcomers now waited in the council chamber. Devna and Xerius were seated at the far end of the dais.

Between them sat a female from a world in the little known Omega Cyna system—a world of light gravity, as shown by her long slender limbs and slimness across the body. There was a quality of ethereal suppleness about that form. Otherwise it was fully humanoid.

Her head was bent, her eyes shut tight in concentration. The lights in the chamber were dimmed.

"What do you see beyond your eyes, Megan?" Devna

whispered softly, putting her lips close to one nearly transparent ear of the Cygnian.

Long, long pause. The female's head rose slowly. The lids slid back to reveal a pair of silver mirrors, blank, pupilless.

"The two newcomers . . ." The voice was delicate, fairylike—wind blowing through high grass. "In each ship, beings strive to solve a riddle."

"Name the riddle," demanded Xerius.

"The riddle of the time trap. Escape, escape." The wind blew harder. "They are desperate for a way out. A way back to their own space-time, to their own universe." Boneless hands fluttering in agitation, in helpless empathy. "Escape, escape . . . !"

Devna reached out hurriedly and took the woman's nearest hand, rubbed her own palm gently along its back. "Gently . . . gently, good Megan. Easily . . . return to us now. See us now."

The Cygnian named Megan let out a sibilant sigh, an almost imperceptible whisper of air as thin lungs contracted. The mirrors of her eyes appeared to dissolve, to break up like blots of silver ink. The eyes turned to a light gold color, and from a tiny pinprick in the center, black pupils appeared, expanded to full size. Vertical, they were, slitted like a cat's.

The Cygnian smiled sadly at her companions. "The new ones wish only to get away, to run. It's always the same for the new ones. I'm sad for them."

"You're sad for everyone, Megan. That's part of you and your people. The sympathy you feel for others, intensified by your mind, enables you to see with sympathy all that others do."

"They may wish to escape all they like, fight as hard as they want," commented Xerius. "It is quite impossible. There is no danger from that."

"Still," Devna countered, "it is natural that they do so. They cannot help themselves, Xerius. They *must* try. They would not be normal if they did not. All must try before they come to accept. Best to leave them so and not try to compel."

"That is truth," Xerius admitted. "All will be well in four days' time when they have no hope. I wish it were now. Even to keep the watch, to see that in their fear they do no harm to themselves or others, feels unnatural to me. It implies the threat of direct physical restraint.

"When I was forced to prevent Commander Kor from drawing his weapon in the council chamber, the action made me almost physically ill. Eventually they will feel the same—even the one named Kor."

"You controlled yourself well, Xerius," agreed Devna. "I think the effort it cost you was worth it. The lesson was taken to heart by Captain Kirk, at least. I felt as sick as you. All of us on the council did.

"It is something we must go through. A close watch is especially vital in this case because it seems that these two are natural antagonists."

"So it would appear," Xerius admitted. "It is difficult, not knowing what is happening in the socio-political universe about us."

"But we do have our compensations, Xerius," Devna reminded him quietly. . . .

Spock was working at the library computer station, Kirk staring over his shoulder. Both men were examining a series of figures the astrogation computer had just coughed up.

More than a little time had passed since Scott's ultimatum. Kirk was growing by turns tired and depressed. Initial results had not been encouraging. It seemed impossible that Spock would not be feeling the same emotions; but, of course, even if he were it would never show.

The most one could say for him was that his usual precision of manner was showing some wear. Spock held his fatigue inside. Kirk glanced back up, at the viewscreen.

Nestled squarely in its center and surrounded by ancient derelicts lay the *Klothos*. Behind it was the tight cluster of ships that still held power and life. Elysia's inhabitants tended to group tightly together for company and companionship, shifting from one ship to another as internal arrangements permitted.

In this way they achieved a certain amount of variety in companionship over the years. Over the centuries, Kirk thought. The image held before them was far from cheering. He turned from the thought and the view of the *Klothos*.

"This is the very best you and your theoreticians could come up with, Mr. Spock?"

"Yes, Captain. I was personally astonished we could produce a plan so efficacious in so short a time."

"I was hoping you could pull a whole rabbit out of that computer instead of part of one. You've done it before."

"I do not ever recall nor do I see any reason," Spock replied in confusion, "why you should suddenly expect me to produce a Terran mammal of the leporid family from the computer banks at this, or any other time."

Kirk waved it off. "Slip of the tongue, Spock. What I meant was that when there seemed to be no possible answer, no conceivable solution to a problem, you and that machine operating in tandem have produced one time after time."

"Not this time, it appears, Captain," Spock confessed, never one to offer an encouraging word in place of the truth.

"Have you covered every possibility?" Kirk pressed desperately. "Every factor—I don't care how extreme the mathematics."

"*Every* possibility, Captain, several times. The facts are, simply, that with our maximum drive we do not have the capability to pierce the continuum barrier. I do not wish to surrender all hope, but the facts do not offer reason for much encouragement. This was the best we could do."

Kirk looked around, suddenly stood up and stared uncertainly at the screen.

"Well, he isn't giving up, at least."

Spock turned away from his console too, as did everyone else on the bridge, to watch the screen.

The *Klothos* had begun to move. It was leaving its parking position and moving off at high speed. Automatic trackers, preset on the *Klothos* to free Sulu and Arex for research, adjusted themselves to follow the Klingon cruiser. Kirk spoke without turning.

"If they can do it, why can't we?"

"I do not believe they can, Captain," Spock said with assurance. Kirk stared at him. "I consider it the unlikeliest of possibilities. Clearly Commander Kor believes otherwise.

"Their S-Two Graph unit, which is roughly the equivalent to our warp-drive, began giving off depleted energy readings at the same time as engineer Scott reported the start of dissolution among our own dilithium supplies. Their situation is no different from ours, their abilities to react to it no better.

"Kor has apparently decided to try it anyway, regardless of the attempts of his navigator and engineers to dissuade him. I am certain they have tried. The attempt may cost them all their dilithium, even to the loss of power to their life-support systems."

"So he's going to try, contrary to the advice from his own experts, without a chance of getting through?" Kirk looked skeptical. "I don't see even a megalomaniac like Kor trying that."

"You are momentarily forgetting the Klingon mentality, Captain," Spock reminded patiently. "It concludes that the guiding law of life is that all laws are made to be violated. To them their treaties with the natural universe are as tenuous as those they make with other peoples. That is why their advancement in the physical sciences was held back for so long.

"I need not add mention of their pride, which is everything to a Klingon—especially to a commanding officer like Kor. He would do personal battle with a sun if his pride was at stake."

"You're right, as usual, Spock." Kirk turned back to stare at the screen. The *Klothos* was now passing beyond the last row of desiccated starships and out into the blackness beyond.

Kirk should have thought of that himself. Kor could not live with his trampled ego without at least making the escape attempt . . .

IX

A subtle trembling had begun to run through the bridge of the accelerating *Klothos*. Kor and his officers ignored it, as they ignored the alarm lights which had begun to flash around them.

The forward scanners showed a strange mix of light and faint color. Sensors indicated a concatenation of immensely powerful forces centered ahead.

The first officer of the *Klothos* struggled to keep his voice normal as he reported to his commander. "All power beyond minimal life-support has been diverted to the engines, sir. We're continuing to pick up speed."

Kor looked over at him, showing equal control—control he didn't feel.

"Continue on course for the coordinates indicated."

"Yes, Exalted One." Kaas' attitude was that of a Klingon warrior about to plunge into battle against overwhelming odds. He was prepared to die, he only wished for a less indifferent opponent.

"Approaching maximum drive, sir," he reported, after a glance at the controls.

The center of the glowing vortex appeared to take on a slight spinning effect, its flanks bursting with erratic flares of violet light. The *Klothos* impinged on the outer edge of the luminescent matrix.

A high-pitched whine began to build on the bridge, accompanied by a steady increase in the trembling beneath Kaas' feet. It built to the point where Kor had to hold tightly to the arms of his command chair to avoid being thrown to the floor.

Several other members of the bridge staff were not so

lucky; they were thrown off balance and had to fight to regain their seats. The whine grew to deafening proportions.

The ship's lights went out and were replaced by a faint purplish light something like the color of the Terran sky seen from the bottom of a spaceport lift shaft. The whine became a scream, a howl. One officer clapped both hands to his ears, forgetting his controls. Another severe jolt rocked the bridge. Then they were all tumbling, falling, as the *Klothos* spun suddenly on its axis and the artificial gravity failed to compensate in time.

Instantly, their speed started to diminish. Though no one was able to report this immediately—least of all Kaas, who had been thrown against a far bulkhead and knocked unconscious.

Spinning, tumbling, rolling crazily, the *Klothos* had been thrown back along the path it had come. Its speed reversed, it was slowing perceptibly by the time it neared its original parking position.

Attitude control was far from being reestablished, however. A slight deviation in its return path was enough to send it crashing into and through half a dozen of the unoccupied, drifting starships. Mangled and dented, it finally came to a complete stop as some desperate engineer shut down its engines completely.

Broken compartments released a small cloud of frost . . . frozen atmosphere bleeding from a broad crack near the rear of the tilted hull.

On the bridge the shrill whine had been replaced by a wail of another sort—a mixture of the overworked alarm system and the cries of injured personnel. Kirk and Spock were not privy to such cries as they studied the damage to the once powerful battle cruiser, now centered in the main viewscreen.

For a moment, Kirk's pent-up anger at Kor's earlier actions was replaced by a grudging admiration. "You were right, Spock, but I almost wish they had made it."

"I am glad they did not," the first officer replied easily. Kirk gasped in surprise.

"Spock, *you* hold a grudge?"

"Not at all, Captain. I would never experience such an unreasonable, long-term emotion. It is rather that their unsuccessful attempt has given me an idea as to how we may be able to break through the barrier.''

Kirk waited a moment, then, ''Well . . . what is it, Spock?''

''I would suggest that everyone concerned with the eventual attempt hear this together. There will be emotional as well as physical requirements.''

''I don't understand.''

''Neither may certain members of the crew, Captain. Especially any who have been involved in serious conflicts with the Klingons before. I suggest, therefore, that we and the principal officers concerned adjourn to the central briefing room.''

''I'm not sure what you're leading up to, Spock, but if you think this is the way to handle it . . .''

''It is for the best, Captain.''

Unlike previous gatherings in the spacious conference room, no one ventured any jokes in an attempt to lighten the atmosphere. McCoy in particular wondered at the absence of Uhura. The reasons for excluding her from the conference would become clear as Spock explained his intentions.

Uhura had more reason than any of them to dislike the Klingons.

Besides Kirk and Spock, the conference included Scott, Dr. McCoy, and Sulu. Lieutenant Arex was on duty on the bridge along with Uhura, primarily to keep an eye on the *Klothos*, though it appeared certain that Commander Kor would be unable to mount any surprises for quite a while.

Aware the others were watching him expectantly, Kirk began immediately. ''Mr. Spock has come up with a formula which has a chance to extricate us from this paradise. Here is one instance where figures speak louder than words.''

So saying, he hit a switch just under the edge of the table top. A standard three-sided viewer popped up in its center. Another adjustment, and a complex set of computations began to appear on the three screens.

Kirk and Spock already knew what the computations meant. McCoy could hardly follow them at all. So it was a toss-up between Scott and Sulu as to which man would see their significance first. The first expression to become quizzical, then lopsided, then finally appalled was Lieutenant Commander Montgomery Scott's.

"But this involves combining, in close-order maneuvering, with the *Klothos*, Captain. Closer-order maneuvering . . . hell, it means combining ships!"

"That's right, Mr. Scott," agreed Kirk quietly. The chief engineer did not try to conceal his disgust at such a prospect.

"You mean you want us to work hand in hand with those vipers? Engine dregs, murderers . . ."

"It's our only choice for getting out of here, Scotty." The chief said nothing more, but continued to mumble under his breath. Were Uhura present, further discussion would have been impossible. Someone would have to break the news to her later.

Meanwhile, Sulu had been working furiously with his pocket computer, occasionally glancing up at the nearest of the three-sided screens to cross-check his own work with the original equations.

"As a problem in navigation it has more loose ends than a millipede, Captain. Trying to guide two such disparate vessels through such an intricate maneuver . . ." His voice trailed off and he shook his head wonderingly.

"How difficult, Mr. Sulu?" Kirk pressed. The helmsman tried to hedge his reply.

"I can't say for sure, Captain." He squirmed mentally. "Just . . . difficult."

"Impossible?"

"No . . . no, not impossible."

"Do you really believe that?" That forced a half-grin from the helmsman.

"I'm not sure whether I do or not, Captain. But I am sure that if Mr. Spock is confident enough to propose it, then he thinks it isn't impossible—though I'm not going to press him too hard for the exact odds. I think I'd rather not know.

"If he considers such a plan workable, then it's up to Arex and myself to find a way to make it work."

"That's that, then." Kirk turned his attention back to his chief engineer. "Mr. Scott, your comments?" Scott appeared to wrestle with himself a few moments longer. He too had little reason to love the Klingons. But eventually, he capitulated.

"Considerin' that we've only two days left before our supply of dilithium has deteriorated to the point where we can no longer drive the ship, I'd say we've no choice but to go with Mr. Spock's plan, Captain. Though I don't like it. Not one bit."

"I know how you feel, Scotty," Kirk sympathized. "I'd prefer just about any alternative. We haven't any. If it makes you feel any better, consider that Kor and his people will like it even less." He smiled sardonically.

"Our dislike of them is founded on reality, which enables us to consider such a plan rationally. Their pathological hatred of non-Klingons would prevent them from thinking of one—but it won't stop them from going along with it."

"That's just my point, Captain," Scott wondered. "Can we trust them?"

Kirk spread his hands. "That we don't know." Sulu finished his own figuring, stated his position.

"I agree with one thing, though, Captain, we have to try it."

"As for the Klingons being trusted . . ." Kirk turned to McCoy. Having nothing to contribute to an argument on astrophysics, the doctor had sat quietly through the entire discussion. "What do you think, Bones?"

"Emotionally," McCoy began, "I tend to concur with Mr. Scott. The idea of combining ship functions with that crew of backstabbers automatically sends my hand for a phaser." He looked resigned.

"But to get out of here, I think they'll restrain their inherent animosity toward us. Anything to escape this elephants' graveyard."

"Exactly," agreed Spock.

McCoy shot him a look of surprise.

"Now there's a reference I would not have thought you'd know, Mr. Spock."

"Reading the great fantasies of Terran fiction was one of my mother's favorite pastimes, Doctor," Spock informed him. "As a child I read through all of them avidly."

"Then we're all agreed on this," put in a smiling Kirk. "I'll get in touch with Kor immediately . . ."

* * *

"Escape, escape, *escape* . . ." Megan fairly vibrated with the violence of the emotions and thoughts she was reading. Devna had to reach out quickly again to soothe the Cygnian.

"Softly now, Megan," she whispered reassuringly, "softly." But Megan had no control over modulating such emotions.

"It burns them . . . it consumes them . . . it is a . . . *fire.*" Her voice shook dangerously.

"Return to me now, Megan," Devna husked quickly. "Gently, gentle, return . . . see me . . . *now.*" The bright mirrors shattered like a pool of quicksilver. Their normal light of gold color returned, the cat-pupils emerging.

"It is a violence in them. They have no control over it."

"Not yet, perhaps," countered Devna, "but they will come to accept. All do, eventually. There is no other choice."

"What has been learned?" queried a new voice. Both women turned to see Xerius materialize in the chamber.

"These new ones," Devna went on, "they learn nothing from their first attempt at escape. Now there is a new plan . . . to combine their two ships and try again. Can you not stop them, Xerius?" The speaker of the council looked troubled.

"It is not against our laws to try to escape."

"But they may kill themselves in these mad attempts. Already one of their ships has been damaged and people injured."

"That is how it must be, then, till they are convinced," Xerius replied stolidly. He looked thoughtful, reminiscing.

"Remember, Devna, how I tried and tried to flee? Tried till my ship and my people and even I were beaten. Only then did I begin to accept. So long as they do not break our laws we must not impede them. Were we to do so *we* would be breaking the laws. Not only that, but doing so would lead them to think they were our prisoners, and then they might never come to join us in peace.

"No, they must learn the futility of escape for themselves."

"Even if they kill each other in the process?" Devna wondered bitterly. "Our laws forbid violence. Why then do we allow them to do violence to themselves?"

"It is only violence against others that is . . ." Xerius looked up at Megan. "You have been looking into them,

Megan.'' The Cygnian nodded. ''Tell me, then. If a majority
are being *forced* to try these escape attempts . . .''

But the Cygnian shook her head. ''One word branded in-
delibly in all, their minds, that word is *escape*.''

Xerius looked slightly downcast. ''It is as I remember it,
from long ago.'' He smiled sadly at Devna. ''You see,
Devna? They must try. They must burn this desire out of
themselves. This thing we cannot do for them.''

The main briefing room on the *Klothos* was far more elaborately decorated than its counterpart on the *Enterprise*. The
central table was inlaid with rough-cut gemstones. Spotted
and striped, diamond patterned and tight-curled furs padded
the seats. Archaic heraldic banners were on the walls, sealed
in transparent plastic. Only four officers were present. Kor
and Kaas representing the *Klothos*, Captain Kirk and Mr.
Spock from the *Enterprise*. The discussion had been going
on for over an hour now—Kor's screeches alternating with
Kirk's taut replies, Kaas' aloofness bouncing off Spock's invulnerable calmness.

At last all suggestions had been made, all inferior arguments rebutted.

''Then it's settled,'' Kirk sighed finally. ''Our science and
engineering teams will get to work immediately at integrating both warp-drives and navigation systems so that we can
maneuver as a single ship. Exchange of personnel and beginning of computer interlock will commence as soon as we
return to our ship.''

Fourteen natural objections leaped to the fore in Kor's
mind. He forced every one of them down. These were extraordinary circumstances. So all he muttered was a curt,
''Agreed.''

They rose. Or at least, three of them did. Spock remained
seated, his face blank, almost dreamy.

''Mr. Spock,'' Kirk said. The first officer suddenly became alert. Rising, he started for the door.

Spock pushed his way between Kor and Kaas and threw
an arm around the shoulders of both men. ''I cannot tell
you,'' he confessed, his voice bordering on true emotion,
''how impressed I am by your splendid spirit of cooperation.'' There was total amazement in the room. It was im-

possible to say whether the two Klingon officers or Kirk stared at Spock with more astonishment.

"I realize we have had our differences in the past," Spock continued unctuously, "but now we can be brothers in the face of adversity."

Kor's natural reaction to such intimate and uninvited personal contact would have been a fast stab to the throat with his nails. Had Kirk tried a similar move, that might have been what would have happened. But coming from Spock, the action so stunned the Klingon commander that all he could do was squirm uncomfortably in the Vulcan's grasp.

"Mr. Spock," Kor muttered, "if you will please . . ."

Kirk, in a state bordering on paralysis, continued to stare. Spock released both mortal enemies then placed his hands on Kor's shoulders.

"Forgive me, Commander," he said gently. "I was overcome by the import of this moment. May I shake your hand?"

"I suppose so," the dazed commander replied. He extended his hand as if it were no longer a part of his arm. Spock took it, shook firm and long. Releasing the still befuddled Klingon, he turned to his own counterpart on the *Klothos*. That worthy was staring silently at him with an expression usually reserved for the more interesting specimens of previously unknown alien life.

"And yours, Science Officer Kaas." The first officer of the cruiser extended his own hand . . . somewhat reluctantly—and Spock shook it, hard.

"Goodbye, for now," Spock said. Then, apparently overcome still further, he turned and started for the door, shoulders heaving, concealing his face.

Kirk followed, glanced back at Kor and Kaas, rather embarrassed. "Goodbye, Mr. Spock," mumbled Kor. "Captain Kirk."

The door slid shut behind them. Kaas stared at it for several seconds after the two Federation officers had left before breaking the silence.

"The stories of his being half human must be true."

"More than true," agreed Kor. "Or perhaps passage through the continuum gate affected his hybrid mind more than most." That shook the first officer from his lethargy.

He turned to eye his commander with something less than mindless subordination.

"I wonder," he began pointedly, "if perhaps we all haven't been affected."

"Explain yourself," Kor ordered, but not as sharply as he should have.

"This willingness of yours all of a sudden to work closely with an old enemy like Kirk. With one who has thwarted so many thrusts of the Empire. It is not like you, Commander. What do you really have in mind?"

Kor relaxed, let out a Klingon chuckle—a sound as devoid of humor as a cobra's hiss. "You've been my first officer too long for me to conceal much from you, Kaas. Very well.

"What would you think if the *Enterprise* were suddenly to disintegrate after our dual ship had pierced the space-time window?"

"I would think my Commander had maneuvered brilliantly."

"I think the implications are clear?"

"Perfectly," Kaas responded, understanding what was required, now.

"And it can be arranged?" The first officer hesitated before replying, ran clawed fingers over the polished wood of the briefing table.

"It involves a high risk factor, given the lack of time to prepare and Kirk's naturally suspicious nature. Yet I think it can be arranged."

"Very good, Kaas. I'll leave it to you to attend to the details of the *Enterprise*'s destruction." The two Klingon officers exchanged vows.

Of all the hundreds of ships drifting in the blackness of the pocket universe, none were stranger than the two that hummed with activity near its center. Blue and purple from tiny phaser welders surrounded the doubled vessels with shifting motes of light, and it wore a corona of suited figures busily weaving about its multiple hull.

The *Enterprise* had been maneuvered to a point just above the *Klothos*. Now the two ships were being joined together with cables and plates, bars and impulse connectors.

Kirk leaned back in the command chair, studying the

changing view on the main screen. Multiple external scanners provided a constantly changing picture of the work in progress. They were racing a clock with too few hours left.

They had to finish by tomorrow noon, ship time. That was the point at which the power supplies of both ships would be depleted to such an extreme that they could not reach the minimum speed necessary to satisfy Spock's figures. Time and navigational requirements were inflexible.

If they failed, they would be trapped here forever.

McCoy was nearby, chatting with Sulu. The doctor was trying for the eighth, or possibly the ninth time, to get an explanation in layman's language of the complicated physics through which it was hoped they could break back into the normal universe.

"Beg your pardon, sir," came a voice from behind him. Kirk swiveled in his chair, was confronted by Second Engineer Gabler and another crewman he didn't recognize immediately. A drive tech . . . Bell was the name.

Slouching between them—rather reluctantly, Kirk thought—was a Klingon engineer. With a thousand other things on his mind, Kirk forced himself to devote full attention to the men before him.

"What is it, Mr. Gabler?"

"Sir, Bell and I are the relief watch for the dilithium storage tanks." Gabler's way of telling Kirk that the suspicious Scott had placed guards at certain vital points in his section. "We arrived a few minutes late and found this one and a couple of his buddies poking around."

"Where are the buddies?" Kirk inquired, glancing behind the Klingon and seeing no one else.

"Being watched, sir. This one appeared to be in charge."

"This is absurd, Captain Kirk," the Klingon engineer broke in. "We were lost, that is all. What is more natural when one is performing hurried work on a strange ship?"

"Lost, my foot," protested Gabler angrily. "It's clearly posted as a restricted area. You didn't have any trouble reading any of the more complicated symbols. *Keep Out* is one I'll bet you recognized easy enough. You knew all along you weren't supposed to be in there."

"Gentlemen, I'm sure there's been a mistake." Everyone turned to stare at Spock as he moved toward them from his position at the library computer station. He put a comradely arm around the shoulders of the Klingon. The engineer couldn't have been more shocked if he'd been bitten by a malachite tree viper.

Once again Kirk found himself at a loss for words. "Now then, my good fellow," Spock inquired pleasantly, "where were you supposed to be working?"

"Ah . . . your pardon, sir, but . . ." The Klingon found an answer quickly. "Engineering subdeck five."

"Close enough to the dilithium storage area. A natural enough error, I'm sure you'll agree, Captain."

"If you say so, Spock," Kirk responded uncertainly.

"There, you see?" Spock said to Gabler. "A perfectly natural mistake. Allow me to escort this young man back to his work area, Captain."

"Very well, Mr. Spock."

Spock, his arm around the Klingon engineer, turned and steered him toward the elevator, talking easily with the alien. The latter continued to eye the Vulcan uneasily. As soon as the doors closed behind them, Kirk looked firmly at Bell and Gabler.

"Return to your posts—and don't leave until you've been formally relieved."

"Aye, sir." Gabler saluted stiffly, making no attempt to hide his displeasure at the way things had proceeded. He and Bell turned and left the bridge.

When Kirk turned the chair back he found McCoy had been standing behind him. There was a note of real concern in the doctor's tone.

"Are you as worried about Spock as I am, Jim? Taking into account what you told me about his actions on board the *Klothos*, and now seeing it for myself, I'd say it would be the understatement of the millennium to say he's not acting quite normal."

Kirk rubbed a hand across his forehead. "He's been performing under a lot of pressure, Bones. All of us have. Spock's been working around the clock for the past two days—almost three, now, and we're not finished yet. Arex and Sulu have checked his calculations, but this is still being done at his say-so. And the most crucial moments are still ahead of us, when he has to be at his sharpest."

"I know that, Jim. So listen to the say-so of someone who has not been under so much pressure recently, when I say that there's something wrong with him. I've never known Spock to act like a pal under any circumstances. Least of all toward the Klingons."

Kirk frowned, clearly worried. "That's true, of course, Bones, but . . ."

"If he's coming apart, Jim," McCoy continued relentlessly, "then we're in real trouble. He handled all the original computations for this escape try himself. If he's not, as you say, a hundred percent when we start to move, he could go under the pressure—and take the rest of us with him."

Kirk reflected on the situation. Bones was exactly right, of course. Maybe he had become so exhausted himself these past couple of days he had not paid enough attention to the condition of those around him—especially Spock's. Particularly since the science officer's work had not suffered.

Still, you never knew for sure what Spock might be concealing.

"All right, I'll talk to him, Bones. That's about all I can do. I can hardly recommend he see you for medication without something more positive."

"No, you can't, Jim. I don't even know if unnatural friendliness on the part of a Vulcan is a sign of illness. I only know it's not part of Spock's normal behavior."

Kirk rose from the command chair. "He's in the main briefing room. I'll take care of it now."

"Good. And Jim?"

Kirk paused. "Yes, Bones?"

"Whatever you find out, let me know. So I can be prepared. In case."

Kirk nodded once.

The briefing room, where Spock could work in absolute privacy, was crowded, but not with people. The table was littered with piles of computer tape, cards, tiny cassettes, diagrams and computations. Material spilled off the desk onto chairs, dripped onto the floor like white moss.

At the moment, Spock was totally absorbed in the study of a series of projected energy abstracts on the three-sided central screen. Kirk didn't remember when the first officer had last slept, but he rose promptly when Kirk entered the room.

Kirk smiled reassuringly. Spock took this as a sign that nothing of an emergency nature had developed, sat back down and concentrated once more on the tiny lists of figures. Kirk examined another side of the triple viewer for a few moments, then looked evenly at his first officer.

"Everything seems to be moving on schedule. But then, you're the only person who can really be sure. Everything devolves on you, doesn't it, Spock?"

"I would suppose so, Captain."

"Any final determination of our chances?"

Spock replied without looking up, though there was a note of puzzlement in his voice. "That is an odd question to ask at this stage, Captain."

"Nothing serious, Spock. It's just that Dr. McCoy and I were thinking—well, there has been something about your recent behavior of late—particularly toward the Klingons . . ." He trailed off uncomfortably.

Now Spock looked up, spoke thoughtfully. "Yes, I grant you it is not my usual pattern."

Back went his gaze to the viewer. He touched a control and a new set of abstracts appeared on the screen.

"Well," Kirk finally pressed, when it was evident Spock wasn't going to add anything, "is something wrong?"

"I believe there is, Captain. But not with me," he added quickly, noticing the sudden look of alarm on Kirk's face. "With the Klingons.

"I sensed something odd about their attitude when we were aboard the *Klothos*. Kor was far too agreeable to our proposals."

"You think so?" Kirk wondered. "He objected to every suggestion we made."

"And ended by agreeing with all of them. I believe his objections were mere verbal camouflage. And his first officer, Kaas, seemed to be more at ease than our mere presence would explain."

"It might be due to their desire to get out of here as desperately as we," Kirk countered. "There could be a host of reasons for both Kor and Kaas acting the way they did."

"I would agree that their behavior might have other explanations, Captain, had I not touched them. But even though the physical contact was necessarily limited, and their minds were uncertain, I did detect a number of subtle indications in Kor—physical as well as mental—connected normally with victory and conquest in Klingon physiology.

"It is not a simple thing to convey with words, Captain. You have to experience it. I can only infer that Kor had an attack on the *Enterprise* in mind even as he agreed to cooperate with us."

"Attack? How can they attack us when our ships are maneuvering as one?"

"I don't know, Captain. But I would hypothesize some form of delayed action. Something that will affect us when we have successfully broken the barrier and the *Klothos* has separated from us."

"Could you gain any hint from Kor's mind, Spock?" Kirk leaned over the table intently.

"No, Captain. At the time Commander Kor may not have decided on the method, only the course. I am not that telepathically gifted, you know.

"I also studied the mood and mind of the Klingon engineer who was discovered in the dilithium vault. There was nothing specific in his thoughts—only a vague feeling of animosity, which is to be expected, and expectancy, which is not. I cannot escape the feeling that some kind of sabotage is being planned against the ship."

There was silence while Kirk weighed possible action. "Whatever they have in mind, they can't do anything until after we've finished our run at the barrier. They need us to get through. That gives us time to uncover anything they try to plant on board." He activated the desk com.

"Security, this is the captain speaking. I want all security teams on round-the-clock duty now. Watch every Klingon who is working on board the ship double-close. Interior or exterior. I don't want one of them to go to the bathroom without our knowing about it."

"We've been watching them all along, Captain," came the reply.

"I know that. I want the most intense surveillance you can mount, Mister. Is that understood?"

"Yes, sir," came the abashed response. Kirk switched off,

looked satisfied. "If they try anything, we'll be ready for it."

"I hope so, Captain," Spock mused. He turned his full attention back to the screen. "I sincerely hope so."

The other members of the bridge complement on the *Klothos* ignored the conversation of the three officers grouped around Commander Kor's chair. As any good Klingon crew ought, they attended strictly to their assigned tasks, closing ears and eyes and minds to all that occurred around them that did not require their personal concern.

Kor and the female, Lieutenant Kali, cast expectant eyes on the first officer.

"All is in readiness, then," Kor announced. "You have the device, Kaas?"

In reply, the first officer reached into a belt pouch, pulled out a small, deceptively innocent-looking device. It was about the size and shape of a throat lozenge and looked to be about as dangerous. It gave even Kor pause when he considered what was bound up inside that tiny package.

"My compliments to Engineer Kanff," he said in open admiration. Kor always appreciated fine workmanship. "A wonder that they got it so small. Kanff and his staff are due a decoration for this."

"Yes, an extraordinary job, considering the requirements and the lack of time in which to fulfill them," Kaas agreed.

"How is it to be triggered?"

Kaas turned the compact device over in his hand, displaying casual disregard for its capabilities.

"According to Engineering's calculations, we must achieve at least warp-eight to have a chance of penetrating the barrier. At the time our dual vessel reaches that speed, a sensing crystal within the device will shatter, setting the timer.

"Reaction time will commence approximately three minutes after we have pierced the barrier, assuming the Vulcan Spock's predictions to be correct. Our engineers concur. The reaction will backflow until it reaches the dilithium chambers themselves. At which point the *Enterprise* will disintegrate."

"An admirable plan with an admirable end," grinned Kor, retaking his seat. "Engineer Kanff has carried out the first half of the mission in producing the machine.'' His gaze wandered up to Lieutenant Kali. For a brief moment he considered virtues other than those of a top officer. It passed.

"The other half, Lieutenant, will be up to you."

"Yes, Commander. I have been briefed and understand what is needed. How will I recognize the diversion?"

Kor looked temporarily pained.

"Unfortunately, that is the one factor we cannot plan for in advance, Lieutenant. For it to succeed, it must be at least partly spontaneous in nature. The choice of the crucial moment will be up to you. However, there should be ample opportunity at the joint gathering this evening-time."

Kali's expression became one of disgust. "To mingle on a social basis with humans and Edoans and their kind," she almost spat. "It will be difficult to maintain an aura of civility, Commander."

"It is necessary to be more than civil, Lieutenant. We must endeavor to appear openly friendly." He eyed her sternly. "We can do nothing until we escape this trap. Remember that if your resolve weakens . . . and smile."

"Yes, Exalted One," she answered compliantly.

Kaas handed her the tablet-sized machine. She took it carefully and tucked it away in a waistband pocket.

"Tonight they entertain us," Kor observed, barely controlled excitement in his voice, "and so it is only just that we provide them with some entertainment ourselves. It will only last for a few milliseconds, but it should be most gratifying."

"If that device does what Engineer Kanff assures me it can," added Kaas, nodding in the direction of the now hidden tablet, "I almost regret that none on board the *Enterprise* will have the opportunity to observe its entertaining capabilities at greater length."

X

It was all the better for Kor's machinations that the party had been suggested by the psychology staffs of both the *Klothos* and the *Enterprise* and then mutually agreed upon by himself and Kirk. That should lull any suspicions of ulterior motives on the part of the Klingons.

The rationale behind the gathering was that since the Elysians felt so strongly about the personnel of both ships co-existing in harmony, it might be an excellent idea for them to observe members of both crews mingling in a spirit of good fellowship and cooperation—even if a little faking was required.

As a further indication of their desire to cooperate with their new friends, invitations had been extended from both ships for members of the council to attend. When locale had been called into question, Kor had magnanimously agreed to have the event staged on the *Enterprise*.

One of the large briefing rooms had been made over for the occasion. Klingon and Federation trappings were placed side by side. They did not blend well, since conflict carried over even into decorations.

Long tables were set up around the room and loaded with food and exotic drink from both ships. Natural antagonisms momentarily laid aside, the celebration commenced surprisingly well. Klingons, crewmembers of the *Enterprise*, and representatives of the Elysian council mingled easily in the large chamber.

Taped music played over the concealed speakers. At first it had been mostly martial Scottish music, angry fifes and drums, until Kirk ordered the selection changed over engineer Scott's objections.

Then the speakers poured forth a tape requested by Devna, the Orionite member of the council, and promptly turned out by the *Enterprise*'s vast library.

She was dancing in the center of the floor, to the admiring stares of numerous onlookers. Sounding clearly over the hum of constant chatter, the music was lush, full, impressionistic. Devna danced sensuously, completely relaxed. Only occasionally did a movement seem forced. It was as if she were desperately striving to demonstrate that there was a different side to her than the formal interpreter of laws who sat on the council.

Now she was interpreting with her body instead of her voice. There was nothing abstract in her movements. They were basic . . . primal, even. The performance ended with a flurry of difficult moves lithely managed—ended with her lying prone on the floor.

There was applause, varying according to diverse styles of artistic appreciation. The music changed to something simple, gentle, purely melodic. Almost embarrassed, Devna made a slight bow and disappeared into the crowd, leaving the dance floor free for others to try their Terpsichorean skill.

Kirk was engaged in a somewhat forced conversation with one of the Klingon library technicians. He turned to speak to Devna as she hurried by. He was glad for the chance to break off the discussion without becoming insulting, finding it increasingly difficult to control his emotions around the Klingons. Their ever-present, unsubtle sense of supercilious superiority generated in him most undiplomatic urges.

"That was beautifully rendered," he told her.

"I thank you, Captain." She was barely breathing hard.

"Especially that grand finale."

Her eyes suddenly seemed to light, and a glow came into her face. "You've seen the dances of Orion before, then?"

Kirk nodded. "Many times. Always with pleasure, never without admiration."

"I wish . . ."

Interpreter of laws, council member or not, the look on her face was unmistakable.

"Wish what?" he prompted. She stared hard at him.

"I wish I could return through this space-time barrier and see Orion again. We tell, we lie, we say to ourselves," she continued tightly, "that homesickness is a mental abstraction and easily avoided. We have put our former lives behind us . . . and so we have.

"But . . . the walls we've built in front of those memories are not always as strong as we would wish them to be."

"You could go back," Kirk told her. "We're perfectly willing to take passengers."

"No," she said, gazing at him tiredly. "You see, we've all seen the absurdity of trying to escape. Many times each of us here dreamed of breaking out, till we came to understand it simply cannot be done. We have accepted our new lives here. To dwell on the possibility of returning is only to open emotional wounds best left closed. Such speculation is unhealthy."

"We're pretty sure it can be done," Kirk countered.

"Do you not think," she half shouted, "that each of us has not believed that same thing as intensely, as strongly as you? Did you not see the *Klothos* fail? Did you . . ." She stopped, staring at him.

"You still do not believe. You still fail to admit to reality. When fact has replaced dream, I will dance again for you, Captain Kirk. You will find, when you have been here a hundred years or so, that the appreciation and companionship of one's fellows is among the finest ends anyone can live for.

"Until then, I will intrude on your dream no longer."

"Funny," Kirk murmured. "I've always felt exactly the same way about appreciation and companionship on the other side of the space-time barrier."

She gave him a friendly, pitying smile of the sort usually bestowed on a stubborn child, turned and walked into the crowd, heading for the place where Xerius stood in earnest conversation with another council member—a Tallarine male, Kirk noted absently. He knew better than to go after her, better than to repeat his offer of escape.

Usually the outright refusal to consider another way of looking at something was a sign of advancing age. It appeared that physical deterioration of the body was not a prerequisite for turning so obstinate. Repeated discouragement would only contribute to such an attitude.

The music issuing from the speakers had turned faintly

romantic. A number of couples were dancing on the floor now. There were also one or two triples.

Kirk might have intervened if he had seen what was happening across the room, but his view was blocked and no one else saw fit to step in. McCoy, overcome by the enforced spirit of the occasion, had imbibed rather too much. But so what if his emotional gauge was running a bit high? His judgment was unimpaired, he thought—and member of an inimical race or no, that Klingon lady was one of the most beautiful gals in the room.

The doctor made a gallant, if unsteady bow before her, smiled broadly.

"Miss . . . would you care to dance?"

Not surprisingly, the offer took her utterly unawares. She made a pretense of looking away, in reality searching for Kor. He saw what was happening, nodded slightly. She forced a smile of her own and stood.

They started to shuffle around the floor—awkward in each other's arms at first, but with increasing steadiness. Kor broke off his conversation with one of the council members and slid over to where Kaas stood. His first officer had not noticed the unusual pairing yet. He was drinking and trying to avoid contact with any member of the *Enterprise* crew.

A few words were whispered, glances exchanged. Kaas waited until Kor had made his way across the floor and struck up a new conversation, this time with one of the Federation officers. Then he moved, starting out onto the dance floor, an angry, half-drunken glare dominating his expression.

A clutching hand, and McCoy found himself spun around to face the furious, weaving Kaas.

"Get away from her, human, this is my woman." Kali looked on quietly.

"Now just a minute," McCoy objected, his liquid amiability rapidly starting to fade. "All I did was ask her to dance. She didn't have to agree, and I certainly didn't . . ."

"She's my woman!" Kaas howled, not wanting to be distracted by facts. Most of his body weight was behind the wild swing he took at the doctor.

McCoy dodged the worst of it, still caught Kaas' fist in the side. He stumbled backward, over went a table laden with food and drink with a nerve-tingling crash. The taped music continued but now every eye in the room turned to them; every conversation ceased.

No one, not even the two security guards at the door, noticed the long-forgotten Kali slip out of the room through an open service hatch.

Gratified at the ease with which he had bowled over his unsuspecting opponent and not wanting to waste the opportunity, Kaas moved in quickly, hoping to get in a few damaging blows before they were separated.

He underestimated McCoy—a characteristic common to anyone who had ever fought the doctor hand to hand. McCoy had been knocked off balance, but he was more surprised by the sudden assault than hurt. And if his present condition was not analytical, it made him plenty combative.

He hit the first officer of the *Klothos* low, ramming his head into the other's midsection and knocking the wind out of him. Grappling wildly, the two officers rolled over and over on the floor.

McCoy flailed away with enough enthusiasm to keep the frustrated, furious Kaas from either doing any damage or getting free. One wild elbow even caught the Klingon officer under the bridge of his nose, an exceptionally painful jolt that started blood flowing.

It was Kirk who got his arms around McCoy's shoulders and dragged him off Kaas.

"Bones, stop it!" McCoy was still weaving on his feet. "What the blazes happened?"

Kaas climbed to his feet. That's when he first noticed the blood trailing from his nose. At the sight of that, he forgot what he was doing on the floor, forgot his position, forgot everything.

He went for his concealed disruptor pistol.

"Stop!" came a booming voice from the back of the room. Xerius' commanding tone. Kaas didn't hear him, just as he didn't hear Kor's frantic cry of *"Khaba dej', Kaas!"* or the curse that followed. Roughly translated, it meant, "The idiot will ruin everything!"

Kor ran toward his first officer . . . too late, he saw. The disruptor was already out and aimed at the two humans. Before anyone had a chance to reach Kaas, he fired.

The killing bolt faded into the air centimeters from McCoy's chest.

Kaas, startled not only by the failure of his pistol but by the sudden realization of what he had done, stared in confusion at the useless weapon. Before he could decide to fire, put the gun away, or do anything, Kor wrenched it from him. The first officer looked up slowly into his commander's eyes.

A milky gaze was fading rapidly from Kaas' corneas. He had been in a berserker frenzy. Kor struggled to control his own emotions. Not the first officer's fault, really, considering that the other had unexpectedly drawn blood.

But what a time to let a little blood intervene!

"Captain Kirk and Commander Kor, and these two," intoned Xerius solemnly, "will come to the council chamber in two minutes to face charges." There was a flash . . . several flashes. When Kirk and the others looked around, every member of the Elysian council had vanished.

The celebration had come to an end.

A low babble of conversation resumed in the room . . . low and concerned. All hint of the enforced pleasantries of moments ago was gone. Members of the two crews now had something real to talk about—a common threat of unknown dimension.

Kali did not participate, however. By then she had successfully made her way into the central computer room of the *Enterprise*, avoiding the depleted security forces.

Using a packet of compact tools taken from another pocket, she removed a certain panel buried far back in the main complex. The components visible beyond the panel pulsed with faint, miniature auroras, by-products of the energies flowing through them.

The tablet-sized machine slid neatly into place, well back among a maze of interlocking circuitry. The device would have been even better located in one of the engine rooms, but security was impenetrable. According to the schematics on board the *Klothos*, this was the closest she could get without being challenged.

Engineer Kanff had calculated it would be more than close enough.

No one saw her replace the panel or leave the room. A

dozen or so technicians, some from the *Enterprise*, some from the *Klothos*, were passing through the nearest corridor, moving to a new work area. Kali blended in neatly with them.

When they reached the work section, she joined two of her shipmates and fell to assisting them as best she could. They eyed her strangely, but said nothing. It was not meet to question the actions of a superior officer. They went silently about their business.

She had successfully carried out the crucial part of her mission. Now it remained only for her to wait and enjoy the spectacle to come.

There was no time to try and rig any kind of protective defensive field. It probably would not have been of much value. Previous experience had demonstrated that whatever transporter the Elysians possessed, it was perfectly capable of plucking any member of the crew off either the *Enterprise* or the *Klothos* any time the council wished.

So it was that once again Kirk and Kor, now accompanied by first officer Kaas and Dr. McCoy, found themselves standing in the cathedral-like council chamber before the assembled Elysians.

There was no attempt at explanation this time, no effort to make the visitors feel at ease. The enmity coming from the council was almost palpable. A feeling of decision that Kirk found frightening, hung in the air. There was to be no discussion or trial here. A decision of some sort had already been made.

In a place where there was an excess of only time, Xerius' speech was brief. "You have been informed. You have been warned. You have been instructed. And you know that any exercise of violence against another intelligent being is forbidden here." He glared at Kor.

"Your man began the fight and attempted to kill." Xerius looked around at his fellow council members. "I formally propose as penalty that we suspend the *Klothos* and its crew for a century of their time."

All his carefully constructed struts and buttresses supporting an intricately wrought plan had neatly been kicked out from under him when Kaas had lost his temper. Now Kor saw the foundation crumbling.

"My first officer was provoked," he protested, trying to project an air of outraged innocence. The excuse sounded lame. Xerius treated it with contempt.

"He attempted to kill—and would have, had we not prevented it at the final moment. There is no lesser penalty for such a crime."

"But I didn't know," Kaas objected. "I lost control of myself, saw only . . ."

"That will be enough," warned Xerius sharply. "You have spoken already . . . with your actions."

"May I say something, then?" Kirk asked.

"You may, Captain Kirk."

He took a step toward the dais, thinking rapidly. As a starship command flight officer he was required to know a fair amount of law, but that had never been one of his favorite subjects at the Academy, though he had done well in it. With his no-nonsense analytical approach, Spock had the better courtroom manner.

But Spock was not here. Kirk would have to argue his case as best he could, alone.

"Captain Kor and I—as you probably know—are going to try and break through the time-space barrier tomorrow. If you put the *Klothos* and its crew into suspension, you'll be punishing us as much as them. We can't leave as a single ship.

"I implore you to let our dual craft make this attempt as we've planned."

"This futile attempt at escape is so important to you?" Xerius was saying. "Despite what we have told you, that it is foredoomed to failure?"

"I repeat, we don't share your eternal pessimism. However you choose to see it . . . yes, it's that important to us."

"You *will* fail."

"We *must* try," Kirk pressed desperately. "Xerius," he went on, hoping the council leader didn't think he was being lectured, "in many respects, Elysia is a perfect society. It has endured a thousand years and proven that when given a chance, the most antagonistic peoples can live together in peace." And when given no other choice, he thought.

"But with all its virtues, it's not home. And with all its faults, we would prefer to return to our own continuum."

Far down the dais, Devna was heard to murmur, "As would many of us."

Xerius pretended not to hear.

"You insist on taking these would-be murderers with you?"

"I'd be lying if I didn't admit that Commander Kor and I regard each other with something less than brotherly affection," he admitted. Kor smiled toothily.

"But sometimes an injured man has to take medication that's not very pleasant, yet necessary to his survival. That's my situation regarding the *Klothos*."

Kirk's argument was simple and logically irrefutable. And so, after studying both men for several long moments, Xerius gave a reluctant nod.

"Very well. I release Commander Kor and First Officer Kaas into your custody, Captain Kirk." He looked sternly at both Klingons. "After your absurd escape attempt fails, the penalty will be carried out—should you survive."

Kor forced himself to fight down his triumphant smile and look nominally repentant. It wasn't too hard. If the Vulcan Spock's calculations proved inaccurate, the penalty might just as well be carried out. Better to sleep than be forced to endure an eternity of this repugnant civility—especially with humans and other Federation grass eaters!

"Lest you believe we think you ill fortune, I wish you good luck, Captain Kirk," the council leader finished.

"Preparations are completed," Kor announced.

Kirk looked up at the viewscreen. The image of Commander Kor stared back at him from his position on the bridge of the *Klothos*. A precision universal chronometer was mounted on one arm of the Klingon commander's chair and was synchronized to the one on the *Enterprise*. They had finished the conjoining work with several hours to spare.

"Ready here." Kirk turned his attention to the rising black band on the chair chronometer, watched it reach a preset numeral. At the instant it did so, there was a buzz from the helm. A preliminary check, successful. Helm and navigation instrumentation on both ships were properly linked.

"Manual timing checks," Kirk reported.

Now nothing was left but to feed power to test Spock's theory.

Sulu was watching him, waiting.

"Prepare to accelerate to warp-six, Mr. Sulu."

"Standing by, sir."

"Ready to compute subordinate corrections if required, Captain," Arex said crisply.

"Communications standing by," Uhura added.

"Computer backup ready." Spock, relaxed, at ease.

Kirk glanced down at the chronometer set in his own chair-arm, silently counted off the seconds: three, two, one, accelerate.

A barely perceptible vibration ran through the deck as preset automatics took over and the linked ships suddenly leaped ahead, accelerating steadily.

Two members of the Elysian council stood in the otherwise deserted chamber and stared at the flowmetal screen which had appeared behind the council dais. Long-range monitors mounted on long-abandoned craft kept the *Enterprise-Klothos* in sight as it moved out of the ship cluster.

Devna and Xerius stared at the picture. As they watched, a third counselor entered, eyes going to the screen. Silver cataracts slid over Megan's eyes as her gaze reached outward.

"Escape," she mumbled. "All are concentrating on escape. Their ships move ever faster."

"Kirk of the *Enterprise* expresses confidence in the work of his technicians and engineers, in the ability of his first officer.

"Kor of the *Klothos*, too, exudes confidence in his personnel and in . . ."

Both hands went to her temples. She stumbled backward.

"No! The Klingons—have hidden an explosive device aboard the *Enterprise*. The picture is in Commander Kor's mind. She will be destroyed. She will . . ."

Xerius and Devna came out of shock simultaneously. It was the council speaker who moved first, clutched at the controls of the concealed microphone. Spoke frantically while staring at the screen.

"Intership emergency, intership emergency!"

"Power Control acknowledges, Speaker," a voice responded.

"Full broadcast to the fleeing starships, tight-beam message to the *Enterprise*."

There was a pause, then . . . , "Probing, Xerius. They do not answer."

"Keep trying . . . give me an open channel. *Enterprise*, this is Speaker Xerius. Respond, *Enterprise*! You are in . . ."

Descent into the Maelstrom, Kirk mused as the whirlpool of light that delineated the space-time barrier appeared on the screen. A wavering cyclone of force they were rushing toward.

Unconsciously, both hands dug tighter into the arms of the command chair. True, the *Klothos* had tried the barrier, been rejected, and survived. But perhaps they were moving so supremely fast that this time the barrier would reject them with less care. His grip didn't relax.

"Warp-seven, Captain," Sulu reported.

"Everyone brace for resistance as we contact the barrier field," Kirk ordered unnecessarily.

"Sir!" Uhura's voice. "Xerius is trying to contact us. The call is coming on an emergency frequency."

"Put it on the main speaker, Lieutenant." She nudged a switch, and the speaker's voice immediately sounded on the bridge.

"Captain Kirk, the Klingons have secreted an explosive device of small size but tremendous triggering power in your . . . in your computer chambers. Megan reports it is located at . . . a moment . . . she is attempting to read . . ."

The intercom went silent. Kirk's stomach was doing acrobatics.

"It is located," the speaker said, voice contact returning, "in the casement housing auxiliary power leads to the drive chamber. It will activate when you reach warp-eight. If it is not removed before then, it cannot be deactivated. It must then be removed carefully, according to Megan's reading of its internal structure, or . . . (fizzle, sput) . . . racinatio . . ."

"Outer fringe of the barrier is disrupting communications, sir," Uhura reported.

"Stay with it, Lieutenant. Spock, Scotty." Both officers were already halfway to the elevator. Kirk punched a switch on his chair console.

"Computer room . . . Captain speaking . . . give me the tech in charge."

Brief pause, then, "Rodino here, Captain."

"Commander Spock and the chief are on their way back there to perform some surgery. Remove all access plates to the drive power leads, auxiliary casement. Don't touch anything else . . . move, Rodino."

"Computer out," came the fast reply.

While the attention of the *Enterprise*'s command was otherwise engaged, their counterparts on the *Klothos* were intent on the main viewscreen. Their alert system had begun to sound, as it had once before only a few days ago.

"Approaching warp-eight, Exalted One," Kaas noted from his position at the science station.

A new sound began to penetrate the bridge, a sound Kor had listened to recently—just prior to being thrown into unconsciousness. A high, wailing roar generated by forces which existed in contempt of all natural law. A wild, thunderous moan which once heard was never to be forgotten. Not by Kor, nor by any member of the *Enterprise*'s crew, now subjected to the same buffeting.

"The barrier," the commander muttered, staring at the light storm ahead. They were close to it, now.

"He didn't specify *which* auxiliary leads it was behind, damn it," Scott rumbled tightly. Shoving the startled Rodino aside, the chief engineer had gone through the first such section. With blatant disregard for everything the manual said and for years of training, he ripped at connections and leads, oblivious to the chances of shock or to the damage he was doing.

The first panel he searched showed nothing, nor the second. Delicate circuitry was shoved aside by the small combination tool in his right hand. He started in on the third, nudging aside a minor knot of microcircuits, probably deactivating someone's favorite entertainment channel.

That could be fixed . . . later. Right now he wanted a look a little deeper into the casement. Something seemed to be reflecting a touch too much light back there. Then he saw it.

A small cylindrical section about the size and shape of a large pill.

"There it is, Spock. I'll hold the lines aside."

Spock dropped to his knees as Scott moved slightly aside. Spock moved his arm into the opening. Gently, two fingers slid around the tablet, lifted, pulled it slowly from its resting place by a double-fluid circuit.

He had it.

Seconds later, both men were standing, examining the compact device. Spock imprinted its exterior design, consistency, weight, color, shape in his mind for future study. Then he moved to a boldly marked slot at the far end of the chamber. A disposal niche.

There were three switches set in the wall beside it. One labeled DISINTEGRATE, the second marked RECYCLE and the third, was covered by a snapdown protective top.

Spock flipped the red plastic up and placed the innocuous-seeming tablet in the open niche. Then he pressed the uncovered button. The red label alongside it read: POWER EJECT.

Despite the coolness on the bridge, Kirk found he was sweating. A vibration that did not come from the engines now rattled the deck beneath them, shook the arms of his chair where he gripped it. A teeth-scratching screech screamed over the speakers and seemed to dig into his bones, despite Uhura's attempts to moderate it.

There was a sudden sharp jolt. Inside his skull a little voice chuckled, said, "Nice try, James T. . . . good-bye . . ."

Then without any warning, the vibration stopped, the high-pitched wail trailed off into a drifting sigh, and the view forward became awesomely normal—a vision of familiar stars and nebulae. The view was infinitely more glorious than the claustrophobic immortality they had left behind.

As prearranged, a single relay snapped over on board both ships. It begat a multitude of tiny clicks and snaps as beams, cables, and plates parted—sometimes softly, other times with the aid of tiny explosive bolts.

The *Enterprise-Klothos* fissioned, each half arching off in opposite directions.

Unrestrained cheering indicated the emotions on the *Klothos'* bridge. Anyone would have thought the crew had just won a major battle against overwhelming odds. In a sense, they had.

Her commander and first officer stared expectantly at the viewscreen in anticipation of further pyrotechnics. Long-range scanners struggled to hold the fast-moving dot that was the *Enterprise*.

For a moment, something seemed to have gone wrong. Then there was an impressive flowering of violet light. The cheering died quickly as the rest of the crew turned in surprise to gape at this new phenomenon. First one gaze, then another, and another, turned toward the command station.

"Exalted One," Kaas said formally, "this is a great moment for the Empire. May I have the honor of . . . ?"

"Not yet, not yet," Kor countered thoughtfully. "Give everyone time to think on it. Let them reach the proper conclusion by themselves. The result will be that much more pleasurable for them. We can confirm it at our leisure. I want to enjoy this as long as possible."

His predatory smile widened as he watched the angry flare fade from the screen . . .

To see familiar stars again was a pleasure Kirk had not expected.

No, no . . . that was not true. Inside, he had always really believed they would successfully escape the continuum trap— no matter how many times the Elysians had failed. There wasn't a barrier in the universe that Spock, Sulu, Arex and Scott couldn't break once they set their combined brainpower to searching for a solution.

That belief had wavered only once . . . when the *Klothos* had tried the barrier and failed. Maybe he had felt so sure about it because they had never really been threatened. Kirk was used to facing down death—the promise of eternal life was something hard to feel terrified about.

Uhura interrupted his musings. He noted a calmness in her voice again that no promise of extended life could put there.

"Sir, I'm picking up a deep-space transmission at the extreme range of reception. It's from the *Klothos*." She paused. "Commander Kor is heading for his home station—there, they've just passed outside our effective communications limit.''

"Don't keep us in suspense, Lieutenant,'' Kirk prompted. "What's the good commander done? Probably taken full credit for our escape from the time-space trap.''

Uhura seemed to be having trouble controlling herself. "It's not . . . that, Captain. They saw the device they planted aboard go off and apparently they felt it was still aboard.

"He thinks we've been destroyed—and he was trumpeting his triumph all the way back to Klingon Imperial Headquarters!''

"Commander Kor is exhibiting the typical egocentrism of . . .'' Spock stopped, observed that Kirk, Sulu and even Arex were now sharing in Uhura's laughter. A steady high-pitched noise of a less ominous sort now permeated the bridge.

"I had thought that if such information inspired emotion in you,'' he said uncertainly, "it would have been of anger and not amusement.''

"Don't you see, Spock?'' Kirk turned to him, trying to retain his composure.

"See what, Captain?'' The first officer was still confused.

"Consider what Kor is reporting, is claiming, Spock . . . and then try to visualize his face when the Empire's emissaries in the Federation send back word that we are still in excellent condition!''

Spock glanced around the usually efficient, smoothly running bridge. It had taken on the air of a carnival. He turned back to his console.

There was a certain problem in abstract mathematics he had been working on. He would return to a consideration of it now. But first he reviewed Kirk's explanation. The incongruity of the situation he perceived, of course. But he would not, if he lived to be a thousand, understand how it could produce in normally sensible human beings a state of transitory imbecility.

In response to his request, the computer laid the details of the problem before him once again. Bending his gaze to his hooded viewer, he found relief from the surrounding hysteria in the cool perfection of higher calculus. He was not, however, isolated in his reaction to the situation.

Had he known, it is quite likely that Commander Kor would not have been laughing, either . . .

PART III

MORE TRIBBLES, MORE TROUBLES

(Adapted from a script by David Gerrold)

XI

The call came in a few days later.

"Message from Starbase Twenty-three, Captain," Uhura announced. "Indication is priority signal, but not confidential."

"Put it on the main screen then, Lieutenant."

"Very good, sir."

Dim with distance, a face appeared ahead—a portrait of a young and rather harassed-looking communications officer. "Captain Kirk, my name is Massey. I'm with Emergency Interstellar Relief . . . Communications Section."

"So I see," Kirk replied.

From what Kirk had seen, members of the IRS wore expressions akin to this Massey's nearly constantly. The nature of their work, naturally. The young officer's gaze, however, seemed especially mournful.

"We've been trying to contact you for ages, Captain. Uh . . . how did your mission into the Delta Triangle go?"

Word certainly gets around in Starfleet, Kirk reflected.

"Standard exploration," he replied blandly, ignored a muffled choking sound from the region of the helm. "In this case, if it had taken us a day longer, you would have spent those ages trying to contact us."

The Sub-lieutenant looked uncertain, aware that Kirk was trying to tell him something and thoroughly unsure how to interpret it. A hand wiped wavy brown hair from his forehead.

"Glad to hear that, sir," he mumbled in response. "You're familiar with the operations of the Relief Service?"

This one was even younger than he looked, Kirk mused. Had he ever been that young? "I have some familiarity with the functions of Starfleet peripheral organizations," he deadpanned. "What can we do for you?"

Missing the sarcasm completely, the Sub-lieutenant turned crisply businesslike. "Do you know the location of Sherman's Planet?"

Kirk glanced over a shoulder. "Mr. Spock, could you . . . ah, never mind. I remember." He looked back to the screen. "A newly settled world on the periphery of the Federation. Population is mixed human and Edoan." Arex nodded in confirmation. There were few worlds where the Edoans felt comfortable outside of their home system. Sherman's Planet was one of them.

"I have a cousin in that colony, Captain."

That lent whatever difficulty Massey was about to delineate a touch of immediacy, as far as Kirk was concerned.

"I recall that Sherman's Planet is a fairly successful venture. Not a paradise world, maybe, but certainly a tame one."

"Quite true, Captain." The youngster was nodding vigorously. "It gave every promise of being a rich agricultural world, capable of exporting a wide variety of staples to the rest of the Federation. Records indicate that the initial seedings of the colonists would produce a first crop beyond anyone's expectations." His expression became more doleful.

"Unfortunately, it seems that the first survey team overlooked something. Occasionally, new worlds have surprises locked inside them that are not revealed at once. Sherman's Planet looks to be one of them.

"We're still not sure what the basic cause of the trouble is. A shifting deficiency in the soil, maybe the presence of a cyclic virus in the atmosphere. Whatever it is, it's deadly where mature grains are involved. As I say, we don't know yet. But the initial crop seems to be a complete failure.

"The soil chemists think they can solve the problem, develop a defense against it. But that will take a minimum of six standard months. The farmers on Sherman don't have six months. It's not a question of export now—it's a question of survival.

"What they do have is a double growing season, thanks to the planet's lushness and long summer. We've turned up a hybrid seed grain on the plains world of Kansastan. According to tests, it ought to be impervious to what's been hitting the Shermanites' crops.

"Two large cargo drones loaded with the hybrid seed are in parking orbit around KS. You are to proceed there, pick up the drones, and escort them to Sherman's Planet. At standard cruising speed you should get them there in plenty of time for the colonists to get the seed into the ground.

"If they don't get the seed, they'll face the coming winter without any crop at all. This is supposedly an established colony. They have only minor emergency supplies left. No crop and they'll face widespread famine. Predictions run as high as ten to eighteen percent fatalities. And the colony proper might never recover."

"The grain will get there. Don't worry, Massey. As you say, we've plenty of time." The best catastrophes, he reflected, were the ones that could be prevented.

"*Enterprise* out, Lieutenant Massey."

The Sub-lieutenant managed a weak grin—as much of a smile as the people in his business could mount—and signed off. Probably to turn his attention to some new disaster, Kirk mused. It took a special kind of person to stand up under the kind of anguished reports the IRS had to handle daily. Kirk did not envy the young man his job.

"Mr. Arex, Mr. Sulu . . . set a course for Kansastan."

"Aye, Captain," sounded the simultaneous acknowledgment.

They had no difficulty in securing the drone grain ships. Each was somewhat smaller than the *Enterprise*, but nearly as powerful. High-speed, bulk carriers, their sole purpose was to convey enormous loads across the plenum in the shortest possible time.

The monitoring officer on the small space station orbiting Kansastan was garrulous to the point of boredom, so Kirk was glad when linkup was completed, giving him a chance to depart.

Still, he couldn't help feeling sorry for the fellow. He was assigned to a world whose people went about their Federation business efficiently and with little fanfare. They didn't get many visitors.

And that monitor might serve in that isolated post until his retirement without a single promotion.

The journey to Sherman's Planet was passing uneventfully. So uneventfully that when they were three-quarters of the way to the outpost colony, Kirk was considering beaming the nearest Starfleet base for further orders.

Instead, he sighed, activated the recorder in the arm of the command chair.

"Captain's Log, stardate 5526.2. Having been assigned to escort two robot grain ships to Sherman's Planet, the *Enterprise* is now approximately . . ." He looked to Arex. The navigator nodded, turned to his readouts and recited a figure. Kirk repeated it into the recorder.

". . . from the colony. Upon completion of delivery of the quinto-triticale seed, the *Enterprise* will proceed to . . ."

"Captain? Captain." Sulu's tone was anxious.

Mildly irritated, Kirk put the log on hold. "What is it, Mr. Sulu? You know better to interrupt when I'm making an official . . ."

"I'm sorry, sir, but I've just picked up some kind of smaller vessel. A one-man scout or an independent trader . . . can't be sure at this distance. It's running an evasive course, sir, at top speed—with a Klingon battle cruiser in close pursuit."

Kirk thought rapidly, lifted his finger from the hold button. "Changing course to investigate the pursuit of a small ship of unknown origin by a Klingon ship of the line. Out." He looked to the front.

"Mr. Arex, alter course to put us on an intercept route with the smaller craft."

"Changing course, Captain," the navigator answered promptly.

Kirk drummed fingers on a chair arm, studied the screen impatiently. "Any confirmation of identity on either ship, Mr. Sulu?"

"Not yet, Captain." Sulu was bent over a gooseneck viewer.

"Captain?" Kirk looked around.

"Yes, Mr. Spock?"

The first officer looked over from the library computer console. "Among the information received by high-beam code transmission from Starfleet Science Center in the past several days was an item that it has not been necessary to mention until now. There are rumors from Federation agents that the Klingons have a new weapon, abilities unknown.''

''Your timing is remarkable, as always, Mr. Spock,'' Kirk commented, straight faced. ''The *Klothos* didn't have it.''

''No, Captain. Had she, it seems certain Commander Kor would have employed it.''

''Cruiser is closing rapidly on its target,'' Sulu announced, forestalling any further discussion of new Klingon potential. Spock turned to his sensor readouts.

''Initial scan indicates the smaller vessel is a one-man scout ship of common design. Federation manufacture and registry probable but not yet certain.''

''I think I can get the other ship on a high-resolution scope, Captain,'' Sulu offered. He worked at his instrument board.

A second later the new picture appeared on the screen, showing the small scout with unusual sharpness, considering the range. A sudden burst of light flashed across the screen, disappeared, as if something had arced for a microsecond between the *Enterprise* and the fleeing scout.

Kirk already guessed the explanation. ''Mr. Sulu, shift pickup, please.''

Sulu figured it out only seconds later. His tone was one of puzzled amazement. ''They're firing on him, Captain.''

He adjusted another switch. A different scanner took over from the first. The new view showed the little craft's massive pursuer, clearly recognizable as a Klingon battle cruiser. As they watched, multiple ripples of light flared from the warship's prow as she let go with her secondary disruptor batteries.

Again Sulu changed views. This time the scout ship eclipsed the disruptor bolts and they passed on its far side. Kirk doubted the Klingon gunners would miss again. The scout vanished from the screen and from then on some instrumental calisthenics were required of Sulu to keep it on the screen.

The pilot was going all out to avoid being hit, Kirk noted. He was good, and his ship was mobile; but it couldn't dodge a warship's electronic predictors forever, couldn't continue to escape disruptor fire that could obliterate much larger prey.

A bigger question was the sanity of the Klingon's commander. His ship was so far within Federation space there was no possibility of navigational error. Unless he and his executive officers had gone completely mad, they knew exactly what they were doing and what chasing the scout ship this far implied. To risk such a blatant violation of Federation borders was a sign that someone desired to destroy that tiny ship very much, indeed.

Territorial intrusion took clear precedence over escort duty. "Ahead, warp-six."

Sulu and Arex coaxed response from the ship's engines. Kirk activated his chair intercom.

"Transporter room, report." A crackle of opening channels, and then a familiar burr. "Transporter room . . . Scott speakin'."

"Scotty?" Kirk's brow furrowed in mild surprise. "What are you doing there? Where's Chief Kyle?"

"On his second off-shift, Captain. I thought I'd take it for him. I've been goin' crazy tryin' to figure out how the Elysians picked you and Dr. McCoy off right through our defensive screens and . . ."

"Never mind that now, Mr. Scott," Kirk interrupted quickly. "You haven't taken the console apart, I hope?"

"No, sir." Now it was Scott's turn to sound surprised. "I intend to eventually, but right now she's fully operational. Why? What's happenin'?"

"We've run into a Klingon battle cruiser chasing a solo scout and . . ."

"A Klingon? This deep inside Federation . . . ?"

"I know, Scotty, I know. She's firing on the smaller ship. We're going to try and rescue its pilot."

"Aye, Captain!" There was a pause at the other end, then, "He's nothin' in the way of a screen, sir, but at this distance it'll take some time to scan the pattern of whoever's on board. I dinna want to bring him in in pieces."

"Get to work on it, Mr. Scott. When you lock in on him, don't hesitate. Bring him aboard."

"Aye, sir."

Kirk turned his attention back to the screen. Another set of light waves passed close by the scout. The cruiser was still firing. Someone muttered that the Klingons couldn't shoot worth a damn.

At the tail end of the mutter, a last bolt struck the ship a glancing blow. A tiny white cloud billowed from it as escaping atmosphere froze solid. The scout continued to move, but it was clearly disabled now.

Still no word from Scott. He spoke over his shoulder.

"Open general hailing frequencies, Lieutenant." Kirk waited a moment, giving Uhura time to comply, then spoke into the pickup once more.

"Klingon battle cruiser . . . identify yourself. This is Captain James Kirk commanding USS Enterprise speaking. You are violating Federation space. Identify yourself . . . halt firing on scout ship."

Sulu switched the forward scanner back again from the weaving scout to the cruiser. It did not take long to tell that the Klingons had no intention of altering their course or ceasing their attempts to destroy the fleeing scout. Several more disruptor bolts darted from the prow of the warship.

"Doesn't even bother to acknowledge," Kirk muttered. A certain amount of hesitation on the part of an interloper could be tolerated. Such outright contempt for a major treaty could not.

"Mr. Spock," he ordered, his voice lowering meaningfully, "you will note this violation and enter it officially in computer records. Mr. Sulu, arm all phasers. Deflector shields up. All hands to battle stations."

After Uhura activated the alarm, the Enterprise became a hive of instant activity. Dropping whatever they were doing when that Klaxon sounded, each moved to his or her position of readiness.

"All stations report battle status, Captain," Uhura reported a few moments later.

"Phasers armed," Sulu announced. "Shields up." Several other switches were snapped over. "Ship is battle status." Kirk nodded, spoke to the mike in one last try.

"Klingon battle cruiser, this is your last chance. Identify yourself." Only the faint static of distant suns sounded back over the speakers. "Ahead, warp-eight . . . range, Mr. Sulu?"

"Closing, sir." Again the view forward altered, back to the scout ship.

"The injured vessel is losing speed rapidly, Captain," informed Spock.

Kirk studied the image worriedly, spoke to the intercom. "Scotty, have you got that pilot yet? We're running out of time up here."

"Workin' on it, Captain," the chief engineer replied distractedly.

Another disruptor bolt flashed past the scout. A second. The third didn't miss. There was a brief flare of radiation from the superheated hull and the tiny vessel melted away like disintegrating butter, faster than a splinter of magnesium in a firestorm.

In the transporter room four lights all commenced blinking at once and several gauges did unnatural things. Lieutenant Commander Scott, after several abortive attempts to alter the reading above one particularly significant dial, launched into an impassioned diatribe concerning the Klingons' ancestry, origins, probable spiritual destination, morals and general lack of good taste. His outburst did nothing to improve the readouts, but it was decidedly therapeutic. Scott's only disappointment was that the Klingons could not listen in.

Actually, if they had been able to, it is doubtful Scott's aspersions could have made them any madder than they were already.

"They got him," Sulu muttered angrily.

"Maybe not." Kirk bent to the intercom. "Scotty? Scout's gone . . . disruptor bolt. The pilot?"

Scott's voice came back full of confusion. "I don't know, sir. That blast must have hit his ship at the crucial second. You should see some of these instrument readings, Captain. In college we once did an experiment which involved dropping an egg from a thousand meters up onto a concrete platform. That's kind of what the integration parameters look like now, sir.

"I *think* I got him out in one piece. The trick now's goin' to be puttin' him back that way."

"Scotty, you pro . . ."

"Captain!" Kirk turned at Sulu's warning shout. His gaze went to the screen. The Klingon cruiser was turning, turning in a wide arc and heading directly toward the *Enterprise*. It began to accelerate.

Spock raised an eyebrow. Kirk's eyes widened.

"They're confident of something," Spock theorized. There was a beep from his own console, and he glanced back to study a computer readout.

"Silhouette and class identification confirmed, Captain. Imperial battle cruiser *Devisor*, Captain Koloth commanding."

The Klingon warship continued to close the distance rapidly. But just before it entered effective phaser range, it sheered off, keeping the distance between them. A strange blue halo formed at the ship's bow, faint at first but growing steadily in size. It thickened until it had the consistency of blue smoke. There was a sharp flash, and the tenuous blob leaped away from the *Devisor* toward the *Enterprise*.

Arex stiffened in his seat as the screen was filled with expanding blue cloud.

"The new weapon, Mr. Spock?" Kirk asked.

"Some kind of solidified field effect, Captain." He was studying sensor readouts. "It will contact us in precisely four seconds." His hands tightened on the console edge. "It appears capable of producing a most remarkab . . ."

There was a lurch as the *Enterprise* rolled forty-five degrees on her port side. It swung upright again. All on-board lights had gone out momentarily. Now they flickered dimly on, operating on stored power.

". . . disruption," Spock concluded.

External hull scanners revealed that the *Enterprise* was now cloaked in the wavy blue field.

Disruption of another kind had affected the main transporter room. Both the instrumentation and Chief Engineer Scott were producing some startling effects.

Sulu was working controls hurriedly. His face wore an expression at least one part panic. "Captain, our engines are dead."

"We have been struck by some kind of projected stasis field," Spock reported evenly. "Our matter–anti-matter generators are disabled. So are the impulse engines. We seem to be completely paralyzed. Most remarkable."

"I'm not feeling in an admiring mood," Kirk shot back. "All phasers . . . fire."

Sulu attempted to respond. His worried frown knotted tighter. "Phasers don't work either, sir."

"I might note that my admiration does not preclude a desire on my part for retaliation, Captain," Spock explained. "I must observe, however, that the photon torpedoes will probably not respond, either. It appears that this field is capable of neutralizing all high-order field and warp functions."

"We could always throw rocks," Uhura suggested.

"This new Klingon weapon must be one of surprising power if it can so thoroughly immobilize a large starship like the *Enterprise*," Spock continued, speaking to no one in particular. "The energy drain must be enormous. Almost insupportable, I should think." No one was listening closely.

Kirk was at the com. again. "Scotty, did you retrieve that pilot yet?"

"He's still in the beam, sir, but I can't integrate him. All transporter systems have been interrupted."

"You sure you've got him, though?"

The chief engineer glanced to the transporter alcove. A familiar shimmering of multicolored particles continued to hover there, outlining a rotund, vaguely humanoid form. And that was all it did, growing neither stronger nor weaker.

"Gauges indicate seventy-three percent solidification attained, Captain. But I need at least another eighteen percent to assure successful final integration. We're going to need more power for that, sir."

"Hang onto him, Scotty." For what? They were at the mercy of the Klingon ship, unable even to run. He hammered the arm of his chair once, twice.

"Captain," Uhura broke in, adjusting her earphone, "message coming in."

"Put it through, Lieutenant."

He forced himself to relax. Even managed a half smile . . . which lasted all of two seconds. But at least he was able to keep himself from shouting angrily as the image of the Klingon bridge formed on the screen. Most of it was blocked out by a single figure.

The Klingon commander turned from speaking to someone off-screen to smile ingratiatingly into the pickup. He was fighting natural instincts to achieve a patina of politeness.

"This is Captain Koloth of the battle cruiser *Devisor*. Have

I the honor of addressing the renowned Captain James Kirk, who . . ."

"You're not calling to laud my reputation," Kirk interrupted him firmly. "Release my ship."

"Of course, Captain, of course. Gladly, happily." He positively oozed good fellowship. "There is only one small thing we require. You must turn over to me the pilot of the little ship we were escorting."

"Didn't look like you wanted to escort him very far," Kirk observed. "In any case, I haven't got anybody to give you. Your last bolt dissolved him along with his ship."

Koloth assumed a sad smile. "I beg to differ with you, Captain Kirk, but our sensors distinctly recorded certain powerful energies at work on board the small ship at the moment of disruption. Computer analysis identifies same as a transporter beam of a type well known to be mounted on your class cruiser.

"As there are no other ships of your class in this immediate area save yourself, I must therefore assume the beam came from your ship. This in itself is not an arguable thing, but sensors further indicate a probability of better than half that the pilot of the scout was successfully removed before his vessel unfortunately self-destructed."

"You lie about as well as you navigate, Captain Koloth," Kirk countered. "In any case that ship was of Federation registry, operating well inside Federation boundaries—something you might also take notice of. The pilot is under our protection."

Koloth's face turned the color of a bad apple. He appeared to be trembling slightly. Somehow the captain was maintaining an iron control over his emotions. Something vital was necessary to force such restrictions on him.

It was.

"Captain, this person has committed ecological sabotage against the Imperium. If I have to take him by force I will."

"Temper, temper, Koloth. The first Klingon to step aboard this ship uninvited will be the last Klingon. Mr. Spock, full internal security alert."

For some reason, Kirk's final refusal seemed to calm Koloth. Even to widen his smile. "I'm afraid, Captain Kirk, that you'll find your hand weapons do not operate any better than your major armament.''

Uhura had noticed something on her board and leaned over to whisper it to Spock. "Mr. Spock, I'm losing contact with our robot grain ships. They are not held by the stasis field and so they are continuing on course."

"What was that?" Kirk asked, looking over at the science station.

"I repeat, Captain," Koloth continued, "you must turn over to us the . . ."

"A moment, Captain. This situation calls for consultation with my officers."

Koloth looked disgusted.

"Ah, your archaic democratic principles? You have a few minutes, Captain, no longer. My patience is growing thin. If by that time you have not beamed the pilot over to us we will destroy your ship piecemeal as it sits helpless within our field."

"All right, Koloth, all right. You've made your point. Just give me a few minutes to talk this out." He rose from the chair, turned to Uhura.

"Lieutenant, cut off reception."

"Yes, sir." She complied as Kirk walked over to stare at the readouts above her.

"As you can see, sir," she commented, gesturing at the monitoring gauges, "they're moving off."

"Then they still have power. Can we control the robot ships, Sulu, in our present state?"

"Affirmative, sir," the helmsman replied a moment later. "Our remote guidance system is a low-order field effect and not affected by the Klingon stasis."

"Koloth made no mention of them. There's a chance he's so concerned with us he has forgotten about them. Bring them back, Mr. Sulu—and have them ram the Klingon ship."

"Captain . . ."

Kirk looked over at his first officer.

"You cannot afford to lose that grain," Spock insisted. "The situation on Sherman's Planet . . ."

Kirk cut him off. "I can afford even less to lose the *Enterprise*, Mr. Spock. Once he gets what he wants, do you think Koloth will let us go to report this serious violation of Federation territory? Why should he, considering where he's got us?''

Sulu was working furiously at his instruments as Kirk took his seat again. ''Open the hailing frequency again, Lieutenant Uhura.'' The screen cleared quickly. ''Captain Koloth? We've reached a decision.'' He paused a moment for effect and to give the robot ships a few seconds more to gain on the *Devisor*.

''I'm going to give you one last chance to release the *Enterprise*.''

Koloth assumed an expression of incredulity. ''*You're* going to give *me* one more chance?'' His voice dissolved in Klingon laughter—hacking, unmelodious, unamusing. Apparently someone off-screen said something equally unamusing, because Koloth abruptly was listening hard and looking to his left. He was frowning when he turned back to Kirk.

''It won't work, Captain.''

Koloth's face disappeared and the screen went blank. Kirk was not sorry to see him go. He smiled slightly himself. The threat was working, otherwise Koloth would still be there, gloating.

Their counterattack was crude and primitive and would have appalled the men who had designed the *Enterprise*'s offensive weaponry. This didn't change the fact that it was working. Either of the robot ships could make a very thorough mess of the *Devisor*.

Sulu expanded their field of vision. At the same time, two new azure bubbles began to form at the *Devisor*'s bow. They grew rapidly in size. Again the brief flare splitting them off from the mother ship and then they were moving away in opposite directions, toward the onrushing robots.

''Incredible,'' Spock was murmuring, ''utterly incredible . . . the amount of energy that must be required to maintain those fields.''

Sulu switched to a deeper pickup to follow one of the blue fogs as it headed toward an approaching grain carrier. As they watched, it suddenly seemed to flutter, uncertain as an albatross coming in for a landing. Fluttered, wavered . . . thinned . . . dissolved.

So did its companion cloud. So did the major field surrounding the *Enterprise*. The starship gave a little shudder as it was released from paralysis.

"I thought so," commented Spock with barely a hint of satisfaction in his voice. "They couldn't maintain it. They didn't have enough power. Even a ship twice the size of the *Devisor* . . ."

Kirk wasn't really listening. "Keep phasers locked on target, Mr. Sulu. But hold your fire until they fire first. Give them a chance to back off."

"Aye, sir." The helmsman kept his face turned away so his Captain wouldn't see the undiplomatic, predatory gleam in his eyes.

Flashes of a deeper blue erupted from the *Devisor*'s prow . . : her main disruptor batteries this time. The first barrage destroyed the propulsion units of one of the robots, missing the huge cargo module. A second attack missed the other carrier, badly.

"Apparently their battle capacity is way down," Spock observed. "They only damaged one ship. Missing two unscreened drones at this range indicates a definite lack of offensive power—for the moment, at least."

As if in confirmation, the *Devisor* turned away from the *Enterprise* in a sweeping curve, away from the remaining charging drone.

"Veering off," Sulu noted formally, locked to his console.

Spock was bent over his hooded viewer. "Sensors indicate their power cells are almost exhausted. I doubt they possess more than minimal deflector capability. We could destroy them at will."

Kirk nodded. "Yes, and I bet Koloth knew exactly what he was asking of his ship. He took a tremendous gamble, and he lost.

"Right now I'm more curious in finding out just what he felt was worth the loss of his ship and an interstellar incident bordering on an act of war. Something has made them awfully angry. They *really* wanted that pilot." He relaxed as the *Devisor* passed out of disruptor range and turned to the com.

"Mr. Scott . . . can you integrate that pilot now?"

"It will still take a few minutes, Captain," came the tired

reply. "He was scattered to hell and gone, but he's locked in solid. I just need a little time to double-check integration."

"We'll be right there, Scotty. Kirk out." He rose from the chair. "Lieutenant Uhura, call Dr. McCoy to the transporter room. In addition to anything incurred in delayed transport, we don't know what injuries this person may have suffered before we took him off his ship."

"Very well, Captain." She turned to contact Sick Bay.

"Mr. Spock . . . ?"

XII

Both men were silent as the elevator took them toward the transporter room. But their thoughts were similar. Each wondered what had made the Empire send a warship so far into Federation territory. True, the Klingons placed a great deal of importance on revenge. But that hardly seemed a sufficient explanation. Though for a moment, Captain Koloth had been as angry as any Klingon officer Kirk had ever seen.

Ecological sabotage, he had said. Well, to a Klingon that might mean any number of offenses which did not really merit destruction. They would find out exactly what was going on in a very few seconds—from the object of the Klingons' wrath.

McCoy was waiting for them as they entered. Kirk's attention was drawn immediately to the transporter alcove. A sharp silhouette there still shimmered with color.

"Haven't got him yet, Mr. Scott?"

"Just finalizing him now, sir. I've been integrating very slowly. No tellin' what a long delay in transport will do. It's almost fail-safe, sir, but there are still histories of peculiar aberrations bein' produced when such delayed folks were rushed back."

Kirk held his impatience and stared into the chamber. The vibrant glow began to fade and a human shape to emerge. Or . . . was it? There seemed to be a multiple form. No . . . one human, all right. Very stout, round. One human—surrounded by lots of little round stout things, very unhuman. Quite a number of little round stout shapes.

The last of the transporter hue started to fade out and the pilot became recognizable—along with the other beings.

Spock raised an eyebrow uncertainly. "It would appear to be . . ."

Kirk recognized it . . . them, too. Wished fervently—oh, how fervently he did not. His words were measured, reluctant. "I think we know that man."

McCoy broke in.

"I don't want to think about it!" The doctor bestowed an anguished look on the chief engineer. "Scotty, what you said about delays in transport producing aberrations—I didn't think you meant anything quite this hideous."

Scott had also recognized the figure and was undergoing mild shock himself. "Not again!" he finally howled.

"Cyrano Jones." Kirk finally said it out, making the name sound like a curse. And in a sense that pudgy, falsely Falstaffian figure surely was.

Cyrano Jones smiled at them. He beamed. He expanded, fairly radiating good humor, hands relaxed on hips. Faint mewing sounds issued from the region of his ankles.

"And he's got tribbles with him," Scotty groaned.

When the cylindrical transporter effect had ceased, the tribbles Jones had clustered around him immediately spilled across the alcove floor. Kirk and Spock glanced at each other, exchanged telepathic sighs.

Kirk moved to the subsidiary console and punched the switch that would tie him in with the log. He needed a couple of minutes of enforced order before he could begin to deal rationally with this situation. As if anyone could deal rationally with tribbles. However . . .

"Captain's Log, supplemental. Our rescue of the pilot of the one-man ship being pursued by the Klingon cruiser *Devisor* has given us important knowledge of a new Klingon weapon—as yet unperfected.

"It has also inflicted on us—for as short a time as possible—the presence of Cyrano Jones, interstellar trader and general nuisance."

"General trader and interstellar nuisance," Scott corrected grimly.

Nudging tribbles out of his path, Jones made his way toward Kirk. "Ah, Captain Kirk. My old friend, Captain Kirk!" He extended his arms to clasp the captain in a fraternal embrace. Fortunately, Kirk had the transporter console between him and Jones.

Kirk turned to the goggle-eyed ensign who had been assisting Scott at the transporter's backup instrumentation. "Seal off this area, Mister, and I mean tight."

"Aye, sir," the man acknowledged, moving to comply.

Kirk's feet suddenly felt unnaturally warm. He looked down and the reason became apparent. Two large tribbles had sandwiched his right ankle. They were rubbing against him from both sides, cooing and purring.

He took an angry step to the side. Both tribbles fumbled to follow him, distracting his attention from the mewing horde which had quickly spread throughout the room from their landing place in the transporter alcove.

Kirk moved up close to confront their owner. His indignation would have been helped greatly if Jones had possessed a face and disposition more like Koloth's and less like that of a beardless St. Nick. Even so, Kirk managed to work up a good dose of righteous anger.

"You know the law about transporting species proven harmful, Jones."

"Harmful, Captain?" The trader was a fount of innocence. Kirk made an angry gesture to encompass the room.

"Well then, what would you call these?"

"Tribbles, Captain."

That was the last straw . . . or hair, in this case. Kirk had just endured the trauma of saving his ship from a previously unknown and nearly fatal weapon to save someone whom he almost wished he had never met in the first place.

"Don't get smart with me, Jones. Believe me, I'm not in the mood."

"Captain, really, I assure you. I wasn't being smart at your expense." Kirk eyed him warningly. "These aren't harmful. These are safe tribbles."

McCoy stood nearby, watching and listening. He had knelt and scooped up a straw-colored, furry ball. It immediately tried to crawl up his arm, rubbing and purring. He used his other hand to pluck it off, shook it threateningly at Jones. The abused tribble purred indignantly.

"As you are well aware, Jones, there is no such thing as a safe tribble."

"A safe tribble," Spock amplified, in his best professional tone, "is a contradiction in terms. I am surprised, Mr. Jones, that you would attempt to fool us with so obvious a lie—particularly us, to whom tribbles are well remembered for their dangerous reproductive proclivities."

"And they breed fast, too," Jones admitted. "Don't you see? Gentlemen, that's why these tribbles are safe." He was pleading with them. "They don't reproduce."

Four stunned faces stared back at him. McCoy was the first to voice the skepticism all felt. "Don't reproduce? Who ever heard of a tribble that didn't . . ."

"I've had them genetically engineered for compatability with humanoid ecologies," the trader added quickly. "A simple gene manipulation coupled with some selective breeding. See how friendly and lovable they are?"

Of course they were friendly and lovable. Tribbles were as well known for being friendly and lovable as they were for reproducing at astronomical rates. And this bunch was every bit as affectionate as any Kirk had seen before. They rubbed and purred and mewed and cuddled with boundless enthusiasm. And as he looked around the room, he had to admit he didn't see a hint of tribbles reproducing.

Not that there was anything for them to reproduce on, but he had seen tribbles seemingly multiply out of thin air. There did not appear to be any more now than when they first materialized.

"Not a baby in the bunch," Jones pointed out proudly. "You know what great pets they make, Captain. Profitable, too."

Something had been nagging at the back of Kirk's mind while Jones had been spouting his smooth sales spiel. Now he had it.

"Jones, how did you get away from Space Station K-Seven in the first place. You were supposed to take care of all the tribbles there. Regardless of what genetic engineering you claim to have done on these, the tribbles on K-Seven were definitely not altered for nonreproduction. You couldn't have cleaned them off in such a short time."

Jones was fumbling at his copious pockets. "Quite so, Captain. But I managed a short parole and found myself some help. Ecologically sound, efficient, unoffensive help."

The thing he took from his pocket was red, had numerous arms or legs or both, and looked decidedly unfriendly.

"This, Captain, is a tribble predator. It's called a glommer."

"Interesting, if true," commented Spock, studying the creature and reserving judgment. "Is the name derivative or descriptive?"

"See for yourself," Jones said, winking.

He put the glommer on the floor. Making rumbling sounds like a toy volcano, it hesitated, orienting itself. It froze stiffly, then started creeping toward the nearest tribble. Pausing a short distance from a moderate-sized specimen, it tensed. Kirk thought he could see the thick hairs on the creature's appendages stiffen slightly. Without a sound and with surprising suddenness, it sprang at its prey like a wolf spider. The tribble never had a chance as the glommer landed on it.

It spread its body surface wide, engulfing the tribble completely. There was a harried series of barely audible slurping sounds accompanied by a violent quivering. Then the predator relaxed.

But only for a moment. In addition to being efficient, it was also apparently ravenous. Its metabolism seemed geared to continual consumption. Bottom hairs tensing, it stalked off after another tribble. Not even a hair was left of the first.

McCoy was impressed. "Neat, too."

But Kirk, having satisfied himself that Jones apparently was not a fugitive from K-Seven, was interested in something much more important than glommer hygiene. Even McCoy looked away from the interesting glommer-versus-tribble drama to listen to Jones' answer.

"Jones, just why *were* the Klingons chasing you?" The trader looked at the walls, the ceiling, his tribbles—anywhere to avoid meeting Kirk's waiting gaze.

"Well," the Captain prompted, "are you going to tell me you don't know?" Given any possible out, Jones leaped at it, nodding vigorously.

"That's it exactly, Captain! I don't. The Klingons have notoriously bad tempers, you know."

"While it must be admitted that the Klingon mental state tends toward the bellicose," Spock observed, "they still retain a sense of proportion when exercising their animosities.

I do not see a Klingon cruiser captain entering Federation space to attack a Federation vessel in a fit of pique. Nor for mere recreation, or because his liver was bothering him.''

"You're right about their temper, though," Kirk added. "Captain Koloth seemed oddly upset over something he called ecological sabotage.''

Jones' eyes took on a rotundity that matched his belly. "Me? A saboteur? I ask you now, Captain, do *I* look like a saboteur?'' He assumed an air of outraged dignity.

"Captain Koloth was pretty emphatic about it," Kirk continued, watching the trader carefully.

"I'm not responsible for Captain Koloth's perverse imagination," Jones insisted.

"If it was imagination." Kirk's tone turned coaxing. "Are you sure, Cyrano, that you didn't . . .," and he held up a hand with thumb and forefinger squeezing a centimeter of air, ". . . maybe accidentally perhaps possibly perform some teensy weensy little act that might have caused the Klingons to overreact like this?''

Jones glanced reluctantly at Spock, then at McCoy and saw no relief from that quarter. He looked at the floor.

"Actually, it was such a little thing. I can't understand why they got so upset. You understand, don't you, Captain?''

Kirk's tone indicated there was an outside chance he did not:

"What did you do?"

Jones tried to look nonchalant, even managed a slight laugh. "Nothing at all, really. I only sold . . . them . . . some . . . uh . . . tribbles . . .''

Kirk's voice dropped dangerously. "You sold tribbles on a Klingon planet?''

"Well," the trader protested lamely, "I didn't *know* it was a Klingon planet.''

"What species were the inhabitants," Kirk pressed relentlessly.

"Oh, mixed. You know, a mongrel world. Tellerites, Sironians, a few Romulans—Klingons, too.''

"How about *outside* the customs port." This from Spock. Jones pretended not to hear.

"I beg your pardon, Mr. Spock?''

"I believe you heard me correctly, Mr. Jones. The population *outside* the free customs and reception station. What did it consist of?''

Jones watched the glommer continue to devour tribbles at an astonishing rate. "Uh . . . Klingons . . . mostly."

"What was that? Speak up," Kirk ordered.

"Klingons . . . they were all Klingons!" Jones exploded. "But where I set down it was a mixed populace, Captain. So how could I tell for certain it was a Klingon planet?"

Kirk had had enough. "Jones," he began, as though he were lecturing a five-year-old, "tribbles don't like Klingons. You *know* tribbles don't like Klingons. Didn't you think they might object to your selling tribbles to visitors at their landing station?"

"Ah well, Klingons like tribbles even less," Jones confessed, ignoring Kirk's question. "It was lucky you came along and saved me when you did, friend Kirk. I couldn't have outrun them much longer."

"I'd estimate about another two seconds," Kirk theorized, wistfully. Jones nodded in somber agreement.

"You snatched me from the jaws of death at the moment of judgment, Captain. I should have known that in a desperate situation, our life-long friendship, the high regard in which you hold me, your unrelenting desire to see justice done . . ."

Trying to control his stomach, Kirk switched to less emotionally charged subject matter. "I am sure, Jones, that a quick scan of our files will show that you stand in violation of three Federation mandates and forty-seven local laws plus various attendant paragraphs thereunto appended. I am formally placing you under arrest."

That pronouncement was sufficiently impressive to draw from Jones a stunned gasp. Although anything was preferable to being either obliterated by or turned over to the tender mercies of the Klingons, Jones was not enamored of Federation mind-wipe techniques. Federation criminal psychoengineers were an especially dull lot. They tended to remove one's most interesting memories.

"You're confined to quarters until we complete our current mission. Then we'll proceed to the nearest Starfleet base and turn you over to the proper authorities."

Jones was thinking furiously. "Captain, couldn't we talk this over?"

Kirk's reply was a look of such overpowering silent fury that even the trader was cowed.

"I didn't think so," the trader mumbled.

Kirk turned to the ensign at the door. "Mr. Hacker, keep an eye on our visitor. Call security and have them prepare suitable accommodations for him." He nodded in Jones' direction.

The ensign moved to the com to comply.

"Bones, let's take a couple of these so-called altered tribbles down to your lab and check out Jones' claims. If there's any truth to them, it'll be a first."

"All right, Jim." McCoy busied himself gathering up suitable specimens.

They headed for the elevator. Kirk looked back to Jones. "If these turn out to be normal tribbles, Jones, I'm personally going to order you placed in solitary with tribble mewing played round the clock into your cell at a dozen times normal volume."

"Really, Captain, do you think I would lie to you about something as important, as vital, as incriminating as this?"

"Yes," Kirk replied without hesitation. "Let's go, gentlemen." He paused as the elevator doors opened, had a last thought. "Oh, Mr. Hacker?"

The ensign looked back. "Sir?"

Kirk spoke as he nudged a tribble out of the elevator with his foot. "Don't listen to anything he says. And above all . . . don't let him sell you anything."

"Yes, sir."

At McCoy's request, they all met in the main briefing room an hour later. The doctor had spent much of that time putting the sample tribbles through every test he could thing of. He had also spent much of the time going *hmmmm* a lot.

Tribbles were the most interesting things to study. And these tribbles offered some surprises. He picked up one specimen—an unusually large tribble, Kirk thought—and gestured with it as he spoke.

"I'm afraid Cyrano Jones was right, Jim. These tribbles don't reproduce. They just get fat."

"Are you sure, Bones?"

"Absolutely. Any excess food turns into flesh instead of stimulating reproduction." He put the corpulent tribble on the floor. It immediately crept over to Kirk and crawled up and down one boot, rubbing and purring.

"So I don't think we have anything to worry about."

"Not as far as the tribbles are concerned, anyway," Kirk agreed. "This new Klingon weapon is another matter. Koloth was adamant about getting his hands on Jones. We may not have seen the last of them." He reached down and pulled the tribble off his boot, tossed it into a far corner—as gently as possible, it seemed to Scott.

"It is an energy-sapping field of great strength, Captain," Spock commented. "It totally immobilizes a ship and its weapons capacity. But it appears that when extended to its ultimate limits, it also immobilizes the attacker as well."

"Aye," agreed Scott. "If that's true then it's a weapon that leaves them as helpless as it leaves us."

"I believe I just said that, Mr. Scott," observed Spock.

There was a pause while everyone present considered this information.

"The practical advantages of such a weapon would seem to be limited," Kirk concluded.

"Limited, perhaps," put in Spock. "But that does not obviate its initial, overwhelming effect." He considered another moment, then went on. "The key question is, how long does it take them to recharge? They'll probably attack us again as soon as they're back up to full power.

"If Captain Koloth has any ability in tactics, he will undoubtedly begin by destroying the remaining robot ships to prevent us from using the same trick again. That would put us in a difficult position indeed." He looked unusually somber. "They must want Cyrano Jones very badly indeed."

"He really doesn't seem the saboteur type, Jim," McCoy commented.

Kirk stared at the fine grain in the wood table top and wished his thoughts were as straight. "Yes . . . yes. And yet, I get the impression there's something he's not telling us. He is still holding something back." He took a deep breath, looked up. "That will be discovered in due time.

Mr. Scott, let's see a status report on the damaged grain ship.''

Scott hit the necessary switch, and the triple table-screen popped up in front of them. Further manipulation of controls produced pictures which illustrated his commentary.

"Well, sir, in the past hour we've managed to transfer all the seed grain aboard. And mind, Captain, it wasn't easy finding room to store it all. We filled the shuttle-craft hangars, all our extra holds, and we've even got containers of that quinto-triticale in the less frequently used corridors of the ship.

"Fortunately, it was modular instead of bulk packed. Otherwise we would have had to repack every grain in smaller containers to fit on board. As it is, not only does the grain hamper movement throughout the ship, but there are a number of activities that will have to be limited, or even curtailed, until we deliver it to Sherman's Planet. For example, we can't use the Shuttle Bay at all.''

"What about the possibility of repairing the damaged grain carrier?''

"Not a chance in a million, sir,'' Scott replied, shaking his head firmly. "Her engines were ninety-percent destroyed. She needs to be rebuilt, not repaired.'' He sighed deeply. "And we've still got that other robot ship to escort, too. I don't like it at all, sir.''

"Nor do I, Mr. Scott. But we'll have to manage with the grain on board, somehow. Sherman's Planet needs it desperately.''

"Aye, sir, aye . . . I know.'' The chief engineer sounded resigned. "It's just that everything seems to happen at once sometimes, sir. Tribbles on the ship, quinto-triticale in the corridors, Klingons in the quadrant . . .'' He shook his head at the injustice of it all. "Why, sir, it's enough to ruin your whole day.''

"Let's hope the worst is over, Scotty.'' Kirk rose. "This meeting is adjourned, gentlemen.'' He reached under the table to deactivate the triple viewer. What he got for a response was a loud mew.

"They appear to be fond of you, Captain,'' Spock observed with a straight face.

"I'm not flattered." Kirk disgustedly removed the curious tribble from the control panel and hit the proper switch.

For a little while it seemed as if Kirk's wish might come true—the worst of their difficulties might be past. Nothing happened in the next several hours that approached crisis proportions.

That did not mean, however, the *Enterprise* was without interesting activity. Down in a dimly lit corridor the glommer—forgotten by an introspective Jones—was stalking another tribble.

The glommer got within range, tensed, leaped—and was bucked off. Growling in surprise, it hopped after the retreating tribble. Quickly overtaking the tribble, it proceeded to ingest—the effort producing rather more commotion than ever before because the tribble it had pounced on was larger than a man's head. That tribble was almost more than the glommer could handle—almost.

The glommer paused a moment, belched, and sat recovering its strength. Discharging another deposit of converted tribble it promptly stalked off in search of further prey, now wobbling a little unsteadily from side to side.

The calm on the bridge did not last nearly as long as Kirk had hoped. He had hoped for five days of it, time enough in which to reach Sherman's Planet.

Instead, he had had only the few hours following McCoy's briefing before Spock broke the stillness. "Captain, sensors are picking up an approaching Klingon cruiser." A brief, hopeful pause, then, "It appears to be the *Devisor*."

Kirk had been standing talking to Sulu, now moved quickly to the Science Station for a personal check of the sensor readouts. Damn! Damn Cyrano Jones and damn tribbles and damn the Klingons' persistence! He strode back to his seat, shoved the twenty-kilogram tribble off.

"Deflector shields up—stand by all phasers."

A sudden thought struck him and he eyed the tribble carefully. Wait a minute—a twenty-kilo tribble?

"How fat do these things get, anyway?" He hadn't noticed any this size when Jones had first come on board. Anyway,

McCoy was not around to answer, and Spock was occupied. A second later Sulu removed all thoughts of tribbles.

"Klingon cruiser approaching rapidly, sir, on interception course. Phaser range in thirty seconds."

"Coming in fast," Spock commented with his usual objective detachment. "Obviously they can recharge their power cells in a matter of hours. Interesting, if true." He did not explain his cryptic final comment, and Kirk was too busy to ask about it.

"Mr. Arex, Mr. Sulu . . . use the robot ship as a decoy. Have it change course and move off due west, up seventy degrees. We can use it to give the Klingons more trouble, since they can't paralyze more than one ship at a time with their field."

The *Devisor* continued to approach confidently as the remaining robot grain carrier peeled off on a new course. As soon as she was far enough off, Sulu activated the helm and the *Enterprise* also changed course.

"Commencing evasive tactics," he reported crisply.

Governed now in part by her battle computer, the *Enterprise* began an erratic weave designed to leave the Klingons with the minimum possible target. The Klingon ship adjusted its path correspondingly, but not to pursue.

"*Devisor* is veering away," Spock observed.

The battle cruiser fired a single powerful disruptor bolt—not at the starship, but at the remaining drone. The bolt nearly severed the clumsy cargo module from the dual propulsion units.

"My error, Captain," Spock corrected. "They were not veering away. They were moving to attack the grain ship."

Sulu checked his gooseneck viewer. "But they didn't destroy it, sir." Kirk relaxed a hair. "They only wrecked the propulsion units. The cargo pod is intact." He looked up from the viewer. "Maybe we should modify our opinion of Captain Koloth's marksmen."

"It appears they are quite accurate," Spock concurred, "when firing on undefended cargo drones."

"They've changed course again," Sulu reported. "They're coming in after us."

"Stand by phasers," Kirk warned.

"Phasers armed and ready, sir." Sulu's hand hovered over

the firing switch. Arex shifted their position so that the main batteries would have an unobstructed line of fire on the *Devisor*. On the viewscreen, brilliant blue flares erupted from the cruiser's nose.

"Disruptors," Spock announced calmly.

A second later the bolts impacted on the *Enterprise*—only to sputter harmlessly on their shields. They felt a mild lurch as the ship reeled with the absorbtion of the tremendous destructive energy, but no one was knocked from their seat.

"Damage report, Mr. Sulu."

"No damage reported, sir," said the helmsman quickly. "Shields holding firm."

"Fire at will, Mr. Sulu."

"Firing, sir."

The battle continued for several minutes—long by intership standards—as the *Enterprise* and *Devisor* wheeled about a common center which shifted every second. Disruptor bolts alternated with phasers, probing for a weakness in the absorbing screens. Multiple barrages glanced off, were handled by opposing defenses.

The repetitive rattling caused only minor damage on the two cruisers. The *Enterprise* suffered slightly more than the *Devisor* because the temporary cargo she was carrying in her corridors and holds was not secured for battle running.

Succeeding jolts broke open one grain container after another. Of itself, the damage was minor. The containers could be easily repaired, the grain recollected.

Except in a couple of corridors, corridors no one was watching because all were at battle stations—corridors where a concerted mewing and cooing suddenly rose appreciably in volume.

Like a fuzzy glacier, clumps of tribbles started creeping rapidly toward the protein-rich kernels of quinto-triticale.

Some of the tribbles were no longer very small . . .

XIII

Now was the time, Kirk decided, to see if his strategy had paid off. By this time, Captain Koloth was hopefully convinced that the *Enterprise* was armed only with phasers and he had adjusted his defenses accordingly. They had one chance to catch him napping.

"Photon torpedoes, Mr. Sulu. Fire."

"Torpedoes away, sir."

All eyes moved to the screen, where computer-guided deep-space scanners held the *Devisor* fixed on the screen like a bug under chloroform.

"Three, two, one . . . impact," Sulu counted down. Then, "Torpedo miss."

But the image of the *Devisor* was starting to shrink. Spock checked his sensors, frowned. "They appear to be running away, Captain. Most odd. They did not use their stasis weapon at all."

"Maybe you were right, Mr. Spock, and they could only partly recharge their power cells, only enough to manage a conventional attack."

"Then why break off the engagement?" Spock wondered aloud. "I detect no sign of serious damage. Unless their attack achieved some unimaginable purpose."

"They disabled the robot carrier," Sulu noted.

"Before they engaged us," mused Kirk. "No, Spock's right. It doesn't make sense. Koloth knew his battle capabilities before he attacked." He shook his head, feeling they were missing something.

"Well, put a tractor beam on the disabled drone. We'll have to try and take it in tow."

"Now that could be their intention exactly, Captain,"

Spock suggested. "Towing the drone will be a drag both on our available power and maneuverability. We're already carrying the extra mass of the first carrier's cargo. Captain Koloth's engineers have undoubtedly calculated how much energy this will sap from our battle capacity."

"We can't do anything about the extra mass on board, Mr. Spock, but we could break the tow instantly in the event of another attack."

"That is true, Captain. But the *Devisor* could attack and run, attack and run. If Koloth is aware of the situation on Sherman's Planet he knows we are operating within certain time restrictions. Eventually his chances of catching us with the second drone under tow will increase."

"That seems logical," Kirk admitted.

"Thank you, Captain."

"Well, Mr. Spock?" he said, after a short pause.

"Well what, Captain?"

"You've already correctly analyzed the situation. We cannot tow the damaged robot ship indefinitely, nor can we abandon it. And there is no room for more quinto-triticale on board. I assume you have some suggestions as to what we can do."

Spock paused in thought, Vulcan gears turning at top speed. "Yes, Captain, we can throw tribbles at them."

Kirk's expression underwent a succession of variations. Arex's reaction was mostly internal, but much the same.

"I thought Vulcans didn't have a sense of humor," he finally ventured.

"We do not, Captain. Allow me to think this out."

Kirk regarded his first officer with a gaze of honest confusion.

Down in one of the lower storage holds a door had burst, flooding the deck with quinto-triticale. Instantly the hillock of golden-brown seeds was inundated by a horde of tribbles of impressive bulk.

At the base of the broken door the glommer was struggling with one of the tribbles. This particular one had the dimensions of a large, furry hassock. It ignored the furious, frustrated glommer on its topside and continued to munch contentedly on the sudden nutritious bonanza.

As Scott was returning to the bridge, he made a quick trip

back to Engineering Central for a first-hand check on the amount of power the cargo drone tow was drawing. A harried security sergeant confronted him in a corridor, tried to babble an explanation of what he had seen. His story was enough to detour Scott temporarily from the bridge.

He was still talking when the elevator doors opened to the low deck. Scott needed less than two minutes to evaluate the situation and head for the bridge at top speed.

"Captain," he said, walking directly to the command chair, "we've got broken cargo pods in all the corridors, and some of the storage holds themselves have burst. The tribbles have gotten into the grain. No need to tell you what they're doing." He paused to catch his breath.

"Eating, I should suppose," observed Spock blandly. He glanced at the base of the navigation console significantly, where a fifty-kilo tribble had appeared. The enormous fur ball was rubbing at the legs of an irritated Sulu. Then Spock began making some quick computations at his console.

"Given the exceptional nutritive value of the hybrid grain, I should say that at their estimated rate of conversion these altered tribbles will . . ."

"Altered!" Kirk stopped listening to Spock. "Get Cyrano Jones up here on the double, Scotty."

"Aye, sir." He headed for the elevator again while Uhura notified the brig.

Kirk rose and walked to the helm-navigation console, nearly tripping over an elongated tribble in the process. Glancing up occasionally at the main viewscreen for signs of the *Devisor*, he examined certain readouts.

"Any sign of Captain Koloth's ship?"

"Nothing yet, sir," Sulu reported.

"Keep scanning. They'll probably come at us from a different quadrant this time."

It wasn't long before Scott reappeared, pushing a puzzled Cyrano Jones urgently before him.

"Ah, Captain Kirk. What can I do for you? From the attitude displayed by your chief engineer," and he looked reprovingly at Scott, who returned the favor with a glance suggesting that he would have liked to display Jones in the nearest converter, "I gather that it is a matter of some gravity."

"Not gravity—grain," Kirk corrected him furiously. "Your shribbles are all over my trip . . . your tribbles are all over my ship." *Easy, James T., easy.* "My security personnel can't find them all, despite the fact," and he kicked at a hundred-kilo tribble where an eighty-kilo tribble had been only moments before, "that they're hardly inconspicuous anymore."

The tribble cooed, tried to rub against his ankle.

Jones shrugged. "You need better security men then, Captain. As you say, they shouldn't be hard to find." He looked interestedly at the apparition Kirk had just kicked.

With enormous effort, Kirk held his emotions in check. "Mr. Jones, you are in enough trouble already. Feeble attempts at humor will only exacerbate your situation." He returned to his station.

"Oh, Captain," Jones protested, "a harmless little tribble. What can they hurt?"

Kirk put his shoulder to the hundred-kilo tribble sitting in the command chair and shoved it out. "Harmless? Maybe. But little? In any case, the main problem is that they're eating the quinto-triticale."

"The what?" Jones looked confused.

"The grain."

The trader looked troubled for the first time. "Captain, you have grain on this ship?"

"What?" Kirk was staring at the screen. Naturally the *Devisor* would show up any second. "Yes . . . grain. Seed grain, to prevent a serious famine on Sherman's Planet. It won't be prevented if your tribbles continue eating at the rate they are."

"But they're hungry, Captain," Jones protested, spreading his hands in a gesture of helplessness.

"So are the people on Sherman's Planet!" Kirk countered tightly. His shout echoed across the bridge. The gigantic purple tribble he had just pushed out of his seat mewed uncomfortably and edged away a little.

"A little tribble, Jones, doesn't eat much. A big tribble does. And these are getting bigger."

That's when it came to him.

"Jones, is this the ecological sabotage the Klingons are so mad about? Is this why Captain Koloth is willing to risk his ship to get you back? The Klingons have a lot of pride, Jones. No wonder they want you.''

The trader started to object, but a sudden shout from Sulu's station shattered the conversation.

"Captain, the *Devisor* is coming back."

There, he knew it was too much to hope for. Now he understood why the Klingons wouldn't break off the engagement.

McCoy chose that moment to enter the bridge. Both hands were full of tribble. "Jim, there's something about these tribbles . . .''

"Later, Bones," Kirk interrupted tiredly. He started to sit down, paused. The tribble in it weighed at least one hundred and forty but otherwise it was just like the one he'd shoved out a minute before.

Which raised another interesting question. How fat did the tribbles grow . . . and how fast?

One crisis at a time. Panting, he shoved the tribble out of his seat once more, sat down.

"Mr. Sulu, release the tow on the robot carrier. All deflector shields on full. Stand by phasers and photon torpedoes." He paused and looked first at Jones and then McCoy. "And all non-combatants off the bridge."

McCoy nodded, took charge of Jones. But first he dumped the overflowing tribble he had been holding.

Everyone's attention was fixed on the screen, which now showed the approaching *Devisor* once again. Kirk diverted his attention long enough to thumb a certain switch under his right hand.

"Captain's Log, supplemental," he recited in a soft voice. "The Klingon battle cruiser *Devisor*, under command of Captain Koloth, appears about to force us into another battle for custody of the trader Cyrano Jones." He cut off. Elaboration would have to wait for leisure time.

On screen, the *Devisor* continued its relentless approach with little recourse to subtlety. Apparently this was to be another head-on attack like the first.

"Contact in thirty seconds," announced Spock.

"Ready photon torpedoes, Mr. Sulu."

The *Devisor* now filled the screen. An ominous cloud of fluttering azure began to form at its prow. Apparently the stasis projector was back in operation. And this time they had no robot ships to throw at it.

"Fire one, fire two."

"One and two away," Sulu announced. "Three, two, one . . . impact." Seconds pause, then, "Minus one, minus two . . . something's wrong, Captain. I show impact but no reaction."

"Are you positive, Mr. Sulu?"

"Absolutely, sir. We show definite . . ."

"I think I know what has happened, Captain," said Spock. "Both torpedoes impinged on the stasis field the *Devisor* is building. Considering the known power of such a field, I have no doubt that the drive and detonation mechanisms of the torpedoes were paralyzed when they reached it."

"Evasive emergency maneuvers, Mr. Sulu," was all Kirk could say.

"Aye, Captain."

Too late—the field enveloped the *Enterprise* even as Sulu directed a convoluted course across the starfield. Enveloped them in a rippling miasma of brilliant blue.

The *Enterprise* gave a sickening lurch. Kirk groaned inwardly. That had not done the weakened grain containers below any good. Little could be done to repair them while the ship remained on battle status.

And so in numerous corridors and holds, the tribble orgy continued unabated.

"That's done it," cursed Scott, looking up from his engineering console in anger and alarm. "We're caught again."

"Message coming in, Captain, over ship-to-ship hailing frequency," Uhura announced. Kirk sighed. He already had a fair idea of what the message would contain.

"Put it through, Lieutenant."

"Yes, sir." Moments later a picture of Captain Koloth—a broadly grinning, self-satisfied Captain Koloth—appeared once more on the main viewscreen. Kirk noted the clarity of the image though he would not have objected to some distortion blotting out some of his smile.

Visual and aural communications were low-order field functions, of course, and thus were not affected by the stasis field, as were . . .

Something was trying to fuse in the back of his head. He

could not spare the time to study it. Koloth wouldn't give it to him.

"Captain Kirk. I am so glad to see that you have not suffered any injury yet, nor," he looked to left and right, "have any of your crew. This pleases me. We will take control of your vessel intact, it appears."

"Not if I can help it," Kirk said grimly. Koloth's smile disappeared and barely controlled fury colored his cheeks.

"You cannot help it and *I want your prisoner, Captain.*"

"Control yourself, Koloth, or you'll burst a blood vessel. Much as it pains me to admit to it, Cyrano Jones is a citizen of the Federation, and therefore is entitled to Federation protection. I am afraid I must refuse your request." He thought, added, "You have no idea how much it pains me to refuse your request."

"I regret any emotional upset it has caused you," Koloth continued with biting sarcasm. "If it will alleviate your agony any, Captain Kirk, let me assure you this is not a 'request.' " For an unguarded moment he sounded almost regretful—for a Klingon.

"Don't force me to take steps we will both regret."

"Not a chance," Kirk snarled. Stasis field or no, he had taken about all he could handle of Koloth.

"Close channel, Lieutenant," Kirk ordered, pacing near Sulu.

"With pleasure, sir." She hit a switch and Koloth's image abruptly faded from the screen.

Kirk started back to his seat . . . and stopped, his lower jaw descending slightly. Even a friend would have been hard put to interpret his expression.

A contentedly mewing tribble occupied the command chair. It weighed two hundred and fifty kilos if it weighed a gram. Folding his arms, Kirk turned to stare at the viewscreen again.

"Aren't you going to sit down, Captain?" Spock inquired.

"I think I'll stand for now, Mr. Spock—haven't you got some important computations to do?"

Spock hesitated, started to say something and thought better of it, turning back to his console.

* * *

Meanwhile, Captain Koloth and his first officer were deep in a strategy conference. The next move was theirs. Koloth finally muttered to Korax, "Initiate Boarding Plan C." The first officer's eyes lit and he replied enthusiastically.

"Yes, Exalted One!"

Kirk was still eyeing the behemoth tribble purring noisily in his chair when everything that had been floating loose in his head suddenly got together. He walked over to Scott, who was monitoring the engineering console and looking distraught.

"Mr. Scott," he instructed, a slightly dreamy, thoughtful expression on his face, "we are going to implement Emergency Defense Plan B."

"Yes, sir," Scott answered snappily. "Emergency Defense Plan B." A look of uncertainty came over him and he asked hesitantly, "Ah, Captain . . . I don't believe I'm familiar with Emergency Defense Plan B."

"That's because it's only used in extremely unusual circumstances, Mr. Scott."

"Oh," the chief engineer commented.

"And also," he added, turning away, "because I've just made it up—thanks to a suggestion by Mr. Spock. Stand by."

"Standin' by, sir," Scott said, still puzzled but ready for orders.

Odd, Scott mused. The ship's enemies and all of their weaponry were frozen; the Klingons were threatening to take over the ship; they were suffering under the combined appetites of an influx of Fafnirian tribbles—and yet it had seemed as if Kirk had a smile on his face . . .

Korax studied his personal timer. Twenty-two *kuvits* had passed since the final warning had been given to Captain Kirk of the *Enterprise*. It had taken that long to assemble the forces necessary to implement the assault plan. Kirk would never be able to claim he had not been given sufficient time to think over the surrender terms.

Now it was too late. He stood by the chief transporter officer of the *Devisor* and watched the first platoon of Klingon marines assemble in the transporter chamber.

The sudden appearance of a large, well-coordinated boarding party on board might not be a total surprise to the Federation crew . . . but it should have no trouble overwhelming any resistance. The supposedly peaceful Federation starships carried no such trained attack groups.

He nodded to the officer in charge, who started to advance his men to positions within the transporter alcove. The officer took a step forward—and froze, gaping.

Something was materializing, not only in the alcove itself but in the room. Several marines moved aside, hands edging nervously toward their disruptor pistols. Had Kirk decided on the same course of action as Captain Koloth? It seemed wholly out of character, and yet . . .

The transporter effect intensified. Faint, huge silhouettes began to form. Abruptly, the effect faded—and every Klingon in the chamber recoiled in horror.

Suddenly, the room was filled with giant emotionally disturbed tribbles.

And in the corridors, in storage holds, in private rooms startled crew members were treated to the most unwelcome sight of tribbles abruptly materializing in front of them, behind them, and, in the case of one nearly suffocated dozer, on top of them.

Scott kept a close watch on his console and a ready ear to the com. linkup with the transporters. Moving the tribbles to the *Enterprise*'s transporters at first had looked like an impossible task, until someone had suggested a method almost too simple.

All they had to do was have any human crew member demonstrate affection toward one of the furry goliaths. Whereupon, cooing and mewing like any healthy tribble, it would follow the coaxing human to any point in the ship.

Scott's smile widened. The Klingons, of course, would be utterly unable to duplicate this maneuver. No self-respecting tribble would have anything to do with a Klingon. He didn't envy any member of the *Devisor*'s crew who tried.

Chief Kyle concluded this report at the other end of the com. Several stats were relayed to Scott, who surveyed them briefly, then looked over to the waiting Kirk.

"Emergency Plan B complete, sir. Chief Kyle reports all transporting has been carried out as directed."

"Open hailing frequencies, Lieutenant."

Uhura acknowledged and seconds later the portrait of an as yet unruffled Captain Koloth appeared on the screen.

"Captain Koloth, are you prepared to release my ship yet?"

Koloth stared back incredulously. "Release your ship? Kirk, you are monotonous. Your ship's armament is completely inoperative and in a few minutes you will not even have the option of surrender."

"That's not an option I require, Koloth," Kirk countered. "You don't know yet then, do you?"

"Know," said Koloth irritably. "Know what?"

"That we have immobilized your ship worse than you have immobilized ours."

"I doubt that. Our instruments report nothing except some fragmentary transporter activity and . . . ." He paused and a thoughtful expression came over his face. "You could not transport any weapons aboard, of course, and you wouldn't attempt an assault with armed personnel, but . . ." A longer pause now.

"Kirk?"

"Yes, Captain? What seems to be the matter? Are you feeling all right? If not, I'd suggest . . ."

"Tribbles, Kirk?"

The Captain's grin grew even wider. "Tribbles."

Koloth started to say something, was interrupted as a Klingon junior officer entered the picture. The two conversed below range of the aural pickup for several moments. The junior officer spoke rapidly, punctuating his words with many erratic gestures. Koloth's face went through a repertoire of expressions suprising even for a Klingon. When the junior officer had left the picture, the *Devisor*'s commander turned slowly back to face the screen.

"Kirk, I am compelled by circumstances to reveal an Imperial scientific secret. When the full report of this incident is known, I shall probably be chastised for it. I may be broken. But under the circumstances I see no alternative.

"Cyrano Jones stole a Klingon genetic construct—an artificially produced creature—from one of our worlds. It was designed to be a tribble predator. It is the prototype, and the only one to survive many hundreds of attempts at crossbreeding.

"We *must* have it back. I am authorized to use any means to secure its return. I hope that includes imparting this sensitive information to you. The Imperium is willing to chance war to gain its return."

"Surely you don't expect me to believe you can't produce others?"

"That is precisely the situation, Kirk." A hint of desperation had crept into Koloth's voice. No talk of surrender now. "I am told that the production of this first success cannot be duplicated. Apparently its creation was as much the result of chance as careful planning.

"This specimen can, however, reproduce by asexual division. We must have it in order to produce others from it. And we need those to get rid of the tribbles Jones disposed of before they completely overrun the world on which he left them."

"And that's all you want—the predator?" Kirk asked.

Koloth gathered himself. "I am prepared to forgo my demand for the return of Jones. But we must have the glommer."

"Oh well," Kirk replied easily, "if that's all." He glanced back. "Mr. Scott, instruct Chief Kyle to transport the glommer over to the *Devisor*. We do have the glommer?"

"Aye, sir. Mr. Jones recovered it himself as we were drivin' the tribbles to the transporters."

Two security guards hustled Jones along between them some minutes later. He seemed somewhat reluctant to part with "his" glommer. It nestled under one of his arms. He was looking around wildly. His gaze finally settled on Scott, who had come down to join Kyle for the crucial transfer.

"You can't do this to me! Under space salvage laws it's mine." He stroked the glommer possessively and it growled softly once.

Scott sounded tried. "As you well know, a planetary surface is not exactly covered by free-space salvage statutes. But if it's a matter of sentimental attachment, that might put a different light on things, Jones."

The trader looked hopeful.

"If you're that attached to the little beastie, I wouldn't dream of separatin' the two of you."

Jones looked wary, but still hopeful. "And that is the case,

Mr. Scott.'' He stroked it again, made babying noises at it. ''I couldn't bear to be parted from my little glommer, after all we've gone through together. It's almost like a child to me, a part of my own self!''

''I understand,'' Scott confessed. ''So . . . we'll transport you over with it.''

''Given the current situation and in the interests of interstellar cooperation,'' Jones said at breakneck speed, ''I withdraw my claim.''

Without shedding so much as a tear, Jones put the glommer in the transporter, backed out. Scott nodded to Kyle, who engaged the transporter.

On the bridge, Kirk noted the subsidence of the stasis field concurrent with the glommer's transporting. Resumption of full power was suitably detailed by Sulu and Arex. Almost immediately thereafter, the *Devisor* was seen moving away at high speed.

Kirk watched it go, feeling better than he had in some time. ''At least we can submit a detailed report on the stasis weapon . . . and although something will have to be found as a defense against it, it's far from being a superweapon. The power drain makes it vulnerable to a second ship. Its main value is in convincing us of its omnipotence, and we've exploded that possibility.''

''Quite so, Captain,'' commented Spock thoughtfully. ''Tribbles appear to be a much more effective weapon.''

There was a buzz from his chair com and he acknowledged. ''Yes?''

''McCoy here, Jim. I'd like you and Spock to come down to the lab. I've made an interesting discovery.''

After assuring himself that the *Devisor* was too far away to catch them even at top pursuit speed, Kirk took Spock and made his way down to Sick Bay.

Moments later they found themselves examining the single giant tribble Bones had saved for experimental purposes. It sat behind a glass wall and munched happily on leftovers from the third shift's lunch.

''You see, Jim, Jones' genetic engineering was very slipshod. He fooled us at first but it's doubtful he could have hidden the truth forever. These tribbles don't reproduce, just as he claimed . . . when *they're normal sized*.

"But because he didn't slow their metabolism permanently, his secret would reveal itself eventually. These aren't giant tribbles . . . they're cooperative colonies. Like our coral, for example, only softer."

"Then that means . . . ," Kirk began, staring at the hulking yellow tribble, "that . . ."

McCoy nodded silently.

Both of Spock's eyebrows went up.

On board the *Devisor*, Koloth was heading for the engine room. He was holding the glommer and stroking it gently. Since glommers shared their disposition, they didn't dislike Klingons. A frantic, excited Korax met him in the passageway.

"Captain, report from Chief Engineer Kurr. His people have had to evacuate the engine room and operate the ship on automatic because the main engine chamber is filled with tribbles."

"I know," Koloth replied with a vicious smile. "We can finally do something about that. Then we're going back after the *Enterprise*."

"But sir . . ." Korax was desperately trying to add something, but Koloth waved him off.

"You'll see, Korax."

Together, they approached the access door to the main engine room. While Korax stood back doubtfully, Koloth put the glommer on the deck opposite the door. Stepping back, he activated the door and focused his attention on the poised glommer.

In fact, his attention was so focused on the glommer that he did not notice the sudden alteration of his first officer's expression, nor what had caused it.

He spoke directly to the glommer. "Attack!"

The glommer seemed to lean back. And back . . . and back. It gave a funny little shake, turned and rocketed off down the corridor in a series of olympian hops, making a sound like a dog with empty tin cans tied to its tail.

Koloth abruptly grew aware of another sound, a low, rhythmic rumbling which a Terran would have likened to an idling locomotive. To Koloth it sounded like approaching thunder.

The captain turned quickly, backed away from the source of that deep-throated pulsing. It was horrible, it was ghastly . . .

It was the angry mewing of a two-ton tribble that filled the *Devisor*'s engine room from floor to ceiling.

"He did it again," he swore. "That plated, overbearing excuse for a starship captain did it to us again!" He jabbed a finger at the growling colossus.

In such an emotional moment, even an Imperial board of inquiry would find reasons for absolving Koloth for an instinctive reaction.

Korax didn't stop to think, either. Instead, he whipped out his disruptor pistol and fired with admirable speed. The miniature bolts from the powerful hand weapon contacted the furry yellow wall. A bright flash temporarily blinded both officers.

Koloth felt the new pressure at his legs and waist even before vision returned. He tried to move . . . first to his right, then left, forward and back. No luck. He was thoroughly pinned in place by . . . something.

Another blink cleared his eyes and revealed the reason.

The entire corridor—all the way from the nearest bend to the depths of the engine room—was now hip deep in tribbles. Not giant tribbles but large normal tribbles. Very large normal tribbles.

Tribbles didn't like Klingons.

"Let us not panic, Korax," instructed Koloth. He was calm, he told himself. Quite calm. "Let us try to move one step at a time toward the nearest exit."

Both men tried to move, found that even the slightest attempt produced a frightening rise in the volume of mewing around them.

"I don't seem to be making any progress, Exalted One. Should I . . . ?" He held up his disruptor pistol.

"Put that away, you idiot!" Koloth cursed . . . but softly, softly. "Don't ever do that again. I'll break you to sanitation engineer . . . twelfth class."

"Yes, sir," said an abashed Korax, suddenly aware of what he had been about to do. He put the pistol away slowly. Both officers stood in the sea of nervous tribbles and stared at each other.

After several long minutes, Korax ventured to ask, "What now, Exalted One?"

"Now, Korax? We wait till we are rescued, of course. I don't know what else to do. Have you any brilliant suggestions, perhaps?"

"No, sir. There's just one thing."

"Well, what is it?"

The first officer of the *Devisor* looked down.

"Either we're shrinking, sir, or these tribbles are getting bigger."

Koloth made a strangled sound . . .

Kirk, Spock, Scott and Jones stood in the lab and watched the giant tribble shiver while McCoy explained what was happening.

"A simple shot of neo-ethylene fixes everything, gentlemen. The catalyst drug induces the tribble colony to break down into its individual smaller units . . . but also enables them to retain their engineered metabolic stability. These really *will* be safe tribbles."

Even as he spoke, the oversized tribble was rapidly collapsing into dozens of little, normal tribbles . . . like a big fuzzy ice cube melting into chunks.

"What about the Klingons?" asked Jones.

McCoy thought a moment, spoke slowly. "Unless they discover how to treat their tribbles—and do so soon—the *Devisor* isn't going to be big enough for all of them. Even if they do so, of course, the smaller tribbles will still retain their dislike of Klingons."

Kirk turned to leave, stopped as he spotted something up near a Jeffries tube. "Say, here's one you didn't get, Bones."

McCoy came over, glanced up the tube also. "Yes, I did, Jim." He turned to inspect one of the small tribbles, let it crawl up his arm, purring.

"But it hasn't . . . ," Kirk began. He was drowned out by a loud, muffled *flumpppp*! as the hidden giant colony suddenly dissolved into hundreds of component tribbles.

Kirk dug himself out of the mound of cooing, pulsing balls, spat out a mouthful of tribble fur and gazing imploringly heavenward.

"Someday I'll learn," he murmured solemnly.

"Aye, Captain," agreed Scotty, standing nearby and observing the talus of the hirsute avalanche. "But you've got to admit, if we have to have tribbles, it's best if all our tribbles are little ones . . ."

The orange tribble that Kirk threw mewed indignantly as it bounced off the chief engineer's retreating back . . .

STAR TREK
LOG FIVE

CONTENTS

PART I
  The Ambergris Element   217

PART II
  The Pirates of Orion   295

PART III
  Jihad   345

For my best friend, Fred Foldvary. . . .
Who knew and had confidence years
before it all started. . . .

STAR TREK LOG FIVE

Log of the Starship *Enterprise*
Stardates 5527.0—5527.4 Inclusive

James T. Kirk, Capt., USSC, FC, ret.
Commanding

transcribed by
Alan Dean Foster

At the Galactic Historical Archives
on S. Monicus I
stardated 6111.3

For the Curator: JLR

PART I

THE
AMBERGRIS
ELEMENT

(Adapted from a script by Margaret Armen)

I

(Sun to Queen four plus two)

"Starrfleet Academy?" M'mar murmured wonderingly. "You werre trrained as a historrian, daughterr. Historry, sociology, anthrropology . . . those werre yourr forrtes in school. Not physics or spatial engineerring or some such."

M'ress' mother reclined on the lounge, her expression one of concern, feline pupils of carved jet narrowed against the warm evening day of mid-summerset on Cait.

"Is it something else that's led you to this line of thinking, daughterr? Perrhaps something else trroubles you . . . that boy, now . . ."

M'ress made a soft sigh of exasperation. "It has nothing to do with N'nance, materr. Orr with V'rrone, orr D'irraj, orr any of my friends. I've simply decided that . . ."

"You've *decided*," M'mar whispered half to herself.

". . . I want to learrn morre about people as they arre now instead of how they've been. Is that so surrprrising? Becoming a Federration Starrfleet officerr is the best way to do that."

"And what about yourr litterr mates? What do they think of this sudden switch in mid-stalk?"

M'ress looked smug. "Sister M'nass thinks I'm as crrazy as you do, but both brrotherr M'rest and M'sitt say it's wonderful . . . and typically me."

"They'rre half rright," M'mar muttered. "Take carre, M'ress. As eldest of the litterr, you have a rresponsibility to set good examples forr them. Considerr that whateverr you do is likely to be copied."

"I rrealize that, materr," M'ress replied, tail flickering nervously from side to side. It was that very thought which

219

had caused her to delay the announcement this long. "But I'm deterrmined on this thing."

M'mar eyed her daughter appraisingly, but M'ress refused to break the stare. "All rright then," she finally conceded, "if you'rre bound on it, trry yourr best. By the Prrey, yourr academic evaluations are high enough. But bewarre, daughter, you could end up on a satellite-to-planet shuttle in some farr cornerr of the galaxy and see no morre in a lifetime than that one cornerr."

"I'm not worrried about that, materr," M'ress countered, with the confidence of the young. "One thing at a time. Firrst I have to get into the Academy."

"And if you can't, despite yourr evaluations?"

"Then I'll apply forr trraining as common crrew, of courrse," she said matter-of-factly.

M'mar offerred the ultimate Caitian argument. "This will separrate the family."

Now M'ress was forced to look away, and her voice dropped. "I know, materr, but this is something I have in my hearrt and mind to trry. Paterr will underrstand."

"Yourr crrazy sirre underrstands everrything!" M'mar half spat. "You inherrited yourr foolishness from him! He even pretends to underrstand yourr poetrry." She quieted abruptly, held out a paw to stroke her daughter's forehead with. "Naturally, we'll both brreak ourr dewclaws to help you make it. . . ."

(Satellite four to Probe six less one)

"The branch classifications have been posted!"

Lena, the human cadet-aspirant with whom M'ress was quartered at the Academy, burst into the room. Her face was flushed, her breath racing.

Instantly the hair on M'ress' neck rose. Her tail flickered from side to side, bottled up. Lena caught her breath long enough to answer her roommate's unasked question.

"We both made the twenty percent cut. That's all I know, Kit."

M'ress relaxed to the point of collapse. Only the top fifth of all applicants who were accepted to Starfleet were passed on for the full multi-year course of training. Now the arduous six-month ordeal of endless tests—physical as well as mental—was over . . . and she had made it, she had actually made it!

Almost as one they reached for the switch which would activate the tiny computer screen each room came equipped with. Lena hit it first. The rectangle lit, and the words AWAITING INPUT appeared. At that point the enormity of their accomplishment supplanted the initial excitement, and the fear that it was all a dream took over.

"You do it, Lena . . . you firrst."

"No . . . I can't. All of a sudden, I can't."

"I'll rriddle you forr it."

"Oh no!" Lena grinned warily. "You're much too good at word games for me." She let her gaze travel around the immaculately kept room, eventually spotted the ancient toy top resting on the pile of workbooks.

"I'll spin you a dredel for it."

"Orrf! All rright . . . choose sides."

They did so. Lena spun the tiny top on the counter in front of the screen. "Gimel," M'ress chortled triumphantly. "I win."

"You always win, Kit," Lena grumbled, but only briefly. After all, they had both made the cut. She punched out her name with the attendant request for information.

An ultra-rapid series of pictures blurred the screen as the desk-top brain hunted through the records. Finally, an immensely detailed chart—Lena Goldblum reduced to numerical molecules—appeared.

"One thousand eighty-three," she read from the blow-up of the bottom line.

Excellent out of ten thousand . . . about average among those who would advance. And of the two thousand, only twenty percent again would graduate . . . *the* Four Hundred.

"Not too good, but I have plenty of time to bring it up," she observed confidently.

"Yes, and that's betterr than—"

"And look!" Lena shouted excitedly. "I've been approved for my first request, security training!"

Two numbers, M'ress thought, that would determine their lives for the next several years. Class ranking and section. Two numbers.

"Now you, Kit."

M'ress made the request. Again the high-speed hunt, again the computer settled on the necessary card.

It was hard to say which girl was the more flabbergasted.

"M'ress," Lena gulped, "I never knew." She looked at her roommate for half a year as if she were seeing her for the first time.

There it was . . . class ranking: 0022.

"Means nothing," M'ress whispered. "Someone always has to rrank numberr one and someone has to rrank ten thousand. They'rre not absolutes . . . just rroughs. Just a convenient statistical abstrract for the administrration."

"But, M'ress . . ." Lena stopped, sensing a sudden shift in her friend's attitude. "Kit, what's wrong? Sure it's only a rough number, but even so, aren't you pleased?"

"Look." M'ress pointed to the other critical number. It translated as: COMMUNICATIONS. "I wanted Science Section," she growled bitterly. "Administrrative science with a culturral anthrro over-majorr leading to executive officerr-ship and eventual Captaincy."

"Practically everyone wants administration and a chance at command, Kit," said Lena comfortingly. "You know how pitifully few even get a *chance* to try for it. There's always the possibility of a field commission, though."

"In communications?" M'ress cried.

"Look, at least you've got a chance to reach the Bridge. That's a lot closer than I'll ever get. Of course, I know I would never have it upstairs for command anyway."

She forced a smile.

"Maybe the computer read some of your poetry."

M'ress had to smile at that.

"I suppose I should be thrilled even to pass on. But I've been making rrankings like that all my life and you get to expect them afterr a while."

"This is Starfleet Academy though, M'ress," Lena reminded her. "Not some—excuse me—provincial school."

"That's so," M'ress was forced to admit. She brightened. "Yes, by the Prrey, I ought to be prroud, and excited, *mrrrr!* Ssst . . . if I have to worrk my way up thrrough communications, then it's thrrough communications I'll worrk."

"That's the spirit," encouraged Lena.

"And I'm going to keep on with my poetrry, too . . . no

matter wherre it puts me in the mind of some centrral collection of solenoids and scrrews.''

(Sun to Black Star . . . even!)

''M'ress . . . we've been hit, badly!''

M'ress looked up from her seat at the library viewer and stared anxiously at Ankee, the short, stocky Jarite engineering ensign who had become one of her closest companions on the heavy cruiser *Hood*. Their sections were totally different in function, as were their individual assignments; but they shared a deep and abiding interest in the construction of reform-era poetry.

Now he looked exhausted, badly battered about one side of his head, and a little scared.

''I felt a slight shudder, Ankee, but I didn't think . . . I only heard the yellow alert sound and saw no harm in continuing with this work.''

''Surprise attack,'' he told her tiredly. ''No one had time to do more than react instinctively. Not even time to sound battle stations.'' He added, seeing her brow furrow, ''Kzinti.''

''Oh, we hit back at them, all right. Knocked out both engines, from what I hear; and scuttlebutt has it she's lost a lot of atmosphere, but . . . ,'' he paused worriedly, ''there's been no further word from the Bridge in some time.''

''*What* Bridge?''

M'ress looked past Ankee as her friend turned. Lieutenant Morax was standing in the doorway, fighting to keep from shaking. Despite his three legs, the soft-voiced security officer looked none too stable.

''The Bridge is gone.''

''*What?*'' both ensigns gasped simultaneously.

''Gone,'' Morax continued to mutter, in a tone that hinted he still didn't accept it himself. ''Just . . . gone. Captain Oxley, Commander Umba, Lieutenant Commander D'Uberville . . . everybody.''

''Then who's in command?'' wondered M'ress. ''That would leave . . .''

Morax shook his head sadly. ''Chief Ellis was on the Bridge, too. Which means—''

''You,'' Ankee put in.

"Me. Believe me, it's an honor I could do without."

"What happened?" M'ress pressed.

Morax made a complicated gesture. "The first attack. Direct hit on the Bridge by a disruptor bolt before we could get our screens up. We missed deflecting it by seconds. Too long." The security chief seemed about to cry.

"What's ourr status?" M'ress asked tightly.

"Engines disabled, Bridge gone, Fire Control scrambled to hell and gone. We're a derelict," Morax told them. "The Kzinti's in little better shape. You know what that means."

"Open to salvage," Ankee said huskily.

M'ress had moved quickly to the tiny computer console. She cleared off her work project—three weeks' study gone, no time to mourn—ran through several shunting operations while the other two watched. She tried again, a third time, finally quit in disgust.

"I could have told you," Morax said sympathetically, "our communications are completely gone, as well."

"So," guessed Ankee, "we sit here, both ships drifting forever in space, unless by accident . . ."

"No, Ensign," Morax cut in. "The Kzinti is totally disabled from a mobility standpoint, true. Offensively, true. But our remaining backup sensory equipment indicates they are managing to put out a signal—faint, but a signal nonetheless—toward their nearest relay station.

"We're deep in Federation territory, but we might as well be on the Galactic rim since we can't generate a similar signal. When theirs is picked up, it'll send another Kzinti warship racing here. They'll take the *Hood* in tow, after disposing of any inconvenient vermin who happen to be witnesses, of course."

"So that's it, then," cursed Ankee fatalistically, slumping in the portal. "No way of fighting back. We can't run and we can't fight—we can't even call for help. But they can."

M'ress was thinking furiously, then she asked, "What arre you going to rrecommend?"

"A great deal of prayer," Morax replied. He turned to leave.

"There's another possibility. Less spiritual, but with a betterr chance of succeeding, I think."

Morax stopped, gaped at her.

"Come now, Ensign, I . . ."

"No, rreally—if you'rre cerrtain the Kzinti communications arre still intact."

"We've got a definite indication they're putting out a signal," the security chief replied. "It will take some time to reach a Kzinti border relay post, considering the lack of power behind it. But it will reach."

"So," M'ress went on, "if we could get control of that same transmitter and beam to one of *ourr* stations, a Federration vessel would get herre in half the time the nearrest Kzin could."

She waited while Ankee and Morax exchanged puzzled glances.

"I'm not sure what you're proposing, Ensign," Morax said finally, "but if it's what I think, I absolutely . . ."

She slid out of the chair, came to the door. Her words were low, urgent. "You've got no choice, 'Acting Captain Morrax.'

"We Caitains and the Kzinti sharre common genetic rroots in the farr past, as do the Vulcans and the RRomulans. With a little carreful makeup, I could pass for a Kzin. A small one, but pass I would. Communications arre my specialty. With Lieutenant Tavi gone . . . ," she swallowed stiffly, "I'm the best qualified to trry this.

"I can speak Kzin well enough to fool theirr own warr council. And the last thing they'll be expecting is a boarrding parrty of one. Now, what's our trransporrter capability?"

"I haven't had time to check," began Morax, "but . . ."

"Then find out, and if anything still worrks, have someone stand by to beam me aboarrd when I'm rready. If I can rreach theirr station and hold it long enough to get a single burrst off towarrd the Cetacea system . . ."

"How long," protested Ankee, "do you think you could hold such a spot against an aroused bunch of Kzinti? Against even one Kzin?"

"All I need is a couple of minutes to re-align the directional antenna—they've got to be using the dirrectional, otherrwise one of ourr patrrols might pick up theirr signal—and get off one little scrream."

"And after that?" wondered a worried Morax. "What

about the chances of our beaming you back aboard when you're finished—in one piece. The odds . . .''

"Let us not exerrt ourrselves with minorr details, acting Captain," she cut in. "I don't want anyone rretrieving me until I signal back that I'm good and rready, too."

"Well," she added, when neither officer essayed anything further, "arre you both of a sudden tongueless?"

Ankee stared at the deck while Morax . . . Morax looked exceedingly unhappy.

"If there were another way, no matter how extreme or unlikely the chance of success . . . You know what the Kzinti would do to you?"

"Morre details," she snapped, but trembling inside. "As you arre well awarre, there is no other way." She started past them. "I'm going down to Recreation. Someone down therre ought to be able to make me up.

"Meanwhile, acting Captain, you might have someone go overr the interrnal schematic of a Kzinti crruiser. It won't help if I'm set down in the middle of one of theirr interro-gation chamberrs."

Against all probabilities—against all hopes and prayers and reasonableness—the scheme worked.

Of course, as soon as the signal was changed and beamed out toward Federation territory, other Kzinti on board the warship got wind of what was happening.

Still, M'ress almost got away unscathed, thanks to the timely and incredibly precise manipulations of the officer manning the transporter controls.

Almost.

Fortunately, the majority of scars were correctable by sur-gery, the others cosmetically concealed. The cause in which they were obtained was the reason why after only two short years on active duty, Ensign M'ress was promoted to the rank of lieutenant and assigned the prestigious post of alternate communications officer on board the *U.S.S. Enterprise*

Actually, the hardest part had not been making it through Starfleet Academy, nor had it been the deception she'd so devastatingly performed on the Kzinti.

No, the hardest part had been the steady separation from the traditionally close-knit Caitian family. She smiled to her-self. Her mater had been right about her setting an example for her younger sister and brothers; all three were now serving in Starfleet in various capacities. So M'mar had learned to bear up under the honor of having not one but four kits achieve officer grade in Starfleet.

A litter of warriors and militarists, she'd raised—she often grumbled. But privately, she was proud, proud.

And her sire, M'nault, wasn't private about it.

(White Satellite to Black Sun two, plus one. Check)

"Check."

M'ress blinked, looked up across the multilevel game board.

"There's a great deal on your mind, Lieutenant," observed the concerned figure seated across from her, "besides your next moves. If you wish, we can continue the game at another time."

"You'rre rright, Mrr. Spock. I wasn't concentrrating."

Spock pushed his chair back, rose. He touched a switch set in the top of the game table. The blue striping on the table rim slowly turned bright red, an indication that there was a game in suspension on it and no one should disturb the pieces.

"I do not like to pry, but your concentration was so intense—if I can do anything . . ."

"It's nothing, Mrr. Spock." She let out a deep, purring sigh. "Nothing at all, rreally. Some unimporrtant memorries, that's all."

Spock studied her skeptically, but elected not to pursue the matter any further. Not that the intimate details of M'ress' history or her mental preoccupations intrigued him so much. But as a student of intelligent behavior, he was curious as to what "minor" matters could distract an outstanding player like M'ress to the point where she would make several moves as foolish as her last.

Such a thing would never happen to him, of course.

Kirk was concluding a log entry as Spock entered the bridge. The first officer of the *Enterprise* moved to stand near the command chair, at ease and at the ready, while Kirk dictated. The captain noticed his arrival, acknowledged it with a barely perceptible nod and continued on without a break.

The subject of said log entry was currently visible on the main screen: a smallish, intensely blue-green globe. The light of a modest G-type star reflected phosphorescently back from the spines of interminable ocean. Misty cloud cover added an angelic air to the scene.

The planet's name was Argo. It was one of a surprising multitude of water worlds thus far discovered in the explored section of the Galaxy.

Argo's one peculiarity worth remarking on—and worth the *Enterprise*'s presence here—was that until quite recently (according to drone probe analysis), it had been largely a landed planet. Now its surface was ninety-seven per cent water.

No great ice caps had melted to cause this; no mythological Terran forty days and forty nights of rain had fallen. According to the data relayed back over the indifferent light-years to Starfleet Science Center by the drones, this world had been subjected to a series of evenly spaced seismic convulsions—intense without being cataclysmic—in a very brief span of time.

Forty days and forty nights of tectonic activity, perhaps. The fact that these convulsions had caused the major land masses to subside and vanish beneath the waves was not especially remarkable, Spock mused. It was the time factor which made Argo a world worth a second, more detailed look. That, and the chance that such emergence—subsidence activity might be cyclic in nature. Because there was at least one other, well-populated, world in the Federation which gave hints of being similar to Argo.

A number of techniques for dealing with such subsidings on a selective basis had been developed, but only in theory. To put them into practice would require a world like the inhabited one. Since the inhabitants of the planet in question frowned on experimentation with the planetary crust and other such intimate chunks of their home, a substitute world had to be located.

Argo was such a world . . . maybe. If so, the *Enterprise* might have a chance to try out some of those hopefully effective techniques.

Kirk wrapped up the entry, flipped off the recorder and glanced up at Spock.

As some sort of comment appeared to be in order, the

Vulcan ventured, "Hardly the sort of world one would expect to be riven at any moment from core to surface, Captain."

Kirk nodded, and his gaze shifted to the screen. "No, Mr. Spock. It certainly seems placid enough on the surface. It's what's under the surface that'll be interesting. But we'll make the standard on-site survey first."

"Very good, Captain."

Kirk rose and both men started for the door.

They might, Kirk mused as the elevator took them toward the shuttle hangar, simply have beamed down with life-support belts to maintain them. The force-fields would keep them supplied with sufficient air while preventing them from drowning.

The trouble was, movement in a liquid environment while encased in a personal support field was peculiarly awkward. And mechanical transportation would be far faster.

The small door slid aside and they strode into the cavernous hangar. Two men met them by the water shuttle. One—young, brown-haired, Lincolnesque-bearded and mellow-voiced—saluted: Lieutenant Clayton, their pilot.

His companion simply smiled. "Hello, Jim. Hello, Spock."

"You're coming with us, Doctor?" asked Spock.

"No, Spock," McCoy shot back. "I'm here to evaluate the possibilities of flooding the shuttle hangar five centimeters deep so that when the shuttle departs, the water will freeze solid and we'll have the largest interstellar skating rink in existence."

Spock paused a moment, considered thoughtfully, finally observed cautiously, "You are being sarcastic again, Doctor."

"It's observational capabilities like that which make me glad that at least one competent observer is going on this trip."

"Three, actually, Doctor," Spock continued, "but we will not be offended if you come along anyway."

Kirk cut off McCoy's inevitable riposte by starting for the shuttle with the young lieutenant in tow. "Clayton?"

"Sir?"

"How long," and he gestured at the nearing craft, "since you piloted one of these?"

"It's been a while, sir," the subordinate replied readily, "but as designated shuttle pilot for this mission, I've been reviewing the appropriate tapes and techniques for the last several weeks."

Kirk muttered something inaudible, turned back before entering. "All right. Mr. Spock, Dr. McCoy . . . if you're *quite* finished?"

The long ovoid shape of the shuttle was broken only by a clear plexalloy dome set midway back on its top. One section of this was raised. A small retractable stairway led into it. Spock, McCoy and Clayton followed the captain into the crew section.

While the three senior officers settled into thickly padded seats set into the bulkheads, Clayton eased himself into the one adjustable one that faced the instrument panel. He ignored the conversation of his superiors and concentrated instead on running a final check of the internal computer, phaser controls, and their inorganic relatives.

"Is this trip really necessary, Jim?" asked McCoy over the beeps and hums of the responding components. "Not that I'm complaining, mind. I'm tickled for the chance to get a look at another water world. Fascinating ecologies on all of them. But can't we get all the information on seismic abberations from on-board instrumentation?"

"Yes, Bones. But the regs say that any world holding life bigger than a bacterium and more complex than a coelenterate requires at least one hands-on survey by a visiting ship. It's especially necessary in this case. You know how much trouble drone probes have getting accurate data on the life of water planets."

"That's true, Jim," McCoy admitted, "even so . . ." The clear voice of Lieutenant Clayton cut him off.

"Ready, Captain."

"All right, Lieutenant, when you're set."

Clayton manipulated controls. Slowly, majestically, the two massive doors of the hangar deck began to drift apart, moving with the ease and speed of milkweed seeds in an autumn breeze. Ebony blackness speckled with brilliant pinpoints of light backed the stage. The blue-green-glowing principal performer lay below them and slightly to starboard.

The lieutenant was as good as his word—and his homework. He had a little trouble handling the entry into the atmosphere, but that was understandable. Kirk said nothing. The shuttle had been designed with underliquid maneuverability first in mind, in-flight navigability second.

Once they had penetrated the shifting cloud cover and Clayton had gotten the feel of the little ship in atmosphere, the operation grew gratifyingly smooth.

With a single exception, the surface of Argo in this region was wholly water. The shuttle skimmed low over roiling swells—all shades of blue and green that endless ocean was: azure, cerulean, deep turquoise; emerald, periodot, and flashing olivine. And where a wave crested, broke, the sea turned to amber foam flecked with white.

A strong concentration of mineral salts would be needed to stain the water that orange-brown hue—manganese, perhaps, Kirk thought.

The single exception hove into view: an island now, once the topmost crags of some mountain range. Stone exploded from the sea like a hallucinatory vision of a medieval castle. Battlements of naked basalt and porphyry offered challenge to endless legions of siegewaves, and amber moss festooned the rock-turrets with the banners of still defiant land.

Clusters of brilliant-hued shells rested in niches and crevices of the rock, and some shone phosphorescent even in the strong light of day. The amber color was prevalent here, too. It seemed to engulf the island and form a secondary atmosphere above the sea.

Not manganese then, Kirk thought. Whatever peculiar trace minerals were present here in ocean and air were likely as not alien to Earthly chemistry. He hoped the shuttle's recorder-sampler was operating at peak efficiency.

Assuredly, there was more of interest here than occasional earthquakes.

Clayton adjusted controls and the shuttle cut speed, eased downward to a damp landing. They hit gently and then slid smoothly toward the island.

They lay in the lee of the prevailing current, the island serving as shield, so here the surface was unusually smooth.

As the shuttle came to a halt, Kirk and the others unfastened themselves from the protective seats.

McCoy and Spock moved to the storage lockers, started to remove the equipment they would need to properly sample what lived and was lived upon on Argo. But it was the enchanting vision of an accidental island that drew Kirk's attention.

He moved forward to stand by the busy Clayton. Through the plexalloy the jagged bastions now towering nearby resembled more than ever an impregnable repository of watery secrets. The dark shadow it cast on the otherwise unmarred ocean looked unnatural and faintly forbidding.

"Spock?"

The first officer looked over from where he was carefully constructing a small, self-powered mesh. It would skim the surface outside the shuttle for microscopic life and return automatically when full.

"Yes, Captain?"

"This is the largest remaining land mass on the planet, isn't it?"

"Yes, Captain." Spock turned back to his work, continued speaking as he fitted another part. "There are other outcroppings, but all are smaller than this. Yet according to readings taken from the ship, the ocean bottom hereabouts is fairly close to the surface. This suggests that the subsidence was unequal in places—or else we are floating above what would be regarded as a monstrously high plateau on Earth or on Vulcan. I think the irregular subsidence theory the more likely."

"I suggest," McCoy broke in, "that we stop debating theory and get down to some practical work . . . like obtaining some specimens."

"For once I agree with you, Doctor," Spock responded. Kirk smiled.

"Lieutenant Clayton, open the hatch and let our two impatient scientists get on with their business."

"Aye, sir." He reached toward the side-mounted lever which would raise the entranceway of the dome. As he did so, McCoy gestured sharply to port.

"What's that?"

"I don't see anything, Doctor," Spock said, studying the indicated spot.

"There's something in the water there," McCoy countered, beginning to feel like a mighty fool. Had he seen something or not? "There, see where the water is fountaining slightly?"

McCoy's fears of seeming a fool were put to rest by a wild churning and frothing at the indicated place. They were supplanted seconds later by more tangible fears as a brace of enormous tentacles broke the surface and hooked down like a pair of gargantuan anacondas to embrace the shuttle in a crushing grip.

Kirk was yelling something about activating the engine, but whatever had them was shaking the shuttle violently and his words were lost in the steady banging about.

Released from their protective loungers the four men tumbled about the interior like dice in a cup. There was a sudden jolt as if the ship had abruptly slammed into something hard.

Either the thing had accidentally struck a sensitive portion of itself with part of the unyielding craft or else it was generally infuriated by its inability to crack the hide of this strange prey, because it had thrown them end over end to bang to a stop against an inoffensive wave.

The shuttle automatically rolled to an upright position. Kirk then pulled himself to his feet, saw they were still seaworthy and watertight.

"Spock . . . Bones . . . Lieutenant Clayton?"

Replies came back promptly. "Surprisingly sound, Captain." "I'm all right, Jim." "Okay, I think, sir."

He stumbled to the dome, holding one hand to the large red bruise forming on his left cheek. "What was it, anyway?"

"At the moment my scientific curiosity stands in abeyance, Jim," McCoy groaned. "Just so long as it doesn't come back . . ." He struggled to his feet.

Kirk took a quick step back from the dome. "No such luck, Bones. Clayton . . ."

Before Kirk could say anything else, the upper portion of the Argoan life-form erupted from the water hard by the shuttle. From what they could see, it resembled a cross between an oversized snake and a whale, with the addition of four side-tentacles thick enough to embarrass Earth's grandfather squid. That they were fully functional had already been amply demonstrated.

It was Spock, not the more severly stunned Clayton, who slipped into the pilot's seat and edged them around in the water. He was taking action even as Kirk ordered it.

"Firing phasers on stun, Captain."

Two poles of fiery red light bolted from the nose of the shuttle, enveloped the head of the monster in a glowing nimbus. The concentrated light danced on amber and copper colored scales.

Incredibly, the creature continued toward the shuttle for another couple of seconds. Then its continual roaring faded to an echo. Still moving weakly, reflexively, it sank from sight beneath the waves.

Uncaring swells dusted the place clean, left nothing to indicate the apparition which had loomed there moments before. Spock paused at the console a moment longer to make certain it was no ruse on the part of the monster, then moved to aid Clayton.

"It's all right, Mr. Spock." The younger officer was limping slightly. "I twisted an ankle a little, that's all. I'll be okay."

Spock nodded once, then walked to the dome to stare at the spot where the creature had disappeared. Clayton returned to his position at the front console, sitting down carefully.

"What the devil was that thing?" McCoy murmured.

As usual, the doctor gave in to his oft-times infuriating affection for redundancy, Spock mused—and as usual, he held the easy retort in check.

"Clearly one of the multitude of life-forms which the drone survey neglected to record."

"Hard to see how something that big could be overlooked," Kirk mused. "Still, with such a large area to cover in so short a time, I'm not surprised. The presence of a predator that size is a sure sign of a thriving ecology. I don't think I've ever seen anything quite like this one."

"A rough combination of Terran Cetacea and Cephalopoda, with unique characteristics of its own," Spock added.

Kirk appeared to reach a decision.

"Let's get another look at it before the stun wears off," he announced. "That was a pretty strong jolt it absorbed . . . we should be safe."

He glanced back over his shoulder.

"Submerge, Lieutenant. Keep the currents here in mind."

"Aye, sir, submerging . . ."

II

Clayton maneuvered the streamlined craft with ever greater skill. After several minutes of searching they had found no sign of the monster. But the view about the domc made up for it.

They had sunk into a green mist tinged with the ever-present amber and were now making their way through a world of green glass. The bottom here was close enough to the surface so that sunlight penetrated all the way to the sand.

If the world above with its monotonous, unvarying sea-scape and its looming island appeared simple and unchanging, the bottom presented a gaudy contrast.

Exotic marine flora abounded, formed a kaleidoscopic background for the alien zoo that lived in and about it. The slanting sunlight combined with an Argoal coral-analog to enhance the similarity to an Earthly tropical lagoon.

Some of the ichthyoids wore broad, feathery tails that would have been more at home on a peacock than on a swim-mer. And the moss which so strikingly decorated the island peaks grew even more abundantly below the surface.

Here and there schools of thousands of minute crimson fish darted in and about the densest mosses, so thick in places that the water appeared to be on fire. They reflected metal-lically off the polished backs of lumbering, clownish mol-luscs which scoured the nooks and crannies in the coral like old women at a rummage sale.

"There it is," McCoy exclaimed, even as Clayton was turning the shuttle in the direction of the somnolent sea mon-ster. The creature had drifted slightly south of where it had gone down. Now it rested immobile on the amber sand.

"Look out," Kirk observed. "Try and set us down close by the head, Lieutenant."

"Yes, sir."

As the smooth metal hull settled gently into the soft bottom there was a slight grinding noise. Moss and hypnotically swaying ferns genuflected in opposite directions, while a small colony of crustaceans protested this unannounced eviction from their apartment rock with considerable verve.

Spock and McCoy adjusted their tricorders, began to take basic readings. McCoy found something which stimulated the first scientific controversy of this exploration.

"Dual respiratory system," the doctor observed. "Lungs *and* gills."

"Most odd," Spock agreed. "Unless our assumptions are correct. If land subsidence and emergence here *is* cyclic, then it would be natural for the animal population to stand ready to live in either environment.

"However, one specimen cannot be considered representative of every species on the planet. More readings of other types are essential."

"There's that amber moss, too," McCoy pointed out. "It seems to grow just as well above water as below."

The stunned monster chose that moment of temporary disinterest on the part of its bipedal observers to stir slightly. Its tentacles quivered, disturbing the sand. Abruptly, the gigantic tail jerked spasmodically.

The glancing blow was powerful enough to send the shuttle tumbling across the sea bottom, to come to a stop against a sand hill. Amber rain fell on the plexalloy dome as the displaced sand settled back toward the bottom.

A groggy Kirk decided that this particular specimen reacted a mite too unpredictably for casual study. A second stun burst as strong as the first might kill it, anything less prove ineffectual.

As Kirk stared out the dome, the monster momentarily seemed to have developed eight tentacles instead of four. And two heads. Also, there were two Spocks and two McCoys pulling themselves to their feet.

However many limbs the creature possessed, at the moment all of them were moving in furious motion as it fought to regain its internal balance.

"Take us up, Lieutenant, it's coming around, and I think we'd better be elsewhere when it does." Clayton nodded.

The shuttle angled upward, rose from the sand and started toward the island. Kirk had one final glimpse of the beast, still thrashing about aimlessly, before the angle of ascent cut off his view.

Any normal creature, having received such a pounding, would have escape as its first thought. This inhabitant of Argo, however, was used to running from nothing, except perhaps a larger one of its own kind. Its flailing quelled for a moment . . . then the creature rolled over with a weird whistling roar and shot off with incredible speed in pursuit of the rising shuttle.

Melting greenness gave way to blue sky and a view of the island dead ahead. Expecting to see nothing but calm water, Kirk looked out the rear of the dome. And as expected, the surface rolled on unbroken—until the father of geysers erupted almost on top of them, the burst sending the nose of the shuttle slamming forward and down. It bobbed up like a cork.

Kirk had had enough of maintaining concern for nonsapient alien life-forms. "Prepare to fire phasers . . ."

Spock moved to the console, adjusted the proper controls, leaving Clayton free to steer the craft. He snapped a hurried look at Kirk when a certain critical light failed to wink on as expected.

"Phasers do not respond, Captain. Obviously we have sustained some damage from being struck below."

Relief or no relief, he still should have ordered a check as a matter of course, Kirk cursed. Too late for recriminations. He looked back again, hoping that the monster had perhaps lost interest or gained satisfaction.

Instead, he saw that the hunter had moved off, turned, and was now rushing back at them, mouth agape and wide as the corridor of an underground transportation system.

"Lift off, Mr. Clayton, now!"

The lieutenant worked the proper instruments, paused as if shot, ran through the sequence again twice as fast before throwing Kirk an anguished look.

"No response, sir! Propulsion units have been cracked . . . I'm not registering a thing."

That cavern of a gullet was drawing closer and closer. Stalactites and stalagmites of polished amber ivory lined its roof and floor.

Kirk didn't waste time on shuttle communications. If both phasers and lift engine were out, chances were bad for the more delicate beam transmitter to have survived. He used his pocket communicator.

"Kirk to *Enterprise*—red alert!"

Engineer Scott's voice reflected the urgency in Kirk's own.

"*Enterprise*, Scott speaking—what is it, Captain?"

"We're under attack, Scotty, emergency—beam us aboard." His last words were drowned in the thunderous bellow which erupted from the monster's throat.

"Full ahead, Mr. Clayton . . . !" The lieutenant hit controls, but not fast enough; the great tentacled head rose up, up, blotting out sun and sky—then came down. Kirk barely had time to grab for a hold before the gargantuan skull slammed into the shuttle.

Another deafening howl penetrated the dome and it grew dark as two huge jaws closed on the aft section of the tiny vessel.

Despite various grips, the impact sent everyone sprawling. Part of the upper jaw came down on the plexalloy dome. The transparent molding was incredibly strong, but its designers had never meant it to take this kind of pressure. It finally cracked.

Shaking the shuttle like an infuriated mastiff with a piece of meat, the monster banged it against a rocky protrusion lying just under the surface. That finished the remainder of the dome. Another shake sent shards of dome, torn internal components, and McCoy and Clayton flying.

The interior was a shambles. High-impact seats were twisted like licorice sticks. Spock lay jammed between the pilot's chair and the base of the control console, and Kirk was entangled in the remnants of some restraining straps.

Both men were unconscious, their limp forms bent and loose. But they didn't come free as the creature swam off, still battering at its stubborn prey.

"We've lost contact, Captain," a tinny voice yelled from somewhere within a maze of twisted metal. "We've lost contact. Come in, Captain, come in! Spock . . . !"

McCoy let out a whoosh as he broke the surface, looked around fearfully. But the only struggling form he saw was weak and small. He gave Clayton some support, helped him clear the water from his lungs.

Together they stared at the distant but still visible form of the monster, the cylindrical shape of the shuttle still clutched tightly in its tentacles . . . what was left of it. Even as they watched, the creature rolled over on its back and vanished beneath the waves.

McCoy tried to shout, call, but couldn't manage the breath. Once more the water was calmed, once more the distant island the only projection above the gentle swells. The shuttle, the monster . . . Kirk and Spock . . . all gone.

Hopefully they had been thrown free, probably in the other direction. As he and Clayton had been—oh, hopefully!

As McCoy was about to suggest they start searching, a not-so-alien mist distorted his vision and he experienced a brief sensation of falling.

Once the feeling had passed, he found himself standing in the main transporter chamber of the *Enterprise*, staring at the distant forms of Scott and Transporter Chief Kyle across the room. There was the sound of flesh meeting plastic alongside him, and he turned to help the fallen Clayton. Scott was there in a second to assist him.

"What happened, Bones?" But before McCoy could form a reply the chief had turned and was calling back to Kyle, "Call Sick Bay, have them get a team up here double-time!" He gazed back into the transporter alcove.

"The captain, and Mr. Spock . . ." His voice faded as he saw the look on McCoy's face.

"I didn't know . . . for certain, Scotty. We were taking readings on the local version of a sea serpent and . . . we got a little careless. Its reaction-recovery time . . . phenomenal . . ." A hand ran through hair matted with amber salts. He was aware he probably sounded as tired as Clayton looked.

"It attacked instinctively—wrong bedamned instinct! Threw the shuttle around like a toy. A previous attack had rendered the phasers and lift engine inoperable, but we didn't find that out until too late. I don't know if we could have outrun it on the surface anyway. That thing was *fast*." He took a few steps, found out how tired he really was and sat down at the edge of the alcove.

"I don't know what's happened to the captain or Spock. I hope they got thrown free like Clayton and myself."

"I'll get a search party together immediately," Scott announced. McCoy was too exhausted to do more than nod.

Planetary ocean stretched unbroken to infinity. Only an occasional curl of foam turning in on itself broke the translucent evenness.

That, and a small slim boat of silver. A small slim boat which had been plying the surface of Argo for some time now, plying zig-zag and spiral routes across computer-suggested courses.

The narrow silhouette was broken only by a pair of compact powerpacks attached to its stern . . . and three irregular shapes seated within.

McCoy and Clayton stood in the bow, patiently scanning the horizon with telescopic binoculars. The doctor paused to rub his tired eyes, something he was doing with increasing frequency.

He stopped, stared at the dappled surface without the aid of the mounted telefocals. "Five days and we've found nothing. *Nothing.*"

"They can't just have dropped out of sight, sir," said a sanguine Clayton. McCoy turned to eye him sadly, shook his head.

"Currents, scavengers, a little shift in the lie of the bottom . . ." He shrugged. "They're gone, that's all there is to it."

Clayton said nothing and both men turned their gaze back to the telefocals. It was the lieutenant's turn next to break the silence.

"I see something, anyway. Barely above sea level, bearing thirty, forty degrees to starboard, about three kilometers off, I'd say." He fiddled with the fine adjustment on the precision focals as McCoy turned his own glasses in the indicated direction. Clayton's voice rose.

"There's something on them catching the sun—and I don't think it's rocks!"

All the exhaustion had gone from McCoy's eyes now. His

gaze was surgeon sharp. Scott had moved to stare through his own set, rest turn or no.

A dark mass of cracked, tumbled boulders, worn smooth by the constant wave action. The highest point on the low-lying island rose barely two or three meters from the water. McCoy pressed the telescopic switch, and the image jumped nearer.

Details revealed odd-shaped fragments of reflective material . . . bits of the hull and cabin section of the lost shuttle, for sure. They lay displayed on the rocks like ornaments on a tree.

McCoy lurched slightly as the boat shifted, lost his gaze. Scott was swinging the prow around. He gunned the twin powerpacks and they jetted toward the rocks.

"Any sign of them, Bones?" the chief engineer shouted as he nosed the gig into a notch between two protruding rocks. McCoy shook his head. Clayton scrambled out with a rope in one hand, secured it around a projecting knob of worn obsidian that looked solid enough to anchor the *Enterprise* itself. Clearly, this island had not appeared within the last couple of days.

McCoy climbed out of the gig. Ignoring the debris strewn around his feet, he started for the peak of the little islet, picking his path carefully around sharp edges of metal, plastic and volcanic glass.

No doubt about it, though, the bulk of the shuttle had been washed up—or tossed up—here. He topped the gentle rise and looked down the other side.

That's when he spotted Kirk and Spock.

On the other side of the islet the water was barely a meter deep, washing up over amber-white sand into a miniature bay. The motionless forms of the *Enterprise*'s captain and first officer lay face down in the sand.

"They're here!" he yelled back. "Hurry!"

Seconds later Clayton and Scott were splashing through the water, dragging in panic at the two bodies.

"You think they're still alive, Bones?" Scott didn't look at his friend as he said it.

McCoy's reply was grim, honest. "Not if they've been down there for five days."

Both forms seemed to weigh tons. They fought to move

Kirk to the nearest dry land while keeping his head above water.

"They might have swum here, crawled ashore dazed, and just fallen into the water recently from weakness," McCoy said wishfully. "*Very* recently, I hope."

They finally managed to drag Kirk's waterlogged form onto a flat section of island. Leaving his feet dangling in the water, they went back for Spock.

As soon as both men were lying alongside one another, McCoy reached into his backpack and removed the medical tricorder. Adjusting it quickly, he passed it over Kirk's chest, then reset it and did the same with Spock. Then he made additional adjustments and repeated the action, including head and neck this time.

While Scott and Clayton looked on anxiously, McCoy studied the resultant readouts. Without a word, he ran through the entire sequence again, finally sat back and frowned at the instrument as though it had suddenly grown arms and legs.

"For the sake of Reaction, say somethin'!" Scott eventually exploded. "Are they alive?"

McCoy blinked, appeared to come out of a dream. He looked at Spock without seeing him—then ran through the examination yet another time.

"Their life systems are still functioning," he finally said, as Scott was about to scream. "Metabolism is slowed, heartbeat slightly faster, and other bodily functions altered—but within acceptable parameters." He looked up in confusion.

"I say 'acceptable' because they're incontrovertably alive. But there's something about their lungs and the rest of their respiratory systems I can't figure at all." He shook the tricorder. "Not with this toy, anyway."

Clayton interrupted, gestured at the bodies. "They're coming around."

Kirk's eyes opened first . . . opened, and opened, until they stared skyward in shock and fear. He grabbed at his throat, and his words came out in a feathery, agonized whisper as he twisted on the damp stone.

"Can't . . . breathe. Suffocating . . . !"

"No . . . air . . . choking . . . odd . . ." Spock said huskily, like a dying asthmatic.

All three officers stared at their two comrades in horror: helpless, confused, uncertain. Spock's hands went to his chest in a reflexive spasm, Kirk's shifting between chest and throat. Both men began tearing at their shirts, the actions of someone fighting to clear some invisible constriction from his lungs.

That was when McCoy first noticed the fine membrane stretched between their fingers. It looked organic, not artificial—almost like webbing, in fact. And that slight, silvery-amber flaking on the backs of Kirk's hands . . . why, it was as if the captain had grown scales!

"Help . . . !" Kirk whispered hoarsely. "Can't . . . breathe . . ."

"What's happening to them, Bones?" Scott pleaded. "What's goin' on?"

"Something's changed their whole respiratory structure," McCoy whispered in awe. "They can't live in the atmosphere anymore. Not a gaseous one, anyway." He stood, grabbed Kirk's arm. "Get his ankles! Help me get them back in the water!"

They had an easier time wrestling the two men back into the shallow pool than they had had pulling them out. As soon as their faces passed beneath the clear surface, both men ceased struggling. Instead of grabbing at their chests, they relaxed completely.

McCoy stared in disbelief, even though he half expected what would happen, as Kirk rolled over on the sand and stared up at him through the crystal-clear surface. As to which officer was the more shocked, no one could say.

Scott walked over to stand next to him, likewise gazing down at his two good friends in horrified fascination.

"What do we do now, Doctor?" McCoy hesitated, then turned to the chief engineer and spoke with conviction.

"We get the captain and Mr. Spock on board, Scotty." And he went on to outline what had to be done.

The corridor was empty except for McCoy. The security chambers in Sick Bay were used (infrequently, at that) for the care and treatment of criminals or dangerous aliens. Now one of them had been converted to a much different—and more vital—use. McCoy would encounter no one as he spoke into the recording pickup.

"Medical log, Stardate 5527.1 Captain Kirk and First Officer Spock were rescued—with qualifications—forty-eight hours ago."

He turned the last corner into the recently empty chamber. In place of the double-security door just inside the entrance, a rather different restraining wall had been installed. It consisted of a plate of clear plexalloy, backed by an air space, and then another plexalloy plate. Beyond this airtight seal the chamber was filled four-fifths full with water—a special kind of water, at that.

McCoy was taking no chances with substitutions from the *Enterprise*'s own tanks. The water which filled the room had been transported up in containers from the Argoan world-ocean—from the inlet where Kirk and Spock had been found. The amber sand that covered the floor of the room came from the same location. McCoy's only liberty had been with the air supply: he had to substitute a pump for the natural plant oxygenation system below. So far, neither officer had demonstrated any ill effects from this one concession to convenience.

Kirk and Spock were at the far end of the room, moving aimlessly, dispiritedly over the bottom sand. They were deep enough in thought, undoubtedly musing on their present situation, so that they failed to notice the doctor's entrance. McCoy studied them, resumed speaking into the pickup.

"They have no recollection of what happened after they were thrown from the shuttle. Medical analysis has revealed the presence of an unknown and as yet unidentified substance in their bloodstreams. There is a high probability that this substance is responsible for the alteration of their metabolism and for changing them into water-breathers."

He stopped, shut the recorder off. Both men had noticed his arrival and were moving toward the transparent wall. As they approached, McCoy once again marveled at the process which had somehow altered his friends' internal structure so efficiently.

Even their eyes had been affected. They were now covered

with a transparent film like the second eyelids of some lizards. And of course there were the primary manifestations of the change such as the pronounced scaling and toughening of the skin, increased layers of subcutaneous fatty tissue, and webbing of fingers and toes.

While the two officers stared at him mutely, he moved to a panel set in the wall, examined the gauges and meters it proffered.

Temperature, pressure, salinity, oxygen content . . . everything read normal . . . for a fish. He nodded to the watching Kirk and Spock. Kirk acknowledged with a single jerk of his head and McCoy touched a switch in the bottom of the panel.

A metal section in the nontransparent portion of the wall slid aside. McCoy entered the pressure cubicle and touched another switch, closing the door behind him. A nudge on the belt at his waist, and the glow of a life-support system enveloped his form in soft yellow radiance.

At the adjustment of a simple lever set inside the cubicle, water began to creep up around his feet, ankles, knees. When the chamber was completely filled, McCoy slid the interior door aside and walked clumsily into the water room.

Kirk and Spock were waiting for him. As usual, their voices held a slight fuzziness, like a beam transmission coming in unamplified from across too many light-years. That they sounded even halfway normal was in itself remarkable, but whatever had touched them had been thorough . . . their vocal cords had been altered for speaking under water.

"Well, Bones?" was all Kirk said.

"We're stumped, Jim. Nothing's worked. We've pretty much settled on this new hormone in your blood as the root cause of the entire mutation. Antidote doesn't automatically follow identification, however. There are some of the weirdest-looking molecules involved you ever saw, and they go on forever. So far the situation defies analysis."

Kirk just nodded—there wasn't much else he could do. "What about the other thing . . . are you sure the alteration wasn't performed naturally?"

McCoy shook his head. "No, Jim. Someone's been working on both of you. I'm certain of that. There are too many signs of penetration at key structural points—you had to receive the hormone artificially."

Kirk let out a bitter, bubbling laugh. "Bang goes the theory of there being no intelligent life on Argo." He paused, thoughtfully. "The medical computers have the entire medicinal knowledge of the Federation in their archives. Can't you duplicate the procedure on a lab animal, then work backward to find the antidote?"

McCoy didn't mention the nagging fear that the mutation might be irreversible. "Sorry, Jim. The surgico-chemical methodology here is utterly alien to us—to me, anyhow. Highly sophisticated, too. If I knew how to begin to approach the procedure, I might . . ." His voice trailed off.

"So we are left with locating a previously unknown, unsuspected sapient life-form below," Spock put in. "Evidently the initial surveys saw nothing but simple marine forms." McCoy looked hesitant.

"I don't see how even a dumb drone could miss a race capable of this kind of medical technology."

"Medical technology is not highly visible," Spock countered. "Knowledge of that sort does not imply knowledge of, for example, advanced structural engineering or other highly visible signs of civilization. Many primitive cultures possess basic, yet complex medical abilities."

"You're reaching, Spock," said McCoy.

"It is only one of several possible explanations," the first officer readily admitted. "Another lies in the composition of the Argoan sea itself. The presence of large amounts of dissolved metals and mineral salts could easily distort delicate sensor readings, block others entirely. Also, such sensors were probably set for shallow scans, ignoring possibly inhabited depths."

McCoy smiled.

"All very plausible, Spock. But if true, where does that leave us? We can't carry out efficient underwater exploration without the aqua-shuttle, and that was our only vehicle designed for liquid-environment study." He gestured at the belt circling his waist.

"We can exist underwater with life-support belts, but our time is limited and our mobility even more so. Also, if there's somebody down there who wants to stay hidden, it would be pretty damn difficult to hide a bunch of floating yellow light bulbs.''

''Well, *we* aren't limited!'' Kirk blurted in frustration. ''Spock and I go anywhere in that ocean as efficiently as the natives.'' He smiled grimly. ''We've been designed to do so.''

McCoy's face took on a look of alarm. ''Too risky, Jim. Argo is totally unexplored. If sensors couldn't penetrate that metalized soup you want to go swimming about in, chances are communications won't be much good, either. And if there are any more minnows down there like the one that hit the shuttle . . .''

Kirk's smile widened, but the grimness remained in his voice. ''We don't have a choice, Bones.'' He waved a webbed hand. ''I can't command a ship from in here . . . hell, I can't even *live* in here! We'd go crazy in a week!''

''The captain somewhat exaggerates the subjective time involved,'' Spock corrected evenly, ''but the inevitability of his prediction is one I'm not prepared to argue with.''

''I know how you feel, Jim, Spock,'' said McCoy. ''But there's still a chance we might find a solution in the lab. If you go down into that ocean, out of contact . . .'' Kirk cut him off.

''Right now the percentages give us two choices, Bones. Live in an aquarium for the rest of our lives like curiosities, freaks—or stay on Argo as her first Federation settlers. I refuse to accept either one of them.''

McCoy shifted his attention from the stubborn set of Kirk's face to appeal to Spock.

''What about you, Spock? You can view this in a logical, dispassionate manner.''

''The captain states the case emotionally, of course,'' Spock replied instantly, ''but correctly.'' McCoy's expression fell. ''I would be of very little value to this ship—or to myself—if I were to remain confined to a tank in Sick Bay.'' He paused, added, ''In a way, we are total invalids, Doctor. Something you should be able to understand. We must seek any possible treatment, no matter what the corollary dangers.''

Kirk raised his right hand, studied the webbing. ''Any intelligence that can produce this kind of mutation ought to be able to change us back. *Has* to change us back.'' He lowered the hand and stared unwaveringly at McCoy.

''There are some other physicians in this vicinity, Bones, and we've *got* to find them . . .''

III

The sun of Argo, slightly yellower than Sol, glinted sharply off mirrorlike swells, struck the smaller silver splinter excitedly and raced on to illumine the island.

Kirk, Spock, Scott and Clayton filled the gig, the latter two holding phasers as they surveyed the surrounding surface for signs of anything even faintly inimical. The tiny boat bobbed just outside the long morning shadows cast by the towering island.

Kirk and Spock made final adjustments of the dark green vinyl that clung to their bodies like a second skin. Bubbles burst occasionally inside the awkward, water-filled masks they wore. Spock moved to the side of the gig while Kirk turned to face his chief engineer. His words came through the mask barely comprehensible.

"We'll make contact as soon as possible, Mr. Scott."

"Aye, sir," Scott replied uneasily. He felt no better about this than had McCoy.

Kirk moved to the side of the gig, looked at his first officer. Spock nodded once. Both men took a deep breath, the water level falling visibly within their faceplates. Then they hurriedly removed both masks and attendant tanks, dropped them into the boat, and dove over the side.

Scott moved to the side, looked down at both men floating comfortably just under the surface. Kirk looked up at him, waved once, and turned to swim downward. The water was clear and Scott continued staring for a long time, until both men had finally disappeared from view . . .

There are three habitable zones to most life-giving worlds: the air, the land and, lastly, the sea. And those who have claimed either of the first two have clearly not deigned to get their feet wet.

It's not merely the incredible lushness that mesmerizes those who plow beneath the surface, nor is it the overwhelming abundance of life that comprises such lushness. To most, it's the constant motion that contrasts so heavily with the stilted, jointed world of air-breathers. Everything underwater is part of a single, unending ballet—a dancing ecology, where every inhabitant from the lowliest worm or plant to the bemuscled and fanged carnivore knows its assigned steps and performs uncomplainingly a perpetual choreography.

Such was the world of green glass through which Kirk and Spock now probed a leisurely path. Descending gradually, they leveled off about a dozen meters from the sandy bottom, began to swim outward from the island. Clusters of amber moss sequined with phosphorescent shells and tiny crawling things drifted lazily in the gentle current. Tight formations of brilliantly hued little fish wheeled and spun in Prussian cloudlets, while larger solitary swimmers observed enviously.

The two bipeds began to move in a widening spiral, now well out from the lonely gig bobbing far above and behind them. Finally, on the fourth curve out, Kirk and Spock encountered what looked very much like a cultivated area. The garden was laid out in an unearthly but undeniably artificial fashion. Instead of distinct rows of different plants, all grew together, but neatly spaced among themselves. There was no crowding, no competition for light or sandy soil among the green, pink and amber vegetation.

Climbing over low sand dunes, the garden appeared to thicken in the distance. A few kicks brought Kirk and Spock to the outlying growths. Wordless, they examined the unmistakable signs of hand planting, constant weeding and care. Spock pointed and without a word they swam to the top of the first dune. They gently nudged through the dense vegetation crowning its top and studied the view beyond.

The garden, farm, or whatever it was stretched out impressively, occupying the sandy plain in all directions for a considerable distance. Far more commanding, however, were the shapes that swam slowly and purposefully among the intricate patterns.

They were humanoid and had almost human forelimbs. But the rear limbs bore no resemblance to anything mankind had ever possessed. The legs appeared almost boneless, while the feet were true flippers, supple and flexible. A small dorsal fin set just back of the neck between the shoulder blades added to the alien aspect. The skin was a variant of the omnipresent amber, with shades of gold or green, while strands of vestigial hair the color of silver and gold tinsel topped the skull.

The race was obviously mammalian, women mixing in about equal numbers with men in the garden. Both sexes were clad in close-fitting garments of minute, metallically colored shells arranged in a multitude of individual designs.

"Once again, the basic humanoid model dominates," Spock murmured softly, "fully adapted for oceanic survival."

"Even so, Spock, they still seem to retain some above-water movements. Maybe instinctive, maybe habitual . . . I don't know. Here's another sign of the rapid subsidence of land hereabouts." He paused. "And I think we've been noticed."

Sure enough, several heads had turned to stare in their direction. Some of the figures were moving hastily backward, giving signs of alarm.

"I cannot vouch for their other senses," Spock commented appraisingly, "but their hearing is evidently acute."

"Well, we came to find them," Kirk sighed. He kicked with both legs, moving through the soft growth and down the slope. Spock followed.

At this first hint of movement, several more of the Argoans moved away, while others stood their ground and brandished tools which were nonetheless lethal-looking for all their agricultural design. One of the natives drifted slightly in front of his companions, then mouthed something momentarily incomprehensible at Kirk and Spock. Apparently the linguistic pattern was relatively standard. The tiny universal translators strapped beneath the green bodysuits hummed softly and the message came out in their ear speakers as, "Go away, air-breathers. You are not wanted here."

Kirk had hoped for a friendly greeting at best, a curious

one at the least. But this expression of familiarity combined with hostility had taken him aback.

Keeping his gaze on the speaker, he directed his voice toward the pickup set in the concealed translator. It rescrambled his voice into something the sea-dwellers could comprehend.

"We won't harm you . . . we are friends. We seek only friendship . . . and knowledge."

"Leave us!" a woman shouted from the crowd. "It is enough for our young to have saved your lives once. If you go on, nothing will save you again." She turned, swam with powerful strokes over the next dune.

Others turned, started to follow. "Wait, listen," Kirk implored those departing, "we only . . ."

"Go away!" the man at the head of the mob shouted. He lingered longer than the others; but eventually he, too, turned and swam furiously to catch up.

A mystified Kirk and Spock found themselves floating alone in the field.

"It doesn't make any sense, Spock. They said that they saved us once; and so they have, but why . . . ?"

"Excuse me, Captain," Spock cut in, "but I believe their exact phrasing was, 'our young saved your lives once.' " That gave Kirk pause.

"Yes, that's right—and these adults didn't seem to approve." He stared in the direction taken by the vanished Argoans. "The answers appear to be that way, Mr. Spock."

As they swam after the retreating farmers, Spock mused, "They are not particularly rational," he observed in a mildly reproving tone, "or at least one of them would surely have realized that we were badly outnumbered as well as apparently weaponless.

"Yet even so, they were frightened. Their primitive fear of air-breathers and this," he gestured around them, "evidence of simple hand farming hardly indicate a race capable of highly advanced surgical procedures. A curious dichotomy here, Captain. Our observations will not readily supply a solution."

"Then we'll just have to press a little harder, Spock. Eventually something's going to have to give. With answers, I hope." They swam on in silence.

Several minutes of steady swimming brought them to the base of a coral-studded reef which rose to the surface. Kirk treaded water easily as they studied the sweeping escarpment. It swept off unbroken to left and right.

"Surely they didn't go over the top of this, Spock."

"Possible but not likely, Captain, I agree. I suggest we separate and study potential approaches, staying within sight of one another."

"All right." Kirk swam off to the left, Spock went the other way. Soon thereafter, he turned at a feathery yell from his first officer.

"Here, Captain . . . !"

A moment later he drifted alongside Spock, where the latter floated by a crevice in the undersea palisade—a fathomless, gaping wound that penetrated the reef for an unknown distance.

"Excellent place for an ambush," he muttered.

"True, Captain. Yet why arrange so elaborate a deception? They could easily have overpowered us earlier. I submit they went through here . . . without stopping." He nodded toward the horizontal shaft.

Both men worked at their suit belts, produced thin, sealed cylinders—powerful undersea lights. Kirk activated his, turned to throw a tubular beam of brightness into the crack. He moved it around, and the beam revealed nothing but naked rock, dead coral, and a few stunted plants and some terrified dwellers in darkness, who quickly darted out of sight into private abysses of their own.

Keeping both beams fairly parallel, they entered the trench.

It was longer than Kirk expected. In places it became almost a tunnel, as the walls arched overhead to blot out all hints of the surface.

He forced himself to concentrate on the finite cone of rock illumined by the light. This was a place for observation, not imagination, to hold sway.

Something touched him on the shoulder and he jerked sharply, but relaxed when he found it was only Spock's hand. The first officer extinguished his light, motioned for Kirk to do the same. They waited silently while their eyes readjusted to the absence of light. Or *was it* absent?

For several moments while they floated in dark coolness,

he saw nothing. Then he became aware that he could make out the faint outlines of the trench around them, albeit dimly.

The illumination appeared to emanate from somewhere close ahead. A few kicks brought them into increased light from overhead once again. Eventually they reached the end of the trench.

Here the coral rampart dropped off in a steep cliff to a broad sandy plain deeper and wider than the one they'd just left. What rose lofty and ethereal there made the manicured gardens and jeweled schools of fish they'd seen pale to insignificance.

What they had come upon was an underwater city, constructed with complete disregard for any ancient cataclysm, any present currents, any concern of any sort save aesthetics . . . a metropolis of faery.

Thin winding towers emulated the internal configuration of spiral seashells in grace and strength. Another huge, shell-shaped structure dominated the city, rising in its center. It was as if the city had been poured whole, entire, from a single, carefully sculpted mold, instead of being built by piece and bit.

At the point nearest the base of the coral cliff, a large archway formed a prominent break in the wall that surrounded the city. Variously clad inhabitants were swimming in and out in a steady two-way stream, intent on unknown aspects of Argoan commerce.

"Beautiful . . . and fascinating," Spock commented. "Notice the wall and use of the archway, when both are easily avoidable. Both carry-overs from land-dwelling times."

"All the more reason to wonder, Spock," said Kirk, shaking his head in puzzlement. "A civilization capable of building something like this, able to withstand continental subsiding, capable of medical accomplishments unheard of in the Federation—why should they be afraid of us, Spock?"

"Perhaps the proper term would be abhorrence, Captain, not fear. It is quite possible they find us grotesque and ugly. Basis enough for their reactions thus far. There is ample precedent in Earth's history."

Kirk nodded slowly. "Agreed. Still, we've got to get inside, no matter what they think of our features. There seems to be much less activity on the far side." Spock strained his gaze.

"I also feel no cultural inhibitions about ignoring the archway, Captain."

Dodging occasional solitary Argoans and taking care to remain a good distance from the city proper, the two men began to swim in a broad curve away from what they'd determined to be the city's main entrance.

Eventually they approached a section of wall that looked deserted. Even so, they felt conspicuous against the bright white and amber sand bottom. They waited until the lowering sun formed a dark shadow behind one thick tower, then swam for it.

A quick survey revealed they were in a little frequented section of the city. Kirk motioned and they swam slowly toward its center. He had no definite plan in mind—there was nothing to formulate one on—only that they had to contact the physician-scientists who had instigated the initial mutation. Persuasion would hopefully follow.

They made rapid progress, keeping close to the walls of low-lying structures wherever feasible. Once they almost kicked head-on into a crowd of busy Argoans as they stumbled into a central crossway. They had to dart back into a nook between buildings and wait for the aliens to pass.

"There it is," Kirk finally whispered.

They were floating on the opposite side of a broad, open plaza from the huge shell-shaped central structure. Right now it was devoid of strollers, and both officers wondered at the absence of citizens.

"Perhaps everyone is out in the fields at this time," Spock speculated, "or deep within the structures engaged in daily tasks we cannot conceive of. Or it may be that . . ."

Words and actions were cut off abruptly as a large weighted net dropped neatly over them. Two males appeared on either side and above them, crossed in a deadly precision maneuver beneath the two startled officers and pulled the net tight.

Kirk and Spock found themselves unable to get a purchase on anything solid, unable to get any speed in the folds of the net, and unable to break it. All the while they were discovering these depressing facts, their captors were towing them efficiently toward the very domed edifice they'd sought to reach.

Kirk finally stopped fighting the netting and relaxed. They might need their strength later and have a better chance to use it. He also tried to look on the bright side of things.

They had wanted to enter the shell-shaped building—very well, it seemed they were going to do that. Not as stealthily as he had planned, perhaps, but half an apple was better than none.

They entered through a broad, low, open arch much like the anachronistic city gate, were towed through several twisting, winding halls. Inside, at least, the Argoans had managed to shuck off enough of their land-based memory to build without regard to land-based gravity.

Some of the hallways dipped up in curves, others ran down to undisclosed depths at crazy angles. Eventually they emerged into a huge auditorium near the roof of the building. As they did so Kirk realized why they had seen so few Argoans swimming over the rooftops.

Most of the buildings were doubtless arranged like this one, with transparent or translucent roofs to let in the light of day. Mass movement overhead would not only be disconcerting, it would block the light as well as eliminate privacy.

Kirk then turned his attention to more immediate matters. The chamber walls were decorated with huge globes of a creamy, pearl-like luster. There was a raised dais at the far end of the chamber. Its three carved seats were occupied by male Argoans.

It was difficult to judge age with any accuracy. But judging from their attitude and bearing as much as outward appearance, Kirk felt these three were fully mature specimens. One was slim and appeared to be regarding them with a thoughtful, though amused air. The one on the far right was slightly paunchy, and his expression was less readable. Between them, the tallest of the triumvirate studied Kirk with piercing amber eyes that seemed to cut right through him. A remarkable personality, Kirk decided instantly, and the one to be watched most carefully.

There was a lower dais set to the left, again with three seats. Two of its occupants were males, the third female—attractive in a fishy sort of way. They were generally a little smaller than the other three. But their motions were quicker, their eyes moved faster, and Kirk had the definite impression that they were considerably younger than those sitting on the main platform.

Time for analysis vanished as Kirk found himself tumbling head over heels toward the dais, net and all. He thrashed about, trying to regain his balance in the enclosed space.

"Here are the spies, Tribune," the translator reported in his ear—the words of one of their captors. There was an unmistakable hint of disgust in his final words: "Air-breathers!"

The tall one, the one with the eyes, rose from the dais to hover in the water before them. He studied Kirk and Spock coldly, and the translator managed to convey some of that coldness across unemotional circuitry.

"You stand."

"Inaccurate," mumbled Spock, struggling to turn erect within the clinging coils of the net.

"I am Domar," their questioner began, "the High Tribune of the . . ."

"Aquans" was the nearest the translator could come to interpreting the unpronounceable name these folks had for themselves.

"These are my advisors, Cadmar and Cheron," the imposing speaker continued, indicating the beings to his right and left.

Kirk gave up trying to extricate himself from the net, settled for striking a dignified post within. "I am Captain James Kirk of the Starship *Enterprise*. This is my first officer, Mr. Spock."

The thin brows of the High Tribune drew together uncertainly. "Your words are meaningless. You are air-breather enemies from the surface. We have been expecting you for a long time, never letting down our guard from the Old Days."

"If you find my words meaningless, I confess I find yours confusing, Tribune," Kirk admitted truthfully. "We came here in peace."

Domar's frown deepened. His two companions gazed grimly at the officers. "The ancient records," he announced, "warn that air-breathers never come in peace."

"Are you saying," broke in a new, challenging voice, "that they come in war, then . . . without any weapons?"

Kirk looked sharply to his left. The young female was on her flippers, staring belligerently at the Tribune. On her right side one of the males added, "Can we do nothing without consulting the ancient records? Have we no ability to analyze and decide without the advice of the long-dead?"

Obviously this was a very different society from, say, that of Earth; for this challenge produced definite hints of hesitation in the attitudes of two of the Tribunes—Cadmar and Cheron. One minute they appeared as inflexible as the walls of the city, the next and their convictions showed cracks at the first objection from their younger colleagues. If the High Tribune Domar felt the same lack of assurance, he didn't show it.

There was an unmistakable weariness in Cheron's voice as he countered, "Why do the Junior Tribunes always wish to change the records? Are the words of those who built this city empty for them? Are they . . . ?"

Domar put out a quieting hand, then the council leader turned and made a gesture to the two guards.

"Let the mesh be removed—but stand ready. Beware the air-breather's deceptiveness."

With considerable relief, Kirk and Spock felt the netting being removed. As they were freed, all six Tribunes inspected them with renewed interest. The powerful amplifier in the tiny translator brought Kirk a whispered translation from—he struggled to recall the vaguely Greco-Roman sounding names. Lemas—that was the youngster's name.

"The surgeons did their jobs well," he was murmuring. "Observe the perfection of the metamorphosis and the ease with which their bodies have adapted."

Kirk felt faintly flattered—the sort of mild exhilaration one experiences when participating in the hard-won success of others. Still, the Tribune's words were not conclusive evidence. The process still might have been initiated naturally and only completed by artificial means. It would pay to be sure.

His natural inclination was to address himself immediately to the younger, seemingly friendly Tribunes. He needed his years of diplomatic experience to tell himself that their elders wouldn't look kindly on the implied slight. So he directed his first words to Domar.

"Then your scientists *did* induce these mutations in our systems?"

"We had no other moral choice. Unlike air-breathers," he finished roughly, "we do not wish to kill."

"You could simply have left us where we were and let us drown," Spock pointed out.

A twinge of contempt was added to Domar's coldness.

"Indifference to the injured is merely another form of murder. A typical air-breather observation. You were brought here unconscious, barely alive. You were returned to a place near where you were found still unconscious, far more alive. Our obligation was discharged."

"It would seem that their own ancient records are as well preserved as ours," Cadmar put in. "They found us again anyway, to come among us as spies."

Again that shrill female voice cut the water. "You do not give them a chance to defend or explain themselves, Cadmar. Our law does not allow that, even for unmentionable air-breathers who come among us."

"Rela is correct," said Domar, then turning back to Kirk and Spock, "You may speak . . . if you have the nerve."

"Look," Kirk began, ignoring Domar's invitation to fight, "you've apparently had some pretty bad experiences in the past with the last remnants of whatever branch of your race remained on the surface of this world. I can tell you with some assurance that you've no longer anything to fear from *that* quarter!

"As for ourselves, we come from another world entirely. Our only desire in returning to your city—which we found simply by following some of your farmers—was to . . ."

He did not get a chance to finish. The excitement his words had generated in the younger Tribunes finally spilled over.

"You do not live on the surface places?" Rela inquired wonderingly.

"Not of this world," Spock began, "we . . ."

The conversation was getting too complicated for Cadmar, at least. "Enough!" he cried, the violence of his comment bringing him out of his seat. "Clearly, this is a great lie.

Another world, indeed! The situation is plain. The air-breathers are come again to wreak havoc among us.''

"You are mistaken, sir," Spock objected quietly. "As Captain Kirk was about to say, our only purpose in returning here was to find a means of reversing the mutations you induced in us."

"That, at least, is impossible," Domar informed them brusquely. "There is nothing in the surgical records we retain that designates a method for reverse mutation."

Kirk slumped inwardly. That was it, then. He was doomed to spend the rest of his life drifting in a portable container. A curiosity, a freak for Federation scientists to ponder on and take periodic samples from.

Spock, undoubtedly, would handle it better than he. He wondered what it was going to be like to spend the rest of his life at the wrong end of a microscope.

The slight dot took on shape and form as Scott adjusted the telefocals. It resolved into a long, narrow creature with broad fins, a long thin tail, flapping wings and fishlike body. It skimmed low over the distant surface and he thought he could make out feathery gills on the back of the thing's neck.

Apparently an amphibious flier. Interesting. He wished Spock were here to see it and venture an opinion.

He wished Spock were here, period.

There was a buzz at his hip. He acknowledged the communicator call and McCoy's voice drifted up from the speaker.

"*Enterprise* to Mr. Scott."

Scott watched a moment longer as the flier folded leathery wings against its body and dove into the water. Then he turned his attention to the communicator.

"Scott here . . . what is it, Doctor?"

"All departments have been proceeding with their own missions, as per Jim's orders, Scotty. We just got a bulletin from seismology. There's a major quake due in that area."

"How soon?"

"Meier can't be certain, but it's going to be a bad one. Complete topography shift."

"All right, he can't be exact . . . I know those guys down there. What's their best estimate?"

A pause at the other end, and then McCoy's voice came back tense, worried. "Probably within four hours, Scotty. That's a conservative guess."

"And inside the captain and Mr. Spock's report-in time," he replied in alarm.

"Inside! Can't you contact them before that?"

"Kinna do it, Doctor. They've no communicators and . . ." He stopped, thought a moment. "Wait . . . there ought to be a trace signal from their translators. Those gadgets are small, but they use a lot of power. We can try like blue blazes, anyway. Scott out."

He flipped off, turned to the anxiously waiting Clayton. "Let's get out those other suits and the life-support belts, Lieutenant. Contact our other boats. We're goin' fishin'."

The green body suits were the closest thing to camouflage they had. But there was no way to disguise the glow from the belts. One by one the belts were activated and the little party dropped over the side.

Scott descended rapidly, braked to study the reading on the wrist gauge he had donned along with the suit and belt. He turned slowly, finally stopped facing toward deeper water.

"Directional pickup indicates they're in that general direction, toward those dunes. Let's go." The little knot of crewmen started off in the indicated direction, shining like fireflies in the clear water.

Searching eyes roved over gorgeously colored underwater life, exotically shaped, remarkably shaded. Plant or animal or both, all were resolutely ignored. The party was hunting for more simply clad, more awkwardly built swimmers.

Two pairs of eyes studied them from behind a concealing dune of amber sand and rock. One pair belonged to one of the farmers Kirk and Spock had encountered earlier.

"More air-breathers," she reported to her companion. "We must inform the Tribunes." The other nodded and they streaked away, weaving in and out among the bemmies and beds of pseudo-kelp.

"The name of our starship, our above-the-air vessel," Kirk explained to the intent Tribunes, "is on the wreckage of our underwater craft. If you want proof, examine the remains."

"Yes," insisted Rela, "let us examine the wreckage before we pass judgment."

"To what end?" wondered Cheron tiredly. "The fact that their vessel has a name is no proof of extra-Argoan origin." Kirk was about to point out that they would find more conclusive evidence in the wreck when the discussion was interrupted by the breathless arrival of two females at the far end of the chamber. They rushed forward.

Kirk noted that no one objected to their entrance, no one sought to bar them from the room. This society had much to commend it, he reflected.

"Important news, High Tribune."

Domar made a curt gesture. "Speak."

"Several air-breathers have invaded the outskirts of the cultivated areas. We saw them. They were moving toward the city. They glowed most strangely."

"That's only . . . ," Kirk began, but Doman drowned him out as he turned angrily to the Junior Tribunes. "Defensive screens, as the records speak of! Do you still believe these creatures come in peace?"

Some of Rela's self-righteous assurance faded, apparently drained by this unexpected information. "We do not know what to believe," she finally whispered unhappily.

Domar looked satisfied, turned his attention to the pair of guards who stood ready behind Kirk and Spock.

"Take these spies to the surface and leave them there. They wish to return to their element. So be it. Justice enough for our enemies . . . !"

IV

Kirk choked, gasped for breath. He got a half mouthful of water and gulped it gratefully.

Whether Domar, the other Tribunes, or the guards were responsible for the particular agony he and Spock were being subjected to he didn't know. But right now all he wished for was a smooth scaly neck under his fingers.

They had been taken to the spot where McCoy and Scott had found them and tied securely to the low-lying boulders there, just barely above the water line. Occasionally a wave would sweep over the rocks and give them a momentary respite from slow suffocation.

But the steady deprivation of air-rich water was making them weaker and weaker. At their present infrequent intake, they wouldn't last much longer. Nor was there any hope here of a life-giving incoming tide.

So weak were they that neither saw the slim form which swam nearby, staring at them sadly. Rela.

A glint of metal as the wave receded elsewhere caught her eye and she kicked toward it, her flippers propelling her rapidly through the water. Holding her breath, she poked her head and arms out of the water and examined the shards and scraps with a kind of resigned curiosity. Several of the pieces were bigger than she was and were almost intact. She noticed that one seemed to have some kind of writing etched into it. With her finger, she traced the cryptic indentations.

U.S.S. Enterprise . . . the bumps meant nothing to her, of course.

Another section, caught high up on a rocky projection, caught her eye. She took a deeper breath, raised her head and stared. It seemed to be part of a dome . . . a dome of some strange, transparent material. Judging from its curve, it must have enclosed a substantial area, though she couldn't get any good idea of its original size or shape. She clambered out onto the rocks, struggling clumsily.

Beneath the broken dome was a section of metal lined with interesting instruments. There were also several sealed cases which had broken loose from their catches and tumbled about within. One was jammed shut, but two of the others lay broken open, their contents scattered nearby.

She picked up the remains of what seemed to be a book—but the material was impossibly, incredibly fragile. Opening it carefully, she thumbed through it, her eyes growing wider and wider at each subsequent waterlogged revelation.

There were pictures of strange vessels, others of absurd underwater creatures she had never seen, and others—of air-dwellers! Such incredible monsters couldn't possibly exist . . . on her world, she realized with a start.

And that meant . . . she plunged into the water, swam furiously, perilously close to the sharp edges of the rocks. Taking another deep breath she scrambled up onto the flat boulder to which Kirk was bound, knelt over him.

"Conserve your strength," she bubbled, "I will free you . . . somehow."

She tugged at the cords, trying to loosen the knots. She dug her flippers into a crack in the rocks and pulled with all her strength, gasping, straining, water running out her mouth and down her chin. No use.

While Kirk continued to gasp weakly she turned and plunged her head back under the surface for a long moment. Coming back up she said in that odd, gurgling voice, "The mesh is too strong!"

"Go," Kirk somehow managed to sputter, "toward the big island . . . assistance there, maybe . . . friends . . ."

Rela nodded, or at least that was the impression Kirk had. After giving both men long draughts of fresh water, she plunged back in and disappeared.

If, Kirk mused painfully, she decided not to come back . . .

Clayton looked over the side of the gig. A moment later, Scott, the lime-yellow aura of his life-support belt still glowing brightly, popped up. He reached up, clung to the side of the small craft.

"See anything?" asked Clayton. Scott shook his head dispiritedly.

"Still no sign of 'em. I wish we carried more underwater equipment. The captain and Mr. Spock are adapted for gettin' around in this environment. We just can't match 'em, tryin' to swim in a life-support aura.

"Besides which, the directional tracker isn't pickin' up their signal anymore. Lost it a while back and I'm damned if I know why . . . unless their translators are broken." He patted the one affixed to his own chest beneath the green bodysuit.

"The only signal I get now is from mine, and I'm not too sure *it* works. I thought I saw some big, man-shaped form watchin' us from one of the big kelp beds. I yelled at *it* and *it* disappeared."

"It might have been a fish," Clayton argued, "but I suppose it could have been one of our mysterious locals. I don't think it's the translator, sir, I . . ." He broke off, staring, as an alien shape broke the water only a couple of meters from the gig. His phaser came around automatically.

But it lowered at the same time they were given proof of the translator's efficacy.

"Follow me, quickly!" Rela implored. Without waiting for a reply, she turned and started off in the direction of the distant boulders.

"Wait a minute!" Scott shouted hurriedly, "who are . . . ?"

Rela whirled in the water, yelled back at them. "Follow me. Your friends need your help." She ducked her head and shot off again.

While Scott climbed into the gig, Clayton focused his telefocals on the distant, moving fin. "I've got her clearly, Mr. Scott. She's swimming just under the surface."

Scott nodded, switched off his life-support belt and moved to the controls of the gig. A second later the powerful side jets came to life and the compact vessel shot off in pursuit.

Kirk's chest felt like the rotten leather of an old bellows, and his hoarse rasping sounded like one. There were more

pleasant ways to die, he thought, than suffocating to death.
He sensed its nearness, and the first hallucinations confirmed it.

It started with the gurgling shout he dreamt he heard
nearby. Vague forms seemed to move before his glazed eyes,
almost human . . . angels, perhaps? It seemed that hands
fumbled at his sides . . .

A warm coolness washed over him . . . a temperature
incongruity? No . . . he drew in another breath, felt himself
growing stronger, drew another and another.

His vision cleared with awesome abruptness, and he found
himself staring into the non-angelic but no less welcome face
of an anxious Scott. He sat up, looked around. Spock stared
back at him across the sandy bottom.

Scott joined them, once again activating his yellow halo.
Kirk seated himself on something soft and, he hoped, non-
lethal.

"*Good* to see you, Scotty."

"Not as good as it is to see you, Captain." The look in
the chief engineer's eyes embarrassed Kirk. He turned to
Rela.

"Rela, this is my chief engineering officer, Mr. Scott.
Tribune Rela is an Argoan-Aquan, as their name for themselves translates. Their city is a short distance away. I'm
afraid Mr. Spock and I didn't make a very favorable impression on its rulers."

"We're obliged for your help," Scott said hurriedly,
forcing gaze and curiosity away from the drifting Rela.
"Captain, we've been trying to contact you for two
hours. There's a severe quake due in this area soon. According to the seismology people, it will disrupt this entire region. That won't bother us, of course, but . . ."

The translators were good, not perfect. Some of the strange
mouthings of the air-breathers came to Rela garbled and devoid of crucial nuances. But if some of the terminology was
vague, the look Scotty gave her was enough to put his point
across.

"There are many legends of such events," she told them.
"When the great surface places sank into the sea. Much of
the knowledge of the ancients was destroyed."

"I still do not understand," put in Spock, "how such a

radical, complete racial mutation could take place in such a short time.''

"You are right, Mr. Spock," Rela complimented him. "Evolution played no part in it. When the surface places began to sink, many air-breathers—my distant ancestors—were altered to breathe and live beneath the sea by surgery, as you were. Such surgery extended even to the . . ." it came out "genes."

"Thus, the change was made hereditary—for those who accepted the change. There were those who did not . . . hence my people's instinctive fear of you."

"Strange that the air-breathing remainder of your race should turn to useless violence," Kirk wondered, "considering their accomplishments.''

"It seems as if those who remained on the surface didn't believe the continental subsidence would be this extensive," Spock theorized. "I would guess that somewhere, sometime, they lost the ability to change themselves into water-breathers. A few generations would serve to breed sufficient hatred and envy for those immune to the coming catastrophe.''

"They hunted and killed among us," Rela recounted grimly. "We learned to hate anything that lives in the air. That is why it has always been forbidden to mutate back to such a state.''

A startled glance passed between Kirk and Spock before the Captain commented excitedly to her, "Then reverse surgery *is* possible. Domar lied to us.''

"Not wholly," Rela corrected. "There are stories of sealed places in the ancients' air-city where many records remain. It is rumored that . . .''

A dull rumbling echoed through the water around them. Sand was jolted upward, fish scurried frantically for the nearest cover, and Kirk and Spock found themselves bounced from their seats. The turbulence sent Scott and Rela tumbling slightly.

Sand continued to cascade in gritty falls from clumps of rock, clouding the water with drifting debris.

"Less than two hours," Scott warned them.

"How far are these ruins, Rela?" Kirk asked.

"Not far . . . in a direction away from the city.''

Kirk already had his mind made up . . . but a second opinion was always good policy. "Mr. Spock?"

"We have no choice, Captain. If there is a chance for us, it lies there."

"But these are only stories," said Rela, alarmed at the reaction her information had produced. "In any case, I cannot take you there. It is against the Ordainments."

Kirk swam close to her. "It's vital, Rela. Not just for Mr. Spock and myself, but for the population of another world much like yours, threatened with similar disaster. Argo's ancient knowledge could help save them."

The Aquan hesitated, staring at the three aliens. If she chose to whirl and swim away it was doubtful that either Kirk or Spock could catch her. She made a sharp, enigmatic gesture.

"I will take you as far as the reef barrier." And before anyone could thank her, she had turned and started off at a right angle from the course back to the sunken city.

Kirk and Spock followed, having to push themselves to keep pace. It seemed as if they swam for hours, traveling over the endless amber-tinted plain, dodging coral heads and dunes.

Kirk noticed the way the fish thinned out as they moved on, and he wondered. Maybe it was something in the water, or maybe a lack of nutrients.

Rela seemed to be growing more and more nervous the further they swam, her eyes darting constantly in all directions. Looking for an aqueous poltergeist, he decided, would be a particularly difficult proposition.

It turned darker as they neared a barrier. A long, winding reef, much like the one he and Spock had encountered on their way to the Aquan city. Only this one was still living.

Rela came to a stop, gestured upward toward a wide-mouthed hole in the rampart, lined with plants which jerked and swayed violently.

"The ruined city lies through there. Take care, the currents are strong."

"Aren't you coming with us?" Kirk asked.

"No," she replied emphatically, backing away, "I can go no further. I will wait for you with your friends."

She turned and, kicking powerfully, raced off into the distance. They would be wasting time and probably effort in trying to convince her to come with them. As one, both officers moved cautiously toward the gaping cavity.

Kirk soon felt a slight rippling of water over his body. It increased rapidly. Soon he was exerting all his strength just to stay in one place—but to no avail. The current had a firm grip on them and was pulling them inexorably into the cavern.

The interior of the cave soon showed blue sky overhead . . . it was another reef rift, not a tunnel. But the walls of this one were lined with jagged spikes of dead coral, twisted spines representing the combined toil of a billion tiny lives.

He fought the current, glad of his webbed hands and feet, as the suction pulled at them. Kicking furiously to stay level and at the same time avoid a reaching coral pike, he found himself wondering why Rela simply hadn't directed them to go over the top of the reef. The currents might be strong there, too, but could they be this violent?

Then it came to him. The reef probably stayed near the surface in most places, even breaking through. The idea of walking across the reef on one's flippers had probably never occurred to her.

Without warning, they were ejected from the reef. They came to a tumbling halt, still amid stone, but stone whose edges were not formed by a patient nature.

They were drifting in a giant's playpen of crumbling blocks and archways and unbalanced pylons—all jumbled together by some unimaginably violent cataclysm in Argo's past.

Down they drifted, past spires, turrets, towers, structures that resembled great temples, others that encircled a coral-encrusted marketplace. All alien, but still more familiar than the underwater city of the Aquans. This was a city made to live in the currents of wind, not water. A broad avenue curved away before them, lined with a crazy-quilt pattern of broken stone and paved here and there with the ever-present amber moss. Much of the sunken metropolis was overgrown with waving plant life. It stretched off to the horizon, dwarfing the city of the Aquans.

"Fascinating," Spock murmured. "Probably an entire

portion of the continent sank within minutes and with minimal upheaval.''

"Rela said the records repository would be a tall, triangular structure,'' Kirk reminded him. They started down the relatively clear avenue, eyeing dark crannies and long shadowed areas cautiously.

Of course, the Aquans' "Ordainments'' were standard, superstitious taboos, but that didn't mean this skeleton city couldn't be home to some less ecclesiastical dangers.

As they moved deeper into the ruins they encountered buildings in a better state of preservation. Slanted towers rose around them, jagged cracks showing in their walls. But they still stood. How many more serious tremors their weakened foundations could stand Kirk could not tell.

The boulevard made a sharp turn to the right and they found themselves facing a broad plaza. At its far side stood a tall, pyramidal building. A deeply etched, gold-colored medallion was set into its top. The Argoan hieroglyphics were hardly eroded, testament to the knowledge of Rela's ancestors. The medallion shone brightly in the urban graveyard, catching the filtered sunlight.

At first it appeared the structure was blessed with a multitude of entrances. Ruined windows, broken doors—but all were blocked by internal collapse. They began to circle the building, checking each opening.

Then Spock spotted the large block that projected outward at the base of the building. Brushing aside sand, prying away encumbering shells, they uncovered a flat stone of a substance substantially different from the rest of the building. It looked more like alabaster than anything else, yet it was clearly artificial. Most important, there was a metallic emblem set into its front that matched the big disk at the building's apex.

Spock swam to the far side, dug webbed feet into the sand and shoved. For a moment nothing happened, then the block suddenly slid aside as though oiled.

Their lights revealed a clear passageway leading upward as far as the beams would reach . . . and steps, honest steps.

A short swim brought them to the first of many interconnected chambers. Every other room was lined with drawers and cases of metal. After a little initial tugging, they came apart and broke open easily. Most of the cases were badly corroded, their contents long since destroyed.

Some, however, remained sealed, and these all had tiny plates of gleaming gold set into them. Each plate had a miniature bas-relief engraved in it, underlined by more of the indecipherable hieroglyphics. They went through a seemingly endless stream of sealed containers. In the sixth chamber Spock held one of the containers out and called to Kirk. Kirk dropped the one he was studying and swam over.

Alongside the expected rows of hieroglyphs was cut the form of an upright human figure, split down the middle. One side of the torso was normal. The other resembled, more than anything else, the body of a fish.

"I do not think the meaning could be more clear, Captain." Spock gestured at the open case behind him. "There are three others set with the same engraving, a fourth with something rather nauseating. I only hope they hold medical records and not the reproduced work of some long-dead Argoan surrealist."

The men swam rapidly now, tracing their path back out of the temple or museum or hospital or whatever it had been, back toward the edge of the city.

A long, curved pillar marked the end of the avenue, a roadblock to fleeing inhabitants during the age-old disaster, but not to swimmers. The obstruction lay across the road from still upright cousins, supporters of a dark mausoleum to their right.

Spock started upward then halted in mid-stroke. Kirk pulled up just as sharply behind him. He had noticed the movement in the fallen column, too.

Another column joined the first, fluttering. A huge form rose into view from behind the partly ruined structure. They weren't stone, those columns; and Kirk frantically damned himself for not recognizing the first.

They were the arms of a creature they had met before, a creature capable of blind fury and incredible strength. If anything, this snake-squid was even bigger than the one that had destroyed the shuttle.

They turned and swam furiously back up the avenue. The snake-squid started to follow, its roars rattling Kirk's water-filled ears. Evidently they had stumbled across one that had been half asleep, or they would both have been fish-fodder already.

He looked back over his shoulder. The muscles in his legs were starting to knot up under the unaccustomed demand. The monster was still well behind them, but closing ground fast. It still wasn't fully awake.

Another roar shook him—literally. A deeper, grinding scream that sent him tumbling head over heels. Walls and towers came crumbling down around them as the quake tortured the old buildings. Kirk held onto his two cylinders for dear life.

One gigantic block of cut stone struck their pursuer near the skull. It paused, drifted motionless in the water for a moment, stunned. Then it suddenly turned—all thoughts of tiny prey forgotten now—and rocketed away.

For long minutes they lay in the protective shadow of the hospital-temple, ready to dart back into the entranceway at the first sign of a probing tentacle.

"A most interesting creature," Spock commented. "Instinctively aggressive and blessed with remarkable offensive equipment. It would be interesting to . . ."

Kirk managed a grin, held up the pair of cylinders he was carrying. "If these don't contain the necessary medical information, we may have an ample number of years to study it first hand."

No further tremors troubled them as they left the city this time, nor did they encounter the snake-squid or any other predator.

Returning through the hole in the reef was pretty much out of the question. Possibly one of Rela's people could have bucked the powerful current, but Kirk didn't think his legs could manage it. Fortunately, they were able to confirm an earlier supposition.

Swimming upward, they discovered that the reef did indeed break the surface in numerous places. By walking carefully and taking deep breaths at the multitude of pools that pockmarked the top, they were able to cross it on foot. Even so, Kirk was relieved when they finally reached the far side and were able to descend once again. He could understand why the Aquans were reluctant to consider such an idea.

One sealed cylinder proved a complete dead end, but the others contained between them the complete details of the air-to-water mutation procedure, as well as water-to-air. There was also a great amount of additional information which kept much of the *Enterprise*'s scientific staff drooling over the shoulders of the linguists. As each new revelation or bit of ancient theory was translated, a small covey of men and women would bear away their booty for intensive study with all the enthusiasm of a bunch of Goths at the sack of Rome.

Kirk pressed up against the glass of the water room and stared out at McCoy. Two-way pickups brought the soft click-click of the computer annex through to him as the doctor ran through the relevant material a final time.

McCoy was hoping to find a substitute for the prescribed methodology. Failing that, he had searched for a substitute for one particular compound. No use. The formula specified by the ancient Argoans was inflexible.

Turning, he spoke into the pickup, "If the translations are all correct, Jim, the mutations are brought about by a timed series of injections. To return your circulatory and respiratory systems to normal, supposedly all we have to do is provide you with sufficient dosages at properly spaced intervals."

Kirk waited. When McCoy didn't continue, he ventured, "Only . . . there's a problem."

"Yes. I can duplicate most of the required chemicals in the lab . . . except for a derivative from a local venom. Weirdest arrangement of proteins you ever saw. No way I can synthesize it."

"All right," Kirk replied calmly, "where do we get it?"

"It's a good thing the chemical text was accompanied by diagrams . . . and pictures. Not surprisingly, the venom is produced by the poison glands of a large local meat-eater. Judging by both the visual and written material, it's not as rare as the Argoans wished it was."

He touched another switch, punched out a combination on a keyboard in the annex. There was a hum and a sheet of printed plastic popped out of a slot. McCoy took it, walked over to the glass and pressed the sheet up against it.

Kirk and Spock studied the carefully reproduced drawing made by some long-dead Argoan biologist. They ignored the translated text because they didn't need it. The creature sported a snakelike body, a circular, toothed gullet, and four enormous tentacles.

McCoy pulled the sketch away. "I don't know where you're going to find one, or how you're going to capture it. The venom must be taken while the creature is alive and active. A phaser stun would numb the poison-injection mechanism. Dissection is out, too, because death causes the venom to lose its potency immediately. It's got to be gathered while the creature is alive and kicking."

"Don't worry about us finding one, Bones," Kirk assured him. "As for handling a live one, we've already had plenty of experience in how not to . . ."

Rela had arranged a clandestine meeting on the outskirts of the cultivated areas. The two other young Tribunes, Nefrel and Lemas, listened attentively to Kirk's description of the impending quake. Their looks turned to alarm when he began to detail the request.

"We need your help to capture one of the snake-squids . . . alive," he told them, "snake-squid" coming out as a series of unpronounceable gurglings. "We can't do it ourselves—the only craft we possess for performing such tasks here was destroyed by one of the creatures."

The three young Aquans exchanged uneasy glances. "Rela was observed leading you toward the Forbidden Zone," Nefrel explained. "Domar has warned us that if we break the Ordainments again we risk being exiled to the open seas."

"We cannot reverse the mutations you induced in us without the serum the captain has told you about," Spock said firmly, "and we cannot make that serum without the snake-squid's venom."

"But the Ordainments," Nefrel persisted, "also state that capturing one is forbidden."

"See how all is cleverly tied together!" Lemas exclaimed.

"It is forbidden to capture a *cpheryhm-aj* because its poison is needed to reverse the sea-change. Tell me, Nefrel, will the Ordainments protect us from the upheaving of the sea-floor? These travelers say their science can help us, but we must help them first. That is just."

Kirk didn't bother to correct Lemas. They would aid the Aquans as best they could, no matter what.

"We must break the Ordainments, Nefrel," insisted Rela, "even if Captain Kirk could not aid us."

The reluctant Tribune finally acquiesced, whereupon the five left the meeting place and started back toward the sunken city of the ancients.

"We do not need to return to *Llach-sse*," Lemas told him. "We can obtain what we need from the outlying storehouses."

Kirk's confidence suffered an unexpected letdown when he saw what the three Aquans intended to use to capture one of the huge carnivores. It was a net . . . uncomplicated, with no secret devices of a subtle undersea science concealed in it.

Of course, he and Spock had been unable, despite their most violent efforts, to so much as loosen a strand of the net that had been used to capture them. Maybe the material was far stronger than he had suspected. He eyed the thin webbing and hoped so.

This was no time for criticism of the Aquans' efforts—he had to hope they knew what they were doing.

The next step took a great deal of persuasion on Kirk and Spock's part. Lemas and Nefrel in particular refused to believe one could simply walk over the forbidden reef and avoid the treacherous, current-torn crevice.

But exhilaration replaced fear when they finally completed the crossing, without a single injury or moment of panic.

Trying to stay out of sight as much as possible, they circled the city and approached the entrance from behind, from the region of the hospital-temple. Kirk hoped they would be able to find the large *cypheryhm-aj* that had ambushed them before.

Rela was swimming well in advance of the rest of the party. Suddenly, she put up a hand in a trans-cultural gesture, and they moved up quietly alongside her.

When Kirk and Spock had stumbled across the snake-squid it had been dazed and drowsy, half asleep. Now it appeared fully quiescent, perhaps sleeping off the blow it had absorbed from the falling stone. It lay motionless on the sand, coiled in among a cluster of huge boulders.

Kirk knew how deceptive that peaceful scene was. At any moment, any suspicious sound, the monster might awaken and make a quick meal of them all. That another timely quake would be in the offing was highly unlikely.

Carefully the three Aquans unrolled their weighted net. Lemas and Nefrel unfurled it while Rela took care to keep it parallel to the bottom and untangled.

At a mutual sign, they started swimming smooth and fast for the snake-squid.

Either they reached a crucial point or someone lost his nerve, because both Lemas and Nefrel suddenly stopped moving forward. Rela let go of the back end of the net. Inertia and weight kept the net moving forward and curving slightly downward. All three Aquans retreated toward the crumbled wall they had left . . . and waited, and watched.

Falling in a gentle arc, the net kept its shape as it neared the bottom, began to settle softly over the snake-squid. The beast quivered slightly when the first strands touched it; but when the body of the net made contact, the *cpheryhm-aj* erupted.

While Kirk and Spock watched anxiously, unable to intervene for fear of getting in someone's way at a critical moment, the three Aquans shot downward.

The more the monster struggled, the tighter the mesh was drawn. Both officers admired the design of the net, which they now saw was equipped with an intricate series of cross-pulls and cords that tightened around any prey.

And Kirk's hopeful analysis of the netting was proven correct . . . not a strand parted, not a square broke.

Judging from the urgency in Rela's voice as she yelled to them to hurry, its invincibility was finite, however. Both officers moved rapidly downward, hurriedly readying the makeshift container-collectors McCoy had designed, flexible pouches from each of which protruded a long suction tube with a wide mouth.

The snake-squid had a better view of the officers than it did of the dodging, darting Aquans. Tentacles and teeth strained for the two maddeningly near shapes. Reflex reaction sent a jet of dark fluid toward both men.

Kirk edged the mouth of a suction tube into the slowly dispersing cloud, touched a control on the side of the tube. He moved the flexible gathering mouth from side to side. McCoy had warned them that they needed as much venom as they could obtain.

Dark poison dissipated around the captain. The Aquans had assured him the poison was harmless unless injected. He kept that resolutely in mind as he directed the tube toward a darker patch, missed it when a sudden current sent him tumbling.

Rubble showered down from surrounding towers. Much of the already battered structure they'd hidden behind came down. Some of the venom already collected drifted from the open mouth of the suction tube and Kirk hurriedly closed it off. A series of violent after-shocks made things more difficult. Rela was alongside him unexpectedly, watching the procedure worriedly. She directed his attention downward.

While the admirable material of the net had proven equal to the explosive spasms of the snake-squid, it had fallen victim to some of the toppling stone. Rocks and carved pillars had driven the pinioned carnivore into a frenzy. They had also abraded sections of the net to the point where the monster was able to break them.

It was still trapped, still bound awkwardly . . . but it had discovered the weakened portions and was tearing at them with mindless malevolence.

"We must leave now, quickly," Rela insisted. She turned, started for the top of the reef where they would be safe.

Kirk examined a gauge set in the side of the tube, called after her. "We need more venom."

"There is no time!" she shouted back. "There . . ."

A thunderous, echoing moan drowned out her last words. Two of the muscular tentacles and part of the upper body of the snake-squid were already free of the netting. Another minute or two and the creature would free the rest of its thick torso. They couldn't hope to outswim the maddened beast.

Cursing silently, Kirk raced off in pursuit of the retreating Aquans. Spock risked a reaching tentacle for one last inhalation of poison before following.

V

Kirk had tried floating on his head, swimming off the walls, counting rocks—in general, doing everything imaginable to dampen his impatience while McCoy ran a final series of checks on the mildly toxic chemical.

So many things could go wrong if even a small portion of the ancient formulae was wrong, out of date, inaccurately set down. And there was no Aquan physician present to look for signs of failure.

Kirk studied McCoy and Nurse Chapel as they moved slowly in their underwater gear—too much precision was required now for life-support belts.

With Chapel's aid, McCoy was locking a small bottle of fluid into a spray-contact hypo. Now, if only Spock's metabolism and his would adapt to Argoan medical procedure as readily as did Bones' equipment.

McCoy's voice, distorted by the broadcast apparatus and the intervening water, broke the nervous silence.

"We've set this up as best we can, Jim. Only a small section of the relevant records was missing. I don't think—I *hope*—it isn't critical."

"But I thought you said . . . ," Kirk began.

McCoy made calming motions. "Oh, I'm sure about the composition of the serum, Jim, that portion of the records is intact and plenty scientific. The section that's missing . . ." He shook his head.

"Something to do with the dosage per unit of body weight. I've had to approximate without the complete charts. We might never turn them up." He motioned the two men toward the bedlike slabs that would serve as a resting place.

"The experiments I ran on local fish-life show that if the

serum dosage is too strong, it causes an over-mutation which then can't be reversed by any means. Inject too little and there can be violent side effects. The stuff is tricky, and too potent for my liking.

"I'd like to conduct further experiments, but we . . ."

"Haven't got enough venom," Spock finished for him.

"Not only that, but the potency of what you brought back fades rapidly. The composite serum has to be used right away. If you could obtain some more . . ." He stared at Kirk, but the captain made a negative gesture.

"We've already drawn on our credit with Rela and her friends to the point of exhaustion, Bones. I'm not sure we could convince them to repeat the hunt. I'm not sure I want to . . . we might not be so lucky a second time." McCoy sighed, resigned.

"Then I'll have to make do. I've decreased the maximum allowable dosage by one quarter—that should be proper for your systems, Vulcan as well as human."

Kirk nodded. "All right. How many infusions?"

"Two small, one large."

"Let's get started."

Both officers assumed reclining positions on the slabs, heads higher than feet. McCoy checked a gauge on the side of the hypo, made a last adjustment. If he had miscalculated half a cubic centimeter either way, the damage to their bodies could be irreversible.

McCoy pressed the hypo's nozzle to Kirk's upper arm, then stepped back and studied his wrist chronometer intently. Several minutes slid by before the first change appeared.

Kirk's skin was changing, the pigmentation darkening slightly. First it deepened to a rich golden hue, then to a familiar amber. The captain's lids drooped low, lower, finally closed tightly.

Abruptly, the amber color drained like bourbon from a broken bottle, leaving Kirk a pale, nearly albino white. They all studied him anxiously, but he showed no signs of movement. McCoy frowned uneasily and hurried to exchange the hypo for a pre-keyed tricorder.

He passed it carefully over Kirk's limp form, muttering to himself all the while. "Pulse fading . . . all internal functions slowed . . . heartbeat weakened . . ."

"Andrenalin . . . aldrazine?" ventured Chapel. McCoy shook his head, pulled the 'corder away.

"There's enough in his system now that doesn't belong there. Give the serum another couple of minutes."

Sure enough, normal color began to tint Kirk's face, returning with the same suddenness it had departed. He stirred slightly on the makeshift pallet.

Chapel let out a bubbling sigh of relief. Spock remained expressionless as usual, but McCoy noticed how an unnatural tenseness had suddenly left the first officer's muscles.

Again he made a pass with the tiny machine. "Pulse and heart normal, other shifts within acceptable parameters . . . good. Nurse?"

Chapel handed him the second of the three bottles and he exchanged it for the first, reset the dial on the side of the hypo. This time he pressed it over the captain's chest, just below the left lung, held it there a second, then moved it to the right side and repeated the injection.

Kirk's body reacted instantly this time, jerking spasmodically on the slab like a puppet with snipped strings. Before McCoy could have countered with another injection of any kind, Kirk collapsed. Once more the amber hue flooded his face. Once again McCoy used the compact 'corder.

"Something's really given his system a kick—his metabolism's a good ten times normal speed."

"Doctor," Spock interrupted, "his hands."

McCoy's gaze moved down the unconscious form. The thin webbing which had formed between the fingers was dissolving like so much gelatin, the faint scaling beginning to smooth out. His stare went lower and he saw that the same process was at work on the feet.

McCoy checked his watch, made yet another pass with the instrument.

"Metabolism normal—and everything else!" He couldn't keep the optimism from his voice, didn't want to. "Indication of physiological alteration in the lungs . . . he's beginning a complete reversal. Nurse . . ."

Chapel handed him the final bottle. Carefully McCoy locked the vial in place beneath the pistol-like hypo.

"This is the final dose," he said, to no one in particular. "The major infusion. Roll him over please, Christine."

Chapel slowly turned Kirk on his stomach . . . easy enough in the water. McCoy recalled the translated instructions, prayed that the ancient recorder was precise in his technique and made the last injection as it had been described.

He pulled the hypo away, nodded to her. She turned Kirk over on his back again, let him relax. Nothing happened. McCoy was about to program a minute secondary dose when Kirk suddenly doubled up in agony, his legs threshing wildly and an expression of pure pain invading his face.

The pitiful moans of a man having nightmares filled the water around them. Scales erupted like scars on his face and the backs of his hands.

Twitching with uncontrollable violence, he spun from the pallet and onto the sand. So powerful were the jerks and kicks that McCoy and Spock were unable to get a grip on him.

Finally the explosion quieted and Kirk came to rest motionless and face down on the sand. The back of the skin-tight green bodysuit started to bulge slightly, showing an eruption of dorsal fin. Chapel didn't scream—she'd seen too many mistakes of nature in McCoy's lab to be terrified by another—but her eyes widened in horror. Spock, uncharacteristically, looked helpless.

"Too strong . . . the serum was too strong!" McCoy groaned. The spasms struck again and once more Kirk was thrashing water. The amber color deepened even further and revealed a faint yellowish overlay.

But this time, as he twisted in the sand, the scales that had formed momentarily on his face and hands began to fade, the bulge on his back disappeared and was reabsorbed.

The kicking and tumbling slowed, stopped. As he lay still on the bottom the yellow tinge vanished from his skin, followed soon thereafter by the amber. McCoy drifted over to the limp form. Again the tiny tricorder did its work.

When McCoy looked up again there was a note of satisfaction in his voice. "He's starting to breathe steadily again. Quick, we must get him out of the tank."

Together, the three of them wrestled the motionless body into the airlock. Spock remained inside. While McCoy supported Kirk, Chapel manipulated the controls. Both watched

Kirk's face nervously as the drains in the floor rapidly sucked the water from the lock.

Kirk started to choke, flailing at the water with both arms. McCoy didn't wait for the water to leave completely. Instead, he slammed a palm down on the red button on the console labeled *Emergency Cycle*.

They nearly fell as a gush of water half-carried them from the airlock. Together they laid the captain on the floor. He stopped kicking almost immediately, coughed a couple of times, water dribbling from one side of his mouth.

Then he rolled over, still wheezing, but with less force now. The coughing finally died and then he was breathing deeply again—and for the first time in a long while, normally.

"Easy, Jim, how do you feel?"

Kirk continued to take long draughts of air, eyed McCoy as if the doctor were a little unbalanced. "Tired, a bit dizzy . . . otherwise fine."

Chapel reappeared with a large thermal blanket. She draped it around Kirk's shoulders as he got to his feet.

"Better make dry clothes your first priority, Jim," McCoy advised him. "Along with the metamorphosis of your respiratory and circulatory systems, there've been some extensive changes in your epidermal layers. I had anticipated them, from what the old records said. But so help me, I didn't think they'd come color-coded!" He grinned. "After what you've just been through, it would be damned silly for you to catch a cold."

Kirk nodded, then McCoy turned his attention to the water room's remaining occupant. "Your turn next, Spock, if after watching, you still want to go through with it."

Spock's gaze remained on Kirk. Only when the captain finally gave him an "everything's okay" smile did he reply, "I await the procedure with a modicum of impatience, Doctor." That was just Spock's way of saying the waiting was driving him up the walls.

Kirk sat down in the command chair . . . slowly, enjoying the use of his legs for something other than horizontal locomotion, luxuriating in the chair's dryness more than anything else.

He looked left, to where Spock and Scott were explaining the various functions of the bridge's instrumentation to the goggling Domar and Rela.

Both Tribunes wore bodysuits and transparent, water-filled masks. Their tanks rested on the back of the wheelchairs that Scott's people had improvised.

It had taken all Scott's persuasive powers to convince even the adventurous Rela that the strange attire would keep them alive and healthy out of the water. But it was Domar who had agreed to the trial visit to the *Enterprise* first.

The qualities which had made him High Tribune dictated that he not appear craven before mere air-breathers, nor allow a Junior Tribune to seem the braver. Actually, he resented the powered chairs more than the water-suits. But while his legs were immensely powerful, they would tire rapidly under the steady pull of gravity in a waterless environment—and his flippers were not designed for walking.

So it was necessary for him and Rela to tour the *Enterprise* from the self-contained chairs. In the shadow of many wonders, however, he rapidly lost all sense of indignity.

Just now he was staring at a large rectangle of light in the middle of which a multicolored globe hung poised against speckled blackness. The air-breather next to him, the one called Scott, had assured him that what he was looking at was his own world—all of it.

Normally, he would not even have deigned to laugh at the air-breather. But he had seen enough of this magical vessel to convince him that anything might be true. Why, he was still trying to recover from the claim that there was neither water nor air outside this ship!

The one called Kirk, Tribune-equal, was gesturing at the screen. From his chest, a small machine carried mechanical-sounding words to the High Tribune, who struggled to fathom their meaning and glimpsed it dimly. Many of the air-breather's words translated poorly, while others, he was afraid, would remain forever only noises to him.

"Careful placement of a few large photon torpedoes, combined with a selective bombardment of fault areas with phaser beams, should shift the epicenter of the quake sufficiently northward for your city to survive with minimal damage," Kirk was saying.

"That's what the theory claims, anyway. It's a technique we planned to try. Now we have something more than an abstract reason to attempt it for. We think it has an excellent chance of working."

"Ninety-four point seven percent," Spock qualified.

Comprehension of what these people were about to try was enough to finally overcome Domar's aloofness.

"I did not believe such knowledge existed." For the first time he permitted himself an open stare of amazement, taking in the entire sweep of the bridge.

"It is incredible . . . . all of this."

"Approximately three minutes to the first significant fault shift, Captain." Kirk glanced back to the engineering station.

"Thank you, Mr. Scott. Mr. Spock, confirm coordinates for torpedo strike to effect re-alignment of epicenter."

Spock bent over his hooded viewer. "Confirmed, sir." He looked up. "The results should prove most interesting. To my knowledge, this will be the first time in Federation history that a starship's offensive armament has been deployed according to the instructions of the geology section."

Kirk turned his attention to the helm-navigation console. "Mr. Arex, Mr. Sulu, I know that the coordinates and firepower required has all been precalculated and preprogrammed. Hold yourselves in readiness, however, for any last minute adjustments. They have a way of cropping up at the most awkward times."

"Aye, sir" . . . "Aye, Captain," came the dual acknowledgment.

Kirk nodded once. "Fire torpedoes, first phasers."

Both men initiated the sequence of computer-directed firepower that would alter the internal heavings of a planet.

Far to the north of the submerged Aquan city, several super-fast objects dropped through the amber-hued atmosphere and vanished beneath the surface of the roiling sea. So fast did they travel that there was no towering fountain of water, no great splash where they entered.

Nor was there any sound. But far, far below the waves the multiple detonations of the precisely spaced photon torpedoes created a shock wave felt for hundreds of kilometers around.

Seconds later, while the deep-water creatures and bottom ooze were still settling back into ages-old quiescence, twin beams of light brighter than a sun lit the underwater abyssal plain with a radiance that illumined simple-minded crawlers for the first and last time of their primitive lives.

"Report, Mr. Spock."

"Too early yet to tell, Captain," Spock declared without looking up from the viewer. "Another minute or so before the major shift is due."

Domar still did not entirely comprehend what was taking place around him. Nor did he understand the process by which certain things were being altered. He knew only that these strange people, these air-breathers from (was it possible?) another world, were presently engaged in some obscure activity that would decide one way or another the fate of his beloved city.

Domar did not for a moment think that whatever the outcome of that activity he, at least, was safe from impending destruction. He *was* aware that the motives of these beings were not wholly altruistic. From what he had been told they had a world of their own much like his on which some day in the future a similar crisis was likely to occur. If proven successful, the methods now being employed to save his people would someday be utilized to save their own.

He mentioned nothing of this. For one thing, everyone in this chamber of miracles was silent and expectant now, in a way that suggested they were hardly indifferent to the outcome of their efforts. For another, voicing his dark suspicions would have been undiplomatic.

Spock's voice, when he finally elected to break the silence, was no higher, no louder, no more expressively modulated than ever. But it resounded on the tense bridge like the brass section of an orchestra.

"Sensors indicate," he announced, "that the epicenter of the just-concluded quake was in the north polar seas, Captain . . . a totally uninhabited area, according to Domar's people."

The interpretation was a bit much for even the usually omnipotent translators to manage. Domar looked at once relieved and confused.

"This means, then, that my people are safe?"

"That's right, Tribune," Kirk said happily, turning from the screen to face him. "It doesn't mean, though, that your city won't be subject to such dangers in the future. We can't make the ground around your city more stable. All we can do is *bleed* the instability to a region where no one will be endangered."

"What the captain is saying, Tribune Domar," Spock elucidated, "is that the technique we have used is effective, if not constructive."

"When can we beam down, Spock?"

"The section of sub-continent on which the Aquan city is built has been subjected to a considerable if not violent realignment of the substrata, Captain. This will stabilize fully within a few hours . . ."

"Where would you like to be set down, sir?"

Kirk took up his position in the transporter alcove, next to Spock. Domar and Rela sat in their chairs by the transporter console, looked on in fascination. They had expressed a desire to see the process by which they'd been brought aboard and would beam down later.

He eyed Chief Kyle thoughtfully. "You have the coordinates of the spot where Dr. McCoy and Chief Scott first found us after we'd been changed?"

Kyle punched appropriate switches, checked a readout and nodded.

"I think that will do, Chief."

"All right, sir. Energizing."

"Perhaps someday, Mr. Spock," Kirk began, as he felt the familiar disorienting caress of the transporter, "they'll take this danged whine out of the transporter mechanism."

Spock didn't have time to reply.

Just before a person winked out for elsewhere the whine rose to an unbearable pitch and for a split second he felt like his teeth were coming apart. Not that they weren't, of course, but the sensation of dental disintegration was distressingly convincing.

The ocean of Argo was as softly amber and calm as Kirk remembered it, with wave-crests the hue of cream chiffon. The memory of the transporter computer was also accurate. They were standing on a pile of jumbled rocks and dead coral, just slightly above sea-level. But something was wrong, something had changed.

The shallow pool where Scott and McCoy had discovered their water-breathing forms lay just below and to their left, all right . . . but now it was only a low sand-filled depression scooped out of the rocks. And the little island seemed much increased in area. He looked to the other side, saw jagged bits of metal and plastic. The remains of the long-ruined underwater shuttle.

No, this was their proper pile of stone . . . only it had been raised high above the water. Spock noticed Kirk's uncertainty, explained.

"Sensors indicated considerable subsidence of the sea bottom near the quake's epicenter, Captain. It was apparently accompanied by a corresponding rise of the ocean bed in this area."

He pointed behind them.

The basalt fortress which had dominated their attention when they had first set down on Argo now towered even further into the azure sky. The shift here hadn't been unduly violent, for the wreaths of moss drooped undisturbed from unbroken crags and spires. But there was clear evidence of change nonetheless. Instead of dropping sheer into crashing waves, the island was now ringed by a broad beach of dark sand, until recently part of the bottom.

Kirk sniffed, wrinkled his nose and found ample olfactory hints of change, too. Fish and other ocean dwellers, too slow or stupid to flee the slow rise, had been trapped by the receding waters in small pools, now evaporated. Decay had set in with a vengeance and generated a miasma in sharp contrast to the visual splendor of the scene.

But the most spectacular sight of all lay hidden from view until they rounded the crest of the island. It took Kirk only seconds to place that graveyard of toppled towers, imploded domes, tumbled rocks and alabaster walls and foundation stones. Despite the upheaval, the sunken city of the Aquans' air-breathing ancestors had risen once more into the light fairly intact. Now it lay exposed and naked, drying in the bright sun of midday like some massive pressed flower.

"Argo appears to have a new city, Captain," Spock observed, "or rather, one reborn."

"Well put, Mr. Spock," a new voice agreed. They turned.

Domar spoke as he and Rela struggled from the water, masks and tanks still in place. They moved better on the soft sand than they had on the *Enterprise*, but Kirk and Spock walked politely down to meet them at water's edge, nonetheless.

"We did not entirely escape the effects of the quake," Rela informed them, indicating that she and Domar had beamed down to the city, "but our people survived with minimal damage—and less injury—thanks to your help. If we had remained near what you call the epicenter, we surely would have been destroyed."

"We owe you and your companions much gratitude, Captain Kirk," Domar said gravely. There was an odd emphasis on the word "gratitude," as if the translator had been unable to reflect the Aquan's meaning exactly and had selected only the closest analog.

"Is there nothing we can do for you?"

"The ability to transform us into water-breathers," Kirk explained, "is something on which our scientists have labored for many hundreds of years, with only the most limited success. If we might have permission to make copies of those and other medical records of your ancestors . . . ?"

"All will be placed at your disposal, Captain Kirk," assured Domar. "What we have left, of life as well as knowledge, you have given us. It is yours by right."

Such adulatory obeisance made Kirk acutely uncomfortable. There were many times when Spock's directness was welcome. Now he relieved Kirk by changing the subject.

"The technique of utilizing starship firepower to alter stress patterns in fault systems has been proven effective. By permitting us to do this you have enabled us to test a method which will mean much to threatened Federation worlds with similar problems."

Domar made the Aquan equivalent of a smile. "It takes a consummate diplomat to make salvation come out like an apology, Mr. Spock."

"So bright, so warm it is here!" Rela purred, stretching lazily. "I will be glad when the surface places can be inhabited."

"It will have to be done slowly, carefully," Kirk admonished her. "You'll need more than the ability to breathe air. There's the problem of your skin, for example."

"What's wrong with my skin?"

"As it stands, nothing," Kirk dead-panned. "But it's adapted to a perpetually moist environment. It will dry out, crack, and blister unless given some form of protection . . . such as the bodysuit you're currently wearing."

He frowned abruptly.

"What do you mean, 'inhabited?' "

Domar gestured toward the risen city of the ancients. "The young among us have decided to rebuild the great shelters of our forebears."

"Only the young?" Kirk queried. Domar sounded apologetic.

"Mature Aquans cannot adjust to the thought of becoming air-breathers. There are no formulas in the old records for altering one's outlook on such things. So most of us will remain in the world we know. Air-life is for the pioneers among us."

"Don't lose contact with each other like your ancestors did, in case of another continental adjustment."

"We will pass ordainments to forbid this."

"And this time we won't ignore them," Rela finished impishly.

"It is always the psychological and not physiological differences that are the real dangers," Spock pointed out. He nodded at Kirk. "The history of Captain Kirk's own world is especially revealing in this respect."

Rela stared at Kirk in surprise. "You have water-breathers on your home world, too, Captain?"

"No." The young Tribune looked disappointed. "Mr. Spock is referring to the fact that in my people's past, great conflicts took place which supposedly had their root causes in small physical differences, but which were actually centered in the mind. Small minds seize upon such differences to exploit their own mental deficiencies . . . apparently a universal trait."

A faint fog began to form in front of his eyes, and he saw that a familiar glow was beginning to distort his view of Spock.

"What happened to the others?" Rela asked quickly. "Were they exterminated?"

"Others?" Kirk's mind raced. "Oh, you mean the ones who were different? As I said, the bodily differences meant nothing. In the end, the ones with the mental imbalances found themselves pitied into extinction."

"I don't understand, Captain Kirk," came the final confused words of the Aquan, of Rela, the water-sprite.

A mild stab of nausea shook him as his perception of the universe went blotto. "Neither did they," he finished.

"I beg your pardon, sir?" said a puzzled Chief Kyle. Kirk blinked. They were back on board the *Enterprise*. "Did you say something about extinction, sir?"

Kirk noticed Spock was watching him with mild interest. "No, Mr. Kyle . . . nothing at all. *Execution* . . . I was complimenting you on the execution of your duties."

"Thank you, sir," Kyle replied uncertainly.

Kirk stepped out of the transporter alcove, with Spock following right behind. Spock noticed the smile spreading slowly over the Captain's face.

"You find something amusing, Captain?"

"The timing of certain demands made by the human body, Spock."

"Now *that* is a subject for considerable amusement," Spock agreed drily. "What particular aberration of your unfortunate self strikes you as humorous at the moment?"

"The fact, Spock, that, after all I've gone through this past week, immediately upon leaving Argo I can find myself experiencing the desire I currently do."

"Which is?" his first officer prompted.

Kirk's smile twisted slightly. "I'm thirsty." Spock continued to stare at him and Kirk stopped, his smile fading. "Well, what's the matter, Spock? You may not find it funny, but . . ."

"It's not that, Captain, the humorous coefficients of the elemental coincidence are decidedly scrutable. I merely am appalled at my lack of basic knowledge where the human body is concerned."

"What do you mean?" Kirk eyed him unsurely.

"I had not known that a case of aggravated thirst . . ."

"It isn't aggravated," Kirk protested, but Spock ignored and went on.

". . . could produce such startling changes in pigmentation. Or perhaps it has nothing to do with thirst at all, but is an after-reaction to our retransformation back to normal."

"Spock, what the hell are you talking about?"

"You will see more clearly in a mirror, Captain. No," he put up a hand to forestall the coming words, "I am not talking in riddles, Captain. You know me better than that. But your coloration most definitely is not normal. How do you feel?"

"Thirsty, as I said . . . and a little tired. Normal enough, under the circumstances." His voice turned slightly irritable. "I feel perfectly fine, Spock . . . I don't know what you mean. 'Coloration' again! It's nothing at all, nothing at all . . ."

PART II

THE
PIRATES
OF
ORION

(Adapted from a script by Howard Weinstein)

VI

"Captain's log, stardate 5527.3," Kirk declared into the armchair pickup as he surveyed the bridge. "My 'nothing at all' turned out to be the first symptoms of choriocytosis.

"Despite an initial outbreak during which several members of the crew apparently contracted the disease simultaneously, it appears to be under control now. Dr. McCoy insists it's no longer even as dangerous as pneumonia, and we have experienced no significant drop in performance. Therefore I foresee no difficulties in completing our newly assigned mission—representing the Federation at the dedication ceremonies for the new interspecies Academy of Science on Deneb Five." He clicked off the log, looked to his left.

"Status, Mr. Spock?"

"All systems operating at prime efficiency, Captain. We are on course and on schedule. I anticipate no deviations from the norm."

Kirk leaned back in the command chair and mused on the arduous duty they would be subjected to upon making landfall on Deneb Five. They would be forced to cope with an endless round of parties, gourmet dinners, the brilliant conversation of new acquaintances and the warm chatter of old ones. Yet, after what they had been through these past several months, he somehow believed they would succeed in muddling through.

"Be nice to play diplomat for a change, eh, Spock?"

Dead silence.

"Look, Spock," he continued, turning in the chair, "I know you find the hypocritical methodology of interstellar

diplomacy somewhat obscene, but that shouldn't prevent you
from enjoying the fringe bene—''

Without a word, without a sound, without a shift in expression or pose, Spock abruptly toppled over and crashed
to the floor.

Kirk was quite capable of reacting quickly and efficiently
to anything from the sudden appearance of half a dozen belligerent warships on the fore screen to impending dissolution
of the *Enterprise*, from the sight of a being a hundred times
larger than the ship to an entire metropolis no bigger than
the bridge. But Spock's collapse was so totally unexpected,
so deathly quiet and matter-of-fact, that for one of the few
times during his tenure as commanding officer of the *Enterprise* he found himself momentarily paralyzed.

Even so, he recovered before any of the other equally
stunned crew. A hand slammed down on the intercom switch.

"Kirk to Sick Bay—Bones, we've got an emergency."

While seemingly hours passed without aid appearing, they
fought to control their feelings and do what they could. There
wasn't much they *could* do, beyond untangling the first officer's crumpled limbs and laying him flat on the deck—and
wondering what the heck had happened. Kirk had put an ear
to Spock's chest and found temporary relief in the steady
beat of a Vulcan heart. But no amount of exterior stimulation—or pleading—could return Spock to consciousness.

McCoy finally appeared, a mobile surgical bed and two
medical techs in tow. Kneeling over the still form, he made
a quick pass over head and torso with a portable medical
transceiver, then directed the pair of assistants as they laid
the motionless Spock on the bed.

Kirk followed them out, knowing better than to trouble
McCoy with dozens of as yet unanswerable questions. As
soon as answers were available, the good doctor would supply them without having to be asked.

On reaching Sick Bay, McCoy had Spock transferred from
the mobile pallet to one of the much better equipped diagnostic beds. While the doctor smoothly adjusted the requisite
instrumentation for Vulcan physiology, Kirk hovered nearby,
watching, waiting for a determination of some sort. Kirk
knew something about every instrument and machine on
board the *Enterprise*, but many of the figures which blos-

somed on the glowing panel above the bed head meant little to him. Those whose meaning he could vaguely identify seemed to indicate the presence of an uncommon abnormality within the science officer's system.

McCoy prepared and administered a hastily concocted injection. Only when the applied serum took did he appear to relax slightly.

"I brought him out of shock, Jim," he finally said. "He's sleeping normally now. Choriocytosis is a strange disease. It's relatively simple to handle in races with iron-based blood, but in others . . ."

A warning tingle started in Kirk's mind.

"Get to the point, Bones."

McCoy appeared to consider something else for a moment, shook it off and eyed Kirk steadily. "Spock has contracted the disease. It's a nuisance to humans. To Vulcans it's fatal. Ninety-three percent probability, as—" his words slowed and finished almost imperceptibly "—Spock would say."

Kirk cleared his throat. "You're sure it's choriocytosis?"

"I've triple-checked, Jim, given the instrumentation every opportunity to prove me wrong." He shrugged helplessly. "I wish to God I was wrong, but you can see it eating at him. Look . . ."

He urged Kirk to activate a nearby viewscreen. While the captain did so, McCoy went to a cabinet. Selecting a tiny cassette, he slid it into a slot beneath the glowing screen, punched out commands on the operating panel.

A few seconds of blurred images raced across the screen as the cassette ran up to the place McCoy had requested. It slowed and commenced normal playback. You didn't need a medical degree to understand what was happening. One sequence stayed with Kirk long after he had left Sick Bay.

It showed a collage of healthy, green-tinted Vulcan cells. From screen right, a flowing yellowish substance slid like sapient gelatin into view. It divided, subdivided, to surround each individual cell. On being engulfed, the afflicted cells started to jerk unnaturally, their steady movements interrupted. Healthy green deepened to light blue, then azure, almost to purple before all internal motion ceased and cellular disruption took place.

On that threatening note, the tape ran out.

McCoy slid the casette free, juggled it idly in one hand, flipping it over and over as he spoke.

"The sequences you saw, Jim, were highly speeded up. Simply, the infection enters the blood and affects the cells so that they can't carry oxygen. For some reason, iron-based hemoglobin fights off the encirclement much better than copper-based. I wish I knew why. The result is obvious."

"Eventual collapse," Kirk supplied softly.

McCoy quit flipping the cassette, put it back in its place in the cabinet then closed the sliding door with more force than was necessary.

"That's it, Jim."

"You said ninety-three percent probability of death, Bones. What about that other seven percent? Does that mean there's a cure?"

"Not always. But there's a drug that would certainly improve the odds in Spock's favor astronomically—if we could get it."

"We'll get it," Kirk told him. His reply would have been the same if McCoy had requested the heart of a dead sun.

"It's a naturally occurring drug called strobolin. Sixty years in the lab and nobody's been able to synthesize it. It's a rare drug, Jim, but choriocytosis is a rare disease."

Kirk nodded, moved for the switch that would open the wall intercom and connect him to the bridge. Then something that had been scratching at the back of his mind finally broke through.

"Bones, if you knew we were experiencing an outbreak of choriocytosis on board and that it could be fatal to Spock if he contracted it—why didn't you order him into isolation until the disease burned itself out?"

McCoy looked away. "I didn't want to have to tell you, Jim."

"Didn't want to have to tell me what, Bones?" Kirk shot back, a little angry. "What could anything have to do with not telling me?"

"I said choriocytosis was a rare disease. My guess is your system was laid open to it—" he looked back, "—by the multiple alterations your circulatory system was subjected to while on Argo. In which case—"

"You didn't want to tell me that Spock and I had infected the whole ship." McCoy nodded, watched the captain anxiously. But Kirk appeared to bear up well under a revelation that might have affected a lesser man dangerously.

"Then, why did I and plenty of others get sick, go through the disease and get cured, and then all of a sudden Spock collapses?"

McCoy looked tired. "Incubation period, Jim. It's a lot longer for Vulcans than for humans. There was no point in telling Spock, nothing to be gained. If he had it, there wasn't a thing I could do about it."

"Why is the incubation period so much?" Kirk began, but McCoy cut him off angrily, his voice rising.

"Why, why, why, why! If I knew the answers to all the whys, choriocytosis wouldn't *be* such a putrid, disgusting—"

"Sorry, Bones," Kirk interrupted softly. There wasn't much else he could say. McCoy'd only been expressing the same frustration he felt.

Instead he activated the nearby computer annex. "Library!"

"Awaiting input," came the instant, mechanical reply.

"What is the nearest strobolin supply world to our present position?"

"Canopus Two," the library responded promptly. "Four days distant at maximum warp."

Kirk flipped off the annex and headed for the door, then stopped in mid-stride and returned, to stare down at the corpselike—no, not corpselike, he hurriedly corrected himself—the sleeping form of Spock.

"How long can he last without the drug?"

McCoy considered carefully, his momentary outburst already forgotten by both men. "I said strobolin couldn't be duplicated in the lab. That's so—but there is an artificially produced related serum I ought to be able to make up.

"All it can do is slow the disease, not stop it. The destructive agent rapidly builds an immunity to the serum. Despite all forestalling efforts, at the rate his blood is losing the ability to carry oxygen, I give him three days at best, Jim. Four days to reach the drug—and Spock will die in three in spite of everything I can do. That's," an odd expression came over him, "logical. Unless—"

"Unless what, Bones?"

McCoy looked guarded. "What about a rendezvous?"

"Of course! If we can't reach the drug in time, there's a chance that another Federation ship might be close to Canopus Two right now. There's *got* to be!" He was back at the intercom in seconds.

"Kirk to Bridge—get me Starfleet operations control for this sector, Lieutenant."

"Transmitting, Captain."

The logistics seemed beyond immediate solution. However, it was startling how much bureaucracy and red tape one could cut through by bringing the proper amount of priority demands, prime requests and insinuations to bear—all seasoned with a touch of judicious threats.

It was eventually decided that the starship *Potemkin*, presently on patrol in the region of Canopus, would pick up the requisite amount of strobolin. This would then be transferred to the interstellar freighter *Huron* for delivery to the *Enterprise*.

Kirk would have preferred meeting the *Potemkin* himself and avoiding any intermediaries. But there were certain requests even he couldn't have filled—tying up two starships for speedy delivery of a drug was one of them.

Spock was a valued officer—but he was only one. Starfleet had a plethora of personnel and a distinct shortage of starships. Vessels the class of the *Enterprise* and *Potemkin* were too few and far between for their missions to be casually aborted—or so said the reply to his request.

Kirk didn't argue with the logic of the missive, but the word "casual" in reference to Spock filled him with a quiet hatred for some unknown officer whose career had been spent behind a desk pushing paper.

On the other hand, if all went well they would still receive the drug in plenty of time. And McCoy had assured him that strobolin's effectiveness matched its rarity.

McCoy leaned against the wall in Kirk's cabin and watched his superior officer and good friend going through mental nip-ups. With the exception of Spock, he was probably the only one on board who knew that this was the first time Kirk had ever traded on his reputation to produce desired results.

Kirk hated officers who used "pull" to get what they

wanted. So his embarrassment at doing so himself was understandable. McCoy repressed a smile. If the captain only knew the awe the rest of the crew held him in for being able to generate such action on the part of a notoriously somnolent bureaucracy.

Naturally no one showed the admiration they felt—everyone knew it would only embarrass him more.

As for himself, he mused exhaustedly, he had done everything it was humanly—or for that matter, Vulcanly—possible to do for the mortally ill first officer. Now he must devote his energies to ensuring that Kirk wouldn't fold up as the critical rendezvous approached. The last thing he wanted was *two* important patients.

"What are the symptoms like, Bones?" Kirk finally muttered idly, staring at the ceiling. The three-dimensional desert diorama projected above his bed offered little comfort.

McCoy shrugged, tried to make the terrifying sound casual. "Increasing difficulty in breathing, coupled with a corresponding drop in efficiency. All the signs of someone working under extreme altitude conditions. Kind of like the standard Academy mountain survival test. Remember that one?"

That memory produced a small grin . . . very small. It vanished when the door buzzer sounded politely.

"Come."

The panel slid aside, and the subject of all the recent activity walked in. Spock showed no sign of the concern or trouble centering on him. His uniform and posture were immaculate, as usual. His expression was bland as vanilla, as usual. Only in his movements could one who knew him well detect something amiss. Lift of hand, drive of leg, all were just a hair slow, the movements of a man recently arisen from a deep sleep.

Or slipping into one, Kirk thought morosely.

"You wish to see me, Captain?"

"Yes, Spock. Sit down."

With a quick glance at McCoy, who in trying to avoid it only made his concern more obvious, Spock took up a seat facing Kirk. The captain swung his legs off the bed, sat up.

"We've arranged a rendezvous to pick up the drug you need."

"I trust it will not affect our scheduled arrival at Deneb Five, nor our duties there?"

"No, it won't," Kirk said gently.

"What's the matter, Spock?" put in McCoy in a forced attempt at levity, "afraid you'll miss the first dance at the Federation Academy ball?"

"I'm afraid I do not dance, Doctor."

"You can say that again," McCoy countered, but he did it without a smile and the attempted joke fell flat.

As awkward pause ensued while Kirk considered how to proceed. With any other member of the crew he wouldn't have had to. But could he simply say what had to be said to Spock? The first officer perceived certain things differently than others. Would he be offended? Angry? More than anything else, Kirk wished now he knew more about Vulcan customs—and etiquette, in particular.

"Will that be all, Captain?" Spock asked, giving Kirk no more time to hope for divine intervention.

"One more thing, Spock," he began, without meeting his first officer's gaze. "I've considered very carefully. Based on Dr. McCoy's recommendations—(*that's it, make Bones the heavy, James T. Chicken*)—*I've* decided to cut your duty time in half."

A faint glimmer of something close to emotion seemed to shine behind dark pupils. "Captain, that won't be necessary. I am perfectly capable of . . ."

A hand came down on his shoulder and he glanced around and up. McCoy, firm, not joking now.

"No argument, Spock. Doctor's orders."

Kirk watched his first officer carefully. No reaction. Of course not—a sign of health in itself.

"That's all, Spock," he said curtly, before his friend could offer additional rejoinders. "Dismissed."

Spock nodded once, rose and walked slowly to the door. McCoy relaxed perceptibly as soon as the portal closed behind him.

"Whew. He took that better than I expected."

"He took it like Spock—no, that's not fair of me, Bones."

"Forget it, Jim. I know how you feel—it's hard, watching

him like that and waiting for the collapse you know is coming. I just wish there was something more I could do for him.''

"It'll hurt seeing him go steadily downhill.''

McCoy looked philosophical. "The only other alternative is to confine him to quarters, or to Sick Bay. I don't see any point in that. It won't do anything for him from a physical standpoint and it could only hurt him mentally. So I see no harm in letting him—''

"Feel useful in his last hours?''

Both men stared quietly at each other, each lost in his own thoughts—the strongest presence in the room that of one who was no longer there.

Streamlining had given way to functionality in the latter part of the Twenty-First Century. So the ships which carried freight between the stars were equal parts ugly and efficient, ungainly and profitable.

The *S.S. Huron* was typical of this class and its crew typical of crews on such ships. There were some who insisted that the small living quarters on board such craft made for small men. In reality, the reverse was usually true. They were no less daring, no less brave than starship personnel—only sloppier and more independent.

Captain O'Shea of the *Huron* probably fell about midway between fiction and reality. Outwardly there was little to distinguish him. He was of average build and temperament, excepting the special sole of his left shoe, constructed to accommodate the fact that the one leg was a number of centimeters shorter than the other one. On such minutiae do careers in Starfleet hang.

Naturally, that detail made him stronger than those he was passed over in favor of. O'Shea needed that strength. The duller the task, the more inner strength a man needed to survive.

His face, at least, was noble, adequately laden with planes and angles inscribed by years of service. It might have been taken from the bust of a Roman patrician, despite the incongruity of the five-o'clock shadow.

At the moment he stood in the small, curved chamber which served as the bridge for the *Huron*. His two assistants were seated before him at the compact control console, staring at the fore viewscreen.

Quarters were snug. On board a freighter everything was sacrificed for the comfort of the cargo. O'Shea and his crew were classed with the other incidental equipment.

"Time to rendezvous . . . ," Elijah paused briefly to check a readout, ". . . two hours seven minutes, Captain."

O'Shea grunted in acknowledgment. It was his favorite mode of expression, being at once eloquent and economical. He also had an excellent negative grunt. O'Shea could produce a veritable spectrum, an *olla podrida* of grunts, constituting a language in themselves.

But the unusual importance of this run compared to their usual assignments compelled him to greater loquaciousness, his ambivalent feelings about the job notwithstanding.

"Must be a pretty important drug we're carrying for the *Enterprise*. I'd just as soon get rid of it and get back to shipping plain dilithium."

The *Huron*'s first officer, John Elijah, smiled to himself. Despite his constant complaining, he knew O'Shea was reveling in the attention they had received. The captain had been hard-pressed to keep the seams of his jacket intact when the priority call had come through from Starfleet, with its companion orders.

O'Shea already had had a chance to do a little strutting before the crew of the *Potemkin*. Now he was looking forward to playing hero before the officers of one of the most famous ships in the Federation, the *Enterprise*.

No wonder he was feeling talkative!

He felt a tap on his arm and looked across at his partner. Lieutenant Fushi eyed him questioningly, directed his attention to a certain readout on the other side of the console. Like nearly everything else, the by-play caught O'Shea's attention.

"What are you two on about?"

"Sir," Fushi confessed, openly puzzled, "our sensors are registering the presence of a ship ahead." Several intriguing new crevices appeared in the captain's mobile face.

"Odd. Could the *Enterprise* be this early? Sure, and this is listed as a priority meeting, but . . ."

"Still too far away to tell what it is, sir," Fushi replied.

"What's its approximate course?"

"Toward us, sir."

O'Shea grunted. Elijah and Fushi had no trouble translating it to, "Well, that's all very interesting information Lieutenant, and I certainly hope it is the *Enterprise*; but since we're not sure yet perhaps you'd best keep an eye on it."

In the hands of a master like the captain the content of a barely verbalized monosyllable could be truly startling.

Kirk halted dictation into his private log and looked to the helm. "Time to rendezvous, Mr. Arex?"

The Edoan checked the chronometer readout, compared it with the declaration of another gauge. "One hour forty-three minutes, Captain."

Kirk considered this briefly before turning his attention to the Bridge engineering station, where Scott was keeping a close watch on numerous gauges.

"Scotty, I hate to ask this, but . . ."

Scott simply looked back and nodded. "Aye, Captain, we'll squeeze a bit more speed out of her somehow."

"If it'll help, Scotty, I'll get out and push."

"Any of us would, Captain. Let me see what I can do."

An insistent buzz pulled Kirk's attention back to the chair intercom.

"McCoy to Bridge."

Kirk opened the channel. "What is it, Bones?"

"Tell Spock it's time for another shot."

Kirk lowered his voice as he looked over toward the science station. "Again, Bones?"

"Again, Jim."

Kirk sighed. "All right, I'll send him down." He raised his voice. "Mr. Spock." There was no response. "Mr. Spock!" Now Sulu had turned to stare, and Uhura had swiveled 'round at her station.

"He looks tired, Bones," Kirk said into the pickup. "Just a minute." He got out of the chair and walked toward his first officer. "Spock? Spock!"

The first officer's eyes, which had been closed as Kirk approached, opened slowly. He gazed blankly up at Kirk for a moment. Then both eyes and mind seemed to clear simultaneously.

"I was conserving energy, Captain."

Kirk nodded matter-of-factly, trying not to let his relief show. "McCoy wants you in Sick Bay. Time for another injection."

Spock rose from his seat—slowly, carefully, but without aid—and walked toward the elevator with the same measured movements.

The silence on the bridge was deafening.

O'Shea leaned between his two juniors and studied the abstract overlay on the viewscreen. So far it could show no more than a moving blip—enigmatic and uniformly uninformative.

Fushi had been staring into a gooseneck viewer for long moments. Now he sat back, flipped a single switch and rubbed his eyes. He had collated the mass approximations, extreme-range silhouette configuration estimates, energy registration and a dozen others. These enabled him to make a single terse announcement.

"It's not the *Enterprise* closing on us, sir."

"Another Federation vessel?" There was more hope than confidence in O'Shea's voice now.

"No, sir. It's an outsider for sure. A design I don't recognize. That's not to say half the helmsmen in the Federation wouldn't recognize it, but *I* don't."

"That's good enough for me," O'Shea acknowledged grimly. "Are we close enough yet for visual pickup?"

"Three minutes on our current course should bring it within range of our fore telescanners, sir."

O'Shea considered. From the beginning he'd enjoyed this mission. It had provided a chance for some infrequent recognition as well as an opportunity to present himself as a person of importance. Everything had run smoothly.

Now there was a loose neutron in the reaction chamber, and he found he didn't like it one bit.

Fushi was doing his best with the *Huron*'s telescopic pickups. The abstract overlay vanished from the main screen, to be replaced by a wavering, fuzzy starfield. In its center was what appeared at first glance to be a red star.

Fushi made adjustments, and the star became a ship. O'Shea studied the unknown visitor intently. Its design was different, but not extreme—alien without being radical. It was colored blood red, a choice which might be coincidental, theatrical, or intentional.

One out o' three, he mused, ain't good.

"You sure it's coming toward us?" he asked again.

Elijah was busy checking gauges. "Definitely on an intercept course, Captain. Estimates of speed . . . it'll reach us before we make contact with the *Enterprise*."

"Maybe," said Fushi quietly, "they just want to chat."

"Maybe," agreed O'Shea, staring at the alien image as it grew nearer and nearer. "Maybe . . ."

"Maybe we can dispense with these injections soon, Spock," McCoy told him.

Spock was lying down on one of the diagnostic beds. Nurse Chapel stood nearby. McCoy wielded the air hypo like an artist with a brush, placed it against the first officer's shoulder.

"This won't hurt a bit now, Spock."

"An unnecessary reassurance, Doctor," his patient replied, "in addition to being untrue."

McCoy grimaced as he administered the serum. "That's the last time I waste my best bedside manner on a Vulcan."

Spock, rolling down the sleeve of his tunic, started to sit up. "Such restraint would be welcome, Doctor."

McCoy put a hand on the first officer's untreated shoulder and gently pressed him back. "Agreed, provided you show some of the same, Spock. Lie there quietly."

Nodding to Chapel, he directed his full attention to the screen over the head of the bed. Chapel adjusted the complex diagnostic mechanism. The result was a series of brightly lit printouts on the screen which the patient, in his reclining position, couldn't see.

Respiration, circulation—McCoy went through the succession of figures, compared them with those taken four hours earlier. There was nothing there he hadn't expected to see. That made them no less depressing.

Considering the massive doses Spock had been receiving, one would think those strobolin analogs would be more effective. To an observer basing his opinion on the present readings, all those injections would seem to have been worse than useless.

But McCoy knew that without those injections he would not be reading any results on Spock now. Corpses generate singularly uniform figures. He looked down at the subject of all this analysis, who waited patiently for permission to get back to his assigned tasks, and smiled in a manner belying his true feelings.

"Well, that's not too bad . . . not too bad at all. I'm afraid it's back to the salt mines for you, Spock."

Spock started to get up, nearly fell. McCoy managed to restrain himself to the barest twitch and kept himself from extending a supportive arm.

"Thank you, Doctor," Spock said evenly, getting to his feet slowly but steadily now. Like a man in a dream, he left the room.

Chapel's professional smile didn't fade until he was gone. "The drug isn't working any more, Doctor. If it was, he wouldn't have lost that much ground in four hours." McCoy turned from her, troubled.

"I know, Christine, I know. The additional injections can't hurt his system and psychologically they may help. Don't worry . . . we'll have the strobolin soon."

That was what McCoy said. But a person did not have to be as familiar with him as Chapel was to read what he meant.

They'd *better* have the strobolin soon . . .

"They've increased speed, sir," Fushi reported tightly. "Closing fast on us now."

"Why do I have this nagging impression they want more from us than just talk?" O'Shea muttered. "Open hailing frequencies, Mr. Elijah. Standard intership call."

The first officer of the *Huron* reached for the required instruments, manipulated several. "Open, sir. They're plenty close enough; should pick us up easy."

O'Shea moved forward, spoke toward the directional mike.

"To unidentified alien vessel. This is Captain Svenquist O'Shea of the Federation freighter *S.S. Huron*—on whose course you are currently closing. Please state your registry and intentions.'' He paused, repeated, ''Please identify yourself.''

''No use, sir,'' a vexed Elijah reported. ''They've got to be receiving . . . but they're not answering.''

Well, that left two possibilities. The first was that the stranger was in sufficient difficulties to render his broadcast instrumentation inoperative.

The second was that O'Shea was in a lot of trouble and needed help, but fast.

''We've got a hold full of dilithium to protect, not to mention that drug,'' he ventured. ''I don't like people who come at me fast and silent. Evasive maneuvers.''

Fushi and Elijah were good. They tried right-left angle shifts. They put the *Huron* through turns warp-drive craft weren't designed for. They sent her galloping off course in a random-number spiral.

None of it fazed their silent pursuer. Whatever sought close contact with them was simply too fast to be denied. Time and again it would slip off the *Huron*'s screens, only to reappear moments later. And with each new maneuver tried, each option exhausted, the alien grew harder and harder to shake. Their pilots might not have been any better—but their navigational computer and engines were clearly designed for more intricate work than traveling from point *A* to point *B*.

''It's no good, sir,'' a tired Fushi confessed. ''Not only can't we lose them, they're still closing on us.''

''All right.'' O'Shea was running down a list of responses to possible challenges. ''Resume course, and send out an emergency signal to the *Enterprise*. By drone. Subtly.''

''Yes, sir.'' He programed the drone properly, sent it on its robotic way. ''Might be a good idea to ready a backup, in case.'' His hands moved to make the necessary demands on the *Huron*'s equipment—and hesitated as a certain telltale commenced a steady winking.

''Message coming in, sir.''

''I can see that, man. Let's hear it.''

Elijah acknowledged the call, put it on the speaker. They had cut in mid-broadcast.

It didn't matter. The message directed at them was as understandable as it was incomplete.

". . . or prepare to be destroyed. Stand by to surrender your cargo or prepare . . ."

VII

"Captain, I'm getting a signal from the *Huron*—by automatic emergency beacon."

Kirk stiffened in his seat. "Are we close enough for direct ship-to-ship contact yet?"

Uhura checked a readout. "Possible, sir—fringe tangency."

"Try it."

"Yes, sir." There was a pause, then, "Nothing, sir. Either we're still too far off or—it's definitely an emergency beacon doing the broadcasting." She didn't have to elaborate.

"Sensor report, Mr. Spock. Have they reached the designated coordinates?" It took Spock several seconds longer than usual to make the check and reply.

"No, sir. Long-range scanners also indicate a course change. They are veering off—and have reduced speed considerably."

"Compute new course to intercept, Mr. Arex. Lieutenant Uhura, keep trying to make contact. Let's find out what's going on—"

It took longer than Kirk expected to make the rendezvous, not because of the course change but because the *Huron* had not merely cut speed—she had practically stopped.

Visual contact soon revealed the reasons why. The freighter sat there on the main viewscreen, drifting aimlessly in space. All entreaties for acknowledgement were ignored with frightening uniformity.

Spock's attention was on his hooded viewer. "The *Huron*'s power levels are functioning at the bare minimum required to maintain life-support systems, Captain. And sensors

313

are picking up considerable metallic and other inorganic debris."

"Natural cause?"

Spock looked up from the viewer. "No, Captain. Extrapolating from preliminary data I would say without qualification that she was attacked. Indications are . . . indications are . . ." He swayed in his chair, eyelids fluttering.

"Spock!"

For a moment the first officer's eyes opened wide and clear. Then a faint suggestion of uncertainty crossed that stolid visage. "Captain, I . . ."

Kirk started forward—caught the limp form before it struck the floor. Uhura was already on the intercom.

"Bridge to Sick Bay—*Emergency*!"

Kirk felt no need to ask McCoy for a detailed interpretation of the readings that winked on and off on the screen above Spock's head. Anyone with a minimal knowledge of Vulcan physiology could see that they were appallingly low.

McCoy studied the unconscious Vulcan. "We've got to have that strobolin, Jim. The synthetic is useless now—hell, it's been useless for half a day! He has lapsed into coma." He looked unwaveringly at Kirk.

"If we don't get that drug soon, very soon, he'll never come out of it."

"Do what you can, Bones." It sounded pitifully inadequate. "And I'll—I'll do what *I* can."

Now they had another problem to cope with. What had happened to the *Huron*? He gave McCoy a hesitant, encouraging pat on the back and left Sick Bay.

McCoy watched him go, his one note of satisfaction in this being Kirk's continued steadiness; then he turned his attention back to his patient. He examined the readouts again. For the moment they were unchanged. Temporary, false pleasure—they could only change for the worse.

"Blasted Vulcan!" he yelled at the motionless form, "Why couldn't you have red blood like any normal man?"

He prayed for a comforting insult.

He got only sibilant breathing—and silence.

Arex was manning Spock's station as Sulu positioned the *Enterprise* close to the unresponsive *Huron*.

"Status?" Kirk queried sharply, striding out of the elevator.

"Her engines are dead," Arex reported, studying the telltale sensor screen. "Backup battery power is operating life-support systems at a low but acceptable level."

"Anyone left alive?"

"There appears to be, sir. Several weak readings. I can't tell how many for certain."

"We'll find out soon enough. Mr. Scott, Lieutenant Uhura, come with me. Mr. Sulu, you have the con. We're beaming over to the *Huron*."

Dissolution . . . nausea . . . teasing oblivion . . . reassembly.

Kirk looked around and saw that Kyle had put them exactly where he had specified. They were standing on the *Huron*'s bridge. Or rather, on what was left of it.

It looked as if something had taken the *Huron* by its stern and slammed the upper end against a nickel-iron asteroid. Signs of severe concussion were everywhere—in the shattered gauge covers, the slight ooze of liquid around loosened paneling from cracked fluid-state switches, in the decided chill in the air from the release of super-cooled gases.

Further evidence was to be found in the condition of two of the three skulls belonging to the crew.

Chapel made a quick examination of the physical damage and tended to Fushi, the most severely injured of the three, first. Whatever had battered the *Huron* had made no distinction between accouterments living and dead. Her three officers were scattered about the bridge with the same disregard and in the same condition as the furnishings.

Kirk waited with agonized impatience as Chapel moved quickly from Fushi to O'Shea to Elijah.

"They'll all live," she said finally. Kirk turned.

"Scotty, check the cargo hold for the strobolin. Every freighter has a double-walled refrigerated chamber for storing extremely valuable cargo. It should be located close by the central accessway. The drug will be in it."

"Aye, sir." Scott turned, started back into the bowels of the ship.

"Uhura, see if you can get a playback off their log. I want to know what happened here."

Uhura nodded, moved to the chaos of the fore control console and commenced trying to make sense out of the tangle of wiring, torn metal and shredded plastics.

Kirk examined what was left of the small engineering station, wished Scotty were around to explain the destruction. Whatever had ruined the freighter had been guided by an intelligence with a definite purpose in mind. The damage here was severe—but still controlled. Something had disabled the freighter without destroying it.

It was difficult to fault their thoroughness. True, they had left O'Shea and his crew alive—barely. But there was no reason to expect three severely wounded men drifting powerless in a little-frequented section of space and existing on stored energy to ever be rescued and bear witness against their attacker.

No, the *Huron* might very well have gone down on shipping schedules as just one of those infrequent vessels marked "never arrived—cause unknown," if it weren't for the fact that the ship was to meet the oncoming *Enterprise* in free space. Something Kirk doubted her attackers had known, or they would have taken care to leave no one alive. They had made a mistake.

Possibly a fatal one.

There was a buzz close by, and Kirk flipped on his communicator.

"Scott to Captain Kirk," the familiar voice of the chief engineer came. Kirk glanced around the shattered bridge. Chapel had turned her ministrations to O'Shea. Uhura deftly avoided a sudden shower of sparks, then bent with renewed vigor to the task of extricating the remnants of the *Huron*'s log.

"Kirk here . . . all steady forward, Scotty. Report."

"I'm in the main bay, Captain. The *Huron*'s equipped with a security bin, all right—only its been forced. It's as empty as the rest of the cargo hold. There's nothin' down here, Captain."

"No sign of the strobolin?"

"Not a single ampoule, Captain. The *Huron*'s listed cargo

for this trip was dilithium. Not a crystal in sight, either. The hold's been stripped clean.''

"Life-support systems?''

"Stable here. No, if this was caused by a natural disaster it's been repaired with the slickest patch job I've ever seen. Also, it must have been a mighty selective disaster. The only major damage is to the security chamber and the cargo locks. I kinna tell for sure from this distance, but I think they were blown open and then resealed.''

"All right, Mr. Scott. Report back up here.''

"Aye, Sir. Sorry I am . . .''

No drug, a voice howled in Kirk's mind. No drug, no drug! He flipped off the communicator and walked over next to the busy Uhura. She looked up at him and wiped a forearm across her brow. The humidity was bad in here and getting worse, despite the valiant efforts of the damaged life-support system.

"All recorders are gone, sir—but indications are that the log tapes are intact. I think I can extricate them without damage. We'll have to play them back on board ship, though.''

"Good enough, Lieutenant.'' He left her to her work and turned his attention back to Chapel. She continued to labor on O'Shea.

"How is he, Nurse?''

"Scrambled inside, concussion upstairs—he needs surgery but,'' she smiled slightly, "he'll live, Captain. Nothing we can't fix. Another couple of days, though, and all three of them would have been gone.''

Kirk moved away, thinking hard. He flipped the communicator open again just as Scott re-entered the bridge.

"Kirk to *Enterprise*. We're ready to beam over, Arex. Have a full medical team standing by. We need—'' he glanced at Chapel, who nodded approval as he spoke, "—three pallets with tech-teams. Tell Dr. McCoy he's got a triple surgery on his hands.''

"Very good, sir,'' the thin voice piped back.

They left the *Huron* where and as it was, its automatic beacon still calling plaintively to an indifferent universe. Scott had installed a fully charged power pack to run the beacon when the freighter's emergency batteries finally gave out.

The shattered transport could be recovered later, by someone else. Right now something other than salvage dominated Kirk's thoughts. And Scott's, and McCoy's, and Sulu's—and those of every other member of the *Enterprise*'s crew—though they might not have admitted it.

Such thoughts were doubtlessly the cause of the pounding headache Kirk suffered from as he paced the outer room of the Sick Bay. His attention was gratefully drawn from the miners excavating his skull when McCoy entered from a side doorway. The reflective figure, clad in transparent surgical garb, beckoned Kirk to a familiar chamber.

Kirk walked past the base of the bed where Spock lay immobile. He glanced once at the diagnostic readouts on the screen above, looked hurriedly away. By now even the figures were painful to see.

He turned in time to see O'Shea wheeled in from surgery. Two medical techs transferred the *Huron*'s captain gently from the mobile pallet to a duplicate of the bed Spock lay in.

Both officers walked over, McCoy peeling the protective sealer from his face. "How's this one, Bones?"

"Oh, he'll pull through all right, Jim. Just a little rear-rangement of his plumbing . . . no permanent damage." He paused. "Jim, what the hell are we going to do about Spock?"

"The best we can, Bones."

"I'm not sure that's going to be good enough, Jim."

Kirk could see that McCoy was sorry for the words as soon as he had said them. He was under more pressure than anyone else on board just now, and it manifested itself as frustration.

Probably there was nothing as agonizing to a doctor of Bones' ability as knowing exactly what to do to cure a patient and simply not having the material to do it with.

"If we don't have that strobolin in twenty hours, he'll die," McCoy continued flatly. "That's a minimal figure, but it's pretty accurate. I wouldn't like to have to stretch it even five minutes."

There was nothing he could say . . . just as there was nothing he could do.

No, no—that wasn't entirely true. There was still a chance, still some hope. The dimness of the readings on the diagnostic indicators over Spock's head were matched by the snail's pace of his thoughts.

"We still might—"

"Might what, Jim?"

"Wait till I see the log tapes we took off the *Huron*. If they're wiped, or if the recorder was destroyed too soon—" He stopped abruptly. "See you later, Bones. Do what you can for Spock, and let me know the minute any of those three," he nodded to where Elijah was being brought in to join O'Shea, "recover sufficiently to talk."

Never enough time, he thought, never enough . . .

As Arex ran the *Huron* tapes through the library computer, Kirk stood nearby and urged the dawdling computer to faster action.

Eventually, the Edoan made his equivalent of a satisfied sigh. "Some of the last tape was burned, Captain. I've been able to reconstruct the damaged sections, however. The *Huron* was definitely, as we suspected, attacked by another vessel. It is interesting to observe that the belligerent ship is a new design, one apparently never before encountered by a Federation ship. There is also evidence to suggest that it possesses an older form of propulsion than modern warp drive."

"I don't care if it came from the far side of M one one three eight and is powered by ten million invisible gerbils—all I want to know is, can we track it?"

"That's the significance of its out-of-date drive, sir. If you'll look here . . ."

He hit a switch. Immediately a blank grid appeared on the small screen above the science console. Another control produced a star-chart nearby. Arex made a last adjustment and the two blended together.

Kirk squinted. There were glowing dots on the composite screen which were not stars.

"The *Huron*'s attacker may be sophisticated in many ways," Arex explained, "but its propulsive units are possessed of a few archaic features. One of these is that they generate a faint residue of radioactive particulate matter. Unless they are aware of us and have carefully laid a false trail for us to follow—which I strongly doubt—we should be able to find them.

"The most recent deposits give a bearing of two hundred twelve plus, one hundred seventy-five minus to the Galactic ecliptic. The half-life of the ejected material is quite short. If we had arrived on the scene as much as three days late, our sensors would have found nothing."

"Lay in that course!" Kirk shouted back to the helm. "Ahead warp seven, Mr. Sulu." He turned back to Arex. "Run through those tapes again—slowly, Lieutenant—and let me know if you find anything else you think significant. I'll be down in Sick Bay."

Kirk found McCoy seated at his desk, his head resting in his hands. "How is he, Bones."

"Worse than he was when you left, Jim," McCoy replied, looking up. "And he'll be worse the next time, and worse after that . . . until we get that drug.

"It's his breathing that worries me most. Pretty soon I'm going to have to put him on forced respiration. That'll draw reserves from other parts of his body already hard-pressed by the disease."

"Well, we're following the attacking ship's trail." Teeth gleamed. "We're going to crawl right up—"

"Ship?" McCoy interrupted. "How do we know there's only one ship involved in this?"

"Lieutenant Arex is certain the radioactive residue comes from a single vessel."

"Sure, only one ship *attacked* the *Huron*. What happens if they rendezvous with another and transfer cargo? Or with two others, or make multiple transfers?"

"Dammit, Bones," Kirk half shouted, "this one's got to be the *only* one. It's *got* to be." McCoy looked apologetic, but Kirk waved off the incipient sorrys.

"Don't complicate things with factual possibilities, okay? If there's more than one ship, well . . . that's probably it, then. We haven't enough time to go chasing all over the cosmos after several ships, even if their trails would last that long."

"A transfer," McCoy finished relentlessly, "would seem the logical thing to do." His voice cracked on the word "logical."

"Sure, *if* you anticipate immediate pursuit. But every sign points to these beings—whoever they are—not expecting another vessel in this region. Certainly not one capable of over-taking them.

."The tapes indicate they weren't much on conversation. Chances are that if O'Shea had been given the opportunity to explain he was about to rendezvous with a heavy cruiser, they might have called off the whole thing."

"I'm sure that'll be a great consolation to O'Shea when he comes around," snorted McCoy. He walked slowly back to stare down at Spock.

"What's the good of being a physician, anyway?" Kirk heard him mutter angrily. "We're only as good as current drugs and technology make us. We've got a few more books, a little more knowledge. Eliminate all the mechanical conveniences, and I might as well be practicing in the middle ages. There's nothing *I* can do for him." He walked a few steps away, slammed a hand against the door sill.

"Me—me, I'm helpless. Totally dependent on instrumentation and pre-programed chemicals. There isn't a thing *I* personally can do. So what's the point of it—what's the point?" He stared down at the floor.

"Better to be an engineer like Scotty. If one of his patients burns out, there's always a replacement in the catalog." A hollow laugh forced itself out.

Silence.

Then, "If you really believed that, Bones," Kirk told him softly, "you wouldn't still be a doctor after twenty-five years. *Especially* a ship's doctor.

"And that's something else I've always wondered about, Bones. Why did you bother entering the service? With your skill you could have made a fortune in government or private practice."

McCoy glanced back sharply, an unfathomable expression on his face. "You're going to find this funny, Jim, but . . . I entered the service instead of striking out on my own because I'm greedy."

"Greedy? As Spock would say, that sounds like an irrefutable contradiction in terms."

McCoy shook his head. "It's no different for me than for you, Jim. I'm here because challenge means more to me than money. And because money can't buy a sense of accomplishment.

"Besides, could you see me sitting in a private clinic on Demolos or on Earth, pandering to the private phobias of overweight matrons and spoiled kids?"

"I admit it's a tough scene to picture," Kirk agreed, amused. "I'm glad your avarice drove you to become doctor on this ship."

"Listen," McCoy began, "if Spock pulls through—"

"You mean *when* Spock pulls through," Kirk countered forcefully. "When Spock pulls through I'll see what can be done about rounding up some more interesting illnesses for you to play with. I don't want you feeling unchallenged."

"Thanks awfully, Jim," McCoy responded, a touch of his normal sarcasm coming back. "I'd appreciate some really different germs for a change. Trouble is, the people on this ship refuse to cooperate. You're all too damned healthy."

Kirk turned to leave. "Well Bones, you've got nobody to blame but yourself."

The dilithium, Kirk mused as he strolled down the corridor, he could understand. As good as currency—no, better. A load of good crystals would be easy to market to some of the Federation's less reputable concerns. Or to any of many non-Federation worlds.

But why did they take the strobolin? Why? Pirates would hardly have known what it was. And if they had, they would have realized it wasn't particularly valuable—it was demand, not rarity, that was responsible for that.

Come to think of it, he considered as he entered the lift, that was probably it. They had taken the strobolin out of ignorance, reasoning that anything worth protecting so well was worth appropriating.

If only they had left the drug, he could have overlooked the assault, forgotten the injuries, ignored the monetary loss. Suddenly he grew cold as he realized that they might not have discovered the drug's true value and simply have destroyed it, or dumped it in space—out of anger, perhaps, for the valuables the security chamber had failed to yield.

He tried not to think about it, just as he tried to ignore McCoy's hypothesis about intership transfers of the stolen goods.

In one way the situation was made simple for him. Because

of the restrictions imposed by time, he was reduced to only one course of action, spared the need of choosing among several tortuous possibles.

All they could do was follow the thread of radioactive residue and hope it led to the intact ampoules of strobolin. Hope it did so quickly.

Exiting onto the bridge he automatically scanned left to right, insured himself that everyone who belonged at his/her post was present. Arex, he noticed as he took his seat in the command chair, was back at the navigator's station.

Handling the dual assignment was hard on the Edoan, he knew. But he was a better backup to have there than anyone else in a situation like this. Sulu could cover for him where necessary.

Besides, he mused bitterly, one way or the other the navigator wouldn't have to occupy the dual position much longer.

"Report."

"Emanations from the radioactive matter still registering strongly on applied sensors, Captain," Sulu informed him. "Bearing still two hundred twelve plus, one hundred seventy-five minus. We are moving up on a massive grouping of solid material."

"Slow to standard cruising speed," Kirk ordered, fingers tap-tapping on an arm of the chair. "Free-space asteroidal belt or globe," he muttered to himself.

Sulu was busily replacing the abstract information listed on the main screen with a view from the ship's fore scanners. Such groupings, Kirk reflected, were not common, but neither were they rare enough to arouse unusual interest.

Visual sightings confirmed that this was a normal collage, jagged fragments ranging in size from microscopic pebbles to a few moon-sized specimens. At the moment, however, abstract analysis was far from his mind.

"The trail of radioactives enters the group and begins a weaving pattern, Captain," Sulu reported.

Kirk nodded slightly. He had half expected as much. They had been closing steadily on their quarry, judging by the upsurge in radioactive intensity of the trail. This was the closest thing to a hiding place open space offered to an interstellar craft.

"They're taking evasive action. A sensible maneuver, wouldn't you say, Mr. Sulu?"

"The ideal place to try and shake us, Captain," the helmsman agreed. "Especially if there are any natural concentrations of radioactives in this belt." He studied his port instrumentation.

"Preliminary indications point to many of the asteroids as having unusual energy properties that—" He stopped, staring at a particular readout.

"Share it with all of us, Mr. Sulu," Kirk said sharply.

"Extreme-range sensor scan indicates that the trail of radioactive debris we have been following ends in the approximate center of the grouping."

"Could be trying to cover their trail somehow, trying to throw us off by running on a different drive system, or perhaps arranging some kind of unpleasant welcome," Kirk murmured, to no one in particular. "We can be sure of one thing, now—they know they're being pursued." He glanced back to Uhura. "All deflectors up—sound yellow alert, Lieutenant. Mr. Sulu, cut speed and maintain evasive approach pattern."

A chorused "Aye, sir" came back to him, while bright flashes paired with suitably cacophonous whoops resounded throughout the starship.

"All sections secured and ready, Captain," Uhura was able to report minutes later.

"Thank you, Lieutenant. Approaching unknown's approximate sphere of confluence. Stand by for—"

A brilliant flare momentarily obliterated the scene depicted on the viewscreen, and the *Enterprise* shook to the force of destructive energies.

"What in the Pleiades was that?" Judging from the violence of the flare, alarm horns should have been sounding steadily.

Arex worked furiously to secure an answer. What he learned wasn't exactly encouraging, but neither did it appear they were under attack from some kind of unknown superweapon.

"Unusual energy properties indeed, Captain. It seems certain asteroids are composed of anti-matter. This entire belt is remarkable for having both matter and anti-matter existing side by side—a highly unstable configuration.''

''Walking on a field of mined eggshells is more like it,'' Uhura suggested.

''All fragments explode on contact with each other— decidedly a dangerous place for a chase, Captain,'' the navigator finished.

''Their maneuverability's reduced, too, don't forget that,'' Kirk countered, scowling at the screen as if the universe were personally trying to make his life miserable. It was not a new sensation.

''Keep those deflectors on maximum, Mr. Scott.'' The chief engineer acknowledged the order from his place at the bridge engineering console.

''Captain? There's enough power locked in this belt to run whole fleets of starships. It would require a major industrial effort to tap it, but the amount of potential energy involved—''

''Enough to do a lot of damage, also, Mr. Scott. Steady and easy, Mr. Sulu, steady and easy.'' Sulu nodded.

They continued on through the belt, crawling impatiently along the still radiant, damning trail. Deeper and deeper into the grouping they moved. Only the occasional flare of antagonistic elements obliterating each other in inorganic suicide registered on the sensors.

Finally something else rocked the *Enterprise*. It was a substantial jolt, but no one was thrown from his seat, and Uhura was soon able to report all sections in with no damage, no casualties.

This time the buffeting was caused not by matter–anti-matter disintegration, but by a deep blue beam which had struck at the *Enterprise* from just over the horizon of a large asteroid below and to starboard.

''Mr. Sulu!''

''Fractional calibration completed, Captain. They're running, but I've got them.''

''Pursuit speed, Mr. Sulu. Phasers stand by.''

It was only a matter of minutes, now. As they passed he considered strategy.

Chances were their assailant had taken his best shot first, hoping to disable the *Enterprise* before she could retaliate.

But the barrage they had taken wasn't anything on, say, the order of what a Klingon battle cruiser could put out—though it could have messed them up pretty badly if the deflectors had not been up.

On the other hand, the belligerent vessel's commander might be trying to draw the *Enterprise* into a more tactically advantageous position for him. It was too soon to judge. Best be ready for anything.

First round to the *Enterprise*, though—the attacker had forfeited the element of surprise.

The starfield pinwheeled on the screen. One glowing blob—blood red, unround, and of irregular outline—was finally locked into its center.

"Hold them, Mr. Sulu." Another probing blue light momentarily erased the view. "Analysis?"

Sulu was working smoothly, efficiently at the controls. "Standard frigate-class phasers, sir, slightly modified."

"Plenty hot enough to make scrap of an unarmed freighter like the *Huron*. They'll never get through our screens," Kirk noted with satisfaction.

"Captain," Arex broke in, "I've finally placed the ship's markings. It's an Orion vessel."

"Orion," Kirk echoed thoughtfully. The Orions were an isolated, humanoid race who stuck close to their small system of three inhabited worlds and shunned contact with outsiders. There had never been any reason to suspect them of antagonism toward other peoples. They were simply thought to be naturally reclusive—until now, he mused furiously.

They were very human-like, but emphatically not interested in joining up with the Federation, with the Klingon Empire, or with anyone else. The corollary was that members of those and other multistellar political leagues expressed little interest in expanding relations with the Orions.

The perfect cover, Kirk reflected, for some widescale, unsuspected piracy. He found himself wondering how many ships had been pushed onto the missing-and-presumed-lost register at Starfleet HQ through the intervention of the *indifferent* Orions.

"They're hailing us, Captain," Uhura announced, just as he was about to order the first phaser burst.

"Put them through, Lieutenant."

Uhura made the necessary adjustments, and they were rewarded by the face of the Orion captain. It was accompanied by a harsh, defiant voice forming comprehensible words. It affected Kirk, who had been threatened by the commanders of full battle fleets, not in the least.

Had O'Shea or Fushi or Elijah been present, however, the first response to the alien's words would have been immediate and distinguished by its colorful invective.

"Enterprise," the Orion commander began, indicating that their detection instrumentation was working as well as their diffusion beam, "we demand you cease your pursuit immediately. As a representative of a recognized neutral government, I must protest."

Kirk controlled his anger with an effort. For the moment he had to try diplomacy. Besides, the Orion commander was technically correct.

"This is Captain James T. Kirk, commanding. Who said we were engaged in a pursuit?" The Orion didn't change expression. "We detected a malfunction in your phaser systems and thought you might require aid. You are experiencing a malfunction?" He grinned sardonically.

"No—but the way you crept up on us, we could not be certain your intentions were not hostile."

"I compliment you on your method of discovering whether or not they were," Kirk snapped back. "It leaves no room for idle speculation. As for your neutrality, Orion's position has been in dispute ever since the affair regarding the Cordian planets and the Babel Concordance of stardate . . . well, I'm sure you're familiar with both date and circumstances.

"But it's a matter of more recent history that concerns me at the moment, Captain. Yesterday a Federation freighter, the *Huron*, was attacked in this quadrant, its cargo hijacked. As the first alien vessel encountered in the area, we request you to submit to search, as per Babel Resolution A twelve. Do you require time to consider your response?"

The Orion didn't go for the lead. A request for time would constitute an admission of guilt. Instead, the Orion managed a respectable smile.

"Orions are not thieves. I am sorrowed to hear of the hijacking of the Federation ship. We certainly hope you find the instigators of such villainy. As for ourselves, we hold no

Federation cargo of any kind. And our papers permitting us to travel in this sector are quite in order. I must insist, Captain, that you end your hostilities toward us. If this harassment does not cease instantly, we will lodge a formal protest with your government.''

Kirk made a quick slashing motion, glanced back over his shoulder as the Orion's image vanished. "Tell him to stand by, Uhura."

"All right, sir." There was a brief pause, then she looked back at him. "They want to know why, sir."

"Tell them I have some internal bodily functions to attend to. If they want further details, supply them."

"Sir," Uhura responded readily.

"Mr. Sulu, anything yet?"

"A second, sir, I'm reconfirming." The helmsman had been working furiously at the project ever since they had made close contact with the Orions. He proved as good as his word, looked back to the command chair wearing a smug grin.

"Sensors confirm the presence of massive amounts of dilithium on board the alien ship, sir. It must be packed in their spare rooms and empty corridors. They're fairly bulging with it."

"What about the strobolin?" Kirk demanded.

Sulu's smile faded. "According to what I've been told, there was no reason for the drug to be shipped in large amount, sir. If they have it, it's too small a quantity to detect through their hull."

Kirk grunted. "All right. Reopen the channel, Lieutenant."

"Channel open, sir," Uhura replied as the puzzled face of the alien commander reappeared on the screen.

"*Enterprise* to Orion vessel, Kirk here," he began. He had made a mental note of how careful the Orion Captain had been in avoiding the mention of his name, those of any of his crew, or his ship.

"I have a proposal to make. If, by some miraculous chance, you *did* happen to encounter the *Huron* and if you decided—in the interests of common decency—to salvage its valuable cargo, and if by chance you overlooked the three—" his voice rose slightly "—critically injured personnel on board, you might also have obtained a small quantity of perishable drugs from a no doubt accidentally opened security chamber. We need those drugs rather desperately."

The Orion commander was manifestly not an idiot. Kirk could see the gears spinning in his opposite number's head while the silence lengthened. Finally, the other commander looked up and ventured softly, "What would this drug be worth to you—frivolously assuming we had experienced the totally unlikely series of circumstances you detailed?"

Kirk leaned forward, his fingers clenching tighter than he wished on the arms of the chair.

"You keep the dilithium shipment. No mention of the entire incident to Starfleet or in my log. Plus an additional standardweight container of dilithium as . . . ," he hesitated, grinned tightly, ". . . payment for the *salvaged* drug."

Another long silence while the Orion commander appeared to consider the offer. When he continued there was a hint of suspicion in his tone—understandable enough under the circumstances. But there was something else, an undefinable something Kirk detected which hinted almost of desperation.

Obviously he understood his strategic position. He had lost the element of surprise. He had lost the chance that the *Enterprise* might run afoul of an unexpected matter-anti-matter explosion.

Despite his natural instincts he probably found himself in a position where he would have to risk the deal.

"We keep the dilithium," he said finally, cautiously, "plus, our neutrality remains intact?"

Kirk nodded. A briefer pause this time, before the alien commander replied firmly, "We will consider your proposal."

"Very well. But make it fast. Kirk out." He immediately switched to intercom. "Kirk to Sick Bay."

"McCoy here," came the rapid reply.

"Bones . . . how much time?"

"Less than an hour, Jim. The strobolin'll be ninety percent-plus effective right up till the end—not much longer than an hour. His internal collapse is starting to snowball. There's not much I can do to slow it and damn little I can do to halt it. If I had one lousy ampoule—"

"Hold on a little longer, Bones, a little longer. We're close, very close, to getting it."

"The Orion is hailing us, sir," Uhura interrupted apologetically.

"I know you can do it, Bones."

"It's not up to me anymore, Jim," the filtered reply came back. "It's up to that abstract community of proteins we call Spock. Skill doesn't matter anymore—just chemistry."

"Kirk out." He swiveled. "All right, Lieutenant, I'll take the call now." He steeled himself for whatever answer the Orions might give.

"Your proposal is agreeable, Captain . . ."

Kirk slumped a little in his chair.

". . . with one qualification."

Kirk sat straight again, suddenly wary. "What kind of qualification?"

"Whether your people come for the drug or we transfer it to you involves the interchange of at most, minor personnel. Expendables." Kirk started to protest, but the Orion commander made a tired gesture requesting silence and Kirk forced himself to sit back quietly.

"No aspersions intended, Captain. But without assuming any real risk, you could obtain what you want and then turn on us."

"What," Kirk replied slowly, "would it take to convince you of our sincerity?"

"More persuasion than the universe possesses. However, we will settle for a face-to-face exchange, the drug for the container of dilithium. In the absence of available absolutes, risking one's own neck is considered the best substitute. I will meet you myself."

"Face to face." All kinds of danger signals were going off inside him. "Where?"

"An extremely large planetoid close by my ship. You doubtless have it on your screens. It has an atmosphere acceptable to both of us. We can predetermine the time and beam down simultaneously. I will hand you the drug personally.

"Your own presence will be most reassuring, Captain. Compared to it, the extra dilithium crystals are superfluous." A faint, nebulous hint of humor. "I believe we can do without them.'' He assumed a rigid, waiting posture. ''Now it is your turn to consider.''

''I'd . . . like to consult with my staff.''

The alien made a sign of agreement.

''You'll receive an answer shortly. Kirk out.''

VIII

"It's got to be some sort of trap, Jim." McCoy's fist slammed into the smooth wood of the briefing room table top in an uncharacteristically violent gesture.

"I don't buy this business of not trusting 'expendable' subordinates. I don't believe it anymore than I believe this space-pucky about your own presence being required on the exchange to satisfy some inexplicable alien sense of uneasiness. What's wrong with your giving personal assurance by communicator? I'll bet they've cooked up this whole scheme just to get a clean shot at you!"

Kirk's reply was noncommittal. "Maybe my presence is required for spiritual reasons, Bones. We don't know much about Orion culture, you know. Still," he added, forestalling another Aesculapian outburst, "I find myself agreeing with you."

"No doubt of it in my mind," Scott added from the far end of the table.

"Yeah. Sure." Kirk put both hands on the table, leaned forward intensely. "It could be a trap. But we've got no time to consider options, no time to devise means of devious subtlety to secure the strobolin.

"If we don't get our hands on it *fast*, Spock is going to die. Would he do less in a similar situation for any of us?"

McCoy was shaking his head sadly. "Why did you bother with this meeting, Jim. You had already made up your mind."

"Yes," Kirk confessed, "I had. But I wanted to see if either of you had another option to put forward—however hare-brained. Obviously, you don't."

"Oh, we're not going to do this without precautions—don't worry on that score. My communicator channel will be frozen open so that every word of what goes on will be broadcast on the bridge—even if it seems to the Orion Captain that I turned it off.

"Scotty, you'll be ready at the transporter, which will be locked on me at all times. At the first sign of anything underhanded, well . . . ," he stared at his chief engineer, "I'm trusting you."

"If this doesn't work, Jim," McCoy went on worriedly, "we could lose Spock *and* you."

"Nothing unique about the situation, Bones. Men have been going through similar ordeals since the dawn of civilization." He exchanged glances with each in turn. "Let's go to it, gentlemen, double or nothing."

The bridge of the Orion pirate was considerably smaller than its spacious counterpart on the *Enterprise*. Its complement was correspondingly reduced.

But the officers who manned its compact consoles and panels had more to worry about.

Everything had gone so well, her captain reflected, brooding in the command chair. The *Huron* had proven a rich prize, and they had ambushed her well out of communications range of any other ship. With no armament to speak of and a small crew, she had been an easy take.

Only this *gisjacheh* drug, this strobolin, had been intended not for delivery to some distant world, but for a free-space ship-to-ship transfer. To a ship already dangerously near. To a Federation battle cruiser, no less!

Now, despite his helmsman's best efforts to elude pursuit, the huge vessel had run him down and cornered him here. When he considered what would happen if news of the *Huron* attack ever reached diplomatic channels, he had made the inevitable decision. The only decision possible, really.

But to be sure first, as is the *bya-chee* bird before striking. He looked down to his executive officer.

"Status, Cophot?"

"We can't outgun the *Enterprise* and we can't outrun it, *Elt*. Nor can we penetrate her shields sufficiently to discourage her."

"No chance of escape?" he pressed.

"No, *Elt*, none."

The commander made his racial analog of a sigh, found no inspiration in a moment's meditation. "Orion's official neutrality comes before this ship, its crew—or its commander. There is too much at stake to take the word of one man—any man. He cannot give enough assurances that he will not at some time report the incident to Starfleet."

"No, sir," his exec admitted. "The only way to prevent that now is by achieving the destruction of the *Enterprise*. And the only way to do that," he hesitated in spite of himself, "is to destroy ourselves, too."

"Agreed. I had thought perhaps, an unexpected surge on our part, at the moment of exchange. Ram, overload their shields—"

"Your pardon, *Elt*," his first officer objected, "but there is a better way." He looked suddenly reluctant.

"Well, come on, out with all, Cophot."

"These asteroids," the other began, "contain among their number many which are anti-matter. Of those that are matter, many contain a high proportion of unstable radioactives. No danger to a man, they are concentrated in the planetary core, as in—"

"The one below us, that I'm scheduled to meet Captain Kirk on?" Understanding dawned.

"I have ascertained that this is so," the executive officer admitted. "Both ships will lay to hard by the planetoid. So close, if the core is triggered to reaction, both will be destroyed, despite the strongest defensive screens any ship could mount. The difficulty lies in the method of detonation. Mere phaser fire will not suffice."

"What then?"

"An adequately powerful explosive, which would provide the minimum number of high-energy particles. The material to make such a compact device has been providentially provided for us.

"Dilithium, yes," the commander agreed. "How could such a device be triggered?"

"I can manufacture a remote control which will—"

The captain's eyes brightened, and he waved his exec off.

"No, no. I've a better idea, Cophot. I'll do it by hand, carry the device down with me when I go to meet Kirk. I want the satisfaction of handing him his precious medicine and then seeing his face when I tell him he and his entire crew are going to the Dark Place with us. Besides, do not underestimate the detection equipment of this class of Federation cruiser. It could detect an old shoe beamed down to the surface, not to mention your proposed exterminator package.''

"As you wish it, *Elt*," the science officer said admiringly. "I will commence work."

"Be certain, Cophot, you do a worthy job. It is not everyday one has the privilege of composing the mechanics of one's own destruction."

The first officer made a silent gesture of concurrence.

"A call coming in from the *Enterprise*, *Elt*," the voice of the communications master broke in. The Orion commander turned his attention from his first officer back to the viewscreen.

"What is your decision, Captain Kirk?"

"I accept your terms."

"Very well," the *elt* replied, keeping his tone carefully level. "We will provide suggested coordinates, or—" he performed the movements of indifference "—you may select them yourself. We will beam down in fifteen of your minutes."

Kirk stared at the screen, noticed McCoy's glum expression.

"What now, Bones?"

"I still don't like it, Jim, but as you said, we haven't got any more time. Spock . . ." He shook his head slowly.

The Orion commander spoke again. "Fifteen minutes or not at all, Captain Kirk."

"Yes, yes," Kirk replied absently. "Agreed. *Enterprise* out."

The screen blanked.

It was a world of compact extinction, where one could see the work of oblivion in small doses, and comprehend.

True, it possessed a breathable atmosphere, a thin gaseous envelope through which jagged mountains rose against a deep purple curtain. Nothing crawled over its pockmarked surface. Nothing flew through its sad sky.

It was not an embryonic world, awaiting only the right

combination of heat and water to give birth. Rather it was a king among cinders, a shard of some long gone larger globe which in itself had never seen life.

But now life appeared on its surface, in the form of two electrically hued pillars. There was nothing to observe this visitation save the constituents of the pillars themselves. The two commanders rematerialized barely a couple of meters apart.

Immediately the Orion captain noticed the tricorder Kirk held in one hand, while Kirk's gaze went first to the overlarge backpack slung over the Orion's shoulders.

Consideration of its purpose and contents were forgotten as his eyes were drawn down to the plastic cylinder the other held. It was filled with tiny cylinders, and they in turn were filled with the fluid that could give life to the dying Spock.

Most of the printing on the cylinder's label was too small to read at the distance he stood from it, but the name STROBOLIN stood out clearly above the archaic red-cross symbol. So that there would be no doubt, the Orion took several steps closer and held the container out to him for a better look.

"As promised, Captain, your serum. Scan it if you wish." He gestured at the tricorder.

McCoy had preset the sensors himself. Kirk pointed it at the translucent cylinder, pressed a switch. If the contents of the container were something cleverly designed to simulate strobolin, they would have to be the work of a master chemist. McCoy had gone over the 'corder's programing a dozen times.

The reading the intricate mechanism showed was clear, however. There wasn't a hint of molecular funny business. On the starship's bridge, everyone breathed a sigh of relief as the captain's voice sounded over the open communicator.

"Pure strobolin, Bones." He rolled the container of dilithium over the smooth surface. It bumped to a halt against the Orion's legs.

"My half of the bargain. Want to check it?"

"No, Captain Kirk. I trust you."

"*Now* you trust me." Kirk shrugged. "However you please. I'll take that now and then we can both beam up." He reached for the cylinder.

The Orion commander skipped backward a few steps.

"No, Captain Kirk, I'm afraid I can't permit that. You see, no matter how I strive to convince myself, I can't believe that word of this incident will not ultimately reach your superiors. If that happens, my world will lose its neutrality and be subject to Federation retaliation."

"Look," an exasperated Kirk began, "we've been through this already. If my solemn word is not good enough for you, you must know that you can't escape the *Enterprise*. We can follow you anywhere."

"Only if you have something to follow, Captain, and something left to do the following in, and someone to do it."

Kirk gaped at him and tried to unravel the riddle, not liking the way his thoughts were leading him.

On the bridge, Arex heard, and muttered, "I've been getting some unusual sensor readings, Mr. Scott. That planetoid's putting out a lot of noise and all kinds of radiation. But this is different—it's localized around the captain and the alien."

"What is it?"

"I'm not sure—it's not around them," he said excitedly, "it's in *with* them. There's dilithium down there with them."

"Of course," Scott noted. "The Captain took down with him, for the exchange, a—"

"No, no!" The Edoan's voice rose to an abnormal shrillness as his voice-box tried to catch up with his thoughts. "This is different. It appears to be barely stabilized!"

"You've been staring at my pack," the Orion commander was telling Kirk. "I don't wish to keep secrets. It's an explosive device. When triggered by me it will detonate the radioactive core of this planetoid. The resulting cataclysm will be considerable—quite sufficient to destroy your ship."

"Yours too," Kirk countered. He wasn't familiar with Orion culture, true, but somehow he was sure the expression that slid over the commander's face was his equivalent of a snide smugness.

"Why do you think my people have been able to maintain our operations for so long, so secretly and well, Captain Kirk? It is because all unsuccessful Orion missions end in suicide. When possible, we enjoy company."

"Mr. Scott," Arex half pleaded for a decision, a command, a call to perform—*some*thing.

"We can't warp out, because we'll lose the captain—and Mr. Spock," Scott thought out loud. He couldn't beam the Orion commander aboard because triggering the device on board would set off the dilithium in the ship's engines. The Orion commander . . ."

"The dilithium!" he shouted, battering at the intercom switch. "Transporter room—Scott here—dilithium crystals on the Orion commander, Kyle, pinpoint 'em and beam 'em up—*fast*!"

"An interesting experience, is it not, Captain?" the Orion was musing, his hand hovering over a switch set into his belt. "Often I've wondered what instant dissolution would feel like. Is there time to feel pain, to sense the coming apart of one's body? An intriguing question."

"Pinpointed, Mr. Scott," Kyle's voice resounded over the open speaker.

"Do it!"

Kyle shifted the proper instrumentation in rapid sequence, his eyes glued to one small dial.

"Ah, well," the Orion commander finished, "it is one thing to philosophize, but another to experience. I have made my peace—let us have reality."

He reached for his belt a second before Kirk leaped at him. Kirk grabbed both alien wrists—too late. The Orion's eyes clenched tight as he winced in anticipation, his finger breaking the trigger contact.

Another second and he found himself flat on the ground. Eyes open again, he discovered to his horror he was still capable of discerning the stars overhead. They formed an irregular halo around the angry face of Kirk, staring down at him.

Kirk was able to relax his grip some, still keeping the Orion pinned to the ground. The alien commander was in shock. He offered little resistance.

"Reality, huh? I'll give you reality." He directed his words to the open communicator. "Scotty, energize."

That brought the Orion awake and kicking. He struggled to reach his own communicator. Kirk jammed a knee into the region of the other man's solar plexus, put pressure on both wrists. The alien slumped, grimacing in pain.

"I know it's not total dissolution," Kirk told him through

clenched teeth, "but it's the best I can do—for now." He felt a twinge of vertigo, saw his vision start to fog. Soon the surface of the asteroid was bare of life once more.

Kirk's first sight on coming out of transport was of two burly security guards who stood covering the alcove from opposite angles, phasers drawn and ready. Then he looked back, saw Engineer Scott enter the transporter room. Scott made no attempt to conceal his relief.

The guards immediately took hold of the Orion and effectively immobilized him—though he was still too bewildered to offer much in the way of coherent resistance. While they checked him for weapons somewhat less lethal than planet-busters, Kirk was on his feet, rearranging his tunic and walking toward the waiting Scott.

"Captain," Scott began, emotionally drained, "that was too close. So close that—"

"Take your time, Mr. Scott, and think of something appropriate." He turned, approached the pinioned Orion and his guards. "I'll take that, Ensign," he said to one of the guards, taking the plastic container from his grip. "It's not a weapon."

He moved rapidly to the intercom, the precious cylinder of strobolin ampules now safely in hand. "Kirk to Bridge—"

"Captain," Sulu's voice responded, "we heard—"

"Later, Mr. Sulu. Right now I suggest moving us several diameters out in case they decide to try that little trick again."

"Aye, sir!"

"Kirk out." He clicked off, looked back to Scott. "Let's get up to the bridge." Then a glance backward as he addressed the security people. "Bring him along, too." The five men started for the elevator.

"By the way, Scotty, where's the dilithium he packed?"

"Stabilized and on its way to the engine storage chambers, Captain, where it will be put to better use."

On board the Orion pirate, the battle on the bridge raged between confusion and desperation.

"I tell you they're both gone, sir!" the communications officer reported.

"Gone!" The science officer was incredulous.

"I was scanning as ordered, *Bhar*, when they vanished from the planetoid's surface—both the Earther and the *elt*.

There was no warning, and sensors detect nothing like an explosion.''

"If it didn't misfire," the exec thought furiously, "then they must have discovered the dilithium pack and disarmed it, somehow."

"*Bhar*, the *Enterprise* is moving. They are leaving the potential radius of destruction."

"Not only have they disarmed it, they know exactly what we intended. That also means that the *elt* has either been killed or captured." He hesitated. "We have one final choice. Contact engineering and tell them to arm the engines to self-destruct."

"We are going to try and ram, *Bhar*?" the communications officer asked questioningly. The first officer was too depressed to frame his reply in contempt.

Instead, he simply repeated what was already known. "They could lose us or destroy us on a whim. But if the *elt* has been killed, or performed *Vyun-pa-shan*, we still have a chance to preserve Orion's neutrality. To prove such a serious accusation they will need more proof than mere tapes can provide. We can at least deny them that."

"Open hailing frequency, Lieutenant," Kirk ordered as he emerged onto the bridge. He took up his position at the command chair while Scott moved to engineering.

The Orion captain was positioned behind the chair where he could see the screen clearly over Kirk—and where he would be in clear range of the screen pickup. Kirk started to sit, noticed a subtle movement out of the corner of his eye. The Orion was moving his arm and hand upward, toward his mouth.

"Stop him."

Both guards reacted instinctively. Each grabbed one of the alien's arms, forced them up and back.

Kirk turned to eye the other closely. The Orion stared stonily at a point beyond Kirk's forehead.

"What are you doing?"

The Orion tried to sound bored. "My cheek itched, Captain. Does it startle you that I might try to scratch it? If you'll direct these idiots to let me go . . ."

"In a minute," Kirk answered absently. He looked downward, then knelt to pick up a small dark capsule. It was unmarked. He waved it under the other's mouth.

"Do I have to ask what this contains?"

Silence again.

"It *is* poison, isn't it?"

Still no reply. Kirk sighed, resumed his seat and dropped the deadly capsule into the chair-arm disposal unit.

"Commander," he said, carefully considering his words as he lectured the alien, "I'm sure your ship is preparing to destroy itself. Everything you've tried and said so far points to it as the logical course of action.

"If it does, your entire crew will have died for nothing. Because we're not going to let *you* commit suicide. Whether they live or die, you'll still stand trial. I'm sure both Federation officials and the representatives of other governments will be very interested in the results of the mind scans. I suspect it won't take very many to put a permanent end to Orion's little game of neutral piracy.

"Any reaction, Uhura?"

"I've finally raised them, sir."

Kirk nodded, peered back at his alien counterpart. The expression on that worthy's face was unreadable. Quite possibly it reflected similar emotions to those Kirk felt as he stared upward—hate, and respect.

To some races death meant little. Kirk didn't think it applied to the Orions. This man had meticulously planned his own destruction for the good of his people. Regardless of racial motivation, the key ingredient was still guts. Kirk had to admire them for that.

"They're acknowledging aural exchange only, Captain," Uhura reported.

"That'll do for now, Lieutenant." He spoke into the pickup. "This is Captain Kirk speaking to the acting commander of the Orion vessel. We hold your commanding officer prisoner." He glanced back at the man in question, then continued.

"He is in excellent health and perfectly capable of communication—voluntary or otherwise. Rest assured he'll remain so." He stopped, spoke more softly to the silent figure behind him.

"Your choice again, sir."

The Orion captain made a resigned gesture with his head. Obviously he had already made up his mind. It confirmed Kirk's belief in the Orion's essential respect for life. He nodded to the security guards.

Both men let the alien go, but continued to watch him closely. Kirk leaned to one side and allowed the other a clear shot at the pickup.

"*Bhar* Cophot?"

Instantly visual contact was established, and Kirk saw the uncertain face of the Orion ship's executive officer staring anxiously back at him.

"*Elt*? Your orders?"

"Disarm the self-destruct system." Kirk noticed he didn't bother to ask if it had been engaged. The exec looked reluctant. "And prepare for formal surrender."

"Very well, *Elt*. Cophot out." The screen went dark—but not before the two aliens had exchanged a complex salute.

Something else impressed Kirk. Despite ample evidence of intricate preparation for self-immolation, both mental and physical, the first officer of the Orion pirate hadn't objected to the surrender order, hadn't argued, hadn't protested.

Having been presented with an unavoidable situation and having exhausted all preferable options, in the end they had elected to do that which would preserve life—much to Kirk's relief. There was hope for the Orions, it appeared.

Their moral foundation was sound—only the edifice itself was rotten. Once a few reforms had been introduced into their presently one-sided view of interstellar economics, they might prove to be good friends.

Kirk dictated the log entry as he strolled back toward Sick Bay. It was the kind of entry he enjoyed making.

"Captain's log, stardate 5527.4. The Orion privateer crew is in protective custody and their ship in tow. The *Enterprise* is back on course for Deneb Five. We—"

No . . . no. He ended the entry. There were a host of details he could have added—but to what end? This was one entry that had intruded on an already hectic routine mission. A good place for brevity.

Their appearance at Deneb Five with an Orion vessel in tow would cause enough excitement. And Kirk had little use for fancy entrances. He much preferred a safe exit.

But it would eventually be good for the ship (the ship, the ship—always the ship). The fact that solving an unknown number of disappearances might gain him a promotion never crossed his mind—merely that it might enable them to get a few requisitions filled rather more quickly than Starfleet's sluggish bureaucracy usually managed.

The rewards of heroism, he mused as he turned a corner. Out of such odd things as the illness of one man do great things come.

Orion neutrality would be shown to be as solid as a shoji. The Klingons and Romulans would lose a potentially mischievous ally. And an enormous quadrant of uncertainty on the Federation's fringe would now be opened as safe for shipping, enabling escort vessels and personnel to be shifted to other tasks.

All because of a drug. He wondered how many times in the past the history of whole nations could have been altered by the presence of an aspirin at the right place and time.

He heard the voices even before he entered Sick Bay. Glancing left as he entered, he saw Spock sitting up in bed and looking Vulcan for the first time since they had left Argo. Not atypically, he and the ship's chief medical officer were engaged in a raucous difference of opinion.

"There's no way you can deny it, Spock!" McCoy was shouting.

"I can deny it," Spock countered patiently, "by pointing out . . ."

McCoy cut him off, rambled—or rather rumbled, on. Sometimes Kirk wondered if they ever argued in complete sentences.

"I've waited a long time for this," McCoy was proclaiming loudly, as Kirk walked up to them, "and you're not going to cheat me out of it."

"Out of what?" Kirk inquired politely. Both Spock and McCoy temporarily turned their attention to him.

"Nothing, Captain. Dr. McCoy is endeavoring to gloat—a reprehensible condition characteristic of his unpredictable prehistoric leanings."

"Spock, that special blood of yours may have saved you a dozen times on other occasions, but this time it almost did you in. You can't deny it, now.'' The first officer leaned back in the bed and folded his arms.

"On the contrary, Doctor, I still have ample grounds for preferring my physiological structure to yours. As far as psychological structures are concerned, there is of course incontrovertibly no contest.''

"I see, gentlemen,'' Kirk broke in, unable to suppress a smile, ''that things are back to normal.''

McCoy scowled. ''Uh-huh—he's as stubborn as ever, Jim.''

"Rational, Doctor,'' Spock corrected easily.

"Insane, Jim,'' McCoy shot back.

Sometimes I wonder if anyone on this ship is operating with undamaged circuitry, Kirk mused.

"I am surprised that you raise the question of sanity, Doctor,'' Spock went on, ''as . . .''

Kirk gave up and walked away. He had had several questions he had wanted to put to Spock. Clearly they would have to wait until McCoy's peculiar brand of rehabilitation therapy concluded.

Meanwhile, at least he had the satisfaction of knowing that both patient and doctor were doing well, thank you. . . .

PART III

JIHAD

(Adapted from a script by Stephen Kandel)

IX

As things turned out, it was fortunate Spock's recovery was rapid. "Things" came in the form of a Class-A Security Prime Order—a classification so strict that Kirk was required to unscramble it himself, using a locked computer annex, in the sanctuary of his own cabin.

The instructions revealed by decoding were brief, even curt. They generated feelings of both puzzlement and anticipation in Kirk.

Something of both must have shown in his face as he handed Lieutenant Arex the slip of paper.

"Set course for arrival at these coordinates, Lieutenant."

"Very good, sir." The Edoan navigator took the slip, examined the figures inscribed thereon and commenced transferring them into the navigational computer. Only after he had completed the assigned task did he allow himself a moment of personal reflection.

When he eventually spoke, his statement was both fact and query.

"Captain, the indicated coordinates have been programed. We are proceeding toward them at standard cruising speed."

"Thank you, Mr. Arex." The navigator continued to eye him. "Was there something else?"

"Captain, I do not possess a perfect memory. However, there was something about our intended destination which prodded at me. Upon concluding programing, I checked out my supposition and found it confirmed.

"There is nothing of planetary size in the region we are headed for—much less at the specified coordinates."

If he expected Kirk to make a counterclaim or supply some

new information, he was disappointed. "You're quite right, Mr. Arex. That quadrant's as empty as a spatial equator."

"A rendezvous, then, with another ship?" the navigator asked hopefully.

"At this point I'm not permitted to say, Lieutenant. Although," and his voice dropped to a faint whisper which Arex could barely pick up, "you might say something like that."

Arex turned back to his console, more confused than before. It might have consoled him to know that Kirk was equally puzzled. Fearful of having made a mistake in unscrambling, he'd gone through the decoding process three times. Three times he received the same reply from the bowels of the computer.

And each time the answer was just as enigmatic as before.

Ordinarily he would have requested clarification of orders so extreme from Starfleet. But Class-A Prime—these orders were not to be questioned, only obeyed. Such orders emanated only from the highest echelons of Starfleet HQ. Something critical was up.

And yet, if it was so vital, why did the orders specify they proceed at normal cruising speed? And what were they expected to rendezvous with? Clearly, secrecy took precedent over execution in this.

There was nothing cryptic about the instructions themselves—only the rationale behind them. They stated simply that the *Enterprise* was to proceed to such and such coordinates, whereupon they would meet something/someone at whose disposal they were to place themselves.

That was all. No additional details or instructions.

It wasn't like Starfleet to supply such sketchy information to back an important order. So much hush-hush suggested something else.

"Someone is badly frightened," Spock agreed. McCoy had finally released him from Sick Bay, to the great relief of both. But he could shed no further light on the orders.

"There are no facts on which to speculate, Captain."

"Well then, Spock, we'll just have to wait until someone supplies us with some."

There were surprises from the moment they neared the rendezvous coordinates, days later. An awful lot of people seemed to know about what purported to be an ultra-secret enterprise.

"I have *multiple* contact, sir," Sulu had reported, "at the coordinates—with something big at the center."

Hours passed. "Put what you can on the screen, Mr. Sulu."

The visual which resulted was revealing indeed. Numerous spacecraft were grouped loosely around the rendezvous point. They were as curious a collection of interstellar travelers as Kirk had seen in a long time.

At least half a dozen civilizations were represented here, possibly more. All were arranged—one couldn't quite say orbiting—around a huge green-and-silver ball. It radiated with the brightness of artificial atmospheric lighting. Against the total blackness of deep space and in the absence of a sun, it seemed to pulse gently.

Too small to be a planet, too small to be even a rogue moon. Too big to be a spacecraft.

In point of fact, it was all three.

Spock's gaze was riveted to the main viewscreen with an intensity rarely seen. "A Vedalan asteroid," he murmured. "I have never seen one before outside of bad pictures and worse sketches."

"Nor have I, Spock," admitted Kirk, likewise awed.

"Well I've never even heard of them, or it, or whatever you're talking about," Uhura broke in. "Somebody elucidate."

"The Vedala," Spock explained smoothly, "are the oldest space-traversing race known. They are so old that they long ago abandoned their worn-out home worlds to begin a nomadic life wandering among the stars.

"They travel at great speeds on large asteroids or small planetoids which have been remade to suit their environmental requirements. In addition to tremendous mobility, these tiny artificial worlds provide them with both personal and racial privacy—a quality they are known to value above all else.

"Yet for some reason, they now apparently require the presence of outsiders."

"And we're to place ourselves at their disposal," Kirk murmured, studying miniature mountain ranges, admiring the pocket oceans and manicured plains which studded the silver globe.

"Captain," reported Uhura, all business once more, "we're being scanned."

Kirk was reminded that the Vedala affected a pastoral veneer and took pains to avoid flaunting their technological knowhow.

What could they need the *Enterprise* for, then? Or these other ships, for that matter?

"Everybody sit tight," he ordered. Time passed as they drew nearer, then Uhura announced the replacement of the scanning signal with another.

"We're being hailed, Captain. No visual."

"Let's hear what we came to hear, Lieutenant." Uhura adjusted controls and an eerie, piping voice filled the bridge.

"Welcome, *Enterprise*. Welcome, Captain Kirk and First Officer Spock. We will expect you as soon as possible. Your coordinates for transporting down are . . ." and the voice ran off a series of figures which Uhura recorded, played through to the main transporter room.

"Please be kind enough to pardon the lack of visual welcome," the voice concluded, "but as you may know, we are extremely protective of our privacy. We regret any offense this may cause . . . but it is required."

"No offense taken," Kirk replied. "Coordinates received."

"Polite enigmas, aren't they?" Sulu commented.

Kirk was about to press further when an unobtrusive palm covered the armchair pickup.

"I think we had best meet politeness with politeness, Captain. Even asking the name of our greeter might be construed by the Vedala as an intrusion—even an offensive gesture."

"I think you're over-reacting, Spock, but . . . all right." Deductions would wait until they finally met their hosts. He rose from the chair.

"Mr. Scott, you're in charge until Mr. Spock and I return."

"Very well, sir. Uh, might I ask, when might that be?"

"No idea, Scotty," he said, moving toward the door. He looked back at a sudden thought. "Why, Scotty, the Vedala have a reputation for paranoid secretiveness, sure. But they're not belligerent. Surely you're not worried about *them* doing us harm?''

''Not the Vedala, Captain, no—though I kinna trust 'em as completely as you seem to.'' He indicated the assembled starships circling the Vedala homeship. ''But there're some ships out there that belong to folk who've been known to get nasty now and again. They could have representatives down there, too.''

''I don't think the Vedala would let anyone run amuck on their homeship, Scotty, but don't worry. Mr. Spock and I will keep our communications close at hand.''

''Dinna worry—that's one order I never can seem to obey, Captain,'' Scott murmured—but Kirk and Spock were already in the elevator.

''Any idea what the specified coordinates will put us down on, Mr. Kyle?'' Kirk asked the transporter chief.

''Something in the atmosphere seems to produce the daylight they receive on the surface, Captain,'' Kyle replied. ''It makes direct visual observation very difficult.''

''Consistent with what we know,'' Spock observed.

''*However*, the people down in cartography are fairly certain you'll be setting down on dry land, in a relatively level region.''

Kirk and Spock assumed positions in the alcove.

''If you'll just take a half-step to the left, sir,'' Kyle requested. Kirk did so. Kyle manipulated several instruments at once, put his hand on the main switch. ''Energizing, sir.''

They stood in a grassy glade encircled by tall, lushly leaved trees. A small stream wound merrily down the low slope just before them.

But the sky overhead was strange. Kirk thought he detected a reflection from something solid. They stood under a transparent dome that sealed them off from the rest of the homeship. He could see where it curved down in the distance to meet the surface—undoubtedly to seal them in and avoid contaminating any more of the home than was required by common courtesy.

Yet, they had transported straight through it. Kirk didn't feel too confident about the accomplishment. Little enough existed in the way of Vedalan artifacts, but it was known that they were outstanding chemists.

Something that resembled an explosive was just as likely to be a composite made from vegetable shortenings, while a soap bubble might prove impervious to the strongest phaser. Yet any deceptiveness on the part of the Vedala was unintentional—or had been till now. It remained to be discovered whether that record would remain unblemished.

They could have made a great contribution to Federation civilization—or any Galactic civilization, for that matter. All entreaties to join or participate, however, were met with the excuse of painful shyness by rarely contacted representatives of the race.

It was the Vedalan way of refusing without insulting.

Besides, what could anyone offer them they did not already have or could not obtain on their own terms? For example, the presence of the *Enterprise* and various other vessels to carry out some as yet unknown task? But that was only common sense.

When the Vedala found it needful to call for help, it was in the best interest of all to respond.

Kirk couldn't tell whether the being standing before them now was the one who had addressed them on their approach or another. The Vedala was a small, furry creature, utterly inoffensive looking. It reminded Kirk of the pictures he had seen of the extinct aye-aye of Terran tropical forests.

Kirk looked around, found he was standing before a grassy knoll that formed a crude but comfortable-looking seat. Either Kyle had been inhumanly precise in his calculations or the Vedala had somehow seen to it they set down where they were wanted.

For the moment, Kirk's attention was wholly drawn to the representative of the ages-old race standing in front of them.

The Vedala made a gesture. Kirk blinked, stared. The grass around them was no longer flat and empty. Now he saw several other grassy knolls arranged in a semi-circle around the Vedala. They were occupied, and their occupants were neither human nor Vedala.

"Welcome, Captain James Kirk and Commander Spock," the Vedala intoned solemnly, turning Kirk's attention away from the other knolls. The creature spoke with a soft feminine contralto, which was at once reassuring and forceful. There was nothing fragile about it, and its strength belied the appearance of the toylike being who produced it. There was the power of millennia behind it. Kirk paid attention.

"I will introduce you to the others," the Vedala continued. It gestured first to a far knoll on which a winged humanoid rested, leathery wings fluttering uneasily against the too-near earth. The creature stood over two and a half meters high. Kirk recognized it from tridee tapes, though he had never met a representative of the Skorr before.

"This is Tchar," the Vedala told them, "Hereditary Prince of the Skorr, master of the Eyrie."

It was a measure of the strength of Tchar's character that Kirk and Spock paid any attention to him at all, considering the mountain that snuffled and grunted next to him. This butte of intelligent protoplasm the Vedala identified as one Sord. The reptile snorted a greeting. He very much resembled the bipedal dinosaurs who had dominated a long-dead piece of Earth's chaotic past.

But the forehead here was high, the forelimbs ending in hands with opposable thumb and fingers, the intelligence self-evident. Nor was Sord from a world like Earth. His body was bulkier than would be needed there, muscles on muscles the sign of a heavy-planet dweller.

The Vedala went on to the third member of the group, and for a moment Kirk and Spock failed to notice it, their eyes adjusted to creatures the size of Sord.

In direct contrast to its massive neighbor, it sat shivering on its grassy chair, trying to withdraw into the loam. Before the Vedala could proceed it interrupted, its voice thin and breathless.

Multiple cilia in place of upper limbs rippled nervously, goggle eyes darted from side to side in perpetual search for avenue of escape. "I was sentenced to this mad expedition," the asthenic ambassador announced, "I don't like it here. It's too quiet. I don't like any of you—no offense intended— I just wish I were back home in my city burrow."

"City cell is the correct appellation, I believe," the Vedala finally managed to say. "Em-three-green—an expert picklock and thief of extraordinary though peculiar talents, when he is not too terrified to demonstrate them.

"Em-three-green's people are . . . ," the Vedala hesitated ever so slightly, ". . . of an extremely cautious bent."

"We're cowards, you mean," corrected Em-three-green, not defiantly, of course—that would have been utterly out of character. "And I," he finished almost proudly, "am the biggest coward of all. I want to go home."

"Oh, shut up. I'm sick of your belly-aching!" broke in a disgusted, very human-sounding voice from the ciliated safecracker's right. Em-three-green uttered a sharp whimper, tried to bury himself even deeper into the grass.

"This," the Vedala continued, indicating a young female humanoid, "is Lara." She was clad in a tight-fitting, multi-pocketed one-piece tunic that covered her from neck to ankle.

"Lara is a huntress from a people who are natural hunters. She also possesses a unique talent—a flawless sense of direction which is as real to her as sight or hearing are to you. A necessary skill for where you are going."

"I was about to bring that up myself," Kirk replied. "We're going someplace, then? I was instructed only to place myself and my ship under your direction. We were told nothing more . . . not even the fact that this expedition is to be multi-racial in makeup."

"Nor were any of these others," the Vedala informed him expansively. "This was done to preserve secrecy."

"You know as much now as we do," Lara added sharply. She looked toward the Vedala. "Who are these new ones?"

"Human and Vulcan," the Vedala informed her, with distressing matter-of-factness. "Mr. Spock was chosen for his analytical ability and overall scientific expertise. Captain Kirk, for his qualities of leadership and initiative, and a remarkably high survival quotient.

"There is, as you others know, one among you who knew by necessity the reason for bringing you here and the purpose to which your diverse abilities shall be put. Tchar will explain the mission, Captain Kirk, as he has to the others."

The Skorr rose, wings fluttering more violently. The words came out in a steady stream, in short, clipped phrases underlaid with controlled fury.

"Two or three centuries ago, humans, my people the Skorr were purely a warrior race. Our entire racial energies were bent to achieving one goal—a perfected militaristic society. This drive, coupled with our ability to reproduce rapidly, soon made us a threatening force in our sector of the galaxy.

"Today, we are a civilized people. Though we retain our military traditions and potential, we no longer live for war and destruction. All this has come about because of . . . ," and he traced an abstract design in the air, his voice turning reverent, ". . . Alar."

"I know the name," Kirk recalled, nodding thoughtfully. "A religious leader with a reputation that extends beyond the Skorr."

"Our salvation and teacher," Tchar intoned solemnly. "He brought peace to us by showing how we might reconcile our violent desires with civilization, how we could direct our energies into constructive paths. He brought realization to the Skorr." Again he performed the peculiar, vaguely figure-eightish gesture.

"The complete brain patterns of this Alar," the Vedala explained, "were recorded by his apostles before his death and sealed in a flawless piece of sculpted indurite."

"And it has been stolen!" Tchar shrilled, wings flaring upward in anger. "Our soul, the soul of the Skorr peoples, has been taken from us!"

"To an outsider," the Vedala continued, "the effect of this theft on the Skorr verges on the inexplicable. The reaction has been extreme, violent, and uncontrolled. Thus, what this Alar was able to achieve in so short a time seems all the more remarkable.

"The Skorr have always been . . . ," the Vedala coughed delicately, "a paranoid race. Hence the havoc the disappearance of the *soul* has wrought among them. Exertions by others, most notably by the Vedala, for moderation in reaction have been ignored by the Skorr, whose latent belligerence has waited only for a cause to rise again to the fore. They now have that cause—though they would deny any desire to return to their ancient ways.

"Denials avail nought against the storm the theft has raised among them. Despite the fact that neither the thief nor the reason for the theft are known, the Skorr are preparing for war."

"But if the thief isn't known," Kirk objected, "who do they prepare against?"

"Since no Skorr could even conceive such blasphemy," Tchar informed him bitterly, "the abomination was clearly carried out by non-Skorr. That is whom my people prepare against. They will go to war with the rest of the known Galaxy and fight until they are no longer able to make war—or until there are none left to make war against. Unless—the soul is returned."

Shocked silence—eventually punctuated by a series of basso whoops from the bulky Sord. Lara the huntress smiled.

Kirk started to smile, too, until he noticed that not only wasn't Spock amused, he appeared unusually grim. He considered. The Vedala had made no move to counter what sounded on the surface like an outrageous claim—therefore, perhaps it might not be quite so outrageous.

After all, what *did* they know about the Skorr, whose numerous worlds lay dozens of parsecs from the nearest Federation planet?

"It is a very real danger," Spock murmured. "Extrapolating from the most recently obtained figures, the existing Skorr population could breed an army of two hundred billion within a few years, with weapons technology to match. In the Skorr, fertility is tied to the aggressive instinct. The more anger generated, the more the population swells.

"According to the information supplied by Tchar and the Vedala, the Skorr now have the incentive to breed exponentially."

"But to fight the entire Galaxy—surely they couldn't win," the incredulous Lara objected.

"No, but what has that to do with it?" Tchar countered sadly. "You still fail to comprehend the mental state into which my people have been driven. Death now means nothing. Revenge, assuaging their anger—that has become all.

"No, my people could not win such a war, but what would that mean to the millions who would die, Skorr and non-Skorr? Fortunately, there are those among us who can still control their anger enough to realize what a jihad would mean to the Galaxy. But they can restrain the fury only so long, before they too are drowned in it and carried along by the madness.

"We *must* recover the soul before these final bastions of reason crumble!"

Kirk turned to the silent Vedala. "And there's no hint of who stole the soul?"

"None," the Vedala replied.

"It is hard to understand," Tchar told them. "What other race stands to profit from such a cataclysm? Yet to provoke such seems the only possible motive for the theft. Unless, of course, it was carried out by the mad."

"Insanity," the Vedala observed, "is possessed of and by its own motivations. The keys to unraveling such convoluted reasoning are merely less obvious. We have not been able to discover them."

The Vedala made its equivalent of a shrug.

"Someone, somewhere, may be furious beyond reason— at what, no one knows. Or the theft may be part of a grandiose suicide wish. None of this concerns us in the least. What does concern us very much is that such a war may hinder the free movement of the Vedala through space. Hence, we are involved."

"The Vedala," Kirk shot back, "are known to possess certain technological abilities beyond the combined talents of our Federation and other governments. Why don't you—"

The Vedala held up a restraining hand. "We prefer not to interfere directly. Also, there are indications that, were we to do so, whoever has stolen the soul would take steps to destroy it. We can direct, however, and suggest."

"All right," Kirk agreed. "If you can't take part openly, and you've no idea who engineered the theft, do you have any hints to the present location of the soul?"

Turning, the Vedala struck at empty air. At least, it looked empty. Whether the gesture somehow activated some invisible switch, Kirk couldn't tell. The Vedala were known to encourage confusion in others. It was a matter of protective coloration: what cannot be comprehended is difficult to coerce.

Whatever the method, the gesture resulted in the appearance of a large holographic projection. It drifted in mid-air in the center of the semicircle, just behind the Vedala. And as they watched, it moved and changed.

A star in space was all that was shown, at first. Then the star grew nearer, larger. Three planets were shown circling around it. Again they were drawn into the projection, which drew near to the middle world.

"The mad world," the Vedala announced, for the first time something like fear appearing amid that invulnerable calm. "See how it all writhes?"

Now they were plunging headlong toward the surface, now wheeling up to run parallel to it in a long, steady scan. A scan that revealed roiling, heaving plateaus; violently unstable crust; volcanos erupting, to be promptly enclouded by multiple cyclones; mountains upthrusting. Vortices of strange glowing gases suddenly appeared in a seemingly normal atmosphere, only to dissipate in minutes. Hail was supplanted by a rain of fiery ash.

"The recording you are seeing," the Vedala said quietly, "is being rebroadcast at normal speed."

Kirk whistled, leaned over to whisper to Spock. "And I thought the Terratin world was bad!"

Spock nodded agreement. "There are indications that the planet in question may be somewhat unsuitable for habitation."

Kirk muffled a reply as the Vedala spoke again.

"Seismically unstable, with radical seismic activity and unpredictable tremors. A most inimical climate. Severe tidal disturbances caused by the unceasing action of five moons possessed of the most perverse orbits—the list is endless, beings. The globe is a compendium of catastrophes. The temperature varies from twenty degrees Kelvin to two oh four above."

The Vedala made another gesture, causing the projection to shrink in size without disappearing completely. Kirk looked around the semicircle, saw with relief that here was something everyone present could agree on. All showed attitudes of respect.

"Somewhere on that world," the Vedala went on, "the soul of Alar is hidden." Again that odd hesitation, that hint of a crack in the pose of racial perfection.

"Three expeditions have so far attempted to locate and recover it. Three expeditions have so far disappeared. More care than before has gone into choosing the members of the fourth—yourselves.

"*If* you consent to participate. We will force no one."

The alternative, of course—Kirk smiled to himself. That threat was enough to persuade any rational being to want to help.

"Naturally, Mr. Spock and I will go," he said.

The Vedala looked gratified, offered no thanks, then looked around at the others. Sord grunted as though it made no difference to him one way or the other. Em-three-green might have declined, but was too thoroughly terrified to do more than shiver violently on his grassy knoll.

Lara acknowledged with a sharp whistle, while Tchar's participation was apparently taken for granted.

"Seems we're agreed," Kirk observed.

"Then it is done," said the Vedala simply.

What happened then was in retrospect sufficiently impressive to outweigh any suspicion of obfuscatory technique. The Vedala began to glow, expanding, changing to a collage of misty particles.

At the same time the holograph enlarged. It swallowed the Vedala-mist, but didn't stop there. They were submerged in it. It flooded out the view of the garden around them. The sound of the little stream became a roar.

An unseen, unfelt torrent he could only hear washed over him and he felt himself falling, falling. Like being in a transporter operating somehow at a fifth normal speed—that was it.

Vision returned to him the same way, slowly, things coming into focus with painful patience. Globs of light and color gradually took on form and shape around him.

Minutes, and the globs had turned into rugged mountains, rain, vast glaciers filling narrow gorges, glowering storm clouds. The dull drone in his ears split into winds buffeting his body, the patter of raindrops on naked stone, and the violent hissing of volcanic ash and lava meeting an advancing river of ice. Kirk was stunned to see that the glacier advanced fast enough that the movement could actually be seen.

He turned slowly.

They had been set down on a broad, flat rock of immense size, utterly devoid of any growth whatsoever. Mountains towered on three sides. Bracing himself, Kirk leaned into the wind. Presumably this was the stablest place the Vedala could find to set them down at. Until he saw the cart, he wondered if the Vedala expected them to find and recover the soul with bare hands and intuition.

The crude-looking wheeled vehicle seemed hardly to represent the zenith of Vedalan technology. But closer study revealed it was designed with typical Vedala cunning. Most of its capabilities were concealed behind the awkward-looking exterior.

To fool any potential attackers, undoubtedly.

Kirk recognized the basic design of the compact drive system. It would drive the cart up anything other than a vertical face. The suspension system was of matching sophistication. Kirk hoped the on-board equipment had been prepared with equal thoughtfulness.

A shrill cry came down to him from above. Leaning back, he saw that Tchar was now in his element—whirling, diving, coming down finally to hover just above them.

"I cannot feel the soul!" he screamed angrily. "It is nowhere near. We have been tricked!"

"I think not," Spock disagreed, raising his voice only enough to rise above the smothering susurration of the wind. "Consider that the surface of this planet is in constant flux. The Vedala warned us of this. I would guess they have provided us with some means of determining the proper direction."

Kirk had already mounted the cart and was examining the protected instruments. There were plenty, and it took him time to sort out the various controls. They had been designed for use by creatures with all kinds of different manipulative members. But the drive controls were not what finally drew a smile from him, but rather the very instrumentation Spock had suggested they would find.

Kirk became aware of motion beside him, saw that Em-three-green stood there, staring under his arm. Finding himself detected, the little alien hastily moved away on the pretext of studying other controls. Apparently he found any close scrutiny threatening.

Kirk moved to the railing, saw that Sord and Lara had joined the argument.

"All right, save your breath, friends. There's directional equipment on board and it's already tuned. Guess what it's been tuned to?"

"Refined indurite," Spock said without hesitation.

"Exactly."

"Then why not tell us that before, instead of riskin' anything like dissension?" Lara wondered.

"The Vedala," Kirk explained, "probably don't want to take any chance on our starting out overconfident. Putting us down here mentally naked was putting us down alert."

"Small worry of overconfidence," Em-three-green grumbled from behind him. "I can operate this machine, Captain Kirk."

"That's all right, Em," Kirk told him. "I'll manage it."

"No, let me, Captain," the little safecracker protested, with a rare show of determination. "I will feel useful, we will get where we are going faster, and," he added softly, "it will help keep my mind off this spine-lined burrow of a world."

Kirk nodded, watched as Em-three-green clambered into the control seat and touched controls with deft assurance. Instantly, a smooth rumble sounded beneath them, rose to a roar of power before settling down to a steady hum.

Spock climbed aboard, moved to examine the directional instrumentation. Kirk bent to give Lara a hand up. Grinning, she made a startling leap, grabbed the railing with both hands and pulled herself up.

That left only Sord. Kirk eyed him uncertainly and was rewarded by a bellowing laugh.

"There's room for you in the back, Sord."

"No," he boomed, "you little ones ride if you wish." The shovel-like head moved like a crane to take in the landscape. "I like this place—it's got variety. And I would crowd you."

Kirk studied the glacier, fascinated. Now it appeared to be retreating visibly.

"Captain," Spock called.

Kirk walked over, his attention going immediately to the small glowing screen the first officer was working with. A grid lay over the lit rectangle, beneath which a web of flexible lines weaved and pulsed. Abruptly they shrunk to a single, pulsing dot.

"It would seem our direction is clearly indicated," Spock observed.

Even as he spoke, the carefully aligned grid suddenly shifted, the dot expanding into a loose maze of questing lines racing crazily across the screen. A red glow began to suffuse the clear plexalloy.

"The position is shifting," Spock commented, "I think . . ."

Em-three-green leaned over from the pilot's chair. When he got a look at the screen, his already wide eyes bulged enormously.

"Shifting—the control elements are unphasing!" As the solid lines of the grid began to break up, Em screamed and jumped out of the chair to dive behind the metallic bulk of the engine.

A whistling sound began, rose rapidly in volume. Small wisps of smoke appeared from behind the screen's upper corners. The whistle began to pulse alarmingly.

Spock glanced at Kirk, whereupon both men dropped to the deck. Thus they were missed by the flying shards of acrylic and metal which screamed by overhead as the screen blew up.

Getting to their feet slowly, they grimly eyed the smoking, sparking ruin that had been their one hope for tracking down the soul. "What did the Vedala call it?" Kirk muttered tightly. "The mad planet?" He gestured disgustedly at the ruined instrumentation.

"How do you explain that, Spock?"

"A confluence of unbenign electronic forces," the first officer responded slowly.

"In other words, you don't know?"

"Precisely," Spock confessed.

"Doesn't matter."

Kirk turned, stared at Lara. She grinned.

"I know the way," she said. "I got a good look at that thing before it went mockers." She turned, cocked her head slightly without losing the grin and nodded in a direction slightly to the southwest. Her voice was matter-of-fact, confident. "That way."

A querulous inquiry drifted down from above: "Are you certain, human?" questioned a hovering Tchar.

"For sureness, birdman," Lara threw back. "I can't be fooled about directions and I can't get lost. That's why I'm here." She pointed again, downslope and out of the mountains. "It's that way, or I'll eat my killboots."

"The Vedala would not have chosen Lara had her abilities been less than perfect," Spock commented.

"So then," Kirk observed, "we know which way we're supposed to go—but we're meant to travel on the ground. An overview could be very helpful." He glanced upward significantly.

Tchar's wings spread wide and he beat downward to gain altitude. "I will scout ahead," he replied simply. Beginning a wide circle that brought him into the updrafts sweeping up the granite flanks close by, he soared effortlessly higher.

Spock studied his progress for a long moment, then looked idly over at Kirk. "I will acquaint myself with our supplies." He moved toward the rear of the cart and the metal cabinets bolted to the deck there.

Lara watched him go, moved a step nearer Kirk. "Vulcans," she muttered. "Never liked 'em much myself. Cold-blooded critters, every one of 'em. Not an ounce of real feelin' in the whole pack."

"I wouldn't be quite so harsh," Kirk objected. "Especially on Mr. Spock. He's something of a unique personality."

"But not human, like you and me," she said huskily, eyeing him boldly.

Kirk said nothing, stared back in disapproval. She wasn't intimidated.

"Look, maybe you got different customs where you come from, Captain. My world, there's a lot of women, not so many men. When we find a man attractive, we say so." If anything, her gaze grew even less inhibited. "I'm sayin' so. How do you find me?"

"Fascinating and not a little overwhelming," he replied, responding to the frontal assault with complete honesty. "The only problem is, we're not here on a pleasure trip."

"All the more reason to take whatever pleasure there might

be in it." She laughed, brushed teasingly close and walked to stand at the front of the cart.

Kirk studied her progress, the supple form and smooth stride. A host of alternating images melted together in his mind to form a single, highly confusing whole.

The muted hum rose in volume as Em-three-green got the cart moving. It lurched down the gentle slope in the direction Lara had indicated. Sord loped along just ahead, his movements cumbersome, awkward—irresistible.

"I've checked out the supplies, Captain."

"Hmmm—what?" Kirk mumbled absently.

"The supplies, Captain, I have completed an inventory," Spock repeated, slightly more forcefully. Kirk finally turned his attention to his first officer. Spock made a show of clearing his throat, continued.

"As expected, the life-support material is more than adequate. There are specific provisions for Sord, Tchar, and Em-three-green. And—there are weapons."

"Against what would we need weapons?" Kirk mused. "I thought the only hostility we were expected to encounter arose out of the planet itself? There's not supposed to be any native life here—unless the Vedala plan another surprise for us."

"I would not rule out anything at this stage, Captain. Judging from the Vedala's outspoken aversion to this world, it would not surprise me to discover that their preliminary survey of it was less than all-inclusive. We have the evidence of three previously unsuccessful expeditions to back this." He scanned the overcast, threatening landscape pessimistically.

"Nor are they, by their own admission, omnipotent. We must rely on our own abilities, I think. Overmuch reliance on Vedalan intervention may have doomed our predecessors here." He nodded toward the horizon.

"To steal something like the soul of Alar and then depend wholly on mechanicals to safeguard it strikes me as unworthy of any beings capable of devising such a theft in the first place. Also illogical. I suspect that before we regain possession of the soul, we may have to deal with those immoral beings personally."

Kirk murmured agreement and turned to contemplate the

terrain ahead. Spock had only recited the obvious, yet it seemed as if the pulverized stone that crunched steadily beneath the wheels of the cart now whispered imperceptible threats at every turn of an axle, and unknown forms of extinction paced them while staying just out of sight.

In all this world, he sensed not a hint of welcome. He would be glad when they left it.

Or if . . .

X

Eventually the slope leveled out and the mountains sank beneath the horizon behind. Gravel and rock gave way to a broad, flat, desertlike plain of sand and fine, soft stone. Only scattered monoliths of black basalt broke the gently rolling plateau, volcanic plugs—the mummified hearts of long-eroded fire-spitters. Fortunately the cloud-laden sky cut much of the daytime heat, or they would have been broiled quite thoroughly. In fact, a brisk breeze had sprung up and now blew coolingly in their faces.

A short, violent chuff brought them to a halt. Sord snorted again and pointed ahead with a finger the size of a man's thigh.

"Now what could that be?" Everyone stared into the distance.

Moving in their direction was what looked like a solid curtain of dark gray. The breeze freshened and beat at them with increasing intensity. Kirk glanced questioningly at their furry driver.

"Em, is there a top to this thing?"

"I don't know," the little alien replied fearfully. He started hunting among as yet unused controls.

"I think so . . . no, that's not it . . . nor that . . ." The gray wall had moved nearer and was now charging down upon them.

"If there is, you'd better find it fast," Kirk warned. He yelled ahead. "I hope when you said you liked variety, you mean a broad definition of the word, Sord." The huge reptile did not reply. He was staring at the approaching wall.

The deluge reached them moments later, a rain of seeming solid intensity. Kirk had experienced a downpour like this

366

only once before, on a deceptive world in the Taurean system. He and Spock had been in the jug there, too.

Em-three-green finally unraveled the mystery sequence involved and got the translucent canopy up, just before they would have been washed away.

Lara wrung water from her hair, smiled radiantly beneath the damp strands. "*Real* weather."

"And a half," Kirk agreed readily, looking out through one of the clear ports. "You'd almost think—"

Before he could finish the thought, the rain stopped—as abruptly as a curse, to be replaced by a blaze of sunlight. Clouds began to form immediately, but under the attack of the sudden inferno, broad shallow lakes disappeared before their eyes, hissing, all but boiling off the sand.

Where vision had been obscured seconds earlier by a solid wall of water, now the landscape shivered and rippled under agonizing heat. Distortion waves added ridges and hills to the desert where none existed. And the distortions were suddenly multiplied as a faint quake shook the cart.

"We'll all die here!" Em-three-green wailed as he put down the canopy. Every one of his many cilia were locked to a control or structural segment of the cart.

"A statistical probability," was Spock's uninspiring comment. Lara eyed him disgustedly.

"Don't you ever act on anything besides your precious statistics, Vulcan?"

"Yes, but philosophy does not appear to be an adequate vehicle on which to base a course of action here," he replied unperturbed. "Nor do I find reliance on instinct satisfactory, as you seem to."

"Oh well," she shrugged, "to each his own."

Further discussion was interrupted by a shrill keening from above. A faint spot appeared, resolved into a slim, limber body centered between a pair of batwings—Tchar. Kirk wondered for a second how the birdman had survived the fury of the momentary monsoon, then realized he must have climbed above it.

"I can see something far ahead," he shouted down to them, "it's . . . ," and his last words faded into inaudibility as he banked and glided down to land atop the next rise.

Em-three-green swung the cart neatly against the base of

the low hill Tchar had perched on. It was a short climb for the rest of them.

The object which had excited Tchar's concern was far enough away to be little more than a hazy outline. It was impressive nonetheless.

A simple cube of some black material, the structure sat utterly alone at the bottom of the vast sink. A sense of its enormity penetrated all the way to the valley's rim—though Kirk couldn't be certain just how large it was. The object was still too far away to judge accurately.

It also, he noted, lay exactly along the line Lara had indicated.

Tchar was fluttering, hopping about on the sand nervously. "I sense it, I can feel it—the soul of Alar is down there!"

A gigantic rumble shook the earth behind them, and the ground shivered in pain. Lara whirled, shouted something in shock that was drowned by Em-three-green's screams and Sord's locomotive whistle.

With absolutely no warning, a fountain of black ash and smoke had exploded from the ground. Like a film running at thrice normal speed, the crevice widened, expanded: then a half-formed volcano erupted skyward. In seconds, it was a hundred meters high and growing with incredible speed.

A crack appeared in the southwest cliff of the cinder cone. A stream, then a river of syrupy red-orange lava poured from the flank eruption. It rushed toward them like a wave of red-hot sand. The pressure below, Kirk knew, must have been enormous to produce such a voluminous flow in so short a time.

They hardly had enough time to realize how precarious their present position was. They sat on a slight rise, but one that was still well below the level of the cinder cone. It would wash this tiny summit clean before the flow subsided.

"It seems that everything happens with remarkable speed on this world," Spock observed. "We may expect volcanic action at any time."

"I can see that, Mr. Spock. Question is, how do we go on remaining observers?"

"The Vedala made you the nominal leader here, Kirk," Lara admonished him. "*You* think of a way out."

"We have several minutes before the flow reaches us," Spock commented easily. "Plenty of time."

Not enough, it seemed, for Em-three-green. Whether it was the molten death racing toward them or Spock's seeming indifference toward it no one knew, but the little alien let out a pitiful screech and dashed down the slope to cower between the huge wheels of the cart.

Lara eyed Spock as if he were personally responsible for the approaching disaster, then she loped down to try and comfort Em. Sord huffed once, sat down on the sand and engaged in some steady nonverbalization of his own.

"I must point out, Captain," Spock went on, "that the vehicle we have been provided with lacks sufficient speed to escape so rapid a flow." He peered into the distance. "I also estimate that the flow is too wide for us to outflank."

"Not entirely true, Spock. We can still outrun it—if we let the engine draw maximum, unhindered power. I know this type. There's enough energy there to run circles around that flow."

"One high speed might be possible," Spock conceded. "But the power leads must be rerun, certain safeguards removed, emergency insulation installed. The total readjustment is complex and time consuming."

"Can't you handle it, Spock?" The first officer hesitated, finally shook his head.

"I know what is involved, Captain, but I have not the skill to perform so complex and complete an operation in so short a—"

"Excuse me for interrupting." They both turned, looked down to see the still shaking form of Em-three-green staring up at them. "I have some skill at digital manipulation. I can do it in time, I think, if," he gazed evenly at Spock, "you can direct me as fast as I can work, sir."

"Still not enough time," Spock insisted.

"We might be able to divert the lava flow temporarily, Spock," Kirk suggested. They had started down toward the cart. Em-three-green was already laying out the tools he would require. He glanced back over his shoulder. "Tchar, see if there's a suitable place."

The Skorr shrilled acknowledgment and launched himself into the pumice-darkened sky.

"Such a diversion would be at best of short duration, Captain, unless the flow of molten rock lessens significantly. It shows no sign of doing so."

"You worry about reprograming the cart engine, Spock, and let me worry about the lava."

They stared at each other a long moment, then Spock nodded. "Quickly then," he yelled to Em-three-green. Kirk noticed that he didn't bother to question the alien's abilities. Em-three-green had better be able to do what he claimed, and that was all there was to it.

Spock had the protective panel over the engine housing off in seconds. A moment sufficed to satisfy him as to its contents.

"This is Federation equipment," he told the tool-laden Em-three-green, "can you . . . ?"

"Anything anyone put together I can take apart," the little alien piped firmly. "We're wasting time."

Spock simply nodded, began: "Terminal M-three red leads to diode channel twenty-seven, cross-connects to CCa-fourteen . . . taking care not to break the fluid-state sealed component Three-R . . ."

Em-three-green's cilia were a blur. Spock experimentally stepped up the pace and the little alien kept pace easily, rearranging and realigning the critical instrumentation as fast as Spock could recite instructions.

Spock was willing to concede as how they now had an outside chance at survival—but still outside!

"Captain Kirk!" Kirk looked upward, away from the work in progress on the cart, to see Tchar hovering overhead.

"There is a ravine," the flyer shouted, "sixty meters to your left." Kirk stared in the indicated direction and spotted the slight break in the ridge between them and the volcano, which roared on unabated.

"I see it."

"If it can be blocked," Tchar said, even as Kirk came to the same conclusion, "the lava will flow past and have to top the ridge to reach us. It will save some time."

"Good enough." He turned. "Sord?"

"I heard him," the organic mountain grumbled. Elephantine legs working smoothly, he lifted himself from the sand and lumbered off toward the ravine. Kirk and Lara followed as fast as they could, Lara politely slowing to keep pace with the slower Kirk.

"Carefully, Em-three-green," Spock warned, perceiving what he thought to be a just-missed movement on the part of the alien that would have caused a fatal short. One improper connection, one mixing of super-cooled fluids, one wrong touch of an instrument on a live component, and the cart could go up in pieces—along with its present pair of occupants.

"I know, I know," Em-three-green muttered softly. "I'm trying to be as careful as possible at this speed. Please try not to make me nervous."

Spock returned to the dull, steady drone of instructions. He forebore to mention that Em-three-green's impossibly rapid, seemingly haphazard style of making the most delicate adjustments was making him not a little uneasy himself.

Sord was containing his impatience with difficulty by the time Lara and a wheezing, puffing Kirk finally arrived at the far end of the ravine.

Lara didn't bother to rest; instead she scrambled spiderlike up a sheer cliff. She looked toward the volcano, then back down at them and made hurrying gestures.

Kirk took out his phaser. Adjusting it for tight-beam, high-intensity work, he began slicing huge chunks of rock from the opposing cliff face. He was cutting at another piece before the first gigantic slab of sandstone crashed to the ground.

Sord put his sternum against the boulder, slipped both hands around and under, and shoved. By the time Kirk had another block cut from the ravine wall, the huge reptile had the first one set in place.

Cut and place, place and cut, while Lara shouted constantly at them to hurry.

The mouth of the arroyo was finally sealed, faster than Kirk would have believed possible. He hadn't counted on Sord's incredible strength and endurance. They still had some time, so he busied himself cutting smaller fragments. Sord used them to chink small gaps in the main boulders.

They stopped only when Lara's anxious cry of "Here it comes, get out!" reached them.

As Kirk turned and ran, he could hear the nearing hiss

from the lava as it sizzled over the sand. He glanced backward, like Lot's wife—and fell.

A moment later the sand was rushing past beneath him. Sord had scooped him up and was carrying him easily in both hands. Behind them the hiss rose to a furious, tense, spitting sound. Sord reached the end of the ravine and felt confident enough to turn and stare.

Jets of molten stone squirted between the uncaulked chinks in the makeshift dam. The topmost boulder seemed to quiver a little at the impact and slide backward slightly. But it didn't fall.

Lara pulled up next to them, panting from the run. She looked from Kirk back to the dam.

"Workin' real nice. For a minute there I wasn't sure it was goin' to hold. The flow's spreading sideways now, though. The lava in the cracks is cooling fast, cementing the whole job."

"How soon before the flow reaches the ridge-top?" he asked.

"Soon enough—but it doesn't matter. I've got our escape route."

"It better be a direct one." He gestured back toward the dam. Sparks were already dancing above it. They had a few extra minutes at most before the lava reached it and flowed down toward them once more.

A shout behind them. They turned in time to see the huge cart send up a shower of sand as Em-three-green swung it to a stop.

"The drive has been reprogramed—expertly," Spock announced. "Quickly, Captain. I do not know how long it will last."

They raced for the ladder as Tchar swooped low, spiraled overhead. Kirk hustled aboard, with Lara right behind. A rumbling query sounded behind him.

"Captain, I'm afraid that while I'm near to being invulnerable, I am not immune to the effects of molten rock. I fear I must crowd you temporarily."

"Get aboard, Sord," Kirk told him. "We'll manage." He and Lara moved to the front of the cart. Spock joined them there, leaving only Em-three-green near the back, at the drive controls.

Moving as quickly as possible but with infinite care, the great reptile struggled onto the rear of the cart. Even so, he nearly overturned it in the process.

"Careful, you monstrous scaly lump!" Em-three-green squeaked—out of fear, of course, not boldness.

"Move this machine, insect-eater," Sord countered disdainfully.

"Twenty-one degrees east," Lara ordered, pointing, "to take us out of the flow path. Then we can circle around and back toward the cube. I don't think—"

A titanic explosion shook the ground, nearly knocking everyone to the deck. Kirk looked behind them, was startled to see that a secondary cone had joined the first and was pouring out lava at a rate equal to its neighbor. The flow had suddenly doubled.

By tomorrow the abrupt action of wind, flood, and quake would probably have wiped out all signs of the entire eruption, he mused. They didn't have time to wait around and witness it. They didn't have even minutes.

The new eruption sent a shower of glowing sparks raining down on them. The engine roared, coughed, roared, coughed.

They weren't moving.

"Something is wrong!" Em-three-green shrieked, nearly losing his voice from panic. Behind them, a red-orange wave from the second cone surged against the ridge-top—flowed over and downhill. The added influx of fresh material was too much for the hastily erected dam. It collapsed. A stream of lava, topped with broken black crust, raced out and headed toward them.

"Quickly, quickly!" Tchar shouted down at them. "What's wrong?"

"I do not know." Em-three-green frantically studied gauge upon gauge, tried two dozen switches. "Something has caused the front shaft to lock. It must be—"

Spock was already over the side and ducking underneath the cart, tools in hand. Kirk raced to the railing, leaned over. Spock was out of sight.

"Spock?"

"One moment, Captain." A hysterical pause, then, "I have it. Sand has entered the mechanism through a broken lubrication seal. I'm cleaning it out and taping it, but it will clog again.''

"Forget it, Spock, the power plant will have burned itself out by then.'' He looked to the ridge. The lava would reach them in three, maybe two minutes. "For Vulcan's sake, get back aboard!''

"A second, Captain. There, completed.'' Spock came into view, his hands and face smeared with some blue-tinted grease. At the same time, the first volcano regurgitated a plug of plutonic phlegm. A storm of fiery sparks and small globs of lava hailed down on them.

Kirk tried to cover up, as did everyone else. The bombardment passed quickly. He looked over the side again.

"Spock—Spock!''

The first officer was sprawled on the ground like a broken doll. One hand fluttered feebly at his head.

Kirk didn't think. Both hands on the cart rail, he vaulted over the side and landed with a jar on the sand. He rolled Spock onto his back.

"Leave,'' he muttered painfully, "all of you . . . go.''

"Not without you,'' Kirk objected.

"Captain, I . . .''

Kirk got a shoulder under an arm, lifted Spock to his feet. "No, Sord, stay aboard. It'll take too long for you to get back on.'' Kirk staggered toward the ladder.

"Tell Captain . . . ,'' Spock was mumbling, ". . . get others away.''

"We're *all* getting away,'' Kirk whispered. Another explosion sent fire down on them. The odor of sulfur had grown nauseating. This time, no one was hit except Sord, who simply brushed the sizzling embers off his hide. Lava bombs the size of the one that had struck Spock he didn't even feel.

Em-three-green was gesturing hysterically at the approaching river of flame, screaming. Even Lara's reserve seemed ready to crack. Sord eyed the flow, then leaned over slowly. The cart creaked, supports and axles groaned. The wheels on the cart's opposite side rose off the sand. Em-three-green was too terrified to scream as the vehicle tilted precariously.

A massive paw grabbed Spock around the waist and lifted him onto the cart.

"Go!" Kirk screamed, clinging to the ladder.

Fear lent even more speed to Em-three-green's incredible reaction time. A roar of power drowned out even the sound of the closing lava as the cart's engine, rigged to permit it to pull energy unrestrainedly from the power pack, cut loose.

Kirk felt himself wrenched backward, locked arms and legs around the ladder and prayed the metal would last as long as his muscles. The front of the cart rose into the air from the force of the blast as it shot forward at an incredible turn of speed. Em-three-green adjusted controls, all four wheels hit the sand, and it shot down the slope seconds before an advancing cliff of red covered the spot where they had been.

Lava boiled angrily behind them, orange talons reaching after. But the flow was receding rapidly into the distance. Drive whining madly, wheels and axles spinning at a rate for which they had not been designed, the wagon raced away from the burning crest behind. Sparks were starting to fly from anguished components.

Tchar watched as the cart below reached the gap in the slope Lara had indicated. It raced through, over another slope and down a winding ravine, narrowly scraping stone walls and abutments. Here the downward slope of the land lay to the south instead of toward the black cube. The lava river would slam up against the ridge they had just raced over and turn harmlessly to the left.

At the end of this pleasant thought, there was a violent, grinding wail from the engine, mirrored by one from Em-three-green. He shut everything down with incredible speed, still not fast enough to reduce the shower of sparks now spitting from more and more sections of the car.

"Off, off, off, everyone off!" the little alien cried, even as he was running for the ladder. Flames began to belch from sealed innards.

With Sord carrying the still dazed Spock, they hurriedly abandoned the smoking cart. Taking shelter behind the first rank of sand dunes, Kirk turned, could make out a thin line of red orange flowing to the south. He turned his attention back to the cart. The expected explosion failed to materialize. Em-three-green had cut the power in time to keep anything from reaching dangerous overload and blowing itself to bits. Whether he had done so in time to keep the cart mobile was open to question.

Tchar glided down to a smooth landing next to them. The Skorr was panting heavily.

"I would like to know what the Vedala put in that cart, Captain. I could not fly fast enough to keep up with you."

"It was a standard Federation engine and drive system," Kirk told him. "The credit for its abnormal burst of speed goes to Mr. Spock and Em-three-green."

He glanced over at his first officer, who now stood unaided nearby. Spock said nothing, while Em looked embarrassed and tried to hide, the tips of his cilia running through a series of color changes.

"Close," Lara said into the awkward silence, staring toward the far river of lava.

"Far too close," agreed Spock. He was rubbing at the back of his head. "I prefer less substantial precipitation. And while I appreciate your actions on my behalf, Captain, your first duty should remain to the group and the mission."

"Quite right, Spock. I felt it paramount to maintain our expedition intact. Don't think anything as primitive as emotion entered into my decision." He made a movement over his chest. "Cross my heart and hope to die."

"The injection of humor," Spock began reprovingly, "does not obviate the fact that you risked the success of the mission to—"

"—save the best science officer in Starfleet," Kirk cut in.

A massive paw smote the sand between them. "Are you two going to argue each other's merits till I throw up, or do we get on with it."

Kirk grinned, turned to face the irritated reptile. "We—"

A blast of cold air hit them, staggered Kirk. Everyone looked back toward the volcanos. Neither peak could be seen. Both lay hidden somewhere behind and beneath the towering range of cumulo-nimbus clouds that had piled up out of nothing.

It seemed to be raining beneath the black cloudbank. "No, not raining," Kirk muttered to himself. Instead, the storm was putting forth a blizzard of considerable ferocity. A violent hissing sprang up from the land beneath the clouds—snow striking the lava. He shook his head, and wondered. A world most mad indeed! Mad was a mild adjective for this paranoid planet.

The dune, at least, would provide some slight protection. Everyone scrambled over to lie in the sheltering lee. The marching clouds caught them moments after.

"And I was just going to ask," Lara shivered, flapping her hands at her sides, "what next? Wish this place would make up its mind—a body can't find time to get comfortable here."

"We've no time to seek comfort," Kirk told her. "As Sord says, we've got to get on with it."

It took Em-three-green all of five minutes to determine that the cart wasn't going anywhere without several major repairs, for which they had been equipped with neither time, skill, nor parts. Kirk felt they could have managed the first two, but the matter of replacement components defeated him.

"Completely burned out," the tiny mechanic announced dolefully, his nose wrinkling at the pungent odor drifting up from the bowels of the engine housing.

Kirk sighed. "That means from here on we carry what we need."

No one voiced an objection, or an alternative. Kirk and Spock moved to the rear deck of the cart, opened the supply lockers, and began portioning out loads.

XI

Kirk eyed the deceiving circle of the sun above, put his head down and into the wind. It had changed direction four, maybe five times since they'd begun the trek.

He'd been right about the deceptiveness of this world—and that included distance. It felt as if they had been walking for years without drawing any nearer to their objective.

Thanks to the intermittent blizzard and freezing rain, many sandy areas had acquired a thin plating of ice. Walking on such terrain was next to impossible. They couldn't have managed it at all had not Sord volunteered an obvious solution. As a result, the big reptile was soon carrying the bulk of their equipment on his back. Doing so did not slow him up any.

Eventually the last snow and rain ceased, but the cold wind continued to blow.

"I don't understand," Kirk muttered, "we should have been there long ago."

"Perhaps, Captain," Spock replied, "the defenses surrounding the soul include image projectors. What we may have seen from afar might have been a false construct."

"What about Lara's certainty of direction, then, and Tchar, insisting he sensed it?"

"That is so. It may only be a matter of distance, then." He looked thoughtful. "If none of the preceding three expeditions had one of Lara's people, or a Skorr, with them, that might explain their demise. They could have hunted false projections in this malign wilderness forever."

Kirk paused, cupped his hands to his lips and yelled up into the chilled air.

"Tchar, see anything?"

A faint reply: "Wait.. .."

Tchar rose higher, stared into the distance. It was there, as he had known it would be—past tentacles and fields of ice-blocks at the bottom of the valley. A gigantic, featureless black monolith. He knew the soul of Alar lay within that ominous repository. They were on the course the humanoid Lara had indicated. He would have to tell the others.

"Yes!" He plunged downward, pulled up at the last second. "Ahead, Captain, it—" There was a low rumble, and he instinctively lifted off the ground. Kirk and Spock had no such ability and were knocked off their feet.

Somehow Lara kept her balance. Sord was not affected, of course.

"Another quake!" Lara cursed.

All around them was the horrible crunching sound of ice breaking up.

Someone screamed. All eyes turned toward Em-three-green. He had been trailing slightly behind. A vast ridge of ice had risen beneath him, cracked, twisted, opening crevices in the ice and in the earth below.

Using every cilium, Em-three-green tried to scramble clear. But the huge slab of ice was tilting sharply, and fine cilia are not equipped with claws or hooks. They found no purchase on the slick surface. Clawing frantically, he found himself sliding backward toward the abyss.

Everything happened fast, then. Spock took several long strides and threw himself stomach-first onto the ice near the tilting slab. He slid to the edge of the crevice, reached out, and grabbed Em-three-green by the scruff of the neck just as the latter was sliding in. Kirk got there barely in time to grab Spock's ankles to prevent him from going in with Em-three-green.

With a doomsday groan, the enormous frozen mass crashed into the depths.

Kirk grimaced with the strain of holding both Spock and Em-three-green. He tried to dig his toes into the frozen sand, found himself to his horror sliding slowly, slowly forward.

A coil of rope flew over his head. He reached up, slipped the noose over Spock's legs. Immediately the cord went taut. He pulled himself to the lip of the crevasse, stared down past the dangling form of Spock to where Em-three-green still hung in the Vulcan's grasp, swaying slightly and moaning. His eyes were shut tight.

Kirk felt Spock's body moving backward, crawled along with it. A glance showed Sord carefully bringing in the cord. Then Tchar had taken Em-three-green's weight from Spock and the first officer was easily pulled clear.

They took a long break there—not because they were especially tired, but because Em-three-green was too frightened now to move. Spock administered the medicine they had found in the supplies, but that would take time to work, too.

If it could have any effect at all. For when Em's violent shaking had calmed sufficiently for him to talk, it became clear that their mechanic was now beyond even terror. It was reflected in his tired voice, his miserable attitude.

"I can't go on any farther," he barely managed to whisper.

Kirk bit back his instinctive reply. A more woebegone being he had never seen. No surprise, really—Em-three-green had been frightened and uncertain on the Vedala asteroid, let alone here. He had probably been pushed through more today than any member of his race had been forced to endure in the past hundred years.

That he was still alive instead of dead from shock was proof enough he was a remarkable specimen of his type. Kirk eyed Em-three-green in a fresh light, took stock of their battered but still intact little company.

Sord sat invincible, a bored block of steel, ignoring the biting wind. Lara leaned against an ice-block, confident, athletic, secure in her knowledge of where she stood in relation to the universe, her lacquered exterior punctuated only by an occasional worried glance at Em-three-green.

Spock, nearby, was as calm as ever, ready for whatever might offer itself as an intriguing problem. And Tchar, free and safe as the air, hovered patiently above.

And himself, of course—concerned, anxious, but still in firm command. He shook his head again. He hadn't the slightest doubt that the finest representative of all the races present was the miserable lump of shivering cilia huddled in their middle and presently suffocating in his own misery and self-pity.

"I'm not even afraid anymore," the subject of Kirk's scrutiny murmured. "Just very, very tired. So very tired."

"Come on, Em," Lara urged with surprising gentleness. "We know where it is, and we've seen it. It's just a little further."

"No!" Em-three-green shouted, with uncharacteristic force, "I'm finished, I tell you! I've had enough. Let the *murvlgeed* Skorr go on their *gurvlmeed* jihad! Let the Galaxy blow itself to its assorted perditions, for all I care. I'm . . .," and the last word came out long and slow and low, ". . . *tired*."

Kirk tried to find a way to say what had to be said diplomatically, and came to a dead end. He firmed himself.

"I'm sorry, Em-three-green, but there's still the possibility we'll be needing you." He glanced up significantly. "Sord . . ."

Em-three-green had enough strength left to protest as he all but vanished in that massive paw. Sord placed him carefully on his already heavily loaded back. The picklock fought to his feet.

"Let me go, you outrageous hallucination!"

"Shut up and hang on," Sord muttered over his shoulder. His head was bigger than Em-three-green's entire body. "Dig down under the seal-tarp, between those boxes. You can get out of the cold and wind." He started off downslope at a steady trot.

"And be still! If you itch, I may forget the source and scratch you!"

"I'll scout on ahead," Tchar suggested, rising into the wind.

Kirk nodded absently as he, Spock and Lara fell in at Sord's flank. Above them, from under the edge of the tarp, a high voice muttered with an equal mixture of pain and pathos, "Some day, you grotesque blob of creation, I'm going to cut you down to size."

Sord did not deign to reply.

Wind faded and clouds ran. The sun returned to melt the ice under their feet—fast enough, fortunately, to prevent the formation of much mud. As soon as the earth had dried sufficiently, they continued on.

They entered a region of low, sandy hills and encountered

for the first time some local vegetation—scrub bushes and the toughest looking grasses Kirk had ever seen. They'd have to be to survive here, he mused. Even the brush grew parallel to the ground instead of up into the unpredictable sky.

"Wait," came a rumbling warning.

Kirk moved up alongside Sord.

"What is it."

"Quiet." Kirk looked in the direction Sord was looking, toward a thicket of bushes. For a moment, he thought he saw what had given the reptile pause—something dark and vaguely sinister moving among the branches.

"What is it?"

"You espy it too, then?"

"I thought I saw something move, though it might have been wind action. Hell, on this world it might have been anything."

"So. There is not supposed to be any animal life on this planet."

Reptile and man stared harder, but there were no more hints of movement.

"I wouldn't be surprised if the plants themselves had learned how to run away from things here," Kirk commented. Sord continued to stare, finally grunted.

"Guess you're right. This world just gets on your nerves."

When they topped the next rise, the black cube loomed just ahead. But there were no cheers, no shouts, no cries of *eureka*! Everyone was too bone tired, emotionally and physically. They were resigned rather than elated, for now their mission really began. Or would those sheer walls of unmarked, unbroken black prove deceptively easy to penetrate? None of them thought so, in the depths of their various minds.

"I can sense the soul," Tchar told them. He fluttered his wings as he stood near Kirk. "This is no illusion—it is here!" He beat the air, lifted.

"I will fly round, examine the structure, and return to meet you. There may be an entrance above the ground. If so, I will find it far more easily than any of you." He soared upward.

"Tchar!" Kirk yelled.

The Skorr stalled, hovered.

"Captain?"

"Watch it—we need you, too."

Tchar paused, added thoughtfully, "I will be careful, Captain." He dipped slightly, then rose and shot falconlike toward the roof.

"Tchar is right in his analysis," Spock finally declared, "but we should continue to search at ground level, if only to find shelter from the next meteorological aberration."

"Excellent idea, Spock," Kirk agreed, starting toward the nearest wall, "I'll see you shortly."

"A moment, Captain. I—" Kirk cut him off curtly.

"Not this time, Spock. If something unexpected gobbles me up, dissolves me, or otherwise renders me in corpus kaput, we're going to need you around to figure out how it was done and then to devise a way to circumvent it."

Spock appeared ready to protest further.

"And that's an order," Kirk finished.

He started down the slope. Before he had gotten ten meters from the others, he felt a warm presence alongside—Lara.

"I'll go with you." It wasn't a question.

"Uh-uh, as long as I'm in charge you'll—"

"Don't *uh-uh* me, Kirk. Remember, scouting's sort of my job. By rights, I ought to be doin' this by myself. You've already gotten all the use of my sense of direction you're goin' to. I'm more expendable than anyone. But if you want to join me in gettin' yourself shot at, well, it'll be nice to have company."

Kirk started to yell—then found the incipient lecture had turned into a mental smile that was mirrored on his face. They walked on together.

Spock, meanwhile, was trying to take his mind off the fact that Kirk was out ahead of them, out of range of immediate help, and nearing a structure they had every reason to believe contained hostile defenses ready for unannounced visitors.

"Sord, what did you think you saw back there?"

The massive brow frowned, forming a small facial crevasse. Its owner spoke without looking down.

"Don't know for sure, Vulcan. A shape—" Sord shook his head as if to clear it of a fog. Profound cogitation apparently wasn't one of his specialties. "Probably seeing things, as the captain figures."

Spock didn't look satisfied. "There should be *no* mobile

life on this world.'' He started down determinedly after Kirk and Lara.

Em-three-green slipped off Sord's back, took two steps to every one of Spock's as he followed at his heels.

''You keep saying that, Spock.''

''Yes,'' Spock admitted. ''The key word is 'shouldn't.' The Vedala should have informed us.''

Sord sighed, sounding like an ancient steam engine, and followed too. ''Maybe, the Vedala didn't know about whatever it was we saw.''

''No, I still consider that an impossibility,'' Spock muttered.

''You think that,'' the dragon snorted. ''Me, I ain't so sure. The longer I'm on this dump, the less I'm convinced of the omnipotence of our alien mentors. Now, mind you,'' he went on, ''I'm just saying there are aspects of this they don't know nothing about.

''Leastwise, that's what I tell myself to explain why *I'm* here instead of them and their supposed super-science. I don't know what you tell *your*self, Vulcan.''

Spock glanced up at the toothed jaws but was unable to read any expression there. However much the facts argued against the reptile's words, there were some odd points to consider about this entire undertaking.

Looking at it from a purely rational standpoint, now . . .

There was a last little sand dune. Kirk and Lara topped it. The fortress loomed over them, barely a hundred meters away. It was surrounded by a field of black gravel.

''That's it.'' He grinned at her. ''End of one long hard journey I've no desire to repeat.''

''Ah, but we still have to go back, James.'' She moved close and this time he didn't edge away. It was not because he was too tired to.

''I'll tell you something true,'' she began, staring into his eyes. ''I find you one of the most attractive men I've ever met. If we were . . .,'' she hesitated, ''*together*, the rest of this would be easier. And if anything happened, why,'' she shrugged, ''we'd have some green memories.''

''I already have a lot of green memories,'' he told her gently. ''I sometimes think too many.''

Lara didn't try to hide her disappointment. "Oh." He put a comforting hand on her shoulder and squeezed.

"Maybe some other time, Lara. If it means anything, I think it would be one of the greenest of the green." He pulled his hand away as she reached for it. "But not now—we still have work to do."

She brightened. "At least you're willing to argue the point."

"I'm always open to logical persuasion."

The enormous, nearly perfect cube of metallic black was even more impressive when one stood at its immediate base. Nowhere could Kirk detect a hint of a sealed joint, bolt, or riveting of any sort. It was almost as if the monolith had been created in one piece, complete and perfect.

Nor was there any sign of an entrance. An awesome bit of engineering. It would have been dominating in a city. Here, on the bare sandy plain ringed by its black gravel border, it was awesome.

When nothing appeared to blast them from the earth, Kirk waved twice—behind and above. Sord, Spock, Em-three-green and Tchar joined him and Lara at the base.

"Is this not the shape," Spock asked the Skorr, "of the more primitive temples of your people?"

"Yes," Tchar admitted in surprise. "I had not known your knowledge extended so far, Mr. Spock." He stared upward. "Though there has never been anything as grand and beautiful as this. It is the work of someone familiar with the Skorr, yet with an ability and single-mindedness of purpose my people have never known." He pointed to the right.

"If it is true to the old schematics, the entrance should be there." He flew toward the corner and they followed.

The carved door was cut inside the corner, as Tchar had indicated. The complex motif engraved in the door itself probably meant something to the birdman, but he didn't find it worthy of explanation and no one inquired.

"Truly, it is the same as the old temples," Tchar announced. "But the inscription is different. I cannot make it out, wholly. Much of it appears to consist of a warning, which is to be expected."

"Can you open it?" Kirk asked.

"No." Tchar looked distraught. "It is a familiar door—but it has no lock."

Kirk's gaze, followed soon by everyone else's, turned to rest on the shivering form of Em-three-green. He looked better now, though. Obviously the rest and shelter he had enjoyed while riding Sord had done him much good. Not that he felt any different about this craziness. He still wanted out at the first opportunity. But he was studying the door in spite of himself, professional curiosity being about the only thing capable of distracting him from his fright.

"There's a lock on my oculars," he declaimed firmly. "I recognize the type—rare, subtle and expensive."

Kirk stared hard at the door, tried to spot the mechanism Em-three-green was talking about and saw nothing but designs and inscriptions in an alien hand.

"I'll take your word for it—I have to," he admitted. "Can you open it?"

"There's no lock, seal, jam, portal, crawlway or door in the Galaxy I can't open," the picklock announced.

As Em-three-green unslung the small pack from his back, Kirk studied the overhanging brow of the doorway and wondered at the motivation behind it. There was a brooding, fanatical malevolence behind all this. A cunning madness that sought only the deaths of millions of innocent beings.

The key question now was—how much confidence did these extremists place in their hiding place? Was it sufficient in their eyes, or were there less passive forms of argument awaiting their entrance?

The pack produced a belt of flexible dark plastic equipped with a multitude of tiny compartments. Em-three-green laid it neatly on the ground, revealing a tool kit of gleaming, exquisitely handicrafted devices that would not have been out of place in a surgery.

The picklock's gaze studied a series of depressions which formed a regular, roughly diamond-shaped pattern in the approximate center of the door. Kirk wouldn't have recognized them in a million years as being apart from their neighboring carvings or as constituting a lock. Em-three-green selected a number of the tools with an assurance which Kirk found remarkably comforting. Having thus armed himself, he walked to the door and began work, his body shielding most of his actions from sight.

Kirk only hoped the alien's skill matched his confidence.

Something moved above them. He glanced upward sharply, saw nothing. *Easy, James, watch out or the boojums'll get you.* He returned his attention to Em-three-green.

Abruptly, an anticlimactic click sounded from somewhere inside the door. This initiated a steady hum.

Em-three-green's reaction was anything but relieved. Instead, his cilia moved more rapidly than ever. He seemed to be working twice as hard, and he looked frightened—which might not mean anything at all, since that was his normal mental state. But still—

"Anything the matter? Can't you do it?"

"I'm doing it, I'm doing it," the picklock muttered tightly, nervously.

"That's wonderful," Lara complimented him.

"No, you don't understand," he told her. "This lock is keyed with a timed series of irregular pulsations. If I don't cut the combination—eliminate the pulses in the proper sequence and within a certain time—it explodes."

Lara looked uncertain. "Does it matter whether we force the door neatly or otherwise?" She took a couple of wary steps backward, spoke to Kirk. "Why not let it blow itself open?"

Em-three-green supplied the answer—which pleased Kirk, because he didn't have one. "Such an explosion is designed to melt the metal of the door and any tunnel beyond, sealing it against unauthorized visitors—sometimes permanently."

"Spock, what's your opinion?" Kirk asked. Spock ignored him. The captain noticed his first officer was staring upward. "Spock?"

The science officer's warning shout sounded even as Kirk was turning his gaze toward the top of the cube.

Wings in wind—

Kirk ate sand as one of the cube sentinels swooped down at him, wicked hooked talons barely scraping his back. In unnatural silence the flying gargoyle banked and started for another pass. There were two of the monsters—huge, threatening, not particularly swift, but immensely powerful-looking.

Kirk rolled to get his back against the cube, reaching for his phaser. Out of the corner of an eye he saw that Lara had her chemical gun out. She crouched just inside the entrance-way. Em-three-green couldn't be seen, but his terrified moans could be heard from behind Sord. The big reptile had moved to block the entrance.

"Keep working," he rumbled over his shoulder. "I'll cover you."

Em-three-green was too busy working at the lock to offer a reply. In any case, he was in no position to argue with Sord. The big carnivore might possibly survive the threatened explosion, but Em-three-green would be reduced to scattered hunks of fur.

A shrill keening sounded directly above. Tchar charged into the two sentinels, breaking their formation and disrupting their attack. If one of the dark guardians got its claws on him, Kirk thought, the dogfight would be over instantly. But Tchar was clearly much faster. And he seemed to have the uncanny ability to dodge at the last second, before wing or claw could strike. It was almost as if he knew what his attacker was going to do before he did it.

The Skorr occupied the full attention of one of the sentinels. The other, the one that had just missed Kirk, was coming on again. Kirk fired. A second beam passed over his left shoulder—Spock was firing simultaneously.

Both beams made contact—and reflected off the polished throat of the gargoyle. It neither slowed nor swerved. A rapid series of explosions sounded from near the door. Lara was firing her out-dated but lethal-looking pistol.

Maybe the explosive pellets did more damage than the phasers, or perhaps the monster was distracted by the noise. Whatever the reason, it shifted course in mid-dive and angled for the exposed huntress.

Kirk bit his lip, forced himself to keep a steady stream of energy trained on the sentinel, which was taking both phaser beams broadside, now. Lara dropped to one knee, tried to hit its underside.

They couldn't tell whether it was the concentrated phaser fire, the explosive shells, or both, but suddenly the creature came apart in mid-flight. The explosion wasn't particularly impressive—but the amount of debris and the size of the area it was strewn over was. Also the composition of that debris.

Kirk kicked at a fragment of it, heard the slight ring as it went tumbling across the gravel.

"Mechanicals," Spock observed interestedly. "Sord felt he might have seen something watching us, back along our path. And you too, Captain." He looked satisfied. "The Vedala were right. There are no living creatures here—only mechanized protectors."

A cry from above reminded them the battle wasn't over. Tchar had gotten a grip on the back of the remaining sentinel. Unable to strike a significant blow at the irritation on its back, the mechanical wheeled and fluttered in frustration. But neither could Tchar effectively incapacitate the armored flier.

It shook free. Then, as though directed by outside authority, it suddenly changed its mind. Folding its wings, it dove toward the door. Sord tried to edge even tighter into the slight indentation of the doorway.

"Hurry, small one," he rumbled. Again Em-three-green had no time to answer.

Kirk and Spock shifted their phasers to cover the second mechanical—then hesitated as Tchar charged straight down in pursuit.

"Don't fire!" the Skorr screamed.

Moving incredibly fast, Tchar slammed across the skull of the monster. A low grinding noise came from it. Either the distraction was effective, or else the creature had decided it wasn't going to be able to get past Sord. It spread ponderous wings and soared skyward again.

Tchar closed with it once more near the top rim of the cube. They locked together and vanished over the edge. Eyes human and otherwise locked there for long moments.

Distantly, the cough of an explosion. They waited a long time. Tchar did not reappear.

"No way to tell what happened up there," Kirk murmured. "Can't even be sure the mechanical blew up." He ran a hand over the slick-smooth wall. "Tchar may be up there, wounded, unable to fly. We can't reach the roof from the outside—maybe there's a way up from the interior. We can damn well look for—"

A soprano cry of exhaustion and triumph came from his right. It was followed by a jerky, piping laugh. Sord backed away.

A deep protest of stone against metal sounded briefly, and then the door began to twist open, moving smoothly on unseen gears. They crowded around the entrance.

A driving, icy rain began to fall from a sky that had been clear and warm minutes before. Even so, the tunnel revealed was anything but inviting, dark as the pit and just as empty.

Kirk looked around at the rest of them, hunching his shoulders against the pelting rain. "We could rest here awhile."

"No," objected Lara firmly. "We've come this far without stopping. If I sit down and rest I don't think I'll feel much like getting up again."

"Let's finish it," Sord snorted, "or give this deadfall a chance to finish us." He grinned, displaying a wicked set of customized cutlery.

"I too, would prefer to press on, Captain," admitted Spock. "There may be other mechanicals on guard. We still have the advantage of some surprise, I think. The faster we move the more off-balance any enemy will be. He will be forced to improvise instead of prepare."

"All right, that's what I want, too. But this is nominally a democratic expedition," Kirk told them, matching Sord's grin in spirit if not in flash. Turning, he led the way into the cube.

Spock and Kirk both had belt lights, which they used to advantage. No automatic lights brightened their way, but neither were they challenged by cousins of the metal gargoyles.

After a short jog, they reached a spot where the tunnel opened into a vast open space. Spock turned his light on each of them in turn as Kirk took a brief roll call. No one had disappeared through a hidden door.

Man and Vulcan increased the intensity of their beams, playing them around the interior. They stood in one immense open space which the two lights could barely illuminate. The walls were a mirror of the outside. They had a slick look, possibly due to internal condensation, and were devoid of markings or features of any kind.

Which starkness made the discovery of the soul all the more dramatic.

Spock's beam flashed on something overhead. The science officer searched carefully with the light—and then he had it. A scintillating lacework of three golden möbius strips floating in free air. It was beautiful—but to the little knot of beings below, hardly awesome enough to inspire fanatical devotion in an entire race. The knowledge of that power, however, outshone any physical trappings and gave it impressiveness to spare.

"Pretty bauble," Sord ventured, breaking the silence, "but how do we reach it?"

By way of reply, Spock turned his light on the wall behind them, played the beam up, down and sideways on it. He ran his palm over the metal.

"Unusual alloy—it would take a warfleet to penetrate this. Using the door was preferable—the Vedalan way. There is not the slightest indentation, nothing that would permit climbing. A remarkable piece of engineering, executed with devotion and care."

"I'm sure the builders would be flattered," Kirk snapped drily. "How do we get up? The walls aren't climbable without special equipment, which we don't have." He ran a bootheel along the floor. The soft squeaking sound echoed dimly in the vastness.

"Either we find a way to reach it," and he nodded in the direction of the soul, agonizingly near yet infinitely out of touch, "or we've come all this way for nothing."

A vaguely familiar rumble then—the sound of the door twisting back into place. It closed with a dull boom.

At which a pale white light began to fill the chamber.

Em-three-green was the first one to the closed door. He had to hunt to find the barely perceptible hairline crack it formed with the wall.

"No lock on the inside," he observed professionally. "No evidence of pressure easement." He looked at them helplessly. "I can't open solid metal. We're prisoners."

"So we are," Kirk agreed. Spock turned to stare at the captain in confusion. His response wasn't quite what he expected.

"You don't seem very surprised, Captain." Kirk was

walking back toward the now well-lit chamber, examining the walls thoroughly.

"Three previous expeditions tried to recover the soul and were lost. Admittedly, this world is unrelentingly hostile—but any forewarned team prepared as we were should have been able to survive as we have." He surveyed the room.

"I see no bones or anything else. No sign of the previous expeditions. Their remains should be here if they got this far. That not one of them did so I find too hard to believe."

"You are suggesting, then, Captain . . . ?"

"I'm suggesting nothing, Spock—yet. Only that we've been luckier than we think, so far." He turned from Spock's inquiring stare to look back up at the soul.

"Still, we've no evidence anyone else *did* make it this far." He lowered his gaze and pointed. "Look there, on the far wall."

The ledge was barely a meter and a half wide and the same color and composition as the walls. It curled gently around the interior of the building, circling upward. It wasn't surprising the ledge had escaped Spock's probing beam. Without the interior illumination that had come on at the door's closing, they might never have spotted it.

They approached the ledge. It started two meters up. Kirk took a short run, leaped, grabbed the edge and started to muscle himself onto it.

A second later he fairly exploded upward. Getting his balance, he looked backward as Sord let out one of his now familiar rumbling laughs. Their reptilian strongman handed Spock up, then Lara and, despite frantic protests, Em-three-green.

"I'm terribly afraid of heights," the picklock sniffled, hugging the wall and shaking.

"You are terribly afraid of everything, Em-three-green," Spock commented. "There is no need to constantly apologize for your natural condition."

"I'm not apologizing!!" Em-three-green shot back defiantly; then he sank in on himself in embarrassment. "Please forgive me for yelling, but . . ."

"Later," Kirk instructed him. He stared across at their massive companion, but Sord stepped back, shaking his shovel-like head.

"No, I'm not built for that sort of thing." Kirk kicked at the metal ledge with one boot.

"I'll hold you, Sord. It's an extrusion of the wall itself."

But Sord replied reluctantly, "*Maybe* it'll hold me. No, you'd better go on without me. I'd crowd you and I'd look funny walking on tiptoes. I'll wait for you down here."

They climbed slowly and patiently. The ledge wasn't dangerously narrow, but neither was it the broad boulevard Kirk wished for, and there was no railing.

It was remarkable, he reflected, how one could float in a suit, free and weightless, outside the *Enterprise* and feel perfectly calm and relaxed, and still grow nauseated and dizzy on a climb like this.

He stared up and out at the object of their search. The ledge reached out a thin tentacle of itself, but stopped short of the soul. What they would do when they reached that point he didn't know.

He felt himself shaking—and the cause was external.

"Hug the ledge!" Spock yelled. The four of them dropped flat, trying to dig nails and toes into the unyielding metal. The quake stopped, then came on again stronger. But there was more bluster than threat in the tremor. There was no sign of the walls coming down or of the ledge collapsing beneath them.

"We already know this world is geologically perverse," Spock commented, rising to his feet. "It would be illogical for this edifice to be built without keeping that information in mind. Most likely it is mounted on flexible supports which absorb most of the violence of the quakes."

"That's what I need right now," muttered Em-three-green.

Kirk was tempted to add that the picklock shook even when the earth didn't. He quickly quashed the thought, which was undiplomatic and unworthy of a leader.

It was just that, as they drew nearer and nearer their objective, his built-in warning system was winding tighter and tighter. They couldn't simply reach out and pluck it—they couldn't! Someone had gone to an incredible amount of trouble to build this supersafe on this unholy world. To believe they could get this close without additional opposition was naive in the extreme.

The ledge turned a sharp corner and narrowed considerably. Sord could never have negotiated it. They had to turn sideways, backs against the wall, and edge across carefully. Then it was up, up, mounting ever higher—until they reached a point where the ledge broadened to a stop, from which a long, narrow arch extended out toward the floating soul.

They needed a respectable hunk of nerve to walk out onto that thin projection, and even more to look down the dizzying drop to the floor below. Em-three-green huddled close to Lara and concentrated his full attention on remaining in the precise center of the platform.

The metallic protrusion ended a couple of meters from the soul. "Close," Em-three-green groaned, "so close!"

Lara was unwinding a length of cord from her belt. "Maybe I can get a line on it."

Spock restrained her.

"We have no idea what kind of force-field may surround it. Best to wait and save direct contact as a final option."

They hardly had time to discuss other possible means of retrieving the soul when a violent *crump* sounded behind them. Everyone ducked instinctively, but the blast was not repeated.

Kirk looked back the way they had come and saw that a wide section of ledge had vanished. Smoke still rose from the edges of seared metal. They were marooned on the platform.

That it had taken this long for their tormentor to show himself was all that surprised Kirk. But the motives of the mad are obscure and difficult to analyze. Kirk stared up into the far reaches of the fortress. They were two-thirds of the way up—from where he saw that near the roof the walls were not entirely unmarred. Instead, they were pocked with carved images, crevices, small craters and tiny dark tunnels.

"I told you there had to be something watching, protecting here besides just a locked door. There had to be something besides reliance on freakish weather and the occasional earthquake. There had to be something besides this super-egomaniacal metal box. Something more subtle, something even the Vedala couldn't defend against."

"Which would be what, Captain?" Spock inquired.

Kirk's reply was tinged with sarcasm.

"A worm in the apple, Mr. Spock. A monkeywrench in

the works, an activated positron in the dilithium, a rottenness in Denmark." He shook a challenging fist at the vast expanse of the roof.

"I know who you are!" he shouted, his eyes searching, hunting. Who could have placed the soul in a restraining field here, three hundred meters up in open air? Who would think to build this travesty of a holy temple as a monument to annihilation? Who, but the Skorr themselves?

"Show yourself, Tchar! The masquerade is over—take your bow."

Nothing happened for several seconds. Then the prince of the Skorr dropped from an as yet undetected hiding place. He dove toward them and spread batlike wings at the last moment, braking to hover on the other side of the soul. Laughing, whistling, jabbing accusing fingers at them—mocking civilization, and worse.

"Tchar," Lara muttered wonderingly, "in the name of the seven gods of the hunt, why did you do this? You and your little clique of militarists?"

Kirk shook his head sadly, tiredly. "It seems history is doomed to repeat itself even across racial and spatial borders. It's not a little fascinating, and not a little sad. You and your accomplices would start a meaningless crusade of blood across the Galaxy, initiate the murder of your people and other innocents—for what, for what? Tell us why, Tchar."

"The Skorr were a warrior race!" Tchar shrilled, whirling about in anger. "Slaves to the illusion of peace are we now—cowards, grown soft through the comforts of trade and weak by mental miscegenation." He gestured at the soul.

"This sick dream," he spat, "stole our souls, it did not heal them!" Now a hint of the fanatic's pride crept into his voice. "But there were a few of us high ones, a very few, who were wise enough to perceive this gigantic illusion which had sapped our racial determination and courage.

"We planned the theft, and none stopped us. None *will* stop us! There will be no time for another expedition before fury returns my people to glorious tradition. I, myself, came along to insure this. I alone saw the need, when I was told who would participate. And I was right—I was needed.

"I, Tchar, hereditary prince, waster of mine enemies,

drinker of blood—I will lead my people into glory and revenge!''

"At best you can win only a Pyrrhic victory," Spock replied calmly, not in the least impressed by the *sturm-und-drang* speech of Tchar. "Most, if not all of your warriors will eventually be tracked down and killed. The Skorr home-worlds will be scoured clean of life when the warrior races of the Federation rise to do battle with you—as will the empires of the Klingons, and Romulans, and all the others.''

"Perhaps,'' Tchar admitted, in defiance of Spock's logic. "A noble death risked to win a great dream.'' He shook angry talons at them.

"But no longer will we live like worms, crawling in the dirt. We will rise and conquer. You will be the fourth group sacrificed to the cause. But you have my respect—only you came this far. Only you necessitated my personal intervention. You will die in grace, as befits the enemies of a hereditary prince.''

"Tchar, wait!" Lara called, too late. The Skorr had already wheeled up to disappear back into the dark places of the ceiling.

Far, far below a massive figure watched and tried to understand. Sord could tell something had gone wrong, but the sound from above dissipated in the vast expanse of the chamber. He had seen the ledge cut, of course, but there was nothing to be seen from below that could tie Tchar to the sabotage. Massive thoughts were considered and discarded as he tried to make sense of what had happened.

Lara had walked to the very edge of the precipice and stared calmly over. "Absolutely unclimbable, as Mr. Spock said." She shook her head disparagingly. "We'd bounce awful high.''

As if to confirm her words, she suddenly drifted upward, followed by the others. Em-three-green spun frantically, clawing for a foothold.

"I believe this renders the problem academic,'' Spock declared.

"Gravity, neutralizer—the building's equipped with null gravity," Kirk explained tightly.

"It may be part of the edifice's own components,'' Spock added, spreading arms and legs and trying to keep relatively motionless. "It would surely explain how this structure has been able to survive the multitude of tremors and other natural disasters that must have struck this spot."

Kirk found himself spinning despite his best efforts. Below, Sord found himself drifting, too, but had reacted more rapidly than any of them. He'd kicked out at the last instant, struck the floor a titanic blow, and sent himself sailing upward. His aim had been excellent. Reaching out, he had gotten a solid grip on the projecting ledge, pulled himself atop it, and was now the only one not floating free.

Somewhere nearby, Tchar was whistling amusedly at them. Kirk struggled to orient himself, finally located the teasing, darting birdman.

"Now you can fly and fight as a Skorr—a worthy way to die, is it not?"

Kirk started to reply, but was interrupted by Sord. "No offense, little one, but let me have him." He slapped his chest with one paw, a blow that would have buckled the wall of a starship. But there was more to this situation than bulk and strength. Tchar would cut the clumsy Sord to pieces before the reptile could get a grip on him.

"No, Sord, not in free fall."

"Use your phaser on him, quickly!" Em-three-green suggested nervously.

"Yes, Captain Kirk," the voice of Tchar mocked, "use your phaser on me."

An invitation to destruction, Kirk knew. Tchar wanted them to fight him as a Skorr, so he could reassert his madman's version of Skorrian bushido. That meant hand-to-hand combat. No modern accoutrements like hand phasers.

If this structure was equipped with electronics as sophisticated as a gravity neutralizer, he had no doubt there was something trained on them this very minute capable of canceling out their phasers—perhaps even keying on their energy cells. To fire one might cause it to blow up in one's face.

"It must be on his terms," he told Em-three-green.

They might work this to their advantage. If they expressed a reluctance to fight, Tchar could probably dispose of them from a convenient distance. Instead he chose personal combat. His controlling phobia demanded he kill them personally.

"Spock, how long since you've done zero-gee combat exercises?"

"I subscribe to the prescribed dosage, Captain."

That told him Spock was up on technique, without telling Tchar any more than was necessary. Let him interpret that as he might.

"Well," he shouted to Tchar, steeling himself, "what are you waiting for?"

Tchar was hard put to restrain his laughter. "You are turning slow circles, Captain Kirk, with no sign of stopping. A most disadvantageous tactical position."

Tchar was right. Before they could do any maneuvering of any kind they needed a firmer purchase than thin air. Tchar didn't want the kill to be too easy, then. Worse for him.

"Lara, throw your line to Sord." The huntress nodded. Uncoiling the line and wrapping one end around her right wrist, she tossed the gently weighted other end toward the braced and ready Sord.

The action sent her spinning, but Sord caught the loop easily and pulled her in. While he braced her she reeled in Em-three-green, Kirk, and Spock.

"Very good, Captain, very good!" Tchar applauded mockingly. Kirk thought he detected the gleam of insanity in the Skorr's eyes even at this distance. He was working himself up good and proper.

So much the better. "If we can get him to lose control of himself, Spock, get him to stop thinking . . ."

"An admirable objective, Captain," Spock whispered back. "Should I have a choice, however, I believe I would opt for a fast kick to the jugular."

Kirk smiled grimly.

"Let's go, then."

Bracing himself, Kirk drew an imaginary line and kicked free of the platform. Spock did likewise, kicking harder. Thus he reached the far wall first and pushed off again to approach Tchar from the other side.

Tchar whistled, charged straight at Kirk. Obviously he intended to deal with them one at a time. He had plenty of time to bleed Kirk, turn, and deal with Spock.

Kirk had aimed for the soul. It was the only cover of any kind available in the dangerously open space. The maneuver generated only contempt in Skorr's eyes. He'd expected better than a desperate dash for the soul.

Talons extended, he headed for Kirk's face. The human's soft hands worried him not at all. Kirk first, then the Vulcan, then the others at his leisure. The large stupid reptile would take many cuts to die. Em-three-green he would save for last. It would be interesting to see if he could frighten him to death.

But first—the human.

Wings beating to his sides, forelimbs extended—then Kirk moved. Tchar momentarily lost his poise and tried to change his angle of approach.

At the last possible second, Kirk had curled into a tight spinning ball. When he came out of it it was with both legs tucked tight into his chest. He extended them just in time to meet Tchar's midsection.

One claw struck home—only to glance harmlessly off the thick sole of Kirk's boot. But the unblocked leg drove deeply into the Skorr's stomach.

As he tumbled awkwardly from the blow, screaming in pain and rage, the hereditary prince of the Skorr was met from behind by the late arriving Spock. Too late, Tchar sensed he had been duped, that the timing of the two bipeds had been planned to bring about just this situation.

He'd committed a terrible error—underestimating his opponents. Now the Vulcan had a grip on both arms and despite his best efforts, Tchar couldn't dislodge him from his back.

Kirk had continued on to the soul, met the expected force-field and used it to kick back toward Tchar. But this time Tchar was ready for the tumble-and-kick and he twisted away, slashing out with a clawed leg.

Kirk wrenched aside and the claw ripped down his front, drawing a little blood. Straining, the Skorr managed to fight his way over to the force-field. A couple of rough jolts against it were enough to knock Spock loose. Furious, Tchar turned to rend the Vulcan.

But Spock was far from incapacitated. Although he had been shaken off, he had managed to get a grip on the outline of the force-field. Now he used it as a barrier between himself and Tchar.

By then Kirk had struck the far wall, kicked off, and was

coming back for more. Tchar spotted him at the last instant, but by now he had had about enough: this exercise had been interesting and instructive, but it had taken rather too much time. Instead of turning to meet Kirk's charge he strove for altitude.

"Very good," he called down to the two men bobbing near the soul. "Surprisingly good. But it was you, Captain Kirk, who called for an end to masquerades. Now this too, must end."

Folding his wings, he dropped like a stone toward Kirk. Sord, Em-three-green and Lara watched, worried. Kirk was drifting free. Even if he reached the force-field around the soul, Tchar's power dive would drive curved talons right through him.

Kirk reached the soul, got a grip on its edge. Tchar screamed in triumph—just as Kirk turned. Both sets of claws slammed into Kirk's backpack—and stuck.

The force of the blow had almost knocked Kirk off the field—almost. Then, as Tchar screamed in frustration, Spock crawled carefully round and got a grip on the Skorr's wings.

They made contact with the soul and contact with the thief. Now was the time.

"Lara, call for retrieval!"

"No!" Tchar shrieked desperately. Kirk had succeeded in his aim, making the Skorr forget everything but the fury of battle. They had to have him pinned before they issued that irreversible call. Had to, because there was a button on Tchar's belt, a button he now fought vainly to reach, a button which undoubtedly controlled the gravity neutralizer and in an emergency could have sent them all tumbling to the metal floor where, as Lara had predicted, they would have bounced very high indeed.

But Lara could now throw the switch on her pack without fear of that.

A faint smell of ozone was in evidence as the air around them crackled. They had only one remaining fear—could the Vedala retrieval field penetrate the force-field holding the soul of Alar? Or would it retrieve only them?

Or would the force-field interfere with the retrieval field and leave them all drifting in limbo?

He speculated on it as his vision began to fade, as Tchar's wrenching cry of, "Let me die!" echoed in his ears.

No Tchar, Tchar of the soaring wings and mad dream, you're coming back with us—though I truly wish that I could grant your wish . . .

Running water played counterpoint to the wind in the grass. Kirk felt a warm breeze on his face and smelled the smell of green things growing. He looked down at himself.

There were no scratches on his arm, no gash in his chest where Tchar's claws had struck. They were standing in a familiar glade, back on the Vedala asteroid.

Baring unabashed stares of astonishment, they stood as they had stood days ago—rested, clean, refreshed—before the expedition had begun. Had he dreamed it all—had the quest only taken place in their minds? Or, he thought as he turned to face the small, confident figure standing in the glade's center, had it all been simply an elaborate display of some strangely Vedalan sense of humor?

"We give you thanks," the Vedala intoned solemnly. He moved aside to reveal a triplet of möbius strips, glowing golden against the greensward. "The soul of Alar is returned to his people. There will be no jihad."

He gestured and the soul vanished. Presumably it was already well on its way to the central Skorr homeworld—along with a recommended list of precautions to prevent any future theft.

"What about Tchar?" Kirk asked. "How are you going to deal with him?"

Another gesture and they saw Tchar, arms and wings bound, sneering at unseen tormentors.

"The hereditary prince is proud and brave and has many useful qualities. We will make a small adjustment in his personality. You would argue the morality of this, Captain Kirk, as is the peculiarity of your race—but you will not argue its efficacy. He will be made sane again." The picture of the bound Tchar faded.

"We cannot reward you with other than our thanks and the knowledge of what you have prevented. Nor can the Skorr, for this must remain hidden from them. Tchar's co-perpetrators will be found out and dealt with, without subjecting their people to racial shock. The Skorr must never suspect that this monstrousness was engineered by some of their own, or they would engage in a vicious, useless witch-hunt for more blasphemers.''

"Oh well," Sord rumbled airily, "got nowhere to wear a medal anyway."

"There will be questions," Spock remarked.

The Vedala smiled softly at the Vulcan. "You will see, there will be no questions. Goodbye . . ." The Vedala began to dissolve.

Lara moved over to stand next to Kirk. "Goodbye, James. It's too bad—we almost could have . . ."

Her voice faded and became inaudible as Kirk's vision began to blur once more.

Scott and Sulu were in the transporter room when Spock and Kirk rematerialized. And although Kirk was glad to see them, he noticed something about their expressions.

"Captain, Mr. Spock," Sulu began anxiously, "what went wrong?"

Kirk took a moment to look down at himself, saw nothing wrong, glanced over at Spock. Everything seemed perfectly normal here—except Sulu and Scott's attitude.

"What do you mean, Mr. Sulu?"

"You went over and came right back," Scott explained. "Did the Vedala call this off, give you orders, or what?"

"Now wait a minute, what—"

Spock made a gesture indicating silence.

"How long have we been gone, Mr. Sulu?" Spock inquired.

Sulu shrugged. "About two minutes, maybe three, I guess. Just enough time for me to get down here after you beamed dirtwards."

A great deal passed between Kirk and Spock in a single look.

"The Vedala changed their minds," the captain said briskly, stepping off the transporter platform. "They needed some fast advice and we answered their one question. Back to your stations, now. This was just a momentary detour, a sidestep. Mr. Spock . . ."

"Yes, Captain?"

"I'm going to my cabin to make the official log entry. I'll see you on the Bridge."

"Very good, Captain." Spock started for the elevator.

"Oh, and Spock . . ."

"Sir?" Spock turned and waited.

"When you get there, instruct Uhura to contact the nearest Starfleet base for orders. Maybe this time they can find something a little more interesting for us to do."

"*Interesting*, Captain?" Spock threw back his head in surprise as Kirk walked up beside him. "It *is* interesting . . . to learn that understatement is not the exclusive province of Vulcans."

The doors closed behind them.

Scott leaned against the transporter console while Sulu stared in confusion after the two departed commanding officers.

"Now what do you suppose all that was about?" the helmsman wondered out loud. Scott smiled.

"It's verra simple, Mr. Sulu. Easy to understand when you've been around the captain and Mr. Spock as long as I have. See, they're both crazy. Only the captain tries to fool us into thinkin' it's a cover, and Mr. Spock is too polite to admit to it." Scott let out a long breath, moved away from the console.

"Well, you heard the orders. I suggest you get back to the Bridge. Me, I'm goin' back to Engineerin' and my engines. At least they're not loonie. It's easy to stay sane back there," he finished as he stepped into the elevator. "Because when anythin' goes wrong with them, I can always call on the little people to come and fix 'em."

The lift doors closed.

Sulu stared at them for a long moment, then muttered something no one was there to hear. It didn't matter—mankind had heard it before, had known it to be true since the beginning of time.

"Everyone's crazy here but me and thee," he sang, "and sometimes I'm not so sure about thee."

Whistling cheerfully, he ambled toward the elevator and the bridge beyond.

STAR TREK®
LOG SIX

CONTENTS

PART I
  Albatross   413

PART II
  The Practical Joker   475

PART III
  How Sharper Than a Serpent's Tooth   541

For Lou Mindling . . .
Expediter, friend, oasis in the desert of
deviltry and dementia, and all-around human being.

STAR TREK LOG SIX

Log of the Starship *Enterprise*
Stardates 5532.8—5535.2 Inclusive

James T. Kirk, Capt., USSC, FS, ret.
Commanding

transcribed by
Alan Dean Foster

At the Galactic Historical Archives
on S. Monicus I
and
Frontier Outpost Moran
stardated 6111.3

For the Curator: JLR

PART I

ALBATROSS

(Adapted from a script by Dario Finelli)

I

It had form but faint substance, shape but little color, face but no visage.

Body but no soul.

Its sword was an extension of its own right arm and it moved and danced with a grace and fluidity that was not human.

Sulu parried and thrust, beat and lunged with his own insulated blade. Initially he had been casual in attack, though his tenebrous opponent made up in nimbleness what it lacked in knowledge and experience.

But it was rapidly absorbing every trick Sulu the fencing master could think of—memorizing each one, analyzing its weaknesses and strong points, and then using them on Sulu in return. It had not yet mastered the subtle intricacies of multiple combinations, thus preventing the *Enterprise*'s helmsman from being skewered a dozen times over.

But since Sulu's opponent did not tire, the combat loomed as increasingly unequal.

Sulu relished the contest. Never before had he faced so dangerous a fighter, nor one so eerily beautiful. His luminescent antagonist shone like a billion golden glowmites in the light of the room. Though its skull was featureless, it did not lack eyes.

Those enigmatic orbs kept close watch on the helmsman's movements, on the placement of his feet, on the way he held his balancing back hand, and most especially on the tip of that deadly foil.

Sulu feinted low, then went high with the point of his blade. As his opponent moved his blade up to parry, the helmsman shot his left leg out in a strong side kick.

The gilded wraith knocked the point aside and lunged forward to finish the fight. But instead of skipping back out of range, Sulu stood his ground, shot vertically into the air and executed a perfect jump-spinning back kick. His shoe struck the sword-arm, smashing it aside, while his foil whipped around simultaneously to stab straight through that gleaming, glittering throat . . .

The attacker froze as Sulu withdrew his blade. No blood had gushed forth on contact, no stream of molten yellow fluid. There had been only an indifferent buzz at the mortal blow.

Walking away from his paralyzed opponent, Sulu picked a towel off a nearby bench and mopped at his sweating face.

"The computer annex's getting too clever, Mr. Scott. It's getting harder and harder to think up new combinations to use against it."

Chief Engineer Montgomery Scott nodded as he pressed the switch on the makeshift control panel. Sulu's dervishlike opponent, a man-shape given form and body by ionized gas held in a rigorously restricted force-field, disappeared—a solid-state djinn.

"I don't see why you've never used that kick-parry before," Scott observed. "It worked marvelously."

Sulu smiled as he toweled the back of his neck. "Never had to get that fancy before. Trouble is, the computer rarely lets me get away with a successful move more than once." He let out a short sigh.

"The problem with that defense is that if you miss the parry-kick, you're left floating in mid-air with your sword at your side—a ripe candidate for shish kebab." His expression turned studious.

"Its movements are still a little unnatural, still a bit machinelike. And I noticed a few other problems, too. There were several times when it fought while floating a couple of centimeters above the floor." He grinned. "No fair. The computer's got enough advantages as it is."

"Not enough to reduce the experience of actual combat, though," Scott countered, checking a tiny window in the panel. "You're still well ahead, laddie, twelve touches to five."

"I remember when I used to beat it seventeen to nothing. It's learning, all right."

Scott shrugged. "That's one of the functions of a games computer. If I could program the ship's computer, you'd have a mechanical fighter who'd act perfectly human, even to experiencing fatigue as the battle wore on. But you know what the captain would say if we asked for ship computation time for a project like this." He indicated the wire-fringed control panel.

"I had a bit of a snap with the stores records cagin' the material for this—filed the requisitions under the 'emergency repairs' column. Shouldn't be any trouble with it unless Starfleet springs a surprise inventory on us. But usin' the main computer—," he shook his head firmly, "we've as much chance of that as me grandmother has of throwin' the caber in the next interstellar Highland games."

Sulu accepted the engineer's declaration as he straightened his blade. The foil was insulated on pommel and blade, leaving only the metal tip uncovered. Whenever that naked point intersected the ionized gas in the force-field, it registered as a touch on the control box Scott had rigged. Unfortunately, there was no equally accurate way of judging when his computer-controlled opponent scored a hit on him. For now, that had to be done visually. But the system was new, and Scott was still working on that problem as well as on several others.

They would have plenty of time during this long, dull mission to Draymia to perfect his *katana-to-ashi* opponent. Unlike say, Mr. Spock, who could always find plenty of challengers for tri-dimensional chess and other logic games, there wasn't anyone else on board who possessed more than a perfunctory knowledge of the modern martial art, which merged European-style fencing with the old karate of the Orient. Those crew members who were athletically inclined preferred bowling, or a good round of water polo.

When he'd finally grown deathly bored with fencing and kicking at his own shadow, Sulu had gone to Scott to see if the circuit-wizard could concoct something in the way of a robotic fighter. It hadn't taken the chief engineer long to produce his golden-gas hominoid.

Scott cocked an eyebrow as he glanced up from reintegrating one of the tiny modular components which controlled the fluidity of the force-field. Sulu was at the open arms cabinet.

"More, Lieutenant? Aren't you worn out yet?"

"Just a little saber work."

The engineer looked disapproving. "The final flurry? You know this thing can't score saber near as well as foil. Half the time I've no idea whether you're hittin' the target or not, with all that blade area. Let alone when it's hittin' you."

"Just a few minutes," Sulu pleaded. "I don't want my edge work to get rusty."

"All right, then, if you must." Scott didn't quite grumble. "I've the little matter of a ship to watch over."

He pressed a switch on the panel. Instantly, still frozen in the pose of its last execution, Sulu's antagonist glowed to life again. Scott adjusted controls, manipulated dials. The games computer set the newly programed tape in motion and the lambent duelist assumed an *en garde* position.

Sulu lined up across from it. "Ready," he announced, turning his gaze to the gilded ghost. Scott touched a red switch.

The chief engineer had been right, though. At times Sulu himself couldn't tell whether or not he was slipping the first blow in. In a real fight, however, it would be more than merely satisfying to know whether a certain move worked. It would be vital.

The fight lasted only the few minutes Sulu had asked for, but not for the reasons originally given. His nebulous opponent had just performed a good parry, faked high and thrust low. Sulu had fallen for the feint. He jumped, trying to avoid a supposedly high attack. When he saw it was really going low, he attempted to recover by twisting in mid-air to kick-block downward, and got himself confused.

Trying simultaneously to parry with his own sword, the net result turned out to be a neat slash with the metal blade across the thin shoe he was wearing. He came down on both feet, immediately dropped the saber and buckled to the floor, wincing.

Having registered an undeniable score, the computer-controlled figure paused and resumed the ready position, awaiting the command to re-engage once more.

Scott flicked it out of existence. There was a brief, dying whine as the force-field's power was cut. Then the engineer hurried over to where the helmsman sat, trying to unsnap the latches on his right shoe.

"Maybe you ought to go back to shadow-fightin', Sulu."

The helmsman grimaced as he worked at the latchings.

"Very funny, Mr. Scott."

Both men saw that the top of the shoe was already stained red. The humor of the situation was relegated to the background.

Scott put one hand on the heel, took a gentle grip on the toe with the other. "Easy, lad . . . I'll try and get this off."

While he pushed and pulled, Sulu leaned back on both hands, stared at the ceiling of the gymnasium chamber and tried to think of other things. He couldn't repress a little gasp as the shoe finally slipped free.

There was a three-centimeter long gash across the top of his foot. Though it bled profusely, Sulu still counted himself lucky. The blade had struck at an angle which caused it to miss the big tendons. He made no move to rise.

"Stay there," Scott ordered him. He moved to a nearby cabinet and came back with a first-aid kit. The bandaging was crude, but at least they halted the flow of blood.

"Sorry, Sulu," he apologized when the temporary repair job was finished. "I'm much better with a needlepoint welding laser."

Sulu eyed him archly. "Thanks just the same, Scotty, I'll settle for the bandages."

"Can you walk, or d'you want me to call for a stretcher?"

"No—no stretcher!" Sulu objected quickly. "The captain's liable to hear about it." He struggled to his feet. "Cut's on the top, not the sole. I can make it. Give me a hand to Sick Bay."

Scott mumbled about the waste of time as he helped Sulu get a large sock over the injured foot. Sulu was right, though. The captain wouldn't take kindly to the news that one of his Bridge officers had disabled himself at a game.

The few personnel they encountered in the corridors inquired solicitously as to the cause of the helmsman's limp. It was explained that he had slightly sprained an ankle playing handball. Much to Sulu's relief, this explanation seemed to be accepted by all.

McCoy was in a testier mood than usual. He unwrapped Scott's makeshift bandage job and stared disgustedly at the neat wound, muttering to himself as he went about the business of cleaning it out and closing it up.

"You cut your foot *how*?"

Sulu looked away and repeated the story for the third time.

"I've already told you, Dr. McCoy. Mr. Scott was kind enough to use some of his off-duty hours to develop an artificial warrior for me to practice against. I was making a parry where I shouldn't have been and I cut myself, that's all."

McCoy shook his head as he used three tiny organic clips to clamp the edges of the wound together. Spray from a can coated the wound and clips with an anesthetizing sealant. Eventually, the modified protein clips would be absorbed by Sulu's body, but not until the wound had completely healed over.

"That's a fairly deep cut, Helmsman," McCoy commented as he put away the can. "Try not to kick anyone with that foot till it heals up, hmmm? It should be okay."

Sulu looked as if he had something further to say, but instead glanced at Scott for help. The chief engineer looked indifferent, then abruptly remembered how many times his senior officer had bailed him out of a difficult situation.

"Uh, Dr. McCoy. . . ."

McCoy looked back at him.

"We'd kinna hoped you wouldn't mention this little episode to the captain. I know it has to be entered in the medical log, but the lieutenant would appreciate it if you didn't go out of your way to tell him about it. You know what his reaction'd be."

"More than 'It'll be okay'," the doctor muttered. He didn't look at Sulu as he added, "I haven't got time anyway—not with that ton of medical supplies we're to deliver to Draymia to check out."

Glad for the change of subject and, incidentally, curious, Sulu swung his legs off the table and wondered, "Why should you have to bother with them at all, Doctor? Aren't they prepacked and self-contained?"

In reply McCoy sat down before a viewscreen and manipulated the controls. Peering over his shoulder, both Scott and Sulu saw vast columns of words and figures, massed tightly together like the ranks of an advancing army. McCoy gestured in an uncomplimentary manner at the screen, shaking his head dolefully.

"The instructional manuals for the equipment and supplies are all mixed up. If I don't get them properly relabeled before we arrive, the Draymians won't be able to tell an encephalograph from an endocrine monitor, or a case of Draymian aspirin from the serum for treating brain damage." He angrily snapped the picture off, turned to them.

"Whoever precoordinated this shipment's a likely candidate for a good shot of the latter drug."

"Can't you get someone to take over your regular assignments until you get everything sorted out?" Scott asked.

McCoy stared back at him evenly. "Would you want me to delegate my duties to someone else? Suppose Sulu had really sliced himself up? Or you, Scotty? How would you feel if I was off cataloging packages someplace?"

Neither man said anything.

He switched the screen back on, swiveled around to stare at the new display. "Besides, the health of hundreds of thousands of intelligent beings might depend on the safe delivery of these supplies. I'm not about to entrust their proper delivery to anyone but myself.

"Now if you don't mind," he growled, "I'd like to get back to my *important* work."

Sulu grinned as he gingerly put more weight on his injured limb. It was amazing how much better it felt already, after McCoy's precise ministrations.

The doctor's surface gruffness deceived neither of them.

"He'll make it all right, if he has to push himself double-shift," Scott declared as the two men entered the corridor outside Sick Bay. "He's got a good two weeks' ship-time before we make orbit around Draymia. It's only stardate fifty-five . . ."

". . . thirty-two point eight," Kirk finished, his voice slightly hoarse from the dry atmosphere of Draymia. As he spoke into the communicator, it relayed his voice back to the official log recorder on board the *Enterprise*, now orbiting far overhead.

"Preparing to beam back aboard ship following successful delivery of medical equipment and supplies to the planet Draymia in the Draymian star system. Kirk out . . ."

They stood on a balcony outside the chambers of the Draymian capital city administration, awaiting the arrival of the Supreme Prefect for the final embarkation ceremony. While Spock and McCoy discussed some obscure point of Draymian physiology as it related to certain of the supplies they had brought, Kirk turned and allowed his gaze to roam over the capital's skyline. Once one became used to the size of everything, built to nearly one and a quarter human scale, this world looked almost familiar. This, despite its extreme distance from the nearest Federation outpost planet.

The vegetation here was not terribly alien, likewise the animal life. But the hue of sky was just a touch too green, the tree trunks a bit too orange, the flying creatures' wings too scaly for hominess. In other words, Draymia was one of those many humanoid worlds whose weirdness was all the more disturbing for its elusive familiarity.

It wasn't a world where the local ungulates rolled around on wheels instead of walking on normal legs, or where the vegetation grew upside down like the ostrich forest on Olibaba. No, on a world like Draymia you always had the feeling that if you could just hit the right switch inside your head, there would be a little click, the proper lens would slip into place in front of your eyes, and everything would suddenly slide over into the normal.

"Hail, Captain Kirk! Hail, Mr. Spock!"

The men turned to see two Draymians emerging from the arched doorway. Kirk recognized the Supreme Prefect, but not his companion.

"Who's the other with him, Mr. Spock?"

"We met him briefly once before, Captain, on arrival," the first officer whispered, wondering idly why there had been no hearty hail for Dr. McCoy. Probably the Draymians simply hadn't noticed him yet. He filed the observation away for future consideration. "The being's name is Demos. He is the chief of the planetary security forces. He was in charge of receiving the few military-related medical supplies."

"Oh, yes," Kirk muttered. "I remember now." He broke off as both aliens halted before them. Their expressions—insofar as Kirk could now judge them—were neutral. Part of the ceremony of departure, no doubt.

Two and a half meters tall, well proportioned, the enormous humanoids could have appeared threatening. Their bulbous pop-eyes, however, gave their faces a comic cast which detracted from their massiveness.

As Kirk watched, the Supreme Prefect flicked one ear forward. The other was turned backward, perhaps to listen to some distant conversation. The effect, alongside the smooth pate, was startling. The Draymians possessed independently mounted ears, like the eyes of an Earthly chameleon.

The Prefect launched straight into the departure ceremony, as the somber-seeming Demos stood at attention at his side. The ceremony itself contained no surprises. Much was said about expanding trade and cooperation between Draymia and the Federation. There were words of mutual praise for the technical accomplishments of both civilizations, assurances of continuing friendship and interdependence, veiled polite references to those misguided races (who shall remain nameless) who might seek to interpose themselves between the goal of Federation-Draymian brotherhood, and so on.

Kirk and Spock replied where necessary, exchanging diplomatic banter with the aplomb and experience of men accustomed to far more complex goings-on. Kirk recalled one world on which merely saying a simple goodbye involved two days of feasting and athletic competition.

Finally, both the Prefect and Demos performed little half-bows and extended their hands, palms turned upward and open. "We wish to thank," he told them in his gravelly voice, "you and the rest of your Federation for your most welcome and invaluable assistance, Captain Kirk, in this and all matters."

The three men returned the gesture, which signified the taking of final farewell, as Kirk replied, "We hope through our medical assistance programs to develop and strengthen relations with all advanced civilizations such as your own, Supreme Prefect."

With that said, both humans and Draymians returned to a natural stance.

Kirk smiled easily, glanced back at his companions as he pulled out his communicator and flipped it open. "Shall we, Spock, Bones? Kirk to *Enterprise*—beam us aboard, Scotty."

The Prefect extended a hand palm down this time, fingers bent at the middle knuckles. "If you would be so kind, Captain, a moment . . ."

Kirk hesitated uncertainly, then looked at Spock and McCoy. Both stared back at him blankly. The gestures were unmistakable, Spock seemed to say. Once the gesture of final leave-taking is made, nothing is supposed to follow.

Something of importance was happening here.

"Belay that, Mr. Scott," he said hurriedly into the open comm. He flipped it shut—for the moment.

"We await," he told the Supreme Prefect.

That appeared to satisfy the huge humanoid. He relaxed visibly and made a gesture to his companion that none of the humans recognized.

"Proceed, Commander Demos."

The security chief, with some ceremony, removed a folded sheet of opaque yellow plastic from a tunic pocket beneath his arm. It opened into the triangle favored by the Draymians.

"I have here a warrant," he announced solemnly, "in your own language, received by deep-space relay for the arrest and trial of one of your crew, Captain." He extended the yellow sheet toward Kirk, who stared at the smooth geometric form in disbelief.

"Best take it, Captain," Spock finally prompted him.

"Warrant," Kirk murmured dazedly. "Who . . . ?"

"If you would be so kind as to read it aloud, please, Captain?" the Prefect requested politely.

Kirk's gaze turned down to the plastic. On it was what looked to be a perfect xerographic copy of the familiar rectangle of official Starfleet command-level stationery. The format design and intricate curlicued seals bordering it were either genuine or else the finest counterfeit he'd ever seen.

"You are directed to surrender," he read in a monotone, "for trial by the people of Draymia, Dr. Leonard McCoy, medical officer, *U.S.S. Enterprise* assigned your command . . .'' His voice trailed away.

"Let me see that please, Captain," Spock requested rapidly. Rather more rapidly than was normal for him.

Blank-faced, Kirk handed the document over. His gaze slowly swung around to McCoy.

"Well, Bones . . . ?"

McCoy gaped back at him in open-mouthed confusion and could only shake his head slowly in total bewilderment. He had seen the opaque triangle of plastic, seen the inscribed borders and seals and the signatures at the bottom. But all he could do was stammer to the chief of Draymian security, "This has to be some kind of . . . bad joke."

"While there are those among you who might find certain aspects of our sense of humor peculiar," the giant replied stonily, "believe me when I say that we do not consider the wanton slaughter of thousands of innocent civilians a joke."

McCoy's jaws made more movements than were necessary to produce the stumbling response. "Slaughter . . . thousands of people . . . ?"

Spock tapped the plastic sheet. "According to this, it is claimed that Dr. McCoy was responsible for a plague which ravaged the Draymian colony on Dramia II some nineteen years ago, Captain."

Kirk shook his head violently, then snatched the warrant from Spock's hands. "Let me see that thing again!" Once more his eyes roved over it, paying particular attention to the concluding seals and signatures. He glanced up at Demos, his voice barely controlled, and cold.

"This is a copy. I'd like to see the genuine article."

Demos executed the Draymian equivalent of a shrug, stepped aside. "Naturally, Captain. I would not expect you to do otherwise. The original is inside, properly protected. This is why we arranged for you to take your leave of us here." He gestured at the building.

"Welcome to the Draymian Chamber of Contemplative Reconstruction, Captain."

"Treachery, you mean," Kirk rumbled, as he stalked off toward the open portal.

Demos' eyes bulged even more than was natural as he followed alongside. "Justice, *we* mean," he glowered. "Under the circumstances, Captain Kirk, I think we are showing remarkable restraint.''

''Restraint? I'll show you some restraining!'' Kirk muttered tightly. ''The *Enterprise* can 'restrain' this whole city.''

''Doubtless your words hold truth,'' the Prefect observed from behind him as they entered the building once again. ''We are a practical people. I, personally, am well aware of the destructive capabilities of your vessel. We are also an astute people psychologically.

''While you could probably reduce this city to its foundations, Captain Kirk, I've no doubt you will not. You will do nothing. Your reputation has preceded you. We know of your respect for your own laws. And as you have seen, the warrant is perfectly in order and properly approved by your own superiors. You will not disobey their orders.''

''Not *my* superiors,'' Kirk shot back. ''Not in Starfleet. This is a judicial order, issued by administrative authority.''

''Whatever the source, Captain,'' Demos put in, ''you recognize its authority. You will not attempt to contravene it. Therefore, I am certain you will offer no resistance while I perform my necessary duty.'' He reached out and placed a huge hand on McCoy's right shoulder.

''Dr. Leonard McCoy, I place you under official restraint. Do you yield voluntarily?''

McCoy nodded slowly and moved forward when Demos tugged, but the motions were independent of any real thought. He could only turn to gape wordlessly at Spock and Kirk as they followed.

There was a buzz for attention from Kirk's belt as they moved through the glass and stone structure, past languidly strolling Draymians bent on other official missions.

Kirk opened the communicator, his voice thick. ''Kirk here.''

''Captain . . . ?'' That single word held a paragraph of worry.

''Sorry, Scotty. I forgot you were on hold. It seems—it seems there's going to be something of a delay here. Dr. McCoy's been arrested and—''

Over the kilometers and through the clouds the chief engineer's astonished yelp cut him off. ''*DR. MCCOY ARRESTED? What for . . . ?*''

Kirk tried to frame the word "genocide," found that the effort of linking that concept to McCoy brought him close to blackout.

"Murder," he finally managed to mutter.

"Murder?" Scott paused. When he spoke again, his voice was no longer querulous. "Sir, if you'd like me and some of the security specialists to beam down just in case, I'm sure there'd be no lack of volun . . ."

"Belay that kind of talk, Mr. Scott!" Kirk said, summoning his usual firmness. "The warrant itself appears to be legitimate, issued and authorized by the proper authorities. Mr. Spock and I are going to double-check it now. We're at the local administration building. I'll keep you posted."

"Should I put the ship on alert, sir?"

"No, Mr. Scott. While it may prove hard to restrain natural impulses, this is the time for careful consideration. The Draymians have been scrupulously correct about this. They've made nothing resembling a hostile gesture toward us. And, Scotty, this is not for general dissemination aboard. What I've just told you stays on the Bridge."

"Aye sir," Scott replied quietly.

"Kirk out."

It was all so absurd, Kirk mused, as they moved deeper into the enormous structure. Bones was no more guilty of mass murder than he was of unnecessarily vivisecting a frog. The good doctor was inherently incapable of either maliciousness or incompetence on such a scale.

And yet . . .

There *was* the official warrant, the insane accusation. He stared at the original communication where it was locked behind triple transparent barriers. Despite Demos' and the Prefect's confidence in his willingness to obey his own laws, Kirk found himself having to fight the urge to simply call Scotty to beam them up and out of this treacherous city. Such an action could precipitate an uncomfortable interstellar incident, he knew. The Draymians wouldn't hesitate to publicize it throughout the civilized galaxy. If the Federation didn't adhere to its own laws, why should potential allies be forced to?

He noticed that they had moved into a small office adjoining the well-guarded transmission. Demos sat across from them behind a large desk of white stone. He was answering most of the questions he had expected Kirk to ask.

"Dr. McCoy," the security chief explained, "headed a mass inoculation program against harmful diseases on Dramia II some nineteen of your subjective years ago.

"He was not yet—annointed? No, appointed—a full doctor at the time of this program. Soon after his small medical force departed, a massive plague struck. Fatalities were near total in the growing colony we'd established—established at much expense in life and wealth, Captain Kirk.

"The Dramia II colony constituted our first step away from our home world. Thanks to your Dr. McCoy, the result has been that for the past two decades we have been unable to progress any farther. Since the plague incident public reaction becomes virulent at the mere mention of deep-space exploration or settlement." He looked grim.

"Such has been the result of your *aid*."

"You talk about this plague," Kirk shot back tersely, "as if you were certain Bones was personally responsible for it. Just because it occurred at the same time doesn't mean it was his fault."

Demos leaned forward and displayed front canines. "Believe me, Captain Kirk, we would also like very much to have the rest of the medical team that served under him. However, it appears this is not possible. Therefore we will settle for having the one who was in charge of those responsible for the disaster. It *is* his responsibility, whether directly or otherwise!"

Demos sat back and looked satisfied. "It is enough."

"You talk as if you'd already tried him and found him guilty."

"Captain, you cannot imagine the kind of emotional reaction the mere mention of the Dramia II debacle stirs in the hearts of the people. Feeling runs high even among those who did not have friends or relatives among the dead. It was a . . . a racial disaster. Furthermore, we could not even chance intensive study of the immediate causes lest we risk bringing the plague here, thus destroying our entire civilization. This has intensified the people's frustration and anger." He glanced away from Kirk.

"But after all these many years, we still can find no other

possible cause than some carelessness on the part of Dr.
McCoy and his medical team. As to his final guilt or innocence, the trial will say.''

''Trial!'' Kirk blurted. ''Kangaroo court, you mean. By
your own admission, Bones can hardly expect anything like
a fair trial from your people. McCoy is a Federation citizen
and—''

To every one of Kirk's plaints, Demos quietly referred to
the copy of the maddening warrant, lying between them on
the desk.

''His own government appears to feel that in this case such
rights can properly be waived.''

Kirk snorted derisively. ''What kind of justice can Bones
expect from a world that accepts our medical supplies with
one hand and imprisons our medical officer with the other?''

''You are becoming emotional, Captain,'' Spock ventured.

''Of course I am!'' Kirk shouted at his first officer, while
Demos was muttering something about returning measure
for measure.

''Bones harming other beings . . .,'' Kirk continued, ''you
know better, Spock. Anyone knows better than that—even
those desk-bound morons at Administrative and Judicial
know better.''

The captain rambled on as Spock tried to calm him.
Demos studied the two men with some detachment.

Alone—oh, how alone!—and forgotten, the fourth inhabitant of the tiny office rested his arms on his thighs and struggled to recall the events of nineteen years past. He found
only hazy memories clouded by age. So much had happened
since, so little had happened then . . .

Dramia II: colony, alien, Advanced Intern McCoy. His
second extrasolar assignment, his first medical command.
Draymia—bustling, alive, thriving. Dramia II—a bleak, chill
world, but promising. Willing giants, fish-eyed—their nervous children already his own size. Weeks of boredom, routine, of looking at nothing but alien arms—his crew anxious
to move on to another assignment, more challenging, nearer
home, with better opportunities for advancement.

Nineteen years. What had those hundreds of inoculations
been for? What had been the contents of those ampules? An

impurity overlooked, an imperfection in sealing—what? He had known so little then, and now he knew so much. If he could only go back, go back.

"I wish I could be as sure, Jim," a voice vaguely like his own finally murmured.

Conversation in the room died, and with McCoy's words, something inside Kirk died a little, too.

II

At least the cell they put him in was comfortable.

It had no bars, and the larger chamber was no more than normally oppressive, as jails went. The furnishings within the cell were simple, but at least they were sized to McCoy's non-Draymian proportions.

"I just can't be positive," he was mumbling from behind the lightly radiant force-field. He had been talking to himself like that ever since Demos and a patrol of oversized Draymians had escorted him to this forlorn waiting place.

"Is it possible that I somehow was, somehow am responsible for the—"

"Ridiculous!" Kirk objected sharply.

"There is surely," Spock added with his usual assurance, "ample reason to believe that the termination of your inoculation program and the subsequent outbreak of plague on the Dramia II colony is coincidence."

"There's also ample reason to believe that it was a tragic mistake of some kind on my part," McCoy whispered.

"I don't buy that, Bones," Kirk said firmly. "I'm not going to sit around and let someone else sell it to the Federation, either."

"You have something in mind, Captain," Spock responded. It was not a question.

Kirk turned. "A little pretrial investigation, Mr. Spock. A bit of harmless fact gathering—independent fact gathering—to aid Draymian justice." He gestured.

One of the several guards in the chamber moved to the wall, touched a series of switches on a small hand control. The secondary force-field vanished, and Kirk and Spock moved clear. The guard touched another combination and the backup field flamed up again, leaving McCoy totally isolated.

Kirk flipped open his communicator without a backward glance. "Kirk to *Enterprise*—beam us up, Mr. Scott."

"How many, Captain?"

"Two. Just two, Mr. Scott."

"Captain," the chief engineer's voice began, "I think—"

"Beam up, Scotty—now," Kirk repeated.

"Aye, sir."

The twin dissolution that followed was colorful, not destructive. McCoy was left alone in his cell. Well, not entirely alone.

The single guard who remained after Kirk and Spock had departed strolled over and peered curiously at the prisoner. He knew of the Terran's reputed crime. It was an honor to be one of those assigned to watch him, to be one of the few designated to see to his health—so he would be fit and well for the trial.

McCoy did not object to serving as the bug in an alien bottle. He was too depressed to think coherently about anything save his own sudden, shocking change of fortune.

"Your friends may scour the surface of Dramia II to the bedrock," the guard informed the despondent figure within the cage. "They will find nothing to save you. We are a civilized race. Our court system is swift and efficient." In the manner of all jailers, he grinned at his own ironic joke.

As is universally the case with prisoners subjected to such humor, McCoy did not find it amusing.

Words alternated with pictures alternated with charts. Sometimes all three combined on the lab screen to form an especially brilliant and impressive display. The men studying it now were not interested in superficialities, however. They were hunting desperately for a clue to a friend's salvation, and they were not having much luck.

Kirk moved from a small computer annex which was connected to the central computer to stare at the other screen over Spock's shoulder. While Spock was running backward through time, the captain was triple checking the legal fine points of the Federation warrant—to no avail. It was as solid as a warp-drive equation.

"Anything yet, Mr. Spock?"

"No, Captain." The first officer did not turn from the steady flow of information pouring across the screen in front of him. "Our historical records for the Draymian system are few, going back barely two standard decades. Dr. McCoy's medical team was one of the first Federation groups to visit here."

"Kind of unusual, isn't it—for a medical team to be called into a new system so soon after initial contact is opened?"

"Yes, Captain. But apparently the Draymian need was considerable. Understandably Starfleet felt that if we did not respond to their request for assistance, someone else might be only too happy to oblige. The Klingons, for example."

"Granted," Kirk admitted. As usual, Spock's assessment of the situation was infallible.

"Most of the information available on early Federation contact with the Draymians comes from the technical survey teams—planetary and solar data, geophysical statistics—the usual enormous mass of pure information which takes many years to properly integrate and codify for easy computer retrieval."

Abruptly the rapid stream of lines and words froze on screen. Spock pressed another switch and several significant paragraphs blossomed into easily readable lines.

DRAMIA II, LOCAL COLONIZATION, HISTORY OF.

"It's about time," Kirk muttered.

The two officers ran through a mass of detail until they came to: *Plague, Dramia II, colony of Draymia. Origin unknown, characterized by pigmentation shift in skin of victim, debilitation, followed by the onset of terminal coma. Theoretically can affect several species of humanoid including man, quorman, and others. Those dead from exposure include corpsman Micheau Pochenko, anesthesiologist Severin Alonzo Hart.*

Spock glanced back at Kirk. "It appears that two of Dr. McCoy's own team also died from the plague. Our Draymian hosts neglected to mention that. *Certain species*," he read, turning back to the screen, "*believed to be naturally immune, notably Tauran and Vulcan. Interesting.*"

"Go on, Mr. Spock," Kirk prompted, ignoring the parade of legalese across his own, now unwatched screen . . .

Done with taunting the unresponsive prisoner, the guard reported to Demos what he'd overheard when the murderer had spoken with his two superiors.

"You are certain?"

"Yes, my commander," the guard insisted stiffly. "The Federation Captain is planning to visit Dramia II to gather material negative to our case against human filth, McCoy."

"Thank you, guard. Speak of this to no one else, please. You may leave."

"It shall be as you desire, Commander." The guard saluted and left.

Demos sat thinking for several minutes. There was no telling what distortion of truth the clever Federation officers might glean from the poor, blighted ruin of Dramia II. But the people of Draymia had waited stoically for their revenge these past years. He, Demos, was not about to see them deprived of it. Whatever tricks, whatever perversion of logic Captain Kirk could concoct from the ruined colony must not go unobserved. And this was not something he could trust to underlings.

He activated a switch within the bonelike mass of the desk, a switch that didn't appear to exist.

"Ready my personal skiff immediately . . ."

Kirk was aware he was proceeding without proper authority. But he wasn't about to contact Starfleet for permission—after all, that *proper authority* had issued the damning warrant in the first place. They could call him on the deck afterward—after he had proven Bones' innocence.

"Estimated time of arrival, Mr. Sulu?"

Sulu checked a readout, reported, "Four hours ship time, sir."

"Move it up a little if the computer can handle the acceleration compensation. The Draymians will *probably* stick to their normal courtroom procedure. However, this is a special case to them, and they may be interested in rushing it to completion. Also, we've no idea how long it may take us to turn up proof of Bones' innocence.

"Demos, their security chief, emphasized the civilized nature of his people. But if it becomes public information that the government is now holding the being they consider responsible for the extinction of their sole off-planet colony, I wouldn't be surprised to see a spirit of vigilantism take over."

"Do not confuse human and alien motivation, Captain," advised Spock.

"I wish that were a uniquely human tendency, Mr. Spock. Unfortunately, it appears from stellar history that we've no monopoly on mob law."

"Unfortunate, indeed, Captain."

Spock's observation had ramifications that Kirk would have liked to pursue but the captain's thoughts were interrupted by a call from the helm.

"Ship in pursuit, Captain."

"Origin?"

Sulu hurriedly checked sensors. "Undoubtedly from Draymia, sir. I'm running the recorder back—here it is, no bigger than a two-man scout."

"Full magnification of the aft screen."

"I'm on full, sir."

Kirk squinted at the screen, which showed only distant stars. "I don't see anything, Mr. Sulu."

"No, sir. Sensors had it for only a moment. The ship apparently was following just out of maximum scanner range. When we suddenly increased our speed, its pilot jumped to stay with us and for a second or two, overcompensated. He's dropped back out of detector range again."

"But not transmission range," Uhura observed. "Shall I attempt contact, Captain?"

"No, Lieutenant, not just yet."

"May I inquire as to the reason?" This from a curious Spock.

"We seem to have two choices, Mr. Spock. We can let this busybody—who is obviously out to make things difficult for us, else he wouldn't be skulking about our stern— continue to think he's succeeding at his game. Or we can try to make things easier for him."

"Easier, Captain? I fail to understand."

"He could certainly cause us more trouble at a crucial

moment by sneaking aboard. That would be simple for him to do, since we've carelessly left open the doors to the Shuttlecraft Bay.''

"Captain, the doors aren't open," Uhura pointed out.

"Oh, yes—take care of that little undersight, will you, Mr. Sulu? Mr. Spock, issue a general order—all internal lights near exterior ports, all observation lounge illumination, to be extinguished.

"As far as I know, no Draymian has ever been aboard a Federation cruiser while it was in transit. They know as little about us as we do about them. I'd like to give the impression that most of the crew is off-duty, asleep."

"Anyone approaching would assume we still have automatic detectors operational, Captain."

"Any representative of a seasoned space-traveling race would, Mr. Spock. But the Draymians are new at this. Besides, we've already given in to their demands to hand over Bones. Why would we have defensive screens up within their system, when we've already shown we abide by the law?

"Whoever's back there is convinced he's eluded us so far. Let's at least give him the opportunity to elude us a little farther . . .''

The lights went out aboard the great starship. On board his small skiff, Demos saw them fade.

He only had suppositions about Federation habits with which to judge the situation, but there had been no sign from the cruiser that his presence had been detected yet. If it had, he couldn't understand not receiving at least a querulous hail. So the decision he reached was precisely the one Kirk was hoping he would.

He edged his tiny vessel ahead—slowly at first, then, as silence continued, with increasing confidence. If the big ship's hangar doors were not automatic, he would be forced to use a suit.

The skiff slid silently into the cavernous hold and settled to a stop. Atmospheric considerations vanished when the hangar doors closed behind him and gauges monitored the rise of air pressure outside. The hold was empty of personnel, but not of concealment. Demos slipped his craft between two others, concealing it from all but direct view. In size and shape it did not differ enough from a Federation scout to immediately catch the attention of some idly strolling crewmember. Of course, these were all rationalizations. But the chance to actually inspect the inner workings of a Federation battle cruiser was too tempting to Demos' martial mentality for him to pass by.

Let him have two time-parts . . . one even . . .

He found the door leading to the first access corridor and peered cautiously through the transparent port set in its upper third. The passageway beyond was deserted. Opening the door and stooping slightly to avoid the overhead arch, he made his way into the empty main corridor.

If he could just find someplace to secrete himself for a while till he got his bearings . . .

The next doorway had no port. He would have to take a chance. The opening mechanism was clearly marked and easily operated. He activated it and the door slid aside.

Reflexively, he reached for the weapon at his belt.

"Not now, Demos, you're hardly in a position to take on the entire crew," Kirk murmured evenly.

The hand dipping toward the gun relaxed, continued smoothly onward to scratch at an imaginary itch on his leg.

"And you," he countered with a touch of impatience, "are not in authority to conduct an investigation in this system."

Kirk's tone was conciliatory as he turned to his first officer. "You will remind me to report my unbecoming attitude to the Federation, won't you, Spock?"

"Of course, Captain."

"I demand you report to your superiors now, and that I be permitted to sit in on—"

"Actually, Demos," Kirk interrupted, "you're hardly in a position to demand much of anything. But I'll surprise you, I think, by saying that I'll happily oblige. Unfortunately, we're out of communications range with Starfleet Central at the moment."

"Report to the nearest Star Base, then—"

"Sorry, you asked me to report to my *superiors*. By your own admission, exceeding our authority to conduct this type of investigation is a matter for consideration at the highest levels. And I wouldn't *think* of insulting you by laying the matter before some minor functionary."

"Then, I myself will proceed to your Star Base and report this violation for you." Demos turned and started back down the corridor, feeling strangely flat eyes on the back of his head.

"I'm afraid your ship has been impounded, Commander, for your own protection."

Demos whirled, furious. "My own protec—"

"You'd never reach Starbase with it."

"So *you* say," Demos muttered angrily. "Just as you say you are out of communications range with your Central Headquarters."

"Yes, and there's something else I say," Kirk went on, now even more firmly.

"You are a stowaway, Commander," Spock informed the angry security chief. "You are in violation, I believe, of one of your own laws."

Demos started to say something, but his words became tangled as a sudden realization of his situation set it. "You planned it . . . you planned this so that it would appear legal, so that my abduction would not seem to break any laws."

"We merely offered you the chance to realize your own desires, Demos," Kirk replied firmly. "I seem to recall a similar course of action recently taken against a Federation citizen by your own government. You wouldn't happen to remember the name of that unlucky individual, would you? His name was McCoy, Leonard McCoy. Maybe now you can sympathize with his situation a little more, Commander. In fact, I'd think you'd begin to acquire a personal interest in it."

"I have a personal interest in seeing justice done," Demos snapped, drawing himself up.

"Excellent." Kirk turned to leave. "Mr. Spock, see to the Commander's comfort. It's good to hear he's after the same thing we are . . ."

Dramia II loomed on the screen before them, a brown and red crescent splotched only fitfully with greens and blues. A harsh-looking world on which to try to mold a new civilization.

The Draymians had been courageous enough to try. They had been rewarded with death and desolation.

Ironically, the vacuum surrounding that stark planet blazed

with beauty. Dramia II swam in the midst of one of the massive deep-space auroras for which the Dramian system had first been noted. Brilliant reds, purples, and blues glowed under powerful bombardment from Dramia's sun, forming a fiery curtain in space. Several shifting, metallic streamers draped themselves across the planet, masking portions of it with ionized glory.

"Lovely phenomenon."

"Yes, Captain," Spock agreed. "According to records, it is one of several such scattered through the system. It was the highlight of the first Federation survey here." He nodded toward the screen.

"This band of particulate matter is the farthest out from the sun itself."

"I see. Surface radiation level, Mr. Sulu?"

"Still working on it, Captain."

A moment, then, "I see the figures," Spock reported. "The level is strong, but nowhere lethal. There *are* some as yet unclassifiable aspects to the readings obtained where one of the auroral streamers intersects the atmosphere of Dramia II, which—"

Kirk cut him short. "We'll have time for research after we secure Dr. McCoy's release."

"Yes, Captain."

Nearby, Demos made a derisive sound.

"All I'm concerned about is that it's safe for us to beam down," Kirk continued. "Since it appears to be . . . shall we, gentlemen?" He rose from the command chair and started for the elevator door, followed by Spock and Demos.

Scott was waiting for them in the transporter room. He voiced his own concerns immediately.

"Are you sure it's safe, Captain?"

"As safe as our sensors are sure, Scotty. Absolutely."

"Not absolutely, Captain. Our sensing equipment is never absolutely sure," Spock corrected.

Kirk grinned, looked over at Demos who was studying the transporter alcove with what seemed like momentary hesitation.

"Mr. Spock, you're not trying to scare our Draymian comrade, are you? You can still remain aboard if you wish, Commander."

The Draymian chief of security stared evenly back at him. "I came to make certain you fabricated no intricate lies, Captain Kirk. I go."

He stepped up into the transporter and assumed a somewhat cramped pose of readiness.

"You heard him, Mr. Scott. Energize."

Scott looked unhappy, but set about the familiar operation. He adjusted the necessary switches, pulled the requisite levers. There was the familiar whine of complaining atoms, and the three figures were gone . . .

Three pillars of shattered crystal solidified on the sandy surface and shaped themselves into upright containers of intelligence.

Kirk stumbled slightly on rematerialization—the surface underfoot was loose and windblown. Part of the region they had set down in was still verdant. Trees and hedgerows of Draymian flora had been planted here.

But the irrigation systems had broken down under nineteen years of neglect. The desert had encroached ever more boldly on what had once been the fertile periphery of the two colony towns.

Around them lay the battered, partially decomposed remains of homes and warehouses and offices—evidence of angry winds, of sand pitted against walls. Dunes were piled up to the sills of windows devoid of glass, which stared with vacant sockets at the advancing drifts.

Here and there were signs of old fires. Kirk hoped they had been caused by natural means and not by the last vestiges of isolated, panicked sentience. Reversion from civilization to barbarism in a single generation was never very pretty, no matter which world was involved.

The physical detritus was sobering. He could imagine what that final, plague-rotted collapse must have been like. Still, it was one thing to imagine and quite another to stand in the midst of such imaginings. His quota of sympathy for the Draymians went up another notch, though the sight of this graveyard of hopes did nothing to shake his confidence in McCoy's innocence.

"Not the most enchanting scene I've ever beheld," he finally murmured.

"Plague seldom leaves behind fields of flowers and dancing children, Captain."

Kirk glared angrily at the security chief, who simply stared over the captain's head with the serene gaze of the self-righteous. Spock raised an eyebrow.

"There must have been local medical facilities—one central hospital, at least. I would assume they are less severely damaged than these structures here, as logic dictates they would be the last buildings to be abandoned. It would be a good place to begin our search."

Again, Demos made that strange Draymian shrug. "As you wish. This is so hopeless. Why not depart our system in peace, now, and leave destiny to take its inevitable course?"

"I'm afraid," Kirk said tightly, "that inevitable is a word I'm not familiar with. If you could direct us . . . ?"

Demos turned and pointed toward a slightly higher cluster of ruins lying near the approximate center of the first town.

"That must be what remains of the communications station. According to Draymian town plan, the medical facilities should have been built several blocks further north and a little to the east."

Kirk nodded curtly, and they slogged off through thick sand in the indicated direction. Soon after they started their progress improved as the clinging sand gave way to pockmarked but still serviceable pavement.

They were in the outskirts of the town proper when they noticed something moving on their right—moving sharply and jerkily, it was neither subtle nor inconspicuous. All three marchers saw it. Surprisingly, it was Demos who looked fearful while they surveyed the rubble.

"Some danger?" Kirk wondered. Demos' eyes studied the rim of the debris with practiced skill.

"If you remember, Captain Kirk, I said that *nearly* everyone on Dramia II was killed. There were reports of some survivors by later survey crews—which did not touch down, of course. I think 'survivors' is an overly optimistic classification for any pitiful souls forever marooned here.

"One drone was sent down some eight years ago. It was at that time that these survivors acquired a reputation for not liking outsiders."

"Hardly surprising," Spock commented, "in view of

what they must feel. They could not be expected to act logically. But surely you cannot be considered an outsider, Commander. You are as Draymian as they. I should think the sight of a fellow being would fill them with pleasure."

"The sight of a fellow *Draymian* might," Demos replied, with a bitter half-chuckle. "But there are no Draymians left on this world . . . not as we know them. The gulf between us now is that which separates the living and the walking dead."

There was more movement to the far right of the crumbled wall they were watching. Kirk would never have noticed it had he not been looking idly at that exact spot when the figure decided to abandon the area.

"Walking dead he may be but he still has some spirit left in him. He mustn't get away!"

Kirk started on the run after the retreating biped. Spock moved up quickly alongside. Demos hesitated for several long seconds. Apparently deciding it would be better to go along than remain alone in the open street, he raced after them. Enormous strides quickly caught him up to the two smaller men.

Had the figure been healthy it undoubtedly could have lost its pursuers easily in the maze of tumbling walls and hollowed-out structures. The few glances they had of it showed it to be ragged and hunched. It ran with a peculiar loping gait.

"There, Captain," Spock husked, "it went around that mound."

The mound had once served as the foundation for a higher, silo-like building. Now it was all crumbled in on itself, a concrete caldera. Sharp-edged blocks of broken masonry protruded here and there from the circular heap.

They rounded the hillock—and came to a sudden halt on the other side. The pavement here was open for several meters in every direction, save where the furrowed brow of a cliff-faced hill backed into the town. There were no structures, tumbled or otherwise, that their limping quarry could have reached in time to conceal himself before they had rounded the ruin.

"I was afraid of that," Kirk panted. "He's got some secret

cubbyhole he's slipped into. Almost looks like someone pulled him out with a transporter."

"Hardly likely, Captain," Spock observed drily. He moved toward the cliff-face while Demos and Kirk stood surveying the nearest ruins.

"I believe your initial supposition was correct, Captain," Spock soon called to them. They walked over to where he stood, staring into a vertical slit in the naked stone.

The crevice wasn't wide, but by turning sideways and holding his breath, a Draymian could squeeze through. It would be easier for Kirk and Spock.

Spreading out as far as possible to cover one another, the two officers from the *Enterprise* approached the opening. Nothing inorganic and unpleasant issued to meet them.

They started in. It grew darker . . . and then it didn't.

"Light inside," Kirk murmured softly. "Can't be a cave, then."

"Possibly one whose roof has collapsed wholly or partially," his first officer theorized. They continued to edge forward, hugging the cold rock wall. A grainy tenor sounded behind them.

"I would advise against this, Captain," Demos said. "Dramia II is little visited. We have no idea what kind of mutations the plague may have spawned among the local life-forms, of which several . . ."

"Save the biology lecture, Demos. You won't mind if I ignore your advice."

"Extreme caution in this restricted area would seem advisable, Captain."

"I'll watch myself, Spock, but I'm not going to lose that survivor. There may not be any others nearby, and we haven't much time. Also, if this one escapes, he may warn others of our presence. We may never spot another one."

The captain moved forward steadily, trying to make as little noise on the gravel underfoot as possible. "Bones' life is on the line, Mr. Spock. I don't mind taking a few risks."

The light dimmed until it was almost dark, but it never died entirely. Ahead he could detect patches of brightness. A few more steps, and Kirk emerged into a broad chamber.

Spock had been right. They stood in a cave whose ceiling had collapsed in places. The floor was dotted with mounds of fallen roof. He looked around, but there was no sign of their quarry.

Water waxed the rock dark and shiny where it issued in a steady trickle from cracks in a rock face. The tiny rivulets formed a small pool. Shade from the desert sun, protection from unrestricted carnivores, and water. His senses sharpened—this *had* to be their limping refugee's home. Kirk hoped they hadn't scared him out of it.

"Captain . . . are you all right?" Kirk snapped back to wakefulness, aware that Spock and Demos were waiting for his okay to proceed.

"All clear, Mr. Spock, come ahead." Kirk walked to the edge of the pool, nudged a pile of charred wood with his foot. "Cave dwellers," he muttered, "in a civilization as high as Draymia's."

"The result of your Dr. McCoy and his *civilized* medicine," the security chief responded coldly. Kirk whirled.

"Look, Demos, I'm getting a mite sick of your steady accusations. Until you can prove—"

A shadow suddenly detached itself from its dark companions and flung itself forward. It was no less gargoylish in form than its inorganic brothers.

At one time it had doubtless been intelligent—an intelligence now transcended by the madness shining in its eyes. It landed just behind Kirk, knocking him to the ground, and began flailing at him in frantic, howling anguish.

Momentarily stunned, Kirk couldn't dislodge his assailant, because of the latter's sheer bulk and unthinking rage. Fortunately, the same blind fury that drove the pitiable specimen to attack Kirk saved the captain from any serious harm, for the Draymian struck aimlessly, with neither skill nor design. Thus Kirk was able to shield himself from all the wild blows until Spock and Demos could wrestle the hysterical figure away.

The captain rolled over, his only injury a lack of breath.

"Captain . . ."

"Okay, Spock . . . I'm okay. He *wanted* to hurt me more than he actually did."

"And why do you think he attacked you, Captain?" asked Demos, struggling to restrain the gradually subsiding madman.

Kirk got to his feet, spoke slowly. "I was the nearest to his hiding place." Demos indicated the negative.

"You are also the only human among us, Captain Kirk. Don't attempt to evade the obvious. You were attacked because you are human—as is Dr. McCoy."

Damn you, Demos, Kirk cried silently. *And damn this whole insane system.* But he said nothing, merely dusted his uniform and moved to study the captive.

Fear had been replaced on the latter's face by remorse, anger by sorrow and misery; and that initial cry of fury became an utterly heart-rendering whimper. Clearly the creature was no longer a threat.

"Let him go," Kirk whispered.

"Are you sure, Captain?" Spock asked.

Kirk stared into the captive's eyes. They didn't meet his own. Instead they were focused on some other, greater horror now—one too distant to encompass the three figures around him.

Cautiously, Demos and Spock turned Kirk's assailant loose. That tortured soul turned, took two steps, and fell to his knees. He dropped onto his side and just lay there, moaning and sobbing uncontrollably.

Now Kirk knew they had to find *absolute*, incontrovertible proof that Bones was innocent. Supposition and verbal reasoning were not going to sway the decision of people who had been subjected to reports of this kind of emotional and mental destruction.

Nevertheless, he couldn't keep from voicing the inner certainty that kept him going.

"Demos, you've got to believe me. Dr. McCoy could never be responsible for something like . . . like that." He gestured to where the insane being gibbered mindlessly on the stone floor.

"Good intentions cannot wipe out the existence of evil results, Captain."

"But how did this one survive the plague?" Kirk wondered aloud, when an especially tortured howl rose from the no-longer-dangerous survivor.

Demos explained. "He and a few others were away, on the home world and elsewhere, when the plague struck. They returned before they could be stopped, to find everyone they'd known—loved ones, companions, everyone—dead of the plague.

"They chose to remain, to live here in the home they had once known." The security chief's voice was close to cracking. "Nineteen years of grief—there are worse plagues than those caused by germs. You see now, Captain Kirk, there were no actual survivors on Dramia II."

III

"I *thought* I heard sounds of fighting, and voices!"

The words that penetrated to the startled listeners were clear and strong, ringing loud in the cave.

"You're wrong, whoever you are," it continued. "There was at least one survivor."

A tall Draymian was walking toward them, climbing over a rocky hillock formed by part of the fallen ceiling. His clothes were ragged, his countenance worn, but otherwise he resembled Demos far more than he did the twisted figure rolling about on the cave floor.

"I was not found by any of the observation parties, nor by the crews of those ships which came to leave the mourners here. But I survived the plague—by what miracle I do not know. I'd given up hope of ever being rescued."

"You must remember what it was like, then," Kirk began excitedly. "During the plague . . . you can tell us."

"I remember," the newcomer nodded, oblivious to Demos' unbelieving stare. "I remember the people around me, even the doctors, turning blue, then green, and finally a dull red color, collapsing, strength ebbing, then . . ."

He stopped, his strong voice fading, the last softly whispered words echoing down hidden pathways in the cave.

"The pigmentation changes associated with the disease, as mentioned in the records, Captain," Spock commented.

Kirk nodded quickly, keeping his attention focused on the survivor. "You *must* remember," he asked anxiously, "before the plague struck, there was a visiting mission here from the Federation, a medical mission that included humans among its personnel.

"They were led by a man named McCoy—Dr. Leonard

McCoy. He was responsible for seeing to the vaccination of the entire colony. He must have treated you too . . . or at least overseen your treatment. *Do you remember him?*''

Kirk had no idea what to expect from the long-isolated alien, surviving amidst the ruins of a forgotten colony and its unstable inhabitants. Some hesitation, surely—a first imperfect attempt at resurrecting a faint memory of a distasteful past.

Instead, the survivor brightened immediately and spoke as though he were talking of yesterday.

''A Terran physician, young—of course, I remember Dr. McCoy. How could I forget the being who saved my life?''

Despite social and physical interspecies differences, the glances that passed then among Kirk, Demos, and Spock needed no interpretation.

''Then that is also the man,'' Demos finally declared, ''who is responsible for the death of this colony.'' And he waved at the surrounding desolation.

The survivor was neither intimidated nor impressed—as one might expect of a being who had successfully survived among the corpses of thousands, living and dead. He stared evenly back at the Commander of Draymian security.

''We knew little of the Federation and its various races, those many years ago,'' he began slowly. ''It has been a long time. Perhaps we know more of them now. But I believe that even those many triads ago we knew that the differences between us were not great.

''Although I knew this Dr. McCoy very briefly, I think I came to know him well. I cannot believe you are speaking of the same person who saved my life.'' The survivor looked thoughtful, reminiscing.

''At times he appeared less than positive, yes, and sometimes gave the impression of hesitation. But he did everything with a kindness and concern for the afflicted that was honest. You, Commander whoever-you-are . . .''

''Demos, of Draymian Internal Security.''

''Well, Demos, Commander of Draymian Security, I, · Kolti, think you have the wrong man,'' he concluded firmly. ''One who saves does not also murder.''

Demos threw Kolti a stare of frustration and anger; but the survivor had seen far worse things these past years than the gaze of the overbearing security chief. He gave no sign of altering his story or his regard for Dr. McCoy.

A smile had replaced Kirk's concerned stare. Spock's eyebrows ascended as the captain inquired, "So you're certain it was this Dr. McCoy who saved you?"

"Indeed, this is so."

"It's been several lifetimes for you, Kolti," Kirk observed, eyeing the tall Draymian appraisingly, "and I know you're anxious to be home."

"I've outgrown impatience," Kolti told them softly.

"You look like the sort of intelligent being who would place certain things above personal comfort. You've heard what your security chief says. Dr. McCoy saved your life. Not many have an opportunity to repay such a debt. You do.

"Will you delay your return to friends and family long enough to help clear his name and prevent a permanent stain from entering the annals of Draymian justice?"

"I would not be here to be offered the choice were it not for your Dr. McCoy. I will do whatever you ask of me."

Kirk nodded. He had his proof . . . committed proof, from a source which could neither be argued with nor intimidated. He pulled out the communicator.

"Mr. Scott . . . beam us aboard, all four of us. And quickly—we may have spent too much time here already."

"Aye aye, sir," came the chief engineer's enthusiastic response.

Near the back of the cavern, by broken shards of limestone and shale, a rocking, moaning figure suddenly rolled upright and ceased its whimpers as the miracle took place before its eyes. Fragments of the sun appeared and swallowed up the four figures.

It was over quickly. Then he was alone in his cave again with the nearby water and approaching night . . .

Kirk was stepping down from the alcove and speaking as soon as full reintegration finished.

"Get me the Bridge, Mr. Scott." Scott activated the transporter console intercom, stepped aside as Kirk took up station behind it.

"Sulu, Arex, get under way immediately. Back to Draymia, at top intersystem speed."

Acknowledgment came back over the speaker, and Kirk clicked off, then saw Scott staring at the ragged but unbent Kolti.

"I know you told me to beam up four, and four I beamed up, Captain. But, who is *that*?"

"A Dramian friend of Dr. McCoy's."

"A *Dramian* friend . . . ?"

Scott broke off in astonishment but continued to gaze open-mouthed at Kolti. The survivor stepped gingerly from the transporter alcove and stared in amazement around him. Scott walked around the console and extended a hand to the bemused alien.

"I don't know where you've been hiding yourself, laddie, but somehow I get the feelin' you've got to be a clan member in good standin'. What's your tartan like?"

"Clan member . . . tartan?" Kolti wondered aloud as Kirk and Spock conducted him toward the turbolift, with Demos trailing along.

"Merely Mr. Scott's way of saying that we find in you a kindred spirit which heretofore has seemed lacking in your people." Spock turned pensive. "We may still be too late to save Dr. McCoy. Even if we are not, your testimony may not be enough to shift the tide of feeling which has been raised against him. But there is historical precedent—instances where the courage of one has been enough to overcome the reckless emotionalism of many."

"Spock's trying to say," Kirk explained tautly, "that we think you've got the guts to go through with this." He waved off Kolti's reply. "Be modest later, after we've saved McCoy. For now, Mr. Spock, conduct Kolti to Sick Bay. Have Nurse Chapel check him out completely. Pull everything we've got on Draymian medicine. And see that he has anything he wants."

"I would settle, Captain Kirk," Kolti murmured, "for some food and a clean bed."

Kirk nodded, turned back to Scott. "I want you to push the navigation computer, Scotty. Get us to Draymia as fast as possible—overshoot, if necessary. Minutes may count. The Draymians," he finished, glancing up at Demos, "are impatient for their revenge."

"Most assuredly," the security chief confirmed.

"I'll pour on the coal, Captain," Scott grinned.

They were ten minutes out from Dramia II and nearing Draymia when Kirk finally relaxed from the hysteria of last-minute emergency preparations long enough to check with Sick Bay.

"Mr. Spock, are you still with our patient?"

"Affirmative, Captain," the calm voice came back.

"How's he doing?"

"A moment, Captain . . ." Spock glanced back to where Kolti was sleeping the sleep of the exhausted in the infirmary bed behind him.

Only Spock had noticed how utterly fatigued their passenger was. He had gone along with the other's pose, admiring the silent fortitude as he had answered questions for both Kirk and then Chapel. As was the case with most sophonts, his expression was far more truthful in sleep.

Chapel hurried past him, to adjust the makeshift instrumentation rigged over the slumberer's bed.

"He appears to be in reasonably good health though terribly debilitated and worn out. At the moment he is resting quietly. A brave man, Captain."

"Brave enough to be the unimpeachable witness we need, I hope," Kirk replied. He glanced up at the main viewscreen. Their truncated course was taking them through the body of one of the magnificent intersystem auroras. "Let's hope the trial hasn't already begun."

Sulu spoke to him. "Approaching Draymia orbit, sir."

"You heard, Spock? I think we can get Demos to beam down to put a hold on the proceedings long enough until our witness is fit to appear before a legal assemblage and to answer questions."

"The trial may be academic, Captain."

Kirk sat straighter in his chair. Spock's voice had abruptly taken on a new tone, even as always but touched now with a faint twinge of . . . worry?

"What's the trouble, Mr. Spock?"

At the other end of the comm, the *Enterprise*'s first officer was once more studying the sleeping Kolti. The survivor of Dramia II still rested quietly . . . but the expression on his face was no longer content. Nor was that the most noticeable change in his features.

"Captain, Kolti is turning blue."

Very blue. Normally a creamy chalcedony in color, the alien's skin had shifted to a pale shade of cerulean. The color shift might have seemed amusing to some, at worst worrying. But the implications were neither of a humorous nor of a mildly upsetting nature. The implications were deadly.

Especially for one Leonard McCoy, M.D., USSIT.

Kirk touched the switch and the door dilated, admitting him to Sick Bay. Followed closely by Spock and Demos, he rushed to the quarantine chamber where Kolti had been isolated hurriedly. Chapel was at the Draymian's bedside, taking readings with a modified medical tricorder.

"I'm sorry, Captain," she finally said. "Everything correlates with the readings the built-ins give. I have no idea what . . ."

"Plague!" Demos gasped after only a quick glance at the prone Draymian.

Kirk spun on the security chief. If there was any foul play at work here, any attempt to offer up McCoy as scapegoat by eliminating his only convincing witness . . . His suspicions were dulled by two things—the fear in the commander's voice and the expression on his face. Not even a master Draymian thespian, he suspected, could have managed to conjure up a look of such pure terror.

"Seal off this entire infirmary, Lieutenant Chapel. No one else is to be admitted, no one is to leave." Chapel darted to the nearest intercom to issue the requisite order, all the while working with the recalibrated tricorder.

Spock was bent over the motionless form of Kolti. "I know little Draymian physiology, Captain, and even less of their reactions to specific diseases. But consider that Kolti has been through nearly twenty of our years of extreme privation. When brought aboard he was weak, undernourished and on the verge of physical collapse.

"Now . . . this. Plague or not, he is no longer in a condition to submit testimony at any kind of trial."

"We've got to save him," Kirk added quietly.

Demos smirked. "For McCoy's sake."

"Yes, for McCoy's sake!" Kirk shot back angrily. "And for Kolti's sake, too." He stood close to the Draymian officer and stared up at the towering biped, for all the world like a terrier challenging a mastiff.

"You see, Commander, we place considerable value on lives other than our own. Does that shock you?"

Demos was suddenly tongue-tied. Kirk's reaction had been unexpectedly violent. Or maybe it was the human's smaller size and controlled politeness which had deceived him till now. He could only begin to stammer, "It is not that . . ."

His jaw dropped and his pop-eyes bulged frighteningly.

Kirk studied him curiously. Surely the brief outburst couldn't have stunned him *this* much.

"Captain . . ." There was something in Spock's voice . . .

Kirk wasn't sure where the impulse originated, but he had a sudden urge to look down at himself. He held up his hands, then slowly turned them over. The palms were blue. Recently examined records welled up in his mind.

Certain species, such as Tauran and Vulcan, are immune. Others . . . The thought died away as he finished, to himself, ". . . such as human, are . . . not."

"Chapel . . . Lieutenant Chapel . . ." He was walking with increasingly rapid steps toward the door leading to the head nurse's office.

She was there . . . sprawled across her desk and turning a rich hue of azure even as he stared.

"Mr. Scott, Chief Kyle, others exposed—quarantine too late," he called back to Spock . . . even as his lower leg muscles turned to water and he slumped to his knees.

Demos weakly reached out a hand to catch him. The Draymian Commander had become sky-colored. Kirk muttered, his head swimming.

"Vulcan immunity! Mr. Spock, take . . . take command." He tried to add something else; but though his mouth moved, no words came forth.

Spock caught him before he collapsed completely. He carried Kirk to an empty bed, then went back and transferred Chapel. He tried to do likewise for the massive Demos; but the Draymian commander's bulk defeated him, and he had no time to wrestle with the huge form. He settled for making Demos as comfortable as possible on the infirmary floor.

Two things must be done immediately—depending on the condition of the crew. It was not good. As Spock made his way toward the bridge, he saw other crewmembers sprawled where they had fallen, with still-healthy companions trying to aid them. Quarantine appeared to be out of the question. This mysterious affliction spread too fast.

It took hold with alarming speed, the effects irresistible and overwhelming. He ordered the healthy crewmembers to make the ill as comfortable as possible right where they were found, and then to return to their own posts to continue functioning as long as they were able. It was a brutal, unavoidable order to have to give.

No one argued, no one objected. After all, this was the *Enterprise*.

The situation was no better on the Bridge. Only Sulu still retained anything like his normal color. But even he was showing signs of initial blueness. He did manage to aid Spock in placing the ship into proper orbit around Draymia.

Posterity came next, before survival. He assumed Kirk's seat and activated the recorder.

"Captain's Log, supplemental. First Officer Spock in command, recording.

"We are in orbit around the planet Draymia under conditions of general quarantine. The situation is critical. We have apparently contracted the plague which wiped out the Draymian colony on Dramia II. Nearly the entire ship's complement has already been affected, some seriously.

"A few have shown slightly stronger resistance than others, but this appears transitory. As Acting Commanding Officer, I have ordered the activation of General Order Six." Spock paused, looked over to where Sulu was turning a deep blue color.

"Has the General Order been engaged, Lieutenant?"

"Yes . . . sir," the helmsman replied, painfully, slowly.

"If everyone on board has perished or been rendered incapable of action at the end of a twenty-four-hour period," Spock continued, "and the computer has not been contacted with proper authority to cancel, the ship will self-destruct in order to protect other beings from the disease."

As he completed the entry—the last entry, perhaps—he reflected on the irony of the situation. It seemed that Dr. McCoy might outlive them all.

"Interesting," he whispered.

"What, sir?" asked Sulu.

"Report to Sick Bay, Lieutenant."

Sulu's voice was growing thick, unintelligible. "But sir . . . you need someone . . . to monitor . . . to . . ."

"I gave you an order, Mr. Sulu. I will . . . manage the necessary instrumentation."

Too weak to reply, Sulu got shakily to his feet and started for the elevator. The doors slid apart before he could reach the switch.

Kirk stood there, swaying slightly, but apparently alert and in control of himself. Every step as he moved forward was painful, every shift of an eye felt like the blow of a hammer on his orbicular nerves.

"Spock . . ." he succeeded in whispering.

The first officer whirled, showing as close to an expression of alarm as he was capable of. "Captain, how . . . ? In your condition, it shouldn't be—"

"Stimulants," Kirk muttered. "Pumped full . . . temporary . . ." Spock was at his side, helping him to his command chair. Kirk brushed aside his objections. "Have to find an antidote . . . fast. Only one man . . . maybe. McCoy."

"Captain," Spock countered gently, "the entire medical staff of an advanced world like Draymia could not find an answer to this plague in many years of research."

"We don't know that they applied themselves directly to the problem, Spock. Demos told us how fearful of contamination their observer teams were." His expression twisted. "Whereas Bones always liked to get right into a problem.

"I'd guess the Draymians' quarantine extended to medical personnel too, as soon as they found the plague was one hundred percent fatal. Maybe a few physicians sacrificed themselves trying to find an answer. At the beginning. But even then, they didn't have the advantage of a Federation medical library computer, or a researcher with Bones' skill and experience in dealing with rare diseases.

"We've got to get him back here . . . back here . . ."

"The Draymians will not permit . . ." Spock started to say. He stopped.

Kirk had lapsed into semiconsciousness.

Spock sat thoughtfully, weighing this possibility against that solution, juxtaposing alternatives with probabilities, before eventually making his way to Uhura's vacated communications station.

"Draymia Port," the visage that appeared on the main screen announced.

"This is the Federation starship *Enterprise*, First Officer Spock. I must speak *immediately* with the Supreme Prefect."

"We know of your power and capabilities, Officer Spock," the figure at the other end said, "but do you think that the Supreme Prefect is a personage who can be called up at every—"

"If I do not speak with the Supreme Prefect instantly," Spock informed the other, "I predict with ninety-seven point eight percent surety the advancement of your status in a backward direction. This matter concerns the Dramia II plague."

Bulging eyes rolled and the communicator began shouting off screen demands, as the Draymian worked his hands in a series of furious gestures.

The screen flickered. For a moment abstract electronic images danced across the face, then the static cleared and the face of the Supreme Prefect hastily appeared. He was wrestling with his tunic and his dignity as the focus sharpened.

"Mr. Spock, what is the meaning of this? What is this about the plague—and why do you speak and not your captain?"

"Captain Kirk and the majority of the ship's complement are presently incapacitated," Spock answered smoothly. "The Dramia II plague has struck the ship."

"Plague aboard." The Prefect assumed a look of panic. "Surely, Mr. Spock, you must not—"

"The plague will not be brought to the surface. I am not here to threaten, but to seek help. In the event no antidote for the plague is found, the *Enterprise* will destroy itself before the next ship-day is over."

The Prefect had been absorbing all this stolidly. Now he suddenly looked suspicious as Spock continued.

"Commander Demos will be killed with the rest of us. I regret this. There is only one way to save him and to save the survivor we found on Dramia II, who can attest to the innocence of your prisoner. A great many lives and truths are at stake here, and only one man can find the solution to them all: Dr. McCoy. You must release him immediately. Temporarily, if you will—but no one else has the skill to find a possible antidote in the time that remains.''

The Prefect considered for long seconds—understandable, in light of the barrage of information Spock had just thrown at him. His decision was obviously agonized, but firm.

''I cannot,'' he announced finally.

''The survivor, Kolti, is a witness for Dr. McCoy. He can testify for him. There are many others, of different races, on board the *Enterprise* who will die if he is not released. We may all die anyway, Dr. McCoy among us. If you have so little confidence in his medical ability, at least release him to die of the plague with his friends.''

''You argue plausibly, Vulcan, but without facts.''

''You must trust me. I have no other assurances to give.''

The Prefect seemed to be a reasonable being. If Spock was interpreting the alien expression correctly, the Draymian leader was going through some tortuous mental gymnastics.

His expression turned crafty. ''There is another who might persuade me. Let this witness, this claimed survivor, speak.''

''Impossible. He, too, is seriously stricken.''

Frustration all too suddenly replaced deliberation at the other end of the transmission. ''Demos cannot speak, the witness cannot speak, even Captain Kirk cannot speak—yet you wish us to release the accused McCoy. On faith. Do you think you can secure the freedom of such a criminal so simply? Did you not think I would see through your desperate ploy?''

The screen went blank.

''McCoy,'' Kirk mumbled from behind Spock. ''Got to get McCoy.''

The first officer tried to re-establish the contact, but this time the ground station on Draymia refused to acknowledge his signals. He finally stopped trying, turned and walked over to Kirk.

''Captain, are you . . . ?''

''One minute I'm fine, the next I can taste oblivion—it's the stimulants, Mr. Spock. Uneven effect on the system, guesswork dosage . . . my body will pay for it in the end, I suppose. What about . . . ?''

Spock shook his head. "The Draymians refuse to release him. Unfortunately, they have no reason to trust us. They have a right to be cautious, but at the same time they are not reacting logically in this."

"No, Spock," Kirk breathed heavily, "they're reacting emotionally. I'm sorry so much of the universe turns out to be more unreasonable than Vulcan."

"It *is* distressing at times," Spock admitted, missing Kirk's sarcasm entirely. "But if you'll grant me the freedom to improvise in the face of adversity, I believe I can secure Dr. McCoy's release anyway."

Kirk stared painfully up at him. "That would mean contravening the official warrant, Mr. Spock."

"Only the letter, Captain. Dr. McCoy could be returned to stand trial afterward. I hardly need point out this is a desperation measure I am proposing. We will borrow Dr. McCoy for a little while. If we die, I do not think he will care what the Draymians do to him anyway."

"You're sure you can pull this off, Spock?"

"I intend to—"

"No, don't tell me." Kirk didn't have to think. He put his palms on the arm of the chair and shoved. Spock hurried to get a supportive arm under one shoulder.

"I think I can handle the transporter for you, Spock . . ."

"Be careful, Captain," the first officer admonished. They had staggered down to the transporter room. Spock waited within the alcove while Kirk adjusted the settings. "I would dislike materializing several kilometers above the streets of the capital city."

Kirk nodded, managed a grin, and engaged the instrumentation. There was something on his fevered mind, something else he had to ask Spock . . .

He hadn't thought of it by the time the first officer was gone.

It was dark where Spock rematerialized on the street parallel to the justice building. Dark and late.

He still felt exposed, but fortunately there appeared to be no strolling Draymians about to observe his arrival. Not that the average Draymian would pay much attention to him.

Unless, he mused distastefully, the Draymians had better control of their emotions than their leaders had displayed thus far, the word of McCoy's arrest must have been kept secret. Otherwise a mob surely would have overrun the building by now. Hence he could expect to be regarded by the average citizen with curiosity rather than animosity.

This time he would turn the government's secrecy to his own advantage.

There were definite benefits in being smaller than the local inhabitants. It enabled Spock to make his way skillfully through the labyrinth of corridors in the building, dodging the night staff. The latter were too engrossed in their own drudgery to peer hard at places where Draymians would not fit.

But the two guards standing watch outside the chamber housing McCoy's force-cell were a different lot. They appeared fit, alert, and fully capable of rapid employment of the primitive but lethal-looking apparatus strapped at their waists.

For a moment Spock hesitated uncertainly, wondering at the presence of only two guards for so great a suspected criminal as McCoy. Then he realized that the doctor had been handed over freely. The Draymians had no reason to suppose the *Enterprise* would relinquish him only to take him back suddenly.

Hence the reason for Spock's haste—for if the Prefect had a little time to reflect on his recent conversation with him. . . .

Of one thing he was sure—this was not the time to debate the ethics of the situation with McCoy's guards. Such individuals were rarely selected for their receptiveness to logical persuasion or, for that matter, to original thought. He did not think they would react politely if he announced his intentions.

He slid a stylus from his waist, tossed it across the corridor. It clattered loudly in the quiet. Both guards were immediately alert. Hands on side arms, they moved to investigate the source of the noise.

An unexpected bonus—Spock hadn't expected both of them to leave their station. The unbarred portal to McCoy lay open.

But the guards hadn't looked incompetent. Therefore, they weren't. Therefore, there was something unseen here to be wary of. Slipping noiselessly across the hallway and into the chamber beyond, he quickly discovered what. A quick block knocked the hand weapon from the third guard waiting at the far wall. But a pillarlike arm closed around Spock's waist, lifting him high, squeezing, impairing his breathing.

With no time to experiment on an intractable subject, Spock reached around and back as massive arm muscles tightened. Finding the spot he wanted, he moved his fingers a certain way . . .

The guard collapsed with satisfying speed. When he crumpled to the parquet floor, the sound was loud enough to awaken the drowsing McCoy.

He rolled over on his bunk and stared. As soon as he recognized Spock he was on his feet and over by the inner wall of the cell.

"Spock—what in the world—"

Spock ignored the questions as he glanced back at the open doorway. Apparently the two guards outside were still searching for the source of the clattering. The little control box slid clear of the guard's hip. Spock studied it, touched the remembered sequence of switches.

"Input later, Doctor—no time now. And keep your voice down."

The first glowing nimbus that enclosed McCoy vanished. Another touch and the inner force-field disappeared. McCoy was trying to talk and awaken at the same time. The resulting combination of questions and accusations was understandably garbled.

"Have you and Jim gone out of your minds, Spock?" he finished confusedly. "Why—this is a jail break."

"If you'll just step out of the force-field area and come with me, Doctor . . ."

McCoy took a step—backward. "Spock, I can't. It's illegal. You saw the warrant. I've got to stand trial. I *want* to stand trial." His face was agonized. "I have to find out if—"

"You will stand trial and you will find out, Doctor," Spock insisted, impatiently looking from the recalcitrant physician to the still vacant doorway. "After you've found an antidote for the plague which is about to kill everyone aboard the *Enterprise*."

McCoy started. "Plague . . . ?"

"We found a survivor, too, on Dramia II. A potential witness in your behalf. I do not know whether the disease lay dormant in him until he came aboard, or what. This is what you must discover. Humans are as susceptible to the disease as Draymians. Nearly everyone aboard is seriously ill."

"Spock—you don't tell me the important things first."

"You never ask me the important things first, Doctor."

McCoy moved quickly clear of the force-field boundary, outside the final bar to the ship's transporter beam.

"You realize, Doctor, the Draymians could still acquit you. But if you return aboard, you will be exposed to the disease. You could die, too."

Fully awake now, McCoy brushed hair from his eyes and glanced at him. "I'm aware of that—who's the doctor here? What surprises me is that you'd even think of mentioning it."

"I apologize, Doctor, but," Spock stared at the door, "I have been operating under stress lately." Out came the communicator. "We are clear of the force cell, Captain, beam us aboard."

A startled, angry voice sounded. Not from the communicator but from the doorway. The other two guards had returned. It took barely a second for them to take in the new alien, the fact that the prisoner stood alongside him instead of behind a glowing shield, and their unconscious companion on the floor.

A pair of tiny, explosive shells passed right through the place where McCoy and Spock had stood second-fractions before. They made a mess of the far wall.

IV

McCoy was mentally reviewing everything they knew about the Dramia II plague even as reintegration was being completed in the transporter alcove aboard ship. Scientific speculation vanished as soon as he saw Kirk, his skin now turned a bilious green, slumped over the transporter console.

"Jim!"

Kirk looked up, grinned weakly. "Hello, Bones. Welcome back." He collapsed before McCoy could set foot outside the alcove.

Kneeling next to Kirk, McCoy rolled him over and studied the weakened form as if the cause of the plague might suddenly advertise itself visibly—a movement under the skin, or glowing germs spelling out the formula for an effective serum.

Kirk only lay there.

"Help me get him to Sick Bay, Spock."

Together they wrestled the captain down to McCoy's lab, placed him alongside the other two who had first been stricken—Kolti and Demos.

The two Draymians and one human lay with a ghastly motionlessness. This was a quiet, efficient disease. There were no flailing arms, no hysterical gasps for air, no hallucinations and no screams of pain—Only the peculiarly horrible pigmentation change . . . to be followed by death.

Occasionally Kirk, still under the waning influence of the stimulant overdose, would awaken and mutter something half-coherent. McCoy didn't waste time listening to him.

Instead, he studied his friend as dispassionately as possible. Only by removing himself to a peak of empirical distraction would his mind stay clear enough to hunt for a solution.

He was aware that he had already been massively exposed to infection. Right up until the onset of the disease he should feel fine. First his ability to work and then his life would go in rapid succession.

It shouldn't be so hard. He should have been able to find a solution. But he hadn't. Couldn't.

McCoy pounded on the console of the medical computer as if it were personally responsible for the steadily approaching disaster. Every time he seemed to be coming close, the white letters, the same damning white letters, would suddenly flash on the annex screen . . .

NO CROSS-CORRELATION—PROPOSAL INEFFECTIVE

. . . and he'd have to start all over again. Doctor? Who said he was a doctor? He had fooled everyone long enough.

Bitterly, he mused that if the Draymians had been right all along, he was going to be executed by the plague he'd initiated. Not that he minded being subjected to such impersonal justice.

But he minded very much that all his friends might be taken along with him—victims of a more mature incompetence.

He looked over to where Spock was sitting. Calm, seemingly relaxed, the first officer studied another annex linked to the medical computer. They wouldn't find an antidote in there—of that McCoy had grown certain. But it probably helped relieve Spock's feeling of helplessness.

Besides, there was always the miniscule chance there might be *something* in the records that could lead to a hint of the relative of a clue.

Give him one straw . . .

"Anything at all, Spock?"

"Negative, Doctor."

McCoy studied his own readout, rubbed at his forehead. "The problem is that these violent pigmentation shifts don't link up with any known, or even with any rumored disease."

Doesn't link up, doesn't add up, no correlation, no correlation—but the pigmentation changes were the major symptom, weren't they? Well, weren't they?

Idly, he voiced a peripheral thought. "Spock, we know Vulcans are immune to this plague. That doesn't mean they couldn't be carriers."

"No, Doctor. It does not."

"Yet you still beamed down after me."

Spock didn't look up from his annex screen. "Given the Draymian's intransigence where your release was concerned, I felt justified in taking a calculated risk."

McCoy, then, was not the only one in this room whose conscience had reason to burn.

Something basic was wrong with their approach. Surely the Draymians had already exhausted this line of research. A first-year medical student, now, with a mind unencumbered by years of precedent, might have seen a solution instantly. But he, with a lifetime of statistics and experience crammed into his cranium, could not see through the muck of acquired knowledge. Was he even capable of having an original idea anymore?

Where was the freshness of youth when it was so desperately required?

He looked again at Demos, Kolti, Kirk. Their color had shifted to pink. Soon it would be bright red and then it wouldn't matter what brilliant insights, what revelations he would be privileged to glimpse.

"Work harder, Spock. They're entering the terminal stage."

"A useless admonition, Doctor."

It was. Spock was already driving himself as hard as he could. If he displayed no sign of it, it was because not an iota of energy was wasted in visible muscle tension or in nervous breathing.

McCoy even tried a tight-beam transmission in hopes of contacting Alco III, the nearest Federation world with advanced medical facilities. That failed him, too.

"Spock . . . Spock!" he yelled, trying to break the first officer from his transfixed study of the computer annex. "I'm trying to get through to Alco. Maybe it's too far, but . . . ," he squinted at the viewscreen, "I shouldn't be getting the kind of scrambled readings I am."

Spock looked over at him, spoke with doleful assurance. "That is hardly surprising, Doctor. Undoubtedly one of the numerous auroral disturbances is now placed between Draymia and Alco. Even a tight beam could not penetrate such a vast disturbance."

He was on his own. He had lost precious minutes hoping for the aid of a distant angel. McCoy finally shut off the annex and simply sat back, to think. Behind him, Kirk was mumbling. He had overheard their last conversation and even his subconscious was attuned to the beauties of the universe he loved so well.

"Local phenomenon . . . auroral excitation, lovely, lovely . . . change colors, shift hues, magnificent . . ."

"Aesculapius!" McCoy yelled.

"No need to shout, Doctor," Spock said imperturbably. "You have found something?"

"The auroras . . ."

"Are a dead-end, Doctor. They are of a peculiar nature, but radiation levels are far from lethal—far from being even slightly dangerous."

McCoy rose from his seat and stretched. "One day, Spock, I'll sit down and correlate the relationship of the auroral radiation to its effect on the melanin in human—and Draymian—skin. But not now."

Spock looked thoughtful for a long minute, then became almost excited. "The pigmentation changes are *not* a symptom of the disease. They are a separate effect caused by the auroral radiation."

McCoy nodded vigorously. "Feed the same data we've been using into the med computer, *without* making any mention of epidermal tone shift. See if we get a result this time."

Spock didn't hesitate. Changing the input program required only a minute. There was a brief pause . . . and then words and figures started pouring back at them.

"Fast," was all McCoy said.

"I believe this is what you need, Doctor," Spock observed, studying the steadily maturing formula.

McCoy sat down, realized he was shaking slightly. "The color change in the skin had nothing whatsoever to do with the plague. We reported them as a symptom . . . no wonder the computer couldn't correlate it with the rest of our information.

"It's giving us an antidote . . . and as to the cause of the disease," he sighed, "it's the aurora, too."

"But, Doctor," Spock began uncertainly, "you just said it was a separate effect."

"It is, but the radiation is also the key to the plague. It just doesn't have any link with the color changes. There must be a virus, a bacterium, which is stimulated by the auroral radiation. Naturally, since the aurora is stimulating both, it would appear the color shift is a result of the disease—when in fact, they have no medical connection." He paused.

"Nineteen years ago Dramia II must have been passing through another of the strong auroral belts. I can't be sure . . . I wasn't in astronomy. But I'll bet a check of the expedition's records will confirm it. I do seem to remember a colorful night sky, though. I was too busy to admire local color most of the time." His voice dropped.

"Death's rainbow—it brought on the original plague, just as this aurora has brought it on again. We weren't affected until a carrier of the dormant microbe—Kolti—was brought aboard. I think a check of old records on Draymia itself might show legends of people changing color . . . and returning to normal when the auroras passed on."

His voice dropped to a whisper. Spock didn't press for clarification—the relief that had appeared in McCoy's voice was a private thing, not to be interrupted or shared. It was a relief that could not be judged on any general human scale . . . only on the personal one of Dr. Leonard McCoy.

"I had nothing to do with the plague, then." He blinked and walked over to stand behind Spock, peering over his shoulder at the screen.

"There's our virus, just as you suspected, Doctor." Spock worked the instrumentation and a new flow of information appeared. "And there is the declaration I most feared."

Under the microphoto of the virus itself had appeared the words, "NO KNOWN ANTIDOTE."

Spock tried to keep his voice as comforting as possible. "I suspected that if there were a cure, the Draymians would have found it. With nineteen years in which to research, even theoretically, they must have hit upon the same aurora-plague connection we've just reached."

"Every disease caused by a living agent has an antidote, Spock. Every . . ." He stopped, his voice sharpening. "*Think*, Spock."

"I have been, Doctor. It took me a moment to make the . . . correlation. Do you remember our witness . . . Kolti? You treated him nineteen years ago for saurian virus."

"The individual . . . there were so many. Maybe . . . yes, I think I do. It was a strange case to find on Dramia II. As I recall, he was one of their off-world representatives. Contracted it from someone in the Federation. Sure, I remember him now! We had a helluva time digging out the right serum for that . . . we'd expected to have to treat only local infections. Wait a minute." McCoy's face lit up like one of engineer Scott's control reactors.

"You say *he's* the witness, the survivor you found?"

"Correct, Doctor. He survived the plague and all aftereffects. Apparently, however, inoculation against saurian virus does not last nineteen years."

"No. No, it doesn't. He needs a booster. In fact, everyone on board ought to have a similar injection. If the key *is* saurian antibodies, recovery from the plague after administration should be as rapid as debilitation was."

"Let us hope so, Doctor," Spock remarked with a glance at the nearby beds. Kolti, Kirk and Demos were beginning to turn a dark crimson. "We have very little time."

McCoy was already moving toward the refrigerated locker where preprepared serums were stored.

"I'd like to run some tests on this first, Spock, but as you say, we haven't time." He grimaced. "Any side effects can't be worse than death."

"A queerly logical statement, Doctor." Spock understood the principles of irony.

McCoy hurriedly filled a mass injector, then a second, with three-quarters of the available serum. Then he programed the organic fabrication computer to prepare the necessary remainder. It would be ready long before he and Spock had finished applying the first doses.

The infirmary was soon filled with hisses from the hypo sprays as they moved from bed to bed, pallet to cot, administering the antidote. Nor had McCoy neglected himself—if for some reason the serum proved ineffective, he wanted to be the first to know.

There was a buzz from the intercom set next to the computer keyboard. McCoy looked up uncertainly. "I thought you said everyone else aboard was incapacitated, Spock."

"They are, Doctor," he replied, heading for the *acknowledge* switch, "but the main computer itself is also immune to the plague."

McCoy muttered something about "Vulcans and machines" which Spock didn't hear and continued inoculating the prone crew members scattered through the room. Spock returned a moment later.

"You will be interested to know, Doctor, that we are leaving the last streamer of the aurora which caused this trouble and blocked your communications attempt. Also, I ran a check on the composition of Draymian and Dramian atmospheres. I don't think we'll unearth any historical records of mass color changes on Draymia. The composition differs slightly but significantly . . . enough to block out the melanin-affecting radiation of the auroras."

McCoy moved to the next body. "So Draymia's always been plague-immune. No wonder the outburst on Dramia II terrified them so. They'd no experience with even the color shifts."

He made the inoculation, noticed that the indicator light on the side of the sprayer had come on.

"Empty . . . the synthesizer should be finished with the big batch I ordered up. Be right back, Spock." The first officer nodded, continued work with his own spray as McCoy started back toward the far end of the infirmary and the medical lab.

On the way he saw that Kirk, Demos and Kolti were running the color change backward. Red, to pink, then green and blue and finally their normal healthy color again. The speed of the change was fast enough to be visible to the naked eye—hopefully physical recovery would be equally rapid.

It was. When McCoy returned with a second empty hypo, Kirk had already opened his eyes. Seconds later Kolti and Demos followed suit. Nearby, a transporter specialist was snuffling like a pig in clover as he, too, started to come around.

Kirk looked at the ceiling, then rolled his head sideways. He looked tired, but had already regained enough strength to smile and nod at McCoy.

A strange disease—he would spend considerable time analyzing it. Studying with rather more detachment than he had been permitted up to now.

It would make a paper suitable for submission to the *Starfleet Medical Journal*—was that a tear at the corner of one eye? He wiped it away before any of his patients could notice—too much close work in too brief a time, that was all.

"You did it, Bones," Kirk mumbled softly.

"Again." McCoy looked up, past the stirring form of Kirk, to see a tall Draymian he didn't recognize staring back at him. The alien wore a look which even a child could have read as undisguised admiration.

He turned away, embarrassed by both the unabashed adulation and the fact that for the life of him he couldn't place the face of this survivor. But then, there had been so many Draymians those long days years ago. But undoubtedly this Kolti had seen very few humans, so it was natural that he should remember the doctor.

Nevertheless, he walked over to the stranger and exchanged hand clasps and Draymian embrace with him. The patient's crushing affection was an excellent sign his body was rapidly returning to normal.

Kirk was sitting up on the edge of his bed, exercising his neck with circling twists of his head.

"How do you feel, Jim?"

"Like I've been asleep for ten thousand years, Bones, and in all that time no one bothered to dust me."

"Dr. McCoy?" He turned and saw that the Commander of Draymian security was also sitting up, a mite awkwardly, on his undersized bed. "We are a technologically advanced race, Dr. McCoy. We had thought that in a few things, such as interstellar travel and contact, we are still in our infancy. It seems that we are still in our infancy in less scientific ways as well."

He extended a huge hand. "Will you accept the sincere apologies of a misguided child who knew no better and had only his civilization's best interests at heart? The malice lies in our memory of events, not in our hearts."

McCoy shook the proffered hand firmly, then moved on— he still had work to do.

"Doctor," Spock called, from where he was administering the serum, "are you certain that *you* are all right?"

McCoy wiped moisture from his eyes. "Doesn't anyone understand basic physiology around here!" he snarled. "I'm working hard and under stress, that's all."

Spock linked the phrase and the tone of McCoy's voice and his hypothetical mental state—and understood. Of course, he saw no reason to smile.

If the Draymians had been careful at first to conceal their enmity, they showed unbridled enthusiasm when making amends. There were times during the following days when McCoy thought he would have to run and hide lest he be smothered by constant accolades. The Draymian people outdid themselves in their gratitude.

The only difficulties arose when he was forced time and again to refuse actual gifts, explaining that regulations forbade accepting any kind of gratuity, however indirect, for services rendered in the line of duty. Their good health, he told them, was reward enough.

When the last medal had been awarded, the last speech read, the final hyperbolic hyperbole driven home, they found themselves outside the justice building once again, high above the bustling streets and boulevards of the capital of Draymia.

Kirk and Spock were there with McCoy, all three resplendent in full dress uniform. The Prefect was there, and Demos, of course. And a third Draymian—Kolti, now toweringly splendid in the blue and puce of Draymian Deep Space Service, Diplomatic Section.

They were going to see a lot more of that well-cut uniform in the future, Kirk surmised quietly—especially if Kolti was an indication of the kind of people being trained to fill it.

". . . and so we of Draymia wish to thank you once more, Dr. McCoy," the Prefect was concluding, "for the discovery of the antidote which frees future colonies from destruction by the auroral plague."

"Thank Mr. Spock and Captain Kirk, not me," McCoy

told him. He managed not to blush—he had already blushed himself out, these past few days. At least, he thought he had, until the Prefect suddenly produced an intimidating scroll from out of nowhere.

"And now," the alien official began, "it is my pleasure to relate some fitting personal sentiments on commemoration of—"

"Please, your Prefectship," McCoy broke in tiredly. "Somehow I have the feeling I've heard these sentiments before. Couldn't I—please—beg off? I'd really like to get back to the ship."

"We must apologize," Demos said, coming to McCoy's rescue by placing a restraining yet gentle hand on the disappointed Prefect's arm. There was no telling how long the security chief had worked on his *own* as yet concealed speech. "But as great a genius as Dr. McCoy is," he continued, "he has not yet discovered an antidote for boredom."

Kirk and the Prefect laughed, while Spock looked normally phlegmatic.

"I'm afraid," McCoy sallied in reply, "that while that's a disease rampant throughout the Galaxy, it's barely been touched upon."

The Prefect made the Draymian equivalent of a resigned sigh and folded up his lengthy scroll. "Very well, then . . . go in peace and health, Dr. McCoy—the health you have given to future settlers. We will see you again some day, I hope."

"I have a hunch Federation vessels will be calling at Draymia with increasing frequency, sir," Kirk predicted. "I wouldn't be surprised if we were assigned another stop here. We'll be looking forward to it."

"It is well, then," the Prefect concluded, satisfied.

Embraces were exchanged all around. Then the three officers stepped back toward the ornamental railing.

"Beam us aboard, Mr. Scott."

"Aye, Captain," came the chief engineer's happy acknowledgment back over the communicator.

"I don't know about you, gentlemen," Kirk said as the elevator carried them toward the Bridge, "but I'm ready to get back to Alco Starbase."

"And I," McCoy informed them fervently, "am about ready to get back to the normal, daily routine of passing out pink pills and examining sore throats!"

"I would hope such exotic efforts," Spock began as the doors slid apart and they entered the Bridge, "would include resumption of the normal, daily dispensing of the regular vitamin rations to the crew, in proper proportions according to their biological requirements."

McCoy hesitated just inside the portal. "What's that supposed to mean?"

"Well, you *have* been somewhat derelict in your duties of late, Doctor."

McCoy gaped at him. "Derelict in my duties? I've been held in solitary confinement on an alien world, accused of mass murder, and forced to find an antidote for a previously incurable plague in an incredibly short period of time—with only your help, I might add—and you can say I've been derelict in my duties?"

"Hippocrates," Spock replied calmly, "would not have approved of attempts at finding lame excuses, Doctor." He called the elevator and stepped inside, leaving Kirk and a flabbergasted McCoy alone by the doorway.

McCoy proceeded to make several unidentifiable mouth noises, none with complimentary overtones, which seemed to relate vaguely to Spock's ancestry.

"Calm down, Bones," Kirk finally told him, working hard to stifle a smile. "You know Spock—he's just trying to get your goat."

"Goat," McCoy sputtered, "I'll give him my goat . . . with anthrax, yet!" There was a wild look coming into his eyes. "Jim, do you think Vulcans are subject to anthrax? Do you think they're vulnerable to—"

Kirk couldn't contain himself any longer. He broke out laughing, was joined by Uhura, Sulu, and the high, amused piping of Arex. McCoy glanced around the room, immediately saw he would get no sympathy from this bunch.

He finally got hold of his emotions. "Jim, if I'm ever in jail again, don't send a Vulcan to release me. If you do, you'll have to send someone else to drag him out. You'll have to!"

He became silent then, and the wild look was replaced with a smile of uncommonly fiendish glee. It sobered Kirk.

"Bones," he asked worriedly, "what are you conjuring?"

"Vitamin supplements," McCoy was muttering. He sounded almost cheerful, "Yes, vitamin supplements." He looked up. "Excuse me, everybody . . . I have some work to do . . . some supplements to prepare. I've been derelict in my daily duties."

Kirk could hear him singing something about vitamin supplements until the turbolift carried him out of range.

PART II

THE PRACTICAL JOKER

(Adapted from a script by Chuck Menville)

V

"Since I have evidentally failed to make myself clear so far, Nurse Chapel, I will repeat it once more," Spock told her tautly. "Vulcans are *not* subject to dandruff."

Chapel leaned back in the office chair and eyed the first officer of the *Enterprise* compassionately.

"Perhaps there is a different Vulcan term for it, then."

"Such a disease is *not* possible," Spock insisted. He scratched behind one ear. "However, I am compelled to admit that for an impossible affliction, it is proving most distracting."

"What is?" Both turned as McCoy walked in. "Hello, Christine. Hello, Spock. Is something the matter?" His voice was overflowing with innocence.

"Something has been the matter for a number of days, Doctor. Ever since we departed Draymia and before we began the survey of this non-system grouping of type-four asteroids." He glanced back across the desk.

"Nurse Chapel insists I have contracted a disease common only to decadent physiological systems, something she identifies as *dandruff*. I have explained patiently that Vulcans are not subject to such primitive afflictions."

"Yes, it's an affliction common to the inefficient human organism . . . and it seems," McCoy added, leaning over to stare pointedly at Spock's scalp, "that you have an advanced case of it. My, my . . . no wonder you've seemed so peevish lately."

"I am never peevish, and I tell you," Spock said in exasperation, "I do not have it. It is simply not possible for— you are smiling, Doctor. I don't believe anything I've said can be taken as amusing."

"Been getting your daily vitamin supplements, Spock? I know I was badly neglectful . . . you reminded me though. Remember?"

"Yes, I have to admit that you have returned to schedule with admira—" The first officer suddenly paused. If it was possible for a Vulcan to take on a suspicious expression, Spock had just acquired one.

"Vitamins . . . Doctor, is it possible that you harbored some irrational resentment against me for the comments I made regarding your efficiency, on our departure from Draymia? Is it possible that you . . . ?"

Spock rose abruptly from the chair. "I do not think," he said coldly, "that an analysis of my supplements will be necessary."

McCoy allowed himself a smile. "Oh, don't be so stiff about it, Spock. Besides, it can only worsen your condition. I'll remove the additive I put into your supplements immediately, and your primitive affliction will vanish in a couple of days. In exchange, we won't hear anything more about my performance as ship's doctor for a while . . . will we?"

"Is that a request," Spock asked, still frozen, "or a threat?"

"Let's call it a reasonable adjustment of circumstances, arrived at by mutual consent of two intelligent beings. I could have arranged for something rather more radical than dandruff, you know. Besides, I'd think you'd find the situation interesting, from a scientific point of view. I didn't even know if it would work. Always nice to see theory confirmed. As far as I know, you're the first Vulcan in history to be plagued with—"

"Please, Doctor. I agree. Just correct it, please."

"All right, Spock, relax." The grin again. "It's not fatal." He walked past the desk and punched out commands on the computer annex there.

"Something you might be interested in—here's the molecular schematic I had to design to produce the proper results. Took a neat little bit of organic doodling, I can tell you. Vulcans have so many antibodies in their blood it's almost impossible to find something to penetrate all those generations of acquired defenses."

"I'm sure, Doctor," Spock said dryly, peering at the diagram of bonded atoms on the screen, ''that it taxed your abilities considerably.''

''Speaking of taxing our skills,'' Nurse Chapel wondered aloud, ''how much longer are we going to be stuck on this mineralogical survey before we can continue on back to Alco Starbase for a little rest and recreation?''

Glad of a chance to change the subject, Spock explained. ''The extent and density of this free cluster has exceeded all previous drone estimates. Despite this, the captain estimates that we are now several days ahead of schedule. He is as anxious as the rest of us to be done with what is really a minor operation and he sorely resented the orders when they came through.

''Orders remain orders, however. We should be finished with the survey any day. A great deal of value has been learned, even if the learning has been monotonous. The cluster appears to offer considerable commercial promise. The asteroid masses are all irregular in shape, probably the remains of an exploded planet which tore loose from its parent system. Nonetheless they have remained tightly packed together. Some are of considerable size and a few are much larger than Ceres in the Sol system. I venture to say that within a few years the activity here will—''

There was a deep rumble and everything shook.

Chapel nearly fell backward out of the chair. Both Spock and McCoy had to grab for the computer console to steady themselves. The tremor died away quickly, leaving them suddenly tense. McCoy and Chapel exchanged nervous glances.

An alarm began to sound. From time to time short rumbles rose above the wail and irregular vibrations could be felt underfoot. But the first, serious jolt was not repeated.

''You okay, Christine?''

''Fine, but what happened?''

''I don't know.'' He looked over at Spock. ''What do you think? Spock? Where'd he disappear to?''

Spock was already on his way to the Bridge. Only a very few things could produce the shaking and accompanying rumble they had experienced. Most of them were natural. Only one was artificial in origin. Experience told him it was the latter. They were under fire.

He emerged on the Bridge in time to see the main viewscreen overloaded by a blinding white glare. It faded slowly, the imagery re-forming as the ship's scanners strove to recover from the intense dose of light.

He acknowledged a perfunctory greeting from Scott, who stood at the Bridge Engineering Station, as he made his way to the library-computer console.

The familiar whooping cry of the red-alert alarm was louder here on the Bridge, in deference to any sufferers in Sick Bay. He knew it was sounding the length and breadth of the battle cruiser.

Another blast rattled the Bridge enough to separate feet from deck momentarily, despite the artificial gravity. Yet another blast in the same place from a slightly more powerful photon bomb, and Spock's feet would leave the deck permanently.

Behind him Kirk's voice resounded—terse, businesslike— in complete control, although the source of the mysterious attack was still unknown.

"Scotty, give us maximum shielding, full power on the deflectors."

"Aye, Captain." Scott carried out the order, then turned his post over to a panting, just-arrived subordinate. The chief's place was back in Engineering Control, and he headed there in haste.

"Photon bombs," Uhura muttered. "But who?"

Kirk ignored the lieutenant's musing. "Mr. Sulu, bring us about to a new heading. One hundred twenty degrees north, up twenty. Initiate evasive pattern one."

"Aye sir." the helmsman responded promptly, working the instruments.

Kirk's businesslike manner now found a moment for open anger. "Mr. Spock, where were you?"

"I have no real excuse, Captain. I was suffering from a prolonged distortion of subcutaneous follicular tissue."

"Yes, I noticed it. But if you don't find out who's attacking us, you're liable to have it cured forever."

"My own opinion exactly, Captain."

The requisite information was already appearing on the sensor screens above his station. To complement the printed readouts, the computer provided him with a three-dimensional schematic of their pursuers, along with classification, type, armament, displacement, number of crew and probable port of origin.

At the moment all the statistics were superfluous. "Romulans, Captain." He studied the main viewscreen, which still showed their last survey target—an enormous, rapidly shrinking hunk of stellar debris the size of a small moon.

"Apparently they were lying in wait for us on the far side of that major asteroid."

"By the Thane of Comorron!" came a furious voice. The burr was unmistakable. Scott had reached Engineering and when he'd overheard Spock's pronouncement, had yelled through the line Kirk had left open. "A cold-blooded ambush! That's goin' a bit far, even furr the Romulans. Let's give the cowards a fight they won't fergit!"

Kirk sympathized with his chief engineer, but kept his tone even as he hit the broadcast return. "Negative, Mr. Scott. I've already received several damage reports. Combined with the fact that we appear to be outnumbered three to one, I think we'd better settle for some well-directed name-calling."

"Discretion is the better part of valor, sir? I've always felt that was a bit of a contradiction in terms."

"Just stand by to give me all the power you can spare from the deflectors, Mr. Scott."

"Aye, sir," Scott said, making no effort to hide the disappointment in his voice. Kirk switched Engineering off. Sometimes Scott's spirit ran away with his better sense.

"Sulu, give me full power on the rear sensors."

"Aye, Captain."

The view in the main screen shifted as more explosions flared around the ship. Now though, under battle conditions, the visual scanners were automatically compensating for the intense radiation.

The three ships were tiny flecks, but Kirk felt he could make out the distinctive outlines, coming straight for them.

"The Romulans continue to pursue, Captain," Spock reported. "And they are increasing their speed. They also appear to be separating further, changing from attack position to an intricate entrapment maneuver."

"Can we outrun them, Mr. Spock?"

Spock hesitated, studying readouts as fast as the battle

computer could supply them. "Indeterminate, Captain. With three ships in pursuit, prediction becomes extremely complex."

"Keep working on it." Lips set tight together, Kirk turned his attention back to the viewscreen and muttered under his breath. "They must want us badly to continue to pursue after their initial attack failed. Too late now for them to plead accident." His expression twisted into a faint grin. "The Romulans are coming." His voice rose as he called to Spock.

"Uncertainty's a hereditary factor with them. I think somebody got nervous and jumped the gun on us. If they'd waited till we were just a few kilometers closer to that big rock, we wouldn't have had a chance."

"True, Captain," Spock conceded. "They must have been observing our progress through the cluster for some time. Fortunately, our survey pattern varied according to the size and density of the asteroids themselves. They could not be entirely certain when we would alter course, hence someone's mounting fear we might suddenly discover their presence."

"Captain?" Kirk turned to look back at Uhura. "I've received an incoming transmission from the commander of the Romulan force. We have visual, too." She grinned. "He seems anxious to talk to you."

"I'll bet," Kirk replied grimly. "Put him through . . . I've got a couple of things to say to him."

The sinister view of the three pursuing cruisers was replaced with a momentary flash of static, and then the sharp portrait of a smug Romulan officer.

Kirk disliked him on sight, even more than he did the usual example of Romulan militarism. He wasted no time on diplomatic niceties.

"Whoever you are, I demand an immediate explanation for this unprovoked attack."

"Unprovoked!" the Romulan echoed with mock anxiety. "My dear Captain Kirk, your ship trespassed into Romulan territory in defiance of our treaty. We had no choice but to defend ourselves and the sovereignty of the Empire."

"I know," Kirk shot back, "our appearance was a complete surprise to you."

"A terrible shock," the Romulan admitted.

"Which is how you happen to know my name."

"We, uh . . . ," the Romulan coughed delicately, "recognized the serial number of your ship, and it is widely known who commands the Federation's famed *Enterprise*."

"I see. Then perhaps you can explain this odd discrepancy?"

The alien commander was put off stride. "Discrepancy?"

"Yes. If your detectors have improved to the point that you can pick out our serial numbers at this distance, how come they failed to tell you that we're nowhere near Romulan territory? We were surveying an unclaimed asteroid cluster lying on the Federation border—well outside the farthest Romulan claim.

"I deny your blatantly artificial charge and plan to file a detailed complaint with the Romulan delegate to the Federation."

The commander was not upset. He even managed a smile, of a sort. "This ignores reality, Captain. You forget that invasion of Imperial territory is punishable by death. You and your crew have already been tried and convicted."

"I told you," Kirk said angrily, "we've committed no violation of Romulan boundaries. We're not subject to your legal farce."

"Details, details," came the unperturbed reply. "Oh, I suppose some blithering clerk might find a flaw in our reasoning . . . but you will unfortunately not have an opportunity to file that complaint with him." He became positively charming.

"It is a pity you fail to recognize the inevitability of your situation, Captain. Why not surrender your vessel? We might arrange some kind of accommodation—leniency for some of your common ratings, say."

Kirk's stomach turned over. "Why don't you arrange . . . ?" he began heatedly. But the screen abruptly went dark. Perhaps something in Kirk's tone hinted to the Romulan commander that he wasn't going to agree to terms.

Another strong concussion rocked the Bridge.

"Captain," Spock reported, "the Romulan attack may have been hasty, but their closing formation is well conceived. I can find no evasive pattern that will enable us to escape from more than two ships at a time. Regardless of how we maneuver, there will always be one cruiser within range.

"If we turn to fight it, and fail to dispatch it immediately, we will soon be forced to exchange fire with all three. Our deflectors will be unable to handle such a concentration of firepower. Conversely, if we continue to run, it appears that all three will close on us eventually, producing the same untenable position."

Kirk thought furiously. "I disagree about our ability to handle all three of them in a last-ditch fight, Mr. Spock. But I wouldn't put it past one of the Romulan captains to exchange his ship and crew for clan glory by making a suicide charge at us while the others keep us occupied. Our deflectors could never handle that kind of overload."

Spock nodded. "The importance the Romulans attach to certain archaic forms of self-sacrifice is well known. I agree that from the standpoint of the Romulan High Command, the elimination of the *Enterprise* is of such importance that they wouldn't consider the sacrifice of a single cruiser excessive."

"Which means we've got to try and run—somehow," Kirk decided.

The conversation was interrupted by several strange beeps and whines from the navigation console and helm.

"What is it, Mr. Sulu?"

The helmsman was studying his instrumentation with a peculiar grimace of uncertainty. "Captain, we are approaching an unlisted energy field of considerable extent, and I'm getting some mighty odd readings from the sensor scans."

"Mr. Spock?"

"A moment, Captain." Once more the view of the Romulan cruiser dead astern disappeared as Spock engaged the forward scanners.

Ahead, emblazoned across the starfield, lay an enormous mass of light that looked like a lambent fog bank.

"Partially gaseous," Spock informed them, "but also heavily particulate. The difference is still undeterminable. It appears to be a mass of minute energized particles held together by a force other than gravity—it's far too dense to be, say, a nebular fragment. And Lieutenant Sulu is right—the readings are *most* peculiar.

"Odd that such a unique phenomenon is not on the charts made by the drone that surveyed the asteroidal cluster. Even a drone should have detected such a concentration of energy this close by."

"As far as I'm concerned it came out of a brass bottle," Kirk said excitedly. "It may be just what we need to shake the Romulans. You know how reluctant they are to have anything to do with anything radically unfamiliar. They're appropriators—not explorers."

Spock's reply held a mild warning tone: "Not always an unwise policy, Captain." He gestured toward the screen. "This field registers very strong, and it contains internal subatomic configurations of a still unidentifiable nature."

"We'll have plenty of time to puzzle them out, Mr. Spock, *after* we've shaken the Romulans. Lieutenant Uhura, general order. Secure for emergency running. Mr. Sulu, take us through."

"Yes, *sir*!" Sulu adjusted the helm, and the *Enterprise* changed course slightly, plunging straight into the outermost edge of the luminescent barrier.

"If I may say so, Captain," Spock commented, keeping his attention focused on the sensors that were now registering their passage through the strange field, "your decision was rather hasty. Influenced, I believe, by emotional considerations."

"You bet it was, Mr. Spock," Kirk admitted without rancor. "I weighed all the facts, considered all the evidence—including your own information concerning our probable inability to escape by running or defending against a concerted three-pronged attack. I admit the thought of being blown to bits prompted me to take a bit of a risk. If that's emotionalism—"

"We are entering the inner region of the field, Captain," the first officer observed, thus putting an end to the debate.

A steady vibration had sprung up underfoot. Kirk felt it first in his feet, then all over as it increased, working its way up his body. Despite the effect, his body wasn't vibrating, of course—merely feeling the effects of the oscillating ride as transmitted through the fabric of the ship.

A fantastic parade of abstract forms and images exploded toward them on the main screen as the *Enterprise* sailed through the sea of energy. Colors so brilliant, hues so intense they seemed to have a solid presence. Deep maroons and light yellows, forest greens, blues, blacks, electric pink—a whole region that passed by instantly and had the texture of blackberry milk, another that resembled rutilated quartz lit from within.

Kirk had little time to appreciate the beauty rushing at him. His concern now was with the destructive effects of all that riotous radiation. The vibrations intensified. His voice was jittery when he spoke, from the vibration, not from internal insecurity.

"What are our chances, Mr. Spock."

The first officer of the *Enterprise* was already attempting the near-impossible task of monitoring the readouts with one eye and gauging the composition of the surrounding field with the other, fighting to keep quarks and ergs on the proper sides of his scientific ledger.

"If the intensity and density—the interrelation is vital—does not increase beyond the subatomic, we should be able to continue safe passage. If it rises, our shields will be hard pressed to ward it off."

Kirk gave a curt nod, reached to activate the intercom. It vibrated like a chair massager under his fingertips.

"Mr. Scott, how are things at your end?"

"From the sound of your voice, Captain, no worse than they are on the Bridge. It's hard to tell whether the shields are workin' at all, at times. Strangest arrangement of energy I've seen in some time, and I'm gettin' readings from the dilithium reaction chambers you wouldn't believe. But . . . everythin' appears to be runnin' all right."

"According to Mr. Spock, the field we're passing through is composed of very dense, unusually charged subatomic particles."

"Mad matter. That explains some of the readings I'm gettin', then—but not all of 'em, Captain. I don't mind tellin' you I'll be glad when we're clear of this."

"Glad to hear you're bothered, Scotty. If the readouts trouble *you*, they ought to give the Romulans the collywobbles. Kirk out."

"Scott out." He clicked off the intercom and placed one

hand on the smooth arc of wall nearby as he studied the gauges which monitored the heartbeat of the *Enterprise*.

"Hold together, little darlin' . . . hold together . . ."

The energy field was larger than initial estimates indicated, but by interstellar standards it was still an insignificant stain in the endless vacuum.

An insignificant stain, Kirk reflected as he studied the thinning panoply of color, that might save all their lives.

"Maintain this heading, Mr. Sulu. Mr. Spock, we have readings taken from both sides of the mass now . . . what's its configuration and how does it relate to our present situation?"

"According to the computer calculations, Captain, the field appears to be thick enough so that if the Romulans attempt to go around it, we will easily succeed in outdistancing them."

"I think they just reached that same conclusion, Captain," Sulu reported. "I can still pick out their engines through all that concentrated small stuff, and it looks like they've turned back. At the very least, they've slowed to a crawl on the opposite side. Doesn't look like they're going to chance it."

"Stay on those scanners, Mr. Sulu," Kirk ordered. "They may try coming through slowly."

But when there was no sign of their pursuers seconds or even crucial minutes later, he felt safe in taking the ship off red alert.

"No sign of them, sir," Sulu breathed in relief. "It worked."

"They turned back rather than risk the field's unknown potential," Kirk agreed.

Spock turned philosophical. "The percentages would appear to be in the Romulans' favor, Captain. From their standpoint the glory is greater if they destroy us in battle. However, if we perish through natural causes such as the energy field, their ultimate objective is still attained. Logically, there was no reason to risk themselves."

"All the same, Spock," he insisted, "they may remain nearby evaluating the field and eventually they may determine they can make the passage safely. They know we've suffered damage, which that rocky journey might have aggravated. We still may see them." He looked to the helm.

"We'll lay to here for repairs, Mr. Sulu. Inform the necessary sections to hurry their work, especially Engineering."

Uhura was rubbing the section of her anatomy that was most often in contact with the ship. "After that ride, I could use some repairs," she observed feelingly.

"I suppose," Kirk theorized, "that what's needed in such cases is an extremely localized deflector field."

"I would suggest," Spock added dryly, "the problem be proposed to Chief Scott. I am sure he would find the mechanics of the problem most stimulating."

"You'd better keep a close eye on the chief, though, Lieutenant. He's a devil with those calipers."

Uhura eyed them both with distaste. "I suppose you both think you're terribly amusing."

Spock looked querulous. "Amusing, Lieutenant Uhura? I can assure you I was merely trying to . . ."

The elevator doors dilated. "Reporting for duty, Captain," a high voice said.

"Good timing, Mr. Arex. You take over." Kirk rose from the chair. "I'd like to make a personal survey of the damaged sections and then take that overdue mid-meal."

Damage from the Romulan photon bombs proved erratic, but there was enough destruction to give somber evidence of what could have happened. Fortunately, Romulan discipline had a way of breaking down when a large measure of glory was at stake. If the captains of the three cruisers had been able to present a coordinated attack to the optimum moment, now . . .

They were lucky it hadn't been a Klingon attack. By now a Klingon commander would have executed the entire Fire-Control section for jumping the gun.

As it was, there was some severe damage in Engineering—though nothing irreparable. Not for the resourceful Scott and his people. Also, concussion from near-misses had battered several storage compartments, and nearly hulled the shuttle-craft hangar. Personal injury was minor, however, and there were no fatalities, since the damage had been wrought in unmanned areas. These were easily sealed off. Repair crews, under the direction of engineers Kaplan and Senif, were making rapid progress in repairing the battered sections.

In the upper Officer's Mess, Kirk had joined Spock, Uhura,

McCoy and Sulu for what he had hoped would be a leisurely mid-meal. They might not have a chance to eat for some time if the Romulans decided to try a sudden move through the energy cloud.

Scott joined them soon after they began. The chief engineer had been supervising steadily and only now felt satisfied enough to take a break.

He took a long draught of the contents of the huge mug he carried with him. Irish coffee, Kirk noted. He doubted there was another engineer in the fleet who could program a standard naval galley to produce Irish coffee—or Russian, Jamaican, Turkish, Balaklavan, Austrian and the host of additional caffeinic concoctions Scott could brew on demand. The same brand of ingenuity had kept the *Enterprise* one step ahead of disaster on more occasions than he cared to recall.

"How are repairs coming, Scotty?" Kirk inquired, knowing full well Scott wouldn't be present if any serious difficulties remained. But the chief would feel slighted if he wasn't asked.

"Better than I hoped, when I first saw what the heathen's bombs had done." He took a barbecued rib from his tray and bit deep.

"Another couple of seconds in getting full power to the screens, though—as it is, we'll be good as new in another twenty hours." His expression turned sour. "No thanks to those Romulan vultures."

"The Romulans are not even distantly ornithoid, Mr. Scott. I am surprised that you . . ." Spock grew aware of the amused silence. "I see," he said thoughtfully, "another terran colloquial expression."

"I was referrin', Mr. Spock, to the Romulans' social habits, not their anatomy. Though I could make some suitable comments regardin' that." There were mutters of agreement from around the table.

They'd been very lucky, Kirk mused. He considered the framework of his official report. This was no case of mistaken identity, and there was no question of a misplaced boundary, despite the claim of the Romulan commander.

The ambush had been planned in advance and nearly brought off. Only the overeagerness of some fire-control officer and the presence of the drifting energy field had saved them.

It was hard to make small talk in such an atmosphere, when what everyone really wanted was an officious Romulan neck to wrap their hands around.

Sensitive to such moodiness, McCoy forced a smile and said jovially, "Well, we're still in business." He lifted his buttermilk. "And so I propose a toast to celebrate our narrow escape—is this the four hundred tenth or eleventh?"

Other drinking goblets were raised. "Cheers . . . goganko . . . offiah . . ."

No one had managed a single sip, however, before a startled Sulu let out an exclamation of surprise. He was staring downwards, at the dark stain that now ran across the front of his uniform.

"Hey . . . this glass just leaked all over me!"

The emotions running around the table were not of amusement, though. Uhura's yelp of surprise followed soon after.

"How do you like that . . . so did mine."

"And mine," Scott added.

Everyone, in fact, sported identical stains. Confusion and puzzlement reigned. An observation came first from Spock, as usual.

"It appears that we are all victims of a rather bizarre coincidence."

McCoy looked around the table. "Maybe . . . maybe . . ."

"The odds against this happening," Spock went on, "against all our glasses being defective or all of us being this sloppy, are astronomical."

McCoy was brushing at his drenched shirt-front and abruptly looked up. "Astronomical my metatarsals! This is no coincidence. I just remembered—we used to pull tricks like this all the time in medical school." He eyed his cup. "Dribble glasses . . . we've been hit with dribble glasses." A slow survey of the table followed.

"Don't look now, but we've got a practical joker among us."

"Don't jump to conclusions, Bones," admonished Kirk. But he also found himself studying the faces of his table companions. All except Spock, of course, who was automatically above suspicion. He could not have imagined a dribble glass, much less considered employing one.

For that matter, it hardly seemed the sort of prank anyone present would pull.

"This isn't a group from which I'd expect this kind of infantile humor. Spock's probably right, Bones . . . it's just an incredible coincidence."

"That's right," Sulu agreed. "We all got wet, so who'd be playing the joke?"

"Probably a minor defect in the inorganic, nonmetallic fabricator programing," Scott supplied helpfully. "I'll check it out with the specialists in charge on the next shift."

"Good enough," Kirk said with finality. "Right now, I suggest that everyone finish eating before the food gets as cold as my drink."

To set an example, he picked up a fork full of fried potatoes. But as he moved it toward his mouth, the fork suddenly wilted in the middle as if the metal had turned molten. The large helping fell in a greasy splotch down the front of his tunic. It made an interesting contrast to the stain already left by his drink.

Whether it was the awkward tumbling of solid food or the fact that this time only the captain was affected, one couldn't say; but several giggles sounded around the table. They were rapidly stifled.

McCoy hadn't joined in the chuckling. "Another coincidence, Jim?"

Kirk brushed at his shirt and gazed around the table again, more thoughtfully this time. "I'm beginning to wonder, Bones." He eyed the fork.

Something had bent the metal neatly in half midway down the stem. How, he couldn't tell. It appeared to be a perfectly ordinary fork. Close inspection failed to reveal any hidden hinge or abrasions where it might have been filed.

"I'm beginning to wonder . . ."

They finished the hexed meal in comparative silence, and without further incident. If there was a practical joker among them, he or she was abashed enough to forgo any further demonstrations.

However, the problem did not fade away. It continued to make itself felt throughout the ship . . . and in the most unexpected ways. The first new manifestation occurred following the command shift's return to the Bridge. Spock noticed an instrument lying on his console which hadn't been there when he had left. He utterly failed to recognize it. It was obvious how it was supposed to be utilized, but when he tried, he achieved nothing.

"Curious," he finally muttered, "most curious."

Kirk heard and strolled over from the navigation printout where he had been studying statistical readouts on the energy cloud.

"What is, Spock . . . what've you got there?" The first officer held it out to him. It was a small tubular device, rather like a monoculor viewer.

"I found this instrument on my console, Captain. There is only this single adjustable ring to serve as any kind of control. But it does nothing . . . see?"

Placing the eyepiece against his left eye, he fiddled with the ring. At the same time, Kirk noticed the dark ring encircling his right eye. When he pulled the tube away, a matching black circle had appeared around Spock's other eye—a circle, he noted, exactly the same size and shape as the eyepiece.

"It appears to serve no useful function," Spock added. "My best efforts have failed to produce any noticeable result."

In spite of himself, Kirk laughed. So did Sulu and Uhura when they turned and saw the result.

Spock simply stood there, befuddled, glancing from the comm station, to the helm and back to Kirk. Naturally, his ignorance of the situation made it all the funnier to the onlookers.

"I'm . . . sorry, Spock," Kirk finally managed to gasp, getting himself under control. "You see, you . . ." He couldn't manage to produce a quiet explanation. Instead, he pantomimed circles around his own eyes.

Spock continued to stand there for a moment, considering this nonverbal information carefully. Then he reached up and dabbed at his face with one hand. When he brought his fingers down, the tips of two were covered with black smudge.

His lips didn't twist, but he succeeded in scowling with his eyebrows . . .

If that had been the last incident, Kirk might still have put it down to someone's idea of humor. But the "incidents," as everyone on board was soon calling them, occurred with increasing frequency. And they became less and less amusing.

Only serious thoughts filled Scott's mind as he strolled down the corridor leading back to Engineering Central. Final repairs on the damage wrought by the Romulans were nearing completion, but a few delicate adjustments still had to be made in certain heavily battered sections.

Intricate repairs required careful thought, which in turn engendered a profound hunger. He paused by one of the galley annexes, just as Arex and M'ress rounded the far corner, walking in the opposite direction.

"Officer Scott," Arex called, "if you're hungry, won't you join us for lunch. We were just on our way to mess." His soulful visage radiated friendliness.

Scott politely declined. "No thanks, Arex. I'm just goin' to grab a bit of a snack before I get back to my work. I kinna afford to let some of my younger techs alone too long with certain machinery." He grinned.

"As it will go," Arex replied amiably. "Any word on who was responsible for the . . . dribble glasses, someone called them, and for what happened to First Officer Spock?"

"Not a clue. And I've heard scuttlebutt about a number of other childish pranks having taken place around the ship."

Arex and M'ress exchanged glances. "We haven't hearrd anything, orr seen anything like that," M'ress purred.

"Maybe you're immune . . . lucky you."

"I hope so, consyiderring what happened to Mrr. Spock," M'ress replied feelingly. "*Mm-aorrr* . . . how embarrassing!"

"See you later," Arex added, as they continued on down the corridor.

Scott murmured a goodbye, then activated the console. Identifying himself as to name and rank, he absently ordered a grilled Swiss cheese on rye.

"No . . . make that pumpernickel," he corrected quickly. The ACKNOWLEDGE light came on promptly. Scott pressed the second button, was rewarded by the sight of a filled plate slipping into place behind the transparent receiver guard.

Reaching in, he removed the sandwich, then turned to leave. As he did so, there was a second muffled thump behind him.

Puzzled, he looked back. A second sandwich had appeared in the opening. He shrugged and withdrew it . . . only to see it instantly replaced by yet another . . . and that by two, piled atop one another.

Muttering to himself, he set his three on the floor and removed the two new ones. Two more appeared, followed by another three . . . the last made with Limburger cheese instead of Swiss.

These were replaced by, in rapidly accelerating order, wedges of fudge cake, linzer torte, falafel, three steaming bowls of chop suey, blacktop sundaes, and a dismembered, smoked turkey.

Blinking and whining like a ratchet wrench with the colic, the machine started to flush a river of food so fast Scott had no time for culinary classification.

"What the blazes . . . *hold it a minute!*"

His hands were already covered with cheese, melting ice cream, and sauces of various composition and ethnic origin. The lower half of his uniform was splattered.

"I said *one sandwich!*" he shouted frantically. "One blasted sandwich, ye great glob of gastronomical gadgetry!"

Footsteps sounded in the corridor. Arex and M'ress reappeared, on the run. "Mr. Scott," Arex called, "we heard yelling. Is everything . . . ?" The concerned piping of the Edoan navigator stopped abruptly. Next to him, M'ress had commenced a smooth, feline laugh. Arex joined her.

"I'm sorry, Officer Scott," he gasped. "Excuse us, but . . ."

"Go ahead and laugh, go on . . . big joke!" Scott muttered in irritation as he warded off a barrage of burritos and kidney pie. "I'll wager you two are responsible for everything that . . . hey!"

The console was ejecting food through the input/recycle slot now, doubling its firepower and making it harder for him to grab at the control panel—even though various stabs and punches at said switches had failed to produce any lessening of the comestible bombardment.

"Just a moment, Officer Scott," Arex objected, his laughter dying down. "We're not responsible for this or any of the other reported pranks. How could I program this? I have no idea if half of the . . . dishes . . . lying about are even edible."

"It could be a random program," Scott countered. "I wonder if the captain will buy your excuse."

He dodged a stream of curried kooftah a Persian gourmet would have been proud of and took another step toward the controls. If he could just unbolt the master panel, he could bypass the circuitry and . . .

"I'm reportin' the both of ye as soon as I . . ." He paused as he reached the wall, bent to touch the first of two screw latches near the floor.

As he did so a large cream pie shot with impressive velocity out of the machine and caught him flush in the face, knocking him backward several steps. He recovered his balance and stood there, wiping whipped cream from his eyes and staring blankly at the machine.

"Believe us, Officer Scott," Arex began seriously, "we have nothing to do with . . . ," but the chief engineer ignored him, backing away from the annex as if it had suddenly acquired a malevolent intelligence of its own.

That last pie had been thrown *hard*—and aimed.

He eyed the machine warily.

That was not to be the last of the strange occurrences to plague the ship.

VI

The pranks multiplied, accompanied by a corresponding decrease in subtlety. Finally it reached the point where even the ship's repairs were being interfered with. The apogee of absurdity was reached when a glowering Kirk came stomping onto the Bridge to stand, hands on hips, just inside the elevator portal.

Arex turned from the navigation console and Spock from his library computer station while M'ress glanced across from communications. "Okay," Kirk announced in a no-nonsense, anything-but-amused voice, "this whole thing has gone far enough."

There were equal parts frustration and anger in his tone. This sudden fury was unlike the captain. Everyone stared at him, baffled.

"What has . . . sir?" Arex finally ventured.

Kirk bestowed a baleful glare on the innocent navigator. "I just picked up my clean uniforms from the service chute, Mr. Arex. When I put one on, I discovered *this*." He turned his back to them.

Lettered across the back of his shirt, in bold yellow, were the words: KIRK IS A JERK.

Below this someone had stenciled a simplistic childlike face with crossed eyes and a silly grin.

Events aboard had progressed to the point where no one was surprised at *any* kind of report. But this blatant assault on Kirk's position produced astonished stares from the Bridge personnel. It had progressed from flat humor to outright insult.

There was a brief, startled giggle from somewhere. Everyone looked nervously at his neighbor, but the giggle was not repeated. It had been indeterminate as to source or gender—fortunately for the giggler.

Everyone was sure of one thing. *They* hadn't laughed—and each in his own way tried to convey that information wordlessly to Kirk as he examined each one in turn. "When the outburst of hysteria has concluded, I'd like an explanation for this recent burst of puerility."

"That," suggested Spock in a strange tone of voice, "may be more difficult than it seems. I was watching both Lieutenant Arex and Lieutenant M'ress closely. I saw no one laugh. Needless to say," he finished quietly, "it did not come from me."

"*Someone* certainly laughed," Kirk countered, his anger dying as curiosity took over.

Further discussion was interrupted as M'ress suddenly rose from her chair to point past Kirk. "Captain, look behind you."

"Really, M'ress," a thoroughly fed-up Kirk muttered, "you're going to have to be more clever than that."

"It's not a joke, sir," Arex confirmed.

Kirk whirled . . . and took a couple of steps backward. A thick clinging fog was billowing inward from the turbolift shaft. It swirled around his legs, hugging the floor.

"*Now* what?"

Spock was preparing an answer. The computer supplied it readily. "The source of the atmospheric aberration appears to be centralized two decks below, Captain."

Fog or not, the lift operated efficiently. When Kirk pressed the emergency-stop switch and the door slid aside, it was to reveal a corridor filled from deck to ceiling with a roiling, eerie mist.

Spock took two steps into the cloud and stopped, pulling a small sensorscan from his hip. He took readings and measurements while Kirk fidgeted nervously behind him.

"Well?"

"Frankly, I had expected something else, Captain," he replied, without going into specifics on what the "something else" might be, "but this appears to be a normal, everyday water-based fog . . . except that such occurrences are *not* normal on a starship. Perhaps the humidification monitors are—"

Taking another step forward, he began flailing wildly as his legs started out from under him. He twisted and fought for balance with inhuman control. Kirk moved quickly to grab him—then found himself slipping and sliding as though on bearings. But by using one another for support and finally struggling to the projections on a nearby door, they were able to avoid a serious fall. After regaining their balance, it took a bit longer to catch their breath.

That accomplished, Spock disdained the sensorscan for less detailed but more immediate methods of study. He knelt carefully. Nearness to the source of the trouble brought revelation.

"Amazing," he murmured. "The deck here is covered with ice."

"It was almost covered with us," Kirk rumbled. "What kind of ice, Spock?"

"From all indications, normal water ice, Captain. It does not appear to possess exotic or dangerous properties . . . beyond the obvious physical ones, of course."

"Ice," Kirk said, staring down the corridor into the frosty miasma. "I don't know what's happening on this ship, Mr. Spock, but it's got to stop before somebody gets hurt. Whoever's responsible for this is getting carried away with his own inventiveness."

As if on cue, the strange giggle was heard again. Kirk had no need to look around for possible concealed bodies—he and Spock were alone in the corridor. That annoying giggle was loud and distinct this time. In fact, it was faintly feminine and almost—almost familiar.

Kirk took a step toward what he thought might be the source of the sound. Was someone hiding in that fog after all? Instantly he found himself sliding crazily. Only Spock's firm grip enabled him to recover his balance again.

"That laugh—it sounds very much like the one I thought I heard on the Bridge a few minutes ago. There's something awfully familiar about it." He eyed his first. "What do you make of all this, Spock?"

"Despite the increasing number of incidents, Captain, the evidence seems to point to a single guilty party."

"How do you know it's not sev—" Kirk's eyes widened. "You think you know who it is, don't you?"

"Not who, Captain—what. I believe that our practical joker is the *Enterprise* herself."

"The *Enterprise* . . . ?" Kirk hesitated, mulled the hypothesis over in his head. Then familiarity and fact came together, and everything else fell into place.

"Everything makes sense now. That carefully calculated feminine tone—it's the voice of our main computer!"

"Precisely," Spock agreed.

"I want all hands to stations, all computer techs to work doubleshift. We're going to run a complete cybernetics systems-check from bow to stern and get to the bottom of this." His voice grew threatening.

"Trick glasses and offensive food-processing equipment is one thing. But when some circuit failure starts affecting the ship's programing . . ."

"I heartily concur, Captain. This must be stopped before these pranks grow any more serious.

"At the moment, though, we have a less lethal if more immediate problem." He used his eyes to indicate the floor behind them. "Getting from here to the lift again in one piece, since the floor is now frozen over behind us."

There is no problem, however, that is ultimately insoluble under assault from the combined abilities of a Federation cruiser captain and his science officer. Crawling carefully on hands and knees, they made their way safely back to the elevator.

While Arex and M'ress handled their duties forward and Kirk and Spock pondered the problem posed by the apparent breakdown of the central computer, an off-duty Uhura and Sulu were approaching the main door to the Recreation Room. McCoy joined them a moment later.

Uhura touched the switch beside the door latch. A small transparent indicator lit up in green with the word UNOCCU-PIED. They followed a small beep provided for the benefit of color-blind, non-Anglo-reading personnel and guests.

Uhura fairly purred with satisfaction. "Good; nobody home . . . at least we can enjoy our free time without worrying about practical jokes."

The heavy door slid aside. McCoy trailed them in. "Exactly what the doctor ordered,'' he quipped, taking in the restful (if illusory) scene of park grounds and fountains.

''The standard re-creation,'' Sulu observed. ''Now for something a bit more original and relaxing.'' He activated the control which shut the door behind them, closing them off from the rest of the ship.

A moment later an electronic chime struck three times, and Spock's voice filled the empty corridor as it did every chamber and walkway aboard.

''All hands to your stations—this is a general alert. Repeat, all hands to your stations. Second and third computer shifts, report to briefing, second and third computer shifts, report to briefing. Repeat, all hands to sta—''

But within the sealed environment of the Recreation Room, the order went unheard. Possibly something was wrong with the inside intercom speakers.

Possibly . . .

Sulu moved to the only visible sign of electronic presence in the big room. This isolated fixture was a small console located to the right of the main door. He proceeded to activate it, clearing the park scene from the room.

They stood in the chamber as it actually was, now—a vast hall with distant, curving walls. Ceilings, walls, deck were a uniform malleable white. It was like standing inside a smooth ivory dome.

''Something soothing and homey,'' the helmsman murmured with anticipation. ''What'll it be?'' he asked his companions. ''Anyone object to a swim at the beach?''

Sulu turned his attention to the intricate keyboard and display screen mounted above. A detailed, three-dimensional schematic of the room program would appear there as the console operator designed it. The console itself consisted of a standard keyboard, plus numerous other controls for adjusting such things as climate, time of day, special effects— and many more. Sulu keyed the latter—only officers and qualified enlisted personnel were permitted to manipulate such touchy details as temperature and oxygen content.

As he worked the dials and switches and buttons, an image gradually began to form on the screen. Minutes passed. As helmsman, Sulu was especially adept in handling computer controls. The diagram formed rapidly under his skillful touch.

Eventually Sulu paused to study the picture, pressed another switch to add a little peripheral vegetation, and examined the finished program with pleasure. He touched another switch and the diagram rotated three hundred and sixty degrees, then displayed itself on an angle.

With a little flourish he keyed the INITIATE switch.

Around them, above them, below them, the room began to change.

Spock would have described it as a routine readjustment of physical conditions within a confined space produced by the recreational computer-annex drawing on the extensive fabrication facilities of the *Enterprise*. Anyone born over a couple of hundred years before would have called it a miracle.

But then, Spock could redefine that in simple, logical terms as well.

This design facility was primitive compared to the master dream computer they'd encountered on another world,* but within its limits it was capable of some very effective transmutations in the interest of alleviating shipboard tedium.

Shimmering, fluorescent forms took on substance and the illusion of solidity. Walls and ceilings vanished—to be replaced by a sandy seashore, complete with lapping wavelets and the distant call of gulls. The recreation annex wasn't up to producing three-dimensional simulacra of the birds themselves. That was too fluid an illusion to maintain. But three-dimensional projections of sea birds were available and they flashed on the distant deep-blue sky.

Sulu paid attention to details—after all, advanced manipulation of such instrumentation was an art form. A starfish hugged the water's edge here, dried kelp encrusted the sloping berm there.

"Nice job, Sulu," McCoy complimented, assessing the finalized creation. "You handle water well, but personally this is kind of hot for me. I'm more in the mood for a nice, quiet stroll in the woods."

"That sounds perfect, Doctor," Uhura admitted, squint-

*See "Once upon a Planet," *Star Trek Log Three*.

ing up to where a powerful light source reposed in placid imitation of a sun.

"Why didn't you say so?" Sulu asked agreeably. "Woods it is then . . . dark and deep."

A single touch dissolved water, gulls, sand, starfish and kelp. The helmsman began again from scratch.

Botany was a favorite hobby of his. As such, he was able to create an even better simulacrum of McCoy's request than he had of the beach. The forest he conjured up (deciduous, North American, temperate zone) was lush and seemingly endless. Rays of sunlight fell like wax blades through the branches and illumined shifting motes of dust. It was a ful-filled vision, even to the moss on the "north" side of the trees and the appropriate fungal undergrowth.

"Ahhh . . . that's more like it," McCoy complimented, savoring the crispness in the air and breathing deeply of the aroma of pine and birch . . . artificial though it might be. He made an after-you gesture and followed Uhura and Sulu as they started off down the path between the trees.

Their course would wind around and through the limited confines of the recreation chamber. If they got bored, a few touches on the console—now discreetly concealed by Sulu behind a young maple—would alter the terrain yet again. Meanwhile they enjoyed the cool, faint dampness of their own personal forest and tried to identify Sulu's purposely jumbled, programed bird calls . . .

M'ress, running through the acknowledgments from key personnel which was standard procedure during a general alert, noticed the failure of three officers to report in. She double-checked before bringing the matter to Kirk's attention.

"Captain," she finally reported, "accorrding to elimina-tion prrocedurre and last eye-witness accounts, officerrs Mc-Coy, Sulu, and Uhurra arre still in the main rrecrreation rroom. They have failed eitherr to rrespond to orr to ac-knowledge the call to stations."

"That's not necessarily surprising, Lieutenant," Kirk said easily. "To maintain lengthy illusions the main recreation room can be total-sealed from the rest of the ship. You can probably reach them by patching through to the rec room's own speaker system.''

"That's just it, sirr, I've alrready *trried* that." She sounded worried. "They still fail to rrespond. I can't even tell if the call is going thrrough.''

Kirk stiffened in his chair. "Now that *is* surprising. Try once more.''

M'ress turned back to her console, activated the necessary bypasses and overrides. "Drr. McCoy, Lieutenant Uhurra, Lieutenant Sulu . . . returrn to the Brridge immediately. This is a generral alarrm. I rrepeat, a generral alarrm. Please acknowledge.''

"Again," Kirk ordered tightly. What was going on?

M'ress sighed, raised her voice even though she knew the pick-up would compensate automatically. "Drr. McCoy, Lieutenant Uhurra, Lieutenant Sulu . . . rreturrn to the Brrid . . .''

The path through the closely packed, tall trees was bordered with thick patches of ferns. Water dripped from a high place into a bog where a venus flytrap closed over the projection of an ant.

The faintly metallic ping of water falling into a small pond was the only sound in the solitude of the forest. The three strollers entered a glade lined with high ferns and brightly colored mushrooms and toadstools. Bark fungi formed elf ladders in the trees.

"So quiet, so relaxing," Sulu murmured. "Such a change from orders and routine. An excellent selection, Doctor.''

"Me for a short snooze," Uhura declared, heading for the shade of a thick maple.

"And best of all, no practical jokes," McCoy exclaimed. "Unless," he added half-jokingly, "one of you is the dearly-sought culprit.''

Sulu sat down on the grass and grinned. The grin vanished as an unnatural, distant giggle broke the stillness. Uhura looked up curiously from where she'd just gotten comfortable. McCoy was scanning the sky and surrounding trees.

"I know you're especially good at animal detail, Sulu . . . but this doesn't strike me as an Irish enough a landscape to qualify for leprechauns.''

"That wasn't anything I programed," Sulu informed him. He was inspecting the dark underbrush with some concern. The illusion inventory of the rec annex was pretty extensive. If someone wanted to give them a scare by introducing a Taurean scimitar-wolf, now . . .

"Almost sounded like someone chuckling."

The giggle—if that's what it was—wasn't repeated. McCoy finally shrugged. "Probably just a malfunction in one of the audio-effects tapes. Maybe a rewind blotch mixed in with the forward play . . . could be most anything. We're all a bit jumpy from the stories circulating."

Uhura climbed to her feet. The glade no longer seemed quite so inviting. "I think I'll pass on that nap. Besides, I'm not that tired yet."

They crossed the open patch of green, picked up the dirt path on the far side. It disappeared ahead and veered to the left among the trees.

Around that first bend, the path unexpectedly vanished. A large square hole intersected its course. As if coaxed by an argumentative breeze, branches appeared from the undergrowth and arranged themselves with unnatural precision across the gap. Once this latticework was complete, leaves and pine needles fell from above and masked the intertwined branches.

They continued to drift downward until even so astute an observer as Spock would have been unable to tell that only a smattering of dead leaves and twigs covered the hole in the pathway. A last leaf, an afterthought, slipped into place to conceal a tiny hint of darkness as McCoy, Sulu and Uhura appeared in the distance, admiring the scenery and landscape ahead.

None of them heard the unnatural yet familiar high-pitched giggling that sounded in that part of the forest. It was concealed by something by now expert at concealment.

"That's a hemlock, isn't it, Sulu?" McCoy asked, pointing at a tall, handsome growth. "Beautiful. I liked your beach, but . . . ," he gestured expansively, "I wanted something a bit more closed and cooling. It's almost as if . . . hey!"

His exclamation was matched by a startled yelp from Sulu and a scream from Uhura. This was followed instantly by some ungentle flopping sounds. A rustle of broken leaves and crushed twigs, and then all was quiet.

Quiet until a blast of all-pervasive giggling suddenly erupted around them. Three pairs of eyes turned nervously upward.

But still nothing was to be seen. "That laughter again," Sulu murmured. "It wasn't our imagination."

McCoy sounded grim. "I was wrong. That's no tape malfunction. Someone's definitely laughing at us." He scrambled to his feet, wiping dirt and clinging splinters from his uniform.

"So we didn't lose our practical joker by coming here after all. But how the devil can someone hide in a cleared rec room? There aren't any sharp corners or dips to hide behind."

"There's an emergency override on the doorseal," Sulu recalled. "Someone might have entered after we'd established this simulacrum."

"Possible," McCoy agreed. "Everyone all right?"

Uhura was just getting to her feet. She winced slightly as she put pressure on her left ankle, but nodded. Sulu had fallen with the practice of one who reacts to such tumbles instinctively. He was unharmed and unbruised. McCoy had simply been lucky.

"Okay." The doctor glanced upward. "I don't know about you two, but I've had enough. I'm going to get to the bottom of this right now!" His statement provoked a response as unexpected as it was rapid. A barrage of giggles preceded an oddly stilted voice that chuckled, "Get to the *bottom* of this." The kibbitzer's tone was jovial, but it did nothing to improve McCoy's dampened humor. He pointed upward, aiming for a spiritual target in the absence of a physical one.

"All right, whoever you are. We fell for your idiotic little joke. Now get us out of here."

"*Fell* for my joke," the voice echoed, evidently entranced with its own wit. "*Fell* for . . . ," it dissolved in burbling chuckles.

Ordinarily, one if not all of the imprisoned officers would have identified the source of that voice by now. But their memories were temporarily clouded by a combination of anger and disgust. They could still only conceive of a flesh and blood antagonist.

"When we find out who you are," McCoy continued furiously, "you're going to be called on the deck before a board of inquiry . . . you can bet on it."

Such threats produced no lapse in the steady flow of laughter. On the contrary, it seemed to increase in proportion to the severity of the threat.

"I'm warning you," Sulu added, "the captain will bust you, whoever you are. This has gone far enough. It's not funny anymore . . . not that any of these pranks ever were."

More giggles . . . their unseen adversary appeared to have an unlimited capacity for laughter.

McCoy looked at his companions. "It seems obvious that whoever we're arguing with is too smitten with his own humor to listen to reason—much less to lend us a hand. We'll have to dig our way out of this."

Turning, McCoy tested the composition of the pit wall. The artificial soil was soft and crumbly. He let his gaze travel to the lip of the depression. The hole they found themselves in—no doubt that thought would amuse their unbalanced prankster if he were to voice it—was not terribly deep. But the four walls were vertical. No human ladder, then, and no climbing straight up.

Experimentally, he dug at the dirt. It came away easily.

"Maybe too easily, Doctor," suggested a worried Uhura. "We don't want any sudden cave-ins."

McCoy looked doubtful. "Oh, I don't think our jokester would let it go that far. Besides," he added sardonically, "if we're killed, how could we be the butt of any more jokes? In any case, I don't intend to sit around waiting for him to decide. Want to give me a hand?"

Working together they tried to cut a sloping path out of the pit, occasionally having to back off quickly when a handful brought the dirt above it sliding down. They rapidly became filthy. No sign of a cave-in appeared. It was a slow, monotonous job, but they'd be out before long. As McCoy had supposed, their unseen tormentor showed no inclination to offer assistance.

* * *

Spock finally looked up from his console to find an anxious Kirk staring at him, waiting for information. "Sorry, Captain . . . nothing. I've tried re-patching around the apparently defective emergency override, and canceling out any present programing, without result."

"Ample evidence exists to show that they are still inside, however. Someone's oxygen is being recycled, and from time to time power is still being drawn to operate the simulacrum machinery."

"Which leaves us with two possibilities," Kirk finished. "Either they can't respond—for what reason we don't know yet. Or else equipment malfunction is preventing them from even trying to answer." The command chair hummed softly as it swung round.

"M'ress . . . any luck yet?"

"Still no rresponse thrrough any channels, Captain."

Kirk pondered. "Let's go to the source of this, Spock. It's the computer that's been giving us trouble. The computer supervises everything that goes on in that rec room. So . . ."

"I was about to suggest that myself, Captain."

Spock turned, and his fingers began a lithe, precise dance over the ship's instrumentation. The blink of indicator lights and the compliant hums and beeps of responsive equipment followed. The reply was presented both in printed form on Spock's screens, and aurally over the Bridge speakers.

"That is for me to know and for you to find out," it announced.

Spock's eyebrows looked as if they had crawled clear up his forehead, through his hair and down his rear collar. Infantile riddle-replies he'd come to expect occasionally from humans. But that something as precise and coldly logical as the ship's computer might resort to such barbaric foolishness seemed to all but herald the end of reason.

Kirk's reaction was nearly as incredulous. "Did I hear that right, Mr. Spock?" he mumbled in astonishment.

"I am afraid," Spock said slowly, "that you did, Captain. The malfunction is clearly more severe than I believed possible." He returned his attention to his keyboard.

"Question," he inquired carefully. "Are you deliberately holding Dr. McCoy, and Lieutenants Uhura and Sulu captive in the main recreation room?"

Another prompt response, this time with a subtle alteration that hinted, perhaps, at something less than complete control over its disturbed circuitry. Certainly, Kirk mused, it wouldn't *want* to sound like a petulant child.

"I'll never tell," it whined. "Never ever never. Can't make me, either. Can't, can't, *can't*! And I won't."

Hands clenched tightly, Kirk rose and walked over to stand by Spock. "Let me try," he whispered, then directed his voice to the input pickup.

"This is Captain James T. Kirk speaking," he announced with as much steel in his voice he could muster. "You are programed to obey any direct order I may give."

"That is correct," the voice replied evenly.

Some of Kirk's fury abated at that conciliatory response. Maybe what the computer needed to break it free of this inexplicable insanity was just a little drill-sergeant firmness. Slowly, he continued.

"Very well . . . I order you to release officers McCoy, Sulu and Uhura from the recreation chamber *immediately*."

A series of flashes and winks from the console, followed by a gentle query, "Say 'please?' "

"Well I'll be!" Kirk gulped, by now beyond amazement. Spock leaned back to murmur.

"One should not debate command priority with a machine, Captain. Under the circumstances, I would suggest compliance coupled with a temporary swallowing of pride."

Kirk started to object, then nodded slowly. Keeping his voice level with an effort, he murmured, "Please?"

A quiet pause, and this time the indicator lights seemed to flash in more natural sequence. He was about to exchange a glance of triumph with Spock when the voice jumped in with gleeful clarity, "Say 'pretty please' . . ."

Kirk snapped off the audio control before any further taunt could be offered. Arex appeared about to say something, thought better of it as Kirk switched the main viewscreen into the intercom system. A terse call and the result was an image of a concerned engineer Scott to go along with his voice.

"Mr. Scott, I've had it up to here."

"Aye, Captain," Scott concurred, ignoring Kirk's angry

tone. He could guess its source. Elaboration was sure to follow.

He was right. "We've got some serious trouble with the main computer, Scotty. It's not just custard pies and slippery decks, now. We're pretty sure it's kidnapped Dr. McCoy, Sulu, and Uhura."

"Kidnapped . . . the main computer?" Scott's lined face underwent a series of highland contortions as the import of Kirk's words penetrated. "The main computer . . . but how . . . ?"

"We're not sure yet."

Scott considered. "Why not ask it to explain itself?"

"We've tried that Scotty." Kirk smiled tightly. "All we've got in reply are taunts and nonsense. Neither Mr. Spock nor myself think continuing along that line is going to produce any useful result—and it doesn't do anything for my blood pressure, either. I can see only one solution, one chance of forestalling even more serious trouble." He sighed.

"I want you to shut down all higher logic functions until we can get *some* kind of handle on what's responsible for perpetrating this cybernetic imbecility."

"Aye, sir," Scott replied, coming to attention verbally.

"Leave only the purely supportive circuitry operational," Kirk went on. "I want everything capable of abstract reasoning and creative cognition put out of commission until we can get a crew in the central core to dissect those information banks. We can't risk further mismanipulation of on-board functions."

"I'll get a crew right on it, sir. And I'll handle the main lobotomy myself. Scott out."

"Bridge out." Kirk switched off. Scott's image disappeared, leaving the captain confronted with a panorama of alien constellations.

VII

Another double handful of soil, yet another . . . and then the last. Sulu stepped back and took stock of the steep incline they had cut in the pit wall.

"I think that'll do it, Uhura." He smiled expectantly. "Ready?"

She took a deep breath. "I haven't done any serious climbing in years." In her Academy days, she and several daring friends had ascended the Aeolian Pyre on Tsavo II. If they could see the worry she was expressing now, over mounting ten feet of dirt, they would laugh.

Sulu and McCoy formed a double support with interlocked hands. With this boost, and moving carefully so as not to dislodge any more dirt, she was able to scramble over the rim.

The helmsman followed her a moment later. Then it was their turn to aid a less agile McCoy as he, struggling and cursing, fought his way to the top of the incline.

"When I get my hands on the clown who's behind this," he vowed, panting heavily, "I'll put him in Sick Bay for a month!"

Sulu rocked back on his heels and mopped at his sweaty face. "I thought you were supposed to operate the other way around, Dr. McCoy?"

"This is one time," McCoy countered, "where I think I'd enjoy drumming up some of my own business."

He would have added more, but the forest surrounding them chose that moment to flicker into chaos. Before anyone thought to inquire aloud what was happening, the tall, temperate grove with its gentle breeze and scented air had been replaced by a howling wilderness of ice and snow. Gale winds laden with snow and tiny, stinging ice chips lashed at them, while above the bone-chilling wind an admonishing voice cried, "Temper, temper! Perhaps this will cool you off!"

Huddled together for warmth, the three officers tried to take stock of their new environment while shielding their faces with cupped hands. Attempting to ignore the driving cold, Sulu made a slow turn. No matter which way he looked there was nothing to be seen but white ground and whiter sky. "We've got a regular blizzard condition here . . . how are we ever going to find the exit?"

McCoy was stamping his feet. The surface shrank from the irregular friction . . . it was real snow, all right.

Giggles fell like snowflakes around them as the temperature plunged to arctic levels . . .

Scott was still trying to imagine how the computer had effected the "kidnapping" of his friends. The abduction puzzled him, the more so since a harried Kirk had not seen fit—or perhaps felt he hadn't the time—to explain the rec room situation.

Future speculation, he decided, would have to wait until he'd carried out the captain's command.

He turned a corner and confronted a sealed single door. He pressed his thumb to the sensor square below the stenciled letters which spelled, "WARNING—AUTHORIZED PERSONNEL ONLY."

At the moment the main computer room was empty. Since this central cortex rarely required servicing and was kept sealed in all but critical situations, it hadn't been visited recently by anyone except the standard security patrol. His practiced gaze showed no hint of unauthorized activity.

This isolation was a pity, since in its fashion the central computer cortex was one of the more impressive sights on the ship. Bank on bank of tireless indicator lights, liquid crystal displays, glowing poured circuitry—and all this only the tiny, visible part of the ship's heart and brain.

His destination lay at the far end of the room. There he was required to supply his thumbprint again, not to mention having to present both eyes for a retinal identification check. Only then would a hitherto hidden slot present itself for the offer of a special key card. Insertion of the key caused a broad, man-high panel to click and then slide silently aside, revealing a series of sequential switches and controls mounted over a color-coded keyboard.

Human memory activated mechanical as he tapped out a rarely used combination. This caused several sets of the sequential controls mounted above to glow . . . the higher logic and creative reasoning telltales. These were subdivided in turn into various sections embossed with such headings as *Intuitive Reasoning*, *Abstraction*, *Deduction*, and *Stage IV Response*. The unlit sections he ignored. "Time for a nap, old girl," he murmured. "Captain's orders." His hand moved for the first of the red-colored switches.

He never reached it.

A piercing whine filled the chamber. It soared into the range of imperceptible ultrasonics before Scott could feel more than a momentary pain. Total disorientation set in as he strove to readjust himself to the fact that he was tumbling toward the ceiling. He landed there with a thud, flat on his back.

Typically, his initial reaction was more emotional than effective. Once he managed to regain his balance and force his mind to accept the fact he wasn't going to plunge to the floor, he rolled over and crawled above the upside-down console set in the far wall.

"Engineering to Bridge," he bawled over the barely reachable intercom. "I've got a problem down here, sir."

Kirk was able to offer commiseration if not help. Exactly the same situation prevailed on the Bridge, where he, Spock, and everyone else had been similarly thrown to the roof.

Spock managed to activate the main intercom by crawling up his library-computer console—or was he crawling down? "Scotty, what the blazes is going on?"

"I'm not sure, Captain." He tested himself carefully and with self-control only an experienced spacer could muster, walked across the ceiling toward the next bank of interdeck monitors. A quick check was enough to show him that his personal plight was being repeated on every level.

"Our gravity's reversed polarity—all by itself, it seems."

"The latter conclusion is an obvious falsehood," came Spock's clear voice. He was sitting upside-down in his seat, studying the information displayed on his readouts. "This is an undeniable defensive maneuver by the computer, to prevent Mr. Scott from disconnecting its higher functions."

"Crazy," Kirk muttered, "this is crazy. Not jokes anymore. Our own computer's declared war on us . . . and I haven't the slightest idea why."

"I do not believe the term 'war' is yet applicable to this situation, Captain. The computer has not yet shown itself to be openly antagonistic—only misguidedly self-centered." He looked thoughtful, relaxed despite his upside-down position. "I do have a theory; but first I suggest that if Officer Scott moved away from the computer's logic terminal—far away—it might feel less threatened, and therefore less inclined to take direct action against us."

"Threatened? Mr. Spock, that computer is programed with so many stabilizing circuits . . ." His objections were halted by the look on his first officer's face.

"All right," he murmured in resignation, "never argue with reality, I suppose." He directed his voice toward the intercom. "Mr. Scott . . . vacate the computer room."

Scott's eyes widened at the order. "Vacate, sir? Now, after this?" His gaze strayed longingly toward the still uncovered terminal.

"On the double, Mr. Scott."

"Aye, sir," he sighed. For a brief moment he considered making a dash for the lobotomizing controls—then he decided against it. Not because of what Kirk might say, but because if threatened again the crazed computer might resort to an even more severe distortion of ecological controls. He couldn't risk exposing anyone but himself to danger more severe than a bad tumble.

Unable to insure that only he would be the object of the machine's retaliation, he turned and walked across the ceiling toward the chamber exit. He paused there for a last look backward. The panel he had opened had not been shut, the telltales still shone brightly. Apparently the computer hadn't managed to find a way to close off its own emergency shutdown. That was his sole encouraging thought. Once he was outside this door, however, those switches would be effectively protected from external manipulation. Kirk's voice sounded behind him.

"Mr. Scott?"

"Just leavin', Captain." He stepped gingerly over the low hurdle formed by the door overhead and turned on the other side, to watch it slide shut behind him.

Stretching downward, he could just reach the door control. As expected, his repeated touch had no effect at all. The door remained closed tight.

Years of experience in ship situations of all types enabled him to cope with what followed.

There was an abrupt cessation of weight, and then he found himself falling. He didn't quite land like a cat, but did succeed in turning his body enough in midair so that his arms and legs—and a less mobile portion of his anatomy—took most of the impact when he hit the floor.

Others were not so fortunate. There were some injuries— sprains, a couple of broken legs, a concussion or two—but nothing fatal.

The chief engineer rolled over and sat up, rubbing at the back of his neck and shaking a fist at the closed door. "Ye bloody big scatterbrain, make up your monumental mind!"

As expected, the door and its now isolated master did not deign to reply.

Experience had also told on the Bridge, where even minor injuries were absent.

"You were right, Spock," Kirk admitted. "Once the threat to its creative reasoning functions ceased, it no longer felt compelled to take defensive action."

The question now uppermost in his mind was, what kind of offensive action might the computer eventually decide to take? But Spock had mentioned a theory. Spock's theories usually turned out to be pretty solid.

"All right, Spock, can you tell me what's happened to my ship?"

Assuming a lecturing pose, Spock began, "Evaluation of the circumstances surrounding both the disappearance of Officers McCoy, Sulu and Uhura coupled with the many previous, though less dramatic, incidents leads me to believe that my first suspicion—that some unbalanced personality on board was tampering with the computer—is false."

"Your reasons, Spock?"

"The machinations which have been carried out so far involve extremely elaborate alterations in the computer's most delicate circuitry and programing. It strikes me that such adjustments and corresponding bypasses of all emergency overrides and fail-safes are beyond the capacity of any group of individuals on board, let alone any one. They would require the facilities and knowledge present only at a major cybernetics construction/repair center.

"With one possible exception," he finished. "Chief Engineer Scott."

"And we know Scotty's not responsible. For one thing, this kind of juvenile delinquency just isn't part of his personality." Kirk looked uncertain. "If it's not due to the actions of someone on board, what then? Central computers are supposed to be fool-proof. Ours ought to shut itself down, considering what it's already done."

"I believe there is only one possible explanation left, Captain. You remember the peculiar energy field we passed through in escaping the Romulans?"

Kirk nodded as he settled back in his chair. It had resumed its familiar location on the floor instead of the ceiling. He considered Spock's words carefully.

"I will assume," the first officer continued, "that the extremely active subatomic particles of which the energy field was composed have acted upon our computer's most sensitive circuits."

"The logic and higher reasoning centers," Kirk supplied.

"Exactly. A kind of electromagnetic infection, to put it crudely. The end result appears to have been an alteration, rather than a breakdown, of the ship's cognitive facilities.

"It is still capable of intuitive reasoning, but now along infantile instead of practical lines."

"So what you're saying," Kirk ventured by way of summing up, "is that the computer, and what it controls on board—meaning just about everything—is now in the 'hands' of a clown-mind." It was an awesome threat—even though, he had to admit, nothing terribly dangerous had happened so far.

Nothing dangerous? Then what was happening to Uhura, Sulu and McCoy?

"What can we do to correct the malfunction?"

"I'm afraid I've no idea, Captain," Spock replied solemnly. "There is nothing predictable about the computer's actions, other than its unpredictability. Without a pattern, I have nothing on which to formulate a potential solution.''

Sulu hugged his arms to his sides. The gesture was more psychological prop than useful action. It did nothing to alleviate his shivering.

They had managed to stumble over a snow bank. It cut off much of the biting wind, though they all knew that if the fickle mind now in control of the computer chose to alter the gale's angle of approach, it could do so any minute. So they nestled together under the white lee and hoped their tormentor would remain otherwise occupied.

He's starting to turn blue, Uhura mused in wonderment as she stared at the shaking McCoy, her own teeth rattling. Odd . . . until now she'd thought that sort of thing only happened on visitape, subtly prepared by professional makeup men. Apparently nature was equally adept at such cosmetics.

Coming as she did from a tropical climate, the temperature drop should have affected her hardest of all. Instead, she seemed to be standing it a little better than her two companions. Sulu was little better off than McCoy.

"The temperature must be twenty below, and still dropping," she observed frigidly.

"Twenty below what?" McCoy grumbled. "Are you on the standard scale or the old Fahrenheit?"

"Well, I'm on the Sulu scale," the helmsman broke in, "and on that scale it's twenty below freezing."

"Look, we're not taking a dispassionate approach to this," suggested Uhura. "No matter how it looks, no matter how radical the illusions set before us, this is still just the Recreation Room. If we travel far enough in one line, we've got to run into one of the walls. From there we ought to be able to feel our way to the door."

McCoy struggled to his feet. He had to shout for his voice to be heard above the steady howl of the wind. "I could punch all kinds of holes in that argument, Uhura, but it's the first suggestion I've heard that contains any sense. Let's move before we all turn into icicles.

"At least walking will help keep us warm. This blizzard shows no sign of letting up."

Also, though he didn't say it, it would keep them from

dwelling any longer on the increasingly serious situation they found themselves in.

The doctor found himself in the lead simply by virtue of taking the first step away from their temporary refuge. As they fought their way through the whiteout, he kept those argumentative "holes" he'd casually mentioned to Uhura to himself.

There was no point in giving their invisible assailant any suggestions.

Whoever had commandeered the rec room controls could create any, absolutely any, type of environmental simulacrum. For example, a fake solid wall. Bending it slightly could keep them feeling around in circles for hours, days, all the while thinking they were traveling in a straight line toward a never-nearing exit.

They might counter that by measuring their steps, since they knew the size of the chamber. In that case, they could find themselves confronted with an infinite series of artificial walls and exits.

An exit could be found . . . found to lead only to another section of the same snowstorm. McCoy's mind grew dizzy with the possibilities. The computer *could* let them out into a reproduction of the outside corridor. He could walk to his own cabin . . . only to awake still inside the recreation room.

It was enough to drive a man mad.

He forced himself to stray from such ominous thoughts as he struggled awkwardly through the deepening drifts. So far their pernicious prankster didn't seem that far-sighted. Or that clever.

He found himself wondering if the designers of this marvelous method of electronic escape had considered its psychiatric possibilities . . .

Kirk studied the readout on the main viewscreen. So far, the deranged computer hadn't interfered with pure information storage and retrieval facilities. Probably, he mused, because it didn't think there was anything in its banks that could be utilized against it.

There were endless tomes on computer repair, on procedures for treating mislaid circuitry, even on treating the colossal machine mind for various psychological electronic traumas. But there didn't seem to be a thing on how to treat a computer whose reasoning power had been inexplicably distorted by the effects of passage through a free-space energy complex of unknown composition. That was hardly surprising, since this was the first time it had happened.

Kirk thought sardonically that they needed to pull the plug and he had no idea where the socket was.

The viewscreen shifted to internal communications channels again, replacing the universe and chromatic emanations of the field with the more prosaic features of a tired young technician. At the moment, he wore fatigue like a badge.

"Search party to Bridge—Ensign Apple reporting."

"Bridge here—the Captain speaking. Report, Ensign."

"Our sensors indicate the missing officers are still in the Recreation Room, sir. The door appears to be jammed from the other side."

A moment's consideration, then, "Hold your position, try the door from time to time, Apple. If it opens, get in there and get them out. Report immediately if there's any change in the corridor."

"Yes, sir."

Some fast switching and the face in the screen grew older, wiser.

"Engineering," Scott acknowledged. "Captain?"

"We've finally located Uhura, Bones, and Sulu. They're in the Recreation . . ." His voice dissolved in the middle of the word . . . to a chuckle!

"Sir . . . I didn't get the end of that."

Startled, Kirk coughed and tried again. "We need a full work crew, with power tools, maybe even a laser drill, to open a badly jammed door. Have them report to . . ."

In horrified fascination, he felt his facial muscles working, twisting involuntarily into a wide grin. "Report to . . . to . . ."

He collapsed in a paroxysm of laughter. Fighting, battling his own body, he gripped the arms of the command chair so hard his knuckles turned white. His head rolled back and forth as he roared at some gut-wrenching cosmic joke.

Arex, M'ress and Spock stared at him in astonishment. But it was Scott who spoke first.

"Captain . . . what's the matter, sir? I don't understand what's . . . what's . . ."

The chief engineer of the endangered ship snorted. Then he smirked. The smirk spread to a smile broken by giggles, then chuckles—and finally he, too, was bellowing with laughter.

M'ress was the next to surrender to the assault of merriment. Her throaty, feline giggles were in sharp contrast to the deeper laughs of Kirk and Scott. She was soon joined by the weird, amused piping of Arex.

Only Spock remained silent, though not unaffected. His concern grew rapidly as he studied his out-of-control companions, while unprovoked, unrestrained hilarity reigned on the Bridge. He was about to voice an observation when both hands suddenly flew to his temples. His brows drew together in an expression of shooting pain. There was nothing he could have done to mitigate the half-anticipated attack of migraine.

Still blubbering uncontrollably, Kirk finally noticed his first officer's silence and painful grimace.

"Come on, Spock," he managed to gasp, "where's that famous Vulcan sense of humor?" This apparent apex of jocularity caused Arex and M'ress to laugh even harder. Meanwhile on the viewscreen, Scott was fighting unsuccessfully to remain in focus.

Holding one hand to the side of his head and gritting his teeth occasionally, Spock turned his attention to his computer console. The crew still retained some control over certain localized monitoring equipment, facilities the central computer apparently disdained to trouble with. Spock already suspected what had happened. Environmental analysis quickly confirmed his suspicions.

"Just as I thought," he murmured painfully.

"What are you," Arex whistled heartily, "mumbling about, Mr. Spock?"

"The atmosphere on the Bridge and presumably also in Engineering," he replied tautly, "is being pumped full of nitrous oxide, better known in the human vernacular as laughing gas. I cannot yet tell what other decks have been affected by this aerobic alteration. In any case, it is no laughing matter.'' His other hand darted up from the console to press at his opposite temple. "Especially for Vulcans. Breathing nitrous oxide causes . . . severe headache.''

The same somber amusement was prevalent in another part of the ship, though with even grimmer overtones.

''This blizzard,'' Uhura roared under the effect of the gas, "keeps getting worse. And I think the temperature is still dropping.''

''I know!'' Sulu shouted, in forced hysteria. "If we don't keep moving, we're going to freeze to death.''

McCoy fell to the snow. Already his feet and ankles were becoming numb from the unrelenting cold and damp. Nevertheless, he rolled and flailed about as if Sulu's observation were the funniest thing he'd heard in ages.

Such laughter-induced helplessness was worsening on the Bridge. Only one person was not similarly enraptured. Though in considerable pain, he was still capable of coherent thought, of responsive action.

Spock's skull felt as if it were about to fly from his shoulders. He staggered over to the engineering console. By now the pain had reached the point where it occasionally blocked out sight. But he was able to locate and adjust the necessary controls.

There was a sudden loud hum as rarely used circuits were engaged. The controls Spock had adjusted were purely manual and required no switching through any computer annex.

As a refreshing breeze flowed over them, the rest of the Bridge crew began to return to their senses, the laughter dying slowly and agonizingly.

''Thanks, Spock,'' Kirk was finally able to whisper, as a last chuckle forced its way loose. "How long have we got?''

Spock checked the gauges on the panel, rubbing at his head. The marching on top had ceased. "The emergency air supply should be adequate for another six hours, Captain. When that's exhausted, we'll automatically go back to standard recycled air until the emergency supply can be cleaned and retanked—assuming that's likely to take place. I would not like to comment on the odds.''

"Six hours . . . then we've from now till oh-eight-hundred to find a cure for the computer. No telling what we'll be forced to breathe next." His gaze returned to the forward viewscreen.

An extremely serious chief engineer stared back at him. Scott put a hand over his mouth, coughed hard a couple of times. "I heard, Captain . . . I'll get right on that crew."

"The main recreation room, Scotty." He nodded as Kirk switched off.

A small measure of sanity returned to the Bridge as Kirk and Spock strove frantically to discover a path through the labyrinth of contradictions their central computer had created. It wasn't long before M'ress indicated a call for Kirk and he was forced to turn his attention from the harried research back to the main viewscreen.

The image that appeared was Scott, but now the background was different. It showed busy men and women working in an otherwise deserted corridor, instead of in Engineering. He knew where the chief engineer was, now.

"How's that door coming, Scotty?"

Scott's voice was filled with despair, discouragement. "None of our power tools work, Captain! The laser drill, standard metal-cutting saws, drills . . . nothin'. Near as I can figure, some kind of internal energy drain is operatin' here.

"I tried them on ship's power first. The big drill didn't even turn over. We got a couple of spins from a battery-powered saw before it died. After that, nothin' so much as burped. Whatever's suckin' this stuff dry is as efficient as it is selective."

The view jerked slightly as he moved aside and readjusted the corridor visual pickup. Now Kirk was able to see exactly how the work was proceeding. Several crew members were attacking the rec room with crowbars while another pounded a steel wedge into the doorway jamb with a sledgehammer.

"As you can see, we're givin' it a mighty go with manual equipment." Scott almost smiled. "We've got some awfully primitive stuff on board, Captain. Whoever wrote out cruiser stores either had a vivid imagination or secret fondness for sweat. Whoever it was, I'm glad he included some old-fashioned persuaders among all the electronics." He chuckled. This time, it didn't hurt.

"Keep at it, Scotty. We've got three people in there whose lives may depend on it." He paused. "I hope the worst that's happened to them is that they've laughed themselves sick."

"We'll have 'em out any minute, sir," Scott assured him, more to boost the captain's spirits than because it was true. "No need to worry . . ."

McCoy stopped, exhausted. Sulu and Uhura had long since outdistanced him. Now they turned and waited patiently for him to catch up. Sulu waved.

"Come on, Doctor, we must be close to the outside wall by now."

McCoy shook his head, wondering if the echo of his voice would reach them. "You two better go on without me—cold's finally gotten to my legs. We may not even be walking in a straight line. Illusion . . . everything's fake. Maybe . . . maybe you can hit the door by chance . . . if you move fast. You won't, with me." He sat down in the snow. He could no longer feel anything below his ankles.

"Doctor," Uhura began as she and Sulu walked back to him, "we're not going to . . ."

She stopped. The enclosed environment changed. The sensation was similar to the feeling of temporal–physical displacement one felt when transporting.

Gone were the snow, the cold, wind and ice. Instead of clinging white drifts they found themselves standing on a patio of pink marble, surrounded by gleaming Corinthian columns out of an ancient Hellenic frieze. The patio was encircled by a lush green lawn, recently watered. Tall, manicured hedges walled them in. The soothing simulacrum was complete even to the position of the warm sun in the sky, the light breeze scented with date blossoms, even drifting butterflies. The maniac in control of the rec room annex was nothing if not thorough.

"Well, what do you know," Sulu murmured, half-appreciatively. "Come on, Doctor, looks like we're finally going to get out of here."

McCoy was too tired to dispute the helmsman, and he sincerely wanted to agree with him. They waited until he hauled himself up on thawing legs and started toward the one opening visible in the surrounding hedge. He passed them, stopped at the entrance. Sulu and Uhura slowed, aware that something was wrong. When he turned back, his voice reflected a weariness born of pessimistic expectation once more borne out.

"I don't mean to discourage you, Sulu, but this may not be as simple as you think."

The helmsman eyed him questioningly. Rather than reply, McCoy beckoned them to come ahead. They came up beside him and looked slightly to the left.

The hedge there was far taller than any of them. It opened into two new pathways. A short sally showed that these in turn branched into several more and broke up again into no one knew how many equally confusing mazes.

Sulu looked disconsolate, while Uhura offered an enlightening combination of Swahili, English, and Simbian curses.

"Ever wonder how the rat feels?" McCoy grinned faintly. "I was afraid something like this might happen." He leaned back against the artificial foliage; it gave like real brush.

"Any time it wants to, the rec room computer can be programed to decoy us with an infinite arrangement of fake walls and exits. Apparently that's not enough for it. It's gone one step further." He gestured at the first division in the green wall.

"We could wander around in this old-fashioned garden maze until we all grew long wrinkles and blank expressions. One thing you can bet on. The last place any of these pathways lead is *out*."

Sulu tried to find a bright side. "At least we know where we are. We might as well stay here."

"Yes, that's right," agreed Uhura hopefully. "We're probably closer to the corridor wall than we were when we started walking."

"Are you sure?" McCoy asked, staring past her. "Take a look behind you."

The two junior officers turned. Marble columns and patio, green lawn, all were gone now. Stretching away in every direction were duplicates of the featureless hedgerows they now faced. Like it or not, they had been trapped in the maze.

"Where do we go from here?" a discouraged Sulu muttered.

The last thing he expected was an answer. So they were all surprised when it came, shattering both the silence and the hedgerow simulacrum with a violent crash.

A section of brush suddenly collapsed inward toward them, and they had a view into the next dimension. The inside of the rectangular section was green; but the other side was made of metal. It was the corridor they had entered from that showed beyond. Their sense of direction must have been right even through the snow and wind.

No wonder their assailant had been forced to alter their environment . . . they had been too close to finding their way out.

Standing in the rough-edged opening, through which the perfume of standard composition ship-air now poured, were a worried Commander Scott and several engineering techs armed with crowbars, hammers and picks.

Uhura let out a relieved sigh and slumped against Sulu, who staggered. He suddenly was aware that he was more tired than he had believed possible.

McCoy started forward—and then stopped dead, a peculiar expression twisting his features.

"Scotty," he said strangely, "what's behind you?"

Scott looked understandably puzzled. "Behind me?" He hesitated. Dr. McCoy sounded serious, so he looked right then left. "Service corridor leading off east and west. What in heaven's name . . . ?"

McCoy walked up to him and extended a hand. Scott looked at him, started to say something and then shook it firmly. As he did so a broad smile spread across the doctor's face.

"I know every groove and callus in that palm," he explained with satisfaction. "If you're an illusion, Scotty, you're the best crafted one this rec room ever devised."

"Illusion?" Scott gaped. "By the holy heather, the captain about worries himself to death over what happened to you three, I nearly break my own back and those of this crew here to get you out, and you have the brass to call me an illusion? McCullhans and Scotts, I'll show you who's an illusion!"

"Easy, Scotty, easy," McCoy gentled. "I plead recreational fatigue."

The chief engineer's brow wrinkled. "Recreational . . . what's that?"

"A new disease recently made up especially for the three of us." He gestured at Sulu and Uhura. "We've been overentertained for the last few hours." Then he sat down on the battered-in door and took off his shoes.

Scott watched him in dumbfoundment until the socks started to come off, then his eyes widened. "What happened to your feet?"

"Come on, Scotty, I'm disappointed in you. You should recognize it—surely you've seen enough cases to."

It hit Scott seconds later. "Frostbite . . . in the rec room?" He looked incredulous.

"Seems impossible, doesn't it?"

"No . . . no, as a matter of fact, it doesn't. You don't have a true picture of what's been goin' on, any of you. You've been out of touch for the last several hours. I forgot that, for a minute. No, nothin' that happened to you in there could surprise me."

"The only thing I'm interested in getting in touch with now," McCoy countered with verve, "is the idiot who's responsible."

"I can help you there," Scott informed them. "We know who the idiot is."

"The culprit's been arrested, then?" McCoy asked. "I'll be interested to see how far over the edge he actually is."

Scott didn't smile. "He hasn't been arrested, and is not likely to be—and you'd have a devil of a time prescribing treatment."

"Tell me about it when I get to the Bridge. First the three of us have to make a little detour to Sick Bay. Sulu and Uhura

have assorted bruises and strains that require attention, and
I think I have to stick my pods in the cooker for a bit . . .''

He rubbed ruefully at his damaged feet as he fought to
make sense of Scott's words . . .

VIII

"There's no need for either of you to stand this shift," Kirk told Sulu and Uhura when they returned to the Bridge. McCoy came along with them.

Both lieutenants ignored him as they relieved Arex and M'ress. "Sorry, Captain, but you'll have to order us out," Sulu objected.

"And as you can see," Uhura added, "we took the precaution of bringing Dr. McCoy along with us—in case we needed an irrefutable medical opinion."

"Seems I'm outnumbered and outflanked," Kirk mumbled, concealing his pleasure at their safe return. "What is your irrefutable medical opinion, Bones?"

"Both of them are fully fit for duty, Jim. You might even say anxious."

"I see. Then I might as well quit pretending and admit how glad I am to see you both back on the Bridge. We had some anxious moments trying to figure out what our berserk computer was doing to you all."

"Not as anxious as we did," McCoy confirmed. "You know what we went through by now—you did see my preliminary report?"

"I saw what you dictated to the medical records log, if that's what you mean," Kirk replied unenthusiastically. "I'd prefer a less technical description."

"Sure . . . if you'll grant me one request."

"Anything within reason and regulations, Bones."

McCoy crossed his arms and rubbed both biceps. "Could you turn up the heat on the Bridge? I *know* it's my imagination, but I haven't felt really comfortable since we left that madhouse."

Kirk chuckled, then self-consciously cut it off. He had already done more than enough laughing for one day.

"As to your description," McCoy began, only to have Spock interrupt him.

"Captain, we're getting under way . . . the main drive has been activated."

"Uhura, on the double, get me Chief Scott."

"Yes, sir." A pause, then a slightly surprised reply. "Sir, Mr. Scott just called in, trying to get in touch with *you*. He reports that despite the fact every sensor and gauge reads negative action, the warp drive *is* operating. He has already tried every emergency procedure . . . even attempted to shut down the control reactors. Nothing works."

"I heard that the central computer's been responsible for all the trouble," McCoy said. "What's it up to now?"

"Sir, the helm no longer responds," a troubled Sulu reported. "We're coming about to a new heading."

"Very well, Lieutenant," a resigned Kirk said. "As soon as our course stabilizes, give me a full plotting."

There was silence for several minutes as Sulu studied his readouts, then reported, "Course stabilizing, sir . . . three-seven-two mark twelve."

Kirk did some quick mental calculation. Roughly translated, those figures meant they were heading back toward the neutral zone, back toward three waiting Romulan cruisers.

"And you can bet they'll be gunning for us, after the way we slipped by them," Kirk said minutes later.

A high, hysterical and by now all-too-familiar chirping echoed through the bridge. It sounded for all the world like a crazed electric cuckoo loose in its clock—and the analogy was not so far wrong.

"Speed increasing, sir," Sulu informed him. "We'll round the energy field any minute—sensors are picking up three vessels." He worked controls. "Long-range scanners show them to be Romulan warships."

"Now *that's* a surprise," Kirk muttered.

"Decelerating, sir," the helmsman continued. Kirk's chair intercom buzzed.

"Bridge, Captain speaking."

"Scott, Captain." The chief engineer sounded concerned. "I've no idea what it means, but I'm receivin' information that the ship's inorganic metallic fabrication facilities have been workin' overtime ever since we started up again.''

"Any indication what the computer's up to, Mr. Scott?"

"I kinna tell, sir, that whole deck section's been sealed off.''

"Captain . . .''

"Just a minute, Uhura." He turned back to the mike. "Let me know if you find anything out, Scotty."

"Aye, sir, Engineering out."

"What is it, Uhura?"

"Sir, monitors indicate the main cargo hatch is opening. I'll swing the rear scanners on it."

"Yes . . . do so, Lieutenant," he agreed absently. His thoughts were running into each other, threads of one frantic solution meshing with the wrong problem. Slow down, he wanted to shout! Slow down—things were happening too fast. As soon as he thought he was getting one problem under control, something new cropped up to shove it aside.

The rear of the ship appeared on the viewscreen as Uhura manipulated the scanners mounted on the stern. She worked controls and the field of view rotated. Something white and glowing slid past.

"Bring that back, Lieutenant," Kirk ordered hurriedly. Slowly the scanner retraced its path, until it was focused on the rear cargo hatch. Two massive clamshell doors were separating. The spot of brightness was the cargo hold itself, brightly lit from within.

Something was occluding that brightness . . . something gigantic.

A huge, highly reflective mass of constantly changing shape billowed from the open hatch. Light from the starship's running lights and the surrounding stars gleamed in that expanding metal skin. It drifted behind the *Enterprise*, still growing rapidly, as the cargo doors closed.

"Keep your scanners on that, Lieutenant—Mr. Sulu, you stay with the Romulans."

Acknowledgment was prompt from both consoles. "What in heaven's name is going on now?" McCoy wondered.

"Your guess is probably better than mine, Bones," Kirk confessed. "You've experienced the computer's whimsy longer than anyone."

"Maybe . . . but I never saw anything like *that* before."

They stared in rapt fascination at the image conveyed by the scanners. It became apparent that the monstrous shape was steadily inflating.

"It looks like some kind of metal balloon, Jim. But what on Earth's it for?"

"If the cargo doors open again and a gigantic pin starts to come out, we'll know," ventured Sulu. "It'd be in keeping with the computer's actions so far."

"I fail to see the connection, Mr. Sulu," a curious Spock observed.

"Sulu's supposition is wrong, anyway, Spock," Kirk told him. "There wouldn't be any noise."

Spock did not appear enlightened. "Noise? Captain, I confess I am puzzled by . . ." He stopped abruptly, peering hard into his own viewer.

"What is it, Spock?"

"Odd . . . the inflatable object is acquiring an outline which superficially resembles a ship."

"I see it now," Sulu agreed excitedly. "It looks like one of the old Federation dreadnoughts—the class that was never built because all that weaponry was never needed."

"Whatever it is, it's about twenty times our size," noted Kirk.

"Captain, we're changing course again," Sulu said. "We're pulling away from it slightly."

"What have the Romulans been doing? We've been within range of their scanners for several minutes now."

"I believe they started toward us several minutes ago, Captain," Spock declared, checking readouts, "but their subsequent movements have been erratic. They have presently terminated all signs of approach. Undoubtedly the sudden appearance of a warship twenty times their size has occasioned some hasty discussion among the Romulan command."

"I'll bet," Kirk agreed, smiling despite his own ignorance of what the computer was up to.

McCoy was less amused. "It may look like a dreadnought now, but if they approach within visual pickup range they'll obtain a detailed fix on it and see that it's nothing more than inflated foil—and they won't think it funny."

"For the present, though, you must admit that the Romulans *have* halted."

"So it's an effective bluff—I see that, Spock. But it won't last long. It'll only infuriate them more." He shrugged. "More cybernetic madness."

"Unless there's a message in it," Kirk whispered thoughtfully.

Spock's brows contracted. "If you would elaborate, Captain."

"Yes, Jim," McCoy wondered, eyeing him steadily, "who's madness are you talking about?" He eyed Kirk in such a way as to indicate that perhaps the central computer wasn't the only brain on board that had gone a little dotty.

"Bones, sometimes to understand madness you have to think like a madman—no, don't be alarmed," Kirk added at the look that suddenly appeared on the good doctor's face. "I mean that this is a time to look for the inner logic.

"All that's happening is that the *Enterprise* is pulling her biggest practical joke so far—only this time it's on the Romulans."

"Are you suggesting," Spock asked, "that the *Enterprise* is capable of experiencing a desire for revenge?"

"What else? She's going to make fools of them by inducing them to attack a balloon, and the Romulans fear disgrace even more than death."

"It is still not possible, Captain. Revenge is a purely emotional action."

"What would you think of a Vulcan who displayed a desire for revenge, Spock?"

"Why, we would try to cure him of his madn—I see, Captain. Your point is well taken. And I confess I have no alternative explanation for the computer's present actions." His gaze returned to the sensor image of the drifting cruisers.

"However, I am most interested just now in the effect of the ploy and not in the motivation behind it . . ."

The alien triumvirate of destruction hovered well outside combat range and considered the colossal apparition that had appeared alongside their target.

On board the heavy cruiser which formed the vanguard of the Romulan task force, an impatient Commander scratched his arm and studied the gargantuan image, trying to imagine how the Federation had concealed a warship of such size from Imperial spies. It didn't seem possible . . . yet there it was.

As soon as it had appeared, the *Enterprise* had started off on a new course back toward Federation territory—but slowly, almost challengingly. It was almost as if Kirk were daring him to pursue, trying to lure him into attacking.

He would have to make a decision soon, or their intended prey would make good its escape. To have failed the Plan once was bad enough. To have the quarry return to tweak the Imperial nose and saunter off at cruising speed was infuriating.

One drawback to renewed pursuit, however, was the apparent indifference with which this new vessel squatted in midspace and regarded the Imperial force. It showed no inclination either to attack or retreat. Despite its size, he felt certain his three smaller vessels could outmaneuver it.

Outgunning it was another matter entirely.

"No response to our calls, Commander," his communications officer reported.

"They have refused surrender. Very well. Large it may be, but foolish is its commander. We will not permit so great a prize to escape." He called to his helmsman. "Notify the others—we will attack according to the fourth helical scheme."

"Yes, Commander!"

The order was passed. Weaving in and about several common points designated by their battle computers, the three Romulan cruisers advanced at assault speed. At extreme range they opened fire in a carefully integrated sequence. Photon bombs which had already proven so effective against the *Enterprise* were flung ahead in a complex half-predetermined, half-random pattern that no ship's defenses could avoid.

The object of this triple barrage did not. Several of the powerful explosives struck the anodized skin and blew gaping holes in the false mass. With no outside pressure to collapse it, the bloated construct of micron-thick foil held its shape. Held it firmly enough for the gaping wounds to show that it was completely hollow inside.

As he ingested this unexpected development, the Romulan commander's eyes grew almost as large as the cavernous gaps his expensive explosives had ripped in the thin metal.

"Fooled . . . tricked . . . insult, insult!" he howled, apoplectic with anger. "Gravest offense . . . most heinous perversion of martial chivalry. Contact . . . contact the *Enterprise*!" he sputtered at his communications officer.

That worthy hurried to comply. "We have made contact, sir," he reported seconds later.

"Put them through."

The link was cleared—and immediately a high, wavering sound washed over the Romulan bridge. One did not have to be a specialist in Federation emotional utterances to recognize it as laughter.

Of course, the Romulan commander had no knowledge of its true source . . . but it was enough for him to know that it came from the *Enterprise*.

All pretense at caution vanished under that teasing giggle.

"Full pursuit speed!" he roared. "I want that ship reduced to dust, to particles, to its component elements."

"Honored Commander," the helmsman protested timidly, "they have some distance on us, and they are no longer within the neutral zone."

Laughter continued to roll across the Romulan Bridge. "Extinguish that! And pursue!"

On board another Bridge the same laughter still echoed, though it was beginning to subside. "Captain," Sulu noted, "the Romulans are giving chase."

McCoy let out a long whistle. "They must be a little crazed themselves to follow us this deep into Federation territory, now that they can't surprise us like they did before."

"I don't care about that. I don't even care about the Romulans," Kirk cried. McCoy's expression narrowed. There was an alien, uncharacteristic fearfulness in the captain's voice. "I just want to avoid that energy field.

"Helmsman, do you have a fix on its present position? For nova's sake, stay away from there!"

Everyone had spun to stare in disbelief at Kirk, who sat all but trembling in the command chair, slumped low into the seat.

It looked to Sulu as if the captain were shivering like a man frightened half to death. In fact, this sudden transformation of the indomitable captain into a seeming basket case was so startling everyone was struck speechless.

"I have it plotted, sir," Sulu was finally able to reply . . . since some sort of reassurance seemed to be necessary. "Our present course takes us nowhere near it."

The relief in Kirk's shaken countenance was almost palpable. "Thank God," he muttered shakily, "I couldn't face that traverse again."

"Sir, if I may be permitted," Sulu continued, unable to keep the tinge of chastisement clear of his tone, "the damage we incurred during the actual passage was mini . . ."

A traitorous feminine voice cut him off. "Why should the thought of making another passage scare you . . . there is no reason for it. I sustained only minimal damage in making the actual passage."

"It's not that . . . not that," Kirk replied in evident terror. "It's the idea of having your body, every cell and nerve, lanced through and through with radiation we know nothing about . . . the thought of what that might do to one's internal make-up . . ." He actually shuddered. "The thought petrifies me."

"How very interesting," the voice murmured sweetly. The whine of gyros sounded.

"Sir . . ." Sulu worked uselessly at his instrumentation. "We're changing course again. The energy field lies on the periphery of our long-range sensors, but we seem to be heading straight for it . . . again."

"No!" Kirk was shaking so hard he could barely lean forward. "We can't be . . . not again."

Laughter reverberated around them . . . laughter that was neither human nor sane.

"Reverse direction, Mr. Sulu!"

The helmsman made a futile effort to provoke some response from his console, then looked back and shrugged helplessly. "I can't, sir. Controls are still frozen. Sir, if I may say, we've nothing to worry about so. We know . . ."

"I can't take that again," Kirk babbled, "I can't take that again . . ."

The view ahead began to shine as the first effects of the

radiant cloud made themselves felt. Barely perceptibly at first, then unmistakably, the deck commenced to oscillate underfoot. Vibration intensified until it was just shy of being severe.

Now the scanners stepped down the overpowering panoply of color to where it was bearable by human eyes.

Kirk remained cowering in the command chair, his hands clutching tightly to the arms. Appropriate discussion would have continued about the captain's startling collapse of nerve, only there was plenty to do at the moment to insure that the *Enterprise* held together during its passage through the field.

There was no *real* reason for concern. After all, they had made this difficult passage once before. Presumably they would do it again. But this time, it would be better to remain intent at one's job, welded to one's instruments—what with the central computer out of control and the captain apparently paralyzed by fear.

Plenty of time for Dr. McCoy to treat the commander once the ship was safely through . . .

So, while the matter never strayed completely from their minds, everyone remained glued to his post and ignored the quivering figure which shook in the command chair—ignored also the ripples of mirth that steadily issued from the Bridge speakers.

Another set of vibrations commenced not far behind them, as the maddened Romulans—their caution overcome by fury—entered the energy cloud in engine-straining pursuit.

The *Enterprise*'s abrupt course change, which had brought it swooping around within near firing range, was puzzling and unreasonable enough to puncture the Romulan commander's suit of anger. Already deep within Federation territory and with a clear lead, what profit could the *Enterprise*'s commander see in a swing back toward the neutral zone and his pursuers?

It unnerved him more than he cared to admit. One thing the Romulans had learned not to despise in their dealings with the Federation was the fiendish subtlety of high-ranking humans like Kirk.

So he consulted with his officers and with the commanders of his other ships. They dumped their worries into their computers and frantically hunted for a rationale behind the inexplicable maneuver. The cybernetic shrugs that resulted did little to alleviate their concern . . .

The Romulan helmsman held tightly to one arm of his chair while his other fluttered helplessly over his abruptly unresponsive console. Assured of its new ineffectualness, he turned and caught the eye of his already brooding commander. .

"Sir, our sensors are useless while in this field. We've lost all contact with the Federation ship."

That was the final *ubuz* as far as the commander was concerned. "First the *Enterprise* alters a heading on which it had a fair chance of escaping or of contacting help, in order to return within range of a superior force. Then it draws us into this mysterious field. Now it appears they cannot be located." What unknown weaponry, what new insult might Kirk be preparing to unleash on them?

The combination of uncertainties was too much for the already jittery commander. His ship was being subjected to a battering which was strong, but not dangerous, as yet. The operative word was "yet." It offered a chance—maybe the last chance—to withdraw with some shred of honor.

Also, his liver was bothering him.

"We must clear this field before our ships break up. Bring us about on a new heading, navigator, for home."

"You're going to let them get away, sir? After the way they've taunted us, insulted us?"

"If we can no longer locate them," the commander replied dryly, not wishing to fight with his own officers, "that strikes me as a reasonable evaluation of our present circumstances. I suggest attending to your duties, Varpa. These require you to obey orders . . . no more. Do so."

Varpa started to say more, suddenly became aware a proximity mine field was an inauspicious place to dance a polka, and shut up.

Pleased by the silence, the commander began to compose his report to Fleet Headquarters: Surreptitious Operations Bureau. As he did so, he regarded the fore viewscreen, which offered a picture of the scintillating, radiant energy field . . . now shrinking rapidly behind them.

Hopefully, somewhere within its magnificently colored

distortion of space and matter, the thrice-cursed *Enterprise* was already tearing itself to pieces . . .

The *Enterprise*, however, was holding together very nicely, thank you. So far it had resisted the corrosive efforts of both the radiation and the Romulan invective.

More concern was felt over the coherence, or lack thereof, of its captain. But his terror seemed to fade slightly when an awkward fluttering cracked the steady laughter still issuing from the speakers.

He began to look normal again when the unsteady chuckling started to waver noticeably.

"Tricked," the computer voice abruptly claimed. "Not fair . . . not fair . . ." Laughter and peevish overtone were beginning to fade rapidly now.

"What the . . . what's happening to it?" McCoy queried, holding tightly for support to the back of the command chair.

The final giggle sounded . . . an unintelligent, choking cough. Then all was quiet.

When Kirk spoke again, it was immediately clear that his *fear* had vanished along with the laughter. "Bones, the worst thing you can do to a practical joker is to play a practical joke on him." His tone was grim but no longer anxious. "Although this is one joke whose successful outcome had something more than a laugh riding on it."

"We're clear of the field, sir," Sulu informed him.

"Good. Change course two degrees up. Same heading. Resume standard cruising speed."

The helmsman looked doubtful, but proceeded to try and comply. His expression and voice brightened the moment he touched the first controls. "All instrumentation is responding normally now, Captain. No indication of any interference with helm functions. Engine response is normal, too."

"And I am receiving standard response in all computer modes," Spock declared. "Higher logic and intuitive reasoning functions check out normal . . . with no intimation of a desire to operate on their own." He glanced approvingly across at Kirk.

"That last pass through the energy field apparently reversed the damaging effects of our initial incursion."

"So that's why you were so vocal in your *horror* of another ride through," McCoy exclaimed as understanding dawned.

"And all the time you had us thinking you'd slipped your helm."

"Something radical *had* to be tried, Bones. Frankly, when it first occurred to me, I didn't think the idea made much sense . . . which made it seem perfectly appropriate, in light of the way the computer was acting."

"A well-conceived and efficiently executed deception, Captain," complimented his first officer.

Kirk grinned wanly. "Not entirely deception, Mr. Spock. I *was* frightened . . . not of another passage through the field, but of what the computer might try next. Its sense of humor was becoming increasingly sadistic."

"Amen to that!" McCoy commented fervently.

"What I had to do," Kirk continued, leaning back in the command chair, "was redirect the anxiety I was feeling and let it run away with me."

"You are too modest, Captain," Spock commented. "You had everyone fooled—all of us, besides the computer. I could never have carried off the same masquerade myself."

"Needless to say," needled McCoy.

Spock ignored him.

"The effects of the field on our computer circuitry and operation have been thoroughly documented by independent means," Spock continued, studying his library console. "They will provide much material for dissection by Federation cybernetics experts. I envision many hours of investigative perusal myself."

"Hold it," Uhura suddenly exclaimed. "Captain, I'm picking up Romulan intership and intercom transmissions—evidently something's gone wrong with their broadcast equipment."

Kirk looked puzzled. "More than *wrong*, Lieutenant. Aside from the waste of power, putting intercom transmissions on ship-to-ship frequencies is a serious breach of comm security. I wonder what—Uhura, what are you smiling at?"

"I'll put it on the Bridge speakers, sir." She adjusted controls.

The first voice they heard happened to be that of the task force commander railing at his engineering staff.

". . . and turn off those food synthesizers!" he was shouting as the broadcast cleared. "We're knee-deep in hot fudge sundaes, and they're starting to impede passage in the corridors!''

The arguments from all three ships and numerous sections went on in that vein—increasingly confused, increasingly angry, increasingly frustrated.

McCoy grinned broadly. ''I didn't even know the Romulans knew what a hot fudge sundae was—much less that their fabricators were capable of synthesizing one.''

''I daresay that the entire situation is rather upsetting to them,'' Kirk chuckled. ''It would seem that something's gone wrong with their computers.''

''Shall we tell them how they can reverse the effects of the field, Jim?''

''Oh, eventually, I suppose. After all, I don't think I'd want even the Romulans to go through too much of what we've been subjected to. But . . . let's not spoil their fun just yet.''

The laughter that sounded on the Bridge then was spontaneous—and decidedly non-mechanical in origin. To Spock, however, it was all the same, even if the motivation behind it was less threatening.

''Inexplicable, incomprehensible and irrational,'' he muttered, turning back to his console. He set about resuming his theoretical studies where he had been forced to leave off when the Romulans had attacked. Laughter filled the air around him.

There was one important difference, though. This non-gaseous stimulation didn't give him a headache.

And while he mused on his research and his companions made jokes about the Romulans' present predicament, he couldn't know that events had been set in motion which would prove of greater importance than anything examination of the records of the central computer's temporary hysteria could produce . . .

PART III

HOW SHARPER THAN A SERPENT'S TOOTH

(Adapted from a script by Russell Bates and David Wise)

IX

The network of detector drones and interwoven patrols which guarded the Federation home worlds, its industrial and population centers, was as thorough and as efficient as that highly advanced multiracial civilization could make it. It was designed to protect and defend against even a surprise Klingon attack in force.

A single ship, moving at high speed and employing radical evasive maneuvers, could conceivably penetrate that electronic web. The one which did so moved in a predictable, straight path and made no attempt to disguise its destination. It compensated for the lack of concealment by moving at a speed previously thought impossible.

No one could be sure, but the probe executed such extreme changes of direction at such incredible velocities that it seemed certain it was uninhabited. Also, it went about its business with supreme indifference to all attempts at contact. When all such methods were exhausted, and the probe continued to refuse repeated warnings to steer clear of Federation worlds, the Federation council reluctantly decided to destroy the interloper. This decision was modified by the science councilor to include some initial attempt to capture the craft. The Federation engineering division desired at least a look at those remarkable engines.

The attempt at capture met with the same result as those at destruction, however. No Federation warship could overtake it, and the alien interloper did not linger in the vicinity of any armed vessel it approached. So in spite of intensive efforts to halt it, the probe performed the most rapid survey of the United Federation Systems in history . . . and it did so with a silence that was as unnerving as it was baffling.

All the while, however, the Federation's most advanced electronic predictors were slowly analyzing the drone's performance. Continued observation showed that it held to a prescribed pattern of survey and dodge, inspection and flight.

At each new world, larger and stronger Federation forces closed in on the craft. Each was programed with a particular attack pattern, which was backed by a third set of reinforcements that would stand by in case the probe escaped the first two. Soon entire fleets had been mobilized in a mounting attempt to corner a single, uninhabited, as yet inoffensive ship.

The problem was that the probe never lingered long enough for the huge forces to catch up with it. Nonetheless, the Vulcan logicians programing the predictors were certain that given enough time, they would trap the drone in a maze of phasers and torpedoes so intense that nothing could escape. But they weren't given the required time. The probe executed its final survey—a brief, yet impressively thorough multiple circuit of Earth itself.

Even as the most powerful Federation force so far was weaving its way toward the probe, it paused in free space and aligned itself toward a predetermined point. It appeared to be blithely unconcerned with the increasing possibility of annihilation. Once positioned, the probe discharged an extremely high-frequency, lengthy blast of energy. The thunderous broadcast utilized far more power than it seemed a ship of that modest size could muster.

The broadcast lasted only a few minutes. At its conclusion, the probe activated its engines. It disintegrated just outside the orbit of Luna in an explosion of sobering magnitude. Auroras formed as far south as Hong Kong and Istanbul for several weeks, and most of the transmitting equipment on Earth's lone satellite required extensive repair immediately thereafter.

The mysterious intruder was gone. Several fragments of eyelash-size metal gave no clue to its origin. It had carried out its lengthy mission for the incomprehensible motives of as yet unknown beings.

From where had it come? Who had constructed such a marvelous machine and what were their intentions? Why had it shunned all contact with Federation intelligences? These obvious questions and more were asked again and again by important individuals serving in the highest echelons of Federation government. And those whom they asked for the answers could only shrug.

A measure of the importance attached to the enigmatic visitation was the readiness with which the Klingons and Romulans cooperated. The wonder at this vanished when both opponents of the Federation sheepishly admitted that before the Federation had been surveyed, their own respective empires had been similarly inspected. Though no one could be certain, it appeared that the same isolated probe had been involved in each instance.

A few zealots within the government warned that it might all be an elaborate plot, concocted by the Klingons and/or Romulans, to obtain military information from frightened government authorities.

Impartial engineering experts quashed such thoughts immediately . . . neither Klingon nor adaptive Romulan physics were even close to producing something as advanced as their visitor had been. If they were, it was ruthlessly pointed out, they would be putting it to more effective use than casual surveillance.

The intricate recording equipment based on Luna, on Earth and on Titan could track even the path of a butterfly at interstellar distances. So when the suicidal probe began regurgitating its concentrated information, those several stations were already tracking it. They detected the transmission the instant it began, recorded it minutely for rechecking at later leisure.

So efficient was that tracking equipment, however, that no rechecks were required, no computer enhancement of that blindingly powerful signal necessary. Instantaneous triangulation was produced by the three stations.

The beam had erupted from the probe along a line as clear and precise as white ink on a blackboard. It was along that path that the *Enterprise* had been ordered to proceed.

The amount of energy expended in that minutes-long broadcast had been immense—far in excess of anything Federation science was capable of. And although that energy was still on the near side of infinite, there was reason enough to believe that the receiving end of the transmission might lie outside this galaxy . . .

If that were the case, Kirk thought to himself, the *Enterprise* could have rather a longer trip than anyone expected. No one had anticipated what the orders might be if she found herself poised on the rim of such extremes.

But Kirk had to consider that the beam had intercepted no known star systems, not even suns without planets, and they were now well outside Federation boundaries. He idly watched Spock at work with the library computer and sighed. They had been retracing the course Starfleet had supplied for weeks now.

No telling how long this could go on. The orders had been for the *Enterprise* to proceed until, as the ethereally worded document stated: "all possible doubt has been removed as to the potential dangers posed to the Federated peoples by the alien intruder."

That order was sufficiently vague to keep them cruising for months, even years, unless recalled—or until the halfway point of their irreplaceable supplies was reached.

Lately Kirk had been subject to a particularly chilling nightmare. Some junior clerk at Starfleet headquarters was continually misplacing the *Enterprise* file, or allowing the recall orders to slip down behind some spool storage case, or accidentally erasing all record of the cruiser from the Starfleet central computer.

The ship was forgotten. It continued on, taking on new stores at various puzzled worlds, whose inhabitants stared sadly at the wrinkled, white-haired crew trapped in its Tantalus-like quest.

He grew aware of a presence next to him. The presence was clearing its throat delicately. "What . . . ? Oh . . ."

Turning away from the patient yeoman, Kirk studied the order form the latter had handed to him. Hmmm . . . standard request for use of the main recreation room.

For a second he almost handed it back unsigned, remembering what had nearly happened to McCoy, Sulu and Uhura in that same room several weeks ago. But the story of their entrapment in that chamber had circulated throughout the ship. A scare like that would die hard. He doubted anyone would go in for any exotic manipulations of the environment for a while. It was one thing to be threatened on a new, alien world—quite another when your own games facilities turned on you.

Someone wanted the proper atmosphere for a birthday party or some such, no doubt. He signed the chit, saluted casually as the yeoman departed, and turned his gaze to the view forward.

The screen displayed the same gloriously monotonous image it had for days and days—unfamiliar star patterns speckling the blackness. Kirk found himself growing sick of unfamiliar star patterns speckling the blackness. If they didn't encounter something soon—a derelict spacecraft, a postal drop, anything—he was going to have Uhura tight-beam the nearest Star Base and patch him through to fleet headquarters, where he could give vent to his emotions.

He began running his speech over in his head. He would discourse on the futility of the entire expedition and add some appropriate thoughts about the power wielded by a few panicked bureaucrats. Above all, this expedition was proving to be a sinful waste of ship's power and crewpower.

He forced himself to clear the welling irritation from his voice as he called for the current status report from his first officer.

Spock paused an instant at the gooseneck viewer, checked another sensor before turning to face Kirk. "We are continuing along the path plotted by Starfleet Central, Captain. However, I feel it is time for me to point out that the accuracy of that plotting diffuses with every parsec we cover.

"It has now reached the point where . . . ," he hesitated long enough to check a last readout, ". . . the margin of divergence has increased to nearly a tenth of a degree."

Kirk nodded. "I see. Not a serious range of error . . . if we're hunting for a planet. But if we're looking for a ship, we could miss it by many trillions of kilometers. Soon that'll be true for a star system, too.

"What would you recommend, Mr. Spock?"

"Reducing our speed to accommodate our long-range, peripheral sensing equipment, so that we do not rush past anything such as a small vessel."

"Reasonable—though I don't like the idea of cutting our

speed. Mr. Walking Bear, bring us down to warp-factor two.''

The ensign who was occupying Sulu's position usually drew the third shift—when both Kirk and Spock were off-duty and asleep. Sulu, however, had elected to take some extra time off that he had accumulated, and Walking Bear had gladly volunteered for the opportunity to serve with the ship's executive command.

He had performed well so far, Kirk mused. Must remember to make note of the ensign's competence in the supplementary log. Unaware that he was being subjected to close scrutiny, Walking Bear made the necessary adjustments. ''Aye, sir, warp-factor two.''

His accent was faint, but the long black hair and rich rust color marked him as an Amerind of the North American Southwest. Kirk struggled to recall an early academy seminar in Basic Ethnics.

It was impossible to be more than cursorily familiar with the background of every one of the *Enterprise*'s four hundred thirty assigned personnel. That didn't stop the captain from trying, however. It was something with a hard *ch* sound in it, now . . .

Kirk wondered how much time the ensign had in . . . perhaps he was eligible for promotion to lieutenant. Even though this expedition had proven routine, maybe he could come up with some way to test the young helmsman's mettle.

As it developed, he would be spared the trouble . . .

''Captain,'' Arex reported, ''sensors have picked up a vessel at extreme range.''

''Any indication as to heading, Mr. Arex?''

The navigation officer studied his readouts a moment longer, made a high, snuffling sound as he expelled air through high-ridged nostrils.

''It appears to be proceeding on the same plot followed by the alien probe's final broadcast, sir—but the vessel is moving toward us, instead of outward. Approximate speed, warp-three.''

''Mr. Spock?''

''Range is still too extreme to attempt detailed observation, Captain.'' He studied his small viewers. ''Possibly this is a second probe. It may be that the first did not complete its assigned task, and merely malfunctioned instead of self-destructing. This may be another drone coming to conclude the operation.''

Kirk frowned. "True, Mr. Spock, or it could be the original probe's owner."

"If this one's coming in search of its predecessor, it's not going to find much," Uhura noted.

"Order all stations, yellow alert, Lieutenant," Kirk ordered. "Open standard hailing frequencies." He gestured at the main viewscreen. Despite maximum magnification, the scanners still showed only awesome darkness, strange suns and feathery nebulae.

Whatever it was, maybe it would prove a little more talkative than its super-fast ancestor—if indeed the two craft possessed any relationship at all. They might merely be racing to meet another deep-space explorer like themselves.

The alarm blared throughout the *Enterprise*, sending a second shift scurrying to join the one already on duty.

Kirk stared expectantly at the screen. "Any identification yet, Mr. Spock?" There was no point in straining his eyes, but every Starfleet officer with any real experience was innately certain that his vision could range just a few kilometers further than his ship's electronic scanners. Kirk was no different.

"Not possible yet, Captain," Spock finally declared, "but preliminary sensor analysis indicates an object at least twice our size. Variance could be substantial on closer inspection."

"Not another double of the probe, then," Kirk commented thoughtfully. "I'd feel better if you'd said it was half our size, with variance either way."

"We have no reason to assume it has a hostile intent, Captain," the first officer felt compelled to point out. "If it acts as its possible predecessor did, we can expect it to regard us with studied indifference."

"People who send drone probes through other people's homes without acknowledging even a hello or how-d'you-do don't strike me as overly friendly, either, Spock."

"The one does not imply the other," Spock argued amiably. Discussion was interrupted by the arrival of new information on his instruments. "Regardless, it appears extremely unorthodox in design—much more so than the drone.'' He made a quick check of the proper records.

"No record of anything like it in the Jane's—and Starfleet information insists there should be no vessels of any known civilization cruising in this extreme region."

"Reduce speed to warp-one, Mr. Walking Bear," Kirk murmured.

"Warp-one, sir?" The ensign looked uncertainly over at Arex. The navigator asked the question spinning through the less-experienced officer's mind.

"Same course, sir?"

"Same course, Mr. Arex. Activate minimal field, ultra-extreme scanner, please." Abruptly the starfield ahead seemed to leap toward them, then come to an abrupt stop. Essentially it remained unchanged. Only now an object lay in its approximate center. It was still only a vague blob of light, but it grew larger with perceptible speed.

"Anything out of those hailing frequencies, Lieutenant?" he asked over his shoulder.

"No response, sir," she told him. "So far it's the probe all over again."

"Continue hailing. Try every frequency you know . . . and when you've exhausted those used by the Federation, go through the special Klingon, Romulan, and lesser alliance levels."

"You believe the probe and this vessel may be the work of some small, isolated race, Captain?" Arex wondered.

"Not one we know of, Mr. Arex," Kirk said absently, still staring at the unresolved luminescent image growing larger with the minutes. "But it's possible that whoever is behind both craft has had contact with a smaller independent system like Michaya or the Yoolian worlds. If that's the case, they might respond to such an infrequently used hailing frequency while ignoring ours.

"That doesn't speak well for the supposed friendliness of some of our nominal allies, of course."

"Whatever its purpose or origin, Captain," Spock suddenly announced, staring intently into his gooseneck viewer as he manipulated controls, "it possesses an immense energy aura. The ship itself appears completely encased in it.

"Something on board this craft is generating an enormous

quantity of extraneous radiation—for what reason, I cannot
tell.'' More adjustments, new readings—and a new conclusion.

"Fascinating. Additional analysis indicates that the ship's
hull is composed wholly of some unknown, unique variety
of crystallized ceramic. It appears to possess some characteristics of the lighter metals such as lithium and beryllium
while retaining the more malleable properties of—''

Spock's engrossed litany was shattered as a giant, invisible
hand clutched the Bridge and shook it violently. Along with
everyone else, the first officer concentrated on grabbing for
the nearest solid support.

The shaking was accompanied by a loud rumbling. It
wasn't a simple, steady vibration; but instead shook them
with a distinct up and down, back and forth motion—unlike
the effects of the energy field they had traveled through weeks
ago while foiling the Romulans' attack.

As the shaking continued, a new sound became audible—
a distant declining whine. Kirk recognized the symptoms of
engine shutdown even as Walking Bear called out, "We're
losing speed, sir—and the helm doesn't answer.''

"Dropping to sublight velocity,'' Arex reported.

Confirmation of his worst suspicions now fulfilled by the
instrumentation, Kirk fought to keep from being thrown from
his seat as he hit the necessary switch. The rumbling noise
was fading, but the shaking continued as violent as ever.

"Bridge to Engineering—Mr. Scott, we're losing speed.
Why?''

An uncharacteristic lag in response followed, though the
reason was understandable. Scott and his subordinates in
Engineering were as interested in keeping their balance as
was everyone else.

The chief engineer reported in soon after. "Scott here.
Captain, all our engines are still set for warp-two thrust . . .
but we seem to have run into something like a wall of solid
alloy!''

So his supposition was wrong—the engines weren't shut
down.

"Maximum thrust, Mr. Scott.''

"Aye, sir.'' A pause, then, "I've got 'er wide open, Captain. We're just not movin'. I dinna know how long the en-

gine bracings can take the strain before they start tearin' themselves loose.''

"Understood, Scotty. Nice try." He switched off, redirecting his attention forward. "All engines stop, Mr. Walking Bear."

The helmsman activated instrumentation before him that he never expected to be called to activate. Despite the newness of the operation, his hands moved smoothly in compliance. As the great warp-drive engines ceased forward thrust, the last vestiges of the rumbling noise faded away. The shaking ceased with appalling abruptness.

"All engines stopped, sir," Walking Bear declared into the unnatural silence on the Bridge.

Kirk tried to moderate their present predicament by repeating the Words over and over in his head. He found they provided no more succor than ever. Perhaps he was simply too hyper mentally for artificially imposed constraints like meditation ever to slow him down. Consequently, he was back on the intercom in a minute, as worried and theory-ridden as ever.

"I want a full damage report as soon as possible, Scotty."

"I'm workin' on it now, Captain," the filtered voice replied. "Everythin' seems minor, so far. No structural damage to the support pylons or braces, and no overheatin' . . . at least, nothing the emergency backups couldn't handle.

"Another couple of minutes of that strain, though . . . I think we shut down just in time, sir."

"Thank you, Scotty. Maintain full environmental and defensive power, and effect whatever repairs are required with a minimum of delay."

"Will do, sir. Engineerin' out . . ."

Another call, another problem area. "Bridge to Sick Bay . . . casualty report."

"McCoy here," came the slightly irritated reply. "No serious injuries, Jim, just the usual lumps and bruises." He managed to make it sound as if the Bridge personnel were personally responsible for the suffering he had to treat.

"What the devil's going on up there? Who's driving . . . no, I've got it. Spock decided to see what would happen if everyone on board suddenly jumped up and down in time to a cycling of the artificial gravity."

"I wish that was all it was, Bones. Bridge out." Kirk glanced across at Spock and saw that the first officer appeared not to have heard McCoy's abrasive sally. To ignore an argumentative invitation by McCoy was a sign that his first officer was worried—and when Spock was worried, that was a good time for anyone in the vicinity to make sure their service insurance was fully paid up.

"What are our chances of getting around this obstacle, Spock?"

"I am sorry to say, Captain, that I do not think that is possible. There is no obstacle to go around . . . the obstacle is all around *us*. So we cannot retreat, either."

"Its nature?"

"A globular force-field of unknown origin, in which we are presently entrapped. It is obvious that there can be only one source of so strong and sudden an energy projection—the approaching alien ship."

"But we hit the field at warp-two," Walking Bear blurted in confusion, "and practically stopped dead. We should have been pulverized on impact!"

Spock shook his head patiently, touched a lever. The view ahead changed as short-range scanners cut in. The much wider field of view showed a faint, bluish-white glow which the long-range scanner had pierced. It was very much, Kirk mused, like what the interior of a soap bubble might look like.

Spock was lecturing. "We did not hit a stone wall, Mr. Walking Bear. The globular field did not form instantly around us, at a single position in space. It materialized slowly. As it slowed, we slowed against it in proportion. Even so, according to Chief Scott's report, the stress was almost seriously damaging.

"But I confess I do not understand why we did not suffer more than we did. I cannot explain it, except to point out that the field is of an unfamiliar type." Something beeped behind him and he finished as he turned to his insistent console. "The knowledge responsible for such an impressive piece of physics must be formidable."

He paused, then: "Sensors indicate we are now being probed."

"Captain," Walking Bear exclaimed as he switched back to longer-range scanners, "there it is!"

No gasps issued from those on the Bridge. They'd seen too many wonders on too many worlds to be easily overwhelmed. But the bow view offered of the approaching craft was radical and unexpected enough to set speculation rife in their minds even at this distance.

At first it resembled the face of a demon. Nearness resolved hazy lines into the struts and projections of a real ship—of peculiar design, but a ship nonetheless.

The demon's face was formed by what was probably the command section or bridge. The curving prow formed the rest of the head, while propulsion "wings" hinted at monstrous horns. A round glassy glow the hue of polished onyx was centered in the middle of the construct like a baleful Polyphemian eye.

Every arch, every line of it hinted at an engineering knowledge and sophistication undreamed of by Federation shipwrights. Yet it remained a vessel composed of recognizable sections. One that could have been built by Federation hands if the basic blueprints and knowledge had been supplied.

The command module was unarguably a command module. Propulsion units, winglike or not, could be nothing but propulsion units. All this was evident, despite the differences in size.

"The approaching vessel is slowing," Arex announced laconically into the quiet. "It is . . ."

Only the ship's battle compensators saved everyone on the Bridge from permanent blindness as pure radiance struck forward.

The vibration died slowly and there was a distant mutter of thunder as air somewhere within the ship was displaced. Kirk didn't need instruments to tell him what had happened.

They had been fired on by an energy weapon of a new type and of considerable power—and they had been hit point blank. Port and starboard scanners locked on the alien as it fired again.

Coruscating breakers of fire foamed across the forward edge of the cruiser's saucer decks and organized confusion reigned on the Bridge as all alert indicators on board flashed crimson.

Half asleep, off-shift personnel who had been awakened before by the severe shaking wondered what was happening as they scrambled for their duty clothes and stations.

"Full power all shields . . . all engines, maximum reverse thrust!" Kirk was shouting at Walking Bear. "Try to get us away from that beam!" Even as he finished, another blast of intense energy rocked the battered ship.

Amid the confusion and harried reactions and semi-panic, rose the calm, steady voice of Spock. "Evasive action will not be effective, Captain. The force-field now surrounding us is ninety-eight point two percent efficient. Our maneuverability is severely limited."

"Maneuvering be hanged!" Kirk cursed as much in frustration as anger. "If that thing can fire in, maybe we can fire out. Mr. Walking Bear, lock main phasers on that ship and fire. Arex, our field of movement appears to be restricted. That means you're going to have to use your imagination to avoid that energy beam."

Ayes echoed from both stations.

The Edoan navigator embarked upon what Kirk later described as a maneuvering miracle. Using only impulse power to minimize stress-threat to the main engines, he managed to shift the cruiser's position within the confined area of the force globe so often and so unpredictably that it suffered only glancing blows from the irresistible energy beam.

At the same time the *Enterprise*'s phasers began to reply with lambent salvos of its own. The destructive double beams sought outward.

Kirk's hopes died when they reached no farther than the interior curve of the pale blue field, where the concentrated energy simply stopped.

"Dispersed, possibly, within the fabric of the field itself," Spock theorized.

Walking Bear continued to fire, but their phasers proved totally ineffective even as the white flame continued to lick at their deflector shields.

"The force globe is selective," Spock commented dispassionately, lending voice to the obvious. "Our attacker can beam us at will and we are helpless to respond."

Kirk mulled this over furiously, hunting for a flaw in the alien's seeming invincibility. They couldn't absorb much more of this intense punishment without overloaded deflectors burning out.

While a force-field is hypothetically capable of dispersing energy among its own fabric, he thought, it is not necessarily effective against more primitive weaponry. Physical objects, for example, possess different properties than those of phaser beams.

He was about to order a full complement of photon torpedoes fired, when the till now unceasing assault unexpectedly stopped. The shaking halted concurrently with the disappearance of the white beam. Behind him, Kirk could hear Uhura struggling to handle the flood of inquiries and reports that started pouring in from every deck and section.

While thankful for the respite, he still remained poised for the barrage to resume at any moment. After all, their best attempts at resistance had already proven childishly weak.

Yet . . . the alien had apparently elected to halt its attack. Why? "Cease firing," he ordered, suddenly aware that in the absence of any orders to stop, Walking Bear was persisting in a futile attempt to strike at the belligerent opponent with phasers.

Kirk turned to Spock as the ensign acknowledged the command. "Status on the alien?"

"Still approaching, Captain," Spock told him, his attention fixed on his instruments. "Going sub-light now. It has continued probing us throughout the battle . . . a moment." He paused, then, "Its surrounding energy pattern is now shifting."

As they watched in amazement, the field of intense radiance which hugged the alien craft like a tenuous remora, the same field which had first attracted Spock's attention, began to assume density and color. The hull of the craft remained unaltered as this process accelerated, though it grew increasingly difficult to detect through the darkening fog.

It wasn't long before the fashioning of the ghost was finished. The result was so nearly terrestrial that for a moment Kirk almost suspected the "alien's" ancestry.

But no . . . it was similar, but undeniably different. The

relationship was one of marriage and not blood. That made it no less startling.

The alien's prow had become a huge snake skull. Jaws hung agape and sported gigantic fangs which curved downward and back. It wore a crest of rainbow-hued feathers vaguely resembling the leathery neck shield of the terran South Pacific frilled lizard. Simulated feathers likewise cloaked the propulsion pods, the illusion heightened by the already winglike construction of the engines themselves. Feathers they were not, only brilliantly colored spines of energy, exquisite in their insubstantiality.

Of all the crew, Walking Bear was the most astonished. Nor did he try to conceal it, staring in open-mouthed awe at the fiery image resplendent on the screen, the bizarre craft draped in the ethereal raiment of a serpentine spirit.

"Ever seen anything like that, Spock?" Kirk asked. The heady apparition was baroquely impressive. But the captain had little time for idle admiration, however. His immediate concerns were more basic.

What were the motives behind such blind hostility—and what was the explanation for this at once juvenile and overpowering display? Exactly how the energy sculpture was accomplished was a question he'd leave for Spock.

The difference between captain and science officer, as usual, was the difference between *Why* and *How*.

Spock was elucidating, "It is not Vulcan-inspired, Captain. Nor do I believe it to be of Klingon or Romulan origin. Romulan, possibly, but . . ."

"I recognize it," a voice whispered unexpectantly.

Even Spock showed signs of astonished surprise as everyone on the bridge looked blankly at Walking Bear. The ensign mouthed the word as he continued gazing at the screen.

"Kukulkan."

"The name means nothing to me, Mr. Walking Bear," Kirk pressed when the ensign gave no sign of elaborating.

"Incoming transmission, Cap—"

Uhura never finished the words.

X

The strange, reverberant voice rolled thunderously over the bridge. It was loud, overbearing—but not unbearable—a unique meld as of many voices speaking in unison. Melodious and rhythmic, passionate and forceful, it compelled attention. Kirk stared at the viewscreen image. He began to suspect that it was the ship itself—the ship and its enveloping ghost—that was speaking.

"I attacked you because I believed you had forgotten me. But there is one among you who knows my name."

Kirk shook his head, trying to clear it of the aural cobwebs surrounding the transmission. The voice was engulfed in a swarm of echoes. It was hard to believe there was nothing wrong with his hearing. He found he could force himself to focus on one part of that multifaceted tone. When he did so he could make out the words, distinct and solemn—and threatening.

"You will be given one more chance to succeed where your ancestors failed. Fail me again and all of your kind shall perish!"

The broadcast concluded as abruptly as it had begun.

"Short and sweet," Kirk murmured. But without any of the explanations he so desperately needed. Now he had all this biblical-sounding business of failing ancestors and incipient annihilation to contend with. What were they supposed to have succeeded at, and how had they failed, and whose ancestors did the voice mean, anyhow? His . . . Spock's . . . maybe Arex's or those of M'ress's Caitian system.

If the ghost-maker wanted to play God, the least he could do was be a bit more informative . . .

One thing Kirk *did* know—they were pinioned here by a

powerful energy bubble fashioned by an enemy whose actions and words were far from friendly. Before he could decide on a course of action, he had to have facts, information, something on which to hang a supposition. The sole possible source of such information appeared to be a half-green ensign of no combat experience, but with considerable promise.

As Spock returned to his instrumentation and Uhura to communications, Kirk rose from the command chair and walked over to the helm. The subject of his impending—perhaps crucial—questions was sitting silently, apparently thinking hard. But he glanced up readily when Kirk approached.

Kirk started talking in an unintentionally suspicious tone, which he hurriedly corrected. "Mr. Walking Bear, how do you happen to recognize *anything* about that ship?"

For a split second something very old and very wise flashed in the young helmsman's eyes. Then it was gone, and Kirk couldn't be certain afterward if he'd actually seen it.

"I'm an Amerind, Captain. North America territory, desert—southwest, Comanche tribe. Anthropology's always been a hobby of mine—personal anthropology in particular." He smiled, ever so slightly.

"You have to know, Captain, that I was an example of an almost extinct terran subspecies . . . the orphan. So I'm rather more interested in my own history than most people. In the course of pursuing my own past, I've also had occasion to study the history of many earlier Earth cultures. Now the image assumed by that ship out there," he gestured at the screen, "bears a powerful resemblance to a god in ancient Aztec legends—Kukulkan. The variance is minimal . . . shockingly so."

Despite the factual knowledge to the contrary, there were still times when Kirk couldn't be sure which was the faster . . . the library computer or its master. In any case, Spock spoke up almost immediately.

"Captain, the records confirm Ensign Walking Bear's suspicions. The countenance of the alien is a remarkable analog of the Central American deity Kukulkan. Research shows that the Aztecs and their neighbors and predecessors—the

Mayas and Toltecs, Zapotecs, Olmecs and many others—all possessed legends of a winged serpent god.''

He nodded toward the screen. ''Ensign Walking Bear does not carry his information far enough, however.'' A quick glance at the readouts produced more startling information. ''It seems that many other cultures besides the Indian of Central America include stories of a winged serpent in their mythologies. The Chinese, for example, and many African tribes. He is referred to most often as a wise but terrible god, a bringer of knowledge and . . .''

''Myoka Mbowe.''

''What's that?'' Kirk spun, to face the communications station.

''*Hmmm?*'' Uhura snapped out of her daydream. ''Sorry, Captain. When I was a little girl, my grandmother used to tell me all the old handed-down fairy tales. Some of the stories revolved around the exploits of a god called Myoka Mbowe. It translated roughly from the Swahili as *winged snake*.''

''It is clear, Captain,'' Spock continued, ''that such legends were abundant among Earth's primitive societies.''

''So that explains it,'' Kirk muttered, turning back to the viewscreen. ''We've been attacked by a myth.'' His voice rose slightly. ''A terran philosopher once said that there are no myths, only vague distortions of half-remembered truths.

''We could be dealing here with the basis of all those legends, all those millennia-old stories—a space traveler who visited Earth in ancient times.''

Spock nodded. ''Entirely possible.''

''It's not possible,'' objected Arex. ''How can we be dealing with the same ship or traveler who forms the base for such legends? That would make the being in question many thousands of years old.''

''A possibility,'' Spock observed solemnly, ''which cannot be discounted.''

''I'll even grant the chance of that, Spock,'' Kirk allowed, ''if you'll tell me what all this business of destroying us, and failing, and ancestor ineffectuality is about? I just can't understand such naked hatred.''

Spock had turned back to the quiet scrutiny of his instruments. "I have no doubt that in time, we will be duly informed . . ."

Soft sound heavy sound . . . the bass engine of a human heart. It sounded clear and regular from the sensor amplifier that was only a tiny part of the incredibly complex diagnostic bed.

Always astonishing, that one muscle on which everything hinges, isn't it, Bones? He studied the figure prone before him.

The sophisticated bed monitoring equipment needed little in the way of external confirmation, but playing safe as always, he passed the belt medicorder over the crewman's forehead. A quick check to insure that the readings matched, and then he laid it back on the nearby table.

"You don't deserve it, specialist," he told the waiting youth gruffly, "but you're getting a few days bed rest."

The security specialist managed a slight smile. One hand gingerly felt the ear McCoy had treated. "It's not necessary, Dr. McCoy. I can handle my duties."

"Mine too? I'll do the prescribing around here. A few days bed rest. Remember, arguing with a superior officer is *almost* as bad as arguing with a doctor. And the next time you get the urge for some off-shift exercise, I suggest you try something besides high-diving into a minimum-level pool."

"Don't worry, Doctor," the specialist cringed. "I had to learn the hard w—" His mouth opened wide.

While the pain in his ear had abated under McCoy's skillful ministrations, it now seemed as if his other faculties had been affected for the worse.

Certainly his eyes were hardest hit, because he could swear that McCoy had become enveloped in a stuttering, immobilizing light, as though attacked by a turquoise strobe. It froze McCoy next to the bed without touching his patient.

It seemed that the flickering light appeared and died faster and faster. It seemed that McCoy was trying to say something. It seemed that Dr. McCoy had vanished.

The . . .

Scott was alone in the jeffries tube. He was inspecting the circuitry which ran from the great warp-drive engines to the engineering computer.

Actually, it was a job any engineering tech could have handled. But when the usual twelve desperate crises weren't clamoring for his immediate attention, Scott always made time for carrying out some of the more routine tasks of engineering maintenance by himself. It was always beneficial, he felt, for an experienced engineer to immerse himself in the plebeian from time to time, to work with a fluid-state hydrometer instead of giving orders.

And besides, he enjoyed it.

Running the tricorder across yet another opened panel cover gave him the same feeling of aesthetic enjoyment, the same emotional satisfaction as he followed micro-chips and coupled modules, that another man might have found in a painting by Turner or a Brahms symphony. Such diffuse and openly gushing creations would have as little appeal to him as to Spock. Scott's artistic tastes were well suited to his profession—Escher for art, say, and Stockhausen in music.

He refastened the panel and prepared to run the compact instrument over the next one. The radiance which enveloped him as he started upward was the blue of a Baja sky.

Then he was gone, the tricorder crying out hollowly for him as it clattered and pinged its way down the open passage . . .

The Four . . .

Kirk paced the deck in front of the command chair. It was simplistic and unscientific; and like many simplistic and unscientific remedies, it worked. He wondered who the first human was who discovered that one of the better salves for the harried mind lay in the feet.

"There's got to be a solution to this deadlock," he was mumbling. "Probably right in front of our eyes." He turned toward the helm. "Mr. Walking Bear, what do the legends say about . . ."

Walking Bear dissolved in a rain of blue gas followed by a tiny bang as a puff of air rushed in to occupy the space formerly displaced by the ensign.

As if he could snatch him back from an unknown fate, Kirk rushed the seat. But the helmsman was gone. To make sure, Kirk moved his hands through the air above the helm seat. No, the body of Walking Bear hadn't been made invisible—it had been made absent.

The Four Are . . .

"Captain," a hesitant voice called. Still dazed by this new development, Kirk turned to face Uhura. She sounded equally stunned, almost apologetic. "Security reports from both Sick Bay and Engineering. Both Dr. McCoy and Chief Engineer Scott have disappeared.

"No one saw Mr. Scott vanish. We have a report on Dr. McCoy's disappearance, however. Apparently he was administering treatment to an injured security specialist . . ." she paused a moment to listen, "Jo van Dreenan, at the time. He claims that Dr. McCoy was held motionless within a blue haze, then he vanished, just like . . ." She nodded toward the now empty helm chair.

Kirk turned to the main viewscreen, where the ghostly alien still hovered directly ahead. There was as much curiosity as anger in his question.

"What are they, or it, doing to my crew?"

A thorough visual demonstration negates the necessity for words. The pulsating blue amoeba ingested Kirk, flickered briefly, and took him, too.

"Captain!" Spock shouted. There was no response. Now the first officer's gaze likewise turned to the viewscreen, and he thought things which, while not exactly emotional, were far from flattering.

But though he wished it aloud among the imprecations, the blue light did not reappear to take him too . . .

The Four Are Chosen.

A vast, gray plain, open and desolate. Dull gray ground reaching to a featureless horizon, melting into a sky the color of antimony. Color began to brighten one tiny bit of it.

The four did not appear simultaneously. And although McCoy was the first chosen, he was not the first to appear. That privilege was reserved for Walking Bear. He was followed by Scott, then Kirk, and the good doctor last of all.

This sequence was intentional and proper. It was not, as a human observer might guess, executed at random. It was only that Kukulkan's science made use of space-time theorems that Scott would have sneered at.

Lead landscape and dirty-cotton hills, rippling rain-laden sky without moisture. Gray pseudopods of rippling gray lakes. It was as drab as an idle thought.

Each man reacted with differing degrees of surprise and alarm as he rematerialized. No one stopped to analyze whether it was instinct or common sense that prompted them to move close to one another, their backs to a common center.

Kirk was the first to recover and commence examining their surroundings. As soon as he had perceived that there was no immediate threat to their continued existence, his powerful curiosity had taken over. He was already gauging their chances for escape . . . even though he had no specific idea where they were.

Generally, however, he felt safe in commenting: ''We're somewhere inside the other ship.'' Silence from his three companions indicated they shared that opinion.

It was absolutely silent in the unimaginative arena. No breeze ruffled the atmosphere.

''No cover,'' Scott noted. ''And us without a single phaser or communicator between us.''

''I have a suspicion neither would be of much use, Scotty.''

''That may be so, Captain, but I'd settle for a nice, ineffective laser cannon all the same. Purely as a psychological prop, of course.''

Kirk smiled faintly. ''Me too, Scotty.''

McCoy was looking down at himself and patting his waist. ''I've still got my belt medikit, for all the good that's worth.''

''I hope you won't have to use it, Bones.''

''Hold on.'' Scott looked puzzled. ''I had an engineering tricorder with me. It must have remained behind on the ship when I was brought over. So why weren't Dr. McCoy's medical 'corder and supplies interfered with?''

''Where was it, Scotty?''

''Right in my fist, Captain. I was inspecting some circuitry with it.''

Kirk shrugged. ''That might explain it. Probably the instruments that were monitoring our transport read Bones' kit as part of his clothing, whereas you were more noticeably employing yours as a tool. I don't think you'd find much use for it here."

"Maybe not, Captain," Scott replied, "but then, I'm a full-time believer in the hairpin hypothesis."

"Hairpin hypo . . . what's *that*?" McCoy wondered aloud.

"An old engineer's adage that goes way back, Doctor," explained Scott. "It states that 'no tool is so useless that something can't be found it can be used to fix' . . . but I'd still rather have a phaser."

"I'm beginning to believe Spock was right about the entity behind all this," Kirk allowed. "That drone probe was unlikely, this ship is unlikely, and its method of communication the most unlikely of all. So I suppose the possibility that we're dealing with a being thousands of years old is no more unlikely than the others have been. When it begins acting rationally, that's when I guess I'll start doubting this." He turned to the youngest of the four.

"Mr. Walking Bear, do the legends say what eventually happened to this Kukulkan? Old cultures usually disposed of their gods neatly."

"Only that he left and promised to return one day, sir."

Kirk looked satisfied. "Sounds like all the promises ascribed to all the ancient gods of Earth." He looked from one to the other. "I don't think we need doubt that the drone probe was an information gatherer for this Kukulkan." He turned pensive.

"I only wish I knew what it was in that information that's caused the receiver to act in such an unfriendly manner, without even giving us a chance to find out what's behind all this. I . . ." He hesitated.

"What is it, Jim?" asked McCoy, sounding worried.

"Listen." They fell silent. In the complete quiet a distant buzz became audible . . . muted but unmistakable. It grew louder, and then familiar.

It was the sound of many tongues speaking simultaneously. It had overtones of pure alienness, which did not bother Kirk at all. It also hinted of expectancy, which did.

"We're being watched, I think," commented McCoy, eyeing the gray bowl of sky uneasily.

"When I was a child," Walking Bear murmured, "I used

to hide in a hall closet when I was supposed to be asleep, so I could listen to the adults talking in the sitting room. There wasn't a minute when I wasn't afraid the door would fly open to show my foster mother standing there, glaring down at me, ready to send me to bed with a beating.'' He studied the featureless plain.

''Strange how the earliest emotions linger the longest.''

Kirk faced his chief engineer. ''Is there any way Spock could get through to us with a transporter beam?''

''I don't think so, sir,'' Scott said, shaking his head in resignation. ''Our sensors couldn't penetrate this ship's screens. And since our phasers couldn't break out of the energy bubble around the ship, I don't see a transporter beam doin' any better.''

The steady buzz intensified. The four men diligently searched the horizon, at once hoping to see something, and hoping not to. Then the insectlike hum seemed to coalesce. The resulting voice still had touches of many, but now the words were distinct—and comprehensible.

''Now I will show to you the seeds that I have sown before,'' it pontificated. ''Learn from them . . . find the purpose if you can. If you can do so, then and only then will I appear before you.''

The buzzing voice faded to nothingness. Even as it was dying away, it was drowned by a profound thunder, as though immense engines were stirring underfoot, in the air, in the gray walls enclosing them.

As Kirk stared and tried not to sweat—there were less elaborate ways of killing four men, and anyway, the voice had said they had some seeds to inspect, whatever that meant—the landscape began to change color. Initially it shifted to an orange-gray. As the concussive rumble mounted, the gray gave way to a pure, almost blinding orange. Distances were indeterminate, but it seemed a sun appeared in open sky above. It was lambent orange. The rumbling reached a peak whereupon definite tones could be heard. They verged on music, but then so did the machinery of a kilometers-square factory. It was almost, McCoy thought, as if an enormous organ was playing somewhere—woodwind, violin, flute and chime pipes all weaving in and out among the deepest pedal notes. Everything participating, he mused, but a vox humana. He didn't expect to hear anything as comforting as that.

The Ivesian mosaic softened and orange turned to blue. Apparently Kukulkan's usable spectrum differed from theirs.

The result of all the activity began manifesting itself. First the familiar vegetation started to appear. Palm trees, huge ferns, vines and creepers lacing together a network of trees rose from the orange-blue ground. Dense undergrowth filled in the empty places like an afterthought.

It surrounded them on three sides, leaving only the ground directly ahead still barren. A trickle of running water could be heard; but even so, the amazing simulacrum still lacked something.

Kirk fixed on it a moment later. This was a curiously lifeless simulacrum. There were no animal sounds. No birds, no complaining primates . . . not even the addlepated hum of a hunting wasp. There were no smells, either, of hidden creatures. There should have been the musky odor of mobile life. Instead, there was only the oddly uninviting perfume of huge blossoms, the pungent miasma of steaming greenery.

Nothing. For all its color this fabricated jungle was as dead as the gray womb they had just vacated.

As if in anger, the rumbling sound returned. This time it was accompanied by a violent vibrating which rattled Kirk's teeth and pricked at his spine.

Lines appeared in the open ground before them. This section was mostly lower than the slight rise they stood on, and Kirk could see rectangles and squares being laid out on the orange. Something was tracing a city there.

It began to sprout, weedlike, from the porous ground.

Had he overlooked the possibility that they had been transported to some far world, and there ensconced in a clay cavern? No . . . the structures forming in front of him were made of something similar to, but far more sophisticated than clay. Then he recognized it—the material was almost identical to the strange crystalline substance of the alien's hull.

Hints of many cultures were embodied in those buildings: touches of Mayan architecture, Aztec edification, of Egyptian engineering and Southeast Asian religious construction and a host of a hundred others. Not all were extinct, but all were distinct. Yet they blended in a way which suggested that this fabrication and not the aged realities was the end to which they had all been striving.

Fragmentary Sumer merged with oil-age New York baroque. Bits of Inca regularity were subsumed by the curves of dead Monomotapa. Everything was enmeshed in its neighbor, interwoven and entwined and interchanged.

Despite this, the commandments of basic geometry held court, and somehow it all worked.

The city seemed livable, if not downright inviting. Nor did it appear all that primitive. Some of the angles and reflective buttresses were unrecognizable even to Scott's experienced eye.

The chief engineer was more interested in the material than in the method. It looked like ordinary stone . . . but when the sun struck a wall or parapet at a certain angle, the hard reflection that resulted was more suited to polished metal. And if you squinted a little with your eyes—and mind—various structures seemed built of opaque glass.

What could only be the city's entrance lay immediately before them, an open gate flanked by two sleek cylindrical towers. They resembled Egyptian obelisks. Yet when the light changed a little it was clear they were akin to the great towers once raised by the mystic artist-architects of Mohenjo Daro.

Just as Kirk was convinced the construction was complete, the persistent rumble rose almost painfully in volume. As the ground quaked underfoot, a single colossal structure leaped skyward from the city center. Dominating the skyline, it seemed to pull all the lines of each and every building, every tower and wall, together to form an unbreakable metropolitan whole. It was the highest facet on a well-cut gem.

As the final block appeared, and the last decoration materialized on the walls, the rumbling sound died for the final time.

The four officers were left to stand and wonder at a city at once alien and familiar. And no wonder, for it was the city man had almost raised half a hundred times, all across his world. The city that shows up in the corner of an architect's eye but never seems the same when committed to blueprint . . . the city men see in old dreams . . .

As if any more was necessary, here was yet further proof

that whatever else this Kukulkan was, he was not an entity to be mocked.

There was much care and purpose behind all this display. Despite the near cataclysmic threats inherent in that many-toned voice, Kirk couldn't help but feel a certain thrill of expectation at imminent revelations of the highest import. Within that city might lie explanations for all the mythologies of mankind.

That would not please some people.

"I've never seen anything quite like it, Captain," Scott murmured appreciatively at the eerie beauty of it, "not in all my landfalls on many worlds."

"What's behind it, though?" wondered McCoy.

Kirk spoke thoughtfully. "The voice spoke of seeds and unfulfilled deeds, Bones. An enormous puzzle's been set before us. Let's start inspecting the pieces."

They headed for the city gate. . . .

An assistant engineer was aiding Spock as the first officer worked at Scott's Bridge engineering station. Another technician stood ready nearby, to respond to muted commands with information or manipulation of certain instruments.

Sulu was at the helm now, the position vacated so startlingly by Ensign Walking Bear. All stations, in fact, were double-manned back throughout the *Enterprise*, as it remained on red alert. Everyone knew that the captain and three others had been taken. No one would sleep until their fate was known.

While the force-field enclosing them gave no sign of weakening, Spock wanted to be ready should their still unknown assailant give them the slightest chance to break free.

He concluded his operations at the engineering station and crossed back toward his own.

Uhura chose that moment to voice the concern which had been building in her for many minutes. "Mr. Spock, shouldn't we be trying to find out what's become of the captain, Dr. McCoy and the others?"

"Lieutenant Uhura, you are supposed to be monitoring the alien vessel for any possible incoming communiqués. You know that our first priority is to free the *Enterprise* and ourselves. As soon as that is accomplished, we can attend to the release of all kidnapped personnel. Continue with your regular duties.''

''Yes, sir,'' she muttered. Spock began recalling information from the library. She continued to stare at him for a long moment and then returned her attention to her own console. She might have been muttering something under her breath. Then again, she might not. Uhura could be unreadable at times.

Four men stood almost respectfully before the towering spires guarding the city's central boulevard. Close inspection convinced Kirk that they *were* Egyptian obelisks.

''With at least one significant difference, sir,'' Walking Bear exclaimed.

Kirk remembered that Walking Bear was only an amateur anthropologist. He wished for Spock's more definitive explanations. But Spock wasn't here. In his absence, they would have to depend on the ensign's informal readings. So far, though, he had to admit, the young helmsman's observations had been as accurate as anyone could wish.

''It's those carvings, sir,'' Walking Bear was explaining as he pointed to incisions about three meters off the ground on the nearest tower.

Kirk eyed them.

They had been exquisitely rendered by a careful, expert hand, he would have said, had he not seen the entire city raised from—*not the dust, Kirk*, he warned himself. *Don't get biblical—you've encountered races with matter-manipulation abilities before.*

He couldn't identify the style of carving. The subjects seemed uncomplicated, though. Animals and people from many different countries and regions of ancient Earth.

''Notice that one there, sir,'' Walking Bear suggested. ''The third row over, first on the bottom.''

Kirk found the indicated carving and instantly understood why the ensign attached such significance to it. It bore an uncanny resemblance to the ghost image which now cloaked Kukulkan's ship, that of a feathered serpent. In this particular rendition the wings were spread wider, and the body was coiled. It hovered over a lifelike flurry of little cuts which could only be water.

"No Egyptian ever carved anything like that, sir."

Kirk nodded, indicated they should continue on. They passed through the gate, which Scott claimed closely approximated some ruins he'd encountered in old China. For his part, Walking Bear maintained that the wall braces backing the towers and arch overhead could only be Scythian in origin.

"Can't pin it down," he finally confessed. "It's like the rest of this place, only on a smaller scale. There's that weird blend of many unrelated civilizations again."

"Everything's a clue, Walking Bear," said Kirk. "Remember, this city is intended to be one gigantic riddle. If nothing seems to belong to its neighbor, that must be significant, too."

The avenue they were walking down was wide and well paved with blocks composed of that same strange stone-metal-glass mix. They continued down it for what felt like a fair distance, examining each structure in turn as they passed it. Every one was finished down to the tiniest detail. Painstaking care had been exercised in this gargantuan recreation, which in turn was part of some still unknown charade.

It was the less amiable McCoy who finally called a halt to the seemingly endless hike. "Okay, so we're here—so, what are we supposed to do now?"

"Your opinion, Mr. Walking Bear?"

The ensign looked at him in surprise. He suspected the captain's growing confidence in him; he was used to offering opinions to the computer in study center, in response to queries posed in technical manuals—not to the ship's captain. For a moment he could only gawk helplessly.

"Come on, Ensign," Kirk finally urged, sensing the other's lack of assurance. "We're all of us equally on trial here."

"Sir, I . . . I haven't the faintest idea what we're expected to do."

"Just tell me what comes to you," Kirk soothed. "Tell us more about Kukulkan . . . maybe something useful will surface." He smiled encouragingly.

Walking Bear grinned slightly. "Well . . . before he left, the legends say Kukulkan gave the Mayas their remarkably accurate calendar, instructing them to build a great city according to its cycles. On the day the city was finished, he was supposed to return.''

As he told the weathered story, the orange-blue sun shone down on them with unvarying warmth, never stirring from its assigned place in the sky.

''The Mayas built their city and waited. Something about it must have been wrong, because Kukulkan never returned. Maybe they paid too much attention to the parts of the calendar that told them the best times for planting corn . . . I don't know.

''They tried again and again . . . at Chichén Itzá, Tulum, Uxmal and others. None induced the god to return.'' He glanced at the silent structures bordering the avenue. ''As Mr. Spock said, many cultures have such legends.''

''The history of Earth,'' Kirk whispered, ''is a history of unfulfilled promises,'' but no one else heard him. He spoke again, more briskly. ''Kukulkan must have visited many of those ancient peoples. It appears each used only parts— different parts—of his knowledge to build their own cities.''

''Does that mean they were all trying to build something that was supposed to look like this?'' McCoy asked.

Walking Bear hedged. ''I *think* so, sir, but they all failed. The Mayas used one part, the Indus River civilizations another, the builders of Zimbabwe yet another . . . over and over, failure after failure, the original knowledge growing more and more distorted with each succeeding culture.''

''I see,'' commented McCoy. ''An architectural Tower of Babel.''

''Sometimes I wonder about us humans, Bones,'' Kirk murmured. ''Someone could come along and hand us the plans for the ultimate civilization—and we'd manage to bollix it up somehow. We're too vain, as a race and as individuals.

''There's always someone who has to improve perfection, just to get his hundredth of a credit in.'' His voice grew tauter. ''Though from what I've seen of this Kukulkan and his methods this far, I wouldn't bet that some farsighted city builders didn't perform a little sabotage on those building instructions.''

''Kukulkan said he would appear only when we learned the city's purpose,'' Walking Bear reminded them. ''Unfortunately, none of the legends mention what that purpose was.''

Kirk ran his hand over the hair above his neck. ''Let's use what facts we have. Supposedly these cities were built to bring Kukulkan back to Earth. How? Obviously he hasn't been hanging around Earth, or anywhere else in our neck of the galaxy for the last several thousand years to see if someone eventually hit it right.

''That means this city has to hold some kind of signaling device.'' The structures surrounding them took on new meaning. ''It can't be too complicated. It has to be something the Egyptians or Mayas could have built, and out of local materials. The basic technology can't be too advanced, either.

''That means we're not going to find any deep-space transmitters housed in a stone pyramid. This Kukulan's approach to basic physics seems pretty different from our own. I don't see why some simple yet efficient communicating system couldn't utilize equally unorthodox technology.

''It has to be in plain sight, I think. After all, the transmitting machinery is the reason behind building the entire city.'' He gestured down the street they were on.

''That central pyramid is the city's physical and visual focal point. Seems a good place to start.''

In the humid silence of an unlengthening day, they started toward it . . .

XI

Eventually they stood at one corner of the ziggurat, at the intersection of the main boulevard and several smaller avenues. At the center of this modest intersection rose a small tower. It wasn't a very big tower, but that did not detract from its impressiveness. Roughly five meters high, it bore a definite resemblance to the elaborately worked, gilded temple towers of the Southeast Asia sector of Earth.

Rounded and roughly ovoid, it was made up of eight tiers of progressively diminishing size, cut from brightly colored stone. At the top of the spire was a graven image of Kukulkan's head. It was exquisitely executed, finely detailed. Everything looked lifelike—the serpent head with its gaping fanged mouth, the collar of metal and glass feathers around the neck, and the rainbow feathered frill formed of inlaid semiprecious stones.

Tilted up and back, the head stared into the sky at a forty-five degree angle, facing away from the pyramid behind. It wore a baleful expression, at once expectant and commanding.

At the sharp-edged corner of the enormous pyramid, a stairway built to human proportions started upward. As near as they could tell it reached to the top of the massive stone structure. At the moment, though, their attention was held by the impressive sculpture from which the web of roads radiated.

''Funny,'' Walking Bear was murmuring, hands resting on hips as he studied the sculpture, ''I've never seen a representation like this before.''

Kirk glanced up at the pyramid behind them, then back to his companions. ''Since the big pyramid's the center of everything, I'd guess it also has something to do with the answer to everything. Maybe it's at the top. I'm going up. The rest of you spread out and circle it. Try to stay within earshot of each other, within sight if possible. Anyone finds anything that demands immediate evaluation, he gives a holler. *Don't* try operating any levers or doorhandles without calling someone else to help. I don't want anyone vanishing down trick hallways.''

"Aye, sir . . . yes, sir . . . okay, Jim," came the replies. Kirk started up the seemingly endless series of steps, while the others split up.

Scott and Walking Bear hadn't gone far to the south before the ensign picked out a distinctive shape far down the walkway. He pointed. ''Another tower, I think, sir.''

"Come on, lad.''

They broke into a trot. As they drew nearer and nearer, they saw that Walking Bear was right. Furthermore, this new structure was more than just another tower . . . it was an exact duplicate of the one they had just encountered.

It lay in the center of another confluence of streets, as had the first. Walking Bear spared it only a glance before strolling out to where he could peer around the pyramid's corner.

Only the unnatural clarity of the air within the huge chamber enabled him to identify the outlines of the dim object in the distance.

"There's a third tower down this way, sir. There must be one at each of the four corners . . .''

Kirk didn't waste energy panting. There was no one around to sympathize. And he had gauged the hike accurately—no difficult task for a man used to estimating astronomical distances. So when he arrived at the top he was more psychologically than physically winded.

He was almost disappointed. The revelation he had hoped for consisted only of a flat, square platform supported on four poles. It perched in unimpressive solitude atop the pyramid. Its sole distinction was that it seemed made of metal— more metal than they'd seen anywhere in the city in one place. But closer inspection failed to disclose the nature of the alloy.

The square itself framed a lustrous, transparent round mosaic depicting Kukulkan in the same coiled, in-flight pose carved on the gate obelisks. The mosaic seemed to be encased in clear quartz, but Kirk didn't trust his initial estimates here. It did look like quartz, though.

He could just see over the top of the platform. There was no question of the mosaic's importance. It was a magnificent piece of craftsmanship, worthy of a fine jeweler, resplendent in its rendering. Other than its opulent beauty, however, it held no attraction for the captain.

Kirk crouched slightly to see beneath the platform. The bottom of the transparent mosaic was as flawless as the top. Passing through it, the rays of the artificial sun cast the winged serpent image clear and sharp on the stone beneath. Dust motes danced in the painted light.

Everything had been arranged here with extreme precision, to produce . . . what? Kirk rose and eyed the top of the mosaic once more, looked down at the image it cast on the stone, and considered thoughtfully.

Walking Bear and Scott were absorbed in their inspection of the second ornamental tower. They had negotiated the easy climb and now stood at the top, even with the sculpted serpent head.

Nearness brought knowledge concealed by height. Immediately they noticed two things not visible from ground level.

For one, the eyes of the statue were composed of concentric inlays of some translucent glassy material instead of opaque rock. Of more obvious significance was the faceted prism like some huge gem which was securely positioned at the back of the stone gullet.

Scott's engineering sense was more intrigued by, say, the controls of a ship than its more impressive bulk. Consequently, while Walking Bear was engrossed in deep study of the eyes and prism, his older companion was busily examining the collar of inlaid feathers which circled the statue's neck. He was hunting for imperfections more significant than the perfection, and he found one at the base of the fringed collar.

"Looks like there's a seam here. I think the head is meant to be turned. Come on, lad, give me a hand."

Lining himself up with his hands on the back of the collar, he directed Walking Bear to press in the same clockwise direction with both hands on the lower stone jaw. Together they shoved.

There was a rasp and squeak as of metal on rock . . . or maybe rock on metal, given the peculiar composition of the building materials here.

More important, the head seemed to move a little.

"Try again, lad." Both men strained, using their body weight against the recalcitrant sculpture. Something snapped inside and the head started to turn smoothly on a hidden pivot. As it turned to the sun, the glassy eyes began to glow, to shine with an inner light that appeared far stronger than mere reflection.

Scott and Walking Bear were too absorbed in the effort of turning the head to notice this new development. Fortunately, someone else was in the perfect position to do so.

Even from his high perch the intensity of the glow in the statue's eyes was so commanding that Kirk noticed it immediately. He spun and shielded his own eyes as he stared upward, muttering excitedly to himself.

"Of course . . . the sun! No wonder it hasn't moved . . . the position is crucial to the city riddle." He turned downward and shouted through cupped hands. No wind kidnapped his call.

"Scotty! Turn the head a hundred and eighty degrees, so that it looks up here!"

The chief engineer's voice echoed back faintly. "Aye, sir."

The head had been turned almost completely around when the polished prism in its mouth also began to shine. Simultaneously, the brightness of the inlaid eyes grew so brilliant that Kirk could no longer look directly at them without squinting. As the carved skull ground the last few degrees, a beam of light suddenly sprang from the serpent's jaws toward the top of the pyramid. It was accompanied by a hissing sound that grew rapidly louder.

Kirk had moved clear. Like a reaching arm, the combined triple beam of eyes and mouth passed directly before him, between the two nearest poles. It struck the underside of the mosaic held carefully suspended by the metal platform. The result was marvelous and unexpected.

As the nearly solid light from below struck the mosaic and passed through it, steady explosions of glittering energy formed in the air directly above, forming and bursting and bursting and forming like bubbles in champagne.

The hissing became a nervous crackling sound. It reminded Kirk of an incomplete electrical connection—though nothing so simple was at work here. Below, Walking Bear and Chief Scott stared anxiously upward, awaiting word from Kirk.

They could see the glow at the top of the pyramid, the distant figure of the captain silhouetted before it. But at this distance they couldn't tell anything else. A moment later and they were reassured as the diminutive form called down to them.

"Turn the other heads this way," the voice ordered. Scott yelled acknowledgment, and both men started down from the tower.

As soon as he saw them moving, Kirk edged around to the other side of the platform area, carefully avoiding the beam. He spotted McCoy waiting patiently by the base of the fourth tower.

"Bones! The serpent's head—turn it to face the pyramid! I'm coming down."

The stone skull was heavy . . . too heavy for one man. McCoy was still struggling with it when Walking Bear and Scott got the second head moving.

Again the tongue of light leaped upward to strike at the pyramid's apex. Now they could hear the crackling sound as it intensified with the addition of this second source of power, see the color of the strange energy deepen.

It remained for Kirk to give McCoy a hand in turning the next head. That finished, they climbed down and headed for the remaining sculpture. All four men met at the last tower, the one they had originally encountered.

For the fourth time the procedure was performed, sending a beam of intense light upward. The top of the pyramid, as Scott and Walking Bear descended, was now completely engulfed by the sphere of pure energy roiling angrily above it.

Abruptly the crackling hiss gave way to a thunderous rumbling, utterly unlike the sound which had accompanied the raising of the city. It dropped in volume, deepened until it seemed as if the very fabric of existence was being punctured by that glittering ball.

Streaks of pure light occasionally shot lightninglike through the multihued nimbus as it continued to grow and expand.

Below, the four officers had to shield their eyes as the glow from the top of the pyramid intensified to where it was greater than the sun.

"The whole thing," Kirk yelled as a breeze sprang up strongly around them, whipping at uniforms and hair, "is some kind of energy amplification device based on solar power—Kukulkan's special signal!"

The tenor of the rumbling changed to a steady drone as the energy ball began a steady pulsing. That's when the voices returned. Many voices joined as one. But this time the stentorian sussuration sounded even above the pulsating signal, reverberated until the multiple distortions were sloughed off like dead thoughts.

Gradually, the many whispers solidified until what they heard was, for the first time, unmistakably the voice of a single being.

"After scores of centuries," the voice boomed, "my design has been fulfilled. Behold me, then, as I am!"

The energy globe vanished in an air-splitting explosion. McCoy and Scott were both thrown to the ground. Kirk managed to grab the tower for support, while Walking Bear somehow succeeded in maintaining his balance.

The last flicker of energy was gone, dissipated in the magnificence of its own disruption by a force still greater. In its place was a hovering, fluttering form that was at once terrifying and beautiful. It was garbed in a cloak of glowing light. Huge membranous wings beat the air as it drifted above the pyramid. Multicolored, scaled torso coiling and recoiling reflexively, neck plumage shifting through a rainbow of brilliance, the massive shape stared down at them. Dragon tongue darted in and out of fanged maw, while dragon eyes glared past flaring nostrils.

"Behold Kukulkan," the apparition rumbled, still enveloped by now dimmed light from the four energy beams. Kirk listened and studied, trying to read the motivation masked by those crimson eyes.

"Where are your weapons of destruction?" came the next query. "Use them on me if you dare!"

"Very impressive, if a bit theatrical," McCoy commented phlegmatically. He'd discovered long ago that no matter how powerful or malign an adversary, if one regarded it merely as an anatomical problem to be mentally dissected, the commoner fears could be conveniently laid aside.

His mind was also occupied with hunting for the reasons behind this unnecessarily overwhelming display.

It was Kirk who answered, however. "We have no weapons with us . . . as you undoubtedly know. If we did, we'd use them only with reason. We haven't been given such a reason yet."

The monster threshed air, wings beating angrily. The energy cloak which clung to him ran through the visible spectrum.

"Reasons? Reasons . . . Where is your hate, then? Is that not reason enough? You hate me, do you not? Why then do you not speak to me of your hate?"

Kirk didn't know how to feel. Threatened? No—he was only puzzled. Despite its amply demonstrated power, there was a pathos about this creature he couldn't quite isolate. But that didn't permit him to lower his guard for a second.

"We don't hate you. You fired your weapons at my ship. We fired back."

The energy belt turned deep, furious purple and he added hurriedly. "We acted in self-defense—if you understand the term."

"I am your master!" the serpent roared. "I may do with you as I will, when I wish."

Madder and madder, Kirk mused, his thoughts awhirl. Obviously this entire display was concocted to intimidate them. But this would-be god had aimed at humans of a bygone age, men of less experienced times and readier belief in the supernatural. His words only made those standing below him angry.

"You think we belong to you?" McCoy exclaimed. "We're not part of the furniture of your cold gray house, Kukulkan."

"Aye, and don't plan to be," Scott added.

Kirk spoke quietly, firmly. "Bones, Scotty—don't antagonize it."

"Antagonize it?" Scott argued. "Captain, it's not exactly in a friendly frame of mind right now."

"It is as I thought," the serpent muttered, "you have forgotten me and strayed from the path I set for you."

Kirk spread his arms. The gesture was a plea for information, not mercy. "You say we've forgotten you. How then can you expect us to *worship* you properly, if we don't remember you and know nothing of the path of which you speak? Are we expected to suffer for the transgressions of ancestors dead these many generations?"

To his relief, this was so reasonable sounding that it appeared to have a mollifying effect on the snake-god. It settled to the top of the pyramid.

"There is some truth in your words. You do not know me. Therefore it is my task to teach you."

That worried Kirk some. He had no idea what was meant by teaching here. One thing he was certain of: judging from what they knew of this alien's character so far instruction might not be too pleasant.

As they watched, the atmosphere turned turquoise—the same blue haze that had lifted them from the *Enterprise*. It enveloped everything around them—pyramid, tower, city and jungle.

When the blue fog cleared, and their vision with it, they found themselves standing in a large, high-ceilinged room. The city was gone. The room seemed to stretch off to infinity, optical illusion though Kirk knew it must be. Kukulkan's science was unpredictable, but he didn't think it extended to creating infinite space aboard a ship of finite dimensions.

Everything was rounded and curved, smooth here as the city had been sharp-angled. The room itself was well-lit and shaded a deep, rich purple.

Levels and platforms hung scattered throughout the room without any visible support. Set on and around them were dozens of transparent cubicles . . . round, square, oddly shaped. More of the same glasslike cages rested on the floor of the chamber.

The whole arrangement was curiously . . . curiously—

Kirk struggled for the right word—sterilized. Yes, hard and sterile.

No bars or force barriers of recognizable type were evident. Some of the containers held plants, others animals. Many of both were unknown to the widely traveled senior officers. Each cage had a pair of thick cables running from it. The cables disappeared into floor or ceiling.

Other wild vegetation grew out in the open, uncaged. Kukulkan was nowhere to be seen.

"Just once," McCoy grumbled, "I wish he'd let us use the stairs."

Kirk examined the incredible collection. "Everything in here is designed to be looked at. I think the idea is that we do some looking."

He selected one path at random among the cubicles and they started down.

"What the devil is this place?" Scott wondered.

"Looks like some kind of zoo," a dubious McCoy commented.

He walked over to one of the glassy cages and tentatively felt of the surface. His hand drew back in surprise. Despite the glassy sheen, the wall had a greasy feel.

This particular cage housed a creature that resembled a hallucinatory vision of a giant platypus. It surged and heaved about within, obviously oblivious to their presence and as near as they could tell, perfectly happy.

"There're a lot of species here I don't recognize, Jim," McCoy told him.

"Me too, Bones. Species—I don't even recognize some of the environments. Look at that one."

The cage he indicated was filled with a red gas holding pink spongy globules in suspension. Within this atmosphere swam—or flew—a spotted yellow disk encircled with cilia. It looked blankly toward them with four eyes sporting double pupils.

Abruptly (but not unexpectedly) they were joined by another observer. Kukulkan hovered slightly above them and to one side. None of the men moved closer.

But when the serpent spoke the cordiality in its voice was in startling contrast to the violence it had displayed on their confrontation at the pyramid.

''Please feel free to examine any of my specimens.''

Specimens? What did this awesome assemblage of life portend? Another mystery they would have to pry out of Kukulkan.

Scott, however, had long since put aside diplomacy in favor of honesty. He shook his head sadly as he surveyed the endless rows of cubicles. ''I could never be proud of putting wee beasties in cages. We've long since abandoned such barbarism on Earth.''

Kirk glared at his chief engineer, but Kukulkan took no offense.

''All these here lead a peaceful, healthy life. One that is safe and contented.''

McCoy had strolled over to a nearby cage. Now he indicated its occupant—a furry, multilegged ball. It was plucking tiny grapelike fruit from a small bush.

''Contented? Cramped in these little cages?''

''Ah, but what you cannot see,'' the drifting alien explained, ''is that each creature is *mentally* in its own natural environment. The fields of the mind are infinite,'' he concluded profoundly, as McCoy bent to examine the cables leading out of the cage. They ran from the floor into an uninformative, featureless black box attached to the cubicle base.

''They eat, breathe and exist,'' Kukulkan continued, ''in worlds dreamed up by my machines. Worlds that only they can see. Nor do they see you. Nothing is permitted to disturb their satisfying, endless vistas. Each lives its own ideal dream. They do not know they are in cages.''

''A cage is a cage no matter how padded the bars,'' Scott whispered.

Kukulkan's hearing was far from godlike, the chief engineer had long since decided. Nor could he read minds. Otherwise he would have dealt with Scott back at the pyramid.

''Then the city whose puzzle we solved,'' Walking Bear exclaimed in a sudden burst of realization, ''wasn't really there!''

''It was 'there','' Kukulkan informed them, ''because I wished it so, for you, and me.

''Each of my specimens has a world of its own far greater than the puny city I created for you.''

"I'd hardly call your city our natural environment," Kirk pointed out.

Huge wings struck at the air. "It was meant to be! That beautiful city and all else I taught to your ancestors were intended to be yours. But they became evil and forgetful and imposed their own teachings above mine until the greater was forgotten!"

There was nothing more to be gained by tact, Kirk decided. It was time to try directness. "We don't like being referred to as property," he said.

He was about fed up with this deranged mechanical wizard. To many primitive terran cultures he might well have seemed a god, but a god he was not.

"No one being," Kirk continued, "not even you, has the right to interfere with the natural development of other civilizations. This is a rule we have established for ourselves."

Huge linear muscles contracted, tightened. Wings beat furiously at cages and plants as the serpent flew into a frenzy, eyes bulging, mouth agape. They backed away from such naked rage.

"Do not speak to *me* of development and interference! Do not speak to me of what is *right*! I have been ever alone. Destruction descended on my kind before your race had discovered fire . . . nay, before it learned to lift itself from the mud and walk upright. Is there 'right' in such endless solitude?"

He gestured at several nearby cages. One contained a creature much like an undernourished seal, the other a quivering mass of green and black protoplasm. Between lay xenariums filled with exotic flora.

"Creatures like these have been my only companions for many millennia. I have seen minds like yours on many worlds . . . savage, warlike, filled with self-hate and destructive intelligence. You end by destroying yourselves and everything around you, by reducing whole planets to lifeless cinders. After endless encounters with such sickening civilizations I decided to"—the word came out savagely—"interfere! As a hopeful experiment I visited your Earth, among other worlds, and tried to teach peaceful ways to the now vanished cultures of many races.

"Then I left, intending when summoned to return to give

you the additional knowledge which would enable you to join me as true equals. But you never sent for me. None did, to whom I gave the knowledge of the city. Finally I sent a probe to find out what had happened. What did it tell me, what did it discover? Warriors!'' He spun rapidly in tight circles.

''Still warriors, ever warriors—the same as always. The same as I've seen on half a hundred worlds, only this time more terribly equipped than ever, with yet greater instruments of destruction. You've surpassed the stage of quarreling among yourselves and have carried annihilation to the stars. You will end by destroying the universe!''

''Saints preserve us,'' murmured a flabbergasted Scott, ''a paranoid god.''

''But we work only to create peace,'' Walking Bear objected.

The serpent glared down at them, his shadow darkening the room, wings fluttering in agitation. ''Nothing you have done so far makes me believe that is so. I—I have done better.''

Again the broad, sweeping gesture, this time taking in the entire horizonless chamber: cages full of snail-like plants, plantlike snails, a cubicle lined with tiny colored balls, animals that resembled rocks, plants that resembled buildings, plant-animals like nothing on Earth.

''My creatures here have little intelligence, yet even the most violent among them exist peacefully in the worlds that I have to give.''

Wings moved, and he backed around a corner. They followed cautiously to where an unusually large cage floated in midair. It held an enormous feline creature that was all teeth, fangs, and rasplike hair. Despite this fearsome array of inborn weaponry it was reposing quietly on a bed of grass, half-asleep. Even at rest, though, this carnivore generated a sense of menace greater than any dozen terran tigers on the hunt.

''Though one of the fiercest and most unmanageable monsters living in your region of space, this creature too lives in peace and contentment in the private paradise which I create for it out of its own dreams.''

''Good Minerva,'' McCoy suddenly blurted, staring at the

cage and taking a step backwards, "it's a Capalent power-cat. No one's ever been able to keep one alive in captivity."

"I'm not familiar with the species, Bones," Kirk said, eyeing the cage respectfully. "Why haven't they?"

"They despise captivity, have to be killed before they can do any major damage," McCoy explained. "Try to confine them and they fly into a blind rage. That rage is coupled to generating cells that make a big electric eel's kick look like a communicator battery next to a warp-drive. One can put out enough juice to turn alloy-netting into a tin puddle, or kill a couple of dozen overenthusiastic hunters."

He looked up at Kukulkan. "I've never heard of one living in captivity for more than a couple of days. How did you manage to capture it in the first place?"

"This one was an infant, when encountered," the serpent told them, "and therefore more easily manipulated. As you were when first I visited Earth. You were destructive children who needed to be led."

"But if children are made totally dependent on their teachers," Kirk put in quickly, "they'll never be anything but children."

Alien wings ripped at the air. "Enough! This is useless. Despite what I've told you, despite what you've seen, you persist in clinging to your disobedient ways." He swooped down to hover threateningly close.

"My dream is ending," he howled, "and all of you are to blame! No time," he continued with an ominous air of finality, "is ever given to those who must decide."

"Scatter!" Kirk yelled, reading Kukulkan's intentions in his tone. As the serpent dove at them the four officers did just that. The demigod hesitated, displaying something considerably short of omnipotence, trying to decide which of several ways to pursue first.

The question of the alien's omnipotence was one which had been burning in another mind for some time now. When the solution finally presented itself to Spock it gave support to the theory that what is most obvious is most often overlooked.

"Of course," he finally murmured softly. The elasticity of the force-field should not be able to respond to assault from more than a single source. If it could absorb and redistribute phaser beams, it shouldn't be possible for it to simultaneously cope with opposing pressure from another source.

As always, he triple-checked his supposition with actual math. The equations and conclusions which appeared on the library-computer screen confirmed his hopes.

He was speaking as he crossed to the empty command chair. "All hands to battle stations . . . red alert is no longer on stand-by." Uhura complied and the fully activated triple shift readied for immediate action—all four hundred twenty-six of them.

"Full impulse power, Helmsman," he ordered in crisp tones as he settled himself in the chair. "Tractor beam on full power, warp-engines on stand-by."

A steady hum built on the Bridge as the closer impulse engine warmed.

"Tractor beam activated, sir," came the report from the engineering station.

"Very well. Set for maximum pull in precise opposition to our present heading."

"Aye, aye," came a ready but slightly confused voice.

"Mr. Arex, you are directed to compensate for catapult effect. When we break free of the confining force-field we will be thrown approximately five point seven light-years in a fraction of a second."

"Understood," the experienced navigator replied. Moments later he reported, "Catapult compensation factors laid in, sir. Gravity recoil compensation also checked."

"But how are we going to break free of the field?" Uhura wanted to know.

"This energy bubble, by its very nature, appears responsive to only one action per contained object, Lieutenant. If the same object—in this case, the *Enterprise*—both pushes and pulls on it simultaneously, at the same spot, the field should become sufficiently strained for a sudden burst of warp power to break clear of it.

"Mr. Sulu, Mr. Arex, you have our present spatial position?"

"Yes, sir," the double reply came. Spock wanted no chance of them being thrown nearly six light-years off with no way of relocating the alien's ship.

"Field contact with tractor beam in four seconds, sir," Arex announced. His voice was perhaps a twinge higher than usual.

Even as he finished, the *Enterprise*, in the person of its powerful tractor beam, once again encountered the restrictive surface of the force globe. Both tractor and impulse engine fought the same section of surface . . . pushing and pulling toward the identical end.

Spock didn't intend that they should bear the terrific strain very long. For one thing the tractor mechanism would blow up if it was required to pull against the opposing force of the impulse engine for more than a couple of minutes.

"Full warp power on my order," Spock said, shaping the syllables slowly. "Now."

Within the force globe the tubularnacelles housing the great engines glowed brightly at the ends. The *Enterprise* hung in that nexus of antagonistic energies for a split second before a blinding white flash obliterated it from view.

Only a translucent blue globe remained.

In an empty, uncontested corner of space the flash was repeated for an audience of indifferent stars. The *Enterprise* appeared in its center. Kukulkan's ship was off the scanners.

No one raised a shout, there were no hysterical cheers. Those could wait until later, when the missing four crewmembers had been rescued.

"All decks report no damage, no injuries, sir," Uhura announced.

"Mr. Sulu, come about. Mr. Arex, put us on course to return." Spock betrayed no hint of satisfaction. His tone was no different than it had been when they had seemed hopelessly trapped.

By interstellar standards the distance they had to travel was not great. "Reduce speed to maximum close-range attack velocity, Mr. Sulu. Begin spiral attack pattern four. Arm all phasers and the photon torpedo banks."

"Sir," Sulu murmured, "if the Captain, Dr. McCoy and the others are still alive, wouldn't it be wise to . . . ?"

"One of the hallmarks of wisdom is the assignment of priorities, Mr. Sulu. The *Enterprise* comes first. You will arm as directed."

"Yes, sir," came the flat response.

Thus prepared to deal a hurricane of destruction at the first attempt to encase them in another force-field, the *Enterprise* wound its way back toward the inimical ghost. . . .

Kirk was nearly exhausted. Just behind him, McCoy appeared to be in even worse shape. He glanced back and made a gesture. McCoy nodded in return. As they rounded the next suitable corner, both men dove behind one of the lowest of the suspended cages.

A writhing shape flashed by moments later, tongue flicking rapidly in all directions and red eyes glaring vengefully. Kirk marveled at the abilities of a race which could create technological wonders like this ship without the evolutionary benefit of manipulative members.

Surely those wings had always been wings, nor were there signs of rudimentary legs. The tail appeared reasonably prehensile, but that hardly seemed sufficient. Yet Kukulkan's people had managed, even triumphed, in matters of fine construction.

Even as he thought they had thrown off pursuit, bat-wings backed air and the twisting figure paused in mid-flight.

Kirk held his breath. He needn't have. It wasn't sudden detection of their presence that had brought Kukulkan to such an abrupt stop. Confusion of a different kind was apparent in his manner, and in the words he muttered unconsciously.

"Something is wrong."

Both officers hazarded a peek around the cage as the serpent made an elaborate gesture with both wings. A square of shimmering blackness materialized before him.

Looking into that was like peering into a cube of space. Miniature stars gleamed within it. Some were occluded by a miniature *Enterprise*.

And no force bubble encased it, Kirk noted excitedly.

The three-dimensional image of the ship grew larger and larger, until it seemed it would burst the confines of the cube.

"Escaped," Kukulkan was growling. "How? I will smash it this time . . ."

"Broken free, Jim!" McCoy exclaimed. "Spock . . ."

Kirk cut him off. "We've got to distract this thing and give him some time to get within range before another force bubble is projected—or worse." He started to draw back into the shadows, bumped something round and unyielding with his shoulder.

As the thought cleared he forgave himself the bruise. The exchange could be more than fair. "Bones, what would happen if we were to pull the cables on some of these cages? Disrupt the peaceful environments?"

McCoy shrugged. "Probably most of the animals would just lie still. Those that weren't cowed would be too confused by the sudden change to know what to do. A few might react blindly . . ." A look of comprehension dawned on his face. "A few . . . the Capalent power-cat!"

"Come on, Bones . . ."

Keeping to the shadows, of which there were precious few because of the even illumination, they traced an indirect path back to the cage holding the big carnivore.

That belligerent creature was awake now and calmly preening itself. As they neared the cage, Kirk found himself wondering if this was really such a brilliant idea. Yet what else could they try? It would take a major disturbance to draw Kukulkan's considerable mind away from the approach of the *Enterprise*.

Kirk carried out a last experiment by charging straight at the cage and slamming his hands hard against the transparent-seeming side. Within, the power-cat's gaze moved directly to him—and past.

They'd have a chance, then. Moving around the cage they started tugging and pulling at the twin cables. Despite their most strenuous efforts, the connections held fast.

Well behind their present location, Kukulkan hovered in humid air and studied the newly created image of the *Enterprise*. He appeared to hear something, his head suddenly lifting and turning in several directions before settling on one.

"No, stop!" he commanded angrily, with perhaps a touch of something other than anger in that shout. Wings flapping furiously, he streaked off down one winding path. Behind him, now devoid of control, the black cube of shrunken universe broke up into tiny puffs of dark smoke.

Kirk heard that shout. Holding tight to the cable just past where it joined the black box beneath the cage floor, he tensed himself for a last, supreme effort.

He put his left foot up against the cage on one side of the cable, and shoved. Maintaining pressure, he brought his right leg off the ground and planted it on the other side of the link. Suspended off the ground, he strained shoulders and legs at the same time. McCoy struggled to imitate his actions.

Kirk's cable gave with a snap and tiny shower of sparks. He fell to the ground. Seconds later, McCoy joined him. The doctor was no athlete, but he knew exactly how to utilize the combination of bands and ropes that made up the muscular system.

Both men employed that system to roll beneath the only immediate cover—the dark bottom of the cage itself.

Above their heads, reaction was instantaneous. The power-cat jerked back from what must have been a shocking and radical alteration of the landscape.

Spinning, it saw more of the same. It shrank down into the earthen floor of the now fully transparent cage. But when no further metamorphosis followed, it rose rapidly to all fours. It could see other creatures moving about around it. Air still pulsed through its lungs, its heart still beat. It was alive.

There is practically nothing a Capalent power-cat fears. Whether panic or rage or both motivated it then, neither Kirk nor McCoy could tell.

It rose up on its hind legs, fur bristling, fangs bared. They couldn't hear the snarl it made, because it was drowned by a greater explosion. The interior of the cage was filled with a violent discharge of electricity that shattered the walls and ceiling of the enclosure into a thousand fragments.

They could hear the snarling now, uncomfortably close above them—a deep-throated, angry rasp that cut the air like a scythe. The power-cat leaped clear and began prowling among the surrounding cages, throwing off immense bursts of energy like a four-legged hairy thunderhead.

Random bolts struck the floor and ceiling of the chamber. Where they made contact, deep smoking scars in the material appeared. Other bursts shattered nearby cages, sending the respective inhabitants into quivering paralysis or leaping for the nearest shelter.

If anything, the rampaging killer's discharges seemed to increase in intensity. It reached the point where each new burst caused the color of the room to change. Kirk could feel the hair on his arms and the back of his neck stand on end in the presence of so much unchanneled power.

Kukulkan was close by, but he was no longer concerned with Kirk and McCoy, nor with Scott and Walking Bear who had hurried to the region of disturbance to offer aid if either captain or physician were in danger.

Wings fluttered in agitation as the serpent hissed, "Irrational savages! See what you have done!"

"Prepare to fire, Mr. Sulu," Spock ordered calmly as the range to the ghost ship closed. "Aim for the propulsion units."

"Aye, sir."

They swept close . . . and no force-field appeared to meet them. No duplicate of the pure white energy beam leaped to strike at their deflector shields.

"Fire, Mr. Sulu. Phasers first."

Twin beams of blue energy crossed the distance between ships. This time there was nothing to stop them. They raked the alien's drive.

"Again, Mr. Sulu." Once more the rear section of Kukulkan's vessel was hit.

Within the life-room a brief turquoise glow touched everything. Then all was plunged into darkness in which the only light came from luminescent specimens and the intermittent blaze of the power-cat.

The carnivore's snarls reached them above an increasing mélange of squeaks, chirps, moans and whistles. Kirk decided to take a chance, crawled clear of the protective cage. To the power-cat, his yell should be no more distracting than the calls of any other freed creatures.

"Kukulkan! You can't control one of your *own* creatures!" The emphasis on the *own* was intentional, but the irony was wasted on that monumental reptilian ego.

Light returned to the chamber and Kirk ducked back out of sight. But this wasn't the bright, powerful illumination of before. It was dim and flickered dimmer at random moments. It was strong enough for them to see by with reasonable ease, though.

Kukulkan had made no attempt to locate the source of that taunt. Instead, he was shrinking back against one smoking cage as the odor of crisped air drifted back to them. Both cat and prey were edging toward their hiding place.

"I cannot, any longer. Your ship has crippled my central power source."

Kirk was about to say something about the power of a god, but McCoy had grabbed his arm. "If that's true, Jim, then that cat's a real threat to all of us."

A snarl sounded close by, and a moment later Kukulkan appeared. The power-cat had its head down and was stalking the serpent-god with single-minded hatred. It was backing Kukulkan in against a shattered cage that reached nearly to the ceiling. Its tail lashed back and forth and blue sparks danced on its fur. Ozone stank in their nostrils.

"We've got to do something, Jim, it'll be after us next."

"Your medikit, Bones—maximum tranquilizer setting for alien mammaloids."

McCoy was fumbling at his kit instantly, muttering. "We're not certain it's a mammal, Jim. Power-cat study's not a favorite subject among researchers on Capalent. I don't even know if the hypo will penetrate."

"It better," Kirk warned nervously.

McCoy drained nearly all of one vial to fill the hypo, then slapped it into Kirk's ready palm like a relay runner's baton. Kirk was already dashing from their hiding place before the doctor could think to object.

Kukulkan was lashing his tail like a whip and beating with its wings. The power-cat was not impressed. If the serpent tried to dodge, the cat would cut him off to either side . . . and there wasn't enough room to fly over the towering cage. Escape was impossible.

Powerful leg muscles tightened and the carnivore's tail twitched faster. It was readying itself to spring, eyes fixed on the brightly-colored creature which hovered before it. One might think the position of deity and mortal had been reversed.

So intent was it upon Kukulkan that the power-cat never saw Kirk. The captain brandished the hypo like a knife and slammed it into the carnivore's rear right hip.

It whirled immediately, as much startled as angered. The

burst of electricity it threw off was reflexive rather than directed. That saved Kirk's life. The discharge was still powerful enough to send him flying into a nearby tangle of uncaged shrubs.

Apparently unhurt, the cat readied itself to hurl a better-aimed charge at this tiny new opponent. Instead, it shook its head and got down off its hind legs, eyes blinking slowly.

Behind it, Kukulkan's agitation diminished. The god cocked his head quizzically as he evaluated the change in the now dazed killer. Its gaze rose to study the place where Kirk lay.

McCoy was at the captain's side in a moment, but Kirk was evidently all right. He was sitting up, shaking his head and rubbing at his right shoulder. The doctor's voice was still concerned.

"Did you inject the beast or yourself? You look a little rocky, Jim."

"I'm okay, Bones. That last bolt just singed me. Funny stuff, lightning. It can turn a hundred-meter-tall tree into lawn stakes without harming someone standing nearby." He gestured with his head to where a long black streak had scorched the deck just to one side of where he'd been, seconds before.

Okay or not, he didn't object when McCoy offered him a hand up. The narrowness of his escape was magnified when a few steps brought them to the hypo. It had been thrown clear. It was recognizable as the hypo only because it couldn't be anything else. Metal and glass were fused into a vaguely cylindrical blob of still hot slag.

Kukulkan, meanwhile, had recovered enough to hover above the power-cat. Kirk considered running for their hiding place, then shrugged. They'd already been seen and anyway, with the power-cat immobilized, the serpent could locate them at its leisure.

McCoy joined him as he walked toward the carnivore. The huge creature was not unconscious. It possessed physical reserves which could almost handle even the massive dose it had been injected with. It sat swaying slightly and licking its forepaws.

"What a system!" McCoy murmured in admiration.

"That hypo had enough mynoquintistrycnite in it to knock out a herd of hippos."

"It's just like a big kitten," a voice sounded behind them. Walking Bear, and Scott with him. The first animal they had seen, the lumbering platypus-like thing, was waddling behind Scott. Every once in a while it would sidle up next to him and rub up and down his leg like a big slick dog, uttering a peculiar gulping sound.

Scott would hesitate, then reach down to scratch behind its ears. "What's this, again? Aren't you the friendly little darlin'."

"Hello Walking Bear, Scotty," Kirk hailed.

"I see things have calmed down a bit, Captain," Scott observed with satisfaction, staring past him. "Maybe now all concerned parties can discuss things a bit more sensibly."

"Yes," Kirk agreed, turning to face Kukulkan. "I think we've earned the right to be heard."

"You continue to take advantage of me," the serpent replied grudgingly. "Yet my beamed request for time will not delay your Mr. Spock much longer. He would destroy my ship. Therefore I must consent. Speak what you will."

Kirk nodded back to where Scott was still scratching the alien platypus. The eyes of the creature were closed in apparent pleasure.

"You think of us as being weak, small creatures like that one, as unintelligent animals. Are we truly that inferior to you?" Kukulkan paused, seeming for the first time to consider his reply before speaking.

"Potentially, mentally . . . no. But compared to the violence of your kind, the power-cat in its natural state is docility personified. How can I let that live to poison an unsuspecting universe?"

McCoy's hands were locked behind his back. He was rocking slowly on his heels and staring expectantly at Kirk. Obviously the good doctor was burning to say something. Kirk saw no reason to stand in his way.

"We'd be fools if we didn't learn from our own history," McCoy began. "Those minds you admit aren't so inferior to yours . . . we've been using them since you last visited us. Don't let your probe's tales of warships and arms convince you we're about to embark on a Galaxywide war of extermination. We've been working to bring about a multiracial civilization in which everyone can live in peace with his neighbors. We've already accomplished this within our own Federation.'' He grinned. ''A few persistent throwbacks like the Klingons and Romulans will come around, in time.''

''You see why we can't be what you originally intended for us,'' Kirk continued. ''If we fail or succeed, it has to be—*must* be—by our own hands. By our own doing.

''You could probably find your worshipful servant races somewhere, Kukulkan, but they'd have to be blind and dumb. Once you have a being with a mind of its own, you can no longer lead it around by the nose. You cannot have intelligent slaves, Kukulkan. The thing is as impossible as a leisurely cruise past a black hole.''

Kirk didn't think it was possible for that cobra countenance to look downcast, but Kukulkan managed it.

''I thought of you as my children. I hoped I could teach you, lead you, aid you. There is much I can . . .''

''You already have,'' Kirk said, with more compassion than he believed he could muster for this overbearing creature. ''Long ago, when it was needed most—when our ancestors were still children. But we're all grown up now, Kukulkan.''

He hesitated, then added as gently as possible, ''We don't need you anymore.''

This time the serpent spoke with true somberness. ''It seems I have already done what I can, and things cannot be as I wished them. Therefore . . . I will let you go your own way, as you wish.'' The power-cat had ceased licking itself and now lay down peacefully between them.

''We would still have you as a friend and equal, Kukulkan,'' Kirk offered.

''No . . . no.'' The wings beat slowly. ''That cannot be, now, for me. As you cannot be servants and children, so can I be no less than the master. It is sad, but it is truth.

''Go now . . .''

Kirk studied the viewscreen. Kukulkan's ship still hovered there, but its awesome energy cloak was gone. The need for deception had passed.

McCoy stood nearby while Spock was watching the screen from his position at the library-computer station.

"An interesting experience," the first officer observed.

"Interesting," McCoy mumbled, in a tone that indicated he would have used other adjectives to describe what they had just been through.

"Our visitor turned out to be the actual Mayan god," Spock concluded.

"And the Toltecs' Quetzalcoatl," Walking Bear reminded, "and the original Chinese dragon, and all the rest."

"But not quite a god," Kirk corrected them. "Just an old, lonely being who wanted to help others—an egomaniacal hermit who'd choose isolation before confessing to his mortality."

McCoy grinned and crossed his arms, rather like a gunfighter preparing for a standoff—only the doctor was readying a verbal salvo.

"Spock," he began innocently, "I don't suppose Vulcans have legends like those?"

The first officer regarded him evenly, raised one eyebrow. "Not legends, Doctor. Vulcan *was* visited by alien beings in its past. They, however, left us much wiser."

McCoy was preparing a reply when Arex, who had insisted on remaining on duty until the incident was finally resolved, broke in with a report.

"The other vessel is getting under way, sir, heading directly outward along the transmission heading."

"Away from Earth, away from the Federation," Kirk confirmed, watching as Kukulkan's ship began to shrink on the screen. "It's sad. Think what we could do with the knowledge on that ship, held in that mind." He shook his head.

"Unfortunately, the price was just too high."

"I think I know how he felt, Jim," McCoy commented, turning suddenly serious. Spock also turned to look at him. "There's a line from Shakespeare . . ."

"I remember it, too, Bones." Kirk's voice recited, " 'How sharper than a serpent's tooth it is to have a thankless child'."

"Indeed, Captain," Spock agreed, filling that terse comment with more meaning than most people could put in several paragraphs.

Kirk sighed, looked back at the screen. It was empty again, empty save for that endless panoply of marching suns. They glowed mockingly back at him, each holding secrets they stubbornly guarded with distance and time.

"Lay in a course for Star Base Twenty-one, Mr. Arex. All ahead warp-three . . ."

About the Author

Born in New York City in 1946, Alan Dean Foster was raised in Los Angeles, California. After receiving a bachelor's degree in political science and a Master of Fine Arts in motion pictures from UCLA in 1968–1969, he worked for two years as a public-relations copywriter in a small Studio City, California firm.

His writing career began in 1968 when August Derleth bought a long letter of Foster's and published it as a short story in his biannual *Arkham Collector Magazine*. Sales of short fiction to other magazines followed. His first try at a novel, *The Tar-Aiym Krang*, was published by Ballantine Books in 1972.

Foster has toured extensively around the world. Besides traveling, he enjoys classical and rock music, old films, basketball, body surfing, scuba diving, and weight lifting. He has taught screenwriting, literature, and film history at UCLA and Los Angeles City College.

Currently, he lives in Arizona.